Walking Through Dreams

Walking Through Dreams

Part One of Lands of Red and Gold

Jared Kavanagh

SEA LION PRESS

First published by Sea Lion Press, 2020
Copyright © 2020 Jared Kavanagh
All rights reserved.
ISBN: 9798367793673

Cover artwork by Jack Tindale

This book is a work of fiction. While 'real-world' characters may appear, the nature of the divergent story means any depictions herein are fictionalised and in no way an indication of real events. Above all, characterisations have been developed with the primary aim of telling a compelling story.

Prologue: First Contact

February 1310
Grey Sea [Tasman Sea, offshore from Kiama, Australia]
Blue sky above, blue water below, in seemingly endless expanse. Dots of white clouds appeared on occasions, but they quickly faded into the distance. Only one double-hulled canoe with rippling sail cut a path through the blue emptiness. So it had gone on, day after day, seemingly without end.

Kawiti of the Tangata [People] would very much have preferred not to be here. The four other men on the canoe were reliable enough travelling companions, so far as such things went. Yet being cramped on even the largest canoe made for too much frustration, and this was far from the largest of canoes. Only a fool would send out a large canoe without first exploring the path with a smaller vessel to find out what land could be discovered.

Of course, only a fool would want to send out exploration canoes at all, so far as he could tell. The arts of long-distance navigation were fading back on Te Ika a Maui [North Island, New Zealand]. That was all to the good, so far as Kawiti was concerned. Why risk death on long sea voyages to find some new fly-speck of an island, when they had already discovered something much greater? Te Ika a

Maui was a land a thousand or more times the size of their forefathers' home on Hawaiki, and further south laid an island even greater in size. Their new lands were vast in expanse, and teemed with life on the earth, in the skies above, and in the encircling seas.

Still, here Kawiti was, on a long voyage like his grandfather had spoken about. He had learned the old skills, and now he had been made to use them, whether he wished it or not. He would much rather be hunting moa in the endless forests than chasing ghosts in this endless water.

"Remind me why I'm out here," he said, to the air around him.

His cousin Nene took the statement seriously. "Because Rahiri wants us to be out here, and so here we are."

"If there's exploring to be done, the Big Man should do it himself," Kawiti muttered.

"That's the point to being the Big Man; you get to tell others what to do, instead of doing it yourself," Nene said.

Since that was manifestly true, Kawiti changed the subject instead. "No matter what Rahiri wants, we can't keep exploring much further in this wind."

As any sensible navigator would do, Kawiti had steered his canoe into the wind for this exploration. That would make it safer to run for home if they needed to, rather than risk being becalmed until they died of thirst.

"We have enough water to explore for another sunrise, maybe two," Nene said. "If-"

He never finished that sentence, since Kawiti pointed to the skies instead. "Gulls!"

That brought exclamations from all the men on the canoe. A half dozen or so white-and-silver gulls circled in the skies to the south-west. Kawiti took hold of the steering oar and turned the canoe in that direction. Sure enough, when they got closer, they saw that the gulls were just like those which crowded the shores of Te Ika a Maui and flocked like so many winged thieves to the site of any moa kill.

Gulls meant land nearby, of course, as any child knew, yet what kind of land? As the canoe swept south-west, Kawiti looked for the build-up of cloud which was often associated with islands. He saw no low-lying clouds, just the same occasional high white puffs which had been their only company for days. Yet the sky to the west did look different. It had turned into a kind of blue-grey haze, instead of the usual clear blue. Strange indeed.

When they went a little further west, Kawiti realised that he could smell something. A striking, tangy odour unlike anything he had ever inhaled. Piercing, somewhat sharp, not entirely unpleasant but most definitely unfamiliar. Land had to be near, but what could produce such a sharp smell that carried over the horizon?

Soon enough, he had his answer. The azure expanse of sea was replaced by an endless stretch of brown-green land in the distance. As they drew near, it covered the entire western horizon. Not a small island, then, rather something worth discovering. Another new land, surely not as large as Te Ika a Maui, but still worth visiting.

Trees grew near to the shore along this entire coast, it seemed, but Kawiti steered the canoe toward an open expanse of sand. The canoe landed easily enough on the beach, as it was designed to do. The men quickly dragged it up past the high-water mark. No telling how long they would be here, and they could not dare lose their only way home.

"Another island of forests," Nene said. "And smell those trees!"

Kawiti could only nod. Those strange white-barked trees were the source of the odour which they had smelled even out of sight of land. They looked tall, but they were more widely-spaced than he would have expected of a forest. The ground between the trees was suspiciously empty, too. A few shrubs grew here and there, with grass elsewhere. Why hadn't those bushes grown to cover all the ground between the big whitebarks? There was light enough for them to grow, surely.

"We need to find water," he said. No stream or spring was obvious, but there had to be something. There was always water somewhere. "And somewhere to camp. And then-"

A strange man seemed to step out of the ground. A man with skin black as night itself, who had somehow concealed himself well enough that neither Kawiti nor any of his crew had noticed. The man held a spear in his hand, although he pointed it at the ground rather than Kawiti and his fellow Tangata. The black man rattled off a few words in a speech which made no sense whatsoever.

Kawiti held his right hand, face up, to show that it was empty of a weapon, then said, "We mean no harm." The words would probably mean nothing, but at least his tone should sound peaceful.

The black man flicked his head upward, as if biting at his own earlobe. A gesture of frustration, or something else? No way to know, not in this strange land. The black man wore some sort of woven cloth around his waist which went halfway to his knees, and had a head-dress of grey-brown feathers covering black, curly hair. The black man spoke again, more loudly, in words which sounded slightly different to his previous speech, but just as meaningless.

Softly, Kawiti said, "No-one raise any spears. There's five of us, and only one of him."

"Two of them, at least," Nene said. "I'm sure I saw someone else back there behind the trees."

The black man looked from one of them to the other, then thumped the butt of his spear on the ground. More black men appeared from behind trees or stood up from behind bushes which by rights were too small to conceal anyone. The other strange men came to stand beside their fellow, moving quickly but not running. They all had spears of some kind or another, and the same night-coloured skin, but there the similarities ended.

Each of the men was dressed differently. One had a feathered cloak wrapped around him, another wore the hardened leather skin of some animal about his chest in what had to be armour. When the cloak shifted on one man, Kawiti saw that the skin beneath was much lighter in colour; still darker than the colour of a Tangata, but not black. When the armoured man adjusted his spear, the skin briefly revealed beneath part of the armour had the same lighter tone. Perhaps the men had dyed their skin black.

One man, apparently the leader of the strangers, had a round shield attached to his left arm. Not made from wood, as a few of the Tangata used, but some kind of strange substance that was yellowish-brown, and *gleamed*. It looked harder than any wood, but obviously lighter than stone, from the way the black man held that shield. Belatedly, Kawiti realised that each of the black men's spears were tipped with heads not of stone, but of the same yellow-brown substance. Those heads did not have the same shine on them, but they still looked strong.

Who were these strange men?

* * *

August 1619
D'Edels Land [Western Coast of Australia]

Commander Frederik de Houtman stood on the deck of the *Dordrecht*, beneath stars which always struck him as unfamiliar. Even though he had named some of these southern constellations himself, in his voyages of half a lifetime ago, to this day he still found them strange. In the moonlight, the coastline was only a murky shadow on the eastern horizon, but its shape filled his thoughts.

For several days he had watched the shore here. It appeared so inviting, yet he had been unable to land. The roughness of the seas meant that he did not dare to let the ships go closer, not even to launch boats - if any boats would survive that treacherous surf. If his ships had not been so heavily laden with goods due in Ambon, he might have risked venturing closer. As it was, he could only wait, and consider.

He did not wish to delay for much longer, but he was intrigued, and more than intrigued. The southern route to the East Indies had only been in use for nine years, since

Hendrik Brouwer discovered the strong winds in the southern latitudes, and reduced the sailing time by two-thirds. With more ships taking that route, some of them were bound to overshoot and end up on the coast of this land. His old friend Dirck Hatichs had been the first, and left an inscribed plaque on what he had privately called a "God-forsaken stretch of emptiness." Other ships had landed here since, and said much the same thing - but none of them had come this far south.

A few days before, he had found an island he named Rottnest, for the strange rat-like creature which lived there. It hadn't been the same as the rats of the Netherlands – it didn't look quite right – but close enough for that name.

Of course, that had only been a small island. This land, Terra Australis, the unknown great southern land, seemed to be much larger. No-one knew much of anything about the people who lived here, but surely there was more of interest here than that little rat. De Houtman wondered about what lay here, but he had limits to his curiosity. He thought for a moment longer, than decided that he would wait until morning. If the seas had not calmed by then, he would give the order to turn north. With that decision made, he retired below to some well-earned sleep.

The next morning, de Houtman came out on deck and looked at calm seas. The wind had eased, although some breeze remained for the sails. The ocean swell was mild enough for him to venture close without a guilty conscience. He gave the order, and the ship came near into shore. He raised a telescope to his eye and searched the new land. He saw strange trees, some with white bark. A flock of black birds flew above them. Even through the telescope, he could not be sure, but he thought they looked like swans.

"*Black* swans?" De Houtman had been trained in logic as a child, even if he spent most of his time daydreaming, and he remember Aristotle's triumphant example of inductive reasoning. No swan should be black, but he knew what he had seen.

Further ahead, they reached an inlet, in what looked to be a river. He gave instructions, and the crew sailed into it. It clearly was a river. "The Swan River," he murmured.

*

"Commander, we found something ashore you should see," Pieter Stins said.

De Houtman looked up from his chart, shrugged, and gestured for the sailor to lead the way back to the boats.

"Ah, you might want to find yourself a musket first, sir."

"Did you find people here?" De Houtman asked. If so, the sailor should have told him at once. If they found people here whom they could trade with, the East Indies Company would forgive almost anything, including late ships.

Stins went pale beneath his sunburnt skin. "Not yet. But there must be people about, somewhere. Best if you see it for yourself."

"Wait by the boat; I'll join you in a few moments." He found another sailor, and gave a quick order. "Send this message to the *Amsterdam*: Reports of strange people on land. I am going ashore to explore." The *Amsterdam*, another one of the eleven ships in his expedition, was commanded by Jacob d'Edel, Councillor of the Indies, who despite his status had the sense to leave navigation to professionals like de Houtman.

D'Edel, in fact, was a man worthy of having his name commemorated. After a moment's thought, de Houtman wrote the name *D'Edel's Land* on the chart.

After getting himself a musket, de Houtman took a boat with a few sailors and landed on the bank of the river. Another group of a dozen sailors waited on the shore. "Where are the people?" he asked.

Stins said, "Somewhere inland, I presume, sir. Shall we go?" The sailor gestured away from the shore.

"Not so fast," de Houtman said. "Load your muskets, men," he said. The sailors did. De Houtman offered a quick prayer of thanks that his men had wheel-locks, not the old matchlock muskets that many sailors still used. He wouldn't want to face hostile natives while trying to light a fuse.

Just above the river, the low scrubs gave way to what had to be cultivation, although it looked little like any farmer's fields he knew back in the Netherlands. There were some scraggly areas of grass, but the field was dominated by a staggered series of sticks dug into the ground. As they got closer, he saw that some of the sticks were forked branches, while others had smaller sticks tied across. Vines had started to creep up the lower parts of the sticks, twirling around and extending dark-green leaves outward. The vines had also started to spread along the ground, and were beginning to shade out the grass.

"Strange plants," he murmured. Grapes were the only crop he knew of that grew on vines, and these things did not look like grapes. He wondered when they fruited.

One of the sailors said, "I've seen something like them grown in the Gold Coast [Ghana]. The roots grow large and sweet. They call them... yams, I think."

De Houtman nodded. Whether these vines were yams or not – just because something looked similar did not prove it was the same – they were obviously important to the natives. There were a *lot* of vines in this field. And that wasn't all.

"What are those trees around the edges of the fields?" he asked. Two kinds of trees, now that he looked more closely. The left and right edges of the field were marked with lines of trees that all reached to about nine feet tall, and had clearly been trimmed to keep them at that height. What looked like a shorter line of trees – large shrubs, really – marked the far end of the field. Those shrubs' lower branches had been trimmed to stop them touching the ground. And the shrubs were in the early stages of flowering, with golden blooms emerging from many of the branches.

"Another strange thing, sir," Stins said. "The seasons are backwards hereabouts. What kind of tree flowers in winter?"

"That one, I presume," de Houtman said, allowing himself a touch of irony. "Have you looked further inland?"

"Not much, sir. There's another row of fields. Do you want to explore further?"

"Is the King of Spain a bastard?" de Houtman replied. "But carefully. The natives have to be here somewhere." Wherever they were, they didn't seem to spend much time tending to these fields. Or maybe it was just the wrong time of year. Who could tell, with crops like these?

The party moved further across the fields. A few brightly-coloured birds flew up from amongst the trees at the field's edge, but de Houtman gave them little notice. They reached a couple more fields, with more of the yams or whatever those vines were planted. Each of the fields was lined with the same rows of pruned trees.

At the third field, one of the sailors called out, and gestured toward the nearest row of trees. At de Houtman's curt nod, the sailor went over and carried back a tool and a small woven basket. The tool turned out to be some kind of spade, with a narrow iron blade beaten flat and attached to a smoothed wooden handle. The basket held many small brownish-red winged seeds in the bottom.

Stins said, "Odd. Why would the natives be planting seeds when their crops are already growing?"

"No way to tell, yet," de Houtman said. "May as well put the spade and basket back; not worth taking, and it would annoy the natives for little gain."

While the first sailor was returning the goods, de Houtman led the rest for a closer look at these strange trees. The nearer trees had thorns on the branches. The trees were carefully-pruned, too. They had the look of something which had been shaped for harvest. "They look almost like olives," he said. Well, the trees themselves looked nothing like olive trees, but they were pruned to a similar height and shape to what he had seen of olives in Spain during his one visit to that country. Whatever fruit was harvested from these trees was probably gathered like olives, too. And it was obviously valued, from the way the natives had shaped these trees.

"Look up there, sir," Stins said. He indicated a hill rising above the fields. It was covered in regularly-spaced trees and shrubs. The eastern side, lit by the morning sun, had what looked to be the same kinds of trees as the thorny ones here. The western side of the hill had the shrubs, and those were blooming golden.

"Beautiful flowers," one of the sailors murmured.

"Never mind the flowers," de Houtman said, although he thought that they were an impressive sight. "Where are the natives?" They had to be somewhere nearby, if they had these fields here. "Muskets ready, men, and let's go find them."

De Houtman led the sailors further inland past the fields, looking for glimpses of the natives.

*

Marri, daughter of Yunupungu, had slept badly the previous night. A twisted night, with whispering just beyond the edge of hearing; one of the *kuru*, perhaps, cast adrift by some waves in the great water's eternity and trapped for a time on the dry mortal lands. If so, and if the *kuru* kept her awake for too much of another night, she might have to visit the triangle-keeper and find out what he could hear. Luckily, Sea-Eagle Tree was a town whose triangle-keeper had not been carried away as tribute by bearded Atjuntja warriors.

Or maybe it was her own spirit that was troubled; she had not dreamed last night, after all. Not all nights need have dreams, of course, but still, their lack could be ominous. If she had let her own spirit stray from the liquid harmony, then no amount of straining her ears for the whispers of *kuru* would prove useful.

For the morning, though, she could do nothing. If there were a *kuru*, the light of the Source would have driven it to hide within the earth, lest its essence be evaporated and returned to eternity in a myriad of raindrops. If the poor sleep was from her own troubled spirit, then she would have to find a new harmony, but that was not something that could be done in a single day, or even a week.

So, with cautious heart, Marri left town in the earliest hours of the day, to go about this day's task of checking the yam-fields. The Source had still not risen properly when she collected her shovel and basket of yam seeds and set out. The first hints of golden light were just beginning to drive away the stars as she walked past the nearer fields, and true dawn had come when she reached the fields near the ever-ocean.

She started to walk along the rows of sticks in each field, checking for any yams which had died over the winter and not regrown with the spring. She found none in the first field, which was a fortunate sign indeed. She walked between the wealth-trees to the corner of the next field, and caught a glimpse of *something* which had appeared out on the ever-ocean.

Marri stashed her shovel and basket beneath one of the wealth-trees, and crept across the fields to find a vantage point where she could watch without being seen. Two *things* had appeared out from the shore. Things like gigantic boats created by the flow of the ever-ocean itself. They had no space for oars, only what looked like an incredibly large tree growing out of the centre of each boat, with immense leaves of white rustling in the breeze. Some kind of giant white-and-blue possum scrambled amongst the leaves, climbing down the tree.

Only then did everything snap into perspective, and Marri saw that it was a man climbing down amongst the leaves. Then she saw that the boats must be a creation of men too, but much larger than any she had ever seen or heard of. Not even the finest-masted boat that travelled the great storm roads to the south could compare to these giants.

After a time, a more normal-sized boat descended from the side of these monstrosities, with men aboard. Marri moved slightly further back into the shrubs, trying to keep herself hidden. The men rowed their smaller boat to the shore and then climbed onto the sand. They were strange men indeed, with clothes of blue and white and with strange clubs of wood and iron.

The strange men started to walk inland toward the fields. Marri shadowed them, as best she could. She was no hunter born – that was the province of men – but she thought that she could still move more quietly than these stumble-footed strangers. They were men, sure enough, but like nothing she had ever seen. Beneath their clothes of blue and white, their skin was so pale, so pink and raw. Like men who had been served raw into the world rather than being baked by the Dreamers into a proper colour.

Raw Men. Yes, that was what they were. But why had these Raw Men come to these lands?

#1: Old Land, New Times

Consider, for a moment, the land which in certain times and certain places has been called Australia: smallest, driest, flattest and harshest of the globe's inhabited continents. Geologically, this is an old land, whose few once-high mountains have been eroded to mere stumps of their former selves. Long ages of weathering have worn down the mountains and borne away most of the soils into the sea. Lying mostly in the desert belts, this is a continent where the sun burns brightly and life-giving rains seldom come.

Life here would seem to be among the harshest on earth. Save for a few of the northern extremities, where monsoons bring seasonal abundance, this is a land where water is scarce. Even in those regions which are not desert, the rainfall is erratic. Some times will see year after year of punishing drought, other times will see the rain fall so quickly that floods wash away ever more of what remains of the thin soils. Every summer, the scorching heat brings the season of bushfires which sweep across vast areas of the continent, consuming everything in their path.

Yet despite the rigours and trials of this harshest of continents, it has been inhabited for tens of thousands of years. Aboriginal peoples have made it their home for millennia, adapting their lifestyles to suit the land, while also changing the land to suit their lifestyles. Their methods of managing the land are different to what many peoples on other continents call farming, but these methods produce plentiful food to suit their needs.

Among other methods, they have mastered the use of fire as a system of land management. They have long burned the bush regularly in patterns which fit their needs, creating open woodlands and grasslands to feed the kangaroos which are their prime game animal. The patterns of fire changed the nature of the continent's flora, burning out some plants and encouraging others. The towering, fire-loving gum trees will become the most well-known of these plants, but there are many others. Regular burning encourages the growth of plants which store nutrients below the ground in the form of tubers, bulbs or tuberous roots, since these let the plants quickly regrow into land which has been fertilised by wood ash and cleared of competition. Aboriginal peoples value these plants, since their underground stores are tasty, easily harvested, and a reliable source of food over most of the year.

For despite living in such a rigorous land, Aboriginal peoples have acquired the knowledge they need to survive here, and survive easily. Fire-created grasslands and woodland allow them to hunt for an abundance of kangaroo. If the hunt fails, one person can spend three or four hours digging for tubers and find enough food to feed a family for a whole day.

Yet for all their extensive knowledge of the plants of this land, the Aboriginal peoples' methods of land management are not the same as the traditional methods of farming used on other continents. They manage the land in a manner which sustains their lifestyle, but they have not domesticated any of the native plants. Some writers have deemed that the flora of this continent lacks plants with the necessary range of qualities to develop a system of agriculture and domesticated plants.

Yet this need not always be so.

Consider the river which in a particular time and place is called the River Murray. Fed by rainwater and snowmelt in the highest reaches of Australia's remaining mountains, this river flows for 2500 kilometres until it empties into a complex system of lakes, sand dunes, saltwater lagoons and

sand bars called the Murray Mouth. The Murray a[nd its]
tributaries drain a seventh of Australia's land su[rface,]
making it by far the largest river system on this
continent. Most of the basin is flat and not far abov[e sea]
level. The rivers that meander through this basin [flow]
slowly for most times of the year, except when rising i[n one]
of the irregular floods. After extended droughts, [the]
Murray tributaries have been known to dry up complet[ely.]

Yet by Australian standards, this is a well-watered [land,]
the heartland of a region which is the breadbasket of
modern Australia. It held the same fertility since long
before white men first visited this land where water means
life. The early white explorers who ventured along the
Murray wrote of seeing acre after acre of wild "yam fields"
encouraged by Aboriginal peoples who managed the land to
suit these plants. These peoples harvested tubers for food,
often leaving part of the tubers in the earth so that the
plants would regrow and there would be more food next
time. In places, the earth was so full of holes from their
digging that explorers found it too dangerous to take horses
across.

Imagine now, for a moment, what could happen if
history were to be turned back and allowed to move in a
new direction. Look far enough back into the long-
vanished past, and you might see a new plant arise along
the Nyalananga [Murray River]. A new breed of yam, a
plant much like its historical forebears, but whose qualities
have altered in a few ways. The most obvious change is
that the white-yellow flesh of these yams has changed to
orange-red. Their tubers grow slightly larger than their
forebears, and the plants are quicker-growing, with larger
leaves. In time, this new breed of yam spreads throughout
much of the Nyalananga Valley, displacing the other kinds
of yams which grow in this region.

This change happens long before the ancestors of the
Aboriginal peoples arrive on this continent's shores. The
newcomers reach this land some time at least forty
thousand years ago, when the sea levels are lower, and

make landfall on a place which has now been concealed beneath the waves. From here, they quickly spread out across the continent, in time reaching the Nyalananga where the red yams grow. They quickly discover the value of the red yam, and it becomes one of the common plants they gather.

The time when the ancestors of the Aboriginal peoples arrive in this continent is a time of glaciers, lower sea levels and climatic instability. Like humans across the rest of the world, Aboriginal peoples will maintain a hunter-gatherer lifestyle until the glaciers start to melt, sea levels begin to rise, and the climate enters a period of relative stability known as the Holocene.

In this new era, people around the world who are gathering wild plants create changes to many of them, in processes which will end in domesticated plants and independent origins of agriculture. First among these will be in the lands which will later be called the Fertile Crescent, where an abundance of founder crops such as emmer and einkorn wheat, barley, peas, chickpeas, lentils, bitter vetch and flax means a very early development of agriculture. Peoples in other parts of the world will develop agriculture independently, with the speed of their development related to how easily domesticable their founder crops are. In China, in the New Guinea highlands, in Africa, the Andes, Mesoamerica and along the Mississippi, agriculture will develop independently. In other regions, agriculture will spread from its first point of origin, until agricultural societies are spread around most of the globe.

Along the Nyalananga, Aboriginal peoples make increasing use of the red yam. Its large, nutritious tubers are a valuable component of their diet. They harvest the yam tubers each year, and leave parts of the tubers in the ground to ensure that there is more food for next year's harvest. Slowly, they take control of its breeding, until with the passing of generations they develop forms of the red yam which are spread exclusively by human activity. They have created Australia's first domesticated crop.

* * *

The red yam (*Dioscorea chelidonius*) is a plant which evolved in allohistorical Australia, and which is unknown in real history. Like most yams, this is a vine with a large, starchy, tuberous root. The vine itself is a perennial plant, with well-established roots. The above-ground portions of the plant often die back in winter, with regrowth in spring or after bushfires.

Like many related *Dioscorea* species, the red yam is domesticable. Like a much smaller number of yam species (such as white and yellow yams from Africa), the red yam is also suitable as a founder crop. That is, a plant which can be independently domesticated even in a region which has no pre-existing agriculture. Founder crops are much rarer than domesticable crops; the real, historical Australia has plenty of the latter but none of the former. Agriculture can't get started without founder crops, no matter how many other domesticable plants may happen to be in a region. Without founder crops, there will be no agriculture in a region unless farming and crops spread from elsewhere.

The particular mutation which has happened in red yams is polyploidy. In this mutation, the entire genome of an organism is duplicated. Polyploidy is generally associated with lusher and more vigorous growth, particularly in domesticated (or domesticable) plants. For example, many of the domesticated forms of wheat and bananas are polyploid.

Events of polyploidy happens reasonably often. This can create a new species in one generation, since a polyploid plant is not fertile with its parent plants, but is fertile with other polyploid mutants from the former species. There have been documented instances of polyploid species arising in different regions and being fertile with the new polyploid plants from different regions, but not with their own parents.

Polyploid plants often have evolutionary advantages, since they possess multiple copies of the same genes, which can evolve in different directions. This led to a greater range of traits within red yams, and in time meant that they were a suitable plant to be domesticated.

Polyploidy is more likely to create new species in plants which can self-pollinate (like wheat) than in plants which have separate male and female plants (such as most yams). However, it can still create new species if a male and female plant both turn polyploid in the same area, and if one fertilises the other. In allohistorical Australia, events diverged from real history when two yams turned polyploid near each other, fertilised each other, and created a new species.

#2: What Grows From The Earth

Think not of the present time, but of an older era. Step back in time, if you wish, to the time six thousand years before the birth of a man whom the world's largest religion will credit with being divine. Far from the place of this birth, in the continent which will much later be named Aururia [Australia], live a great many peoples. Long before the peoples along the Nyalananga discovered how to make the earth bear regular bounties of red yams, one other people had developed their own method of farming. A method which did not involve growing plants, but rather farming eels.

The Junditmara people live in a region which in another time and place would have been called south-western Victoria. Their home country includes areas of natural wetlands, but what is found there now is far from natural. The Junditmara have transformed the landscape to suit their needs. They construct stone dams and weirs across rivers and streams, creating man-made ponds and expanding existing swamps. They dig channels through rock and earth to join the ponds and lakes into a complex system of waterways. These waterways are naturally abundant in fish, but the Junditmara do not stop there. From the nearby ocean, they catch young eels which they release into the waterways. These eels grow for up to twenty years, and are then harvested in woven baskets which form eel traps.

The Junditmara have, in fact, developed a system of aquaculture. The eel harvests are abundant and predictable enough to let them develop a sedentary lifestyle. They have no need to move around in search of food. With the harvests of eels, hunting of eggs and waterbirds, and collection of edible plant roots and tubers which grow along the fringes of the waters, they have more than enough food to sustain their population. Indeed, the Junditmara have such a surplus of eels that they smoke eel meat for later consumption or as a desirable trade good that is sent along trade routes that stretch for hundreds of kilometres.

For in Junditmara country, Australia has its first people who build in stone. Junditmara society is a complex of hierarchical chiefdoms, with chiefs controlling the lives of their peoples, assigning them to roles and arranging all their marriages. The chiefdoms sit on a confluence of trade routes; the Junditmara export smoked eel meat and possum-skin coats, and import quartz, flints and some high-quality timber which cannot be found in their own country. Collectively, the Junditmara chiefdoms oversee the lives of some ten thousand people[1].

Forget for a moment the Junditmara living alongside their waterways and look further north, to the peoples who live along the Nyalananga. When last we looked at them, the peoples of the Nyalananga had been harvesting red yams from the wild and turning them into Aururia's first domesticated crop. With the red yam, they have learned the idea of farming. This is not enough to turn them into full-time agriculturalists, not by itself, but it is a beginning.

The gradual domestication of the red yam has turned these peoples from hunter-gatherers into hunter-gardeners. They hunt and fish for food, they gather other wild plants,

---

[1] The changed history of Aururia has led to different events and in time, different peoples. Cultures, languages and beliefs across the continent have changed compared to their historical counterparts. The lands which the Junditmara inhabit in this history were in real history inhabited by a group of cultures variously called Dhauwurd Wurrung or Gunditjmara. The historical people had similar practices of creating artificial wetlands and farming eels.

and they have established gardens of red yams which they plant and tend.

Still, red yams alone are not sufficient to let them maintain permanent settlements. Wild yam tubers can be stored for up to nine months; not enough to form a year-round store of food. Instead, the peoples of the Nyalananga have established gathering places where they assemble and reside for up to nine months out of each year. During that time, they live together in organised groups of hundreds of people. For the remainder of the year, they disperse into smaller groups to hunt and gather wild foods.

Of course, these societies are not static. The population of the Nyalananga peoples grows, and they start to develop new tools, new social structures, and new beliefs. With their growing population comes more contact with their neighbours outside the Nyalananga Valley. Ancient trade routes connect the Nyalananga Valley with regions both to the north and south. In a land without beasts of burden or good roads, most trade goods are passed between many hands rather than having one person move along the length of a trade route, but where goods move, sometimes ideas do, too.

One of the major trade routes is to Junditmara country, far to the south. This brings in eel meat and other goods, but it also gives opportunity for travellers. With the increasing population of the Nyalananga peoples, some of them visit their neighbours, and in time travellers bring back tales of the elaborate dams, weirs and channels of the Nyalananga chiefdoms. And with these tales comes inspiration.

For one of the Nyalananga peoples call themselves the Gunnagal[2]. Their country is around where the Anerina [River Loddon] flows into the Nyalananga. They call this

---

[2] In keeping with the changed peoples within Aururia, the Gunnagal are not the same culture who lived there historically. The real historical inhabitants of Swan Hill and the surrounding country were the Wemba-Wemba people.

place Tjibarr. In another history this locality would see the founding of a town called Swan Hill. The town would have been named for a lagoon at the joining of the two rivers, which teemed with so many waterfowl that the first European explorers who visited there could not sleep properly at night, even though they were camped half a mile away.

The Gunnagal know nothing of these explorers in a time-that-was-not, but they do know of the lagoon that is one of their richer sources of food. Inspired by travellers' tales, and with a population boosted by farming red yams, the Gunnagal begin constructing works of their own. They do not have the same bountiful rain which feeds the waterways of the Junditmara, but they do have a river which floods prodigiously if irregularly. With stone, wood and determination, they create their own systems of ponds and lagoons, connected with channels to the Nyalananga and the Anerina. In most times those channels are dry, but when the rivers rise they bring enough water to the new ponds and lagoons to sustain them as standing water.

With the new waterworks, the Gunnagal have a greatly expanded source of food. In the lagoons they hunt for swans, ducks and other waterbirds. In the waters, they lay traps to catch a variety of fish[3]. Around the watery fringes, they harvest plants with edible tubers and leaves. On the nearby fields, they farm red yams, and in the more distant reaches, they hunt kangaroos and gather wild plants.

Like the Junditmara before them, the Gunnagal have established a lifestyle which allows them to maintain permanent settlements. Unlike the Junditmara, the Gunnagal live on a river system where these practices can spread over a wide distance. For with the establishment of yams and fishing, of agriculture and aquaculture, the

---

[3] The most common species of fish they catch are Murray cod (*Maccullochella peelii*), golden perch (*Macquaria ambigua*), and Australian smelt (*Retropinna semoni*), but there are many others.

Gunnagal will develop the first year-round settlement large enough to be called a city. As a people, they understand the principles of farming, and with their continued gathering of a wide range of wild plants, they can turn their attention to domesticating other Aururian plants.

That is, if there are any other Aururian plants which can be domesticated.

* * *

It has been claimed that the Australian continent lacks any domesticable plants apart from the macadamia nut. This claim has the advantage of being simple, easy to repeat, and offers a plausible explanation for why Australia did not develop any full-scale indigenous agriculture. This claim has only one major disadvantage: it is completely wrong.

For several Australian native plants have, in fact, been domesticated. While today the most widely-known native Australian domesticate is the macadamia, other Australian native plants were domesticated much earlier. The first such domesticate was the plant which today is marketed in Australia as Warrigal greens (*Tetragonia tetragonoides*), and which has been variously called Botany Bay greens, Australian spinach, New Zealand spinach, and Cook's cabbage. This plant was brought from Australia and established in Britain in the later eighteenth century as a domesticated vegetable. It is harvested as a root vegetable and used much like spinach.

Another Australian plant was also taken to Britain and became domesticated. The mountain pepper (*Tasmannia lanceolata*), a plant with peppery-flavoured leaves and berries, was established in Cornwall and domesticated under the name 'Cornish pepperleaf.' The cereal weeping rice (*Microlaena stipoides*) has recently been turned into a domesticated crop. Recent selective breeding efforts have also produced domesticated strains of several Australian fruits, such as quandong (*Santalum acuminatum*), muntries (*Kunzea pomifera*), and various native Australian *Citrus* species (relatives of oranges and limes).

More intriguingly, there are several domesticable plant species which are native both to Australia and nearby parts of Southeast Asia. The water chestnut (*Eleocharis dulcis*) is an aquatic vegetable which is native to China, Southeast Asia and northern Australia, and which was domesticated in China. Two species of yams (*Dioscorea alata* and *D. bulbifera*) were likewise native both to Southeast Asia and northern Australia, and were domesticated in the former, but not the latter. Common purslane (*Portulaca oleracea*) is a succulent plant widespread in Australia and much of the Old World, was domesticated on multiple occasions in several parts of the world as a leaf vegetable, yet was not domesticated in Australia. All of these plants are clearly domesticable, were known and used by Aboriginal peoples within Australia as wild-harvested sources of food, and yet were not domesticated on Australia's shores[4].

More intriguingly still, Australia possesses native plants which are easily cultivated into staple crops. Trees of the genus *Acacia* are widespread throughout the tropics and subtropics of the globe, and are abundant in Australia. The Australian acacias, usually called wattles, are well-adapted to the harsh conditions and are widespread throughout the continent. They produce large quantities of edible seeds which are collected by Aboriginal peoples as a rich source of food. Recently, several species of wattles were introduced into various parts of tropical Africa (*Acacia colei, A. torulosa, A. tumida, A. elachantha* and *A. saligna*). The seeds from these wattles are being increasingly adopted

---

[4] There are several domesticable plant species which are common both to northern Australia and parts of Southeast Asia, and which were probably carried between the two regions by birds. The plants listed above are those which are known to have been present in Australia before European contact and which were used by Aboriginal peoples. There may well have been others (e.g. the domesticable herb and leaf vegetable common self-heal, *Prunella vulgaris*), but it's not always clear whether these arrived before or after European contact.

as staple crops, and domesticated strains of wattles have been developed.

In short, Australia has a variety of domesticable plants, including some which have recently been domesticated or which were domesticated millennia ago elsewhere in the world. Given this, the question which naturally arises is why these plants were not domesticated within Australia itself over the last few thousand years.

The answer lies in the fact that there is a distinction between domesticable plants and founder crops. Domesticable plants are any plants which can be bred to human uses, but most of them first require a human population to be at least semi-sedentary and acquainted with the concept of farming. Founder crops are much rarer plants, since they possess appropriate qualities (either alone, or in a package with other crops) to enable people to move from a hunter-gatherer lifestyle to a farming lifestyle.

Domesticable plants are relatively common throughout the world; founder crops are much rarer, and they need to become established first before many other plants can be domesticated. The quintessential founder crops were found in the Middle East, which possessed eight Neolithic founder crops which allowed agriculture to be established there. Founder crops were also found elsewhere in the world, although in most cases they needed longer to domesticate than in the Middle East[5]. Notably, however, the Middle East possessed several domesticable plants which were not domesticated until well after the Neolithic founder crops. Plants such as olives and date palms were domesticable, but the process took several thousand years after agriculture had already started.

---

[5] Independent agriculture has arisen in a number of areas: definitely in Mesoamerica, China (at least once), New Guinea, the Andes, West Africa (at least once) and in eastern North America. It is also quite likely to have arisen independently in Ethiopia, in two locations in China and West Africa, and possibly in India. There have been a variety of founder crops in these areas; potatoes, squash, sunflowers, millets, sorghum and rice, among others.

In Australia, historically, there were no founder crops. Australia possessed several domesticable crops, including some yams which were domesticated elsewhere in the world once agriculture had started, but never in Australia. Some yams are suitable as founder crops, such as the white and yellow yams of West Africa (*Dioscorea rotunda* and *D. cayenensis*, respectively), but others are not.

In allohistorical Aururia, the red yam (*Dioscorea chelidonius*) is a suitable founder crop. It is not enough to form a complete diet in itself, but it is enough to encourage a semi-sedentary lifestyle and an understanding of the principles of farming. This leads to a stationary population who are still gathering wild plants as a significant component of their diet, which in turn means that more plants will be domesticated[6]. In time, this will lead to the development of a full Aururian agricultural package of crops, and farming cultures will follows from that.

---

[6] In real history, recent domestication efforts for Australian native plants have needed to compete with long-established domesticated plants from elsewhere around the world. This is often a difficult challenge. The establishment of new fruit crops is hard, for instance, because wild fruits are usually small and have irregular yields. Domesticated fruit plants have had thousands of years of selective breeding for larger size and improved flavour. Despite this, some Australian plant species have been domesticated. Naturally, if agricultural cultures had been in Australia for longer, they would have domesticated a greater range of crops since they would not have the same competition from overseas crops.

#3: Yams of Red, Trees of Gold

Picture a time four and a half thousand years ago in a history that never was, then picture a place along the banks of the river that is here called the Nyalananga. Along this river, in the region that is here called Tjibarr, live a people called the Gunnagal. Like many of their neighbours along this river, the Gunnagal have domesticated a plant called the red yam. An extremely valuable source of food, this crop has let the Gunnagal and other river peoples become hunter-gardeners. They establish seasonal settlements along the river to live off their yam harvest for up to nine months, then disperse for the remaining months to live off what they can hunt, fish, and gather from the earth.

Beyond their lives as hunters and gardeners, the Gunnagal people have developed new methods. Inspired by travellers' stories of the distant Junditmara chiefdoms, the Gunnagal have turned their attention to expanding their natural lagoon into a system of wetlands. From this, they harvest fish and water plants. So successful are the Gunnagal that they can live year-round in stone dwellings and enjoy an abundance of food. With their harvests of yam and fish, they have no need to wander seasonally.

From their first settlements, the Gunnagal begin to expand along the river, bringing their methods of yam- and fish-harvesting with them. They have food, they have numbers, they have prestige, and they displace and absorb many of their neighbouring river peoples. Along a length of the river of some eight hundred kilometres, the Gunnagal language becomes a *lingua franca*, and their culture becomes predominant. Not all of their neighbours have been expelled, but those who remain do so because they have taken up Gunnagal farming and fishing methods, and in time their speech and many of their beliefs.

Along the river, amidst the expanded country of the Gunnagal, people still gather wild plants to supplement their regular sources of food. They have knowledge of farming, now, and a sedentary lifestyle which inclines them to replant their most favoured wild foods rather than keep moving in search of new food supplies. Selective human gathering of favoured plants started even before the Gunnagal adopted a fully sedentary lifestyle, and in time this process leads to the domestication of other crops.

* * *

The early Aururian agricultural package consists of several plants which are native to the Nyalananga, and which have good potential for domestication:

The red yam (*Dioscorea chelidonius*) is a perennial vine. The foliage usually dies back over winter and regrows in spring, although the leaves sometimes remains year-round in warmer and wetter climates. Red yams produce an edible, slightly sweet tuber as a food store. The tubers are formed quite deep in the ground (up to a metre down), and so take a reasonable amount of digging to extract, but they are large enough to justify the effort. In their wild state red yam tubers can grow up to 1 kg in weight (or more in wet years); domesticated red yam tubers are often much larger. Domesticated red yams have been artificially selected both for larger tubers and for a sweeter taste[7].

---

[7] Selection for relatively sweeter varieties is common to a lot of domesticated varieties of plants. This has an additional benefit of providing a higher nutritional yield for the domesticated yams, since more of the tuber is formed from digestible starch rather than water or indigestible fibre. Domesticated varieties of red yams have a lower water content (which means that they store longer) and it also means that they provide a higher calorie intake per unit of weight.

Like many (but not all) Aururian wild yam species, red yams can be eaten raw but are usually roasted or cooked in other ways. In culinary terms, the red yam can be cooked in a variety of ways similar to the potato or sweet potato. It is a staple crop which for most people forms over half of their daily calorie intake. Red yams are native to the central Nyalananga Valley, but domesticated forms can be grown without too much difficulty in regions of adequate rainfall between latitudes of about 25 to 45 degrees. Cultivation of red yams at more tropical latitudes is impossible, at least for current cultivars, because the plants cannot adapt to tropical growing seasons and are also less tolerant of high humidity[8].

Wattles (Aururian species of the genus *Acacia*) are a diverse group of shrubs and trees with nearly a thousand species across the continent. Wattles are fast-growing, can tolerate extended periods of drought, and grow even in poor soils. Indeed, they are legumes whose roots provide nitrates to revitalise the soil. They produce large numbers of protein- and vitamin-rich seeds which are a valuable source of food. Wattle seeds are pseudocereals; while not true cereals, their seeds can be used in a similar manner.

---

[8] The red yam has evolved into a form which is well-suited to the periodic droughts and semi-arid conditions along the Middle Nyalananga. The most important of these is that red yams have evolved a process called crassulacean acid metabolism (CAM), which allows plants to store atmospheric carbon dioxide in their leaves at night, and then photosynthesise during the day. This means that CAM plants keep the stomata in their leaves closed during the heat of the day, and lose much less water than non-CAM plants. This makes red yams well-suited for semi-arid conditions, and combined with their deep roots, makes them resistant even to long and persistent droughts. CAM photosynthesis comes at a price, however; CAM plants are less efficient at absorbing atmospheric carbon dioxide. This means that in areas which do have higher rainfall, the red yam is likely to be out-competed by non-CAM plants. Thus, the red yam does not grow naturally in the wetter areas of Aururia's eastern coast, although domesticated red yams can grow there provided that the soil is well-drained. (Red yams, like other yam species, do not tolerate waterlogged soils very well.)

Wattle seeds also remain viable for many years; over twenty years for some species.

The early Gunnagal domesticate three main species of wattle, the mystery wattle (*Acacia difformis*), the bramble wattle (*A. victoriae*) and the golden wattle (*A. pycnantha*). Domesticated wattles are distinguished from wild varieties by having larger seeds, more regular yields from year to year, and also for flowering reliably at around the same time each year. While each individual wattle species has its own qualities[9], their main uses are similar. Wattle seeds are used similarly to cereal grains such as wheat or barley; the seeds are ground into flour for baking into flatbreads, cakes and similar products. They have a much higher protein content than cereal grains, which is particularly valuable in a society which does not have many domesticated animals. They are extremely important as a food reserve; the long life of wattle seeds means that they are ideal for storage until drought years.

---

[9] The first domesticated wattle, the mystery wattle (*Acacia difformis*), grows in the old Gunnagal homelands around Tjibarr. As the Gunnagal expand west along the Nyalananga, they domesticate the tree variously known as bramble wattle, gundabluey or elegant wattle (*A. victoriae*). As they move east along the Nyalananga, they domesticate the golden wattle (*A. pycnantha*). These three wattles form the early domesticated wattle species, although other wattles will be domesticated elsewhere in Aururia when agriculture spreads.

Of the early domesticated species, bramble wattle is tolerant of a very wide range of soil and weather conditions, grows very quickly, and usually produces the overall largest yield of seeds even in drought years. Mystery wattle produces a sizable seed yield, with very large individual seeds which are easy to harvest from their pods, tolerates a range of harsh conditions, and produces large quantities of edible gum. Golden wattle produces a tolerable crop of seeds, but it is slower-growing, and when grown in close cultivation, is more vulnerable to pests, disease and death. Domesticated golden wattles are usually planted alongside the edges of yam fields rather across whole fields. Golden wattles are on the whole less reliable as a source of food, but they have the advantage of growing much taller than other domesticates wattles, which makes them a source of longer timber. Golden wattle bark is also the richest source of tannins and provides the greatest volume of fibre.

Apart from their seeds, domesticated wattles have many other uses. They grow very quickly and can be used as a valuable source of timber. Wattle bark produces fibre which can be used for rope and clothing, and also contains tannins which can be used to tan animal leather. Their roots replenish the nitrate content of the soil, which means that they can be used in a system of crop rotation or companion planting alongside red yams and other crops. The empty seed pods and dead leaves of wattles can be used similarly as compost or mulch to maintain soil fertility; they are often mixed back in with the replaced soil after yam tubers have been dug out. Wattles produce a very useful gum, which is sweet and edible either immediately or dried as stored food. The gum also has many other uses, such as being added to water to make a sweet drink, sometimes used as a kind of candy, or for non-food uses such as an adhesive or binding agent in paints[10]. Even the pests of wattles have their uses; the galls formed by wattle pests are edible, as are the witchetty grubs which burrow into wattle trunks and roots. In time, domesticated wattles become as important to the Nyalananga civilization as the olive tree is for Mediterranean peoples, or the date palm is in Mesopotamia; the Gunnagal word for wattles, *butitju*, will also become the root of their words for "wealth" and "prosperity."

Murnong or yam daisy (*Microseris lanceolata*) is a perennial flowering plant which produces an edible radish-shaped tuber. Like the red yam, murnong has perennial rootstock but its above-ground foliage usually dies back every winter. Murnong tubers are much smaller than those of red yams, but murnong can be grown much closer together, and their tubers are nearer to the surface and thus require less digging. Wild murnong has one or two tubers,

---

[10] Wattle gum is similar to gum arabic, although true gum arabic comes from related African *Acacia* species (*A. senegal* and *A. seyal*).

while some domesticated varieties will have four or eight tubers.

For culinary purposes, murnong tubers are treated similarly to the red yam or more familiar crops such as potatoes. In most areas, domesticated murnong are a secondary crop when compared to red yams. They do not produce as high a food yield per hectare, but add different flavours to the diet. It is customary to have some land under murnong cultivation in case disease or pests affect the main yam harvest. In the highland areas of south-eastern Aururia, murnong will become a more important crop since hybrids with the related alpine murnong (*M. scapigera*) are better suited to upland growing conditions than most red yam cultivars.

Purslane (*Portulaca oleracea*) is a succulent annual flowering plant which tolerates a wide variety of soil conditions, and is resistant to drought. The leaves, seeds, stems and flowers are all edible. Purslane is abundant throughout mainland Aururia and much of the Old World. It has been independently domesticated on multiple occasions throughout the world. Amongst the Gunnagal, multiple varieties have been developed. Some cultivars are grown as leaf vegetables; the leaves can be harvested all year round and are a useful source of some vitamins and essential dietary minerals. Other cultivars are grown primarily for their edible seeds, which are ground into flour and used for similar purposes as wattleseed flour.

Spiny-headed mat-rush (*Lomandra longifolia*) is a perennial sedge-like plant, with many stiff leaves that grow close together and are suitable for weaving. Mat-rush is a hardy plant which can tolerate a wide variety of soils and weather conditions. Domesticated mat-rush is grown primarily as a vegetable fibre to make baskets, nets and the like. Mat-rush is occasionally used as a source of food during lean times; its seeds and the base of its leaves are edible, and its flowers are a source of nectar, but its primary role is as a non-food fibre crop.

Scrub nettle (*Urtica incisa*) is a relative of the stinging nettle (*U. dioica*) of North America and Europe. It is a perennial plant which dies back to the ground every winter. As with its northern hemisphere relative, the leaves and flowers of scrub nettle are covered with hollow hairs loaded with formic acid, which produces a nasty stinging reaction if it comes into contact with the skin. The main use of domesticated scrub nettle is harvesting high-quality fibre from its stems, which is mostly used to make textiles, ropes and other cordage. Scrub nettle is occasionally used as a vegetable, too; its leaves are tasty and quite nutritious, provided that they are cooked first to neutralise the formic acid.

Native flax (*Linum marginale*) is a close relative of common flax (*L. usitatissimum*). Native flax is a perennial plant which, like many Aururian plants, often dies back during winter. The wild version has long been used by Aboriginal peoples as a source of fibre and for its edible seeds. Domesticated native flax, like common flax, is used as a source of fibre for textiles; the Gunnagal will rely on linen for most of their clothing and other weaving. The seeds are edible on their own or sometimes added to wattleseed flour. They are also used to make linseed oil, although this needs to be managed carefully since once extracted the oil has a short shelf life under Aururian conditions.

Tufted bluebell (*Wahlenbergia communis*) is a perennial wildflower which produces bright blue flowers which are edible. The plant persists for five or more years, making it a useful low-labour crop. The Gunnagal sometimes consume the flowers directly, but their more common practice is to boil the petals in water to produce what they call blue-water. This is used for a variety of purposes, such as a sweetener in cooking, for medicinal and cosmetic purposes, and later as the basis of some perfumes.

* * *

The Aururian agricultural package has quite a different range of characteristics from most other agricultural packages which have arisen from other independent origins of agriculture[11]. Perhaps the most noteworthy of those is that all of the staple crops, apart from the relatively minor purslane, are perennial plants. That is, they are planted once and then produce a harvest each year for a number of years. This is in contrast to most of the staple crops grown around the globe today and historically, which are annual plants, that is, planted, harvested once, then they die or are removed.

Annual plants are the basis of most modern agriculture. Staple crops such as wheat, barley, maize, rice, and potatoes[12] are all harvested as annual plants. Annual plants have a variety of advantages which have made them easy to domesticate and then use. As annual plants, they have a fast generation time which enables selective breading to happen more rapidly. There are a wide variety of annual plants which are domesticable and offer good food yields. In particular, there are many annual cereal crops which produce grains which can be stored for several years, which is vital for preventing famine during drought. Moreover,

---

[11] Collectively, the Aururian agricultural package is most-suited to latitudes between 25 to 45 degrees at low altitudes, with long-term rainfall between 300 to 500 millimetres. Their nature as perennials means that rain does not need to fall in a particular season; the plants can cope with irregular rainfall. Established plants can tolerate drought reasonably well, although a prolonged drought is likely to mean that new plantings do not grow. Growing the full package of crops with long-term rainfall below 300 millimetres is marginal; the main crops will tolerate areas where the long-term rainfall is anything above about 250 millimetres, although the yields will be lower. Rainfall above 500 millimetres can be tolerated, and to a degree this will increase the yield, but soils need to be well-drained; waterlogged soils will cause problems for yams, in particular. The plants grow best at low altitudes, although they can be grown at higher elevations, particularly at latitudes between 25 and 30 degrees. Some of the domesticated plants can grow at lower (tropical) latitudes, particularly the bramble wattle, but the early agricultural package as a whole does not grow well in tropical latitudes.

[12] Potatoes are actually perennial, but are usually grown as annuals.

with an annual plant, if the harvest is lost due to disease, drought, flood, fire or warfare, then only a single year's production has been lost, and it can be replanted next year.

However, annual plants also have a number of disadvantages. They have quite high labour requirements, since the soil needs to be plowed and plants resown every year. The type of soil cover used with annual plants – light roots, soil often exposed to the weather during planting – means that topsoil erosion and other environmental damage is quite likely. The soil loss is often severe enough that annual crops can no longer be reliably grown. For example, the Greek highlands were originally deforested to plant wheat and barley. After the topsoil was mostly washed away, farmers there switched to perennials such as grapes and olives. Similar processes caused desertification in much of what used to be the Fertile Crescent. Apart from these problems, many annual crops also have to retain a considerable part of each harvest as seed for next year; in classical harvests of barley, wheat and other small grains, up to half the harvest had to be kept as seed grain.

While annual plants have been the foundation of most agriculture, there is a potential alternative. Some perennial plants also offer rich sources of food. As crops, they have several advantages over annual plants. The labour requirements for collecting food are much lower, since there is no need to plow and replant each year. Perennial plants also have established root structures which allow them to take advantage of out-of-season rains or the standing water table, which is very useful in drought-prone areas such as Aururia. The same established root structures, combined with much more limited plowing, and more frequent (often permanent) plant cover means that the soil takes much less damage. Since perennials do not need yearly planting, it also means that there is no need to retain large amounts of each year's harvest for seed crops.

Nonetheless, perennial plants also have some significant disadvantages. There are not as many easily domesticable perennial crops. This problem is compounded because the longer generation time of perennial plants means that it takes longer to selectively breed new strains. Many perennial crops produce food which is difficult to store long enough for the next harvest; fruits are tasty but hard to preserve, as are many root crops. Probably the biggest disadvantage is the longer growing time for most perennial plants. If an annual crop is lost, more can be replanted for next year's harvest, and a society has lost only one year's worth of food. If a perennial crop is lost through warfare, raids, or fires, it may take many years for the trees to regrow. This may make it difficult for a perennial agricultural society to feed itself in the interim.

For these reasons, it seems that perennials are rarely used as staple crops, despite the considerable labour savings. There are a few perennial crops which have been used as staple crops, such as plantains and breadfruit, but these have usually had a limited distribution. Most agricultural societies have used annuals as their main staples, with perennial crops such as fruit trees taking on a supplementary role rather than providing the bulk of people's daily calorie intake. There have been occasional societies which have used perennials as their main source of food, such as parts of Sardinia which used chestnuts.

The perennials which are grown in Aururian agriculture have some traits which minimise many of the disadvantages of perennial crops elsewhere. These plants are relatively quick-growing. Red yams and murnong can both be planted in one year to be harvested in the same year, then keep on producing a fresh tuber every year. Wattles grow quickly enough that they start to yield useful harvests of seeds within two to four years. Wattle seeds are also excellent as a food reserve for long-term storage.

Aururian perennials are also well-adapted for recovering from damage, thanks to evolving on a landscape regularly visited by flood and fire. Yams already die back during winter and regrow in spring, and they can recover from fire in the same way. Wattles have the ability to regrow from their roots after fire or other damage, which will mean that domesticated wattles can regrow if raids by neighbours means that the trees are burnt or cut down.

The nature of Aururian perennials also means that their farming methods are quite different from early farming methods elsewhere around the globe. The overall labour requirements for Aururian farming are lower than for most agricultural systems with annual crops. As perennials, there is minimal need for plowing. Wattles and yams are harvested at different times of the year[13], which means that farmers can rotate their work between crops without too much difficulty, and there is not the same intensity required to have all available workers available to help during the harvest. Outside of harvest time, Aururian crops still need some ongoing tending – pruning of trees, tapping of gum, replacing individual plants when they die, and the like – but this can be spaced out over most of the year.

Overall, the perennial nature of Aururian agriculture means that its farmers have a much higher food yield per worker than with most annual crops. Living in a dry and uncertain climate as they do, they do not have a particularly high yield per hectare, but individual farmers are quite productive. This makes it easier for them to accumulate food surpluses for storage. In turn, this allows Aururian farming societies to sustain a much larger percentage of their population as urban dwellers than in most early agricultural societies. Most early agriculture needed ten or more rural farmers to support one non-farmer, be it a smith or a priest. Australian perennial agriculture means that

---

[13] Aururian wattles as a group flower year-round; there is almost no time when there is not a wattle blooming somewhere on the continent. However, the domesticated wattles fall into two main divisions. Early-flowering wattles (such as mystery wattle) flower around August-September, and their seeds are harvested around October-November. Late-flowering wattles (such as bramble wattle) flower around November-December, and their seeds are harvested around January-February. Red yams and murnong are harvested in late autumn, around April-May.

only four or five farmers are needed to support non-farmers. This means that they can support more specialists, more division of labour, and, in time, much more besides.

#4: What Lies Beneath The Earth

Archaeology, it has been said is the Peeping Tom of the sciences. It is the sandbox of men who care not where they are going; they merely want to know where everyone else has been[14].

When the time comes for future archaeologists to fossick through the buried remnants of Gunnagalic culture – the Nyalananga Valley Civilization – they will discover a great many things. They will find a series of settlements, some large, some small, some ephemeral, some built to endure. They will argue over the details, placing too much emphasis on some, and disregarding others. They will understand some things correctly, and others they will misinterpret. But in time, a picture of sorts will emerge, a story complete with stratigraphy, estimated and often disputed dates, some accurate observations and some misconceptions.

The first phase of the Nyalananga Valley civilization is what future archaeologists will call the Archaic Era. The dates are often contested, but most scholars date the Archaic Era from 5000 to 2500 BC. This period is a time of the first glimmerings of agriculture, of the increasing cultivation of yams as a staple part of the diet, and the first indications of semi-permanent settlements throughout the Middle Nyalananga; some of these are large enough to contain a dozen or more families. Construction of

---

[14] Originally said by Jim Bishop.

dwellings in those settlements becomes more advanced as the Archaic Era elapses; in the early phases the dwellings were usually pit-houses dug out of the earth, by the Late Archaic timber houses were built above ground.

The Archaic Era is the time of the development of the first arts of civilization, as those future archaeologists define it. This is the time when the cultivation of red yams spreads along the river. This is the time when the Gunnagal first discover the use of ceramics, with pottery, bowls, and other cooking and storage vessels emerging in the archaeological record. Late in the Archaic Era, archaeologists report the first evidence of loom weaving, with textiles such as blankets and clothes woven from nettle and flax fibres.

The next phase of the Nyalananga Valley civilization will be called the Formative Era by most archaeologists, and the Preclassical Era by a few holdouts. The Formative Era is the first flowering of the Nyalananga Valley civilization, the time when the first full agriculture is developed, closely followed by the rise of the first towns and cities, and the emergence of complex hierarchical societies. This phase of the Nyalananga Valley civilization is comparable to what later archaeologists were familiar with in the development of other ancient river valley civilizations such as the Sumerians along the Tigris and Euphrates, Predynastic Egypt along the Nile, the Harappans along the Indus, and the early Chinese along the Yellow River. While the Nyalananga Valley civilization started later than most of those cultures, the archaeologists will note that the emergence of large towns and cities followed much more quickly after the development of agriculture than it did in the other early river valley civilizations[15].

The start of the Early Formative (or Early Preclassical) period is dated to 2500 BC, with the emergence of Tjibarr,

---

[15] This is because the nature of Aururian permaculture (perennial agriculture) allows the accumulation of much larger food surpluses per worker than most annual forms of agriculture.

the first permanent large agricultural settlement to be found in the Australian archaeological record. As with most prehistoric sites around the world, the Tjibarr culture is recognised principally by the development of a new pottery style. The older Archaic pottery was usually decorated with simple patterns of lines and crosses. The pottery at Tjibarr is decorated with pointillist images, usually of animals such as kangaroos and possums, and sometimes fish. Archaeologists will argue at length about the purpose of these representations. They are not something used to depict what was stored or cooked in many of those bowls and pots, since the decorations show only animals, not the plants such as yams and wild-gathered wattle seeds and murnong which formed much of the diet, and traces of which could be found amongst the pottery. Perhaps they had some ritual significance, some archaeologists argue, while others see these pottery decorations as merely the surviving example of what was presumably a flourishing artistic tradition. As it happens, the latter archaeologists are correct; the early Gunnagal decorate almost everything that they use indoors. Their house walls are painted too, and most of the early Gunnagal paint their skins in ochre too, but these other artworks are not usually represented in the archaeological record.

In Tjibarr, future archaeologists will have trouble excavating the heartland of the earliest buildings, since so much of what was built there is overlaid with the buildings of later towns. But they are able to discover that a sizable town emerged in the region by about 2400 BC, with at least five hundred people living in or near its walls. The inhabitants built in wood and mud-brick, not in stone. Evidence excavated from cooking sites indicates that these early Gunnagal were not just yam farmers; they had abundant meals of fish, duck, kangaroo and emu, among other meats. They also find enough evidence to indicate that the Gunnagal had started to build channels, weirs, and other works to create the first improved wetlands.

One detail which the archaeologists will get wrong is that they think that the development of a full agricultural package – yams, murnong, purslane, and wattles – is what leads to permanent settlement and the development of these wetlands. In fact, the development happened the other way around; the Gunnagal learned the practice of improved wetlands from the Junditmara far to the south, settled into a fully sedentary lifestyle, and only then started to cultivate a greater variety of plants and eventually domesticated them.

While the archaeologists will get this detail wrong, and a few others, they will be correct in the broad picture they draw. Tjibarr is the first permanent settlement, established around 2500 BC, but it will be followed by several others. The distinctive Gunnagal style of pottery spreads along much of the Nyalananga over the next few centuries, associated with the development of several other towns and cities. Some of the pottery itself spreads much further afield, both north and south. This is evidence of considerable trade routes with other peoples who are still living as hunter-gatherers, but there is no doubt that the peoples along the Nyalananga itself are farmers. This is still a time before the development of metallurgy; apart from a few knives and axe-heads of hammered meteoric iron, the Early Formative urban centres use only stone tools.

The end of the Early Formative period will be conventionally dated at 2000 BC. By this time, Tjibarr has turned into a burgeoning town of some five thousand people. There are four other major urban centres along the Nyalananga during this period, and several smaller towns. They produced a variety of artworks with what will be described as "ritual significance." The most common of these artworks are clay figurines, cast into human form but always with some aspect of their anatomy exaggerated; long legs or arms or heads. Archaeologists note that these early cities clearly had some kind of elite class; a few houses in each city are much larger than others, and some of the surviving burials show men and women interred with considerable adornment. Since there was no writing during this period, they cannot be certain, but it does not look like these early cities had a single ruler; rather, they had some kind of council or other oligarchy. As it happens, they are right in this conjecture.

Following the Early Formative period comes an era which most archaeologists will call the Middle Formative, but a persistent minority will call the Middle Preclassical. As with most prehistoric sites, this period is recognised in the archaeological record by gradually evolving pottery styles, but it has two particularly distinguishing features: building with rammed earth, and the emergence of metallurgy with the first smelted copper tools.

Construction in rammed earth is the most distinctive aspect of Middle and Late Formative cities. In the Early Formative, buildings were usually constructed from mud-brick prepared and dried in the sun. Mud-bricks were easy to make, but lasted only three or four decades before they crumbled. Rammed earth is a more laborious construction method, but the results are worth the effort. Gunnagal labourers gather soil which has an appropriate composition of clay, gravel and sand, moisten it, add a stabilising blend of lime and wattle-gum, then pour the mixture into a wooden frame and compress it. When the rammed earth dries, the wooden frames are removed and then left to cure for up to two years. The resulting walls are almost as strong as stone[16]. Rammed earth construction will be used in most major buildings throughout the Middle and Late Formative periods, although some smaller dwellings are still built out of timber or mud-brick.

---

[16] Rammed earth (or *pisé de terre*) is a method of construction which has been independently invented in several parts of the world, such as Mesopotamia and China. It is labour-intensive, but in reasonably dry climates, allows for long-lasting buildings. In a civilization which lacks domesticated animals or hard metal tools, it is also easier to develop strong building walls with rammed earth than it is to quarry and transport stone. (Copper is too soft to be of much use quarrying hard building stones.)

The Middle Formative is also the time when archaeologists will first recognise the use of copper metallurgy in the Nyalananga Valley civilization. The first copper-working emerges not in Tjibarr, but much further to the west. Gunnagalic peoples slowly moved along the length of the Nyalananga during the Early Formative, and by 2000 BC they had established a small settlement in the region of Goolrin [Murray Bridge], in the lower reaches of the Nyalananga. This is a region of moderate rainfall, barely suitable for yam farming, and less useful for wetlands, but with enough potential to allow settlement. The region of Goolrin includes some of the richest copper ores in Australia, including some easily accessible surface deposits, and the people of Goolrin are quick to discover and exploit them.

Knowledge of copper-working spreads quickly throughout the Nyalananga Valley during the Middle Formative, and copper tools will take their place alongside stone tools. Copper as a metal is not strong enough to replace all the uses of stone, but copper battle-axes and knives become common finds in the archaeological record from this period. Copper also becomes a valuable decorative metal; bangles, beads, pendants, earrings and other jewellery are well-represented in the archaeological record. The most abundant discovery of all is copper-tips shaped for digging, which were once attached to wooden digging sticks, but where the wood is almost always rotted away. Copper-tipped digging sticks will gradually be developed into spades during the Middle and Late Formative as copper becomes more abundant. This will greatly enhance the productivity of yam farmers, and allow a substantial growth in population during these periods.

The Middle Formative will be conventionally dated to end in 1400 BC, although the date is largely arbitrary. The archaeological record of the Middle and Late Formative periods blends into each other in a series of smooth transitions; there are no dramatic changes in the culture. The trend throughout both periods is the same; increasing urban and rural populations, the development of commerce and more complex social organisation, increasingly impressive public architecture which would have required the mobilisation of a considerable labour force. The first evidence of proto-writing emerges during the later stages of the Middle Formative, with simple marks on large ceramic containers which are thought to depict either ownership of those containers, or their contents. These written marks develop into more complex patterns during the Late Formative, and sometimes appear on other surviving goods such as jewellery and weapons, although they remain indecipherable.

The Late Formative period is a time of increasingly sophisticated metallurgy. Many copper ores contain arsenic as a natural impurity, including those around the Lower Nyalananga. Smiths in Goolrin discover how to melt and reforge increasing concentrations of arsenic from copper ores, and produce the first arsenical bronzes. From a metallurgical perspective, arsenical bronzes are perfectly functional, and about as useful as bronzes made from the more familiar alloy of tin and copper. The toxic fumes from molten arsenic mean that many Gunnagal smiths go lame, crippled, or into early graves, but such is the price of progress. The development of arsenic bronze tools is credited with increasing stonework in the Late Formative. While rammed earth remains the main building material, statues and other decorative stone facings are added to many buildings.

The Gunnagal also learn to work with other metals during this period. Travellers moving along the spreading trade routes reached Gumbalong [Glen Osmond, Adelaide], where in time they discover a rich source of lead and silver ore. In keeping with their earlier traditions, the main early use which Gunnagal smiths find for these new metals is for decorative purposes; lead beads become valued adornments, and the first silversmiths discover how to fashion a variety of jewellery.

The Late Formative also marks the time when domesticated animals become a major component of the Gunnagal diet. Domesticated dingos have long been used by the Gunnagal as hunting dogs and fireside companions of the elite, but during the Late Formative, excavation of middens reveals the first evidence of dingos consumed as meat. Artistic evidence from surviving murals, along with the same excavation of middens, reveals that domesticated ducks were also important as a source of meat, eggs and feathers[17]. Archaeologists interpret the domestication of these animals as a sign of growing sophistication amongst Gunnagal farmers. This is true to a point, but what is less easily realised from the archaeological record is that the switch to domesticated sources of meat was adopted because of growing population straining natural resources. Gunnagal peoples during earlier periods were able to support their dietary needs for meat through fishing and hunting waterfowl in their artificial wetlands, supplemented by hunting kangaroos in fire-managed rangelands further from the river. During the Late Formative, the Gunnagal have reached the limits of how many wetlands they can construct given their existing technology and scarce supply of bronze tools, and over-hunting has decimated kangaroo numbers within the rangelands.

In the matter of Gunnagal animal domestication, as in so much else, the future archaeologists can make only limited inferences about the nature of Gunnagal society and technology. They can recognise the main urban centres,

---

[17] The Gunnagal have domesticated the Australian wood duck (*Chenonetta jubata*). This duck is easily kept and bred in captivity; captive birds can raise up to three broods in a year. Wood ducks need minimal contact with the water; they spend most of their time foraging for grass, clover and other plants on land. Domesticated wood ducks are easily fed by grazing with occasional supplements of wattleseeds or waste seed pods, and can be used to pick out insects and other pests from crops. Domesticated wood ducks are a valuable source of meat, eggs and feathers in a culture which otherwise lacks many domesticated animals.

they can salvage some tools and remains of crops, they can recognise the pottery carried by trade far beyond the Nyalananga, but so much more will be lost to the ravages of time. For instance, archaeologists will assume correctly that the Gunnagal used many more tools of wood than they did of stone or copper, but most of those wooden tools have decayed into oblivion.

Excavators of the early Nyalananga Valley cities cannot find the written records they would need to tell them what language these people spoke, or what they believed. Based on the languages spoken by their descendants in the Nyalananga Valley and elsewhere, future archaeologists make the inference, correctly as it happens, that those people spoke a language which they call Proto-Gunnagal. But there is so much more which they can only guess at, such as the nature of Gunnagal religion. Archaeologists find small shrines in most well-to-do homes, but not the same large temples which were common in the comparable stages of many other early civilizations.

Another question which puzzles researchers is why knowledge of domesticated crops took so long to spread beyond the Gunnagal heartlands in the Nyalananga Valley. The Gunnagal had developed a useful agricultural package by 2000 BC, but even a thousand years later, traces of farming had scarcely spread beyond the Nyalananga.

Still, there is one conclusions future archaeologists will draw which is entirely correct. The Gunnagal are the first Aururian agricultural civilization. In their language, their beliefs, their learning, and their social organisation, they will influence all who come after them...

#5: Life As It Once Was

Future archaeologists excavated much of what remained of the culture they called the Nyalananga Valley civilization. Yet even the most detailed excavations can only reveal a small fraction of the lives of vanished times. To find out what life was like for the Gunnagal in what will be called the Late Formative period, archaeology alone will not suffice. Another way is needed to look back in time, to imagine what happened in this world that never was. If the pages of history can be turned back for a time, then you might picture the Nyalananga Valley as it existed one thousand years before the birth of the man whom some would call the Christ.

 In that time, if you looked from above the Nyalananga, you would see a thin ribbon of blue winding its way from east to west across an otherwise dry landscape. Near the river, fields of yams spread their spread their foliage across the landscape, dark green leaves and stems winding up the forked branches planted for them, or spreading across the soil. If watched over time, the yams die back to the ground in late autumn, regrow in late winter and early spring, display small purple flowers in late spring, then grow vigorously for most of the summer, before the tubers are harvested in late autumn, and the cycle begins again. Wattles grow along the edges of the yam-fields, or are planted in rows on sloping or hilly ground. The trees grow quickly when they are planted, regrow vigorously if damaged by fire, and in season are covered in sweet-smelling golden flowers, which are then replaced by abundant seed pods which start green but ripen to brown before they are harvested.

In between the yam fields, or closer to the river, lie the marks of the other main achievement of the Gunnagal civilization. They have shaped the land to be a home for water, with channels running amongst yam fields to connect to ponds, small lakes, swamps and other wetlands. Maintained by a system of weirs, dams and other stonework, the wetlands usually thrive even through the irregular droughts which can last for several years. Rushes, reeds and other water plants grow vigorously throughout these wetlands, and the Gunnagal sometimes harvest them for food. Mostly, though, here is where traps are laid to catch fish, and sometimes to catch the swans, ducks, and other water birds which visit.

From the fields and the rivers, the Gunnagal draw almost their complete diet. The core of the Gunnagal diet is yams, murnong, and wattleseeds; everyday labourers often eat little else. Yams are usually peeled and then roasted alone or with murnong. Sometimes yams and murnong are boiled in water and then pounded into a paste-like porridge called *benong* which can be eaten alone or with soup. Wattleseeds are ground into flour, which can be baked into flatbreads and served alone or alongside roasted yams. Ground wattleseed can also be used to flavour *benong*, along with some other seeds such as purslane and flax. Leaf vegetables such as purslane and nettle leaves are baked and served as part of the same meal. This is what the Gunnagal call the 'farmer's diet'; adequate from a nutritional point of view, sufficient to avoid starvation, but low-status food which the upper classes will try to avoid.

Meat is the preferred delicacy amongst the Gunnagal, eaten by elders and other high-status people whenever they can, and usually available to common citizens only on feast-days and other festivals. Fish is their most common meat, harvested in traps from their wetlands. The traps are only permitted to be large enough to catch fish of specified size, and even then the harvests are controlled by order of the Council of each city. Ducks and dingos are also farmed for their meat, although this is less available than fish. Wild-harvested meat from waterbirds in the wetlands is an occasional delicacy, also subject to control from the Councils.

The rarest meats are wild-hunted animals such as kangaroo and emu, which can be gathered from the rangelands designated by city Councils. The rangelands are in theory subject to Council hunting controls, but in practice kangaroos and emus are being increasingly harvested 'against law and custom.' The Councils appoint rangers to police the rangelands, but the expanses of the rangelands make effective control difficult, and in many cases the rangers themselves are the illegal harvesters. All of this makes kangaroo and emu meat increasingly rare and expensive. Amongst city-dwellers, usually only elders can afford it.

While meat is the most common Gunnagal delicacy, they also have other valued high-status foods. For those who cannot afford meat, the most common substitute is 'beefsteak fungus' (*Fistulina hepatica*), an edible fungus which in appearance is remarkably like a piece of raw meat. In the wild it grows on living or dead wood, and with their abundant sources of timber from wattles, the Gunnagal grow this fungus as a delicacy[18]. A variety of wild-gathered plants are available from the wetlands and cherished for their exotic flavours; the most common of these are cumbungi and water-lily roots. Duck eggs are much enjoyed but rarely eaten, at least in the cities; one of the ironies is that city-dwellers view eggs as a luxury food which is above a 'farmer's diet,' but actual Gunnagal farmers eat eggs regularly. The Gunnagal have also

---

[18] Beefsteak fungus exists in the wild both in Australia and on several other continents. It has historically been (and sometimes still is) cultivated as a meat substitute.

domesticated a few native fruit species, such as native raspberries, which are treasured seasonal delicacies, and sometimes dried for later use. The Gunnagal also cultivate a variety of plants which are used as flavourings or spices, such as river mint, sweet peppers, and sea celery[19]. Consumption of spicy food is another mark of the elite; duck in river mint sauce is particularly popular, as is pepper kangaroo steak, for those who can afford both the kangaroo and the sweet peppers. For those who lack the wherewithal to procure spices, sweeteners such as wattle gum and blue-water are sometimes used instead.

Of all the delicacies treasured amongst the peoples who live along the Nyalananga, the rarest and most expensive is wattleseed oil. Wattleseeds themselves are abundant and a staple food, particularly in hard times; silos of wattleseeds are found in every Gunnagal city as a vital protection against famine. Wattleseed oil, however, requires extensive processing to extract. Wattle seeds contain most of their vegetable fat in a small aril attached to the main seed. The Gunnagal have learned to separate this aril from the seeds before they are ground into flour, using a particularly fine knife of copper or obsidian. This is a laborious process, usually done by children who have smaller fingers and keen

---

[19] The Aururian native raspberry (*Rubus parvifolius*) is a close relative of domesticated raspberries (*R. idaeus* and *R. strigosus*), produces similar-tasting fruit and has similar growing requirements, although it is much more drought-tolerant. Aururia also has a variety of plants which are suitable as spices. Aboriginal peoples harvested many species as flavourings, and several of them have been cultivated or used by recent immigrants as well. River mint (*Mentha australis*) is a widely-distributed plant in south-eastern Aururia whose leaves have a distinctive spearmint flavour. Sweet peppers are known in real history as pepperbushes, such as mountain peppers (*Tasmannia lanceolata*) which have been cultivated both in Aururia and overseas as a spice. Sea celery (*Apium prostratum*) is an Aururian relative of common celery (*A. graveolens*), which grows along much of the coast of Aururia. Sea celery is used as a vegetable and flavouring by the Gunnagal, in much the same way as common celery is used in other parts of the world. (Sea celery was harvested by early European colonists as a celery substitute).

eyesight to cut the arils from tens of thousands of seeds. The fat-rich arils are then turned into a form of vegetable oil, which is mostly used for flavouring, and even then available only to the elite. The most ostentatious use of wattleseed oil is for frying. One of the favoured methods is to cut yams into small wedges and then fry them in wattleseed oil on a hot metal pan for a few moments, until crispy brown. Only a few among the Gunnagal are wealthy enough to use wattleseed oil in such a profligate, but tasty, manner.

While the fields and lakes supply their food, the Gunnagal are bound to the river. It supplies them with a rich lifestyle; six cities and more than two dozen smaller towns and settlements are dotted along its length. The Nyalananga is a source of life-giving water for drinking and for their wetlands, and it is their primary means of transportation. All their main cities are on the Nyalananga, and no town and few farms are more than a day's march away from the river or one of its tributaries. Without beasts of burden and few decent roads, the Gunnagal rely on the river to move their goods. The great river is crowded with boats large and small, some with sails, some with oars, and some towed by men on the banks. Only riverine transport can supply the city-dwellers' insatiable demands for food, wood, and clay; only boats can support such a volume of long-range trade in metal, textiles, pottery, dyes, spices, and other trade and manufactured goods.

The Gunnagal have become a numerous people beyond the imaginings of their forebears who lived alongside one swan-inhabited lagoon, and of those people, about one in four live in towns or cities. The easternmost outpost of the Gunnagal civilization is a small town at Kamilay [Tintaldra], where workers often harvest timber which is easily floated downstream, and where miners have started to explore some of the copper deposits in the region. Kamilay and some other smaller nearby towns are under the aegis of the largest of the Gunnagal cities. Gundabingee is located a little east of the place which in another history would become the town of Corowa. Gundabingee is a flourishing city at the heart of some of the best agricultural land in Aururia, and it has a permanent population of around thirty thousand inhabitants.

Gundabingee is one of the Wisdom Cities, and while it is the largest, there are five more, each of which has a population of ten thousand or more. Bangupna [Tocumwal], with some of the most extensive wetlands along the entire Nyalananga, has some eighteen thousand inhabitants. Yalooka [Echuca] has about fifteen thousand people, while the ancient centre of Tjibarr has around twenty-two thousand dwellers. Downstream of Tjibarr, as the river moves ever westward, the surrounding countryside becomes drier and the wetlands harder to sustain.

Tapiwal [Robinvale], the fifth of the Wisdom Cities, has about ten thousand inhabitants, but it draws from a much larger agricultural hinterland than the cities further upstream. Tapiwal controls a series of smaller towns, with its westernmost outpost around Kelliga [Mildura], beyond which there is a large region of only thinly-inhabited land. This area is the driest part of the Nyalananga Valley, where the rainfall is poor enough that even the drought-tolerant farming of the Gunnagal is marginal. They do not irrigate crops in any meaningful way, with their waterworks more focused on supplying fish, and so there is only a small population in this area. Yet this is not the last of the Wisdom Cities. The last great Gunnagal city is Goolrin, separated by a considerable distance from the other main Gunnagal centres, but which has grown rich from the flourishing trade in copper, lead and silver.

The Gunnagal have many towns and settlements, but the Wisdom Cities have an exalted status which goes far beyond merely large size. Each of the Wisdom Cities has a recognised body of religious government, a Council of Elders, which is honoured even in their rival cities. The elders are those whose houses will be recognised by much later archaeologists as indicating signs of social stratification, with the accumulation of high-value goods and individual shrines, but no excavation can reveal the full function of the councils. Elders win that distinction not because of advancing years, but because of recognised wisdom, and age is not considered an automatic guarantee of wisdom. Many elders are indeed advanced in years by the standards of early agricultural peoples, but there are those who are young and considered wise, while many city-dwellers are old but are not considered wise.

Government by Council has some variations between the Wisdom Cities, but at least in outward tradition it is similar. The office of elder is not formally hereditary, and a new elder must be recognised by the combined consensus of the existing elders. In many cases, the rank is nonetheless inherited, for elders are not just the nobles and priests of this era, they are also the merchants of the times. They trade in goods moved along the Water Mother (Nyalananga), and sometimes in the rarer goods like alabaster, ochre and opals which are moved over land.

With inherited wealth comes power, and it is a rare occasion when a council will spurn the son of a current elder, although not unknown. Politics within the councils are complex, fractious, and full of factions and rivalries; the intrigues often defy the comprehension of ordinary citizens within their own cities, let alone those who try to understand them from a distance of three millennia. While formally the decisions of any council need a consensus, there are many ways of achieving agreement. Some are dominated by a smaller group of oligarchs who hold the true power; in the case of Bangupna, there is a single family which rules the Council in all but name, and whose leading member would be considered the monarch if the Gunnagal had such a concept. In the case of Tjibarr, oldest of the Wisdom Cities, the institution of the Council has stayed closest to its roots, and it remains governed by the principle of equality of mistrust. The elders are heads of rival merchant and religious families who sometimes find it necessary to cooperate and strike compromises, but who will always act to bring down any individual elder who is thought to be accumulating too much power.

As priests and merchants, the Councils are responsible for following the established law and customs of their predecessors. They oversee marriages, resolve disputes between individuals and families, and in theory are the guardians of traditional lore. Many of these duties are delegated to a smaller caste within the elders, whose rank translates as 'stick-men.' Named for the ancient means of communication between distinct peoples[20], the stick-men have made an art of memorisation, using chants, mnemonics and other practices to allow them to recall the accumulated oral law of their city. Once a year, in the Goldentime of autumn which marks the passage of the new year, each of the Wisdom Cities holds a great festival which lasts for three days. Most of this time is taken up with feasting, social gatherings, dances, song and the like, but at the dawn of each day, the stick-men take turns to recite passages from the oral law code of their city, in such a way that over the three days, the entirety of the law code is retold for all listeners to hear.

In keeping with their wealth, elders have a much greater variety of clothes to choose from than the average citizen, but on formal or religious occasions (which are often synonymous) they wear possum-skin cloaks as a mark of their rank. Ordinary citizens usually wear an all-purpose linen kilt around the waist, knee-length for men and ankle-length for women, dyed into a personalised pattern. During

---

[20] Message-sticks were a form of communication used by Aboriginal peoples to transmit information between different groups, particularly those who spoke different languages. They consisted of solid sticks of wood with patterns of dots and lines to convey information, and which could be carried by messengers for hundreds of kilometres. They could be used for a number of purposes, but one of the most common was to announce a gathering of many peoples for religious or social events. This sense of using message sticks to announce gatherings has carried over into the Gunnagal, where the stick-men open the yearly festivals which announce the laws and customs which all of the peoples follow.

colder weather they wear a linen cloak with a similar pattern. This not all the decoration that people wear, for the Gunnagal decorate everything: skin, jewellery, household walls, tools, everything. Every citizen will have some form of personal decoration which is the symbol of one or more of their totems, but they have decoration almost everywhere else, too. Painted clay figurines are common, murals are on most walls, and everyone uses the most elaborate jewellery which they can afford. Even their copper and arsenical bronze axes and knives have patterns of fine lines etched into them when they are forged, not enough to weaken their primary purpose, but to give them a more aesthetically pleasing appearance. Indeed, even city walls are decorated; ochre is mixed into the upper layers of rammed earth in each wall to give a decorative pinkish-red tint to the tops of city walls.

The Gunnagal systems of decorations are complex, often adopted merely for the aesthetic appearance, but they also serve important social functions. The Gunnagal have an intricate set of social relationships, kinship patterns, and customs of respect and mutual avoidance. The core of this system is the division of all Gunnagal people into a set of eight kinship classes called *kitjigal*.

* * *

The codes of the *kijigal* are complex. Every Gunnagal is born into a particular *kitjigal*, which changes over the generations, based on their father or mother's *kitjigal*. All members of the same *kitjigal* are considered to be relatives; members of the same *kitjigal* who are born into the same generation will refer to each other as 'brother' or 'sister,' and there is an intricate vocabulary of social terms to refer to members of the same *kitjigal* who are of different generations. Since all members of the same *kitjigal* are considered relatives, they will support each other even if their own cities are at war; warriors of the same *kitjigal* will refuse to fight each other, for instance. Marriage between members of the same *kitjigal* is always considered to be incest, and there is a complex set of relationships which allows marriage only between certain *kitjigal* and forbids others.

Each of the *kitjigal* is named for a colour, and each has its own set of totems. Every adult Gunnagal, and most children, will wear the representation of one or more of their totems at all times, and their personalised decorations for their clothing will usually include their *kitjigal*'s colour as part of the pattern. The totems often match the colour-names, but not always the colour-name represents an underlying concept. The totems are linked with the concept, not necessarily the colour itself. For instance, the Gunnagal associate (medium and dark) blue with water and rainfall, which for them for them is an occasion welcomed with joy and laughter. So one of the totems for blue is the laughing kookaburra, a bird which sounds like it is laughing, but which is not blue. (This is comparable to common connotations of colours in English, where green is associated with envy, for instance).

The eight *kitjigal* and their associated totems are:

Grey has three totems, the eastern grey kangaroo (*Macropus giganteus*), sandstone (regardless of colour), and a type of cloud which the Gunnagal call rain clouds (nimbostratus).

White has four totems, the long-billed corella (*Cacatua tenuirostris*), the little egret (*Egretta garzetta*), granite, and lightning.

Black has four totems, the snake-necked turtle (*Chelodina longicollis*), the raven (*Corvus coronoides*), the perentie (*Varanus giganteus*), and the new moon.

Gold has four totems, the golden perch (*Macquaria ambigua*), wattle flowers, obsidian, and shooting stars.

Blue, to the Gunnagal, is a colour which includes shades which English-speakers would classify as medium and dark blue, but not light blue. Blue has four totems, the laughing kookaburra (*Dacelo novaeguineae*), sand goanna (*Varanus gouldii*), the morning star (Venus ascendant), and raindrops.

Azure (or light blue) is a colour which the Gunnagal consider to be separate from blue in the same way that English-speakers distinguish between red and light red (pink). Azure has four totems, the wedge-tailed eagle (*Aquila audax*), the short-beaked echidna (*Tachyglossus aculeatus*), orchid flowers, and strong wind.

Green has four totems, the common wombat (*Vombatus ursinus*), quartz, eucalyptus flowers, and the crescent moon.

Red has four totems, the dingo (*Canis lupus dingo*), the common brushtail possum (*Trichosurus vulpecula*), the evening star (Venus descendant), and northerly winds. Northerly winds are associated with red since these hot winds, blowing from Aururia's arid interior, fan the worst summer bushfires.

The social codes of the *kitjigal* create many intricacies about which people can marry each other, and dictate terms of address when interacting with people. For instance, all members of the same *kitjigal* as a person's father will be politely referred to as 'father.' For descent, a child's *kitjigal* shifts according their parent of the same gender. In the male line, the *kitjigal* are divided into two groups of four, with the pattern repeating every four generations. Blue fathers have red sons, red fathers have black sons, black fathers have gold sons, and gold fathers have blue sons. The other group sees azure fathers have white sons, white fathers have green sons, green fathers have grey sons, and grey fathers have azure sons. For women, the corresponding groups are blue to black to white to grey (then back to blue), and red to gold to azure to green (then back to red).

* * *

The social codes of the *kitjigal* dictate both individual and political relationships throughout the lives of every Gunnagal. Marriages and inheritance are the most obvious example of these, with children of one *kitjigal* changing to another in every generation as part of a complex pattern. Yet the relationships are broader; in politics it is considered important for each *kitjigal* to be represented equally amongst each city's elders, and rivalries are often shaped by kinship cycles. Marriages amongst the Gunnagal are often arranged from birth as part of these social arrangements; even when marriages are individual love-matches, the marriage ceremony requires the approval and then the participation of an elder from the *kitjigal* of both bride and groom.

Even during informal social and recreational events, the codes of the *kitjigal* predominate. The most common sport amongst the Gunnagal is well-represented in their artistic traditions, and archaeologists will christen it, with inspiring mundanity, as the 'ball-game.' Depictions of descendant games will be recognised amongst many successor cultures to the Gunnagal, and it will usually be inferred to have had some religious significance. In fact, the ball-games – there are many variations – are used purely for recreation, and are played at most social gatherings. In their basic form, the ball-games are played used a ball (usually of possum skin), which is kicked between a large number of players. The aim of the game is usually not to let the ball touch the ground, and the last player to catch the ball drop-kicks it again. Sometimes the game is played for points, other times just for entertainment, but in all cases, people of the same *kitjigal* will automatically be on the same team whenever the game is played. The same principles apply to other Gunnagal sports such as wrestling, where even in championships wrestlers of the same *kitjigal* will not compete against each other.

The social system of the *kitjigal* links the polities of the Gunnagal. Since all people of the same *kitjigal* are considered relatives, even from rival cities, this allows for channels of communication and hospitality to remain open even during troubled times. Such occasions are relatively rare; while the Gunnagal cities are often rivals, they have customary limits on the practices of warfare. Each of the six Wisdom Cities has recognised borders marked by boundary stones, and the Council of each city is supreme within those borders. Warfare, when it does come, is usually border warfare, for rangelands or other territory. Even then, warfare is usually ritualised. Gunnagal elders themselves do not take up arms, but many of their younger sons join a dedicated warrior caste, who are recognised and trained from childhood. During peacetime social gatherings between polities, warriors will fight honour duels with each other to first blood, or occasionally to the death. Formal warfare follows similar rules, with battles often being decided by a set number of duels between the two sides, although these duels are usually to the death.

Military tactics are not particularly advanced; even when rival cities cannot agree on terms for a contest of duels, the two armies will usually meet on a chosen field. Battle tactics generally consist of both armies forming a rough line of battle, flinging taunts and boasts at one another, until one warrior decides to charge, and his comrades will follow him into a battle which rapidly degenerates into individual contests. Even during the middle of a battle, it is considered extremely poor manners to interrupt two individual soldiers who are fighting, or to strike quickly without recognising one's opponent, in case it turns out that the two warriors were of the same *kitjigal*. For the same reason, ranged weapons are frowned upon during warfare; throwing spears and other missile weapons are considered tools for hunters, not warriors.

Underlying the traditions of the *kitjigal*, of warfare, and indeed all of Gunnagal society, are their religious beliefs. The beliefs of the Gunnagal are complex and not always coherent; in a culture with no writing system and no overall religious hierarchy, there is nothing to enforce total conformity. In its essence, though, the Gunnagal religious world-view is shaped by their concept of time and of fate. To them, time is non-linear; they do not see the world in terms of past, present and future. They see the immediate world as being the present time, but which is touched by what they call the Evertime. The Evertime is both what was and what will come to be. A person's current actions are reflected in the Evertime, but not in a linear way; the

Gunnagal see no functional difference between a person's actions affecting the past as much as the future. Dreams are considered to be extremely important, as they are the most direct link between the present time and the Evertime. One of the most important roles of elders is to interpret dreams, which are variously seen as omens, as warnings, as visions of the past or future, or as answers to questions which the dreamer has been pondering.

The Gunnagal see the Evertime as populated by a variety of beings, some powerful, some mischievous, and some insignificant. The most powerful of these are a set of beings regarded as being responsible for the shaping of the world. To the Gunnagal, the world itself is eternal, but the creator beings have made the world into its form. In keeping with their non-linear view of time, the Gunnagal see creation as a continuous, ongoing process. For instance, they view the Nyalananga as the Water Mother, who has shaped the river's course, but they speak of the Water Mother as if she were still creating the river every day. Some days, the Water Mother makes the course of the river anew, which is why the Nyalananga sometimes shifts its course slightly. Lightning Man is another important creation being, who shapes the storms and brings down lightning and thunder, but to the Gunnagal, all storms past, present and future are part of the same act of creation. The Gunnagal see all the creator beings – the Fire Brothers, the Rainbow Serpent, the Green Lady, Eagle, Bark Man, She Who Must Not Be Named, and several others – in the same way.

Aside from the great creator beings, the Gunnagal also believe that their extended family (both ancestors and descendants) live in the Evertime. Until they are resurrected, at least; the Gunnagal believe in reincarnation of the spirit, in human, animal or plant form. The Evertime is also inhabited by a variety of lesser beings, which are thought of as mischievous and which sometimes cross over to the present time and interfere with human affairs. Elders are responsible for knowing the traditional lore needed to placate, bargain with, or drive away such beings. Elders are also seen as responsible for communicating with the greater creator beings, although these beings are seen as more distant and often implacable. The Water Mother is seen as the most important of the creator beings; the Gunnagal do not like to wander far from the Mother's embrace. They are reluctant to settle anywhere far from the Nyalananga or one of its tributaries; traders and travellers who leave the Nyalananga swear an oath to return as soon as they practically can, and ask that their body be carried back even if they die elsewhere[21].

In their religion, then, as in so much else, the Gunnagal appear to be flourishing in the Late Formative. They have several large cities, and their agriculture supports a total population of nearly one million. They know how to work in copper, silver, lead, and are starting to work with arsenical bronze. They have a dynamic tradition of artwork in paintings, figurines, dyes, and other mediums. They do not have a system of writing, but they have a developing tradition of proto-writing. The archaeological record will not show all of the details, but it will confirm their apparent success.

Which makes what happens next all the more puzzling for archaeologists to explain.

---

[21] This is one reason why early agriculture spreads only slowly from its heartland in the Nyalananga; the spiritual attachment means that very few Gunnagal want to abandon the vicinity of the Water Mother. The Gunnagal possess a dryland agricultural package which is not limited to areas of irrigation or high rainfall; their crops are drought-tolerant, and their main domesticated animals (ducks) do not need significant contact with water. Indeed, the Gunnagal themselves do not usually irrigate their crops even when living along the Nyalananga; their efforts at waterworks are more focused on aquaculture. This means that knowledge of Australian domesticated crops does not spread readily beyond the Nyalananga Valley until the Gunnagal themselves find a reason to leave their homelands.

#6: Collapse and Rebirth

The history of archaeology, like so many of the sciences, is replete with disagreements and unanswered questions, with established consensuses which are overturned by new discoveries or new theses. Unsolved mysteries are an appealing target for applying the scientific method, and an intriguing unanswered question raises interest and often tempers. To be a useful question, there need to be several elements. A good archaeological question requires enough information to propose detailed explanations, but insufficient information to provide a definitive answer. Preferably, there should be strong-willed personalities amongst the researchers; all the better to ensure heated arguments and vehement testing of proposals. Ideally, a good question also needs to be about a civilization which people care about, one which is well-known enough or has enough popular appeal so that arguments over an archaeological controversy spill over into the wider world.

The fate of the Nyalananga civilization will produce one of the most long-lasting questions in the allohistory of archaeology.

The archaeological record of the early Nyalananga civilization is one of gradually growing population, flourishing cities, and developing technology. At the beginning of the Formative Era in 2500 BC, there was one urban centre with a population of roughly five hundred people. At the conventional date for the end of the Formative Era, in 900 BC, there were six major cities with a combined urban population of about one hundred thousand people. Yet over the next two centuries, the cities along the Nyalananga collapsed. Four of them were abandoned entirely, and the remaining two were reduced to mere villages in comparison to what they had been. Many of the smaller settlements were similarly abandoned or depopulated. The three centuries between 900 and 600 BC will usually be referred to as the Interregnum, a time of severe population decline along the Nyalananga, of near-disappearance of trade, of the abandonment of many of the old cultural icons. This was the time when most of the old artistic styles vanished almost completely, along with so much else. It would take most of another millennium for the population of the Nyalananga basin to recover to its former levels, and some of the cities would never be rebuilt.

What caused the collapse of the Nyalananga civilization? There will be many theories, many ideas, and many conflicting interpretations of the evidence. A few authorities will argue that there was no complete collapse at all, emphasising the continuity of culture, while a few authorities will go to the other extreme and argue that the new civilizations which arose owed very little to their forebears. Yet most researchers will agree that the collapse was severe and wide-ranging, but that that it did not involve complete cultural replacement. Unfortunately, that is the limit of their agreement.

The number of proposed explanations for the collapse of the Formative Gunnagal is immense; over sixty different theories or variations of theories will be proposed to account for the mystery. Setting aside esoteric and supernatural proposals, five main groups of theories are proposed, although archaeologists are unlikely to ever reach a definitive answer. Such are the problems of conducting archaeological research on sites which pre-date the invention of writing.

One group of theories ascribes the collapse of the Formative Gunnagal to destructive warfare, either from foreign invasion or from increasing internecine struggles between the Nyalananga city-states. This proposal finds some support from archaeological evidence; excavations have found that the great city of Goolrin was systematically looted and burned at about 900 BC, right at the beginning of the Interregnum. A few of the smaller urban centres show similar destruction, at dates which are spread throughout the Interregnum; among them, the easternmost outpost at Kamilay was similarly burned sometime around 810 BC. Yet most of the other major urban centres do not show much evidence of destruction, which makes theories of invasion or warfare difficult to support.

Explanations based on destructive warfare will also be criticised on a lack of direct evidence for who these invaders or great warriors might have been. The early Nyalananga civilization was the bastion of farming in what was otherwise a continent of hunter-gatherers (apart from the early Junditmara, who were too far away). There is no evidence of any peoples who might have been numerous enough to invade the Nyalananga basin. Internecine warfare amongst the Nyalananga city-states might have been a possibility, but what evidence is available does not suggest that the city-states were particularly war-like or that they had the military capacity to wipe each other out so thoroughly.

There is some evidence of internal migration within the Nyalananga basin, which might suggest some effects of warfare. During the Formative Era, particular crops such as wattles were usually geographically limited to near the area of original domestication. These agricultural patterns were largely stable throughout the fourteen hundred years of the Formative Era, yet during the Interregnum each of these domesticated wattles were spread throughout the Nyalananga basin. Some authorities argue that this is evidence that invaders moved and brought their crops with them, while others argue that it is more likely that any internal migrations were the effects of the collapse, with survivors fleeing abandoned cities and bringing their crops and other knowledge with them to other areas of the Nyalananga.

Another group of theories relates to environmental or climatic factors. These theories ascribe the collapse of the Nyalananga civilization to famine brought about by recurrent droughts or increased bushfires destroying harvests for repeated years. Surviving examples of Late Formative Nyalananga burials are few, but of those which are excavated, archaeologists will notice a gradual decrease in the height of skeletons, which is taken to be evidence of malnutrition or other effects of famine. According to the environmental collapse theories, droughts or increased bushfires were the underlying cause, and the struggle for limited resources caused some of the destruction attested in the archaeological record.

These theories find some support from studies of tree ring patterns, which show a substantial increase in the number and severity of bushfires during the Interregnum when compared to the preceding period. Critics of the environmental collapse theories will argue that the increased bushfires are more likely to be an effect of the collapse rather than the cause. The Nyalananga civilization had been living in a region with severe bushfires for over a millennium, and should have known how to limit the effects of bushfires by protective burning. These critics argue that the severe bushfires of the Interregnum were the result of the collapsing human population no longer maintaining effective burn-offs on their own, and thus natural bushfires became more severe.

A third group of theories will ascribe the collapse of the Nyalananga civilization to internal revolution or social turmoil. According to these theories, unrest and dissatisfaction with the elites led to social unrest and revolution. Researchers who support these theories point to the evidence of destruction excavated at Goolrin and elsewhere as being rooted in social unrest, not foreign invasion. Direct confirmation of these theories are difficult, due to the lack of written sources, but their critics will point out that, as with the theories of foreign invasion, the evidence of destruction applies to only a few cities. It is difficult to explain how social unrest could have been widespread enough to depopulate most of the Nyalananga cities. Even if the social elites were destroyed through revolution, this leads raises the question of where the rebel populations moved to, and why they abandoned so many cities.

A fourth group of theories will seek to explain the collapse of the Nyalananga civilization in terms of a spread of disease. Some researchers favour a disease explanation because the spread of a new disease or diseases could explain rapid initial depopulation, and persistent endemic diseases as slowing population recovery. While no direct evidence of disease survives in the archaeological record, proponents of this theory argue that the expansion of human-created wetlands throughout the Formative Era created the perfect environment for harbouring pathogens and encouraging insect-borne transmission of infectious diseases. Objections to this theory will come principally from lack of evidence. While later civilizations along the Nyalananga are known to harbour epidemic diseases, none of these diseases can be traced to this era or are known to be linked to insect vectors.

The fifth group of theories will ascribe the collapse of the Nyalananga civilization to systemic ecological collapse. According to these researchers, the history of the Late Formative was one of expanding population placing ever-greater pressure on the natural resources of the Nyalananga basin. Ever more intensive farming is believed to have exhausted the soil, while increased hunting and fishing is thought to have depleted the supply of protein-rich foods. According to these researchers, over-use of the land led to exhausted and sometimes eroded soils, famines, and then competition for limited resources led to destructive warfare and the abandonment of many of the urban centres as the remaining inhabitants reverted to subsistence farming.

What future archaeologists will probably never be able to find out is that most of these theories capture part of the explanation, but that none of them give a complete account. For the truth of the collapse of the Gunnagal civilization is found in a series of unfortunate events, some of their own making, some imposed by nature.

Throughout the Late Formative period, the population of the Nyalananga basin boomed, aided by the development of arsenical bronze tools, and by a steady supply of food from the agricultural package of crops which they had developed. Yet in some respects their farming methods were still quite primitive. Red yams were the basis of their diet, but like all yams, they are hard on the soil. Farmers of red yams faced ever-decreasing yields when working on the same fields, which they could resolve only by moving on to new territory, leaving the land fallow for several years, and which provoked more territorial rivalry between the city-states.

While the Gunnagal as a whole had access to several wattle species, most of them had not spread far from their original area of domestication. This meant that their farmers were more vulnerable to pests and diseases which affected single crops. The Gunnagal farmers had not yet recognised the potential of wattles to revitalise the soil, which would have let them rotate their crops between yams and wattles. Without this realisation, the Gunnagal faced declining farming yields from yams and the emergence of several pest species which preyed on wattles, which made their farming increasingly marginal. The same pressure for food meant that their fishing and hunting grounds were gradually being exhausted, which made their population even more vulnerable to famine and other misfortune.

By 950 BC, the Nyalananga civilization, although still heavily-populated, was nearing its Malthusian limits and merely awaiting a trigger for disaster. Calamity would not be long in coming. The climate of south-eastern Aururia had been relatively stable for the last few thousand years, but in 1000 BC, the region entered a severe dry spell which would last for nearly a millennium. Rainfall declined, droughts became more prevalent, and already marginal farming yields plummeted. Much of the Lower Nyalananga became too arid to support farming, and while in some areas agriculture could continue, reduced yields meant that this could not sustain the large populations seen at the height of the Late Formative.

At first, the western regions of the Lower Nyalananga were the most badly-affected. The great centre of Goolrin, heartland of mining and the only large-scale source of copper and arsenical bronze, became so arid that farming could not be easily sustained. The leaders of the great city responded by trying to force more of the population into mining, to extract more of the valuable copper which could be used to trade for food from the still-fertile areas upstream. This worked in the short-term, but provoked social unrest which developed into revolution. In 898 BC, a revolt in the mines spread to the great city itself, which was burned to the ground. The surviving residents abandoned the city; some fleeing into wetter regions to the west and south, a few escaping upstream, while others reverted to subsistence farming and eking a precarious existence in rural areas around the vanished city.

With the destruction of Goolrin, one of the six great cities had been removed from the map. Tragically for the peoples of the Nyalananga basin, this had been the key source of their metal. A couple of much smaller deposits were known in the highlands in the Upper Nyalananga, but these were insufficient to meet demand. Copper and bronze were now almost-irreplaceable commodities, and re-smelting and re-use of metal would not be sufficient. Intensive farming had required more use of bronze tools to clear land and for digging, and this metal in particular was very difficult to obtain. Civilization gradually fell apart in the Nyalananga, with prolonged famines ravaging the population, and long-range trade declining amongst the Gunnagal cities. Warfare became more intense in competition over dwindling resources, and the eventual result was collapse.

The collapse of the early Nyalananga civilization was relatively swift, although not complete. Of the six great cities, four were abandoned entirely. Goolrin was destroyed through internal revolution. Tapiwal was not destroyed directly, but its position in an already semi-arid area made it vulnerable to prolonged drought. Farming became marginal enough that even the Gunnagal agricultural package could not supply the food surpluses needed to sustain a large city, and the people who dwelt there needed to move on or revert to subsistence farming. Yalooka and Bangupna found themselves caught between the collapse of their wetlands, which was particularly severe given the drought, and the pressure of warfare from the larger centres of Tjibarr and Gundabingee. The end result was that Yalooka and Bangupna were abandoned, although some of the survivors founded a new outpost between those cities, at a place they would call Weenaratta, which in time would grow into a city of great renown.

All that remained of the Nyalananga civilization, or so it appeared, were the former two largest cities of Tjibarr and Gundabingee. Both of these suffered severe population decline during the Interregnum, a result of famine, endemic warfare, and emigration outside the Nyalananga basin. Yet they did survive, reaching their nadir around 750 BC when both cities had only about two or three thousand permanent inhabitants. After that time, they began a slow recovery, although it would take a very long time for the Nyalananga civilizations to regain their former glory.

* * *

History teaches that when it comes to conflict between farmers and hunter-gatherers, farmers almost always win. As individuals, hunter-gatherers were normally much healthier than farmers; the diet of early farmers was more nutritionally limited and the workload much higher. As a group, though, farmers were much more numerous. Unless the climate turns unsuitable for agriculture, then farmers usually have an immense weight of numbers which means that they can displace hunter-gatherers. When one group of peoples adopts agriculture but their neighbours do not, this can often mean substantial shifts in population, particularly if the agriculturalists also have other advantages such as metal tools and domesticated animals.

One of the most dramatic examples of such population shifts is the Bantu expansion which transformed southern Africa. Before the Bantu expansion, the southern half of Africa was inhabited by a variety of hunter-gatherer peoples, including the ancestors of modern Khoisan-speaking peoples and the "Pygmies" of the central African jungles. In a series of migrations from their homelands in West Africa, Bantu-speaking farmers pushed into hunter-gatherer territory and displaced most of the hunter-gatherer peoples throughout southern Africa. There were a few holdouts, mostly in areas where farming was unsustainable, but the Bantu-speakers came to dominate Africa south of the equator.

Allohistory teaches of another dramatic example of a population shift; the Great Migrations which transformed southern Aururia. In 1000 BC, Aururia was mostly a domain of hunter-gatherers. Agriculture was confined almost exclusively to the Nyalananga basin. Here, the Gunnagal had a thriving but geographically limited civilization; almost all of the farmers lived within a day's march of the winding Nyalananga. Some cultivation of crops had started to spread slowly beyond this narrow band of land, but the Gunnagal had a technological and spiritual link to the river which meant that they abandoned it only reluctantly. Apart from the Gunnagal, the Aururian continent held a great many peoples and languages, but the only other sedentary civilization was the eel-farming Junditmara, who occupied a couple of hundred square kilometres far to the south of the Nyalananga.

All of this would change with the collapse of the Gunnagal. This was a time of prolonged drought, of internecine warfare, but it was also a time of large-scale population movements. Some of these population movements were within the Nyalananga basin itself, as people moved up and down the river. This allowed more sharing of ideas, goods and crops, which in time would stimulate a new cultural and technological flowering along the Nyalananga. More of the population movements would be those of people abandoning their ancestral homelands. The calamities of the collapse broke the cultural link to the river, and Gunnagalic peoples began to expand over much larger territory.

The Gunnagalic migrants who abandoned the Nyalananga did so for a variety of reasons, fleeing famine or revolution, defeated in warfare, or pursuing tales of opportunity from their predecessors. Regardless of their motivation, they had the same set of advantages; an agricultural package of crops which could grow on all but the most arid lands, and knowledge of how to smelt and work copper. They had lost access to the great copper mines of the Lower Nyalananga which had sustained the Gunnagal. Still, the Aururian landscape contained many small deposits of copper which were sufficient to sustain the tool and weapon-making needs of the bands of migrants moving out of the Nyalananga in the Great Migrations.

From their homelands along the Nyalananga, the descendants of the Gunnagal expanded in all directions, taking their crops with them. The expansion received its first momentum from the initial flood of refugees leaving the drought-stricken Lower Nyalananga, but it gained a life of its own, with the Gunnagalic farmers still pushing into new territories long after the population along the Nyalananga had stabilised. The Great Migrations transformed Aururia, as agricultural societies displaced hunter-gatherers throughout the southern half of the continent. In the north, the stream of migrants stopped only when they reached the tropics, where the warmer climate and different growing seasons did not suit their staple crops of red yams and murnong[22]. In the west, they stopped only when they reached the aridity of the interior. In the south and east, they halted only when they reached the sea. From the Tropic of Capricorn to the Narrow Sea [Bass Strait], from the Grey Sea [Tasman Sea] to Aururia's red heart, the region was transformed with the advent of agriculture.

The Great Migrations began in 900 BC, and lasted for over a millennium. They were not a continuous advance, but a series of population movements in many directions, sometimes with agricultural peoples moving back into already-settled areas, and a process of warfare with some leapfrog advances far into new territory while the areas in between remained controlled by hunter-gatherers. The first Gunnagalic settlers displaced by war fled eastward past the mountainous headwaters of the Nyalananga [Monaro plateau] to reach Aururia's eastern coast by 600 BC, but most of the eastern seaboard would not be colonised by agricultural peoples for another three centuries. Pioneering Gunnagalic migrants followed the Anedeli [River Darling] and were growing red yams near Nungli [Roma, Queensland] by 500 BC, at near the northern limit of that crop's range, but the full displacement of non-Gunnagalic peoples from this region would take another four hundred years. The conventional date for the end of the Great Migrations is AD 200, although Gunnagalic settlers had reached most of south-eastern Aururia a least a century before that. Most of the last hundred years was a process of consolidation of control over this territory, where the remaining hunter-gatherers were displaced or took up Gunnagal farming ways.

The Great Migrations were a combination of colonisation, assimilation and military expansion. Hunter-

---

[22] A few of the domesticated Australian crop species will actually grow further north than this, particularly the bramble wattle (*Acacia victoriae*). As a complete package of crops, however, the effective growing limit is a little south of the Tropic of Capricorn.

gatherer societies did not survive the migrations, except where the peoples were pushed north into the tropics or west into the arid interior. The pre-Gunnagalic hunter-gatherers were not exterminated as individuals; many of the colonising Gunnagalic peoples intermarried with the local inhabitants. Some elements of old beliefs survived the Great Migrations, especially place-names, and names of unfamiliar plants and animals. Most of their accumulated knowledge of local flora and fauna survived, too. But the diverse hunter-gatherer cultures and languages which had existed before the Great Migrations were transformed into a region of cultural unity. This would later be referred to as Gunnagalia, although the inhabitants at the time did not have any conception of themselves as a coherent group.

Gunnagalia was a common cultural zone, the legacy of having such closely-related peoples expanding over such a wide area. The early Gunnagal spoke one language, although dialects had begun to diverge even before they started leaving the Nyalananga basin. The migrations spread these dialects across Gunnagalia, and the dialects would diverge into separate languages over the next few centuries. The Gunnagalic peoples likewise brought their religion, technology, and other accumulated lore with them, and left this legacy for their descendants. This common legacy would be reflected in all the cultures and peoples who followed the early Gunnagal.

Yet while the Gunnagalic migrations were extensive, they did not quite displace everyone who occupied the south-eastern regions of Aururia. There were three main hold-outs, areas where the pre-Gunnagalic peoples preserved their own language and culture. Far to the south of the Nyalananga, the Junditmara had maintained a settled society with thousands of people long before the Gunnagal had learned to farm yams. Gunnagalic migrants brought yams, wattles and knowledge of metalworking to the Junditmara, but the migrants were absorbed into the Junditmara, rather than the other way around. On the coast, far north-east of the Nyalananga, a hunter-gatherer people named the Mungudjimay occupied the Daluming region [around Coffs Harbour] before the Great Migrations. An early group of Gunnagalic settlers entered that area, and were few enough in number that they became part of the Mungudjimay. With this knowledge, the Mungudjimay took up farming and adopted a settled lifestyle before the main stream of Gunnagalic migrants reached them. The third group of hold-outs were in the region which the Gunnagalic peoples called the Highlands [Monaro plateau]. This is an elevated plateau which includes some of the headwaters for the Nyalananga and one of its major tributaries, the Matjidi [Murrumbidgee]. Here, the altitude meant that red yams did not grow well, and farming developed using hybrids of domesticated murnong and a related alpine species[23], producing a new crop suited to these regions. This meant that the Nguril and Kaoma peoples who lived there had time to take up farming rather than being displaced by Gunnagalic immigrants.

The Great Migrations did not reach all of the fertile areas of southern Aururia. While they covered the south-eastern quarter of the continent, there was another fertile region of the south which they did not touch. The fertile lands of south-western Aururia are separated from the eastern regions by desert barriers, included a land so barren that the first historical European explorers in the region named it the land of no trees[24]. In allohistorical Aururia,

---

[23] *Microseris scapigera*, the alpine murnong, is well-adapted to the highland regions of south-eastern Aururia.

[24] This is the Nullarbor Plain. Its name is sometimes misconceived to be of Aboriginal origin, but is in fact derived from Latin and means "no trees." The Nullarbor is an extremely harsh landscape, consisting largely of a limestone plateau which is so arid that it doesn't really support any trees. Historically, some Aboriginal peoples did live here (the Pila Nguru), although in relatively small numbers when compared to the lands to east and west of there. In allohistorical Aururia, this arid region called the Dry Lands is a substantial barrier to land communication; not totally impassable, but nearly so without local knowledge.

there was extremely tenuous contact between east and west, conducted via the peoples who lived in this arid region. The desert barriers meant that no large-scale migrations were possible, but in time some crops and knowledge did diffuse across the barren lands.

Around 550 BC, the first red yams were being grown in the fertile regions just west of the Dry Lands [Nullarbor]. A few other crops would follow, such as bramble wattle and native flax, though many others did not make the crossing. Yet those few crops allowed the Yuduwungu people of this region to develop sedentary societies, and in time they developed their own agricultural package of crops, including some plants not known further east. The Yuduwungu had some very slight trade contact with peoples across the Dry Lands, enough for knowledge of metalworking and pottery to spread, although they developed their own unique styles. In time, the Yuduwungu would begin their own migrations, spreading farming, their language and culture across the fertile regions of south-western Aururia.

By around AD 200, much of the southern half of Aururia had become a land of farmers. Hunter-gatherers still occupied the arid interior of the continent, but in the east and the west, agriculture was now widespread. In most cases, these peoples were still quite thinly-spread, but the reliable food supply would allow their population to grow rapidly in the following centuries. The foundations had been set for the development of populous societies and advancing technology. Still, the most populous region of the continent remained the Nyalananga basin, where the inhabitants started to recover from the collapse by around 600 BC. The long-term result of the collapse would turn out to be not entirely negative; the changed conditions and internal population movements produced a variety of innovations. In time, the heirs of the Gunnagal would share these new developments with Aururia, too.

Although not all of these new developments would be welcome.

#7: True Wealth

"*Budetju-yu tjimang agu-yiba garr.*" This is an axiom amongst the people of Tjibarr, spoken after the worst of the Collapse. In their dialect, this phrase means "all true wealth comes from the earth." This was a simple yet profound truth, amongst a people who had witnessed two centuries of environmental ruin, social upheaval, migration, and warfare. To the people of Tjibarr, who still called themselves the Gunnagal, the earth was the source of all bounty. Some wealth of stone or rare metal was dug from beneath the earth, but most of the wealth was grown from it.

In an era when a centuries-long drought persisted, there were increasing opportunities for anyone who could find ways to make the earth more productive. The pressure on agricultural yields meant that farmers developed new solutions. Early Gunnagal farmers had possessed only limited knowledge of techniques for replenishing the soil. Amidst the struggle of the drought, they found new methods. Their forefathers had long known of the value of burning areas of forest to promote the growth of their chosen crops, and Gunnagal farmers learned to use wood ash as fertiliser, along with dead wattle leaves and other organic matter.

Gunnagal farmers had often used wattles along the edges of yam fields, as a handy source of timber, to mark farm borders, and to act as shelter for small birds who fed on insect pests. Observant farmers noticed that in times of declining yields, yams grown along the edges of fields, next to wattles, would grow larger than yams in the centres of fields[25]. This led to the development of new techniques for companion planting, where rows of wattles were interspersed amongst rows of yams. It also led to methods of crop rotation, where wattles would be planted across exhausted yam-fields. They would be allowed to grow for four years, producing a couple of harvests of seeds, and revitalising the soil while they grew. The wattles would then be cut down as a source of timber, with their leaves mixed into the soil as further fertiliser, and new crops of yams grown on the revitalised soil.

Wattles, the trees whose name became the root of the Gunnagal word for wealth, were also developed in other ways. The Formative Gunnagal had used several wattle species, but usually only one in a particular area. With the population migrations, several species of domesticated wattles were spread across the Nyalananga. This gave farmers access to more kinds of wattles, including those which flower and seed at different times of the year[26]. The Gunnagal farmers developed a system of planting two different kinds of wattles on their farms, in roughly equal numbers. This meant that they could harvest the wattle seeds in different months, spreading the labour required across the year, and allowing a given number of farmers to

---

[25] Being legumes, the roots of wattles contain symbiotic bacteria which replenish nitrates in the soil.

[26] Wattles can be broadly divided into early-flowering wattles, whose seeds are harvested around November-December, and late-flowering wattles, whose seeds are harvested around January-February. The advantage of harvesting two species of wattles is that the harvesting can be spread over more of the year, while still allowing time to harvest yams and murnong (in April-May). Some of the other farming work, such as pruning wattles, harvesting gum, and so forth, can be spread over the quieter farming months. This allows for an ever higher yield of food per worker than in the previous form of Gunnagal farming, which in turn supports a greater proportion of the population as city-dwellers.

harvest a larger area. This also meant that they had a greater variety of flavours available in their food, and had more protection from pests and diseases, since the same pests and diseases rarely affected both kinds of wattles.

Together, the new farming techniques gave the Gunnagal long-term agricultural stability, allowing them to sustain themselves indefinitely. During the long centuries of the great drought, overall farming yields would still be lower than in former times, but they were more stable. This allowed the Gunnagal of Tjibarr and other Nyalananga cultures to rebuild following the Collapse. The population reached its lowest level around 750 BC, and from there, they began a slow recovery. After this time, the Nyalananga basin again became a source of fresh migrants while the Great Migrations transformed the Aururian landscape.

The Collapse devastated the peoples of the Nyalananga, but the long-term results were much less catastrophic. The new agricultural techniques meant that once the great droughts faded, a higher population could be sustained than before the Collapse. The population dispersals of this era led to intermingling of new ideas, new crops, new artwork, and in time new religions. The strains of the era, and the new resources which were made available with the Great Migrations, meant that in time new innovations and new technologies would be developed.

After the Interregnum, a new civilization emerged along the Nyalananga, which would become known to archaeology as the Classical Era. As in its previous incarnation, the Classical Nyalananga civilization saw the great river become a heartland of urbanisation, innovation, and cultural ferment. Unlike its previous incarnation, the Classical Nyalananga civilization did not stand alone. It formed the heartland of an expanding region of agricultural societies. Trade, technology, crops and ideas could now spread over a much wider region. Ideas born along the Nyalananga were no longer confined to its banks, and could disperse elsewhere. Many of the new crops, ideas and trade would now originate from outside the Nyalananga, and spread to the Nyalananga basin.

During the Interregnum, one of the most pressing constraints on the Nyalananga cultures was the lack of reliable sources of metal. Their pre-Collapse predecessors had possessed an abundance of copper and a reasonable supply of arsenical bronze, forged from natural impurities in the copper found in the Lower Nyalananga. With the pressures of the extended drought, mining had collapsed in the Lower Nyalananga, leaving the surviving peoples to search for alternative supplies of metal. Some copper and arsenical bronze was reused and reforged, but access to fresh supplies of metal was quite poor during the Interregnum. Some limited sources of copper existed in the upper reaches of the Nyalananga, which were used throughout the Interregnum, but these lacked the necessary arsenic impurities to form bronze.

Due to the shortage of available metal, knowledge of bronze-working almost collapsed, but not quite. For while arsenical bronze had served the Formative Gunnagal well, most of the world's civilizations have used bronze made out of tin instead. The upper reaches of the Nyalananga and its tributaries also contained some sources of tin, some as lodes which needed to be mined, but with some secondary deposits in riverbeds which were easily exploited. Late in the Interregnum, the Nyalananga peoples discovered the properties of alluvial tin, and how to forge it with copper to develop a more reliable type of bronze. This discovery revitalised their metalworking; they now had a reliable source of metal which could be used to develop much more effective tools. Farming, warfare, stone-working and a host of other industries would be transformed through the availability of bronze tools.

By 450 BC, the Classical Nyalananga civilization had firmly entered the Bronze Age, although their supplies of tin were limited enough that bronze was still a premium metal. This changed over the next couple of centuries, thanks to events elsewhere in Aururia. Between 400 and 300 BC, some groups of Gunnagalic migrants went northeast from their old homelands until they reached some new highland regions that possessed rich farmland [New England, New South Wales]. They quickly established productive farming communities.

In one part of this region, around the highlands of Toodella [Inverell], the new settlers discovered that they had arrived at an area rich in mineral resources. Here they found gemstones such as sapphires and diamonds which they polished and used as adornments, in the traditional Gunnagalic manner. Here, they also found rich sources of tin, including extremely useful native tin which they could exploit immediately.

Tin mining quickly expanded around Toodella, bringing considerable wealth for its inhabitants. Trade routes carried their tin and gems across much of the continent. Toodella is located among the headwaters of the Anedeli, a long river which eventually joins with the Nyalananga. Transport by water meant that large quantities of tin could be exported to the great cities along the Nyalananga. Tin was valuable enough that it was also carried overland to the eastern seaboard and other areas of the continent. Thanks to exploitation of new sources of copper, bronze-working spread across Gunnagalia; the metal was still expensive, but at least it was available.

Tin was not the only discovery from outside the Nyalananga which would spread back to the old heartlands. The Great Migrations had won the Gunnagalic-speaking peoples access to the resources of half of the continent, sometimes from settlement and sometimes from traders and travellers who ventured beyond the borders of the agricultural regions. The migrants who exploited the new regions found and domesticated new crops which grew there, and in time many of these spread back to the heartland of the Nyalananga.

North of the Nyalananga, the Gunnagalic migrants found lands which grew ever drier, even by the standards of their old river lands. In most of these lands, the Gunnagalic peoples could grow their old crops, although the yields were lower due to the reduced rainfall. But they found new plants here, ones suited to the arid landscape, and some of these plants could be harvested and then domesticated. They found and domesticated the desert lime, a relative of common citrus trees, and whose tasty fruit was occasionally eaten fresh, but which was normally used as a valued flavouring[27].

When desert limes reached the Nyalananga, they were gladly adopted as a fruit, and their juice was used for flavouring food. In time, their most valued use became as an additive to beverages. The early Gunnagal had long brewed an alcoholic drink from crushed yams. Adding the pulp of desert limes to the brewing mixture produced a new kind of drink, *ganyu*, which became the beverage of choice during festivals and other ceremonial occasions. Wealthier Gunnagal drunk varieties of *ganyu* which were further flavoured by spices traded from the eastern coast.

Migrants from the north also found another plant to be worth domesticating, the sweet quandong[28]. This is a tree which also grows in semi-arid areas, and whose fruit is large and sweet, by the usual standards of desert plants. In a land with few large fruits, domesticated quandongs would become a treasured part of their diet, eaten fresh as a

---

[27] The desert lime (*Citrus glauca*) is related to domesticated citrus species such as oranges and limes. It is native to the more arid areas of Aururia, and quite tolerant of harsh conditions such as heat, cold and drought. In historical Australia, it is harvested both from the wild and from commercial plantations, and it is also used to hybridise with other domesticated citrus species.

[28] The sweet quandong or desert peach (*Santalum acuminatum*) is a member of the sandalwood family, and a fairly close relative of Indian sandalwood. It is a hemi-parasitic plant whose roots derive parts of its nutrition from the roots of other trees. The Nyalananga peoples grow domesticated quandongs alongside rows of wattles for this purpose. (A similar practice is done in commercial harvesting of quandong in historical Australia).

seasonal fruit or dried for later use. Quandong fruit contains a relative large nut in the centre (much like peaches). This seed is also edible and highly nutritious. Farmers along the Nyalananga would come to refer to the quandong as the "queen of fruits."

Still, of all of the plants which the Nyalananga peoples would come to cultivate, none would be more treasured than corkwood (*Duboisia hopwoodii*). This is a shrub whose leaves and shoots contain high levels of nicotine. In its wild form, corkwood is widespread throughout much of central Aururia, but the form which was important grew in a much more geographically restricted area far to the north. The early Gunnagal knew of this region only through travellers' tales, which named it the Wonder River [Mulligan River, Queensland] because of the value of the plants which grew there.

Here, since time immemorial, the local peoples managed the land to ensure that they could collect abundant harvests of the leaves of corkwood. The leaves were dried, mixed with wood ash (usually from wattles), and rolled into a form of chewing tobacco, called *kunduri*, which was a highly prized drug. Harvests of corkwood from this region saw *kunduri* become the basis of a trade network which stretched across large parts of the continent. The useful form of corkwood grew further north than the limits of Gunnagalic agriculture, but they had enough contact with the traders to visit the region and bring back the plants back with them to cultivate. Here, they came to apply the name *kunduri* both to the corkwood plant and the drug they harvested from it. In time, both the cultivation and use of *kunduri* would spread to the Nyalananga[29].

---

[29] Corkwood is relatively easy to cultivate, being a plant tolerant of limited rainfall and poor soils. Some species of corkwood are grown commercially in historical Australia as a source of various alkaloids which are used in making pharmaceuticals. The drug produced from corkwood was historically called *pituri*, but is called *kunduri* in allohistorical Aururia.

In the south, in the wetter regions near the coast of the Narrow Sea, Gunnagalic migrants also discovered a variety of new plants which were suitable for domestication. Here, they found new species of wattles, such as sallow wattle and gossamer wattle, which they started to cultivate alongside their more familiar wattles. They found new fruits such as muntries and apple berries, and new vegetables such as Warrigal greens, which they also cultivated[30]. These new crops were treasured in the areas where they were native, and spread widely along the eastern coast of Aururia. In the Gunnagalic heartlands along the Nyalananga, though, they were of only limited value. These new crops needed more rainfall than could usually be relied upon, and even during the Classical Era the Gunnagalic peoples rarely used irrigation for their crops.

Although few crops from the south would become widespread along the Nyalananga, the south provided other things which changed the nature of farming and society across the continent. The Junditmara chiefdoms had been sedentary societies even before agriculture reached them. Now, they adopted not just new crops, but they also domesticated a new animal. The tiger quoll (*Dasyurus maculatus*) is the largest marsupial carnivore on the Aururian mainland, a predator of small mammals, birds and reptiles. It occupies a similar ecological niche as cats do in the Old World, and indeed is so alike in its habits that early European settlers to historical Australia called it the native pole-cat.

The tiger quoll is relatively easy to tame, and even in hunter-gatherer times it was occasionally kept as a pet.

---

[30] Sallow wattle/ Sydney golden wattle/ coastal wattle (*Acacia longifolia*) and gossamer wattle/ white sallow wattle (*A. floribunda*) differ in some of their details from other domesticated wattles, but their main uses are similar. Muntries (*Kunzea pomifera*) and apple berry (*Billardiera scandens*) are both fruits which will be valued along the coastline, and when dried, used as a trade good inland. Warrigal greens/ Australian spinach (*Tetragonia tetragonoides*) will become a useful leaf vegetable.

With the adoption of farming, stored food often attracted rodent pests. Tamed quolls were very useful in keeping down the numbers of rats and mice. In time, this led to the domestication of the species. Much like cats, quolls were mostly used by farmers to keep down the numbers of rats and mice, although a few were also adopted as household pets by the wealthy[31].

Of all the animals which the agricultural peoples of Aururia would domesticate, one would be valued above all. The emu (*Dromaius novaehollandiae*) is a flightless bird which is widespread across Australia, and by height is the second largest bird in the world. Both farming and hunter-gather peoples of Aururia had long hunted emus as a source of meat and feathers. Among the groups of farmers who still hunted emus were the Kurnawal, a Gunnagalic-speaking people who had settled along the coast which they called the Mother Lakes [Gippsland Lakes, Victoria]. Some Kurnawal found it useful to corral emus with ditches and fences until the time came to slaughter them. From here, they sometimes fed and bred them. In time, this led to the domestication and farming of emus[32].

Domesticated emus quickly spread far beyond the lands of the Kurnawal. Farmed emus became called *noroons*,

---

[31] Although unlike cats, domesticated quolls do not get stuck up trees. They climb down on their own.

[32] Emus can be easily kept and bred in captivity (as is done in historical Australia and around much of the world today). However, they took longer to tame than the other main Aururian domesticated food animal, the wood duck. This is because wood ducks are primarily grazers, while emus need a more varied diet. Domesticated emus are partly left to feed on grass and other plants, and some insects which they catch for themselves in the fields. They also need to be partly grain-fed, for which Aururian farmers use wattle seeds. Farmed emus can also be run through wattle fields once the main harvest has taken place. This keeps the emus exercised, and also lets them clean up any stray seeds, discarded seed pods (which emus also eat), and any other insect pests which may be in the fields.

based on the Kurnawal name for the bird. Quick-growing birds, they became a very useful source of meat, but also provided many other products, such as eggs, feathers, hides for leather and parchment, and noroon oil [emu oil]. As the rearing of noroons becomes widespread throughout the Nyalananga, one of the main indexes of a farmer's wealth became how many adult emus they could maintain in their flocks[33].

With the arrival of domesticated noroons, and increasing number of ducks farmed in the now-empty rangelands, the Nyalananga peoples had a replacement for their exhausted hunting grounds. Fishing from their wetlands remained a useful supplementary source of meat, but the primary source of meat for the Classical Nyalananga peoples came from domesticated animals. Combined with their development of new farming techniques, this gave them the basis for building a new culture, with considerable advances in technology and social organisation over their predecessors.

The Interregnum also saw the domestication of one new animal along the Nyalananga itself. After Goolrin fell at the start of the Interregnum, most of its inhabitants moved away, but a few remained in the area. The climate changed around them, becoming drier and warmer, and many of the plants and animals that had lived there retreated south-east, toward cooler and wetter lands. Many more arid-adapted species moved into the vacant lands.

One of those migrants was a mid-sized lizard with a strange "beard" beneath its chin, which another history would call the inland bearded dragon (*Pogona vitticeps*). The former refugees of Goolrin thought that the lizard

---

[33] Emu broods are fairly large, often up to 15 chicks for every breeding female, but most of these birds will be slaughtered at around 12-15 months old for their meat and other products. The index of a farmer's wealth is thus the number of long-term adult birds which they can maintain, not the total size of the flock (which will often include many chicks).

resembled the traditional depictions of the Rainbow Serpent, so they called the lizards *little serpents*. When rendering this name into European languages, it would usually be translated as little dragons.

The new lizards became quite tolerant of people, and in time the locals began to tame and farm them. The little dragons grew larger and more docile under human domestication. Farmers valued them during the Interregnum since they produced a decent amount of meat and leather while consuming relatively little food or water. The return of wetter climes and the spread or noroons means that farming of little dragons was reduced. Use of the lizards persisted in some more small-scale farming where they could be efficiently raised on food scraps, or when farming drier, agriculturally marginal lands where their water conservation was helpful. Some urban households also used little dragons since they could be obtained as hatchlings, fed on food scraps and any insect pests which the lizards found in the house, and eventually butchered as a source of meat.

The Interregnum was a time of considerable cultural ferment and increasing technology. New techniques and technologies were developed in artwork, masonry, construction, metallurgy, ceramics, sundials, textiles, weaponry, and many other fields. Among these was the development of the first true writing system. By the Late Formative, the Gunnagal were using a variety of symbols to mark ownership and contents of some goods, particularly on ceramics. At first, these were mostly according to personal designs and methods, and varied from a few straight lines cut into the sides of pots to elaborately-painted diagrams to represent container contents. The disruptions and population displacements led to the breakdown of many of the trade routes and the people who used some of these symbols. The remaining traders found that it became more practical to have a common set of symbols representing ownership, which could be presented to the Council of a city in the case of disputes.

This was the genesis of the Gunnagalic writing system; a set of symbols used to assert private ownership which was standardised to assist with government resolution of legal disputes. Yet once the first system of writing developed, it did not take governments long to adopt it much more widely. The power of writing combined with abundant clay to make into tablets led to the rise of a literate bureaucracy who began to keep detailed records of many aspects of life in the Nyalananga cities. The spread of bronze tools and increasing stone working also meant that public inscriptions and proclamations could be conveyed to the people. The first surviving inscription (a fragment of a law code) which later archaeologists can decipher will be dated to 117 BC, but writing on clay had been commonplace for more than a century before that.

The Gunnagalic writing system which emerged in early Classical times was shaped both by the preferred writing medium and the variety of personalised designs which preceded it. Early Gunnagalic scribes wrote mostly on clay using a stylus with a sharpened point, which meant that all their characters were formed from straight lines; early Gunnagalic writing was distinctly angular. The Gunnagalic script was fundamentally a syllabary; all of the words in their language (except for a few recently borrowed words) could be represented by about four hundred characters depicting syllables[34].

Thanks to the legacy of symbolic designs, Gunnagalic writing also included a number of stylised pictographs which were originally intended to represent trade goods.

---

[34] The Gunnagalic peoples are fortunate in their syllabary, in that their language is structured in such a way that about four hundred syllables will represent their entire language. (An English syllabary would run into thousands of symbols, since English has lots of consonant clusters and lots of vowels). Most syllables in spoken Gunnagal (at least the Tjibarr dialect) consist of a consonant or consonant cluster followed by a vowel, such as *ki, be* or *tji*. Only a relatively few syllables have a consonant-vowel-consonant arrangement, such as *gal*.

These pictographs originally represented a single word, usually a name. They were soon expanded used to represent ideas as well, and often acquired multiple meanings which needed to be interpreted based on context. The most common pictograph was a stylised representation of a tree with spreading branches. This was originally intended to depict a wattle tree, but which was soon co-opted for other purposes. Depending on context, the wattle-sign could represent wealth, food, a good harvest, the new year, gold as either the colour or the metal, and several other meanings.

In time, the invention of writing allowed the consolidation of government power. The surviving governments of the Interregnum and early Classical era were effectively continuations of the old Wisdom Cities; oligarchic councils which were mostly responsible for the rule of their own city and for a long stretch of the river outside of the city walls. Two of the Wisdom Cities survived the Collapse, Tjibarr and Gundabingee. Displaced migrants within the Nyalananga had founded a third city partway between those two centres, Weenaratta, which started with a similar oligarchic government, and which grew rapidly in population during the later stages of the Interregnum.

During the Classical era, these three cities continued to be called Wisdom Cities, but their governments changed their form. The Councils had been ruled by the elders of the eight *kitjigal*. Their roles often combined aspects of noble families, lawmakers, priests, military leaders, and merchant princes. With the chaos of the Collapse and the subsequent rebuilding, many of these functions changed or became more specialised. The *kitjigal* persisted, but developed into a system of political factions with their own interests in trade and sport, and who also often functioned as an armed militia. Their prominent families emerged as nobles with an interest in trade and warfare, but they lost any functions as lawgivers or priests. Priestly hierarchies emerged in each city, who took over the main religious duties, and who functioned separately from the *kitjigal*.

In time, the factions in each city nominated secular leaders, whose function was originally to arbitrate in disputes between the factions, but which in time evolved into monarchies. During the Classical era, the rule of these monarchs was never absolute; the factions had their own interests and if enough of them combined in revolt, they could bring down a monarch. Still, under the monarchs, the Wisdom Cities become the centres of expansive states, who sometimes fought with each other, and who extended their rule far beyond the bounds of the Nyalananga.

The Formative era had seen rule largely confined to a narrow strip of land along the river, but the monarchs extended their power much further. The monarchs at Tjibarr ruled over a kingdom which at its height stretched as far south as the Murragurn [Grampian Ranges, Victoria], and as far west as the old lands around Goolrin, where they re-opened the copper mines. The monarchs of Gundabingee had a similarly growing realm, expanding their power southward and eastward into the highlands.

Besides the three cities along the Nyalananga, a fourth city was founded by migrants who left the Nyalananga proper and moved along the Matjidi, one of its major tributaries. Here, just upstream of an area of large natural wetlands, they founded a new town which they called Garrkimang [Narrandera, NSW]. Garrkimang never knew the rule of a Council; it had been founded by migrants following a man who claimed to have visions. His heirs became a line of prophet-kings who ruled according to their claim to be best at interpreting the wisdom of eternity. Under their direction, the natural wetlands downriver were expanded and controlled as a source of food, while the rich lands upriver were turned into productive farmland. In time, Garrkimang would grow to become the wealthiest and most populous of all the Wisdom Cities, first as a monarchy, and then in time as the capital of an empire.

Classical Nyalananga civilization centred on the four great cities, but it fit into a much larger network of trade and transportation which sprawled across much of the continent. Some of this was evident even in the changed methods of construction within the great cities. With bronze tools for quarrying and masonry, the Classical Era saw many buildings constructed out of stone. Most notably, the developing priestly and royal classes saw the construction of large palaces and temples, where the earlier Gunnagal had been much more egalitarian in their dwellings.

From these palaces and temples, the developing bureaucratic classes administered life in the great cities. They did not control everything; the faction-riven societies of the Nyalananga did not lend themselves to tight government control. Still, the bureaucrats kept records of contracts and censuses. Warehouses under the control of the temples and palaces stored bulk goods, particularly wattle seeds, yams, and other yields from the harvests. The monarchs and their representatives did what they could to ensure impartial government decisions. Especially when it came to anything involving trade.

Trade, more than anything else, ensured the prosperity of the Classical Nyalananga civilization. Much of the trade was local, carried by boats along the rivers. The greatest bulk came from food, including staples such as yams and wattleseeds, and delicacies such as meat and fruit. Other local trade goods included timber, textiles, metal tools, fine ceramics, wattle gum, locally grown spices such as sea celery, river mint and sweet pepper, ochres used as mineral dyes, and a variety of vegetable dyes formed from wattle pods, wattle flowers, and the roots of other native plants. Even more valuable were the locally grown drugs; *ganyu* and other alcoholic beverages were always well-received. While the Nyalananga peoples did not use much irrigation for crops, they did ensure that their cultivated corkwood grew well enough to provide them with *kunduri* to trade far across the continent.

Indeed, the Classical trade networks reached much further than the environs of the Nyalananga. Some goods could be moved by water along the erratic Anedeli, and others were so valuable that they were carried overland for long distances. From several coastal areas came a blue-purple dye made from the shell of a sea snail, which preserved its colour long after vegetable dyes had faded[35]. Silver and tin were brought down from Toodella and mined in other smaller deposits. Copper came from both the Upper and Lower Nyalananga. Gold was rarely found, but small alluvial deposits were exploited around Guwindra [Bathurst, NSW]. Gemstones were highly regarded when they could be found; opals from the deserts, sapphires from Toodella, and diamonds from a dozen small deposits in the east.

Salt, that valuable preservative, was harvested from inland dry salt lakes or from evaporation ponds in settlements along the coast. The same inland salt lakes supplied treasured alabaster gypsum which was used to make ornamental statues and other stonework. Dried fruits from the southern and eastern coasts were valued delicacies in a civilization with only limited sweet foods of their own. Likewise, a few highly-prized spices grew only on the eastern and southern coasts, where the rainfall was high enough to support them; lemon myrtle, aniseed myrtle, cinnamon myrtle, mintbushes, native ginger, and several

---

[35] This dye is made from the shell of the large rock shell (*Thais orbita*), a predatory sea snail which is common around much of the Aururian coast. It is a relative of the Mediterranean sea snails which produced dyes of Tyrian purple and royal blue which were such valued commodities in classical times.

other spices were carried by people across the mountains to inland trading posts[36].

While trade flowed from and to each of the four great cities, each had its own areas of specialty. Tjibarr, furthest down the Nyalananga, was the main source of the copper, silver, lead, and tin which came from the Lower Nyalananga or shipped down the Anedeli. Garrkimang, from its position along the Matjidi, was the major supplier for the *kunduri* trade, and it also had good access to the eastern spices. Gundabingee, in the upper reaches of the Nyalananga, supplied premium-quality timber from the highlands, and with its relatively abundant rainfall grew most of the locally-produced spices. Weenaratta, in the middle of the Nyalananga, had access to the greatest wetlands, exported fish and other meats, and used its central position to take a cut of all trade which went up and downriver.

From their four great cities, the Classical Nyalananga peoples flourished in ways which surpassed even their pre-Collapse ancestors. About 100 BC, the centuries-long drought came to an end. The return to normal long-term

---

[36] Lemon myrtle (*Backhousia citriodora*) is a tree whose leaves produce a sweet, strong lemony flavour; in historical Australia it is the most widely-cultivated native spice. The related species of aniseed myrtle (*Syzygium anisatum*) and cinnamon myrtle (*Backhousia myrtifolia*) have similar properties, and all of these are cultivated by farmers on the eastern seaboard. Native thyme / roundleaf mintbush (*Prostanthera rotundifolia*) and the related cut-leaf mintbush (*P. incisa*) are members of the same plant family as more common culinary herbs such as culinary herbs such as mint, oregano, sage and thyme, and are similarly used as flavouring. Native ginger (*Alpinia caerulea*) was historically used when roasting food in earth ovens, and gives a strong gingery flavour to cooked food. Lemon-scented tea tree (*Leptospermum petersonii*) is also cultivated for its lemony-scented leaves, which will be used to make an Aururian equivalent of tea (as it is sometimes used in historical Australia). Lemon-scented grass (*Cymbopogon ambiguus*) is an Aururian relative of common lemon grass (*C. citratus*). Drought-tolerant and easily cultivated as a herb for cooking or for tea, lemon-scented grass is one eastern spice which will spread west across the continental divide.

rainfall levels allowed them to recolonise most of the Lower Nyalananga areas abandoned in the great drought. Greater availability of bronze tools allowed for more clearing of land for farming, and for more efficient farming. It also permitted larger and faster boats, which in turn permitted more effective food transportation.

Combined with the new agricultural techniques and domesticated animals, this led to a booming population. By AD 100, the Nyalananga peoples now matched their pre-Collapse levels. By AD 350, the population of the four kingdoms had passed two million people, mostly clustered along the Nyalananga and its major tributaries, but with some subject peoples living further away.

The Nyalananga peoples of this era never thought of themselves as a single group. By this time, the dialects that evolved from Proto-Gunnagal had diverged beyond the point of mutual intelligibility, even for the peoples along the Nyalananga[37]. The only group who still called themselves the Gunnagal were those people who still lived around Tjibarr; the other Nyalananga peoples had different names for themselves. Yet they shared a common heritage, and common bonds along the great river which they still called the Water Mother.

And, in time, common problems.

---

[37] By way of comparison, the difference between the Tjibarr [Swan Hill] and Gundabingee languages is about the same as the difference between modern Dutch and Austrian German.

#8: Of Birds, Bats and Bugs

When Europeans arrived in Australia, they found a continent without any epidemic diseases to greet them. Eurasian diseases like smallpox, measles, tuberculosis, typhus, chickenpox and a cocktail of other killers devastated the indigenous peoples of Australia, but no epidemic diseases waited in the Great Southern Land for foreign visitors.

In allohistorical Aururia, this is not the case.

* * *

Aururia, as a continent, has long been isolated from the rest of the world. Some of the neighbouring islands to the north are part of the same continental landmass, and were connected to each other when sea levels lowered during the ice ages[38], but it has always been a separate landmass to the mainland of Asia. Ocean barriers have protected it, but that isolation has never been complete. Over the millennia, many plants and animals have crossed the seas from the north and established themselves on the Aururian mainland; birds, bats, rats, monitor lizards, and humans, among many others. Still, with the separation of salt water, Aururian agricultural cultures developed in almost complete isolation from the rest of the world.

Almost.

---

[38] Or, strictly speaking, during the glacial periods of the ice age. The world is still in an ice age, just during an interglacial period where the ice sheets have retreated to Antarctica and Greenland.

Direct human contact between Aururia and its northern neighbours is rare. Some sporadic visits have occurred in the north-west or across the narrow strait to the north [Torres Strait], but their main legacy has been the transportation of the dingo to Aururia's shores. Yet some animals do make the crossing, particularly migratory birds. Several plant species are thought to have been established in Aururia when carried across by migrating birds.

Sometimes, birds bring less welcome influences with them. Such as their diseases.

Early Aururian agricultural peoples kept some birds of their own. The most important of these were the domesticated ducks and noroons used for meat. These birds often lived in close contact with humans, especially ducks. Some birds were also kept as pets, such as several varieties of parrots. Where there was such close contact between humans and birds, avian diseases could easily spread.

Avian influenza is a species of virus which has numerous subtypes, like most viruses, but which is primarily adapted to infect birds. Infections of avian influenza are often unnoticed among their main carrier bird species; infected birds often show no symptoms, even when they can infect other birds. Strains of avian influenza can jump between bird species to new hosts, and in the new host species, these strains are often more infectious and much more deadly. Avian influenza is endemic amongst many water birds, and has long been spread to Aururia from migratory birds crossing to and from Asia.

Farmers along the Nyalananga lived in close contact with domesticated ducks, and also lived near to human-shaped wetlands populated by an abundance of wild water birds. Strains of avian influenza regularly afflicted domesticated ducks, sometimes causing substantial die-offs to farmers' flocks. In time, the domesticated ducks would develop resistance, sometimes becoming asymptomatic carriers themselves, and thus be largely unaffected until a new strain evolved.

In AD 349, a particularly harsh strain of avian influenza spread from wild swans in the Bitter Lake [Lake Alexandrina] at the mouth of the Nyalananga to domesticated ducks at nearby farms. As had happened with many previous strains of avian influenza, the disease killed up to a third of the domesticated ducks in the region, and spread up the Nyalananga. In AD 350 it reached Tjibarr, devastating duck populations and farmers' livelihoods. In AD 351 the strain reached Gundabingee, where it also struck farmers' flocks. Most epidemics of avian influenza burned out here; farming communities beyond the Nyalananga were too scattered to allow for easy spread of the virus. But the strain in AD 351 was different. Unlike previous epidemics, this one mutated into a form which spread easily between humans.

This strain of influenza was the first epidemic disease which Aururia had experienced. Some endemic waterborne diseases were spread by poor hygiene, and a few endemic but rarely fatal diseases were transmitted by mosquitoes. But the influenza epidemic was like nothing which had been seen before on the island continent. Like all flu epidemics, this one spread mostly by airborne transmission, particularly through victims coughing and sneezing. In a population with no previous exposure to epidemic diseases, its symptoms were swift, severe, and often fatal. The first visible sign was usually a blue tint to the lips, combined with a sudden sense of weariness, which led the afflicted Gunnagalic peoples to christen the disease "blue-sleep."

Blue-sleep struck quickly; it sometimes took only a matter of hours for newly-infected victims to be too fatigued to move themselves. The most severe symptoms affected the lungs; the virus attacked the lung lining, usually causing haemorrhaging until the victims coughed up blood and died from pneumonia when their lungs filled with fluid. Blue-sleep also affected other parts of the body; it often infected the intestines, which sometimes caused its victims to die from blood and fluid loss. Victims who survived the initial assault of the virus were weakened for days or weeks;

secondary pneumonia often spread from opportunistic bacteria, and victims who had no-one to care for them often died of dehydration or even malnutrition.

Blue-sleep spread throughout the farming peoples of south-eastern Aururia, killing up to ten percent of the population in the worst-affected areas. It spread to the nearer hunter-gatherer peoples as well, but those communities were more fortunate since the virus affected people so quickly that it often prevented them from travelling to spread it further. Blue-sleep killed about five percent of the agricultural population of the south-east, and a smaller percentage of the hunter-gatherer peoples who lived nearby. The Yuduwungu people of south-western Aururia were fortunate to be spared; the desert barrier of the Dry Lands was too thinly-populated to spread the virus.

After its initial ravages, blue-sleep became an endemic disease in south-eastern Aururia. It lost the worst aspects of its virulence, and in evolved into a disease whose symptoms were largely similar to strains of flu seen elsewhere in the world, although it retained the distinctive blue tinge to the lips, and the early onset of fatigue. Like all flu viruses, it mutated rapidly, and new strains appeared every few years. Occasional major epidemics occurred when blue-sleep evolved into a form where people had no resistance. Aururian peoples would never be truly rid of the blue-sleep virus.

When Europeans contact Aururia, they will quickly recognise blue-sleep as a form of influenza. Its symptoms are more severe than ones which they are familiar with, but they will still know what to call the illness. And they will die from it.

* * *

Creating artificial wetlands is one of the hallmarks of early Aururian farming peoples. Wetlands supply them with value sources of fish and meat and feathers from birds. In the wetlands, people gather plants for food, fibre and dyes, and cultivate some herbs and spices which cannot tolerate drier climes. The wetlands even help to filter the water of the Nyalananga and other major rivers. Human waste and other pollutants which are dumped into the waterways are carried into artificial wetlands downstream, which cleanse the water of many of the contaminants.

Yet artificial wetlands are a mixed blessing. Swamps, ponds and marshes are excellent for harbouring fish and birds, but they also offer an ideal environment for biting insects and a host of waterborne parasites. The waters of Aururian wetlands harbour a variety of pathogens such as giardia, cryptosporidium and parasitic worms which often infest human hosts. These parasites are widespread throughout the Nyalananga basin and other areas with artificial wetlands. Fortunately for their human hosts, the illnesses caused by these parasites are debilitating but rarely fatal.

Wetlands also harbour myriads of mosquitoes. Mosquitoes transmit many of the deadliest diseases in human history, particularly malaria, which is thought to have caused more human deaths than any other single cause. Luckily for Aururian agricultural peoples, the worst mosquito-borne diseases were either confined to the tropical north, or never became established in Aururia[39]. They will also be helped by a side-effect of their wetland management practices. Several species of Aururian sundews produce edible tubers which are valued as a food source, and so the Nyalananga peoples cultivate sundews. Since sundews are carnivorous plants which trap flying insects in sticky leaves,

---

[39] Malaria existed in historical northern Australia (until recently eradicated). Dengue fever is also present in northern Australia, but does not spread very far south. Yellow fever, the other major mosquito-borne disease, has never become established in Australia.

this helps to limit the number of mosquitoes in the artificial wetlands[40].

Nonetheless, there are enough mosquitoes in the wetlands to transmit diseases, and Aururia harbours several pathogens which are easily spread by mosquitoes. Ross River fever (also called epidemic polyarthritis) is a virus which produces a variety of flu-like symptoms such as fevers, chills, headaches, fatigue, and sometimes stiff or swollen joints. Most victims recover within a few days, although about ten percent experience a chronic form of the illness which produces ongoing joint pains, depression and fatigue which persists for months or years. It is fortunately a non-fatal infection, but it will become established in the wetlands surrounding Nyalananga cities. While it will not kill visiting Europeans, many of them will be struck down by what they see as a mysterious malady. The Nyalananga peoples will have a long familiarity with the disease, which they will call "old man's curse," from the arthritis-like symptoms which it produces even in the young.

The disease which another history will call Murray Valley encephalitis (MVE) is another virus that is transmitted by mosquitoes. Despite its name, it is historically more common in the tropical north than the Nyalananga basin, but it can become established further south. The wild host of MVE are herons, cormorants and related birds, which are common throughout the Nyalananga wetlands. MVE will become endemic throughout the Nyalananga. Fortunately, most of its victims experience no symptoms more severe than occasional nausea, headaches or vomiting. A small proportion - less than one percent - go on to develop

---

[40] These are the tuberous sundews of genus *Drosera* subgenus *Ergaleium* (sometimes classified as genus *Ergaleium*). The Nyalananga farmers cultivate several species, such as *D. praefolia*, *D. schmutzii* and *D. whittakeri*, and have spread those far beyond their natural range. None of these sundews are domesticated in the botanical sense, but have become widespread through human influence.

encephalitis (brain inflammation), with symptoms such as drowsiness, fits, weariness, and fatigue. Of those so afflicted, a quarter will die and up to half of the rest will experience permanent effects such as paralysis or brain damage.

Still, of all the gifts which Aururian mosquitoes give to humans, the one which will kill the most people is the one which initially was the least dangerous. Barmah Forest virus is related to the Ross River virus, and often has symptoms so similar that it requires a blood test to tell them apart, although Barmah Forest virus is usually less severe. Hosted by a variety of wild birds, it quickly became established in the Nyalananga wetlands, where for centuries it was a minor malady. Like the other mosquito-borne viruses, Barmah Forest virus was originally transmitted mostly between animals, where humans were simply incidental infections. Over time, however, the virus evolved into a strain where humans were amongst its preferred hosts. When it did, the results were deadly.

A virulent strain of Barmah Forest virus appeared along the central Nyalananga basin during the sixth century AD. Victims who were infected by this strain first suffered from chills, then fever and a blistery rash which spread across most of their body. The distinctiveness of the rash, and the realisation that the illness was suffered by people who had been near wetlands, led the Nyalananga peoples to christen the illness "swamp rash." The initial rash would be followed by fatigue and swollen joints. Many victims recovered at that point. A minority entered the toxic stage of the infection, where the lymphatic system was infected, leading to severely swollen lymph nodes over most of the body, extreme pain, and eventual coma and death.

Swamp rash became endemic to the Nyalananga wetlands, although it did not spread far beyond the Nyalananga basin. The virus is well-adapted to infecting humans, although there are also animal reservoirs amongst several kinds of wild water birds, and sometimes domesticated ducks. Birds rarely die from swamp rash, but humans are not so fortunate. When swamp rash first became virulent, the death rate amongst unexposed adults was around ten percent, and up to double that rate for infected children.

Centuries of infection from swamp rash has meant that the Nyalananga peoples who live near wetlands have evolved some natural resistance; the death rate amongst infected children is about five percent, and less for adults. For Europeans, who lack such resistance, the death rate will continue to be around ten percent for adults and worse for children. The higher death rates are not limited to people of European descent; since swamp rash did not evolve into its virulent form until after the Great Migrations, people who come from other parts of Aururia are as badly-affected as Eurasians.

* * *

While the Aururian continent holds relatively few infectious diseases which can be transmitted to humans, there are some potential killers. Of those which do exist, some of the most deadly are carried by bats. Aururian bats harbour several endemic diseases which are fatal to humans. As long as Aururian peoples remained hunter-gatherers, their population densities were too low for any of these diseases to turn into epidemics. With new farming practices transforming the landscape, bat populations were increasingly disturbed, and came into more contact with humans. This sometimes meant that their diseases infected humans, too[41]. With the larger human populations, particularly the larger urban populations, this now meant that bat diseases could turn into epidemic human diseases.

---

[41] A similar process is happening in modern Australia. Australian bats harbour a number of diseases which are capable of infecting and sometimes killing humans. These include: Australian bat lyssavirus, a close relative of rabies which produces similar symptoms; Hendra virus, which can cause respiratory haemorrhaging and fluid build-up in the lungs, and which sometimes infects the brain causing a form of encephalitis; and Menangle virus, which produces severe flu-like symptoms.

At first, these bat-carried diseases were not easily transmissible between humans. Initial exposure was usually either from a bat bite, or farmers accidentally coming into contact with bat urine or other bodily fluids. In many cases, this resulted in the death of the person infected, but rarely infection of other humans.

The first bat-borne disease to become endemic in allohistorical Auurian cultures was the disease known historically as Australian bat lyssavirus (ABLV). A close relative of rabies, this virus produces similar symptoms. The infection spreads slowly along the nervous system until it reaches the brain. Once there, symptoms begin with headaches and fever, and progress to severe pain, violent fits and spasms, extreme weakness, and mental instability. Eventually, the victim dies from inability to breathe properly.

A few early Aururian farmers died from direct infection of ABLV caused by bat bites. However, the disease only became endemic when domesticated dingos were infected by ABLV. In dingos, ABLV produced similar effects to rabies; aggressive behaviour including biting, which often transmits the virus to other dogs or to humans. Aururian peoples did not know that ABLV originally came from bats, but they quickly learned to recognise the behaviour of "mad dingos" that could lead to a fatal bite. The Atjuntja of south-western Aururia had a name for the illness, *drun-nju*, which literally translated as "barking mad." The Dutch who first encountered the disease there would transliterate the Atjuntja name into Drongo disease, the name by which it would be known to the world.

Still, while Drongo disease was almost universally fatal for people infected, it was almost impossible to transmit directly between humans. This meant that it never became a major epidemic disease.

Unfortunately, another Aururian bat-borne virus is both often fatal and capable of easy transmission between people.

* * *

History does not record exactly where the disease that came to be called Marnitja was first transmitted from bats to humans. Written sources do, however, describe the first time it appeared in one of the major urban centres along the Nyalananga. The city of Garrkimang, the former imperial capital, still possessed a fastidious and methodical bureaucracy who recorded all important events that affected the city. No event since the deposition of the last emperor would make a more lasting impression on their city than the arrival of a disease which they called the Waiting Death.

The archives of Garrkimang record that Marnitja first struck the city in 1206. A myriad of clay tablets describe the course of the disease with painful precision. Victims first experienced an initial fever, chills and weariness. These symptoms were reminiscent of the other epidemic disease, blue-sleep, although they lacked the hallmark blue lips of that sickness. However, Marnitja progressed to much more striking symptoms. Victims started to cough and splutter up a pinkish-red, frothy fluid mixed with saliva. Although the archivists in Garrkimang did not know and thus not could record it, the pink fluid was a result of haemorrhaging of the lungs.

The more fortunate victims of Marnitja started to recover from the "pink cough" after a couple of days, although fatigue and milder coughs would continue for another fortnight. The less fortunate victims did not recover, but suffered worsening coughs and increasing weariness. Some of the victims died through difficulty breathing, others from blood and fluid loss caused by excessive coughing. Other victims died of renal (kidney) failure, or simply slipped into a coma from which they never awoke. Survivors of the pink cough sometimes suffered permanent damage to their lungs, which produced life-long breathing difficulties.

Pink cough, the first stage of Marnitja, was devastating enough in itself, but what followed was worse. Victims who had recovered from the early stages of the pink cough, or rare survivals from the later stages, were not completely free of the disease. Many of the survivors started to suffer from strange new symptoms about two months later: headaches, a fresh bout of fever, confusion, seizures, and eventually delirium. Every victim who showed these new symptoms would die from them; a few succumbed to the fever or killed themselves by mischance from the seizures, while most eventually slipped into a coma from which they never recovered. The excruciating period of uncertainty for survivors of the pink cough, waiting to know whether they would suffer the fatal second stage, led the people of Garrkimang to christen the new disease the Waiting Death (Marnitja).

Marnitja spread far beyond its first outbreak in Garrkimang. The archives of the former imperial city and the other major Nyalananga cities do not record precise numbers, but it appears that about a third of the population were infected by the disease. Of those infected, about half died from the first or second stage. Marnitja slowly burned its way across the continent, and in time touched even the hunter-gatherer peoples on the farthest northern shores.

The first epidemic killed perhaps fifteen percent of the Aururian population. Nor would the disease disappear easily. A small percentage (0.2-0.5%) of those who came into contact with the virus became asymptomatic carriers. They would never suffer the symptoms of Marnitja, but remained infectious throughout their lives. So, like blue-sleep before it, Marnitja became established as an epidemic disease. It struck again every generation or two, although subsequent generations started to develop some resistance to the Waiting Death.

* * *

Aururia thus has two epidemic diseases waiting for any contact with overseas peoples: blue-sleep and Marnitja[42]. These diseases first spread to Aotearoa [New Zealand] after 1310 when the Māori made first contact. They caused considerable death amongst the Māori, but in time the Māori developed a similar level of resistance to these diseases as the Aururian peoples.

By 1618, blue-sleep is endemic across Aururia and Aotearoa. Within that region, it mutates every few years, as flu viruses usually do, although these new strains are rarely fatal to people who have survived the previous variants. Blue-sleep sometimes mixes with other strains of influenza from wild birds to create particularly severe epidemics, although even then the mortality rate is usually less than 0.5% of those infected.

As a disease, blue-sleep has become a variant of influenza with a couple of distinctive symptoms. The blueness of the lips remains a persistent and recognisable symptom, and in lighter-skinned peoples will show up as a bluish tint to the entire face. Blue-sleep has an incubation of 2-3 days before the first symptoms appear, although victims remain infectious for up to two weeks while recovering from the illness. European and Asian visitors will recognise it as a form of influenza, but it is a strain of flu virus to which non-Aururian peoples will have no immunity. The death toll when it spreads to the rest of the world will be as bad or worse than the historical Spanish flu pandemic of 1918; somewhere between 2.5 to 5% of the

---

[42] One of the side-effects of having epidemic diseases like blue-sleep and Marnitja (and the other less fatal mosquito-borne diseases) is that Aururian peoples will have developed generally stronger immune systems. Exposure to any infectious diseases during childhood tends to produce a stronger adaptive immune system, which in turn offers somewhat more protection against all diseases. The arrival of Old World diseases will still be deadly to Aururian peoples, but not quite as devastating as the equivalent epidemics which ravaged the Aboriginal peoples of historical Australia.

global population will die when blue-sleep spreads around the world.

While Europeans will have some familiarity with blue-sleep, they will be completely unprepared for Australia's biggest killer, the Waiting Death. Marnitja is a henipavirus related to the historical Hendra virus and Nipah virus, and more distantly to measles and mumps. Its original animal hosts were flying foxes (fruit bats), which became agricultural pests that raided farmers' fruit orchards. The virus was not transmitted directly to humans, but first infected dingos which came into contact with bat droppings and bodily fluids left beneath fruit trees. Infected animals spread the virus to other dingos, and eventually to humans, where it became an epidemic disease[43].

Marnitja spreads through airborne transmission or in bodily fluids. The virus has an incubation period of 7-14 days. Infected people are contagious for most of that time, although more so later in the incubation period. The haemorrhagic (pink cough) stage of the disease can last for up to two weeks, although some victims die within two days of the first signs. Infected people are contagious throughout the haemorrhagic stage, although not once the pink cough has subsided. After the haemorrhagic stage, the majority of the survivors are free of the virus (and have lifelong immunity), but a minority will develop a form of encephalitis over the next two or three months, or sometimes a longer period (up to 3 years). If the virus reaches the encephalitic stage, then it is almost (99.5%) universally fatal.

The Marnitja virus is capable of producing deadly pandemics. Even after several centuries of afflicting Aururian peoples, who have evolved some resistance, fresh epidemics still kill 3 to 5% of the non-immune population.

---

[43] Marnitja is an allohistorical disease, based on the features of the real-world Hendra and Nipah viruses, and what they might become if they evolve into a form which can be easily transmitted between humans.

Elsewhere in the world, virgin-soil epidemics will have considerably higher mortality rates. Depending on their overall level of health (well-fed peoples are more likely to survive), Marnitja will kill anywhere from 10-15% of the population of a given region. Transmission of the disease beyond Aururia's shores may take some time; sea travel in the seventeenth century was often slow. Still, sooner or later, the rest of the world will discover the affliction of the Waiting Death.

#9: The First Speakers

The time of the Collapse was one of great panic and greater upheaval. Harvests failed, droughts persisted for years and stretched into decades, bushfires grew more frequent and spanned ever greater areas of the continent, and the arts of civilization seemed to be failing. In this time of chaos, people sought refuge in whatever consolation they could find.

In 842 BC, Tapiwal, one of the old Wisdom Cities, was a place ripe for new ideas. Uprising and subsequent collapse had destroyed the great city of Goolrin, further downriver. In turn, this had ruined the arsenical bronze trade which supplied most of Tapiwal's wealth. The seemingly endless drought had destroyed much of its agricultural hinterland. More than half of its former territory had already been abandoned, wattles and yams left to run wild while wetlands silted up and returned to semi-desert. Hunter-gatherers reoccupied the former farmlands, while the surviving farmers gathered in Tapiwal itself, growing increasingly unruly.

Wunirugal son of Butjinong was one such farmer among thousands who arrived in Tapiwal in that year. The exact location of his old farm is not known; at least two dozen sites would later be claimed to be the site of his birthplace. He is reliably known to have been a member of the Azure *kitjigal*, and he claimed the wedge-tailed eagle as his personal totem. Beyond that, nothing definite is known about his life before he arrived in Tapiwal in the summer of

842 BC, although a thousand tales have since sprung up to explain how he spent his early years.

Just as with his early life, what Wunirugal accomplished in Tapiwal in that year has been recorded in many contradictory versions. Certainly, Wunirugal was among the more vocal of the farmers complaining about the lack of food, to the point where the city militia took official notice of him. Some say that he spoke so eloquently that the militia agreed to escort him before the Council to plead his case. Some say that Wunirugal outran the militia and entered the Council hall on his own. Some say that he was struck immobile by a vision and was carried bodily into the Council hall for investigation. One account claims that the Council came out to meet him in the main square of Tapiwal, but that version is usually discounted.

No two versions of Wunirugal's meeting with the Tapiwal Council agree on what he said, or even on the names of the members of the Council. There is surprising unanimity about the Council's decision: Wunirugal was deemed a danger to public order, ordered to be expelled from Tapiwal immediately, and not to return for a year and a day, on pain of death. Wunirugal left, but he was not silent along the way. Again, the accounts of his words vary, but all sources agree that he persuaded at least three hundred people to come with him into exile.

Wunirugal led his new followers far from Tapiwal. Accounts of their journey include some fantastic events. The most nearly-universal of those events is an account of how soon after he left the city, Wunirugal received another vision. While having this vision, he was struck by lightning which came from clouds which produced no rain, yet he survived with no ill effects. Scholars will long argue whether this widely-reported event is factual. It might be; some lightning strikes come from thunderclouds where rain is falling but evaporates before it reaches the ground, and some people do survive lightning strikes. Certainly, the reports of what Wunirugal did after the lightning strike are in surprising agreement. He is said to have fallen to his knees and said: "I know now what I must do, O lightning blue."

Whatever the merits of this account, it is clear from the many tales of Wunirugal that he had visions, or what other people believed to be visions. He drew on these for guidance, and led his followers up the Matjidi. This river is one of the major tributaries of the Nyalananga, but it had been a relative backwater since most of the trade flowed up and down the main river. Wunirugal led his followers past a long series of natural wetlands, and reached an area of lush, fertile soils which flourished even in the drought. He declared that this would be the perfect place to build a town. According to most (but not all) accounts, he said, "Here, the earth will always bring forth its yield. Here, we can build a city which will have no rival."

He called the new city Garrkimang.

* * *

Garrkimang [Narrandera, New South Wales] grew to become one of the four great cities of the Classical Nyalananga civilization. Like their contemporaries, the people of Garrkimang could trace their ancestry back to their Formative forefathers. However, Garrkimang developed along a different path from its neighbours. In language, it was much more distinct than any of the other Classical cities. The migrants who founded Garrkimang were a combination of refugees from the former Goolrin and the most westerly areas of former Tapiwal territory. This meant that their speech had diverged much further; while there were clear underlying similarities with other Gunnagalic languages, learning the speech of Garrkimang was considerably more difficult for foreigners than that of any other Classical city.

In culture and religion, Garrkimang was also unlike any other Classical city. The inhabitants called themselves the Biral, a name which means "chosen people." They traced this back to the migration under Wunirugal, believing that they had been chosen to be granted their new land as a sacred trust. Their religion had a similar foundation to the older Gunnagal beliefs; they still shared the same general view of the Evertime and of the spirit-beings who inhabit eternity, although they gave different names and attributes to many of those beings. Yet the old beliefs had been overlaid by a new religious structure, that of the First Speakers and their representatives who interpreted the world.

The heirs of Wunirugal ruled Garrkimang as absolute monarchs. The old cities had been ruled by oligarchic councils, but there had never been such an institution in Garrkimang. The rulers claimed the title of First Speaker, and based their rule on religious authority. They asserted that they were entitled to rule because they possessed the talent of interpreting the wisdom of eternity. They proclaimed their rule through a series of law codes first promulgated in Garrkimang itself, and which were spread throughout every city and town which came under their rule. They also adopted a set of protocols in terms of conduct, dress, and ceremonies to support the view of the First Speaker as the greatest moral authority. This was most obviously shown in the privilege which gave the First Speaker his title: in any meeting or ceremony, the First Speaker was always was the first person to speak. Anyone who dared to speak to the First Speaker unless directly addressed first would be fortunate if they were simply exiled; death was a common punishment for such a social *faux pas*.

The First Speakers were not always direct heirs of Wunirugal; the succession was open to all males in the royal family. It was even possible, although difficult, for those not of direct royal descent to be accepted into the House of the Eagle. Adoption was an accepted method for particularly eminent people to join the royal family and become eligible for the throne. The succession was often decided by the will of the First Speaker, who would designate an heir from amongst his relatives. On some occasions, the royal princes would meet to acclaim an heir when the succession was unclear. Public disputes over the succession were rare, and civil wars over succession would be unknown until the declining days of the monarchy. Incompetent rulers could, however, be removed. If the royal family thought that a First Speaker was very bad at listening to the wisdom of eternity, then that First Speaker would be quietly offered an opportunity to commune with eternity more directly, and another member of the royal family would take the throne.

Despite some internecine intrigues in the House of the Eagle, Garrkimang's monarchs were always much more secure on their thrones than the rulers of any other Classical city. The royal family had the bastion of religious authority to support their rule. More than that, in Garrkimang the old *kitjigal* system had broken down during the time of the Great Migrations. With so many people displaced, two of the eight *kitjigal* were lost entirely, and the rest were abandoned as social institutions. In the other Classical cities, the *kitjigal* evolved into armed factions which preserved their own privileges, including the right to form social militia. Monarchs in Tjibarr, Weenaratta and Gundabingee always feared uprisings amongst the factions, but Garrkimang did not have this threat.

Some aspects of the *kitjigal* were still preserved in Garrkimang, but in much-changed form. From its founding, Garrkimang's armies were traditionally divided into six warrior societies, each of which had their own initiation rites, values, informal social hierarchies, and special duties. These societies were named the Kangaroos, the Corellas, the Ravens, the Kookaburras, the Echidnas, and the Possums. Each of these societies derived their names and some of their values and practices from the old colours and social codes of the *kitjigal*[44].

---

[44] The Kangaroos came from Grey, the Corellas from White, the Ravens from Black, the Kookaburras from Blue, the Echidnas from Azure, and the Possums from Red. The old colours of Gold and Green were lost during the migrations.

Garrkimang also had six trading associations, each of which emerged from the old *kitjigal* colours. These formed into a system of recognised partnership and profit-sharing, and were in effect early corporations which had collective ownership of farming land, mines, trading caravans, and other ventures, who shared the profits and risks amongst all members of their society. The trading societies were powerful voices within Garrkimang and its dominions, but since all military and religious power was reserved for the monarchy, the trading societies never acquired the same political power which the factions did elsewhere.

* * *

Garrkimang occupied what was probably the best agricultural site of any Classical city. It had the convenience of large areas of productive land upriver suitable for the Gunnagalic system of dryland agriculture, and a series of natural lagoons and other wetlands downriver which were easily expanded into their managed artificial wetlands. The wetlands downriver of Garrkimang were productive enough that the First Speakers encouraged the diversion of some water to irrigate a few chosen crops, unlike the usual Aururian farming practices which relied on rainfall. This irrigation primarily fostered the cultivation of their favoured drug, *kunduri*, and was also used for the cultivation of a few fruits and other high-status foods[45].

With productive lands as the foundation of their power, the First Speakers turned Garrkimang into the capital of a growing kingdom. The early core was along the Matjidi. They gradually expanded northward to the Gurrnyal

---

[45] In historical Australia, this region has been transformed into the Murrumbidgee Irrigation Area. This uses a system of weirs, canals and holding ponds to irrigate the area, and which is in turn fed by larger dams further upriver. This has made the area very productive agriculturally. In allohistorical Aururia, Garrkimang engineers have developed their own complex system of weirs and channels to divert floodwaters and feed them into wetlands which are used, as elsewhere, for fishing and hunting.

[Lachlan River], which was a tributary of the Matjidi, and then much further to the Pulanatji [River Macquarie]. By edict of the First Speaker, in AD 256 the kingdom became known as Gulibaga, the Dominion of the Three Rivers. Despite the name, Gulibaga did not fully control any of these three rivers. The upper reaches of the Pulanatji marked their northern border, and the farthest downstream stretches of the Matjidi and Gurrnyal remained under the control of the kingdom of Tjibarr.

While Gulibaga was a powerful kingdom, for most of the Classical era it was only one nation amongst four. The three Nyalananga kingdoms of Tjibarr, Weenaratta, and Gundabingee all flourished during this era. The four nations each had a vested interest in ensuring that none of their rivals grew too powerful, which was reflected in a fluid system of alliances that prevented one kingdom from completely defeating any of the other four.

The alliance system broke down in the Late Classical period, thanks to the social disruptions of the first blue-sleep epidemics in the mid-fourth century AD, and a more than usually faction-ridden aftermath in the kingdom of Tjibarr. This let the First Speakers extend their control to the Anedeli, a major tributary of the Nyalananga, and the key transport route for tin from the northern mines. Gulibaga kept its control over the tin trade from this time, despite efforts to dislodge its forces. While tin was still traded further downriver to the other Classical kingdoms, Gulibaga received the largest share, and from then on they had better access to bronze than their rivals.

It was an advantage they would put to good use.

* * *

In the vanished era of the Classical Nyalananga peoples' ancestors, war was as much a series of raids for honour as it was a contest between nations. The era of the Collapse changed that; wars were now fought for national gain. Still, while Classical military tactics were more organised than those of their ancestors, they were not particularly advanced. The archetypal Classical warrior carried a wooden shield and a bronze-tipped spear, sometimes also with a short sword. Armour was rare, save perhaps an emu leather helmet. Captains might have more bronze armour, but the common Classical soldier was only lightly-protected. Battle tactics and training were not particularly advanced; being a soldier was a part-time occupation for most people, and while the Classical peoples knew how to form a line of battle, their coordination and discipline were both limited.

With a near-monopoly on bronze, Gulibaga's warriors changed the old pattern. The kingdom had the wealth and the resources to equip their leading warriors with better armour, typically a bronze helmet and greaves, and hardened leather breastplates. They could afford to maintain the first large professional standing army, elite units who trained and deployed together. They standardised and extended their tactics with a number of military innovations. Professional Gulibagan warriors carried pikes and rounded shields, transforming them into Aururia's first heavy infantry, who could break almost any enemy line of battle. In battle, the core infantry were supported by lightly-armed skirmishers who used bows with stone or bone-tipped arrows, and who helped to disrupt enemy formations.

By the mid fifth century AD, Gulibaga's military organisation was clearly superior to anything developed by its Classical rivals. The combination of better arms, armour and tactics would prove almost irresistible.

* * *

With its superior military organisation and resources, Gulibaga transformed itself from a kingdom into an empire. In the name of the First Speakers, its armies waged war on its classical rivals, particularly its most powerful opponent, the kingdom of Tjibarr. In a series of campaigns from AD 467 to 482, Gulibagan armies conquered most of Tjibarr's territory, although the city walls withstood siege after siege. In AD 486-488, a long siege finally broke through the walls of Aururia's most ancient city.

In previous wars between Classical kingdoms, similar victories had seen defeated monarchs being reduced to effective vassals, with "advisors" from the victorious kingdoms dictating policy. Such advisors were usually thrown out within a few years, with the support of one of the other four kingdoms. With the defeat of Tjibarr in 488, however, the First Speakers did something unprecedented: they deposed the old monarchs and created a new province with an appointed governor. This action is usually taken to be the start of the Imperial era in the history of the Nyalananga basin. Some authorities use a later date of AD 556, when Gulibagan armies subdued the forces of Gundabingee, the last surviving independent Nyalananga kingdom. After this victory, the First Speaker renamed his nation to Watjubaga, the Dominion of the Five Rivers[46]. This would be the name by which it would be remembered.

With the resources of the Five Rivers at its command, Watjubaga expanded into Aururia's first empire. Its core territory remained the old lands along the Nyalananga and Matjidi, but its armies carried its rule to most of the agricultural regions of south-eastern Aururia. In the north, one of its major early accomplishments was the gradual expansion along the Anedeli until they conquered the Gemlands [New England highlands] directly, taking over the sources of tin and gems. To the south, they faced some determined resistance from the Junditmara peoples, who had their own developing kingdoms and a hierarchical social code based on duty to one's elders, conformity, and rewarding loyalty. Still, the might of professional discipline and imperial bronze saw the Junditmara kingdoms defeated one by one.

* * *

---

[46] The Five Rivers are the Nyalananga [Murray], Matjidi [Murrumbidgee], Gurrnyal [Lachlan], Pulanatji [Macquarie] and Anedeli [Darling].

At its height around AD 850, Watjubaga claimed suzerainty over territory which stretched from the Neeburra [Darling Downs] in the north to the Narrow Sea [Bass Strait] in the south, and to the deserts and the Turtle Gulf [Spencer Gulf] in the west. These northern and western borders represented what amounted to its natural frontiers. In the north, the Neeburra was inhabited by a set of feuding Gunnagalic peoples who dwelt in small villages and raided each other for noroons and honour. Their northern limits were bounded by the growth of the red yam, which does not grow properly in the tropics. The Empire imposed its authority on these peoples, although the distance and the fractious nature of its subjects meant that its authority was perforce rather loose.

Likewise, the western and southern borders of the Empire were largely bound by desert and the seas. Watjubaga controlled all of the thinly-inhabited lands west of the Anedeli, and the more fertile coastal lands around the Nyalananga Mouth, the Turtle Gulf, and the Narrow Sea. They largely ignored the Seven Sisters [Eyre Peninsula], a small, lightly-settled agricultural land beyond the Turtle Gulf, since they deemed it too poor and too difficult to control without decent sailing technology. Direct imperial control did not always end with the desert; imperial forces maintained a few inland colonies to access some key resources such as the silver, zinc and lead of Silver Hill [Broken Hill], and a few salt and gypsum harvesting colonies on some of the dry inland lakes.

In the inland regions of Aururia, imperial influence was minimal, although they did have some contact with the desert peoples. Long-established trade routes stretched across much of the desert; ancient traders had travelled hundreds of kilometres across some desert routes when trading for flints and ochre. With the establishment of imperial outposts along the desert fringes, some of these trade routes were expanded. In a few locations with particularly high-value resources, the local hunter-gatherers found that they could mine a few key goods and trade these for food and metal tools from the agricultural peoples along the coast.

The most important of these routes became known as the Dog Road, which started at the imperial outpost of Dogport [Port Augusta] and ran over five hundred kilometres northwest to Ngarringa [Coober Pedy]. Here, the local Ngarjarli people mined opals from one of the richest sources in the world. The climate was far too dry to support a large population, or even a permanent population, but like most hunter-gatherer societies, the Ngarjali had a lot of under-used labour.

Thanks to the imperial interest in opals, the Ngarjali found a reason to mine those gems and establish a semi-permanent settlement at Ngarringa, where some of their people slowly mined opals throughout the year. Once a year, in June when the heat was least severe, the annual trading caravan set out from Dogport. People and dogs pulled travois loaded with trade goods: clay vessels full of wattle-seeds, smoked meats, dried fruits, and *ganyu*; metal tools; textiles such as clothing, baskets and bags; and *kunduri*. When they reached Ngarringa, they held a great celebration and trading fair with the Ngarjali, and exchanged opals for their trade goods. This reliable food storage allowed the Ngarjali to occupy the same area for a large part of the year, although water shortages meant that they sometimes needed to move elsewhere.

* * *

While Watjubaga had clearly-defined natural borders in the north, west and south, its eastern frontier was more ambiguous. In most regions, imperial authority ran as far as the mountain range which they called the Spine [Great Dividing Range]. The combination of rugged terrain, lack of beasts of burden, and distance from the imperial heartland meant that conquering the less technologically advanced peoples of the east coast was largely deemed not to be worth the effort. Along the southern coast, however, imperial armies had marched east from Junditmara lands and gained control of the lands around the Little Sea [Port

Phillip Bay]. In the headwaters of the Matjidi, the Highlands [Monaro plateau] were occupied by sullen imperial subjects who sometimes paid tribute and often rebelled. Further north, the rich farmlands of the Kuyal Valley [Hunter Valley] were inhabited by city-states who were reluctant imperial tributaries; this was the only region where imperial influence extended to the Grey Sea [Tasman Sea]. Except for the Kuyal, the eastern coast of Aururia remained independent of imperial control save for occasional raids.

As an empire, Watjubaga claimed immense territory, but in many cases its level of control was limited. The empire maintained its predominance through its military strength, and more specifically through a core of well-equipped veteran soldiers who were the battlefield heavyweights of their day. In a land without cavalry, the imperial heavy infantry could be relied on to shatter any opposing army in any battle on open ground. Still, rebels often found ways to neutralise these tactics, particularly when fighting on irregular ground or resorting to raids and retreating to rugged terrain where the heavily-armoured imperial infantry had difficulty pursuing them.

Moreover, imperial manpower was limited. Watjubaga drew its soldiers exclusively from the ethnic Biral, who mostly dwelt in the ancient territories around Garrkimang, formed a significant minority in the rest of the Five Rivers, and elsewhere were either a small ruling elite or inhabited a few colonies established both as garrisons and trading posts. Joining the Biral was difficult for anyone of a foreign ethnicity; marrying in sometimes happened, but otherwise the only way to join was to persuade a Biral family to formally adopt someone, which was rare. These limitations on imperial manpower became an increasing strain with the large territories where Watjubaga tried to maintain its rule. The large distances and slow transportation technology meant that when away from one of the major rivers, even the local Biral elite often partially assimilated into the local culture, and the long lines of communication meant that local garrisons in distant territories were perpetually vulnerable to revolt.

* * *

At its height, Watjubaga ruled over vast territories, but it did not create much of a sense of unity amongst its subjects. With the Biral forming an elite ruling class, the subject peoples were rarely inclined to adopt Biral language or culture. Some people learned Biral as a second language, since it was the language of government, but it did not become the primary language of any but the Biral themselves.

Still, while relatively few people could speak or write the Biral language, an increasing number of people in the Empire were literate. Later archaeologists discovered this due to the wealth of written information preserved in clay tablets. Written accounts preserved considerable details about life within the empire, preserved in government records, legal documents and other archives, and also through an abundance of private documents such as letters, trade records, and religious texts. Within most regions of the Empire, government administrators could simply place tablets announcing new proclamations or other news in town squares, and be confident that they would be read, understood, and the information conveyed to everyone in the city.

The nature of imperial rule varied considerably amongst the imperial regions. Watjubaga's core territories were the heavily-populated areas along the Nyalananga and Matjidi, and the almost as heavily-populated area around the Nyalananga Mouth and eastern coast of the Turtle Gulf. Here, imperial administrators exercised considerable control over everyday life, using a system of labour drafts which required every inhabitant to perform a certain number of days service for the government every year. This labour was required outside of the core harvest times, and was used to construct and repair public and religious buildings, maintain artificial wetlands, and sometimes to grow high-value crops such as *kunduri*, which were subject to imperial monopoly.

Outside of the core territories, the labour draft system was much less prevalent. The imperial government tried to enforce it amongst the Junditmara in the south, with only limited success; this was one reason for the repeated revolts in that region. In the more thinly-inhabited regions along most of the Upper Anedeli, power was usually delegated to local chieftains instead. In the Gemlands, the Empire ran the mines using a system of labour drafts, but otherwise imperial control there was limited. In most other regions, the Empire did not even attempt to directly rule the territories, but simply collected tribute from local leaders.

In terms of religion, Watjubaga likewise exercised only limited control over the views of its subjects. The imperial view of religion was syncretic; like all of the Gunnagalic religions shaped during the Great Migrations, it had assimilated some indigenous beliefs from the hunter-gatherers displaced during the population movements. The underlying structure of their religion remained similar to their ancestors; they viewed the present world as only one aspect of the Evertime, the eternity which controlled everything and was everything.

Within this framework, the actions of individual heroes, sacred places, and of spiritual beings were all adopted in a cheerful mishmash of beliefs. The Empire had no qualms about recognising other religious traditions as simply being aspects of the same underlying truth. Their only concern was for the religious role of the First Speakers, who had always maintained the claim that they were best suited to interpret the wisdom of eternity. Obedience to imperial authority was treated as accepting this religious duty; civil disobedience or outright rebellion were both treated as blasphemy. Beyond that, what individuals or peoples believed was of no concern to the imperial administration.

* * *

The Imperial era spanned several centuries, and it brought immense wealth to the royal city of Garrkimang. Extensive use of labour drafts usually meant that much of this wealth was invested into public architecture. The First Speakers and other noble classes amongst the Biral had a fondness for large, ornate buildings. At the height of imperial rule in AD 850, Garrkimang had five separate palaces reserved for the royal family, and three dozen smaller palaces used by other noble families. They also built several large temples and many smaller shrines dedicated to various spiritual beings or former First Speakers. The royal city also held several large amphitheatres used for sporting and religious events.

Imperial engineering techniques were not particularly advanced by Old World standards, although they had developed considerably from their Classical ancestors. Imperial engineers built very effectively using a wide variety of stones. They had not discovered the arch, and lacked both the wheel and beasts of burden to help with moving building material around, but they had waterborne transport and lots of determination. Imperial construction techniques tended toward large, solid stone buildings, with the walls supported by buttresses at key points. They could build some very large columns, but they mostly used them for freestanding monuments or as aesthetic elements of building design, rather than as the main structural support. In the most elaborate imperial buildings, the solid buttressed walls were overhung with large eaves, and the eaves themselves were supported with elaborately-carved columns.

Imperial aesthetics placed great value on elaborate displays in architecture. This meant that imperial buildings were covered both within and without by a great many decorative elements: intricate ornamental stonework, sculptures, glazed tiles, murals, and above all bright, bright colours. Some valued stones were transported large distances because their appearance was preferred; the marble quarries at Guwindra and Mullagamba [Orange, NSW] were far from Garrkimang, but that was of little concern to the imperial engineers who ordered large quantities of marble to decorate the exterior of the palaces and temples. Colour was an integral part of most decorations, from some coloured stones, or glazed tiles, or from a variety of paints. While the individual stylistic elements were wholly alien to European building traditions, the overall impression of imperial architectural styles would be reminiscent of the Baroque period. In technicolour.

* * *

In technology, the advent of the Imperial era did not mark any dramatic improvement over the preceding Classical era. While the First Speakers were not hostile to new learning, the focus of imperial efforts was on administration, aesthetic improvements, and organisation, rather than any particular sense of innovation. Outside of engineering, architecture, and military technology, there were no fields where the First Speakers would be particularly interested in supporting experimentation or the application of new ideas.

Still, the spread of literacy allowed more communication of ideas, as did the growth of trade under the imperial peace. This contributed to some technological advances during the Imperial era. Metallurgy became considerably more advanced during this period, particularly in the development of many copper-based alloys. The exploration of the Silver Hill ore fields led to the isolation of zinc ores, and these were used to create brass. With imperial aesthetics being what they were, most brass and many alloys of copper with precious metals were used for decorative rather than functional purposes. Brass also came to be used in various musical instruments such as horns and bells. Imperial smiths knew of iron, both from ancient experience of meteoric iron, and as a waste product from their extraction of zinc ores[47]. However, their smelting techniques did not produce sufficient heat to melt iron ore, and so they did not make any significant use of the metal.

The spread of literacy allowed the beginnings of the development of a medical profession in the Empire. Doctors in the Imperial era began to make systematic studies of symptoms of sickness and injuries. Clay tablets found by later archaeologists included some handbooks of illnesses, of their diagnosis, prognosis and recommended treatments. Many of these recommended treatments did not actually work very well, since internal illnesses such as fevers, epilepsy and parasites were believed to be spiritual phenomena which required treatments by priests. Still, the early Imperial doctors had some capacity to assist in the treatment of physical injuries, using some basic surgical techniques, bandages, and a variety of lotions and herbal remedies derived from several plants. They also had a basic knowledge of dentistry, using drills to deal with cavities, using forceps and other specialised tools to extract teeth, and using brass wires to stabilise broken jaws.

Imperial scholars had some knowledge of mathematics and astronomy, although their methods were often basic. They used some rudimentary trigonometry and related methods to assist with calculating engineering requirements, but they had little interest in algebra or other more advanced mathematical techniques. They kept astronomical

---

[47] The process which the Imperial smiths have used to develop brass is distinct from that used elsewhere in the world. Early brasses elsewhere were produced from calamine, which is an ore which contains zinc carbonate and zinc silicates, and which were melted with copper to produce brass. In Aururia, the Imperial smiths have explored the massive Silver Hill [Broken Hill] ore deposits, initially for extraction of lead and native silver, both of which are abundant there. Mining in this deposit will also mean that they discover sphalerite, an ore of zinc sulfide which has also has impurities of iron. This can be melted to produce brass in the same way that calamine was elsewhere, but it also means that iron will frequently be encountered as an impurity in the waste products.

records on matters which interested them, but they ignored some other aspects. They were aware of the movement of the planets, although they believed that both Venus and Mercury were each two separate bodies, not having made the connection between their appearances in the morning and evening. They kept enough of a watch over the constellations to recognise novas and supernovas. They kept particularly detailed records of comets, which they believed to be a visible representation of the reincarnation of a 'great soul' who would make their mark in the material world in the near future. Being born during the appearance of a comet was a highly auspicious omen, to the point where heirs to the imperial throne would sometimes be chosen based on that fact alone. They kept some occasional records of eclipses, although not systematically, and did not make any practical application of those records. Imperial scholars had no real conception of the shape of the earth; they still assumed that it was flat.

* * *

The Imperial era marked a period of common administration with fewer barriers to trade or exchange between peoples. Among other consequences, this meant that some domesticated crops and animals became much more widely-distributed amongst imperial territories. For example, the different species of wattles were freely exchanged across imperial territory, giving farmers more options about the best trees to suit particular circumstances. Noroons had spread among much of eastern Aururia already, but during the imperial administration they became much more commonly raised and spread to all parts of imperial territory.

One plant became so widespread it almost became synonymous with imperial administration. The tufted bluebell (*Wahlenbergia communis*) was a sweet, edible blower which had been farmed since earliest agricultural times. However, during the Great Migrations, most of the migrants who left the Nyalananga basin did not bring the art of bluebell cultivation with them. This meant that use of the bluebell was largely confined to the four Classical kingdoms along the Nyalananga, and only rarely was the flower cultivated outside of that region.

In the Classical city of Garrkimang, the practice developed that tufted bluebells were grown in large, publicly available and royally-maintained gardens. This meant that any town dwellers who wished to collect some flowers to eat or use to make sweet blue-water could freely do so. As the kingdom and then imperial territory expanded, maintenance of these bluebell gardens became regarded as a mark of civilization. The maxim spread that "a town without a garden is not a town, just a collection of buildings." In any town of significant size throughout the Empire, one or more bluebell gardens would be present within the walls or nearby outside.

The cultivation of tufted bluebells would remain a significant part of Aururian farming from that time onward. The flowers or their products would be widely used as sweeteners and for some cosmetic and medical functions. While not all Imperial successors would maintain public gardens of tufted bluebells, the flowers would nevertheless continue to be widely cultivated for private purposes.

Although the Imperial era meant that many crops and animals spread widely, this did not apply to everything. For two key products, the imperial administration deliberately maintained monopolies on production in key areas within the Five Rivers, and thus controlled the wealth they brought. These two products were *kunduri* and silk.

Kunduri cultivation had begun during the Classical period, and Garrkimang was by far the largest producer. Imperial conquest brought with it regulated *kunduri* production. A number of locations throughout the Nyalananga basin, mostly but not entirely along the Matjidi, were designated as sites for *kunduri* production, with any cultivation elsewhere being expressly forbidden. Specialised imperial administrators oversaw the cultivation in the designated locations, not so much to ensure quality but to ensure that the imperial government received its allocated share of the revenues.

The other main imperial monopoly was on a product which if anything brought even more wealth than *kunduri*: silk. In pre-Imperial times, as far back as the Formative Gunnagal, people had occasionally gathered wild silk from the cocoons of various species of butterflies and moths, and used this to make high-quality, highly-prized textiles. While valuable, wild silk production was unreliable and gave only low yields.

Around AD 450, some farmers upriver of Garrkimang began to deliberately rear the ribbed case moth (*Hyalarcta nigrescens*) on trees on their farms. Case moths are a group of moths whose caterpillars produce woven silk cocoons (cases) which they carry around with them while feeding. The cocoons of most case moths are made from a combination of silk and plant matter, which makes their cocoons far too troublesome to use for silk production. However, the ribbed case moth uses only silk in its cocoon, which means that the silk is much easier to extract for human use.

By around 510, imperial records revealed that ribbed case moth production was being managed under imperial administration "for the glory of the First Speaker." Whether by accident or deliberate breeding – records do not reveal – the farmers had obtained a domesticated variety of ribbed case moth whose cocoon fibres lacked the mineral reinforcements that were found on the wild variety. This meant that the domesticated moths produced a finer silk fibre which could be more easily extracted and more readily woven into cloth[48]. The domesticated moths were also more easily bred and raised on a variety of local trees (mostly eucalypts), which enabled much higher silk yields than wild-gathered silk.

---

[48] A similar change of losing mineral reinforcements is found in the historical domesticated silkworm of China (*Bombyx mori*), which also produces a much finer and softer silk than wild silks.

Silk, too, became an imperial monopoly with designated locations for cultivation and weaving. For silk, all of the cultivation locations were along the Matjidi itself, the heart of the Empire, for better control and for security against cultivation being stolen elsewhere. Silk production remained a major source of imperial wealth, and a jealously-guarded secret which the imperial administration sought to preserve for as long as possible.

* * *

Militarily, Watjubaga reached its largest borders in AD 822. One of their most celebrated generals, Weemiraga, had earlier subjugated the peoples around the Littla Sea, and incorporated them into the Empire. In 821-822, he made his great "March to the Sea," leading an army across the Spine into the Kuyal Valley, and then to the Grey Sea. He imposed tributary status on the city-states in this region. This accomplishment would be recorded in sculptures, murals, and legends, and it saw Weemiraga adopted into the royal family and become First Speaker from 838-853.

At this moment, it appeared that Watjubaga was in a period of ascendancy, but in truth these accomplishments were virtually the last military expansion which the Empire would achieve. Logistical difficulties meant that the Empire would find it difficult to expand further, and the imperial regime soon faced internal problems. After the death of Weemiraga, the succession was contested between three princes, leading to the worst civil war which the Empire had yet seen. The civil war ended in 858, but other underlying trends were further weakening the Empire's ascendancy.

Imperial rule had relied on two pillars of the state. The first was a solid core of veteran heavy infantry equipped with bronze weapons and armour from the continent's main supply of the metal, who could defeat any major uprising. The second was a system of garrison-colonies in the far-flung regions of the Empire to maintain a local presence there and ensure the main army would be rarely needed.

As the ninth century progressed, both of these pillars were weakened. The colonisation of the Cider Isle

[Tasmania] in the early ninth century provided a rich new source of tin and bronze which was outside the imperial monopoly. This disrupted the trade networks and government revenue, and allowed peoples in the southern regions of Aururia to gain access to better arms and armour. Subject peoples were also becoming increasingly familiar with imperial military tactics, and through the legacy of several revolts developed ways to imitate or counter these military tactics. Combined with the increased bronze supply, this meant that rebellious peoples could now field soldiers to match the imperial heavy infantry, and the Watjubagan military advantage waned.

The other main pillar of the state was also being undermined by a slower but more significant process of cultural assimilation. The Biral governors and upper classes formed a small minority in most of the outlying regions, and imperial governors came to look more to local interests than the dictates of a distant First Speaker in Garrkimang. Governors assumed more and more *de facto* independence. Successive First Speakers found it increasingly necessary to settle for payments of tribute and vague acknowledgement of imperial suzerainty, rather than maintaining any effective control.

The weakening of the imperial military advantage was manifested by two successive military disasters. In the 860s, imperial forces were sent to subjugate the Mother Lakes region [Gippsland] on the southern coast. This was inhabited by the Kurnawal, a fiercely independent-minded people whose relatives had been one of the two main groups to cross the Narrow Sea and settle in the Cider Isle. Thanks to that colonisation, the mainland Kurnawal had access to good bronze weapons, and they largely fought off the imperial forces. The imperial commander conducted several raids and collected enough plunder to bring back to the First Speaker as a sign of victory, but the manifest truth was that the conquest had failed.

Worse followed in 886, when a new campaign was intended to launch a new March to the Sea and conquer the

Mungudjimay around Daluming. This time the imperial armies were defeated utterly, unable even to claim plunder. This marked the resurgence of the Mungudjimay as an independent people, and within the next few decades they would begin raids into imperial territory around the Gemlands.

The defeat in Daluming marked a devastating blow to imperial prestige. Another disputed succession followed in the 890s. While this did not turn into a major civil war as had happened four decades earlier, it encouraged already-rebellious subject peoples. The Kuyal Valley had always been a reluctant tributary, and actual payments of tribute had been largely non-existent since the 870s. In 899, the city-states of the Kuyal ceased acknowledging even the pretence of imperial overlordship, and the weakened Empire was in no condition to restore its authority.

While the ruling classes in Garrkimang found it easy to disregard the loss of the Kuyal tributaries, thinking of it as only a minor matter, a much more serious rebellion followed. The Junditmara peoples had long resented foreign rule, requiring substantial imperial garrisons. A revolt over labour drafts in 905 provided a trigger for unrest, and in the next year it turned into a general Junditmara revolt. The imperial troops were massacred or driven out of Junditmara-inhabited territory, and in 907 the army sent to reconquer them was outnumbered and defeated. The Junditmara peoples established their own loose confederation to replace imperial rule. They would take what they had learned of imperial technology, literacy, astronomy and other knowledge, and apply it to their own ends. The loss of the Junditmara lands also made imperial rule over the rest of the south coast untenable, and they lost everything south of the Spine within a few years of the Junditmara establishing independence.

With crumbling imperial authority in the south, the First Speakers turned to one last territorial expansion. The Seven Sisters, beyond the Turtle Gulf, had long been disregarded by the Empire. The peninsula was a small region of fertile land separated by a desert barrier from the nearest imperial city at Dogport. The land was useful for agriculture, and had some very occasional trading links with the Yuduwungu across the western deserts. Still, there was little to recommend a conquest, and the separation of deserts and water made a military campaign difficult.

Keen to restore some military prestige, the imperial government cared little for such details, and despatched forces who marched overland from Dogport. The Mutjing people of the Seven Sisters peoples withdrew behind city walls rather than fight in open battle. While their cities were besieged and captured one by one, the long and bloody warfare did not justify the conquest. The Seven Sisters were proclaimed as conquered in 926, but the loss of imperial manpower would hurt far more than the minor gain in resources.

After the conquest of the Seven Sisters, the remaining imperial structures started to rot from the periphery inward. In the north, the local governors assumed effective independence, although the fiction of imperial control continued for two more decades. The decisive break came in 945. The governors of the five provinces which made up the Gemlands had long been more sympathetic to their subjects than the distant proclamations of the First Speakers. The governors announced their secession from the Empire in a joint declaration in 945, bringing the local Biral garrison-colonies with them, and raising additional local forces for defence. Imperial forces were sent to reassert control of the source of tin (and many gems), and were defeated in a series of battles in 946-948. This event, more than anything else, marked the collapse of the Empire. Apart from some brief attempts to reconquer a rebellious Seven Sisters in the 970s, this marked the last time that the Empire would try to project military power outside of the heartland of the Five Rivers.

Imperial rule over the core of the Nyalananga basin – the Five Rivers – persisted for much longer than the more distant territories, but with the same condition of gradual decline of imperial power. The Biral remained a resented ruling class along the Nyalananga proper, and revolts became increasingly common. The First Speakers resorted to increasingly desperate measures to quell some revolts, including the wholesale razing of Weenaratta in 1043, but in the end, none of these measures were successful. The lands around the Nyalananga Mouth were lost in the 1020s, then Tjibarr rebelled in 1057 and started to encroach further into imperial territory. Gutjanal [Albury] asserted its independence in 1071, taking most of the dominions of the old kingdom of Gundabingee with it. By 1080, the Empire consisted of little more than Garrkimang and its immediate hinterland; its borders had shrunk even further than the borders of the Classical kingdom. The last of the First Speakers were removed in 1124, leaving Garrkimang a decaying city filled with monuments to past imperial glories.

#10: Times of Bronze

February - March 1310
Raduru Lands [The Illawarra, New South Wales]
Kawiti of the Tangata had explored far and wide around Te Ika a Maui [North Island, New Zealand], and once to the even larger island to the south. His father, who had taught him the arts of navigation, had sailed even further, being one of the pioneers who had guided the fleets of canoes bringing the Tangata from the ancestral homeland of Hawaiki. Kawiti had heard many tales, oft fanciful and extravagant. Yet he had never seen or heard of men like these.

Eight of them, no two men alike except that they all carried spears tipped with some strange yellowish-brown substance. When he first saw them, he thought that they all had skins black as night. Now he saw that was a combination of shadows and artifice. Once they stood out of the shadows, the small patches of skin visible beneath their cloaks and armour were darker than his own, but not midnight-black. Some sort of dye must have been used to darken the more visible parts of their skin. To aid in hunting, or through some strange custom? No way to know, not yet.

The leader of the dark men asked him another question in their incomprehensible language, pointing at them, then their boat, then to the water both north and south. After a moment, Kawiti realised that the man was asking where they had come from. He told his comrades to stay quiet –

no point having everyone answering the question. He pointed to himself and his comrades, then the boat, then he pointed east, and made repeated pushing gestures to show that they had come from far to the east.

That provoked a mixed response from the dark men. A couple laughed, as if not believing. Others spoke in raised voices, their expressions showing disbelief. The leader – if leader he truly was – snapped a command, and the arguments died back to murmurs. He asked a single-word question: "*Guda?*"

Having no idea what the word meant, Kawiti settled for gesturing to include himself and his comrades again, then pushing many times to the east, to show how far away it was.

The dark men argued amongst themselves for a few moments more, until they settled down. Their leader seemed to convince the others as much through volume as anything else. He then turned back to Kawiti, and gestured at himself and his comrades. "*Raduru,*" he said. "*Iya Raduru.*"

Kawiti nodded, and gestured to himself and his fellows. "Tangata. We are Tangata."

The leader of the Raduru gestured to himself. "Gumaring. *Uya* Gumaring."

Kawiti gave his own name.

The dark men – the Raduru – all smiled after that. Gumaring gave what sounded like more orders, from the crisp tone, and the Raduru passed over some gifts. They handed over two water skins and some kind of orange, translucent substance which felt slightly soft against his fingers. Almost like kauri gum, but different. Gumaring mimed eating the gum.

"Here's hoping that offering us food makes us guests," his cousin Nene said.

"And here's hoping that this isn't like kauri gum," Kawiti said. Dried kauri gum could be dug from the earth, and was very useful for its gleam and appearance, but no-one ever ate it.

He chewed on a small portion of the gum, and found that it was sweet. Very sweet. He washed it down with a mouthful of water. An unusual taste, but a pleasant one. His fellows did the same.

"We should return the favour," Kawiti said. Except that all they had for food was cold, smoked moa meat and raw kumara [sweet potato]. Explorers were used to such fare, but he did not know if he wanted to offer it to strangers. Did the Raduru see offering any food as a greeting, or would they prefer only something sweet or fine-tasting? No way to know, so would if offend them more to offer no food in response, or to offer food they did not like?

Gumaring solved the matter for him. He quietly regathered the now much-emptier water skins. He gave some lengthy explanation which made no sense whatsoever – maybe wondering if they could learn a few words here and there – and then returned to using gestures. He conveyed the idea that he wanted the Tangata to come with his men to the north, and copied Kawiti's earlier gesture to indicate that it would be a long way to travel.

Using a variety of gestures and signals of his own, Kawiti managed to convey the idea that he and his comrades would travel in that direction, but by water. He would not leave the canoe behind and have no way to reach home without making another, especially with no surety that they could make new sails.

Gumaring appeared happy enough with this, and then had another voluble discussion with the other Raduru. As before, he seemed to settle it as much by volume as by persuasion. After that, Gumaring kept pointing to himself, then to the boat, indicating that he wanted to travel with them, leaving the other men to journey by land. Kawiti was more than happy for that; having Gumaring along would avoid any problems with wherever these people lived at the other end. Still, he asked the other Tangata, preferring to make sure that they were happy rather than have friction on the trip.

"Fine. Just be glad they all didn't want to come," Nene said. The others gave their agreement, too.

All of the Raduru came back to the canoe. They seemed utterly fascinated by it, as if they had never seen a boat like it before. "What would they think of a big *waka*?" Kawiti asked.

The other Tangata laughed. This small exploration canoe could carry a few men a long way, but it was nothing like the much larger *waka* which had carried their fathers from Hawaiki, and which were used nowadays to take settlers further south along Te Ika a Maui. A *waka* could carry eighty men across the seas to a new home.

Even this one? Kawiti wondered, for a moment, but dismissed the thought. He was here to explore, not to raid. The Big Man back home would decide whether to settle or to trade or to ignore this new land altogether. Still, from what he had seen of these Raduru and their shields and strange spears, it would not be easy to push them aside, if they wanted no newcomers. Te Ika a Maui had been empty, and thus easily settled. This land... *Wait and see*, he reminded himself.

Once off the shore, the wind favoured them. It blew from the land, which made it easy enough for Kawiti to take the canoe north by sail power alone. The canoe could be paddled if they absolutely needed to, but he would rather not go to that effort. Who could say how much further north the Raduru dwelt?

Gumaring proved to be a pleasant enough sailing companion. He did not become disturbed or aggressive, and spent most of his time going back and forth with Nene and Kawiti about the meanings of a few words in each other's languages. Kawiti was most intrigued by found the strange yellow-brown substance which these Raduru used. Gumaring had a shield made out of it, which gleamed, and a serviceable knife and spearhead, which were much duller. The substance seemed to be as hard as most stones, and looked to be perfect for making all sorts of tools.

After a few attempts, Gumaring indicated that his people called the substance *dunu*. After even more effort, Kawiti managed to get across a question about where the substance came from. By virtue of lots of gestures, mimes, and lengthy if incomprehensible explanations, Gumaring explained that *dunu* was made from two substances melted together. One was apparently dug from the earth, and the other came from somewhere to the south. A very long way away, from the way in which Gumaring kept making pushing gestures.

Just how big is this island? Kawiti wondered. He knew no way to get that question across, but he was extremely intrigued. The two moa-filled islands which the Tangata had found for themselves were far larger than any other islands *anywhere*, according to what his father and every other navigator had said. How could this western island be even bigger?

They sailed north for a while, enough for the sun to sink noticeably lower over the western land. They passed several beaches, then neared a rather large headland which jutted out into the sea. At Gumaring's indication, he steered the canoe wide of the headland. When they passed, he saw that a building had been built near the highest point on the headland. Even from the distance, he could see that the whole building had been made out of some light yellow stone. As their canoe passed, smoke started to pour from the building. A watchtower and a signal fire, he supposed. Gumaring tried to explain more about it, but Kawiti and Nene could not figure out his meaning.

Once around the headland, he saw a couple of other small canoes in the water, being rapidly paddled toward the shore. Made from some kind of bark sewn together, from what he could see of them, not dug out from a tree trunk like any proper canoe should be. He vaguely wondered why these Raduru needed to do that, when they had so many trees to shape into dugouts, and why they did not use outriggers to stabilise their canoes on the seas. Maybe they knew no better; it would explain why they had been so fascinated by the first glimpse of the Tangata canoe. If those bark-skin canoes were as flimsy as they looked, he would not take one out of sight of land, and given a choice, he wouldn't even take them onto the water.

Thoughts of canoes were driven from his mind as they neared a small sheltered harbour. The people in the other canoes landed them and carried them up the beach, but other people were waiting to meet them. A lot of people. A couple of hundred men lined the shore, waiting for them. It was hard to be sure at a distance, but it looked as if they all had spears and shields. Beyond the beach rose walls of the same creamy-yellow stone which had been used to make the watchtower.

Gumaring leaped off the canoe as soon as it touched sand underneath the waves, even before it was fully ashore. He started shouting at the other Raduru while he ran toward them. Kawiti ignored them for the moment, and made sure that the canoe was brought ashore properly. He needed to ensure that it was above the high-water mark. That much he could do. Keeping the canoe safe from the Raduru could be another matter, but they seemed friendly so far.

More raised voices carried across from where Gumaring spoke to his fellows, but they sounded more excited than angry. By the time Kawiti and the other Tangata had secured the canoe above the high-water mark, the crowd of warriors had separated somewhat. Gumaring gestured for them to follow him. "*Bigan*," he kept repeating, over and over. Presumably that meant something like "come," but who could say for sure?

Gumaring led them toward the walled town, or whatever it was. A few of the Raduru followed behind, while others dispersed. As they drew near, Kawiti's gaze focused mostly on the creamy-yellow walls. It looked something like the sandstone he had seen in a few places in Te Ika a Maui, but not quite the same colour. Whatever it was made of, though, the wall was high. Higher than a man could reach. These Raduru must expect raids from their neighbours, then, especially if they had gone to the trouble of building a watchtower.

"What are those birds?" Nene asked, pointing off to the left. Not far from the walls, a large space of land had been enclosed by a fence and ditch. Inside it crowded a large number of birds. Big, flightless birds, reminiscent of moa. Not the same, though. Bird heads poked over the fence to watch the people outside. Black-feathered heads with patches of naked blue skin. No moa had heads like those.

"Not moa," one of the other Tangata said. "Ever tried to keep moa fenced in?"

Kawiti chuckled, as did the others. A few hunters had tried to herd moa into enclosures to keep them around to be killed during harder times. It never worked. If a moa took fright, it would run in panic. If there was nowhere to run except into a fence, then the moa would run into the fence, either killing itself or breaking down the fence. Sometimes both.

"Don't look as big as moas," Nene said. "Not the decent ones, anyway."

Kawiti shrugged. The biggest moas sometimes weighed more than two men, well worth the hunting, even with the ever-increasing distances needed to travel to find and kill them. These birds looked smaller, but would still make for a fine feast.

Gumaring led them inside the stone walls of the Raduru town. Inside, buildings of stone and wood crowded near to each other, except for one road which ran through the town. Some kind of dark grey stones had been laid into the ground to form a solid surface on the street. That was a marvellous idea – stones would not turn to mud whenever it rained.

"How many people live here?" Nene asked, as they walked along the winding street. Building after building lay on either side, with narrower unpaved streets running off. "Hundreds? Tens of hundreds?"

Kawiti nodded. The entire extended family networks of their *iwi* [clan] numbered less than ten hundreds of people.

This crowded town had to hold at least that many people. How numerous were the Raduru? The more he thought on it, the more he doubted that the Big Man would ever order the settlement of this western island. Not anywhere that the Raduru claimed, anyway.

About a dozen of the Raduru warriors followed them into the town; the rest had returned to whatever they were doing before the Tangata arrived. Gumaring led the way to a large stone building at the top of a small hill. The building was surrounded by an open area paved with more stones, and separated from the rest of the town by a low wall about knee-height.

A man waited inside the paved area. A brief glance confirmed him as someone of high status, with elaborate, colourful clothes and some accoutrements made from the same *dunu* which the other Raduru used for spearheads and some shields. This was clearly the Big Man of the Raduru. He did not bear any shield or other weapons, save for a gleaming *dunu* dagger at his belt. He wore a cloak wrapped around him, dyed in alternating lines of green and light blue, and fastened by a clasp of a material which looked like *dunu*, but which had a yellower, brighter sheen. He had a bracelet on each arm made from the same metal, and several other decorations of *dunu*. His headdress was an elaborate work formed in three overlapping circles, one projecting from either side of his head, and the third just above it. Brightly coloured feathers had been attached to the headdress, an iridescent arrangement of greens, blues, oranges and yellows.

Gumaring dropped down to one knee before the Big Man, and lowered his head level with his neck. He motioned for the Tangata to do the same. Kawiti did so, and the others followed his lead.

When they rose, the Big Man exchanged a few words with Gumaring, but did not try to speak to the Tangata directly. Kawiti did not know whether that was because the Big Man was smarter than Gumaring – who kept trying to speak with them in a language which they did not understand – or whether the Big Man thought he was too important to speak to them directly. No way to know, yet, but Kawiti wanted to find out as much as he could about these Raduru, including what their Big Man thought. Returning to Te Ika a Maui now would mean only a few brief tales, which would not do much to increase his status. Being the first to bring back a detailed account of some of the Raduru learning would be much more useful.

The Big Man turned and walked to the wall of the main building. A fire burned here, with a woman tending to it. A small rounded vessel made of another strange substance hung above the fire, with steam wafting occasionally from the lid. Kawiti was not sure exactly the rounded vessel was made from; it looked almost like clay, but harder and drier, and decorated with patterns of black lines and spirals. They waited while the woman ladled some of the boiling water into six cups made from the same substance as the boiling vessel. The woman sprinkled some sort of bright green powdered substance onto the top of each cup – they looked like crushed leaves – then stirred it in with a smaller ladle.

The Big Man took each of the cups and handed them to the Tangata one by one. He said something which sounded formalised and slow, although the words were as unintelligible as everything else. The scent wafting up from the cup smelled pleasantly sweet, but with a hint of something more tart underneath. At the Big Man's gesture, he took a slow sip from the cup; the water was hot, but not undrinkable. The flavour was oddly pleasant; the drink had more than a hint of tartness, stronger than he had had expected from the smell, but still drinkable[49]. He finished the drink, and the others did the same. At a guess – and he hated to guess – this was how the Big Man welcomed guests. Which was good; being accepted as a guest should give some protection from trouble.

---

[49] These are leaves from the lemon-scented tea tree (*Leptospermum petersonii*), which in historical Australia were used by early colonial settlers to make a substitute for tea. The flavour is reminiscent of lemon, though not as tart.

After that, Gumaring showed them to a building near the Big Man's house, and indicated that they could live here. They spent the next few hours discussing the implications of all that they had seen here. There was much to wonder about, since so much of what they had seen was new and alien. No-one could agree which of these new things was the most important, but they were all sure that what they had seen here could be very useful back in Te Ika a Maui.

That evening, they were invited to a feast. About a hundred people were eating, about half of them women. That was unlike the Tangata, where the women would only eat once the men were finished. He said, "No-one touch a woman here unless she touches you first. Don't let your gaze linger on any woman for too long, either." Among the Tangata, nothing could be more guaranteed to start a fight than over women, and he suspected that the same held true here.

Throughout the feast, he paid little attention to the people, but more to the food. The centrepiece was a couple of large roasted birds, which from their size had to be like the ones they had seen on the way in. They were certainly worth the eating, although he thought that he preferred moa.

Besides the meat, there were a variety of vegetables to eat, spiced with alien flavours which he enjoyed without being able to put a name to them. He recognised one of the plants as a kind of yam, something like those which the Tangata had brought to Te Ika a Maui, but of a strange red colour. These yams grew much larger than anything which could be grown on that island, too. That interested him more than anything else which he had seen so far. Sweet potato, yams, taro and other crops did not grow well on Te Ika a Maui, at least compared to what his father had said about how large they grew back on Hawaiki. And a man could not live on moa alone. Would these red yams and other foods be better-suited to growing back east?

The Tangata's discussions after the feast that night were slower, since it was harder to think on a very full stomach, but they all agreed that they wanted to stay for longer. There were plenty of questions which Kawiti wanted to ask, once he learned the words to use. Starting with how big this land really was.

The Tangata were allowed to stay for several weeks. The Raduru seemed to have endless hospitality for guests. Kawiti was able to find out much more about the Raduru. He found out early on that they had neighbours to the south that they were at intermittent war with, which seemed to consist of a series of raids every few months, but nothing more. He learned of the many plants they grew, of red yams, of wealth-trees [wattles] which produced edible seeds and gum and had many other uses, of flax and nettles which they used for weaving and linen and ropes. He learned of the noroons and ducks which they raised tame, like dogs, so that they could have them to eat without needing to go hunting. He learned how they shaped and baked clay into pottery – such a useful thing! He learned of the metal *dunu* [bronze], the working metal of so many uses, and the sun and moon metals [gold and silver] which they used for ornamental purposes. These Raduru were fond of decorating everything, it seemed. Their Big Man and his wives dressed the most ornately, but everyone had at least one set of brightly-decorated clothes.

Kawiti even had the chance to join them on a couple of hunts. They used rangelands to the south to hunt for a strange hopping animal which they called *gupa* [kangaroo]. These gupas were hard to find, but the meat had a stronger, more welcome flavour than noroon, which was why they still hunted for it. The Raduru he went with laughed at him sometimes when he hunted; Gumaring explained that they thought he was clumsy. The laughter stung at first, but he soon witnessed how effortlessly the Raduru could move without being seen. Even knowing exactly where they were, he still sometimes could not see them. Moa were much easier to hunt than gupas; as often as not a man could walk right up to them. These gupas were another prospect altogether. A man had to learn to camouflage himself well to come near enough to strike them with arrow or spear.

It took several weeks before he or the other Tangata could communicate with the Raduru about anything past the basics. Gestures could only go so far, but they did learn a few words here and there, enough to let him attempt some longer conversations. At one of the evening feasts, after a successful hunt which saw the Big Man give Gumaring the prize cut from the gupa he had killed, Kawiti asked the question he had wanted to ask for so long. "How big this land?'

Gumaring said, "Half the world."

Just when I thought that we understood each other, Kawiti thought, but he persisted. "How long to walk to other side of land?"

"Land go on forever," Gumaring said. "Half world land, in west, other half world water, in east. Little water on land, river and swamp and lagoon, just as little land on water, like island you come from. But most on each half of world. No end to land if go west; it go on forever, like time."

Odd. All lands were islands, in the end. Water surrounded everything, just as in the end of time it would cover everything, but that meant that this must be a very large island. Bigger even than Te Ika a Maui, by everything Kawiti had seen and heard.

He tried a question which might get a clearer answer. "Who else live on this land?"

A couple of nearby people overheard that question, and it provoked another of the arguments of which the Raduru were so fond. Eventually Gumaring won the argument by volume, as he usually did. "People some-like us live north and south. Putanjura live north, snakes of Nyumigal live south. Some times with them both we talk, some times we fight."

"And to the west?" Kawiti asked.

"No easy to cross big up," Gumaring said. A moment later, Kawiti realised he meant the cliffs which lined the interior along this coast, rising up high and leaving only rugged terrain beyond. "High empty country, where few hill-men live, but not else much. Not know who live past that, not for sure. Wanderer-trader-liars go, come back, say what they want make them look brave or see what tales fools believe."

More argument followed, and this time one of the other speakers won, calling someone else over. Kawiti could never pronounce this man's name properly; the closest he could get was Junibara, but that was not quite right.

Junibara said, "Past big up, hills rise high-high. Paths go through for those-know-guide, but long time take. Go far, land flat and dry. River-men live there, in big, big towns. One called... Garr-ki-mung. Hundreds of hundreds live there. River-men no have sea, so make own lakes for fish. Have much-much *dunu* and drink water-that-burns-and-bravens. Each River-Man think he best in world, always speak and not let other man finish talking. Big Man there and his servants store words in clay so always know what-happen-where-when. Dry there, always dry, except where river flows."

Kawiti kept his face still. This land was very, very big, then, and full of people. Rahiri, the Big Man of the Tangata back home, would be very interested in all of this. Kawiti was not sure what Rahiri would want to do once he had heard it. For himself, he thought that coming back here again and again might be the best use for the navigation skills which his father had made him learn, no matter how much he had hated it at the time.

#11: On The Eve Of The Storm

This chapter gives an overview of allohistorical Aururia and Aotearoa as they developed over the millennia since the invention of agriculture, and then a broad overview of their status in 1618, on the eve of first contact with Europeans. Many of the cultures and beliefs mentioned in this overview are explored in more detail in subsequent chapters.

* * *

Sometime in the distant unrecorded allohistorical past, a wild yam growing along the River Nyalananga in southeastern Aururia mutated into a new form. The result was a domesticable plant called the red yam, which grew wild along most of the central Nyalananga. Red yams were just one plant among many until humans arrived in Aururia. When they reached the Nyalananga, red yams became a staple part of their diet.

When the glaciers retreated and the climate entered the current interglacial period, humans around the world started down the road to domesticating plants. The red yam is a more difficult crop to domesticate than some other founder crops, but by around 4000 BC, the plant was fully domesticated. Other plant domestications followed this, most notably another root vegetable called murnong, and several species of wattles, fast-growing trees which bear edible seeds and have multitudinous other uses. These formed the core of an indigenous Aururian agricultural package. These crops are largely perennial, drought-tolerant plants which are well-suited to regions of low or irregular rainfall. As perennials, they also need less labour to produce a useful harvest; the yield per worker for Aururian crops is very high. This allows Aururian agricultural societies to sustain a much higher percentage of their population in non-agricultural roles than other comparable early agricultural peoples.

The Gunnagal, Aururia's first agricultural civilization, emerged along the Nyalananga between 2500 and 1000 BC. Their ancestors were already using domesticated crops, but inspired by contact with eel-farming peoples further south, the Gunnagal developed a complex system of artificial lakes and wetlands. These wetlands gave them an excellent source of food from fishing, hunting water birds, and gathering water plants. The planning and organisation needed to build and maintain these wetlands resulted in the development of hierarchical societies and an organised form of government.

The early Gunnagal flourished for about sixteen centuries. They developed many innovations: pottery and other ceramics; weaving; metallurgy in copper, lead and arsenical bronze; complex oral law codes and an established government; an organised trade system; and some domesticated animals (ducks and dingos). They did not invent full writing, although they had a developing proto-writing system which used symbols to represent ownership, especially for trade goods, and to indicate container contents. Gunnagal culture spread along the length of the Nyalananga. Religious preferences and reliance on artificial wetlands meant that their settlements were largely confined to the vicinity of the river.

The Gunnagal culture of this period (usually called the Formative era) collapsed after 900 BC, under the pressure of depleted soils and prolonged drought. Many of the displaced peoples expanded across Aururia in a series of population movements which would be called the Great Migrations. Gunnagalic-speaking peoples spread their languages, culture, and agriculture across much of south-eastern Aururia. The new farming communities spread almost as far north as the Tropic of Capricorn, and to the eastern and southern coastlines of Aururia; their western border was the deserts of central Aururia. Agriculture spread even further than the limit of the Gunnagalic migrations; red yams and a few other crops spread across the deserts to the fertile south-western corner of Aururia, which in time would develop its own agricultural cultures only loosely connected to peoples further east.

The farming communities formed in the Great Migrations began as isolated settlements, small villages and the like; they would take time to develop into larger political units. Along the Nyalananga itself, the survivors developed better agricultural techniques and through trade contact received a new domesticated animal, the noroon [emu]. In time, their urban cultures recovered into what would be termed the Classical era.

In this time, the Nyalananga peoples developed from small city-states into four kingdoms. They developed a full writing system, mostly used for inscriptions and clay tablets, and this became the basis of a developing government bureaucracy[50]. They perfected the use of tin-alloyed bronze, replacing the older arsenical bronzes. This new metal became an integral part of their increasing technological expertise. They were particularly successful when working in stone; some of the buildings built in the early days of the Classical era would still be standing and in use two millennia later when first visited by Dutch explorers. The Classical Nyalananga kingdoms were at the heart of extensive trade networks which stretched across the eastern half of the continent, and which carried their culture and ideas far beyond their political borders.

Classical Nyalananga culture survived for centuries. It endured the rise of Australia's first major epidemic disease, blue-sleep, a variant of influenza. The demise of the Classical Nyalananga eventually came from within. The

---

[50] Whether this counts as an innovation or curse is a matter of opinion.

kingdom of Garrkimang, centred on the eponymous city, was one of the four nations of the Classical Nyalananga. Unlike the others, it was located on a major tributary, the Matjidi, not the Nyalananga proper. The city had been founded during the Great Migrations, and its social structure was less faction-ridden than the older and more traditionalist cities along the main river. Under the determined and largely capable rule of a dynasty of prophet-kings, the kingdom of Garrkimang grew into the largest and wealthiest nation on the continent.

Garrkimang rose as a cultural and military power and eventually eclipsed the other Classical kingdoms. Trading wealth started its growth, but the kingdom's ultimate success was founded on several military innovations. They had greater access to bronze than any other Classical peoples, and created a system of well-armed heavy infantry which used long pikes and shields. Combined with better tactics and training, these soldiers transformed Garrkimang into an empire. Its armies first conquered the other Classical kingdoms, then expanded much further. After conquering the last surviving Classical rival in 556 AD, the nation took the name Watjubaga, meaning the Five Rivers.

Watjubaga was Aururia's first empire. At its height, it claimed suzerainty over territory which stretched from the Neeburra in the north to the Narrow Sea in the south, and to the deserts and the Turtle Gulf in the west. Its eastern border was mostly formed by the Spine, apart from tributary city-states in the Kuyal Valley. It reached its greatest territorial extent in AD 822, but its primacy did not last long. Economic disruptions formed by the colonisation of the Cider Isle and increase in the bronze supply unravelled much of the economy. Subject peoples learned how to counter imperial military tactics, and logistical difficulties meant that outlying regions grew independent of imperial control. Revolts and military disasters saw most of the outlying regions gain independence by the mid-tenth century. The imperial heartland around the Nyalananga and Matjidi gained independence more gradually, and the last vestiges of the Empire were overthrown in AD 1124.

The Imperial period coincided with the colonisation of the Cider Isle. Seafaring techniques amongst Gunnagalic peoples were not an early specialty, but their technology slowly improved. In time, this led to the colonisation of the Narrow Sea islands, then, in the ninth century AD, the settlement of the Cider Isle itself. The Cider Isle was colonised by two distinct groups of peoples, the Tjunini who entered via Benowee [King Island] in the northwest, and the Kurnawal who entered via Tayaritja [Flinders Island] in the northeast. The Tjunini settled most of the northern coast. The Kurnawal were initially established along the north-eastern coast, but after the War of the Princess (which would become immortalised in song), were driven to the eastern coast. The central highlands and rugged western coast of the Cider Isle were initially left to the previous hunter-gatherer inhabitants, the Palawa. Tasmania has rich reserves of tin, which were quickly exploited. The Tjunini and Kurnawal made more extensive use of bronze than anywhere else in Aururia, and they also exported considerable quantities of tin back to the mainland.

The collapse of the Empire did not mean the decline of agriculture or of the human population over its former lands. Indeed, the growing size of the subject populations was one of several factors which had weakened imperial control. This increasing population inevitably had effects on Aururia's natural environment. Increased farming meant some cases of local deforestation and habitat destruction. Fortunately for the Aururian peoples, their perennial agriculture did not produce the same soil erosion which European farming practices would produce in another history. Still, the changing habitats meant that much of the local flora and fauna were being displaced. Large gupas [kangaroos] and wild noroons [emus] were usually hunted out near any settlements. Some trees and other plants became locally extinct, or even completely extinct if they had a limited geographical range. Other Aururian wildlife was likewise displaced: possums, wombats, wallabies, bandicoots, and so forth became increasingly rare over the agricultural areas of the continent.

While politically fragmented, the cultures of the Nyalananga basin and their southern neighbours flourished in the post-Imperial period. Aururia's deadliest epidemic disease, the Waiting Death (Marnitja), emerged in the thirteenth century and caused widespread death, but the population recovered over time. These cultures were focused mostly on themselves, defining the Nyalananga kingdoms and their Junditmara neighbours as the only peoples possessing true civilization. Save as sources of trade goods, they had little regard for the lands outside. They were vaguely aware of the Yuduwungu and related peoples in south-western Aururia, but only occasional travellers visited those distant regions. The arid interior was a source of some metals, gems and salt, with a few mining colonies and trading contact with some local hunter-gatherers who adopted semi-sedentary lifestyles trading gems and salt for food. Otherwise, this region too was largely ignored.

The major urban areas of Aururia also regarded the eastern coast of the continent as an uncivilized backwater. Separated from the older cultures of the west by the Spine, the eastern coast was for a long time only thinly-populated. A few valuable spices grew there and were traded west of the mountains, but for the most part the rugged geography and lack of effective sea travel meant that the eastern coast consisted of scattered agricultural communities, with few large states. Two developing kingdoms were forming in the Kuyal Valley and around Yuragir [Coffs Harbour], which had some contact with the more westerly peoples, but most of the rest of the remained a backwater. Yet it was in these eastern lands that Aururia's isolation came to an end.

In 1310, voyaging Māori from Aotearoa landed in the region which another history would call the Illawarra in New South Wales. The initial contact was wary, but peaceful. An exchange of crops, animals and ideas followed over the next few decades. The Māori obtained Aururian crops such as red yams, wattles and murnong, and animals such as the noroon and duck. The Māori also learned about new technologies such as metallurgy and ceramics. The Aururian peoples gained new crops such as kumara (sweet potato) and taro. They also received new inspiration in sailing and navigation techniques, first from individual Māori who settled on the eastern coast, and then from diffusion of ideas. Sailing technology slowly spread up and down the east coast and eventually along the southern coast, leading to new trade routes and increased contact between Aururian peoples. Contact between Aururia and Aotearoa continued until the time of European arrival, although the volume of trade was limited; only a few high-value, low-bulk items were worth trading at such distances, such as greenstone (jade), kauri amber, some high-quality textiles, raw tin and some worked metal tools and weapons.

With the advent of new sailing technology, much more effective long-range contact became possible between Aururian cultures. Some societies were more open to these new technologies than others. Most notably, the inhabitants of Gurree Island [Kangaroo Island] took the new sailing techniques and became the leading maritime trading power in Aururia. Their voyagers plied the stormy waters of Aururia's southern coast, bypassing the desert barriers between east and west. In time, they or their successors may well have made contact of their own with Aururia's northern neighbours. However, their progress was cut short on 6 August 1619, when Dutch sailors under the command of Frederik de Houtman landed on the banks of what they called the Swan River.

* * *

Aururia in 1618 is a complex group of societies, ranging from literate Iron Age urbanites to desert-dwellers who care nothing for farming. It is a region with much common heritage, and some vast cultural differences. It is a region where the inhabitants have learned to master the challenges of nature, of flood, fire and drought, but where a much greater storm will soon break on their shores.

The south-western corner of Aururia is a small region of fertile land surrounded by hostile deserts. Some domesticated crops spread here in the sixth century BC, and a trickle of new ideas and technology has continued ever since, but the region developed largely in isolation. Lacking a reliable source of tin, the region had only very limited supplies of bronze, but in the last few centuries, they discovered the arts of working in iron. Iron tools and weapons here are the most advanced in Aururia. The Atjuntja were the most successful people to adopt these new technologies. They created a dominion which stretches from Pink Water [Esperance] in the east to the Indian Ocean in the west, and with its most northerly outpost a salt-harvesting works and penal colony at Dugong Bay [Shark Bay]. The Atjuntja rule over an empire of multiple ethnicities, who speak dialects which are sometimes different enough to be considered distinct languages. Under the watchful eye of their armies, a steady stream of tribute flows to their capital at the White City [Albany]. The Atjuntja pour this wealth into two of their main passions; they are masters of working in stone and arranging the natural world to suit their vision. The carefully shaped glories of the Garden of Ten Thousand Steps and the grandeur of the Walk of Kings would be considered amongst the wonders of the world, if the world knew of them.

Northward of the Atjuntja dominions to the north are lands which they consider barren and useless. North-western Aururia, particularly the coast, is little-affected by the rise of the Atjuntja. The peoples here do not farm, largely because the desert is unsuitable and the wetter regions are too far north to grow the red yams and other crops grown in the south. There is some sporadic trade contact, which has seen the spread of some copper tools and a very few of iron, occasional beads, pendants or other jewellery, and even rarer textiles and ceramics, but the peoples of the north remain largely isolated from those of the south.

Eastward of the Atjuntja lies a treeless, barren plain which until recently formed their only line of communication with other agricultural societies. Now that role has been filled by a people who call themselves the Nangu, but who are known to outsiders as Islanders. They are inhabitants of Gurree Island who have taken the Polynesian navigational package and adapted it to the conditions of the Southern Ocean. The Islanders regularly voyage from the Atjuntja dominions in the west to the Cider Isle in the east, and occasionally beyond; their trading ships sometimes the spice-growing regions on the east coast. Northwest of the Island lies the Seven Sisters, a small fertile patch of land bounded by sea and northern deserts. This land is occupied by the Mutjing, who live in several city-states and care little for the larger states further east, except for their trade with the Island.

On the eastern side of Turtle Gulf is the region which the inhabitants call the Copper Coast. This contains richly fertile land and an abundance of copper and other metals. This is a much-contested region between two of the great powers of Aururia. One of these is the resurgent Post-Imperial kingdom of Tjibarr, which has its heartland along the central Nyalananga but which seeks to control the wealth of the lower Nyalananga and the lands beyond. Tjibarr is the most powerful kingdom to reemerge after the collapse of the old Watjubagan Empire. Most of its inhabitants still call themselves Gunnagal, and are famously argumentative and faction-ridden. The old imperial heartland has never been reunited; Tjibarr shares the Five Rivers with the kingdoms of Gutjanal [Albury] along the Upper Nyalananga and Yigutji [Wagga Wagga] along the Matjidi. Neither of those two kingdoms has ever succeeded in regaining the former imperial control over the Highlands [Monaro plateau] further east. That high country is still occupied by the Nguril and Kaoma, non-Gunnagalic peoples who have learnt to fight in the mountains, and who sometimes raid into the low-lying regions of the Nyalananga basin.

When fighting for control of the Nyalananga Mouth and Copper Coast, Tjibarr is opposed by the most populous empire in Aururia: the Yadji. Named for their ruling dynasty, the Yadji are the descendants of the old Junditmara. With relatively rain-drenched lands and fertile soils, the Yadji dominions stretch from the Bitter Lake and almost all of the land south of the Spine, as far as Elligal [Orbost, Victoria]. The Yadji have a rigidly hierarchical society bound by conventions of religion and tradition, and their government is among the most organised in Aururia. Trade contact via the Islanders has acquainted them with the arts of working in iron. They are particularly adept at building roads to allow swift transport between the key regions of their empire. They have greater population than Tjibarr; the latter usually relies on riverine control of the Nyalananga to assist them in fending off the Yadji's military adventures.

To the north and east of the Yadji and the Five Rivers dwell backward peoples; that is, according to the standards of the city dwellers of those lands. North of the Five Rivers kingdoms lies the dry inland plains of what another history would call New South Wales, and which in Aururia is called the lands of the Panjimundra. A land of mostly flat ground and fading rains as one moves further west, this is not a region to support a large population in any one place. Food is not the limitation; even here, dryland Australian agriculture can supply a sufficient harvest to support a decent population. The limitation is water. Away from the permanent rivers, only limited amounts of water can be collected from wells, small dams, and rainwater cisterns. The open plains of the Panjimundra are occupied by scattered agricultural communities and city-states, each of which defends larger areas of rangelands which they use for hunting and extraction of timber and other resources. At times, the kingdoms of the Five Rivers exercise some control over the Panjimundra city-states, but that rarely lasts more than a generation or two.

Bounded by the peaks of the Spine and the Grey Sea, the eastern coast of Aururia is a narrow stretch of often rugged but well-watered land. By Aururian standards, the rainfall here is high; sufficient to support a great variety of plants which do not grow west of the mountains. Several of these plants produce spices which are traded further west; as far as the Five Rivers kingdoms and the Yadji are concerned, this is the only feature of interest of the eastern coast. A few additional crops have been domesticated here, including additional species of wattles, and a few fruits, but these are mostly unknown further west.

The great length of the east coast is inhabited by a variety of agricultural peoples. The rugged nature of the terrain and the limitations of transportation technology prevented the development of large political entities in most of this region. For most of their history since the Great Migrations, the peoples here lived in small farming communities which are usually separated into distinct valleys or coastal regions.

The diffusion of better sailing technology from the Māori has seen some limited seaborne trade linking the east coast peoples, though in most regions the peoples here remain divided into small communities. Two larger states have emerged in parts of the east coast. One of these formed amongst the Patjimunra people in the Kuyal Valley. Here, after the collapse of the Empire, the former city-states were united into Murrginhi, the Kingdom of the Skin. The Kuyal Valley controls one of the best ways to cross the Spine, and the Patjimunra have become wealthy through trade in spices. The Patjimunra are a Gunnagalic-speaking people, but their culture and religion has evolved along a distinct path from those further west. The *kitjigal* have developed into a rigid social hierarchy that defines all occupations and social contact.

The other major state along the eastern coast is the kingdom of Daluming, formed by the Mungudjimay around

Yuragir [Coffs Harbour]. A non-Gunnagalic people who preserved their own language and way of life despite the Great Migrations, the Mungudjimay have religious beliefs and a social structure which is wholly alien to their neighbours, who consider them to be warlike, head-hunting savages.

Inland of the kingdom of Daluming lies the region called the Gemlands [New England tablelands]. This is a region of high country with reasonably fertile soils and some of the best mineral wealth in Aururia. The Gemlands form one of the two main sources of tin in Aururia. Despite its elevated terrain, its climate is still mild enough that red yams and other crops can grow here. Politically, the Gemlands are divided into competing chiefdoms whose borders shift over time, although they sometimes form defensive alliances against threats from Daluming to the east.

North of the Gemlands, the agricultural population gradually diminishes. These regions are nearing the effective growing limit of the red yam, which was for so long the main staple crop of all farming peoples on the continent. Inland lies the Neeburra, a region of sweeping plains and open pastures which is inhabited by the peoples who call themselves the Yalatji and Butjupa. They live in numerous small agricultural communities, but few large towns.

Around the coast, where drinking water is easier to obtain and seafood supplements the farming diet, the population density is higher. This region is called the Coral Coast [Gold Coast, Moreton Bay, and Sunshine Coast]. This land is the home of the Kiyungu, another society born in the Great Migrations, and who have adapted to life in the northern sun. They are not very militaristic; the Empire never reached this far north, and they face no military threat save occasional raids from Daluming or the Neeburra. The Kiyungu are happy to squabble amongst themselves, while mostly living for trade.

While they call their homeland the Coral Coast, in fact most of the coral reefs are further north. The Kiyungu had long learned to voyage north in small boats and dive to collect corals. This is a valuable trade good which they exchange further south for tin and copper to forge into bronze. The Coral Coast is home to several decent-sized cities, and the Kiyungu have adapted Māori sailing techniques to better their own navigation and trade networks further north.

Beyond the Kiyungu lands and the Neeburra, northern Aururia was until recently almost the exclusive domain of hunter-gatherers. The Kiyungu maintained a few small fishing outposts and trading points along the coast, but otherwise farming and towns were non-existent. In the last century and a half, though, new tropical crops emerged. Kumara (sweet potato) and taro, brought across the seas by the strange Māori, first reached the Kiyungu around AD 1450, and their cultivation has since spread inland.

Another new crop appeared in farmers' fields about half a century before that; a new kind of yam. It did not look quite like a regular red yam; it was smaller, and its roots were twisted. No-one was quite sure where it came from, and it did not always grow well on its own, but farmers learnt to cultivate it through cuttings, and then later through seed. This lesser yam did not yield as well as the common red yam, but it had one valuable quality; it could grow even in the northern fields where common yams withered[51]. The benefits are obvious, and farming has

---

[51] The lesser yam is the product of a hybridisation between the red yam (*Dioscorea chelidonius*) and one of its close relatives, the long yam (*Dioscorea transversa*). This hybridisation occurs occasionally whenever cultivated red yams are bred near wild long yams, which occurs in the regions which in actual history are called north-eastern New South Wales and southern Queensland.

slowly spread further north. The lands around the Tropic of Capricorn are in the midst of a process of transformation. Small agricultural communities have been established, though hunter-gatherer peoples have still not been completely displaced. The only decent-sized towns are on the coast, where offshoots of the Kiyungu are slowly spreading north. Farming peoples are on the advance once more, and absent outside influence, the northern migration will stop only at the northern tip of Aururia [Cape York]. As of 1618, the northernmost coastal outpost is at Quamba [Mackay], though farming inland has not spread that far.

Much further to the south, the Cider Isle in 1618 remains divided between the descendants of the Tjunini and the Kurnawal. Their long rivalry has divided the fertile northern and eastern coasts between them. The more rugged interior of the central highlands and the southern and western coasts remains the domain of the Palawa, who have developed a hunter-gardener lifestyle. The territorial and cultural conflicts between the Tjunini and the Kurnawal has produced two states with clearly-defined borders and patrolled frontiers. It has also meant that both peoples possess a strong sense of nationalism. In their language, their culture, their fashion, and their diet, the inhabitants of the Cider Isle define themselves as citizens of either the

---

Like both of their parents, the hybrid yams have a perennial root system and their stems and leaves die back every year. The hybrid yams have tubers which are midway in size between the larger red yams and the smaller long yams; hence their name of "lesser yam." The first lesser yams were not interfertile with either of their parents, and since yams require both a male and female plant, were effectively sterile. Aururian farmers learned to propagate yams through using cuttings, though, and this allowed them to farm the lesser yams. Since hybrids show up on a fairly regular basis, this eventually meant that they found strains of lesser yams which could fertilise each other and then be grown from seed. As a crop, the lesser yam offers a lower yield than red yams, and is somewhat less drought-tolerant, but from its long yam parent it has inherited the capacity to grow in the tropics.

Tjunini confederation or the Kurnawal kingdom. It is often a mortal insult to suggest to a Tjunini that they act like or a Kurnawal, or vice versa. Their rivalry is not just cultural, but over land and trade. The best tin mines lie in the region of the disputed frontier, and the two nations have fought a seemingly endless series of wars over control of that region, and over other valuable agricultural land. Cider Isle-produced tin and gum cider are held in high regard on the mainland, although neither of the two nations conducts much direct trade. The export of goods to and from the mainland is usually controlled by the Islanders.

In Aotearoa, the Māori have benefitted immensely from the introduction of Aururian domesticated crops and animals, although they also suffered from the arrival of blue-sleep and Marnitja, both of which have become endemic diseases. The Māori have been transformed from a hunter-gardener people into a culture of warrior-farmers. They have acquired knowledge of ceramics, writing, and metallurgy from Aururia, and adapted them to suit their own culture. The Māori are limited in their metallurgy, because Aotearoa has virtually no native sources of tin; all of their bronze must be imported from Aururia, and this is almost prohibitively expensive.

Still, the fertile and well-watered lands of Aotearoa support a much higher population density than virtually any part of Aururia. The Māori population is more highly-concentrated in Te Ika a Maui [North Island], but farming has spread throughout both of the main islands. The introduction of metal weapons and farming permitted an increasing population, and wars between different Māori kingdoms are still common. The Māori are linked to Aururia by small-scale but regular trade contact, and by much less frequent contact with their old homelands in Polynesia. Fortunately for the inhabitants of Polynesia, the travel time required, and the infrequency of those contacts, means that so far they have not been afflicted with Aururian diseases.

#12: Men of Blood and Iron

Historically, the south-western corner of Australia is a complex mixture of fertile coastal land gradually melding into an arid interior. Around the coast, frequent rains fall, creating what by Australian standards is a well-watered climate. Before European arrival, this land sustained forests of towering 90-metre karri trees, among the tallest trees in the world, and abundant jarrah trees, whose timber was so reminiscent of New World mahogany trees that European colonists would call it Swan River Mahogany. Moving inland, the climate becomes gradually drier, although there is enough fertile land to produce half of modern Australia's wheat harvest. Moving even further inland, the wheat-producing regions gradually fade into more arid desert, although the dry interior contains abundant mineral resources, including large deposits of iron and nickel and a third of the world's known gold reserves. Although possessed of abundant resources, this region is extremely isolated from the rest of Australia; the state capital Perth is closer to Indonesia's capital Jakarta than it is to the Australian national capital in Canberra.

In allohistorical Aururia, the fertile south-western corner was for long isolated from the rest of the continent. Although the climate was suitable for growing the Aururian crop package, the separation of desert barriers meant that it took millennia for crops to be transported further west. Fortunately for the peoples of the south-west, the isolation was not complete. Traders and travellers sometimes crossed the deserts, and they brought food back with them. Since any careful desert-crosser brought more food than they needed, this sometimes meant that samples of domesticated crops reached south-western Aururian.

From this source, farming slowly developed in the west. Small-scale growing of red yams started around 550 BC, and other crops followed. The Yuduwungu people around Pink Water became the first farmers of the south-west, adopting red yams, bramble wattles, and native flax from the east. Their isolation from the east remained quite substantial, enough that murnong, one of the key staple crops in eastern Aururia, was not grown in the south-west until carried by Islander ships in the fifteenth century[52]. However, the Yuduwungu farmers developed some new

---

[52] The crops which are brought overland across the desert are only those which travellers would bring with them, and which would survive replanting. Red yam tubers were often taken back by traders, since they were a large and valuable source of food. Red yams are also useful since they do not need to be planted intact; like other Aururian yam species, only the top part of the tuber needs to be planted in the soil to regrow. Western Aururian peoples already knew how to harvest and replant a local yam species (the warran yam), although they had not fully domesticated it. Travellers who brought red yams back with them to the west would cut slices off a yam tuber as they travelled, using it as food. If the top part of the yam tuber survived the trip, they would sometimes replant it. With their familiarity with harvesting warran yams, this meant that they could apply those techniques to a new crop which was more suitable for full domestication.

The other crops which were brought over were seed crops (wattle seeds, flax seeds), which traders also brought with them as food. Seed crops were ground into flour and cooked as seedcakes. Since the seeds were not ground until they were used, this mean that surplus seeds were also available for replanting if they were brought back west. Some other eastern crops were not suitable for transport in this manner; the tubers of murnong are too small to be useful to bring back intact, and the seeds of nettles were not harvested.

crops of their own, such as the tooth-bearing wattle, manna wattle, warran yam, and bush potato[53].

Pre-farming south-western Aururia was occupied by a group of eleven peoples who spoke related dialects and shared a common cultural heritage. The Yuduwungu were just one of these peoples; collectively the eleven groups referred to themselves as the Yaora[54]. Eight of these peoples lived along the coast. Moving clockwise, these were the Yuduwungu, the Wadjureb, the Pitelming, the Atjuntja, the Madujal, the Djarwari, the Inayaki and the Binyin. Three other related peoples occupied the inland arable regions: the Nyunjari, the Wurama and the Baiyurama. Unlike in the east, where farmers displaced hunter-gatherers, amongst the Yaora, farming spread quickly enough that the individual peoples adopted crops and technologies rather than being displaced. By about AD 300,

---

[53] The tooth-bearing wattle (*Acacia dentifera*) is a small shrub which provides a large seed yield for its size, and manna wattle (*A. microbotrya*) produces abundant quantities of wattle gum. The warran yam (*Dioscorea hastifolia*) is a real yam species which was historically used by the Noongar and other peoples of south-western Australia. Warran yams were harvested with the upper part of the tuber being replanted to allow it to regrow and collect a fresh tuber the next year. Warran yams are not quite as well-suited to arid conditions as red yams, and do not provide as large yields per acre, although their taste will be preferred by some Yaora peoples. Australia has a large number of plants which have been called "bush potatoes"; the species described here is *Platysace deflexa*, whose potential as a domesticable crop is being explored in recent plantings. The main role of the warran yam and bush potato is as secondary staple crops which do not yield as heavily in nutritional terms as red yams, but add variety to the diet, and offer some security for food supply if disease or other misfortune affects the red yam harvest.

[54] Historically, most of the fertile regions of south-western Australia were similarly occupied by a group of thirteen related peoples who broadly considered themselves part of the same culture. They collectively called themselves the Noongar (also transliterated with other spellings). The Noongar did not occupy an area quite as large as the allohistorical Yaora; the borders of their country were roughly everything south and west of a line from Jurien Bay to Ravensthorpe, Western Australia.

the eleven Yaora peoples had all taken up farming and sedentary lifestyles.

The allohistorical Yaora peoplesoccupied an area which in terms of historical Australia comprises everything west of a line roughly from Geraldton to Esperance. They called their home country Tiayal, meaning "the Middle Country." In their early religion and worldview, their homelands were the only important fertile country in the universe; to the south and west were endless seas and to the north and east were hostile desert wastelands. They were only vaguely aware of any peoples beyond the Middle Country; trade routes to the north brought pearl shells from the northern coastline of Aururia, while trade routes to the east had brought a few crops and decorative items, but with only very sporadic contact.

The isolation of the Middle Country meant that many of the fundamental elements of Gunnagalic cultures further east were only slowly transmitted to the western outlier. Ceramics were spread relatively early, since storage jars and other containers were among the goods transported across the desert. Domesticated ducks were brought directly across by a returning traveller (and cross-bred with their wild relatives), and this became inspiration for an independent domestication of the noroon. However, many other ideas and technologies did not spread until much later. Sometimes this was to the detriment of the Yaora; knowledge of writing took a long time to spread across the desert. Sometimes the slow transmission of knowledge would turn out to be to their advantage. Nowhere would this be clearer than in metallurgy.

The basics of metallurgy were known to the Yuduwungu and other early Yaora peoples, but only in limited form. They were broadly aware of the process of smelting metal, enough to create copper tools of their own. Yet while they received a few bronze tools and weapons, these came through very long trade routes; the source of tin was not just across the desert, but at the other end of Gunnagalia. This meant that the early Yaora peoples never learnt to recognise tin ore, and in any case they had only one possible source of tin near Corram Yibbal [Bunbury]. The developing Yaora civilizations knew how to smelt and work copper, but their only other metal tools were made from a metal which fell from the sky: meteoric iron.

In the end, this would be an inspiration.

* * *

In the traditional chronology, technology progressed from the Stone Age (Neolithic) to a Copper Age (Chalcolithic), to a Bronze Age, and then finally to an Iron Age. Each of these developments provided some advantages over the preceding age. Copper tools gave more flexibility without replacing stone tools. Bonze was a stronger and more useful metal than unalloyed copper, although it required higher smelting temperatures and a functioning trade network to supply tin. Early ironworking techniques did not provide a stronger metal than bronze, but allowed for much more widespread use of metal; iron ore is much more abundant than the components of bronze, especially tin.

However, the historical record is more complex than a simple progression between ages. Some cultures never went through a copper age, and some cultures did not go through a bronze-working period before they started working with iron (such as in West Africa). It is still an open question as to whether a civilization needs to progress through bronze working before it develops ironworking techniques. Sub-Saharan Africa may well have developed ironworking independently without ever having a bronze-working period; sources disagree as to whether the West African ironsmiths learnt ironworking on their own or whether they were inspired directly or indirectly from ironworking in the region of present-day Sudan.

Ironworking in western Eurasia came later than bronze-working, but the techniques involved in Western ironworking (in bloomeries) are quite distinct from those used in bronze-working. Early bronze-working involved smelting of copper and tin, alloying those metals, and then casting them into tools or weapons. Early ironworking in bloomeries did not involve melting iron ore. Instead, it involved burning iron ore with charcoal so that the iron ore was reduced to iron without ever reaching its melting temperature, then working the iron while it was heated but still solid.

In the allohistorical Middle Country, metalworkers found themselves in a curious position. They knew of metallurgy and had examples of finished bronze products, and knew how to smelt metal (copper), but they did not know the full bronze-working techniques. So some of them began to experiment. As well as copper, they had much rarer meteoric iron, which they could work into useful tools. The techniques needed to work meteoric iron are exactly the same as those used to work iron once it has been created in a bloomery. Meteoric iron was available in the Middle Country, but so were earthly forms of iron ore. In particular, magnetite ore is abundant in several sources near Milgawee [Albany]. Magnetite ore is easily recognisable as being related to meteoric iron; lumps of magnetite have a close enough resemblance to meteorites that they can mislead meteorite hunters. In time, smiths around Milgawee started to experiment with magnetite, and discovered techniques of burning it with charcoal. This gave them an abundant source of iron which they could work using already familiar techniques. The Middle Country had entered the Iron Age.

* * *

With the spread of farming, the Yaora peoples developed into a distinctive cultural zone. While they had some differences in speech – not all of their dialects were mutually intelligible – they remained in close contact with each other. They shared the same broad religious beliefs, including a few concepts which were transmitted from the older Gunnagalic cultures further to the east. These concepts had been changed considerably through travellers' misunderstandings, the difficulties of translation, and the tyranny of distance.

To the Yaora, the universe comprises three "substances," which can be broadly translated as solid, liquid, and gas. All solid objects are only separate flavours of the underlying substance, and all liquids and gases are similarly flavours of separate underlying substances. Each of these substances is mutable into each of the other forms, but through the actions of the universal symbol of eternity: water. To the Yaora, water is the driver of the cycles of eternity, the physical manifestation of time. They acquired the old Gunnagalic belief of the universe being eternal, but they adapted it into their observations of the properties of water. The Yaora know that water can transform from solid to liquid to gas, even though their knowledge of solid water is limited to a few rare instances of snow and frost, and they think that clouds are formed of gaseous water, not liquid water drops. The Yaora believe that the transformation of water between its three forms is what drives the movement of time and eternity.

The Yaora religion is based in part on their understanding of the role of water as an agent of erosion. Living in a flood-prone land, they know how the actions of water can remove soil and stone. They recognise sand as rocks which have been worn away from solid hills, and believe that this sand is in the process of being transformed into liquid over a very long time. In their cosmology, the sun is viewed as the Source which drives the actions of water through evaporation from the oceans and precipitation when rain falls onto the land. They also believe that the Source acts on solid rock, heating the water within it and causing it to expand, which means that hills gradually rise from the earth over time. These hills are then eroded away by water, turned into part of the oceans, and then eventually solidify beneath the waves to be carried back to join the land. All of this is viewed as part of the same underlying cycle of eternity; they believe that the world has always been and will always be.

The Yaora as a whole do not have a concept of a creator deity, although some of the individual peoples will later develop such views. Instead, the Yaora believe in beings called *kuru*, a word which originally meant "reflection," since *kuru* were thought of as reflections in the ever-ocean. *Kuru* are not considered to be eternal beings in themselves; it is believed that they will eventually dissolve back into the ever-ocean. Still, some of them have lifespans long enough that they may as well be immortal, from a human point of view.

Kuru are perceived as varying greatly in power; some are powerful and can be worshipped or appeased, whereas others are weak or mischievous and simply cause trouble for people. Phenomena such as thunder and lightning are thought to be the actions of particularly transient *kuru* which are soon going to dissolve back into the ever-ocean. Some *kuru* are associated with particular concepts such as growth, fertility or courage, and are called on for blessings or favours for people who are in need. One quality which all *kuru* have in common is that they cannot stand directly in the light of the Source without being slowly weakened. Greater *kuru* might be able to withstand sunlight for hours, while lesser *kuru* would be dissolved in seconds. This means that all worship is conducted out of direct sunlight, whether indoors or just under trees or some other covering.

* * *

For centuries after the adoption of farming, the Yaora lived in small communities, and had no larger political entities than city-states. Over time, a few of these developed into small kingdoms. While they occasionally conquered some parts of their neighbours, none of them successfully held onto large conquests.

Things changed with the discovery of ironworking in the twelfth century. Ironworking spread rapidly, with the new technology allowing much greater access to metal tools than anything in previous Aururian history, even more than the abundant bronze of the Cider Isle. Iron tools allowed more clearing of land and more effective farming techniques. Iron weapons could be cheaply supplied to armies in a way which had never before been seen in the Middle Country.

The result was a rapid social and political transformation, particularly amongst the Atjuntja, the first people to work iron, and the ones who would put it to the greatest use.

Writing was unknown to the Atjuntja at the time when iron was discovered, so the early history of the Atjuntja conquerors was preserved only in oral form, and would not be transcribed until many years later, when memory had faded and exaggerations and distortions became commonplace. It is known that the Atjuntja had long dwelt in the country around Milgawee, around the shores of the Sea Lake [King Georges Sound], which formed the largest deepwater harbour in the Middle Country. They were divided into three main city-states: Milgawee, which means the White City [Albany], Warneang [Denmark] and Fog City [Walpole], along with several smaller towns and settlements.

The Atjuntja drew much of their food from fishing, while inland much of their country was covered in trees which were difficult to clear with copper and stone tools. The Atjuntja were less numerous than many of their neighbours, until they discovered how to work the magnetite iron in their territory. With iron tools, they started to clear the forests and plant yams and wattles to feed a burgeoning population. Disputes over this land led to wars between the three main Atjuntja city-states, which were ended when King Banyar of the White City defeated both of his rivals and proclaimed himself the *Kaat-kaat* (King of Kings) of the Atjuntja. His heirs would go on to conquer much further.

* * *

In 1618, the Atjuntja rule an empire which controls all of the Middle Country. The Kings of Kings have even expanded their territory further than the old Yaora lands. The region around Seal Point [Geraldton] is the northernmost area where large-scale agriculture is sustainable, but the rule of the Kings of Kings stretches further; they have a penal colony and salt-harvesting works on the shores of Dugong Bay. In the eastern frontier of their territory, they have pushed into the semi-arid region they call Timwee, meaning Golden Blood [Kalgoorlie]. The land there is poorly watered, but it holds something of great value: gold. The Atjuntja esteem gold; they call it 'sun's blood' and view it as the solid form of the Source. The harsh environment of the desert does not make for long life amongst the miners, but the Kings of Kings care little for that.

Within this vast expanse of territory, the Atjuntja rule over everything, but not always directly. The Atjuntja are only one people amongst many in their empire, by now the largest single ethnicity, but still a minority of the overall population. The nature of their rule varies from region to region, reflecting both the duration of their rule in each region, and the form of its conquest. The Atjuntja began their expansion in the thirteenth century, acquiring writing only when they conquered the Wadjureb people near Red Eye in the mid-fourteenth century, and completing their expansion with the conquest of Seal Point in 1512. There is no longer any need for armies of conquest; the remaining military forces are used as garrisons to preserve the peace.

Rebellions are hardly unknown, although they have been growing less frequent in the last half-century. Their empire includes a patchwork of individual regions, some with explicit privileges established as part of their conquest, and some peoples who have been displaced entirely from their original homeland. The general practice of the Kings of Kings has been to leave local institutions in place unless threatened by revolt. Some peoples have been more accepting of Atjuntja rule than others. The Pitelming rebelled one time too often and were forcibly deported from their homelands and resettled in small groups across the empire, except for those who were sent to the mines. In some regions, the non-Atjuntja populations are gradually assimilating to the dominant culture; the prestige attached to the Atjuntja dialect means that many of the related dialects are being abandoned. In other regions, the other

Yaora peoples still remain attached to their own culture and heritage even if they are quiescent under Atjuntja rule.

Imperial administration is based on a combination of Atjuntja aristocrats and local potentates who have been integrated into the ruling class. They have established a number of garrison-cities which serve both as bastions of imperial military power, and as centres of trade and administration. Most of these garrison-cities have turned into local metropolises, with attached towns developing outside the walls of the main garrison. Among the largest garrison-cities are Lobster Waters [Jurien Bay], Spear Mountain [Merredin] – where an ingeniously-built dam collects most of the water that falls on the mountain – Corram Yibbal, Archers Nest [Redcliffe, a suburb of Perth], and Red Eye. Trade focuses on these centres, and travels along the well-maintained roads which the Atjuntja have built between the garrison-cities. This is the most extensive road network anywhere in Aururia, thanks to the use of iron tools which makes construction much easier.

From the garrison-cities, the imperial administrators oversee the collection of yearly tribute from the subject peoples. This is rigorously gathered, in a variety of forms depending on the region, imperial requirements, and the preferences of the subject peoples. Some tribute is collected in local produce, such as dyes, timber, oils, incense, lorikeet and cockatoo feathers, copper, or iron. Sometimes the tribute is collected in staple crops and foods, particularly to feed the garrison-cities and the imperial workforce. Sometimes the tribute is collected in labour drafts.

The Atjuntja have developed a methodical system for managing labour and the workforce throughout their empire. Much of this labour is used in public works and major engineering projects, such as roads, buildings, earthworks, and the like. Most of the labourers are required to work only at certain times of the year. This is usually in the winter and early spring, which coincides both with the least wearying part of the year for heavy labour, and with the timings of harvests. After the yams have been harvested and the wealth-trees pruned, and before it is time to replant them or collect the first wattle seeds, the imperial administrators demand the labour of tens of thousands of people for a fixed period of time. These labour drafts are widespread, but permanent slavery is much rarer, used mostly for the gold mines in the interior. For regular subjects, the labour draft is a wearying but predictable part of their yearly life. While they may serve on a variety of projects, the single largest use of drafted labour is working in the imperial capital, the White City.

* * *

The White City, some call it, or the City Between The Waters, or the Place of Twin Peaks, or the Centre of Time. Another history would call it Albany, the first deepwater port in Western Australia, located on a large mostly sheltered harbour called King Georges Sound, which contains two completely sheltered harbours inside, Princess Royal Harbour and Oyster Harbour. To the Atjuntja who live in the White City, the Sound is simply the Sea Lake, and they call the two interior harbours West Water [Princess Royal] and North Water [Oyster]. It is the centre of their universe, the largest city in the known world, the dwelling place of the King of Kings. Most of its residents would prefer never to live anywhere else; those who are appointed elsewhere as governors or soldiers treat it as an exile, no matter how important the duty.

The oldest part of the White City was founded between two mountains, the Twins, Un Koit [Mt Clarence] and Un Bennan [Mt Melville]. Strong walls once protected this city, but the walls have long since been torn down, their stone going to new buildings. No foreign army has threatened the White City in over two centuries, and the inhabitants have many uses for building material.

The core of the White City is still in the land between the mountains, including most of the public buildings. Many drafted labourers have worked over long years to produce the great monuments and public buildings of the White City, and their work continues. Here, in the old heart of the White City is the Palace of a Thousand Rooms, for the private use of the King of Kings, his many wives, administrators, and honoured guests. Here is the grandeur of the Walk of Kings, the great avenue which runs between the two mountains. Most of the other public buildings adjoin the Walk of Kings: the Garden of Ten Thousand Steps is halfway along; the public temples to the Lord and the Lady are here, along with smaller shrines to a dozen well-known *kuru*. The public arena of the House of Pain is at the western end, with the private rooms built into the mountain. The House of the Songs adjoins the Walk, where the greatest of musicians in the Middle Country come to study their craft; and so does the Mammang, the great school where the sons of Atjuntja nobility come to receive military and religious schooling.

Everything about the heart of the White City is built to impress. The Walk of Kings runs in a straight line between the two mountains, with fountains every hundred steps, towering jarrah trees planted to shade the walkers, and columns and statues to depict imperial accomplishments and religious figures. The Garden of Ten Thousand Steps is where the Atjuntja indulge their love of the natural world. It is said that with every step there is a new marvel to see, a new flower or tree[55], or a new arrangement of stones and trees, artificial waterfalls, or flocks of sacred ducks bred for bright colours. Disturbing the ducks is punishable with the kind of pain which ends in eventual death. Everywhere in the Garden is the sound of water, flowing, bubbling, or cascading down rocks.

At the eastern end of the Walk is the Palace. Most of it is private, but at the appropriate season visitors can walk up the limestone steps, past statues of cockatoos, lorikeets, and goannas carved so that they appear to be about to jump

---

[55] South-western Aururia is a region of substantial biodiversity, with over seven thousand species of vascular plants. The Atjuntja don't have every one of those kinds of plants in the Garden, but they give it their best attempt.

into the air. At the top, there is a large covered balcony where the King of Kings sits to watch public events. He sits on the Floral Throne, symbolic of the Atjuntja veneration of all flowering plants, which has been carved in a shape of forty petals opening as if part of a very large flower.

The grandeur of the public buildings is what most visitors to the White City remember, but this is a much larger city. The outlying districts extend much further than the old heartland, filled with houses and markets, storehouses, smaller shrines, and the three schools for common Atjuntja men, women, and foreigners. Two hundred thousand people live here at the busiest times of the year, although many of those are drafted labourers who return to their homes outside of draft times. The storehouses are full of the wattleseeds and yams needed to feed the burgeoning population, and the main imperial roads are always busy with traffic bringing in food, other tribute, and trade goods. The people, the gardens and the fountains are watered by several aqueducts which come from the mountain ranges to the north[56].

The White City includes a foreign quarter, built on the eastern side of North Water, to keep outlanders and their influences away from the royal city. This is where Islander ships and merchants visit in regular fleets, and a few of them have settled here semi-permanently. They have their own small temples where they complete the rituals of the Sevenfold Path in accordance with the teachings of the Good Man, but strictly-enforced imperial law forbids them from proselytising within the White City.

* * *

As a ruling class, the Atjuntja are divided into noble families and commoners, although even common Atjuntja are believed to outrank all but the most favoured of subject

---

[56] The source sof water for these aqueducts are two mountain ranges north of the White City, which historically are called the Stirling and Porongurup Ranges.

peoples. Governors and military commanders are chosen exclusively from the Atjuntja aristocracy, although there are protocols whereby high-status nobility from the subject peoples can be adopted into the Atjuntja ruling class. This adoption is subject to acceptance of Atjuntja ways, including learning their dialect and adopting a proper mode of dress and appearance. The most visible mark of this acceptance is the full beard which all Atjuntja men are expected to wear; a man's beard is regarded as a sign of strength and virility.

The Atjuntja system of nobility includes a variety of ranks and offices. The highest of these is *kaat*, which can be approximately translated as "king." In keeping with long-standing tradition, the heads of the thirteen greatest noble families are accorded that title. Each of them is officially a king of a particular place, such as the other ancient Atjuntja city-states of Warneang and Fog City, or the newer garrison-cities. The link of these titles to geographic locations has long since been broken; the leading members of the nobility prefer to live in civilization in the White City and let lesser family members deal with the bothersome business of administration. In any case, governors to the garrison-cities are appointed by the reigning emperor without any regard to which noble family claims the royal title for that city.

Overseeing the whole empire is the emperor, the King of Kings, the Voice of Divinity. The emperor is chosen from among the members of the imperial family, and in theory each King of Kings is confirmed (elected) by the kings of the noble families. In practice most emperors have appointed their own successor from amongst their sons or other kin, and the kings have simply acclaimed the new monarch. In a few cases of disputed succession, or where the King of Kings has died without an appointed heir, the decision of the kings has mattered.

The protocol surrounding the King of Kings is elaborate, based on his divine status. The title of Voice of Divinity is a key part of the recognition of this status. Only those who are "blessed" are permitted to hear the Voice speak. This naturally includes the nobility of all ranks, and palace servants and the like, but otherwise is a rare honour bestowed on those who have performed exceptional service to the realm. Apart from this, people may come in audience before the Voice, or the army may march past his balcony while he sits on the Floral Throne, but they do not hear his voice. The Voice uses a range of gestures to indicate his intent, with meanings such as "tell me more," "you have done well," and "you may leave me." A few Voices have developed their own forms of sign language and use an interpreter to convey more precise meanings, although most Voices have thought that commoners have little to say that is worth hearing.

In 1618, the imperial dignity is held by Kepiuc Tjaanuc. He is the Voice of Divinity, but to be frank, the blessed often wish that they did not have that status, so that they would not have to hear him speak. He can talk, can the Voice. Too many bright ideas, too many questions, and too many whims for the nobles to feel comfortable hearing him speak. Not to mention too many wives. There is no restriction on the number of wives which a man of noble blood can take – commoners are permitted a maximum of three, of course, and then only if they can pay for a separate house for each wife – but the Voice married his 101st wife last winter solstice, far more than any other nobleman in living memory. Some less charitable gossip, carefully repeated out of the ears of any untrustworthy listeners, is that the Voice can no longer remember how to do anything with his wives other than talk to them; certainly, he has not fathered as many sons as would be expected for a man with so many wives. Perhaps he only married them so that they have to listen to him.

* * *

Writing is not a native concept for the Atjuntja, but something which they acquired in the process of expanding their dominions. The first people in the Middle Country to develop writing were the Yuduwungu, who acquired it by stimulus-diffusion from across the desert. While direct contact with the east was limited, some trade flowed across the desert. This included a variety of decorative objects such as pendants and bracelets which were inscribed with messages. Some of the containers for trade goods had labels of their contents. Travellers to the east rarely learned writing themselves; literacy in the Gunnagalic script took years to acquire, due to its complexity. Still, they were aware of the existence of writing, and their tales percolated throughout the Yuduwungu lands.

In the eleventh century, a Yuduwungu artisan named Nuneloc developed a writing system based on what he had heard of the system to the east, and using examples which he had available. Many of the symbols which he used were borrowed from the Gunnagalic script, but used for completely different sounds, and some of the symbols were invented outright[57]. The script was fundamentally syllabic, although also proto-alphabetic because related signs were used for syllables with the same initial consonants but different vowels. Nuneloc had his name immortalised, since it became the root of the Yuduwungu word for writing, and which in time would be passed on to the Atjuntja.

By the time the Atjuntja started conquering, writing had spread as far as the neighbouring Wadjureb people. The Atjuntja adopted the system of writing, finding it extremely useful in maintaining their empire, but its use is limited to preferred purposes. They keep some religious texts and have some of their epic poems and songs written down. They keep detailed records to support their administration of the empire, included lists of tribute collected from each region, the number of people present, and so on. The last Atjuntja census revealed just over 1.75 million people live under the rule of the King of Kings. They have public inscriptions announcing the glory of their rulers, but even

---

[57] There are historical instances of writing being developed in a similar method, such as the development of the Cherokee writing system.

then they rely as much on the carvings and sculpture as on the content of the inscriptions. For the Atjuntja like everything to be a spectacle or festival, or ideally both. Sports, military parades and triumphs, and celebrations of the harvests are all conducted in the most ostentatious manner possible.

As are religious experiences.

* * *

The Atjuntja share the same ancestral religion as all the Yaora peoples, but their beliefs have evolved into an overarching dualism. They believe in the same *kuru* and water-cycles as their kin, but they also worship two divine beings, whose names translate roughly as the Lord and the Lady. Theological interpretations differ (sometimes violently) as to the underlying nature of these beings. One school of thought can be approximately translated as literalists; its adherents consider the Lord and the Lady to be literal beings which have a tangible existence, personalities and so forth. The other main school of religious thought can be roughly translated as abstractionists; they hold that that the designations Lord and Lady are merely a convenient shorthand for what are underlying principles and basic nature of the universe itself.

Regardless of which theological viewpoint individual Atjuntja hold – and the last four Kings of Kings have been careful never to take an official position on the matter – the consequences of these beliefs are similar. The Lady is given a number of titles to represent her essential nature: She Who Creates, the Lady of Goodness, the Patron of Beauty, the Giver of Wisdom, the Incarnator. The Lord is given a corresponding set of titles: He Who Destroys, the Lord of Evil, the Unmaker, the Bringer of Pain, the Harvester of Souls. The Atjuntja believe that the two deities (or principles) act in dynamic unison over the course of eternity. Both are necessary; goodness cannot exist without evil to define it. All that is created will eventually be destroyed; from the shards of what has been destroyed, new things will be remade.

Worship of the Lord and Lady takes many forms, most of them public and ostentatious. Yet the rituals which make the most vivid impression on outside visitors are those associated with some of the more negative aspects of the Lord. Visiting Islanders and other occasional eastern guests are disgusted by them; later European visitors will be similarly appalled.

In Atjuntja theology, a certain amount of misery, pain and death are demanded by the Lord. It is unavoidable, either as part of His wishes (according to literalists) or a fundamental aspect of the universe (according to abstractionists). Since misery, pain and death cannot be prevented, it is best to arrange for them to happen in a form which minimises the effects on the world. Better to inflict pain in a carefully-controlled manner than to leave it to run wild throughout the Middle Country; better to appease the Lord with appropriate ritual torture and bloodletting rather than to allow death to strike where it wishes.

The rituals involved with these aspects of the worship of the Lord are conducted in a building whose formal name translates as the House of Absolution, but which is colloquially and more widely known as the House of Pain. Its priests are titled Appeasers. The House includes both public and private sections, including one large public arena where the major rituals are conducted. The arena can seat over twenty thousand, and it is regularly filled by people who have come to bear witness.

The House hosts two main kinds of rituals, the sacrifices conducted by the Appeasers themselves, and blood bouts performed entirely by guests. The sacrifices are conducted using a variety of techniques which are best not described too closely, but which fall into two basic classes: "to the pain" or "to the death." In either case, the Appeasers work as slowly as possible, gradually increasing the intensity of their efforts. When a person is sacrificed to the pain, the ritual will continue until they signal for it to stop; a sacrifice to the death is self-explanatory.

Sacrificial victims are all volunteers. In theory, at least. The Atjuntja hold that a sacrifice from a person of noble blood is far more effective at appeasing the Lord than that of a commoner. A certain number of members of each noble family are sacrificed to the pain every year. The longer the sacrifice continues without the victim calling it to a halt, the more efficacious it is judged to be. Human nature being what it is, the noble families compete with each other to win the greatest spiritual rewards – to say nothing of public acclaim and honour – by how long their children can last in the sacrifice. Stoic endurance is deemed a major virtue, since there is no better method to appease the Lord. The Appeasers are rarely short of volunteers, both from noble and common stock.

Sacrifices to the death are rarer; in a normal year the standard number is thirteen. In bad years, such as those afflicted by diseases or extended droughts, it is common for the King of Kings to request more volunteers. Such requests are usually honoured; a large part of a region's annual tribute can be in the form of people to be sacrificed to the death. However, this is one instance where the imperial administrators will never demand tribute in this form; such offers must always come from the individuals concerned. This is not out of any sense of squeamishness or even out of any fear of alienating their subjects, but simply a result of their religious beliefs. A forced sacrifice will not appease the Lord; if anything, it will simply invite His attention and risk Him taking a more direct hand in worldly affairs.

Or so commoners and subject peoples believe, at any rate. Many of the upper classes have fewer scruples when it comes to their own kin. It is not unknown for less favoured members of a noble family to volunteer to take the ultimate sacrifice. Even the royal family are not above such requests; being a surplus prince is not an indicator of a long life expectancy.

The other form of religious ritual in the House of Pain is the blood bout. This is a contest between (usually) two volunteers, fought with the objective of inflicting pain, loss of blood, and eventual death. Volunteers for these bouts are usually from the lower classes; most noble families prefer to win honour through sacrifices instead. Blood bouts are usually held only once a year, as part of broader religious ceremonies involved with the start of the new year. Blood bouts are fought using a number of stylised weapons, or (rarely) bare-fisted. Armour is not permitted, beyond basic clothing for modesty. Weapons are designed to make it difficult to inflict a single killing blow. The blood battlers are expected to kill slowly; the most favoured contest is one where the loser dies from slowly bleeding through a large number of small cuts. It is quite common for both contestants to die in a blood bout, although some particularly gifted duellists have survived bouts for several successive years.

* * *

The House of Pain will attract most early attention when Europeans first discover about Atjuntja religion. Still, the Atjuntja beliefs are far more complex than this, a combination of their own special interests and older traditions which have been subsumed into their theology. One older belief which has become integral to Atjuntja religion is their study of the heavens. Several Yaora peoples interpreted the constellations and other heavenly bodies in terms of movements in the great water-cycles, and believed that a proper study of celestial events would yield detailed knowledge of signs and omens to guide the decisions of men. Of the various groups who held these beliefs, none would take them further than the Yuduwungu.

Before the invention of writing, Yuduwungu astrologers established an observation point far inland. They chose a plateau which they called the Heights of Heaven, although it would later come to be called Star Hill [Boorabin]. From this inland vantage, they had much clearer skies to watch the heavens and study the signs and omens. They established a tradition of picking the keenest-sighted people in the land and sending them to Star Hill to become apprentices to study the craft of astrology. The astrologers of Star Hill became dedicated to studying the heavens, and built up a detailed oral system which described the known constellations, stars, planets, and some records of meteors and comets. The sect became known as the Watchers, and the Yuduwungu gave them the same veneration which classical Greeks would give the Oracle of Delphi.

When Nuneloc developed his script, it did not take long for the practice to spread to the Watchers. They added their own system of signs for numbers, and transferred their oral knowledge into written form. The Watchers began to keep a very detailed record of constellations, stellar movements, and new celestial bodies such as comets, novas, and the like. Living in a plateau in the desert, with clear skies and no distractions, they became very good at watching. With much time for contemplation, they discovered a variety of astronomical truths, although these were wrapped up in astrological terms and incorporated into their system of predictions. When the Atjuntja conquerors came, they did not interfere with the Watchers; indeed, several of the Kings of Kings have allocated labour to construct expanded buildings for the Watchers.

Over the centuries, the Watchers have accumulated a detailed body of astronomical knowledge. They have very thorough records of the constellations and individual stars, and their observers are astute enough to have recognised the precession of the equinoxes over the five and a half centuries in which they have been keeping records. They have a detailed record of every comet, solar and lunar eclipse which has been visible above the Middle Country since 1076, except for a twenty-year gap between 1148-1168 where several records were lost due to flooding. They keep a calendar of meteor showers, and have recognised most (but not all) novae which have been visible since their records began.

In common with European and other astronomers, they know of the supernova which occurred in 1604; brighter than any other celestial body apart from the Moon and

Venus[58]. The Watchers are still arguing over exactly what that new star meant, although most of them agree that it was ominous. On their advice, the then-King of Kings requested fifty volunteers to be sacrificed to the death in 1605, to appease the threat contained in this new sign in the heavens. They are aware that the world is round, although they have no particular interest in calculating its size. Their star catalogues and their dedicated observations have allowed them to recognise Uranus, which they include in their list of wandering stars [planets].

In short, if European astronomers gain access to the Watchers' records, they will find much to interest them.

---

[58] Northern hemisphere astronomers also recorded another supernova a generation before in 1572, but this was in the northern hemisphere constellation of Cassiopeia and could not be seen from where the Watchers operate.

#13: Tales Of The Cider Isle

There is a land, the land of bronze, the land of mist, the land of courage, where valiant Tjunini soldiers battle endlessly with crafty Kurnawal warriors, where the wild men still lurk in the highlands, raiding where they may, and where in the long winter evenings honourable men gather to feast around roaring fireplaces, drink endless goblets of gum cider, and hear the bards recite the endless verses of the *Song of the Princess*, and even the smallest boy can recite the names of every captain who led men into that war, while in the courts of cunning kings, poets compete with each other to create ever more complex verses packed with allusions and circumlocutions which only the most learned of listeners can fully grasp...

* * *

The island which another history would call Tasmania held what was for a very long time the most isolated human society on the globe. First settled tens of thousands of years ago when the seas were lower, the inhabitants of that distant land easily walked there. When the ice melted, sea levels rose and flooded what became the Narrow Sea [Bass Strait], and the inhabitants of this southerly island were trapped in isolation. Although their distant ancestors had used boats or rafts to cross the seas and reach Australia, the inhabitants of the Cider Isle had lost those skills. For ten millennia these people, who called themselves the Palawa, lived in complete isolation from the rest of humanity.

The island which the Palawa call home is a cold and wet land, by the standards of mainland Aururia. Much of it is rugged and covered in forests, although there are substantial flat and fertile areas, mostly on the northern and eastern coasts. Lying in the midst of the Roaring Forties, the island is often wind-swept, particularly the western coast. The rugged terrain conceals a wealth of mineral resources: gold, tin, copper, zinc, and iron. The few thousand Palawa who live on the island do not practice metal-working; with a small population and no suitable plants to develop indigenous agriculture, they live as hunter-gatherers.

* * *

The waters of the Narrow Sea are shallow and treacherous, filled with reefs and submerged rocks which hinder navigation. Strong currents move both east and west, and the fury of the Roaring Forties creates frequent storms and wind-driven waves. In a different history, this strait would be notorious for the hundreds of shipwrecks on its islands or along its shores.

For the Gunnagalic peoples who lived along the northern shores of the Narrow Sea, the island beyond the wild waters for so long might as well have been on the far side of the moon. The various peoples who lived along the northern shores – Tjunini around the Wurrung Mountains [Otway Ranges], Giratji around the Little Sea [Port Phillip Bay], and Kurnawal to the east – knew how to build some ships, but their techniques were primitive. Their seagoing boats were mostly small, single-masted vessels built from wooden planks and held together with dowels. In these boats, they carefully fished the coastal waters, always wary for any potential storms, and rarely venturing out of sight of land. At times these vessels would be blown out to sea, where the sailors were often wrecked or drowned. On a few rare occasions a ship would land on the Cider Isle itself, where the crew might be killed by the local Palawa, sometimes be accepted into a local band, or otherwise starve to death in a land where they no longer knew how to hunt.

The long isolation of the Cider Isle might have continued until contact with the outside world, if not for the islands which lie in the midst of the Sea. The shallow waters of the Sea contain a great many small islands and semi-submerged rocks which are hazardous to shipping, but they also contain some larger islands which can sustain human habitation. The largest of these are Benowee [King Island] off the northwest coast of the Cider Isle, and Tayaritja [Flinders Island] off the northeast coast. Both of these islands had held human populations in the distant past, but these had left or died out.

In the late eighth century, a pair of Kurnawal fishing boats were swept out to sea, as so many had before them. Unlike so many of their predecessors, these boats were not sunk or wrecked on the shores, but made a safe landing on the eastern side of Tayaritja. Here they found an empty land with no signs of human habitation, but which abounded with natural resources. In particular, they found large breeding populations of fur seals and elephant seals. Seal colonies had been largely hunted out on the mainland, for they offered an attractive source of meat, pelts, fur, and seal oil. The crews of these fishing boats killed a few seals, collected their pelts and meat, and tried to sail home. Again, unlike many of their predecessors, they successfully returned to the mainland, with news of islands and seals.

News of the seal-filled island to the south caused a considerable stir among the peoples who lived beside the Narrow Sea. Their navigation techniques were not advanced, and the waters of the Sea were always risky. Still, they could recognise general directions from the movement of the sun, and seal hunting offered a considerable source of wealth for those who braved the waters. Over the next few decades, Kurnawal sealers colonised Tayaritja, while further west Tjunini sealers did the same on Benowee.

With their colonies so close, and with several smaller seal-filled islands in between to encourage exploration, sealers did not take long to discover the larger island to the south. The long rivalry between Tjunini and Kurnawal means that both of them claim that they were the first to discover what they first called the Big Island. As such, no date can be firmly established, and the margins of error of radiometric dating meant that later archaeologists would never definitively settle the question. Still, it is certain that sometime in the early ninth century AD, Tjunini and Kurnawal both made landfall on the Cider Isle itself. The Palawa's ten millennia of isolation had come to an end.

* * *

The Tjunini established their first permanent settlement on the north-west coast of the Cider Isle. Here, they found an imposing natural feature: a flat-topped circular headland which seemed to grow straight out of the sea, seemingly defying the power of wind and wave. On the sheltered southern side of the headland lay a useful port. The first Tjunini sailors to see this head called it Hope Hill [Stanley], and built their first mainland town just to the south[59].

From their base at Hope Hill, Tjunini sealers started to explore the Big Island's shores. Along the western coast, they found only rugged coastline; good for harvesting seals, but not much else. To the east, they found that the northern coast was relatively flat and fertile. From their perspective this was bountiful nearly-empty land ripe for settlement. Naturally, the Palawa had a different view.

To the Tjunini, the northern coast of the Cider Isle was extremely alluring. It was only slightly colder than their homeland, and its relative emptiness held appeal. Yet the most attractive feature of this new land was its distance from the mainland and the Empire who ruled there. The Tjunini homeland had been recently conquered by Watjubaga's armies, and many amongst the Tjunini resented imperial rule. For those brave enough to sail

---

[59] Historically, this headland was named Circular Head by the first Europeans to see it (Bass and Flinders in 1798), although it is informally called the Nut.

across the Narrow Sea, they could build new lives in a land untouched by imperial influence.

The lure of new lands proved to be strong. Over the course of the ninth and early tenth centuries, more than twenty thousand Tjunini crossed the Narrow Sea to permanently settle in the Cider Isle. The migration was so substantial that the Tjunini on the mainland would disappear as a separate people over the next few centuries, having become few enough that they were absorbed into their neighbours.

On the Big Island, though, the Tjunini flourished. Most of their early settlements were on the coast, where they could rely on fishing or sealing for part of their food. Some of these early settlements would grow into significant cities; the largest of these were Kwamania [Smithton], Mulaka Nayri [Wynyard], and Mukanuyina [Devonport].

From these early cities, the Tjunini started to settle inland, and push further east. The previous inhabitants could not stop them; outnumbered almost from the beginning, some Palawa were assimilated into the Tjunini, and the rest pushed from the coastal lowlands into the rugged interior. Nor did the Empire ever offer a credible threat to the Tjunini expansion. The first real threat to the Tjunini came when they pushed far enough east to encounter the Kurnawal.

* * *

The Kurnawal settlement of the Cider Isle began near-simultaneously with that of the Tjunini. Like their western neighbours, the Kurnawal had first settled an offshore island, then found a convenient port on the mainland of the Big Island which was first used as a sealing base. For the Kurnawal, this was Dawn Dunes [Bridport]. From here, Kurnawal sealers charted the northern and eastern coasts of the Cider Isle. They established another early settlement at Orange Rock [St Helens]. Unlike the Tjunini, the Kurnawal moved inland relatively quickly. Inland from Dawn Dunes, they found a place where the soils were so rich that yams grew larger than anywhere they had heard of. This place they called Bountiful [Scottsdale], and it quickly grew into the largest Kurnawal town in the Big Island[60].

However, while the Tjunini had crossed the Narrow Sea in their thousands to flee imperial expansion, the mainland Kurnawal were not yet under threat. The apparent emptiness of this new island did attract some settlers, but it was not the main driver for Kurnawal migrations. It would take another discovery to lure large numbers of Kurnawal settlers across the Sea.

* * *

The north-east of the Cider Isle contains many ancient granite mountains, worn down by rain and wind into rugged terrain. Many of the rocks worn down by ages of rain have been carried into river beds, which over the aeons have formed immensely thick alluvial deposits. Kurnawal explorers who travelled along the north-eastern rivers recognised several minerals in the beds, including one which would prove an irresistible lure: tin.

Although the early Kurnawal did not know it, the granite in the mountains they climbed over had rich concentrations of cassiterite (tin ore). Mining the granite itself would have been difficult, but millions of years of erosion had broken down the granite and washed large concentrations of cassiterite into the river beds. The Kurnawal easily recognised cassiterite; similar ores had been carried to their mainland homes from the trade routes.

To the Kurnawal, the alluvial cassiterite deposits offered a source of wealth which made seal-hunting seem trivial. Although essential for forming bronze, tin was a rare metal. At the time, the only significant source in Aururia came from the far-off Gemlands. Some tin did come south along the trade routes, but it was very expensive. The promise of

---

[60] Historically, the first European surveyor who explored the Scottsdale region considered that it had the best soil in all Tasmania. The inhabitants of the region seem to have liked that claim, since they named the town after him. In historical Australia, the region of Scottsdale is a major agricultural centre, especially for potato farming.

tin-based wealth brought several thousand Kurnawal across the Narrow Sea to settle in the Cider Isle. Unlike the Tjunini, though, the mainland Kurnawal did not migrate *en masse* to the Big Island; the majority of them remained in their home country.

* * *

The early history of the Tjunini and Kurnawal settlers on the Cider Isle is shrouded in mystery. Writing was unknown in the Kurnawal homeland at the time that the first settlers crossed the Narrow Sea. It was only barely known amongst the Tjunini, who regarded it as a tool of imperial conquest and bureaucracy, and wanted no part of it. Archaeology can reveal only glimpses of those early days, and oral history has been overlaid by many embellishments and biases.

From what truth can be sifted from myths and legends, it seems that Tjunini and Kurnawal settlers on the Cider Isle had some clashes with each other even during the early days of colonisation, but these did not develop into full-scale war for more than a century. In the early days, both peoples lacked the population to support a major war, and considerable distance separated their main settlements. The two peoples were never fond of each other, but they appear to have tolerated each other's existence for a time.

By the mid-eleventh century, the Tjunini and Kurnawal had both grown considerably in population. The Tjunini were the more numerous people, and were well-established along the north-west coast; later archaeologists will excavate quite a few large settlements. They were a people without political unity; each of their cities had its own king. Mukanuyina was the most populous city, with Kwamania and Mulaka Nayri roughly equal second, while six other cities also had monarchs who claimed descent from the Rainbow Serpent.

The Kurnawal had never received the same number of immigrants from the mainland, but they still had a substantial presence in the north-east coast. By far their most important city was Bountiful. The rich soils supported its large population, and the city marked one end of the Tin Trail which ran through the mountains to Orange Rock on the east coast[61]. Orange Rock was their second most populous city, with ancient Dawn Dunes a distant third, and there were a few other small towns further south along the east coast.

The boundary line between the two peoples was for a long time the Kanamaluka [Tamar River]. Later Kurnawal sagas claim that the Tjunini kept crossing the river to steal their land for farming; Tjunini songs speak of furtive Kurnawal sneaking across the Kanamaluka on winter nights to raid and steal what they could. While the truth of these accounts is open to dispute, it is clear that the two peoples were becoming more hostile. The stage was set for a series of events which would be immortalised in song.

* * *

What happened in the Cider Isle in the turbulent decades of 1060-1080? The short and unhelpful answer is: a war. The long-enduring tensions between Tjunini and Kurnawal came to crisis point during this time, and led to a war which the Tjunini won and the Kurnawal lost. That much can be known, at least with as much certainty as anything is known about history. Beyond that, things are much harder to determine.

About a century after the events of that troubled time, a bard named Tjiganeng took the existing tales and verses and wove them into song. Into a very long song. If written out (which it later would be), it ran to over 25,000 lines in the alternating twelve and ten syllable patterns of Tjunini verse. As far as is known, Tjiganeng gave his song no title,

---

[61] Historically, the Tin Trail starts roughly at the modern town of Scottsdale (western end), runs through the rich tin mines around Derby, Moorina, Weldborough, and Blue Tier, and ends in the modern town of St Helens (eastern end). This was the trail used by tin miners during the Tasmanian tin rush of the nineteenth to early twentieth centuries; there were hundreds of tin mines along the trail, including the Briseis Mine which was for a while the world's richest tin mine.

referring to it simply as "My Song." Some later Tjunini would give it that name, but it was most popularly called the *Song of the Princess*. It told the tale of the War of the Princess, a war which raged for twelve years, and which rearranged the political and cultural borders of the Big Island.

The War of the Princess was undoubtedly a real war; archaeology has confirmed the destruction of Bountiful which was the central event depicted in the Song. Still, for all that memorising the Song became fundamental for the training of all later bards, the historical accuracy of the events it depicts are open to considerable dispute. Some historians think that the gist is accurate, but many details were invented. Some think that only the names of the central characters are accurate, and that almost everything else was artistic licence.

Still, with all the appropriate caveats, the Song records a reasonably credible account of a war. It describes how the Tjunini kings had long fought amongst themselves as much as they fought the Kurnawal, until King Tiyuratina of Mukanuyina established a loose confederation. All the other kings became vassals who could not make war except with his permission. Tiyuratina took the title of Nine-Fold King.

According to the Song, Tiyuratina sought peace with the raiding Kurnawal, and so offered a pact of eternal friendship. This was to be sealed by a dual marriage, with Tiyuratina's son Mulaka to marry the daughter of the Kurnawal monarch, while in turn the Kurnawal monarch's son married Tiyuratina's daughter, Lutana. The Kurnawal king, Anguma, agreed with the peace pact, until the appearance of a brilliant comet the night before the dual wedding, which he interpreted as an unfavourable omen[62].

---

[62] Historians who view the Song as essentially accurate believe that this was the appearance of Halley's Comet in 1066, and so use this to date the beginning of the war.

Haunted by this omen, Anguma betrayed the pact by dressing a servant Palawa girl as his daughter during the double wedding. The subterfuge was not discovered until after the dual marriage was completed. Anguma insisted that despite the deception, Lutana was now his son's lawful wife. Tiyuratina refused to break the oaths of safe-conduct which he had sworn, and so watched his only daughter carried off to Bountiful where she would be both wife and hostage.

When he returned home, Tiyuratina had the fake princess killed then dismembered, sending parts of her body to each vassal city, calling on them to avenge the honour of the Tjunini. Each king brought their armies, and they began a campaign to release the princess and drive the Kurnawal from the Big Island. The Song lists each of the captains of the army, and names several heroes who were to play leading parts in the war. After several battles which are mostly glossed over in the Song, the Tjunini armies reached Bountiful and besieged it. The granite walls held off every attack from the Tjunini armies for seven years, with many clashes of heroes along the way, while the besieged Kurnawal waited for help from their mainland cousins which never came.

Bountiful eventually fell when a Tjunini hero known only by his nickname of the Wombat dug beneath the granite walls and made a section collapse at a well-timed moment. The besiegers on the surface were already attacking, and used the breach in the walls to capture the city. Many heroes on both sides died during this final battle, which ended with the burning of Bountiful and the massacre of most of its inhabitants. Princess Lutana was returned to her father, but Anguma escaped. Tiyuratina vowed that the war should continue until the Kurnawal king was dead and his people driven into the sea. His vassal kings refused to honour his vow, saying that they had come at his calling to ensure that his daughter was returned, and that had been accomplished.

Tiyuratina continued the war with only his own forces and those of a few captains who remained loyal. He divided his armies in half, taking personal command of the forces sent to Dawn Dunes in case Anguma had fled there. The Wombat led the other half east through the mountains until they reached Orange Rock. In Dawn Dunes, Tiyuratina fought his way into the city and met Anguma's son, where they fought a duel where both of them slew the other. On the same day, the Wombat dug under the walls of Orange Rock in a raid, since he lacked the troops to besiege the city. There he found Anguma in a tower overlooking the eastern sea. They fought their own duel, which ended with each wounding the other, then wrestling and trying to push each other out of the tower. The Song ends with the description of the Wombat and Anguma each dragging the other out of the tower window, where they fall to their deaths in the eastern sea.

* * *

Whatever the historical truth of the Song, it is clear from the archaeological record that the Kurnawal were pushed out of most of the north-east during this period. Excavations of Dawn Dunes and Bountiful show a layer of destruction which can be dated to sometime between 1060 to 1080. Below this the record shows Kurnawal pottery and artefacts, above it they are entirely replaced by Tjunini pottery.

Of the major Kurnawal cities, only Orange Rock survived the wars of this period. Still, it appears that much of the population from the defeated cities survived and fled south. A number of new Kurnawal towns can be dated to this period. Of these, the most important were Narnac [Woodbury], Dabuni [Hobart] and Gamoma [Orford]. Here, the Kurnawal would thrive. Despite later attempts by various Tjunini warleaders, the Kurnawal would never be completely dislodged from their new homes.

The main legacy of the War of the Princess was long-lasting enmity between Tjunini and Kurnawal. The Tjunini took control of the rest of the northern coast; Bountiful and

Three Waters [Launceston] became major cities under new kings. The Kurnawal were pushed onto the eastern coast; Orange Rock became their northernmost bastion on the main island. For a time it was the capital, but the Kurnawal monarchs would eventually establish their royal city at Dabuni, far from the Tjunini threat.

In the immediate aftermath of the War, the border between the two peoples ran roughly from Orange Rock to Hunters' Cliff [Millers Bluff], although it was never fixed in one place for long. Friction over the border became a regular inspiration for wars, particularly disputes over the tin mines in the north-east. The long-term trend has been for the Tjunini to push the Kurnawal further south, although there have been several temporary reversals. The most significant long-term conquest has been Tayaritja, which for long held a Kurnawal hold-out population, but which was permanently conquered by the Tjunini in 1554.

The unending war between the two peoples would produce something unusual in Aururia: a very strong sense of nationalism and a view of particular lands as being the inalienable heritage of a particular people. Even though both peoples fought amongst themselves from time to time, cooperation with anyone from the other people was regarded as the worst sort of treachery. They also viewed their own lands as being part of their inalienable heritage, and a call to war to liberate any enemy-occupied lands would always be well-received amongst both the Tjunini and the Kurnawal.

* * *

In 1618, the whole of the Cider Isle is divided into three parts. On the north coast dwell the Tjunini, the most numerous people. Warriors, singers, feasters, and bronze-smiths par excellence, the Tjunini live according to their own code of honour. Memories of the past guide how they think they should live in the present. Writing is known to them, a necessary tool of government, but for their folk memory they rely on the ideals depicted by their bards.

Bards are their most honoured profession, requiring a combination of memory, musical talent, and dramatic flair. The foundation of any bard's skills is the memorisation and appropriate recitation of the many verses of the *Song of the Princess*. Any bard who cannot remember the entirety of the Song is not considered a bard, but at best a student and at worst an imposter. Tjunini bards know a variety of other epic songs, and compose many more topical and light-hearted songs which they recite when appropriate, but it is a rare winter's evening when a bard does not recite a few verses of the Song.

As a people, the Tjunini have done their best to forget that they ever dwelt on the mainland. They see themselves as the heroes of the world, descendants of those who answered the call of Tiyuratina and fought in the great war. What happened before that war means little to them. They adhere to what they see as the standards of behaviour and conduct laid down by the captains who fought in the war. While the bards are the repositories of the full knowledge of the war, even a small child can recite the names of each of the great captains.

In truth, the Tjunini are much changed from their mainland forebears. While they are a Gunnagalic people, like so many others in Aururia, their ancestors mingled their blood with the Palawa who lived on the Big Island before them. About ten percent of the words in the Tjunini language are of Palawa origin, and an even higher percentage of place names and personal names. Even the name of their greatest king, Tiyuratina, was originally a Palawa name, as were the names of his son and daughter. Still, the Tjunini have forgotten this truth; they have pushed the Palawa off the north coast and into the less fertile highland regions beyond. They trade with them from time to time, but consider them wild barbarians who lack honour.

Politically, the Tjunini have not much changed from the old system of petty kings which existed in the days of the War. Or what they believe existed during the war, at any rate. The Tjunini lands are divided into a number of feuding city-states, each ruled by a king who claims divine descent from the Rainbow Serpent. The rank of the Nine-Fold King still exists as titular head of the Tjunini confederation, although there are now more than nine subject kings. There has not been a continuous line of Nine-Fold Kings; there have been periods when no-one has held the crown, and several wars have been fought amongst the Tjunini to determine which head should wear the crown. Internecine warfare is an integral part of the Tjunini way of life; the vassal kings fiercely guard their individual rights, and fighting each other is as much a part of their tradition as the list of the great captains. The Tjunini fight, in essence, because they have always been fighting.

On the east coast dwell the Kurnawal. Like the Tjunini, these are a Gunnagalic-speaking people, but otherwise they have little in common. Where the Tjunini are numerous, fractious and tradition-bound, the Kurnawal are less populous, but more united and less interested in the mores of the past. The Kurnawal are a people who inherited a tradition of survival from the massacres and defeats of the War. To them, cunning and resourcefulness are a way of life, both in war and in peace. A Tjunini merchant will always name his price and expect it to be honoured, while a Kurnawal merchant would think that anyone who accepted the first price was a fool. In war, the Kurnawal place much more emphasis on deviousness, feints, manoeuvres, and surprise attacks.

Where the Tjunini are politically divided, the Kurnawal have been forced by necessity to adopt a united monarchy, except for a renegade outpost at Jangani [Cockle Creek]. Their kings claim descent not from any divine beings, but from the daughter of Anguma, who survived the War. They do not have a bardic tradition, but they inherited some of the old forms of poetry and storytelling which their ancestors used on the mainland. The mainland Kurnawal used a form of alliterative verse to describe the deeds of their ancestors and of modern heroes. The Kurnawal who live on the Big Island have kept up this tradition, and have developed it much further.

Where the Tjunini have bards who speak in song, the Kurnawal emphasise the use of the spoken word alone. Their word for such speakers is *wusaka*, which can be broadly translated as poet, but which encompasses much more. The *wusaka* recite not just alliterative verse, but also sagas and other epic tales, which often include many poetic stanzas as part of the tales. When writing spread from the mainland, the Kurnawal enthusiastically adopted it to record the sagas, although they still emphasised oral recitation.

Most Kurnawal poets recite epics and poems in language which is meant to be easy to understand, since their audiences are usually the general populace. However, there is another kind of poetry, which specialises in using metaphorical language, allusions, and other poetic devices. These poets evolved out of an old Kurnawal tradition which was an equivalent to a court jester. The early Kurnawal kings appointed an individual poet who was given exclusive permission to "scold" or chastise the king without fear of retribution. While speaking rudely to a Kurnawal monarch could mean death for anyone else who was so foolish, the "scold" had free license to criticise the king's action. As part of the same tradition, any scolding had to be done in poetic speech rather than plain speech; the ambiguous language of the criticism made it more difficult for the common man to understand, while the kings had to be adept at understanding the literary language and allusions to understand the nature of the criticism.

The function of this class of poets has evolved considerably, but they are still remembered by their old name, the *scolds*. Now they create poems and panegyrics praising the kings as often as criticising them. They also create poems on a diverse range of topics, from religious to historical to mythical. The best scolds are kept around the king's court, but they also find audiences elsewhere, amongst the nobility or wealthy commoners. Scolds speak in a poetic language which is intricate almost to the point of opaqueness; to the Kurnawal, who esteem cunning and cleverness, the more obscure the poetic language, the more it is appreciated. The scolds pile allusion upon pun upon double meaning in an elliptical, inverted style of language which makes their meaning almost impossible for the casual listener to follow.

In the central uplands and the rugged lands of Cider Isle's south and west, the Palawa still dwell. Once they lived all over the Big Island, but the Gunnagalic invaders have pushed them out of the flatter, more fertile lands on the north and east coasts. What they have left is the more rugged terrain, where the elevation and cool westerly winds means that it is less suitable for agriculture. Both the Tjunini and Kurnawal usually treat them with hostility, calling them wild men, barbarians, uncouth speakers of an incomprehensible language, ignorant of farming and city-building. The Palawa, for their part, often raid the fringes of Tjunini and Kurnawal territory, sometimes for food, sometimes for tools and weapons. The Palawa also have some contact with the Islanders, who have mastered the difficult sailing route into Timber Haven [Macquarie Harbour]. The Islanders have a trading outpost at Yellow Pine [Strahan], and several other timber-harvesting camps along the harbour's shores.

While the Palawa were hunter-gatherers when the Gunnagalic peoples arrived, they have learned much since that time. The Palawa have not taken up full-time farming, but they have acquired some domesticated crops from their neighbours. They plant these crops in suitable areas, and at the right time of the year, they move to harvest them, and they store much of this food for later use. The Palawa are not full-time farmers, but they are hunter-gardeners. With these gardened crops to feed them, the Palawa are more numerous than at any time in the last ten millennia, despite having lost much of their ancestral lands. They are still much fewer than the Tjunini or even the Kurnawal, but they are thriving in their way.

For the Palawa have learned much from their neighbours, not just about farming. The Palawa conduct only limited mining, but trade and raids have given them metal tools, and they have a few smiths who have learned how to melt and reforge bronze. They have learned how to make textiles and ceramics. Above all, they have learned how to make weapons, especially ranged weapons. In some cases, ingenious Palawa have developed weapons beyond anything which the city-dwellers can match. The most significant of these is a kind of longbow, which the Palawa lovingly craft from the wood of the myrtle beech (*Nothofagus cunninghamii*). All Palawa men learn to use this longbow, since it is very useful both for hunting and for piercing even the strongest of bronze armour. Even the boldest Tjunini soldiers hesitate to chase Palawa into the hills when they might receive a barrage of arrows if they get too close to their foes.

Relations between the Palawa and their neighbours are often hostile, but not always; there is intermittent trade contact, for instance. The Palawa lifestyle requires that they become expert hunters, and they are adept at moving without being noticed. This ability makes them very useful as scouts; both Tjunini and Kurnawal have been known to recruit Palawa auxiliaries during times of war. The Palawa are too few to supply significant numbers of longbowmen, even if they were interested in doing so, but they excel at finding the enemy without being spotted themselves.

* * *

For all that Tjunini, Kurnawal and Palawa have so much hostility toward each other, there are three things which they all agree on. Every person on the Big Island knows the merits of bronze, the good taste of a goose, and the worth of the cider gum.

For without a doubt, the Cider Isle is the island of bronze. Indeed, for a long time the name the mainlanders had for the island literally translated as the Island of Bronze. The island has abundant reserves of tin and copper, and its peoples here have a wealth of bronze by the standards of mainlanders. Bronze weapons are abundant; both Tjunini and Kurnawal make bronze swords, daggers, axes, spears, and maces. Bronze tools are extremely common, far more than on the mainland: knives, hammers, chisels, wedges, saws and many other tools. Bronze-based jewellery is popular and widespread, and some people can afford to use bronze nails, screws, horns and other musical instruments, to say nothing of cooking utensils and dishware. Both Tjunini and Kurnawal can afford to protect their common soldiers with full bronze armour which would be considered extravagant even for elite officers in mainland armies.

The peoples of the Cider Isle are aware of iron as a metal, since the Islanders have traded a few iron artefacts. However, they regard iron as inferior to bronze. Wrought iron from the mainland is less versatile than cast bronze, and much more prone to corrosion along the coast. With ample quantities of bronze, both Tjunini and Kurnawal regard iron as little more than a curiosity. The spread of ironworking on the mainland has reduced the importance of the tin trade, but on the Big Island itself, bronze remains the metal of choice.

Of course, while it is a useful metal, man cannot live by bronze alone. The Cider Isle peoples have all become acquainted with agriculture to some degree, even the Palawa, and many of the mainland crops are quite suitable to growing on the Big Island. Still, all of these peoples prefer meat, when they can get it. They are fortunate in that regard, for they have another species of domesticated bird which is still uncommon on the mainland.

The Cape Barren goose (*Cereopsis novaehollandiae*) is a gregarious bird which breeds mostly on offshore islands; it is abundant on several of the Narrow Sea islands. Kurnawal sealers were the first to start it on the road to domestication, keeping semi-wild flocks on some of their sealing islands as a source of food while they were hunting seals. Some Kurnawal brought these geese with them to the Big Island. The biards could be easily bred and reared in captivity, since they are grazers that could be left to feed themselves on pasture. Domesticated geese have become widespread across the Big Island; even the Palawa keep a few semi-wild flocks around as handy sources of meat and eggs. The local cuisine features a variety of dishes based on geese, from simple roasted goose at feasts, to goose fat used as an equivalent to butter, to goose meat sprinkled with herbs and then slowly left to cook in its own fat (which also acts as a preservative).

The third thing which unites the peoples of the Cider Isle is the cider gum. While the Big Island did not provide many new plants suitable for domestication, the cider gum transformed the culture of the Tjunini and Kurnawal settlers. The Palawa had long learned to tap the cider gum for its sweet sap, which is similar to maple syrup. While this was sometimes used as for flavouring, the Palawa also discovered that if the syrup was sealed in a container and left to wild ferment, it would produce a mildly alcoholic beverage[63].

When the Tjunini and Kurnawal landed on the Big Island, they were quick to appreciate the virtues of the cider gum. They brought their own tradition of brewing with them, which was mostly done with various kinds of yam wine. The Tjunini and Kurnawal used ceramic containers which were much more easily sealed for suitable periods to allow fermentation, and they had discovered how to make systematic use of yeast to make fermentation more reliable. With these techniques, they could now brew much stronger ciders than the old wild-fermented Palawa versions (up to about 9% alcohol).

---

[63] The Palawa use of the cider gum (*Eucalyptus gunnii*) for syrup and gum cider is exactly what they did, historically. The cider gum is endemic to the island, growing in both lowland and some highland areas. It grows easily in cultivation, and is established as an ornamental plant in some parts of Europe. Unlike most eucalypts, it can tolerate frosts and subzero temperatures. In the allohistorical Cider Isle, the cider gum has become their most valuable crop.

Gum cider has become one of the Big Island's most valued products, supported by the cultivation of large numbers of cider gums. All three of the Tasmanian peoples drink it to some degree. The Tjunini, in particular, like nothing better than to feast away the long winter evenings, drinking gum cider while bards sing of the heroes of the War. Gum cider is also a valued trade good. The Islanders who regularly visit the northern coast trade it over a wide area. Since the rise of ironworking on the mainland has reduced the value of the tin trade, gum cider has become the most well-known product of Tasmania. No longer do people on the mainland speak of the Big Island or the Island of Bronze; now, they call it the Cider Isle.

#14: Give Me Liberty Or Give Me Cash

History calls it Kangaroo Island. A small island, not even four and a half thousand square kilometres, but teeming with wildlife. Some claim it to be one of the last unspoilt refuges on earth. Kangaroos, koalas, wombats, goannas, echidnas, platypus and other Australian wildlife flourish here, without introduced predators. In truth, it is far from pristine. The native emu of this island has been hunted to extinction, and many of the indigenous animals were in fact brought across from the mainland by European colonists.

Allohistory calls it Guree Island, or simply the Island. A place not of unspoilt scenery, but the crowded home of the wealthiest people in Aururia. In 1618, on the eve of Dutch contact, the Island is home to sixty thousand people. Dependent on commerce for both their food and their wealth, they have turned their small island home into the nexus of the greatest trade routes in the continent.

* * *

Like the much larger Cider Isle, the Island once held a remnant population who were separated from the mainland by rising waves at the end of the last ice age. Unlike the Cider Isle, the Island's native population vanished sometime in the distant past, abandoning their homes and fleeing to the mainland millennia ago. For a time, the Island was left to the kangaroos and wombats, while the mainlanders referred to it as the Land of the Dead[64].

The Island was resettled about 750 BC, during the Great Migrations. One group of refugees from the abandoned city of Goolrin moved down the Headland [Fleurieu Peninsula] and sailed across to the Island. Early Gunnagalic peoples were not good shipbuilders, but the narrow strait between the Island and the mainland was easily crossed[65].

The settlers of the Island called themselves the Nangu. They spoke a Gunnagalic language, one which was quite linguistically conservative. With the relative isolation of their island, Nangu speakers were unaffected by many of the changes which spread across the mainland languages. The Nangu adopted writing from the mainland during imperial times, and their early written records reveal that their language has changed relatively little since that time. Later linguists would find the Nangu language invaluable in their efforts to reconstruct Proto-Gunnagalic.

Living on the Island, the Nangu were for many centuries an isolated, underpopulated backwater. They received some ideas from the mainland, but the spread was often slow. They learned the arts of bronze-working, although the metal was a rare trade good for centuries. They adopted the new mainland farming techniques of crop rotation, and raised domesticated noroons to replace the

---

[64] Historically, Kangaroo Island was inhabited until some time between 3000 – 200 BC. It is unclear from the archaeological record whether the inhabitants died out or abandoned the island for the mainland.

[65] Historically, Investigator Strait, which separates Kangaroo Island from the mainland, is narrow enough that there have been reports of people who successfully swam across it.

wild birds which had been hunted to extinction during the early days of settlement[66].

Still, in many ways, the history of the mainland passed by without affecting the Island. During the Imperial era, the Nangu were a subject people who vaguely acknowledged the imperial hegemony and occasionally paid tribute. Yet the First Speakers never sent any invading armies across the water. During the early tenth century, the Nangu simply stopped paying tribute to the Empire. No-one in distant Garrkimang seems to have cared. Certainly no army was sent in reconquest, even though this was the time when the Empire had its last burst of military expansion and conquered the Seven Sisters. After the collapse of the Empire, the Nangu continued on largely untouched. Warfare and political intrigue on the mainland was of little concern to the Islanders, since the bickering nations lacked the ability or interest to invade the Island.

Of course, the Nangu were never completely isolated. Dependent on fishing for much of their food, they developed good shipbuilding techniques by the standards of early Gunnagalic peoples. During the eleventh century, a few brave Islander captains started to sail directly to Tasmania, which they called Tjul Najima, the Island of Bronze. The voyage was risky, especially the return leg, where they sometimes had to wait for weeks or months for a change in the prevailing winds. Still, the rewards for successful captains were substantial. Bronze on Tjul Najima was cheap enough to trade for Islander dyes and spices, then return home to sell the metal for excellent profits. Previously the Nangu had received bronze only through a chain of mainland intermediaries; now they had much cheaper direct trade.

---

[66] Kangaroo Island held a dwarf species of emu, variously called the Kangaroo Island emu or dwarf emu (*Dromaius baudinianus*) which was hunted to extinction by European whalers and sealers who used the island as a base of operations. In allohistorical Aururia, it will similarly be easy prey for the early Nangu migrants.

Islander ships expanded the bronze trade over the next few centuries. Some more venturesome captains slowly broadened their trade network over the next couple of centuries. Sporadic visits to the Seven Sisters were expanded into regular trading trips to Pankala [Port Lincoln], to trade bronze and gum cider for opals, salt, and agricultural produce. Other captains started to call at Jugara [Victor Harbor], a small town on the most convenient natural harbour next to the Nyalananga Mouth. From here, they traded for goods which had been moved overland from the Nyalananga.

The early Islander trade network was relatively limited, since their ships could move only small volumes of goods, and that at considerable risk. Yet it was enough to bring many new things to the Island, including new technologies and knowledge in medicine, masonry, and many other fields.

Of these new ideas, perhaps the most significant was the adoption of a new religion. Plirism, the religion of the Sevenfold Path, had experienced only limited success on the mainland. In Tjibarr and Gutjanal its followers were a small minority; among the decaying feudalism of the Junditmara and their Empire of the Lake, its followers were treated as infidels.

On the Island, though, the disciples of the Good Man found a receptive audience. The first Plirite temple was founded at Crescent Bay [Kingscote] in 1204. From here, Plirite priests sought to convert all of the Islanders. They met with substantial success over the next few decades. By 1240, about half of the Islanders followed the rituals and beliefs of the Sevenfold Path. There were considerable religious tensions between Plirite converts and the older Nangu beliefs (which were derived from the early Gunnagalic religions).

At this time, the Island had no single monarch or established aristocratic class. Instead, the population were divided into twenty-four bloodlines, which were derived from the old *kitjigal* system. Bloodlines functioned much as extended clans, where the members were expected to defend each other in case of disputes. Belonging to a particular bloodline was not a matter of strict descent; people could seek adoption into a new bloodline if they wished. However, while birth did not always matter, loyalty did; early Islander history is rife with tales of feuds and vendettas between bloodlines which carried on for generations.

To bring order to the Island, the Nangu had established an institution of a yearly assembly by the elders (chiefs) of each of the bloodlines. This assembly met to decide on the law, resolve disputes between bloodlines, and dispense other judicial functions. In 1240, the assembled elders voted to convert the whole of the Island to Plirism. More or less willingly, the remaining adherents of the old beliefs adopted the new rituals. More temples were built, and the Nangu became committed to their new faith. In time, they would seek to spread it beyond the Island.

* * *

Aururia's isolation from the rest of the world ended in 1310, when the first Māori[67] exploration canoe landed in Raduru lands [Illawarra, NSW]. After this initial contact, the Māori started to make trading visits north and south. In time, after chasing after rumours of bronze, they reached Tjul Najima. Here they established what would become one of their major trade routes, exchanging their greenstone [jade], kauri amber, and textiles and cordage made from harakeke [New Zealand flax] for the local tin and gum cider.

With Nangu trading captains also regularly visiting Tjul Najima for bronze and gum cider, contact soon followed between Māori and Nangu. Unlike many other Aururian peoples, the Islanders had a keen interest in better ships for

---

[67] Some of the individual Māori tribes called themselves Tangata, which means "people." As happened historically, Māori developed as a word which collectively referred to all of the Māori peoples, to distinguish them from outsiders (i.e. Aururians).

their own needs, both trading and fishing. With the example of Māori ships, and with a few Māori who were persuaded to live on the Island and share their knowledge of shipbuilding and navigation techniques, the Nangu became the best seafarers in Aururia.

History does not record the precise date of Māori-Nangu contact, but by 1380, Islander records describe the construction of twin-hulled boats. Inspired by Māori examples, these were dual-masted vessels whose twin hulls gave them great stability and speed. These boats also had lateen sails (woven from linen) which were extremely manoeuvrable. Thanks to the Māori, the Nangu learned the art of tacking into the wind; the best Islander captains and crews could sail their ships within 60 degrees of the wind. This meant that their ships were capable of sailing even into the strong winds of the Roaring Forties.

The old Nangu ships had used a shallow enough draft that they could be pulled up onto a beach if one was available, or use a port and wait for a favourable wind. With their new ships, the direction of the wind became less of a concern, although their ships could still be pulled ashore in rough weather if the captain chose to do so.

The basic design of the Nangu ships would be similar for the next few centuries, although they made some refinements. Some Islander captains started to use larger sailing vessels which could not be pulled onto any beach, but which needed to operate from a port. By the late sixteenth century, a few of these ships were steered using a rudder rather than the traditional steering oar. However, even at the time of European contact, most smaller Nangu ships were still operated with a steering oar. There had been some refinements, but the general design would still have looked familiar to any Māori of the early fourteenth century.

With their new ships, and with their keen eye for anything which might turn a profit, the Islanders expanded their incipient trading network into a major enterprise. Nangu ships could carry sizeable cargoes, and their captains regularly sought new markets. One of their major roles was as middlemen who carried tin, gum cider and gold from Tjul Najima to destinations across mainland Aururia. This included the Yadji, the Mutjing in the Seven Sisters, and Tjibarr and the other Five Rivers kingdoms, via Jugara and a road to the Bitter Lake [Lake Alexandrina].

In time, Nangu captains sailed around the barrier of the treeless desert, and made contact with the expanding Atjuntja dominions. This soon became a flourishing part of their trade network, and allowed the exchange of many ideas, crops and technologies between the east and the west of Australia. The Atjuntja acquired a much greater variety of eastern crops. Via the Islanders, the Yadji and the Five Rivers kingdoms learned the Atjuntja technologies for working with iron.

* * *

In 1618, the Island is the most densely-populated nation in Aururia. Sixty thousand people live crowded but happy lives on the Island. Trade and shipping is their lifeblood; not even the most intensive cultivation of Aururian crops could support such a population. The Nangu do grow some food on the Island, and have large fishing fleets which venture across much of the Southern Ocean. Even with this, they rely on bulk shipping of wattle seeds and yams from the Mutjing city-states to feed their people. The Island is not completely stripped of trees, but timber is valuable enough for other purposes (mostly building) that most new Islander ships are now built further afield, either in the Seven Sisters or in timber camps on Tjul Najima.

Theirs is a society in the midst of urbanisation. There are still substantial small holdings in some of the rural areas, and the bloodlines remain socially divided, but the importation of food has meant that more and more people are now clustering in cities. Between them, the two largest cities, Crescent Bay and Deadwatch [Penneshaw] have about twenty-five thousand inhabitants.

The Island's government is divided between the twenty-one surviving bloodlines, each of which preserves its claim to certain lands and trading rights. Competition between the bloodlines is one of the major drivers in their trading network. Each captain belongs to one bloodline or another, and they try to outdo each other in obtaining the greatest profits. The annual meeting of the Council of Elders maintains some order and does its best to resolve disputes amongst the bloodlines. Still, for all that the Nangu have converted to the supposedly peaceful faith of the Good Man, feuds and vendettas are common amongst the bloodlines.

In their lifestyle, the Islanders have abundant metal for tools, weapons and jewellery, all of it imported. Iron tools are used for most purposes on the Island itself, but since iron rusts quickly in salt air, they use bronze on their ships or close to the coast. In their early days on the Island, they lived in houses built of wood and earth, but with access to iron tools, most of their buildings are constructed from the local granite. The Nangu are a people more given to personal ornamentation than to constructing many large buildings; most of the sizable edifices on the Island are the temples and sanctuaries of Plirite priests. Those temples are richly adorned with gold, silver and bronze donated by pious trader captains.

Shipping and trade underlie everything which the Islanders do, in one way or another. Their trade network is the most extensive in Aururia. In direct trade, their ships carry goods from one side of the continent to the other, and via their colony of Jugara, they have links to the ancient trade routes of the Five Rivers.

To the west, the Islanders regularly visit the Atjuntja dominions. Their visits are accepted by the Kings of Kings, who have established a trading quarter for them to use in the White City. The Islanders do not usually sail much further than the White City itself; the Atjuntja do not encourage visitors to round Sunset Point [Cape Leeuwin][68]. A few Islander ships have visited the Indian Ocean from time to time, but their regular trading fleets go only to the White City, Warneang [Denmark] and a small port built south of Red Eye [Ravensthorpe].

To the east, Islander traders regularly visit ports in the Yadji lands and on Tjul Najima. Their visits beyond that are less frequent, but there have been occasional Islander visits as far as the spice-producing kingdoms of Murrginhi and Daluming. These visits remain rare; there are limits to how far Islander ships can reliably sail, and there is enough local and occasional Māori maritime trade along the east coast that spices can often be obtained further south for decent prices. Still, from the Atjuntja Empire to Aururia's eastern coast, the Islanders are the dominant maritime power.

The Islanders are mostly an economic power, but they are also adherents of Plirism, which encourages conversion of other peoples. Receptiveness to this religion has varied remarkably amongst the various peoples who have come into contact with the Islanders. The Atjuntja sternly discourage proselytisation, to the point of executing any would-be converts. The Yadji are also intolerant of other faiths, and persecute any of their subjects who convert to the Islander school of Plirism, though they tolerate some other existing schools of Plirism amongst their subject peoples. Tjibarr had long since made its own accommodation with the disciples of the Good Man, and the Islanders have had little influence there.

However, among the Mutjing city-states and parts of Tjul Najima, Plirite priests have found a much more receptive audience. The Mutjing have converted completely to the new faith. So have many of the inhabitants of Tjul

---

[68] The Atjuntja economic system relies on moving goods and tribute along internal routes. Allowing the Islanders to take over their internal trade would undermine their existing system, so the Atjuntja only permit the Islanders access to a few trade ports on their southern coast.

Najima, although with more reservations. Even those Tjunini and Kurnawal who have adopted Plirism retain most of their old attitudes, especially toward nationalism. The Palawa are prepared to listen to the Islanders who speak of the Good Man and his teachings, but their conversion has mostly been syncretic, where they adopt the Good Man's teachings alongside their old beliefs. In recent times, the Islanders have established a few missions on the eastern coast of the continent, where some peoples have accepted the new religion.

The majority of the Nangu still live on the Island itself, but they do have some settlements and colonies elsewhere. Some of these are under foreign rule, such as the Islander quarter in the White City. Others are independent colonies, such as the trading outpost of Yellow Pine on the Cider Isle, or the Islander-controlled town of Dogport [Port Augusta] which remains independent despite being surrounded by Tjibarri territory.

The Islanders also have an isolated mainland settlement whose name translates rather exactly as Isolation [Eucla]. This is in the middle of the treeless desert [Nullarbor]. Here farming is marginal, but fishing is good, and the settlement can sustain itself. Isolation is mostly used as a stopover point for ships conducting western trade; they sometimes visit if they are running low on supplies or fleeing bad weather.

For all that Islander ships voyage far and wide across the continent, their most important trading destination is quite close to their home island. This is the Islander settlement of Jugara [Victor Harbor]. A few people lived there since ancient times, but the Islanders turned it into a major settlement. Jugara is the closest good harbour to the Nyalananga Mouth, and it has become an essential link in trade with the interior. The Nyalananga itself is not navigable from the sea, but from Jugara the Islanders built a road to Bunara [Goolwa], a port on the Bitter Lake, where goods could be carried by people or by dog-pulled travois. From here, riverboats could move trade goods throughout the Five Rivers[69]. This connected the old trade routes along the Nyalananga and Anedeli rivers with the maritime trade networks of the Islanders, and led to a burgeoning growth in trade.

With the linking of the interior and maritime trading networks, Jugara grew into a bustling port, with a great variety of peoples visiting it. While the Islanders have always sought to maintain a monopoly on maritime shipping, they have never been averse to carrying other people on their ships. So Jugara has grown into a great entrepot where many peoples mingle; a place of vice and wealth. Here the Nangu are the largest ethnicity, and their port-captain is the effective ruler of the city, but they are not alone. In Jugara live haughty Yadji, boisterous Nangu, hot-headed Gunnagal[70], drunken Tjunini and Kurnawal from the Cider Isle, stoic Atjuntja from the far west, wary Mutjing, and even the occasional Māori from distant Aotearoa.

Jugara has been an effective Islander colony since the fifteenth century, despite its politically precarious location. The lands between the Murray Mouth and Dogport have long been contested between the Yadji Empire and the kingdom of Tjibarr. However, while wars have raged and borders shifted, by unwritten convention, neither nation's armies would plunder Jugara, Bunara or the road between them. The benefits of the trade were too valuable. Conquerors would impose taxes, duties and levies, but they

---

[69] Victor Harbor was used similarly in historical Australia; one of Australia's early railways connected it to Goolwa to move goods without needing to navigate the Murray Mouth.

[70] In 1618, the term Gunnagal the name which the dominant ethnicity in the kingdom of Tjibarr use to refer to themselves; a few of these people also live in parts of the other Five Rivers kingdoms. Later ethnographers and historians will use the term to refer to the ancestral peoples who took up farming. *Gunnagalic* refers to all of the languages (and sometimes the peoples) descended from the founding agriculturalists.

never sought to close off trade entirely. This suits the Islanders, who are usually neutral in disputes between Yadji and Tjibarr. The tension between the two nations has another valuable advantage for the Islanders, since it means that the closest mainland ports to the Island are not available as a base for invasion.

So, in 1618, the Islanders are wealthy and flourishing. Military invasion from the mainland is not a serious risk, unless the Yadji can inflict the decisive defeat on Tjibarr which they have been seeking for so long. The only threat to the Islanders' way of life comes from much further afield. With Islander captains always voyaging so far in search of profits, there are always a few Islanders in the west. So when the Raw Men come out of the far west beyond the seas, Islanders will be among the first to hear of them.

#15: The Lords Of The Lake

This chapter provides more information about the history of the Junditmara, the oldest sedentary people in Aururia, and describes the beginning of the rise of the Yadji, who by 1618 would rule the most populous state in the continent.

* * *

Junditmara: an ancient people in an ancient land. Their forefathers and foremothers were among the earliest people in the world to adopt a sedentary lifestyle, based on elaborate aquaculture and eel-farming. They have maintained a continuous cultural tradition since that time; the region around Tae Rak [Lake Condah] has been continuously occupied by Junditmara peoples for eight thousand years.

Long before the ancestors of the Gunnagal started to farm red yams along the Nyalananga, the Junditmara were building in stone and mobilising workforces of thousands to maintain their stone weirs and dams. Their aquaculture was in fact the original inspiration for the early Gunnagalic farmers, who took their techniques and adapted them to the drier conditions but much greater water volume of the Nyalananga.

While an ancient people, the Junditmara were few in number when compared to the farming civilization which emerged along the Nyalananga. Until they had access to crops, the sedentary Junditmara population never rose much above ten thousand, divided into four chiefdoms clustered around Tae Rak. In comparison, the Gunnagalic-speaking peoples had a population of almost a million people by 1000 BC, occupied most of the Nyalananga, and had six major cities and many smaller towns.

The early Gunnagalic civilization collapsed after 1000 BC, and the resulting migrations brought domesticated crops and animals to the Junditmara peoples. The Junditmara absorbed a few of the Gunnagalic immigrants and took up their farming ways. This allowed the Junditmara chiefdoms to expand their territory and started a substantial increase in their population. Unlike most non-Gunnagalic-speaking peoples, the Junditmara maintained their identity, language and religion despite the Gunnagalic tide.

In some ways, the Junditmara became innovators. They were the first people to domesticate the tiger quoll, which they used to control rodent pests and in some cases as a fireside companion. They were also the first people to make widespread use of muntries, a native fruit which the Junditmara learned to grow using trellises to increase the yield[71]. They adopted the noroon as a domesticated bird before it reached the surviving Gunnagal cities along the Nyalananga.

Still, for all of their increase in population, the Junditmara of the first millennium BC remained a relative backwater. They were divided into a varying number of chiefdoms (usually five) who fought amongst themselves, and preserved enough of their own sense of identity that they withstood pressure from neighbouring peoples. They were connected into the broader trade networks around the rest of the continent; most commonly, they traded dried muntries and other fruits, smoked eel meat, and some timber, for tin and copper which they shaped into bronze.

---

[71] Muntries (*Kunzea pomifera*) are one of several native fruits common to southern Victoria which are suitable for domestication. They are used as an occasional "bushfood" today, with some commercial harvest, and have also occasionally been grown overseas. (They were first recorded as cultivated in England in 1889).

The large-scale population movements of the Great Migrations were largely ended by AD 100, at least near the Junditmara. (Population movements elsewhere lasted about a century longer). At the end of the migration period, the Junditmara occupied a region roughly bounded in the west by Gurndjit [Portland] and Narreduk [Coleraine], in the north by the Murragurn [Grampian Ranges], and then by a rough line running south-east to Punyan [Camperdown] and then further south to the Wurrung Mountains [Otways].

Within these borders, the Junditmara were divided into several competing chiefdoms. The borders and even existence of these chiefdoms was fluid, with new dynasties emerging regularly, and older ones being defeated and absorbed. The most important population centres during this period were Gurndjit, which sheltered the best port for fishing, Jurundit [Koroit], whose rich volcanic soils supported the best farming in their region, Tuhonong [Hamilton], whose proximity to their ancestral lake Tae Rak made it their most important spiritual centre, and Nguwurru [Cobden], the largest population centre in the eastern part of Junditmara territory.

The competing chiefdoms fought regular wars for control of territory and the major population centres. However, the Junditmara chiefdoms did not have any clear rules for succession; any male descendant or close blood relative could claim the title of chief. This led to regular fratricidal wars amongst the Junditmara, and prevented the emergence of any long-lasting kingdoms.

Outside their borders, the Junditmara were surrounded by Gunnagalic-speaking peoples on every side. The most important of these were the Tjunini who lived around the Wurrung Mountains to the south-east, the Giratji who lived to the east, the Yadilli and Tiwarang to the west, and the Yotjuwal to the north. While borders were fluid, there was a gradual long-term trend for the Junditmara to slowly expand their borders; their aquaculture allowed them to support slightly higher populations than their neighbouring peoples[72].

During the period from AD 200-400, the population of all of the lands south of the Spine was substantially increased by the diffusion of new agricultural techniques from the Classical Nyalananga cities to the north, such as crop rotation and companion planting. The growing population saw the emergence of the first political entities amongst the Junditmara which were large and stable enough to be called kingdoms. It also meant that their trade and other contacts with the Classical Nyalananga became much more significant. The first indisputable historical account of the Junditmara emerges during this period. While the Junditmara did not yet have writing, records in Tjibarr dated to AD 265 speak of a trader who visited "Tjuonong" and who brought back golden jewellery and finely-woven textiles.

These records make it clear that even at this early stage, the Junditmara were familiar with the two products for which their descendants would be famed. Finely-woven textiles were an integral part of Junditmara society for centuries. Even in their pre-farming days, possum-skin coats had been used both as a sign of status and protection from the cold. With the spread of flax and thus linen, Junditmara weavers developed a variety of elaborate techniques. They used a diverse range of dyes, from copper and other metals, from wattle leaves and roots, from tree sap, from a variety of other plants, from ochre, and from shellfish. They used these to dyes to create intricately-patterned textiles – blankets, garments, coiled baskets, bags, slings – which were markers of status, and also used in a variety of religious ceremonies.

---

[72] While the Gunnagalic ancestors of the neighbouring peoples had practiced aquaculture, these practices were lost amongst the migrating peoples.

Gold-smithing was another venerable Junditmara practice, one which would became known around the world. The early Junditmara did not have much access to gold, apart from one field in the Murragurn on the edge of their territory. However, not far to their east, in the lands of the Giratji, were some of the richest gold-fields in Aururia. Later archaeological investigations in the region of Nurrot [Ballarat] would find the first traces of gold mining here in the first century AD, and gold would be traded from the Giratji both east and west.

The Junditmara esteemed gold far more than the Giratji, and adopted it for both decorative and religious purposes. Junditmara chiefs wore gold masks on important occasions, and other wealthy people used it for jewellery and other ornamentation. In Junditmara temples, gold was the essential metal for a variety of ritual objects, particularly for any lamps or fire-holders.

In time, the Junditmara would combine these two specialities, leading to one of the names which they would be known to outsiders: the weavers of gold. Gold and silver threads were woven into the capes and other garments for the priests and chiefs, or carefully-positioned small plates of silver and gold were added to the woven products. Sometimes these capes were further decorated with brightly-coloured bird feathers, such as those of lorikeets, cockatoos, or other parrots, or the iridescent, lustrous sheen of mother-of-pearl from abalone shells. The variety and splendour of these textiles made considerable impressions on visitors to Junditmara territory, and their descendants were still practicing these arts in 1618.

* * *

The Junditmara chiefdoms developed on a largely independent path for many centuries. While they had acquired farming, domesticated animals and other arts from their Gunnagalic neighbours, they had applied their own interests and specialisations to these technologies. The twin barriers of language and religion meant that they always differentiated themselves from their neighbours, despite ongoing contact.

The rise of the Watjubagan Empire cut short the Junditmara's separate development. The chiefdoms had started to develop into more stable kingdoms, but this did not help them to stave off the advance of Watjubaga's armies. In a series of campaigns which lasted from AD 718-764, the Junditmara kingdoms were conquered by the Empire.

The Junditmara never made willing imperial subjects. At times they were quiet, but even those instances were merely sullen periods of peace. In their religious views and their social codes, the Junditmara were an alien people by Gunnagalic standards, especially when compared to the views of the Biral who ruled the Empire.

The Junditmara had a hierarchical social system based on duty to one's elders, conformity, and the rewarding of loyalty. Imperial rule did not fit into this system, particularly the system of labour drafts where people would be required to work on tasks assigned to suit imperial preferences. Junditmara expected to work to help their own family and local community; they cared nothing for working for others, and viewed labour drafts as forced betrayal of their families. The result was simmering tension, numerous revolts, and the eventual overthrow of imperial rule in AD 907.

While the Junditmara resented the imperial conquerors, that did not prevent them from acquiring a variety of knowledge from their Biral rulers. Writing spread with the imperial conquest; while the Biral used mostly their own language in administration, the Junditmara took the Gunnagalic script and adapted it to their own language. The Junditmara also inherited imperial knowledge in fields such as metallurgy, astronomy, and the Gunnagalic calendar.

After the restoration of their independence, the Junditmara took this knowledge and applied it to their own ends. There were many aspects of Gunnagalic culture which were either explicitly rejected or never adopted, such as their ball sports, their religious views, and the social system of the factions. With the return of their own sovereignty, the Junditmara once again started to develop on their own path.

* * *

The revolts which overthrew the Empire were based on a conscious sense of ethnic nationalism. The Junditmara saw themselves as a sovereign people and sought to remove unwanted foreign overlords. This sense of common purpose meant that what they created what was meant to be a new nation for all the Junditmara-speaking peoples. At Tuhunong, the city near Tae Rak, they appointed the rebellion's leading general to become the Lord of the Lake. This was meant to be an empire; the role was inspired by the imperial rank of the First Speakers of Watjubaga. The Lord of the Lake's role was meant to be to lead all of the Junditmara.

In theory, anyway.

Although notionally an empire, the Junditmara had in fact formed a confederation. The old competing chiefdoms had not been restored, but there were still many local aristocrats who had built substantial local reputations. Moreover, one of the legacies of imperial rule was that the Junditmara had a considerable distrust of too much central authority. This meant that while there was now an Emperor, the local chiefs were disinclined to listen to what he said.

Instead, what emerged after Watjubaga's overthrow was not an empire, but a community of local rulers who first ruled in the name of the Emperor, and after a couple of generations, in their own names. As a people, the Junditmara had always maintained a strong sense of hierarchy, of kinship, and of membership in a local community. They found little comfort in having a distant Emperor, and gave their loyalty to the emerging social class of local rulers.

These new leaders were called *otjima*, a name which translates literally as "golden men." They became the ruling nobility of the Junditmara, each with their own hereditary authority to control a particular region, collect tribute in the form of goods or labour, and defend its inhabitants from all enemies. For centuries, all Junditmara acknowledged the theoretical authority of the Emperor, while in practice their loyalty went no further than their local *otjima*. Even the *otjima* rarely met the Emperor, and except for an occasional instance where the Emperor was asked to mediate between feuding *otjima*, they gave the Emperor no heed either. One of the early *otjima* was reported to have said, "I promise to obey the Emperor in all things, provided he promises not to order me to do anything."

To defend their lands and enforce their will, the *otjima* made use of another emerging social class: the first professional military class within Junditmara society. During the pre-Watjubaga days, the Junditmara had not had much in the way of professional soldiers. Their chiefs had a few household guards, but otherwise their armies were mostly local levies and militia who took up arms at need.

The old ways changed with the new military technology and organisation which Watjubaga brought. Now, to be effective in battle, soldiers needed bronze armour, a bronze sword, and usually a bronze spearhead. Bronze was available, thanks to imports from the Cider Isle, but it was expensive. Only a few people could afford such quantities of metal on their own. Moreover, the new military tactics required considerable training. Soldiering needed to become a permanent profession, not just for ordinary people who were called up at need.

In these circumstances, it did not take long for a hereditary military class to emerge in Junditmara society. They were called the *briyuna*, a word which originally meant "hunter" but which took on a new meaning in the time of the Empire of the Lake. A *briyuna* was born into the life of a warrior, and trained for their craft since childhood. *Briyuna* learned how to use a wide variety of weapons – swords, daggers, maces, axes, spears, bows, javelins, slings – and even techniques of unarmed combat. They had strict standards of physical discipline to ensure that they had the strength and fitness to wear armour for extended periods while marching and then fighting.

As a people, the Junditmara had rigid social codes and expectations, and nowhere would these be more clearly-articulated than for the *briyuna*. The *briyuna* were expected to live according to a warrior's code which emphasised courage, loyalty to one's comrades, and unquestioning obedience to one's lord (*otjima*). They were expected to maintain their skill in arms, and to demonstrate it both in peacetime (through duels and displays of prowess) and on the battlefield. Cowardice was the ultimate failing, and a *briyuna* who was condemned for cowardice or fleeing the battlefield would be spurned by lord and family. *Briyuna* were taught not to fear death; indeed, in keeping with Junditmara beliefs, no-one was better prepared to die than one who had perished while armed.

Briyuna were expected to be honourable men in both peace and war. While there was no obligation to accept an opponent's surrender or to fight an opponent on even terms, it was considered a great breach of honour to harm a prisoner once their surrender had been accepted. Likewise, in peacetime *briyuna* were expected to keep to their sworn word, never lie about matters of honour, and to uphold both their personal reputation and that of their *otjima*. They were expected not to inflict violence on civilians except if deliberately insulted or in self-defence; to do so in other circumstances was a grave breach of honour.

Still, the code of the *briyuna* did not protect everyone. The principle of not harming civilians applied only to ethnic Junditmara; people of other faiths or language were not protected. Moreover, the code only protected civilians' lives, not their property. In warfare, *briyuna* were permitted to plunder and take whatever portable wealth they could with them, as trophies and rewards for war. If civilians tried to resist such plundering, then they were no longer protected by the *briyuna* code.

In their personal lives, *briyuna* were expected to maintain an attitude of temperance and moderation in all things. They were certainly permitted to enjoy pleasures, including the traditional yam wine, women and song (not necessarily in that order), but they were not to let their pleasures control them. A *briyuna* who drank to excess would be considered both personally disgraced for losing control of himself, and also as having failed in his duty to his lord since he would not be able to fight properly while drunk. Likewise, a *briyuna* who sought comfort in a woman's arms was acting appropriately, while one who put concern for a woman above his duties would be considered to have shamed his name.

While the life of a *briyuna* was in theory one of continual preparation for warfare, in practice they spent much more time at peace than at war. *Briyuna* were always expected to be literate, and indeed to have a thorough knowledge of the literary and historical classics of Junditmara society. As such, they often indulged a variety of other pursuits besides purely studying warfare. Many *briyuna* acted as administrators for their lords, since they were considered the most trustworthy of servants. They were also often involved in a variety of cultural pursuits; several *briyuna* became noted singers, poets, and artists.

* * *

The formal rule of the Lords of the Lake lasted for nearly four centuries, from AD 909 to 1289. For virtually all of that time, the Junditmara lived under the theoretical authority of these emperors, but the actual authority of their local *otjima*. At times, this meant that as a people, the Junditmara expanded their territory, as would-be *otjima* pushed into new territory. This meant that the remaining Tjunini around the Wurrung Mountains were absorbed by Junditmara expansion. A similar process saw most of the

Tiwarang people pushed further west as emerging *otjima* claimed new lands of their own.

However, the decentralisation of imperial authority also led to increasingly bloody struggles amongst the *otjima*. There were no formal divisions in rank amongst the *otjima*; in theory each of them had the same status, and answered only to the Emperor. The closest thing to a formal division of rank was that each year the Emperor would name Twenty Counsellors who were meant to advise him for the following year. This normally included the wealthiest and most prestigious *otjima*, but not always; some Emperors named lesser *otjima* to the Twenty for a year as an effective bribe to persuade them to accept imperial mediation in their disputes with their neighbours.

In informal status and control of territory, though, the *otjima* were never equal, and they regularly fought to gain territory or prestige. It became an axiom amongst the Junditmara that "a *briyuna* is loyal to his *otjima*, and an *otjima* is loyal only to himself." Sometimes they formed alliances, but as the centuries progressed, the divisions amongst them became more violently and treacherously expressed. By AD 1200 it was popularly said that each hilltop had its own *otjima*, which in some areas was not an exaggeration.

The infighting and political fragmentation contributed to the gradual decline of the Empire of the Lake. The deterioration was accelerated when the first Marnitja epidemic swept through the Junditmara realm in 1208-09. The first blow of the Waiting Death fell heavily on the Junditmara; nearly twenty percent of their population succumbed to the ravages of the pink cough or the feverish delirium which followed[73]. In its first wave, the virus did not discriminate between fit or weak, young or old, healthy or unhealthy; all were equally vulnerable to the Waiting Death.

The effects of this epidemic were devastating to the Junditmara social order. Many of the more prominent ruling *otjima* died, along with a significant proportion of their experienced *briyuna*. This led to an increase in internecine warfare, as would-be successors fought amongst themselves, or surviving *otjima* sought to take advantage of inexperienced heirs by invading the territory of their dead rivals. With so many experienced *briyuna* dead, these battles were often bloodier and more badly-coordinated than would have been the case under their veteran predecessors. The fractious warfare undermined the already limited credibility of the rule of the Lord of the Lake.

The death toll of the Waiting Death and the subsequent warfare had profound social effects on the Junditmara. Their surviving art and literature of this time shows the emergence of apocalyptic themes, and depicts the first beginnings of a shift away from the martial code of the *briyuna*. The older form of literature was represented in songs, poems and heroic tales which had some similarities to the romances of medieval Europe. In these tales, *briyuna* were invariably depicted as the epitome of honour, devotion, and self-confidence. In the tales which emerged after the arrival of Marnitja, there are new depictions of

---

[73] This death toll is a higher percentage of the population than Marnitja will have on most other peoples (such as Eurasians), for two reasons. Marnitja here is just emerging as an epidemic disease, and is still quite virulent. It will evolve to be somewhat less deadly over the next couple of centuries. The other reason is that since at this point the Aururian peoples have limited exposure to epidemic diseases, and this exacerbates the death toll. Repeated exposure to Marnitja over the next few generations will not only produce some natural resistance to the disease, it will also mean that their adaptive immune systems are somewhat stronger against all diseases.

briyuna as more human and realistic, with human failings and mistakes.

Likewise, the apocalyptic themes of the time resulted in new shifts in Junditmara religion. Unlike their Gunnagalic neighbours, the Junditmara had always viewed time as something with a beginning and an end, not an endless cycle of eternity. With the great dying of the early thirteenth century, their old beliefs were reshaped into a more apocalyptic theology. New religious visionaries appeared, who proclaimed that the times they were living in were the last days of the world, before the time when the Neverborn would break free from His home in the womb of the earth and call His chosen warriors to fight in the last great battle against the Lord of the Night.

Amidst the chaos of these times, one *otjima* family rose to prominence, one whose name would become synonymous with the most populous empire on the continent. The Yadji were one of many *otjima* families who had arisen amongst the Junditmara. The first surviving record of the Yadji is from 1067, when a man named Narryani Yadji led a band of *briyuna* to conquer a small town named Kirunmara [Terang, Victoria] and had himself proclaimed as an *otjima*.

Of itself, Kurinmara held little to distinguish itself from so many other small towns and settlements under the nominal rule of the Lord of the Lake. It had decent rainfall by the standards of the Junditmara, and adequate although hardly spectacular soils. It was toward the eastern frontier of Junditmara territory, but nowhere which offered any strategic significance or even defensibility. A small lake just to the south was about the only feature of interest; to the water-loving Junditmara, this lake could be expanded into a series of swamps and open water which would supply regular meals of fish and waterbirds to the table of the ruling *otjima*.

Still, while the Yadji were for so long just one *otjima* family among many, they were reasonably successful ones. Their rulers were on the whole more capable than most of their rivals, which allowed them to conquer a reasonable stretch of territory by 1150. In this year, surviving records from Tuhunong first include a Yadji *otjima* among the Twenty Counsellors. This was an indication of their success, and for the next century, there would be a Yadji named to the Twenty each year.

When the first great Marnitja epidemic swept through Kurinmara in 1209, the Yadji suffered along with everyone else. Their ruling *otjima* died in a viral-induced delirium, and his heir, Ouyamunna Yadji, contracted the pink cough two days after he inherited the family title. However, while he waited to know whether he would live or die, he had substantial motivation to create a legacy for himself. Ouyamunna is reported to have said, "Soon I will have forgotten the world, but the world will not soon forget me."

In the months while he waited for death, Ouyamunna found a way to create his legacy. He changed the rules of warfare as they had existed among the Junditmara for three centuries. Warfare was meant to be the role of well-trained and armoured *briyuna* who fought for their lord. Ouyamunna decided to recruit a new class of warrior from the men who had survived the pink cough, and who were waiting to know their fate. He is said to have told these men, "Soon you will leave the world, but the manner of your leaving it is up to you."

The warriors who Ouyamunna recruited were mostly not *briyuna*, and they had limited training in using swords or wearing armour. In any case, the Yadji family did not have enough wealth to equip so many new warriors with bronze armour and swords. For weapons, he gave them axes and maces, since they were easier to find and most of the men had used such things as tools. For armour, he gave them nothing, but Ouyamunna would turn the lack of armour into an advantage. He did not have or want men who fought coolly and well-armoured. He wanted men who would be consumed with the fury of battle, and who cared naught whether they lived or died, because they already expected to die soon.

Ouyamunna got what he wanted.

The new warriors he created wore no armour, just clothes of woven flax died crimson to mark the death they already expected. Before they entered battle, these men worked themselves into a trance-like state through a combination of chanting, ritualised dancing, and consumption of native tobacco[74] and certain mushrooms which were known to deaden pain. When they entered the battle, these warriors were consumed in a violent frenzy, howling with fury, rushing headlong at the enemy regardless of the odds, and striking blows with what appeared to be superhuman strength. In their frenzy, they shrugged off wounds, and often became so indiscriminate in their killing that they would not distinguish between friend and enemy. They fought with incredible energy until the battlefield was cleared of any foes, and then as often as not, they collapsed in exhaustion and would not recover for days.

Ouyamunna did not, in fact, survive the Waiting Death. Whether by chance or through natural resistance, he held off the onset of the death fever much longer than most. It took nearly a year before he showed the first symptoms, but in time the delirium consumed him as it had consumed so many before him. He fought off the fevered delirium better than most; it took three and a half months from the onset of the fever until he breathed his last. In that time, though, the death warriors he had created made a legacy for him. They

---

[74] The native tobacco mentioned here is grown from several native Aururian plants in the *Nicotiana* genus (principally *N. benthamiana*) which are related to domesticated tobacco from the Americas (*N. tabacum* and *N. rustica*). These plants were used by various historical Aboriginal peoples as stimulants. They are not the same as the drug *kunduri*; that is grown from a native corkwood species (*Duboisia hopwoodii*) which is only distantly related to domesticated tobacco. The Aururian *Nicotiana* species do contain nicotine, but have a much harsher taste and milder effect than corkwood *kunduri*, and so were not used as a major trade item. They were locally available, though, which is why they were used for creating the first death warriors.

swept battlefield after battlefield clean of foes – and sometimes each other, too. In fourteen months, Ouyamunna defeated and conquered thirteen other *otjima*, and more than tripled the size of Yadji territory.

The rise of the Yadji had begun.

#16: Regents of the Neverborn

The Yadji, their neighbours call them. In 1618, the Yadji Empire is the most populous nation in Aururia; two and a half million people live under its rule. Its dominions include a variety of peoples; the empire is named not after its inhabitants, but for the family name of its ruling dynasty. However, the core ethnicity of the Yadji Empire is the oldest sedentary people in Aururia, the Junditmara, and their empire began its growth amongst that people.

* * *

The Yadji Empire emerged out of the disintegration of its feudal predecessor, the Empire of the Lake. The old Lords of the Lake had exercised only nominal authority for centuries, and the head of the Yadji family was one of the *otjima* [ruling feudal lords] who controlled one of many realms. While most of the *otjima* realms were becoming ever more fragmented, the Yadji were one of three *otjima* families who became significantly more powerful during the twelfth century.

The Empire of the Lake, already in decline, was devastated by the arrival of Aururia's worst native epidemic disease, Marnitja. The first epidemic swept through imperial territory in AD 1208-10, killing approximately one person in five, and the disease returned in a fresh epidemic a generation later (1238-40). The death toll from these epidemics produced major social and religious upheaval, including setting off a long period of internecine warfare amongst the surviving *otjima*.

The Yadji were the most successful *otjima* family to take advantage of this period of warfare. Under Ouyamunna Yadji, who died during the later stages of the first epidemic, and then his brother Wanminong, they launched an aggressive program of military expansion. Ouyamunna created a new caste of warriors who had survived the first stage of Marnitja, and who were waiting uncertainly to know whether they would survive the second stage. In battle, these warriors worked themselves into a frenzied rage, and helped Ouyamunna win a series of battles and subdue his immediate neighbours.

Most of the death warriors died from the fevered delirium or in battle. Some survived the intensive period of battles in the first year, and it gradually became apparent that they would not be consumed by the Waiting Death. Many of the survivors abandoned the death warrior cult at this stage. A few remained in the cult, motivated by the immediate prestige of being raised to a military caste where they had previously been excluded, and by the prospect of a glorious death in battle ensuring that they had a good afterlife.

The surviving death warriors created a new social institution, and they recruited new members from men who were dispossessed or displaced by the internecine warfare of the period. The few men who joined the new elite cult of death warriors shaved their hair and stained most of their faces with white dye, carefully applied to give the impression of a skull staring back at anyone they faced. Under Wanminong (1210-1227) and his son Yutapina (1227-1255), the death warriors were used as shock troops, normally held in reserve during the first stages of a battle, and then used to turn the tide or break the enemy line at a crucial moment. They were never very numerous, but their presence was felt on many a battlefield as the Yadji expanded their rule.

The Yadji were the most successful *otjima* family who expanded during this period, but they were not alone. Two other families, the Euyanee and the Lyawai, had been increasing in prominence before the Marnitja epidemic, and they also gained territory during its bloody aftermath. The Yadji gained control of much of eastern and south-eastern Junditmara territory, the Euyanee consolidated their power in the south-west, and the Lyawai controlled much of the north.

Between them, the three families controlled about a third of Junditmara territory by 1220. After this, while the internecine warfare continued, their expansion was largely halted, due to a shortage of warriors, and the difficulty of controlling so many new subjects. Many of the smaller *otjima* families continued fighting amongst themselves for longer, although over time many of them banded together to oppose the great three families, or entered into tacit alliances with one side or another.

The second Marnitja epidemic swept through the Junditmara lands in 1230-40, and was almost as deadly as the first, killing about sixteen percent of the non-immune population. The overall death toll was lower than the first epidemic, since many of the older generation were immune, and because the total Junditmara population had still not recovered. Still, the social disruption was immense, and the Lord of the Lake [Emperor] took the unprecedented step of publicly asking for the *otjima* to show restraint and calm against their fellow Junditmara.

He was ignored, of course.

All three of the great families made fresh bids for expansion during this time, as did some ambitious lesser *otjima*. Unlike the previous generation of warfare, though, this new round of internecine fighting saw relatively few *otjima* families conquered. The lesser *otjima* were much more inclined to side with each other and resist the advances of the Euyanee and the Lyawai. In this endeavour, they found support from the Yadji. For Yutapina Yadji did not seek to conquer his fellow *otjima*. When he did fight wars against Junditmara, they were defensive wars to protect his neighbours from the Euyanee and the Lyawai, or their supporters.

Instead, under Yutapina, the Yadji turned their attention outward, pushing into non-Junditmara lands. They conquered the surviving remnants of the Tjunini along the shore of the Narrow Sea, and began to expand amongst the Giratji to the east. Here, they had far more success than anyone else had expected; perhaps even Yutapina himself, although history does not record that. The Giratji had internal struggles of their own, due to similar problems with Marnitja. The combination of death warriors and disciplined regular troops proved to be irresistible. Their greatest accomplishment was in 1251, when they captured the gold mines around Nurrot [Ballarat].

By Yutapina's death in 1255, the Yadji had more than doubled the territory they controlled at the start of his reign, although that included much of the thinly-populated Wurrung Mountains [Otway Ranges]. While they had no meaningful census records, certainly close to half their population were non-Junditmara. By comparison, their two main rival *otjima* families had gained only limited territory. The Euyanee made an attempt to emulate the Yadji's external conquests amongst the Tiwarang to the south-west of Junditmara territory, but they had only marginal success. The Yadji were now clearly the most successful *otjima* family.

With their new conquests, the Yadji were no longer a purely Junditmara society. They had to make new accommodations in terms of religion and social organisation, since their old institutions would no longer serve them. They started to rework the fabric of their society into a new form which drew from the old Junditmara social codes, but which had many new features.

Even under Yutapina, they had already started to change the old religious systems. Aided by the many apocalyptic beliefs which were emerging at the time, the Yadji created a new religious system which adapted the old beliefs into a form which suited their rule. Yutapina and his heirs created a new priesthood, with temples at the centre of every community, and who preached of the new faith where the ruling Yadji was the Regent of the Neverborn, and everyone else his subjects.

The Yadji also started to create a strict social hierarchy which was even more rigid than the old Junditmara social codes. Yutapina is reported to have said, "My lands have a place for everyone, and everyone is in their place." In time, the Yadji rulers would decide that the old *briyuna* warrior caste did not fit into this scheme, since they were loyal to their local *otjima* and usually not to the ruling Yadji. They would eventually disband the *briyuna*.

With the new religion and social system they were creating, the Yadji did not fit into the old feudal system of the Empire of the Lake. It made little sense for their rulers to acknowledge the nominal authority of the Lord of the Lake when they claimed divine backing for their own rule. The formal break came in 1255, with the death of Yutapina Yadji. His son Kwarrawa chose to mark his accession in a ceremony where he was ritually married to Lake Kirunmara, rather than paying homage to the distant Emperor. The Yadji would date the creation of their own empire from this moment.

The Empire of the Lake persisted for a few decades longer, but after 1255 it could no longer be considered even a nominal nation. The real power had always been in the hands of the *otjima*, and now it was being concentrated in the three most prominent families. The lesser *otjima* started to formally align themselves with the Yadji, Euyanee or the Lyawai, or were conquered by them. The last Lord of the Lake died in 1289 from the third major Marnitja epidemic to hit the Junditmara in the same century, and he was never replaced. By then, virtually all of the Junditmara were either directly ruled by one of the three great families, or their local *otjima* were effective vassals of one of the three.

In time, they would all be ruled by the Yadji.

* * *

Ouyamunna Yadji, the ruler who created the death warriors, is said to have believed that they would ensure he had a legacy which would be remembered. In truth, four centuries later, few men remember him, but they have not forgotten the death warriors he created. The death warriors have become an elite few recruited from amongst those who have limited life prospects, and who embrace the opportunity for glorious death in battle. The Yadji still use these frenzied warriors as shock troops in their armies, and they have won many a battle. Under their aegis, the Yadji have become the most populous empire on the continent.

In 1618, the Yadji rule over an empire which they sometimes call the Regency of the Neverborn, and at other times they call Durigal, the Land of the Five Directions. For like many other peoples around the world, the Junditmara perceive five cardinal directions, not four. As well as the more familiar north, east, south and west, they also describe a "centre" direction, the point of origin. Within the Yadji lands, the centre is always Kirunmara [Terang], their capital. All directions within the Yadji lands are given in relation to Kirunmara itself; a man might say that he is travelling "north of the centre" or "south of the centre."

From west to east, the Land of the Five Directions extends approximately from the mouth of the Nyalananga [River Murray] and includes all of the coast as far as the River Gunawan [Snowy River]. Its northern border is usually near the Spine [Great Dividing Range]. Some of these borders are fluid; regular warfare with its northern neighbours, particularly Tjibarr, means that frontiers are contested in the north and northwest. For the rest, Yadji rule is relatively secure, apart from some occasional rebellions over religion, tribute, or language.

The Land of the Five Directions is well-populated, with several large cities and a host of smaller towns and villages. The Yadji divide their lands into four provinces, which roughly correspond to the old ethnic divisions at the time of Yadji conquest. The Red Country stretches from the Nyalananga to just west of Gurndjit [Portland]. Its old inhabitants were two Gunnagalic-speaking peoples, the Yadilli and Tiwarang. The borders of the Red Country are the most fluid in the Land, sometimes advancing with military expansion, and sometimes withdrawing due to revolts among conquered peoples or victories by Tjibarr.

The Lake Country is the most populous province; it includes the old Junditmara lands, and some parts of the more contested northerly regions inhabited by the Yotjuwal people. Along the coast, it stretches from Gurndjit to Jerang [Lorne], although its inland boundary is more restricted, and runs generally north-west from Jerang.

The Golden Country consists mostly of the old Giratji lands, although its northern border sometimes includes much of the Yotjuwal lands, except when those areas revolt or are captured by Tjibarr or Gutjanal. The Golden Country includes the gold mines around Nurrot and sometimes those around Djawrit [Bendigo], although the latter mines are sometimes controlled by one of the northern kingdoms. The Golden Country stretches from the border with the Lake Country east as far as Kakararra [Koo Wee Rup].

The White Country is the easternmost province, stretching from Kakararra to the edge of Yadji-claimed territory. Its eastern borders are vaguely defined, because the Yadji claim more territory than they have settled, but their effective line of control is along the lower River Gunawan. The easternmost city of any size is Elligal [Orbost]. Beyond these boundaries lies rugged, difficult to farm territory where the Yadji sometimes raid but do not control. The White Country is mostly inhabited by the Kurnawal, who make reluctant imperial subjects, but who have been largely quiet for the last half-century.

* * *

While the Yadji rule subjects of a great many languages and religions, they have done their best to centralise their whole empire. Based on their inherited Junditmara social codes, they seek to create a strict sense of local community and common religion, and to impose a broader sense of hierarchy where everyone has their place under the Regent.

Every Yadji city and town worthy of the name has at least one temple at its heart. The temples are the grandest part of each city; built of the strongest stone available in any given area, and deliberately constructed so as to appear larger than life. The temple is the centre of all aspects of daily life. Religious rituals are only one part of that control. Each temple governs all aspects of daily life for the town and the surrounding community, from telling the farmers when and where to work the fields, overseeing hunting and fishing, controlling the building and maintenance of waterworks, giving approval to new buildings, approving or rejecting marriages, overseeing the activities of the weavers and craftsmen, and collecting the proceeds of the harvest. Every temple has attached storehouses where the bulk of the harvest can be retained, including storage for bad years. It is considered very poor practice for any temple to have less than four years stored food available in case drought, bushfires, or pests ruin the harvest.

In their religious practices, the Yadji have created a new religion blended out of some of the older Junditmara beliefs and the apocalyptic teachings popularised after the Marnitja epidemics of the thirteenth century A.D. They teach that the first being was the Earth Mother, and the warmth of her body was the only heat in an otherwise cold and empty cosmos. In time, she gave birth to a son, who was known as the Firstborn. The Firstborn served and loved the Earth Mother, until he found out that she was with child. Jealous that he would have to share his mother's affection, the Firstborn stabbed her through the heart.

As she lay dying, the Earth Mother plucked out her eyes so that she would not have to look upon the son who had betrayed her. One eye she hurled into the sky, where it would circle the world and act as a mirror to reflect the warmth of the earth. Her other eye shattered with tears; the largest shard became the moon, the smaller shards became the stars.

With her dying breath, the Earth Mother cursed the Firstborn to be trapped in eternal darkness and cold. Her blood spilled over her body, creating the mortal world and all of its inhabitants. The warmth of her blood meant that things would always grow, but the Firstborn could not endure the heat for long. He was driven from the surface of the world, out into the darkness of the night. (Hence his alternative title, the Lord of the Night). Here he dwells still, waiting and watching. Whenever someone dies, he or one of his servants will descend to the surface of the earth to try to claim the spirit of the recently deceased. The deceased will have to defeat the Firstborn or his servants, or be carried up into the darkness of the night to become another servant. Thus, the Yadji say that one someone has died, he has "gone to fight his Last Battle."

However, while the Firstborn succeeded in killing his mother, he did not kill the child she was carrying. That as yet unborn being still lives, trapped within the flesh of the earth. He is the Neverborn, the true loyal son of the Earth Mother, who waits yet within the warmth of the earth. He is the one who will be born someday to fight his elder brother, and that day will be the changing of the world. All who have died and who won their own last battles wait with him, and will be called to fight at this, the Cleansing, when the universe will be remade.

This, the Yadji teach, is the purpose of the world: to live one's own life in preparation for the world that is to come. They recognise only three deities, the dead Earth Mother, and her two sons, the Firstborn who is scorned, and the Neverborn who is loyal. They also recognise a number of other beings who play a role in the day-to-day world, who are servants of one of the Sons, but they do not view them as gods. Only the Neverborn should be worshipped, since he is pure and steadfast, and the Earth Mother should be honoured and remembered.

To the Yadji, religion is meant to be a unifying force, and indeed many of their subjects have converted to this belief. Not all have done so, though, and religious unrest continues to trouble their empire at times, particularly amongst the Kurnawal in the east. Those peoples who live near the north-western borders are also often more reluctant to follow the Yadji faith completely; they still cling to some of their older beliefs or the teachings of the Good Man (Plirism).

Some Regents enforce religion more strictly, and others care little about the substance of others' beliefs provided that they obey. The current Regent, Boringa Yadji, worries very little about what his people believe. He has concerns of his own; partly staying awake when his generals argue about how best to solve the perennial border wars with the northern kingdoms, and partly how to convince his pet rock to talk. His senior priests have never bothered to dissuade him from his efforts to attain this difficult goal; after all, while the Regent is incommunicado, they can speak for him to the outside world, and this suits them well enough. If he progresses to the stage where he starts to drool too obviously at public audiences, well, they will deal with that problem when it comes. It is a crime beyond hope of atonement to spill the blood of any member of the Yadji family, let alone the Regent, but they will find a solution.

* * *

The temples control most aspects of life within the Yadji realm, and nowhere is their organisation more significant than their oversight of waterworks and aquaculture. This is the Junditmara's most ancient technology; they have developed it to a level unsurpassed anywhere else on the continent and, in some ways, anywhere else on the globe.

Not everywhere in Yadji lands is suitable for waterworks. However, anywhere that geography, rainfall, and water flow permits, the Yadji will have sculpted the land itself to suit their waterworks, creating the swamps, weirs, ponds and lakes which are their joy.

The ancient Junditmara developed their system of aquaculture into the basis of the first sedentary culture on the continent. It relied on the short-finned eel (*Anguilla australis*), a species which migrates between fresh and salt water depending on age. Mature short-finned eels breed far out to sea, and the young elvers return to freshwater rivers where they will swim far upland in search of a home territory. The elvers can even leave water for short periods, traversing damp ground in pursuit of fresh territory. Eventually, the elvers find a home range – a stretch of river, a lake, a pond, or a swamp – and establish themselves there. They feed on almost anything they can catch – other fish, frogs, invertebrates – and slowly grow to maturity. The eels are remarkably tolerant of changing environments, tolerating high and low temperatures, murky waters, low oxygen, and going into a torpor state if conditions are poor. The mature eels can reach a substantial size (over 6kg for female eels), and will eventually migrate back downriver to the sea to repeat the process.

Or the eels try to, anyway.

The early Junditmara system of aquaculture was designed to maximise the available habitat for short-finned eels to live and reach maturity, and then trap them when they had reached a decent size. They did this by creating ponds, swamps and lakes for the eels to live while they grew. This involved not just the occasional pond or lake, but long series of ponds with connected waterways, each with enough water to support one or more eels. The Junditmara reshaped the land to suit their needs, using weirs and dams to trap sufficient volumes of water, and creating a myriad array of canals and trenches to connect the ponds and lakes to each other and eventually to the rivers and the sea. Their lands were crisscrossed by an immense network of these canals, all carefully maintained to allow eels to migrate up the rivers.

Sometimes the Junditmara even trapped young elvers, transported them upriver, and released them into suitable habitats for them to grow to a mature size. Their entire system was designed to allow the eels to grow to their maximum size, then trap them before they could migrate back downriver. The Junditmara made woven eel traps and positioned them at well-chosen points along the weirs and dam walls, so that they would trap larger eels when they tried to swim back downriver, but would still allow smaller eels to pass through.

The early Junditmara built their culture around farming eels, harvesting edible water plants, and catching waterbirds who fed off the abundance of their waterworks. When they received agriculture from Gunnagalic migrants, the Junditmara were no longer completely reliant on eel meat to feed their population. Still, they never lost their knowledge of aquaculture, and they built larger and more complex waterworks wherever geography and their technology permitted them to do so.

The newer Junditmara waterworks are far more diverse in the produce they harvest than the original eel farms, although 'waterfood' remains a high-status commodity. Many of the expanded waterworks are too far upriver to obtain a decent supply of eels; sometimes because of the distance itself, sometimes because most of the elvers become established in suitable habitats created by communities further downriver.

The Junditmara have solved this by farming a much greater variety of fish and other watery denizens. They create a series of watery habitats of many depths to suit particular species, and allow fish to migrate between these ponds depending on their habitats. The shallowest waterworks are kept as swamps and marshes with limited depth, where edible reeds and other plants grow in abundance. Deeper ponds and lakes host a wide variety of fish species; Australian bass, silver perch, river blackfish, and eel-tailed catfish are among the most common.

Some smaller ponds are maintained simply to breed freshwater prawns and other invertebrates to be used as bait by Junditmara fishermen. For some fish species, especially river blackfish, the Junditmara breed them in special ponds and then transport the young fry to stock larger lakes and wetlands. They also keep separate ponds where they breed freshwater crayfish as a luxury food; these invertebrates are slow-growing but are considered extremely tasty. A few Junditmara farmers have even developed farming methods for freshwater mussels (*Alathyria* and *Cucumerunio* species), which are treasured not just as sources of food, but because they occasionally produce freshwater pearls.

The Junditmara have amassed a thorough knowledge of which habitats suit the breeding and living requirements of the many fish species in their country. Some fish prefer locations with underwater cover, so the Junditmara ensure that suitable logs, rocky overhangs, debris, or other places of concealment are available for those species. Some fish will only spawn in flooded backwaters of small streams, and the Junditmara hold some water back in dams to flood in the early spring when those fish breed. Many fish migrate regularly throughout their lifecycle, and unlike the engineers who would dam these rivers in another history, the Junditmara make sure that their weirs and dams still allow enough waterflow for these fish to migrate up and downstream as they need.

As part of their aquaculture, the Junditmara also learned much more about how to work with water, stone and metal. They have never developed anything approximating scientific investigation or philosophical inquiry, unlike the classical Greeks who first started to use mathematics to calculate the shape of the world, of mechanics, and hydraulics. Still, the Junditmara have a long history of experimentation and development of solutions by trial and error. This is not a quick process; there have been many errors and many trials. But slowly, the Junditmara and their Yadji successors have developed a substantial corpus of knowledge of hydraulics and of engineering as it applies to the construction of water-related features.

Junditmara engineers have become experts at controlling the movement of water. They know how to build very good dams and weirs. By trial and error, they have developed arch dams whose curving structure allows them to build very strong dams while using less stone. Their engineers do not quite understand the principles of forces and calculations and stresses, but they know that the method works. Likewise, they have learnt how to build gravity dams, carefully balanced to ensure that they do not overturn under water pressure. Their engineers have also learned how to build cofferdams to keep a chosen area dry while they are building more permanent dams. They know how to build levees against floods or to keep chosen areas dry even if surrounded by waterworks. Around larger river systems, they build networks of levees, flood channels, and secondary dams to trap floodwaters for later use.

On a smaller scale, Junditmara engineers have discovered how to control water for other uses. They use reservoirs and aqueducts to supply drinking water to their towns and cities. Like their neighbours in the Five Rivers, they understand the usefulness of plumbing, but they apply it much more widely. Most Junditmara houses have plumbing connected to sewer systems, and the human waste is collected for fertiliser and other uses. In the temples and the houses of the upper classes, they have flush toilets with a carefully-shaped fill valve which can fill the water tanks without overflowing[75].

The Junditmara engineers have even developed mechanical means of shifting water, thanks to their discovery of screwpumps [Archimedes screw]. They discovered a primitive version of this device more or less by accident, but they have improved its design over the centuries. All of their screwpumps are hand-powered devices; the most typical use is to move water from low-lying ponds into higher ponds as part of maintaining their waterworks. They also make some use of screwpumps to irrigate elevated gardens, drain local flooding, and maintain watery features of their major cities.

* * *

The practice of aquaculture is the most obvious example, but everything in Yadji daily life revolves around the temples and their dictates. Trade, farming, craftsmanship, and everything else is in one way or another dictated by the

---

[75] This is a similar type of mechanism to the ballcock which would historically be developed in the nineteenth century.

reigning priests, who exercise the will of the Regent. In many ways, this is a continuation of the old Junditmara tradition, where their chiefs or other local headmen oversaw their daily lives. The Yadji rulers have applied the same principles, although priests are usually appointed by the Regent or his senior advisers. There is a deliberate policy of moving them between temples throughout their lives, to limit their opportunities to build up a personal power base.

Trade and farming, and many of the other parts of Yadji life, have been eased by the Junditmara invention of what was for them a revolutionary device: the wheel. For many centuries the peoples of this isolated continent had never invented this device; perhaps for want of an inventor, perhaps because with few beasts of burden, it would not benefit them as much. For so long, transportation relied on sleds, travois and other means, rather than the wheel. In the last few centuries, however, the Junditmara adapted their existing potter's wheel into a form which worked upright – and which revolutionised their lives.

The Yadji have applied the wheel to several uses. While they are still hindered by a lack of any large beasts of burden, they have converted their old transport vehicles into carts or other wheeled forms pulled by people or by teams of dogs. These are used in their larger cities to transport people and goods. They are also used along the royal roads. The Yadji road network is not as extensive as that of the Atjuntja, but most of their main cities are connected. There are two royal roads which start at their westernmost outpost on the Bitter Lake [Lake Alexandrina], with one running near the coast and the other in the northern regions, converging at Duniradj [Melbourne], then dividing again as they run east, and finally converging at the easternmost Yadji outpost at Elligal. The Yadji also use small hand carts to help with their farming, and this has been a substantial boost to their agricultural productivity.

Yadji productivity would no doubt have been improved in many other areas if they found out how to apply wheels to them. Textiles, for instance, would be easier to weave if they had developed the spinning wheel. No-one has found out how to do this, and the Yadji rely instead on the ancient technology of the spindle for weaving. Still, elaborately-woven textiles were a Junditmara specialty for centuries, and the Yadji have only expanded their use.

For textiles, the Yadji have only a few fibres to work from, but they put them to many uses. Their basic fibre is the ubiquitous crop, native flax, whose fibres they work into a variety of forms of linen and other textiles.

For higher-status textiles, they use animal fibres. Dog hairs, to be exact. The Junditmara have bred white, long-haired dogs whose fur is thick enough to be turned into a kind of wool. These fleece dogs are carefully maintained as separate breeds which do not have contact with other dogs; the largest breeding populations are maintained on the personal estates of the Regent. The dogs are fed mostly on eel and other fish meat gathered from their waterworks, and they are shorn every year to produce fleeces and yarns used for high-quality textiles.

For even more high-status textiles, the Yadji have learned to weave with silk. This is an expensive fibre; silk is not grown anywhere in the Land of Five Directions, and must be imported from the Five Rivers. Despite the cost, silk is highly desired for its coolness and lightness to wear, and silk clothing is a mark of considerable status amongst the Yadji.

The most precious fibres of all are threads of silver or gold. These metals are under strict royal monopoly, and much of the material collected from the mines is spun into thread and woven into the clothing of the imperial family or very senior priests.

From these few fibres, the Yadji have created a myriad variety of textiles, to serve the many needs of their hierarchical society. The fundamentals of their clothing are quite simple. Men wear a sack-like tunic with a hole for the head and two more for the arms, and which usually reach to their knees. Women wear a sleeveless dress held in at the waist with a patterned sash. Both sexes wear the *anjumi*, a kind of textile headband which has elaborately-woven patterns which indicate a person's home region and their social rank.

Indeed, while the basic aspects of clothing are similar for peoples of all ranks, the Yadji use a wide variety of colours and patterns to indicate status. They use many dyes, some produced from local plants, some imported by the Islanders or from the Five Rivers, and they use these to mark status. The patterns on a person's *anjumi* are an immediate indication of their rank, role in society, and the region where they live. Amongst those of higher status, there are more elaborate indications of status; thread or small plates of silver and gold, lustrous shells, pearls, feathers from parrots and other birds, and other markers to show the wealth and standing of their wearer. It is said amongst the Yadji that even if every person in their realm was gathered into one place, it would still be possible to tell where each person was from, and their rank.

The varieties of clothing which the Yadji wear are only the most visible sign of the careful organisation of their society. For where it has been said that three Gunnagal cannot agree about anything, the Yadji and their Junditmara ancestors have always been a regimented society. The priests act as local rulers, within the broad expectations of the Regent and his senior priests at Kirunmara. To enforce their will, they can rely on both religious authority and the carefully-maintained records of a literate society. For the Yadji make extensive use of writing, using a script derived from the ancient Gunnagalic script. They have never developed clay tablets as their northern neighbours used. Instead, they use parchment made from noroon hide, and a form of paper made from the boiled inner bark of wattle-trees. Literacy is largely confined to the priestly class and a few aristocrats, but that is sufficient to allow careful administration of the many lands under the control of the Regent.

The same desire for control means that the old military structure of the *briyuna* has been completely removed. The *briyuna* were a hereditary class of warriors who were loyal to their local *otjima*, but no further. The reigning Yadji have no tolerance for warriors whose allegiance is not to the Regent, and the *briyuna* who survived the conquest of the other Junditmara lands were retired.

In their place, the Yadji developed a new military order based on the careful recruitment of loyal soldiers. Military discipline is strong, with Yadji units very good at fighting alongside each other. They have also developed good methods for coordinating movements between units, using a combination of banners, drums and bugle-like horns.

The spread of ironworking has also revolutionised their military tactics. The Yadji most commonly use a form of scale armour, which they favour as cheaper to produce than the mail which is preferred by their rivals in the Five Rivers kingdoms. Part of their preference for scale armour is also because it is easier to decorate; the old Junditmara love of ornamentation lives on in the Yadji military. High-ranking officers in Yadji armies are given sets of ceremonial armour, as well as practical varieties. Designs of gold are common in ceremonial armour, for one of the useful properties of iron is that gold designs show more prominently than on the old bronze armour.

Still, for all that the Yadji have changed, the original ethos of the *briyuna* has persisted. Within the Regency's borders, they no longer exist as a separate warrior caste, but many of the retired *briyuna* took up priestly or related administrative roles in the expanding Yadji realm. Their old warrior code lives on in songs, epics, and chronicles, becoming increasingly mythologised and romanticised, and the ruling Yadji have tolerated this development. The code of the *briyuna* is still seen as the standard by which a proper Yadji gentleman should conduct himself, even if this standard is more honoured in the breach than the observance.

As for the *briyuna* themselves, they did not completely vanish when the Yadji dissolved their order. Some of the *briyuna* refused to accept retirement, and fled beyond the borders of the Regency. A few went to the Five Rivers kingdoms, but the largest group fled to the Kaoma, another non-Gunnagalic people who live in the highlands beyond the Regency's eastern border. There, the *briyuna* have become a warrior caste amongst the Kaoma and their neighbouring Nguril, and they still preserve much of their old code and lifestyle. They have not forgotten their origins, and they still mistrust the Yadji who evicted them from their old homelands.

* * *

One of the perennial questions which has vexed linguists and sociologists is whether language shapes society, or society shapes language. Or, indeed, whether both are true at once.

When they come to study the Yadji, they will find a rich source for further arguments. For the Junditmara who form the core of the Regency's dominions have developed their own extremely complex social rules regarding their interactions with each other. The rules dictate who can speak to whom, the required courtesies and protocols needed when people of different status meet, what subjects can be discussed with which people, and a myriad of other intricacies. The Junditmara are status-conscious in a way which few other peoples on the globe would recognise.

The intricacies of Junditmara social codes are reflected in their language. All Junditmara pronouns have six different forms, which can be roughly translated as dominant, submissive, masculine, feminine, familiar, and neutral. Their language also uses a variety of affixes which are added to individual names and titles, and which carry a similar function to the pronouns.

Each of these forms indicates the relationship between the speakers. Dominant and submissive are broadly used to indicate the relative social status of each of the speakers. Using the dominant form with a person of higher rank is a major social *faux pas* at best, and is usually treated as a grave insult. These two forms can also serve other functions, such as when two people of similar rank are arguing, one might use the submissive form of "you" in a form such as "I agree with you" to concede the argument.

The masculine and feminine forms have the fundamental purpose of indicating the gender of the person being referred to, but the customs regarding their use also reflect social rules amongst the Junditmara. When speaking to a person of higher social status, a person will normally use the submissive form rather than a masculine or feminine form. When speaking to a person of roughly equal social status, the masculine or feminine form is typically the form used. When speaking to a person of lower status, a high-status speaker may choose to use the dominant forms, which indicates a greater degree of formality, or the masculine or feminine form, which indicates a less formal meeting. As with all aspects of Junditmara society, these forms can be used in other ways, such as if a group of soldiers wished to condemn another soldier for supposed unmanly or cowardly behaviour, they would typically refer to him using a feminine form.

The familiar and neutral forms are more restricted in their usage. The familiar form is normally used only for relatives or close friends, and indicates that the relationship between the two people is so well-established that questions of status will never arise[76]. It sometimes has other uses, such as being used with someone who is clearly not on familiar terms, which indicates either irony or extreme disrespect. The neutral form is used mostly in ambiguous situations where people have only just met and are not sure of each other's status, or a situation where someone of lower status temporarily needs to be treated as being of equal status. Some subsets of society also use the neutral form if they want to indicate that they are completely equal.

---

[76] The familiar form is used in approximately the same manner as "first name terms," back in a time when being on first name terms actually meant something more meaningful than having said hello. Or the distinction between *tu* and *vous* in French (or similar forms in many other languages).

For instance, amongst soldiers, men of the same rank are expected to refer to each other using the neutral form, rather than the masculine form.

The intricacies of Junditmara language extend to many of their other words. Most of their common verbs have two different flavours, which can be described as directive or suggestive. Directive means that what is said is a command, while the other indicates a request or a preference. "Come here" if said in a directive flavour would have a rather different impression upon the listener than if it were said in a suggestive flavour.

While the intricacies of the Junditmara language are not directly matched in that of the other peoples who make up the Yadji Empire, some of their phrases and meanings are slowly diffusing amongst the other peoples. For the Junditmara language is the effective language of government amongst most of the Regency; even if priests speak a local language as well, they will be literate mostly in the Junditmara tongue. This is one of the many methods which the reigning Yadji use to centralise control over the dominions. Religion, however, remains the most important aspect of their government. Up until the year 1618, this has been very effective in maintaining their rule over a disparate group of peoples. As that year draws to a close, however, a new era is preparing, one in which all of the social institutions of the Yadji will be sorely tested.

#17: The Good Man

In historical Australia, the driest of inhabited continents, water means life. Droughts are common, and even when rain does fall, it often does so in such abundance that it causes floods. The irregularity of this rain is most pronounced in the interior, and naturally enough most of the humn inhabitants of the continent live nearer the coast. The outback – the red heart of the continent – is nearly devoid of water, and nearly devoid of human life.

In eastern Australia, the frontier between the outback and more populated districts is traditionally the River Darling. Rising in the mountain ranges of southern Queensland, the Darling drains a large part of the continent before emptying into the River Murray. The Darling is an extremely irregular river, often drying up completely, and at other times flooding so prodigiously that the waters can take six months to recede. Nonetheless, it became an important transport route during the early days of European colonisation of Australia.

Beyond the Darling lies the red heart, the outback. The nearest part of this is called the Channel Country, a series of ancient flood plains marked by the courses of many dried up rivers. Rain seldom falls here, but when it does, it floods along these channels and drains into Lake Eyre, the largest lake in Australia, which has no outlet to the sea. Most of the time, Lake Eyre is a flat, dry salt plain, but sometimes the rains from distant cyclones or monsoons fill the lake. When it does, fish spawn in great abundance, and waterbirds gather from across the vast interior to feed and breed by the shores. The lake dries out soon enough, leaving the fish to die, the waterbirds to move on, and its bed reverts to a salt plain.

In the cyclically dry country beyond the Darling, Europeans found relatively little to interest them. Some rich mineral lodes have been mined, and sheep and cattle graze in stations (farms) which need very large areas to support their herds on the sparse vegetation, but otherwise they mostly left the country empty.

In allohistorical Aururia, the same river is called the Anedeli. To the Gunnagalic peoples who developed agriculture along the Nyalananga [River Murray], the Anedeli was for a very long time considered a frontier. The lower reaches of the Anedeli drained through country where the rainfall was extremely limited and agriculture almost impossible. In time, migrants used the Anedeli as a transportation route, following its course to the upper reaches. Here, they found more fertile country and a variety of mineral wealth – especially tin – which meant that the Anedeli became a much more important transportation route.

As Gunnagalic civilization developed over the centuries, they came to regard the Anedeli as one of the Five Rivers that watered the known world. An empire arose, Watjubaga, which took its name from the Five Rivers which flowed through the heart of its territory. Some of those rivers had long-established cities and verdant agriculture and aquaculture along their banks. But the Anedeli continued to be used primarily as a transportation route, and it marked a frontier rather than a source of life.

To the Gunnagalic peoples, the country beyond the Anedeli was called the Red Lands, the Hot Lands, or the Dry Country. They did have a few uses for it. Silver Hill [Broken Hill] gave them a rich source of silver, lead and zinc, and other mines gave them some valuable metals and minerals, especially varieties of ochre which they used for dyes. They sometimes mined salt and gypsum from the dry lake beds, and collected a few flavourings and fibres from some of the outback plants. For the most part, though, the Red Lands were a thinly-settled frontier fading into desert which was occupied only by sometimes hostile hunter-gatherer peoples.

Usually.

For the Red Lands had a brief flowering of more reliable agriculture, a time when the Anedeli became not a frontier but a treasured source of water for peoples who lived along its banks. Thanks to a rare shift in the climate, the rainfall along the lower Anedeli became sufficient to support several substantial cities and a separate kingdom. This time of flowering would come to an end, with the yams and wattles withering for lack of water and the cities abandoned to the desert. In that brief time, though, the kingdom beside the Anedeli witnessed the birth of the first evangelical religion on the continent; a new faith which would in time spread far beyond its shores.

* * *

November 1105
Nyalananga, downstream from Gutjanal [Albury]

A steady rhythm of splashing oars carries to his ears as the oarsmen push the barge upriver. Their timing is perfect; he hears only one splash with each stroke, rather than the staggered splashes he has so often heard from less experienced crews.

He stands near the prow of the barge, watching the ever-changing vista that opens before him every time the barge rounds another of the endless bends in the Nyalananga. He does not speak; no-one else stands near him. In any case, none of them have a station in life which matches his own, and so would be unlikely to approach him for casual conversation. He has engaged this barge to carry him to Gutjanal to trade incense for fine pottery, and has been unfailingly polite to them at all times. Yet none of that makes the crew any more comfortable speaking to him.

Instead, he watches the river and the verdant growth along its banks, and lets his mind drift in silent contemplation. These lands beside the upper reaches of the Nyalananga are more well-watered and well-forested than any of the country in his homeland of Lopitja. The change in rains has made Lopitja a land where civilised men can live, but nowhere along the Anedeli is there rainfall sufficient to sustain forests such as these.

The barge rounds another bend, giving him a view of something unexpected. Something large and grey rises above the trees, standing some distance back from and above the riverbank. A statue. A *massive* statue, carved from granite or some similar stone; even from this distance he can see the mottled pattern of grey and white.

The statue is of a man, his face a stern visage beneath a towering helmet, above a body plated in armour. The statue has one arm holding the hilt of a sword and the other folded over its chest.

"Who is that man?" he asks, only half-aware that he has spoken aloud.

A discreet cough sounds behind him. The barge's captain walks up; the only man with the confidence to approach him.

"An old Emperor. From when they ruled here."

"A colossal testimony to their ambition," he murmurs. The captain does not reply, but then he has not asked a question.

"Which Emperor?"

"Lopitja, I think. The one who founded your homeland."

The push of the oars has brought the barge closer to the statue, letting him make out further details. An ornate necklace hangs around the throat, and the eyes are half-lidded, as if in divine communion or in disregard for those it looks down on.

"So many men must have worked for so long to shape and move that statue," he says. Granite is the hardest of rocks, and the quarry must surely have been much further from the river.

Again, the captain says nothing. Only a question will prompt him to speak, it seems. Sailors have too much concern for status.

But then, so must the Emperors, to have built this, he realises. This statue was carved to honour an Emperor, with no care for how many men had to labour for so long to build it. A monument which now looks over land where that Emperor's successors no longer rule. The Emperors parade around Garrkimang, still pretending that the world owes them glory. They forget, or want to forget, that they barely rule beyond the city's walls, where once they ruled the world.

He says, "The Emperor who built this statue cared only for his glory, and not for the harmony of the people he ruled."

"Harmony," the captain repeats, sounding like a man who has just received an insight.

No, the insight is mine. What good comes of having the Empire fall, if we fail to learn from the mistakes it made?

* * *

At the turn of the tenth century AD, during the decline of the Watjubagan Empire, imperial authority was dying outside of the heartland of the Five Rivers. The Mungudjimay in the northeast had defeated imperial armies and were starting to raid the fringes of the tin and sapphire-producing regions of the north. In the east, the Patjimunra had just declared their independence from imperial authority. The Junditmara in the south were rising in perpetual rebellion, and the imperial governors were powerless to stop them.

In the midst of this chaos, it took some time for the imperial administration at Garrkimang [Narrandera] to notice a remarkable shift in the climate. The lands around the Anedeli had always been dry and barely worth farming. Yet over the last few decades, the usual winter rains had been heavier than usual, and reached further and further north. Summers and winters both had grown somewhat cooler, but not intolerably so. Any minor inconvenience that the colder temperatures caused was more than offset by the prospect of bountiful rains falling year after year[77].

Just after the turn of the century, news reached Garrkimang of another remarkable change. They knew, of course, of the distant salt bed that they called Papukurdna [Lake Eyre], and of the cycle of refilling and evaporation. Most of their salt came from smaller dry lakes, but they had sufficient contact with the hunter-gatherer peoples of the interior to hear about this greatest of dry lakes. Tales from these peoples, and confirmed by "civilized" visitors, confirmed the extraordinary tale that this great lake had filled permanently, or so it seemed.

The years turned, with rebellions and defeats plaguing Watjubaga, yet still visitors reported that the former dry lake remained full. The heavier winter rains continued over the frontier of the River Anedeli and the Red Lands it bordered. In time, the existence of these heavier rains came to be seen as the natural state of affairs. In 912, then-First Speaker [Emperor] Lopitja announced the founding of a new city along the Anedeli, modestly named after himself. Farmers started to settle the lands around this new city of Lopitja [Wilcannia, New South Wales]. In time, most people forgot that this country had for so long been arid and too hostile to support agriculture[78].

---

[77] Bountiful rains by Aururian standards, that is. The rainfall in this period still only averages between 300-400 mm. It *is* more reliable than the usual Aururian weather, though; droughts have been reduced in both frequency and duration.

[78] This climate shift occurs within the same broad timeframe as the Medieval Warm Period (roughly AD 900-1300). Around the North Atlantic, this climatic shift produced generally warmer temperatures. It lasted for varying time periods and had different effects in other parts of the globe; parts of the tropical Pacific seem to have been cool and dry, as was the Antarctic Peninsula. In Aururia, the weather was affected by a long-term *La Niña* phenomenon, which produced generally cooler temperatures and increased rainfall. The Aururian climate reverted to a drier phase by the end of the Medieval Warm Period, possibly earlier.

The decades passed, and the Red Lands along the Anedeli became almost as well-populated as any other part of the Five Rivers. Yams and wealth-trees flourished with the rains, and the expansion into this region gave them access to crops which had not been domesticated further south; bush pears and bush raisins as fruits and flavourings, and trees such as blue-leaved mallee as a spice[79]. They were not able to build artificial wetlands in quite the same way as on the other main rivers, but they built some artificial lakes which could store Anedeli floodwaters and allow both fishing and irrigation.

Lopitja became a flourishing city, the largest of several along the lower Anedeli, and an important waypoint in the tin trade. It prospered even as Watjubaga faded; the Empire was first reduced to its heartland of the Five Rivers, then into what was a minor kingdom in all but name. Lopitja declared its independence in 1080, establishing a nation of its own along the banks of the Anedeli. It became the capital of one of the several post-Imperial kingdoms which vied to inherit the mantle of the First Speakers' authority; its main rivals were Gutjanal [Albury-Wodonga], Tjibarr [Swan Hill] and Yigutji [Wagga Wagga].

Lopitja's favourable position along the Anedeli meant that it controlled the best transportation route for tin from the north. This was no longer a monopoly, since tin could also be imported from the distant Cider Isle [Tasmania], but it was still a valuable trade good. It was also close to the mines of Silver Hill, and its control over those lands added to its wealth.

For a brief flowering in the twelfth century, Lopitja was one of the two greatest post-Imperial kingdoms. Its main

---

[79] Bush pears (*Marsdenia australis*) and desert raisins (*Solanum centrale*) are fruits grown on vines and shrubs suited to semi-arid conditions. Blue-leaved mallee (*Eucalyptus polybractea*) is one of many Australian eucalypt species. It is native to semiarid regions such as along the Darling, and its leaves contain high concentrations of eucalyptus oil which make them useful as a flavouring.

rival was Tjibarr, and the two kingdoms fought several wars throughout the century. Lopitja successfully defended itself during those wars. What its people did not know, however, was that their era of prominence was limited. The climate was reverting to its long-term norm of semi-aridity, and Lopitja's place in the wet would be replaced by a more normal place in the sun – the endless heat of the desert sun, to be more precise.

In that brief time, though, Lopitja produced one man who had ideas which would change the world.

* * *

August 1145
House of the Spring Flowers
Kantji [Menindee, NSW], Kingdom of Lopitja
Some have called him the Good Man, although he never acknowledges when people speak to him using that title. Nor does he answer to the name his mother gave him. What is that but an arbitrary set of syllables? Some have called him the Teacher, and he will answer to that name, however reluctantly. He does not want to teach people; he wants to make them teach themselves.

He stands at the double bronze gates that mark the start of the Spiral Garden. The breeze blows out of the northwest, warming his cheeks with the breath of the endless desert. The wind carries the distinctive tang of blue-leaved mallee trees, a scent that for now overwhelms the myriad other aromas of the garden beyond these walls.

In the burnished bronze, the Teacher catches a glimpse of himself. Red-brown skin covers a face which no honest man would call handsome, and which is mercifully blurred in the imperfect reflection of metal. Wavy hair growing bushy and long on both sides of his face, black streaked with white. He is turning old, he knows, but that is all part of the Path on which any man finds himself, willing or not. It matters not what befalls a man, just how he bears himself while events happen.

The image in the burnished bronze reminds him, although he already knows, that his clothing is no different to that worn by any other gentleman of substance in the kingdom. It has to be. Rightly or wrongly, no-one would listen to a poor teacher, any more than they would seek treatment from a deformed doctor. So he wears the same black-collared *tjiming* which any high-status man would wear, fitting loose around his neck, long sleeves dangling beneath his arms, and the main bulk of the garment wrapped twice around his torso and held in place with an opal-studded sash, while the hem just covers his knees. A sapphire-studded bracelet adorns his wrist. Clothes and jewellery are merely appearance, not substance, but a wise man knows when appearance matters.

Four other men cluster behind him, dressed in similar styles although without the ornateness of opals and sapphires. They think that he has brought them to the House of the Spring Flowers to reveal to them some great truth that is concealed within these walls of stone and timber and vegetation.

So, in a way, he is. But it is nothing like what they will be expecting. The carefully crafted forms of the House were built on a spot where, it is said, the Rainbow Serpent rested on his path down the Anedeli. This is meant to be a place of power, a place where a man can stand and feel himself growing closer to the Evertime. The gardens, the pools, the three fountains, are all meant to inspire that sense of serenity.

If only truth were so simple to find that a man could step in here and attain it!

He gestures, and three of the four would-be acolytes move to open the gates. The fourth man does not move, but keeps chewing on a lump of *kunduri*. That man had offered the Teacher another ball of the stimulant a few moments before, and did not seem to understand why he declined the offer. Many men have claimed that using *kunduri* or other drugs brings a man closer to the Evertime. For himself, though, he thinks that such drugs merely let the user hear the echoes in his own head.

He leads the men into the Spiral Garden. He moves at a quicker pace than they will be expecting; he pretends not to notice the occasional mumbles of the would-be acolytes behind him. The Garden is meant to be contemplated slowly, in a careful progression in ever-decreasing almost-circles until one reaches the centre.

The Teacher strides past the places of contemplation; he ignores the niches set into the walls, or the places where gum trees have been planted to provide shade for men to stand and savour the scenery. He walks alongside the stream that traces a path through the centre of the spiral, drawing water via underground passages from the Anedeli. Flowers bloom in a myriad of colours around him, desert flowers from the Red Lands to the far north and west which normally would blossom only in the aftermath of rare desert rains. Here, with irrigation available, the flowers bloom according to the command of the gardeners. There is a lesson there, but not the one which he wants these men to consider today.

He leads them through almost all the Garden, then stops while they are not yet in sight of the central pond, although the sacred bunya trees[80] around that pond grow high enough that they show over the walls. When he stops, it is not to draw their attention to any of the arrangements of plants, but to speak to a gardener's assistant who is methodically pruning one of the ironwood [*Casuarina*] trees.

---

[80] Historically, the bunya tree (*Araucaria bidwillii*), popularly but somewhat inaccurately called bunya pine, is a kind of conifer which in its wild state is restricted to small areas in the Bunya Mountains and a few other parts of Queensland. At erratic times, it produces large yields of edible seeds which were much appreciated by Aboriginal peoples; in the years when bunyas produced seeds, large gatherings of people would congregate to feast on the seeds. Bunya trees can be grown in cultivation over a wide area, although they need considerable water. In allohistorical Aururia, bunya trees are also revered as sacred, and have been spread over a substantial part of the continent. In inland areas, they can usually only grow if supported by irrigation.

The assistant pauses in his labour and says, "Good to see you, Teacher! Are you well, my friend?"

The Teacher says, "Yes, Gung, I am well." He introduces each of the would-be acolytes in turn. Each time, the gardener's assistant gives the same enthusiastic greeting, word for word the same except for the name of the person he is greeting. The acolytes respond to the enthusiasm that the assistant shows, saying their own greetings in a similar energetic tone.

The Teacher says, "We need to see more of the Garden. Stay well, Gung."

The gardener's assistant says, "You too. Have a good day, Teacher!" He offers similar farewells to each of the would-be acolytes.

The Teacher leads the would-be acolytes a short distance away. Far enough that they can talk without their voices carrying, but not so far that they lose sight of the gardener's assistant. They watch as the assistant returns to his task of pruning the ironwood trees, cheerfully completing each step without supervision.

The Teacher says, "Gung is a man slow of wit, but sincere in his heart. If we go back and greet him in a few minutes, he will say the same thing as before, and greet each of us warmly, for he knows but little of how to speak. Yet he does his tasks as the gardeners give them, and will approach all of them in the same manner."

He pauses, then continues, "So, is this man happier than the king? The king is burdened with worry, with our enemies in Tjibarr and Yigutji threatening our borders. Yet this man knows little, and enjoys much."

The would-be acolytes nod and murmur in agreement. "This man is happy, happier even than the king," the *kunduri*-chewing acolyte says.

The Teacher says, "So, if this man is happy, then, what makes him happy? It cannot be wealth, for this man has none." As if carelessly, his fingers run over the sapphire-studded bracelet on his wrist. All of these acolytes know that the Teacher is wealthy, if not quite of the royal family.

"It cannot be praise, for those who work with him neither praise him nor condemn him, but just expect him to work."

"His joy must come from within, then," one of the acolytes says.

"So, then, is joy something which comes from within?" the Teacher asks. "Is it intrinsic to a man, not something which can be granted from without?"

The acolytes nod again.

"Yet if this man were to be punished, condemned, shouted at, would he not feel sorrow? Would he not be deprived of happiness?"

"Maybe happiness comes from within, while unhappiness comes from without?" the *kunduri*-chewing acolyte says.

"Perhaps," the Teacher says. "Yet if a man is praised, would that not usually make him happy? If I were to say to you, "I am pleased with you," would *that* not grant you a boon of joy?"

"It would be the honour of my day," the *kunduri*-chewer says.

"So, then, is joy something which can be found from within, or something which comes from without?"

The Teacher waits, but no-one answers him.

Eventually, he says, "Joy is neither internal nor external; it comes from bringing oneself into harmony with the world around. It need not even be a choice of enlightenment; a man who perceives as little as our gardeners' assistant can still be abundantly joyful. It is the alignment, the convergence of one's own desires with the present circumstances which matter. As circumstances change, as lives change, we must strive to keep ourselves aligned; we must make our own essence the balance on which our world shifts."

* * *

The man whom allohistory would come to call the Good Man was born sometime around 1080; accounts differ as to whether he was born before or after Lopitja gained its independence. The place of his birth is recognised to be somewhere near Kantji, although there are several competing claims for the exact location. He was born into a wealthy family; his father is reported to have been a dealer in incenses and perfumes. A plethora of tales describe his life and his teachings, many of them undoubtedly apocryphal, but there is no doubt that in his lifetime he was regarded as a great philosopher, teacher, and visionary.

Certainly, he spoke of the need to bring harmony to the cosmos, and of the Sevenfold Path which was the best means to achieve harmony. He was presumably a literate man, as most men of his background would have been, but no surviving letters or other writings can be indisputably attributed to him.

Accounts of his life disagree in many of the details; no single undisputed account can be given. Still, in its broadest form the accounts agree that he was born into wealth and in his youth and early adulthood he lived on the path of that wealth. He is reported to have travelled to many destinations across the Five Rivers to trade in incenses and perfumes. Sometime during those journeys, he had an insight, a revelation into what caused struggles and misfortune in the world. He turned away from the path of wealth and set about a path of understanding the world.

In his adulthood and later life, he continued to travel throughout the Five Rivers, though he spent far more time in Lopitja than anywhere else. Accounts agree that he never visited Garrkimang until after the last of the First Speakers had been deposed, and that he made only the briefest of visits to Yigutji. Some Nangu accounts claim that he made a visit to the Island, although that is not recorded in any non-Nangu tales.

In his teachings, the Good Man expounded on his understanding of the cosmos, and of the principles needed to ensure a harmonious life for a person and for society. He attracted many disciples and followers, including some who took up life travelling with him and others who honoured him when he visited.

No two accounts agree on the names of all of those disciples, but three disciples in particular are widely-listed as the Good Man's closest followers. Warrgin is said to have been the first to follow the Good Man, and to have the greatest insight and vision after the Good Man himself. Noolnoo is said to have been the one who took the Good Man's many insights and paraphrased them into the Sevenfold Path as a foundation for understanding, of which the Good Man approved. Marrawalku is said to have been the one who had the strongest memory of any disciple. He could recite the most sayings and stories of the Good Man.

In his travels, the Good Man reportedly offered his teachings freely to all who asked, and made no distinctions of rank or social status. In most accounts, it is stated that he would accept gifts if offered in exchange for teachings, but that he encouraged all of his disciples to work to earn their food and clothing, rather than relying on the generosity of others. Some more disputed accounts claim that for much of his life he followed monastic principles where he would regularly go into seclusion and contemplation to consider the harmony of the cosmos. Other accounts claim that he always tried to engage with people and did not have any periods of seclusion or monasticism; a disagreement which would later lead to competing interpretations of his teachings.

For all of the competing accounts of his life, the tale of the Good Man's death is surprisingly well-agreed. All accounts concur that the Good Man had grown old and had foresight that he would soon be dying. He was then teaching in the town of Yapun [Pooncarie]. He told his local disciples and had them spread the word of his forthcoming death to his other followers scattered across the Five Rivers. A large group of these followers gathered in Yapun – sources differ on whether it was three hundred or seven hundred – to hear the final words of the Good Man. He called them to a great feast, where he advised them to continue to build their own understanding and to spread knowledge of the Sevenfold Path to the world.

Following his last feast, the Good Man retired to die in solitude, accompanied only by his three closest disciples. He gave some final advice to each of these three disciples, then willingly abandoned his life. Per his explicit instructions, his remains were cremated and the ashes scattered in the Anedeli.

The Good Man's death is dated to AD 1151. After his passing, his disciples held a long convocation which would come to be called the First Council. Here, they took it in turns to recite what they could recall of his teachings, and sought to bring them into a coherent message. Marrawalku was the disciple charged with integrating what others had said into his own memories of the Good Man's saying, and preparing an oral account of the Good Man's teachings which others could memorise and repeat. Marrawalku provided such an account, with most stories of the First Council claiming that he took three days to recite it in full.

The First Council endorsed Marrawalku's general account of the Good Man's teachings, but it failed to reach agreement on the governance of his followers. The majority of the assembled disciples agreed that Warrgin should guide the teachings and act as the final source of authority. A few disciples argued that no one person could replace the Good Man, and that only the full assembly of disciples could provide guidance to match his teachings. One disciple argued that the Good Man had designated him to be his heir, and that governance of the faith should fall to himself and his successors in body and in spirit.

The legacy of the First Council was division. The followers of Warrgin formed what they would call the Warrgowite school, named for the word *warrgowee* which means "orthodox" or "standard." The holdout disciples founded what they called the Plirite school, named for the word *pliri* which the Good Man had used to mean "(the) Harmony." The Warrgowite and Plirite schools recognised each other as part of the same community and holding to the same underlying truth; their disagreements were essentially in matters of religious governance and priestly structure. They regarded the Good Man as a prophet-philosopher and the ideal example of how a person should live.

The lone disciple took a new name for himself, Tjarrling, which meant "the True Heir." He taught that the Good Man had been more than just a man, but a semi-divine figure, and that this legacy had passed on to Tjarrling, and would follow his successors. Followers of both Warrgowite and Plirite schools were divided about whether Tjarrling and his followers could be considered part of the same religion, or whether it should be considered as something so misguided that it represented a false truth.

* * *

In the decades after the Good Man's death, his disciples sought both to refine his teachings and to spread the word of his faith to others. The Warrgowite and Plirite schools further divided into different sub-schools, due to ongoing disagreements about the details of the Good Man's teachings, how best to interpret the Sevenfold Path, and other matters of religious practice. They continued to view each other as part of the same broad community – and sometimes, viewed Tjarrling's followers as part of the same – but their religious practices continued to diverge.

In their efforts to convert other peoples, missionaries of Warrgowee and Plirism spread throughout the Five Rivers and beyond. They won a few converts, but also encountered resistance. The syncretic nature of many of the Gunnagalic traditional religions meant that they were prepared to consider the Good Man's teachings as another religious practice, but were less receptive to the idea of one true path.

Warrgowite missionaries had their first major success in 1209, when the new king of Loptija converted to their school. In 1214, he made it the state religion of his kingdom. He also convened the Second Council, where adherents of Warrgowee, Plirism and even Tjarrlinghi were invited to come together to seek to resolve their religious differences.

In practice, all that this Council accomplished was to consolidate the differences. Within the kingdom of Lopitja, all followers of the Good Man were strongly encouraged to convert to one of the Warrgowite sub-schools. Outside of Lopitja's borders, followers of the Good Man largely abandoned Warrgowee; those south and east of Lopitja turned to Plirism, while those in the thinly-populated lands north of Lopitja turned to the Tjarrling school.

Over the new few decades, the Warrgowite schools became deeply established in the kingdom of Lopitja; most of the population converted. The Plirite and Tjarrling schools outside slowly spread, but they had nothing like the same success that Warrgowee had in the land of the Good Man's birth.

Under royal influence, the Warrgowite schools evolved along monastic lines. They held that the best insights were gained from contemplation and keeping away from the world. With royal patronage, many Warrgowite monasteries were established around the kingdom, with the monks spending nine months of the year in seclusion and only having contact with outsiders for three months. In contrast, Plirite and Tjarrling schools both agreed that priests needed to be involved with the world to provide proper insight, and encouraged their priests to have ongoing contact with the people throughout the year.

Unfortunately for the Warrgowites, Lopitja itself was dying. The unusual climatic conditions which sustained the kingdom were fading. Papukurdna was drying up, and the winter rains were becoming more erratic. Farmers abandoned their fields, the population declined, and in time the kingdom lost its wars with Tjibarr. The capital was sacked in 1284, and most of its other cities were abandoned. Kantji returned to desert, its stone walls and roads now an empty haunt of wind-borne red dust, while the wonders of the Spiral Garden were reclaimed by desert scrubs.

By then, however, Plirism had spread much further.

* * *

Over the centuries since the Good Man's death, Plirism evolved into the first evangelical religion which the continent had seen. The early Warrgowite schools have largely been abandoned with the collapse of Lopitja; what remains are the various competing schools which make up the Plirite tradition.

The adherents of Plirism created an organised priesthood, whose emphasis was on the continuity of faith and personal teaching from the Good Man to his disciples and to his priests. While they had a variety of religious writings, to the Plirites, these were treated as supplements to the continuity of learning from teacher to disciple to priest. They taught that following the Sevenfold Path and bringing balance to one's own desires was the only way to achieve true harmony and concord throughout the cosmos. Other faiths and beliefs might have some truth, but they were not the whole truth, and so would thus inevitably bring discord. Only once all peoples followed the Sevenfold Path would there be complete harmony in the cosmos.

Plirism has spread among the Five Rivers, but never become the majority in any of the three surviving kingdoms. Several Plirite schools have become established in different parts of the Five Rivers, with long-established temples which have remained over the centuries. Yet the traditional religion remained strong; the majority of the peoples of the Five Rivers view the Good Man's teachings as simply one path among many.

Plirite missionaries also brought the word of the Good Man to the lower reaches of the Nyalananga. They found some success there, particularly in converting the Yadilli who dwelt south-east of the Nyalananga's mouth. Their most important long-term success, however, came from the establishment of temples on the Island, and the wholesale conversion of the Nangu in 1240. The Nangu embraced Plirism, and as their trade network grew, the faith spread along with it.

The followers of Tjarrling made little progress within the Five Rivers, even after the collapse of Lopitja. But they were rather more successful in carrying their beliefs to the northern headwaters of the Anedeli. There in the Neeburra, the Butjupa and Yalatji peoples slowly converted to the new faith. By the seventeenth century, Tjarrlinghi had become almost universal among those peoples.

* * *

Plirism has developed many competing schools and interpretations. They have different collections of religious writings, but have no universal agreement about what these mean. The schools have different views on all manner of religious questions, from how to apply each of the seven paths, to the nature of the gods (or whether they exist), to the nature of the soul, to what gives priests their authority, and to other religious practices.

Above the level of an individual temple, there is no guiding central authority for the faith, no-one who can make absolute decisions. Some living priests become regarded as influential authorities who should be consulted, and the writings of some former priests have become the foundation of particular schools of thought.

However, in many ways the most influential school of Plirism is the form which the Nangu have adopted. Like all of the schools, it was based on acceptance of the Sevenfold Path which was the core of the Good Man's teachings. It also included considerable elements and influences from traditional Gunnagalic religion. For the Good Man had taken many religious concepts and other aspects of his worldview from the preceding Gunnagalic religions, and some others were inserted into Plirism by his disciples and early converts.

At its core, Plirism views the cosmos as a single connected entity. The actions of every person and every object are connected; nothing happens in isolation. There is no such thing as an inanimate object, for everything is seen as having the same "essence," and both affects and is affected by everything else. All actions, great or small, good or bad, have their place in the pattern of the cosmos. Moreover, all actions have consequences; nothing which is done can be said to have no effect on the rest of the world. The most common analogy which the Good Man taught is of the cosmos being like a pond; anything which was cast into that pond would produce ripples.

According to the Good Man, the foundation of understanding came from recognising the truth of interconnectedness, and the effects of this truth. It is inevitable that actions will change the world, but the question is whether an action is *dandiri* (bringing harmony) or *waal* (bringing discord). Acting in a way which brings harmony is the foundation of all virtues and good things; acting in a way which brings discord is the foundation of all suffering, even if the influence is not obvious to the casual beholder.

The Good Man taught that the key to maximising harmony was to bring balance to one's own desires, and align them with the broader cosmos. This meant that one should follow the Sevenfold Path. The Path was the only true way to bring oneself into harmony with the cosmos. Stepping off the Path unbalanced oneself and reduced harmony in the cosmos, which increased discord and suffering. Other faiths and beliefs might contain some similarities to the Path, and so some aspects of truth, but their correspondence was never perfect. So, to some degree every other faith increases the suffering and discord in the cosmos. If everything and everyone acts in harmony, then there will be balance. That will bring a minimum of suffering, and the maximum of solace.

The Sevenfold Path manifested in seven complementary paths, each of which should be followed by every person, as far as they are able to within their understanding and ability. The interpretation of these paths was coloured by individual societies and pre-existing religious beliefs, but the names of each of the paths was accepted throughout Plirism.

The first path, the founding path, is the path of harmony. All people should act in a way which increases harmony, not in a way which causes discord. There is no universal list of the actions which create discord, but in general harmony can be increased by maintaining standards of courtesy, honesty, and respect for others. Honesty is not an absolute, at least according to some priests, for a lie can be tolerated when it would be less hurtful. Theft and taking of other people's property is condemned unless it is to avoid greater suffering. Violence is generally to be avoided, but it can become necessary if it is directed against something which would otherwise increase disharmony, such as social unrest, preventing murder or theft, and so on.

The second path is the path of propriety. This means that each person should act in a manner befitting their station in society; to do otherwise is to cause disharmony. Rulers and slaves should both act as befits their role. A Nangu axiom restates this path as "to the merchant his profit, to the chief his obedience, to the artisan his craft, to the priest his prayers, and to the worker his duties." This includes the implicit assumption that rulers who act in a manner befitting their status should be obeyed, while those who do not do so should be removed. It also means that workers, labour draftees, slaves and the common classes are expected to obey and serve, not seek to improve their station. There is an implicit hierarchy in a Plirite society. Since Plirism inherited the old Gunnagalic belief in reincarnation, it is expected that people will live in different stations in different lives.

The third path is the path of decisiveness. This is often restated to mean "no half-actions." The principle of balance and harmony means that inaction is often the best course; sometimes doing nothing is the best way to avoid causing discord. Conversely, when action *is* required, it is because something has been done to cause disharmony. In this case, decisive action is required, not half-measures.

For instance, the Plirite principle is that war should not be fought unless there is good reason. Most commonly, this is because a society is causing discord, or against social unrest. Such a war should be pursued to its utmost finish. Enemy soldiers should be hunted down and killed in decisive battles. Sometimes this is also interpreted to mean that prisoners should not be taken, and quarter should not be given. Soldiers should not kill those who are not part of the war, but if someone makes himself a part of the war, then he should be killed without compunction. Likewise, rulers who live according to this path should ignore small slights; there is no need to respond to every complaint and insult. That would only provoke a cycle of retribution and cause endless discord. If action is required against an enemy of the realm, though, it should be swift, decisive, and without mercy[81].

The fourth path is the path of prayer. The Good Man viewed prayer as both a means of personal enlightenment – communing with the Evertime – and as a means of honour, respect and intercession with other beings. People are expected to pray for intercession from beings of power, such as the myriad of divine beings whose existence was accepted as an inheritance from older religions. People are also expected to pray to honour and respect both their ancestors and their descendants; the Plirite view is that the respect of prayer can flow forward to benefit one's future lives.

For common people, the faith has standardised the time of daily prayers as dawn and dusk. These are called the half-times, when there is balance between day and night, and when prayers are most efficacious. Other important times for prayer are at the times of the half-moon (both waxing and waning), and especially the equinoxes, which are seen as the focal points of the year. The Plirite calendar starts with a great religious festival at the autumn equinox, as an ideal time of balance. Priests are expected to spend much of their lives in prayer, since this will increase harmony and preserve the balance of the cosmos.

---

[81] Orthodox Plirite priests would be right alongside Machiavelli's adage of never doing an enemy a small injury, although he would not necessarily have agreed with their common notion of fighting wars without taking prisoners.

The fifth path is the path of charity. The Good Man taught of the need to support and care for others. On the Island, the Nangu traditionally interpret this as requiring a donation of a twelfth of their income to support others; other Plirite schools usually just expect generosity and helpfulness rather than a specific amount. In most cases, this path is followed by donating to the temples, which in turn are expected to support the poor, sick and hungry. Rulers are likewise expected to be generous; earning wealth is perfectly acceptable, but hoarding it while people starve is not.

The sixth path is the path of acceptance. The Good Man taught that the cosmos is larger than any individual; sometimes, no matter what a man's deeds might be, there are larger forces at work which he cannot control. In this case, while a man should do the best he can, he should not express frustration or condemn himself for things which cannot be changed. He should simply accept some things as inevitable, abandon futile striving which will only bring about further discord, and focus his attention on those duties which he can perform. In common practice, this is interpreted to mean avoidance of complaining about outcomes, perceived poor fortune, bad luck, or the like. It is appropriate to advise others on when their actions may be increasing discord, but not to complain about one's own status or present condition.

The seventh path is the path of understanding. The Good Man taught that each person should strive to understand themselves and the cosmos as they really are, not through misunderstandings or illusions. They should achieve this knowledge both through self-reflection and through instruction from those who have achieved greater understanding. In common practice, this means that a person should seek the guidance of their parents or other elder relatives to assist in understanding their daily lives. To understand the broader cosmos, they should seek the guidance of their priests or the written teachings of revered teachers, who can help to build their proper knowledge.

Priests can guide people and help them to recognise the effects of their own actions, and thus better follow all aspects of the Sevenfold Path.

While they are not strictly part of the teachings of the Sevenfold Path, there are also other beliefs which have become integral parts of Plirism. Most of these beliefs were derived from the traditional Gunnagalic religious milieu. These include the existence of a great many divine beings, heroic figures, and other spiritual figures which are part of the cosmos. These can be prayed to, negotiated with, and in some cases consulted to gain greater understanding. However, the Good Man taught that none of these beings were infallible or all-knowing; they were merely powerful beings.

Likewise, Plirism accepts the idea of the Evertime, of the eternal nature of the cosmos, and of reincarnation. However, reincarnation has been somewhat reinterpreted. In traditional Gunnagalic religion, reincarnation could be into a variety of forms, human, animal, or plant, and could happen forward or backward in time. Plirism recognises only reincarnation in human form, and does not accept that people can be reborn into the past. Plirism teaches that people are reborn into different bodies and stations as part of the overall balance of the cosmos. Reincarnation is based not just on an individual's own actions, but on the broader principles of harmony and discord. Everyone will be influenced by the cosmos.

* * *

In 1618, Plirism is the one multinational faith on the continent. Some peoples have religions of state, such as the Atjuntja and the Yadji. There are some traditional syncretic religions which are widespread over some areas, particularly the Five Rivers.

However, Plirism is the one faith which explicitly tries to convert other peoples, and its adherents have slowly become more numerous and more widespread, with even a few converts in Aotearoa. The Atjuntja kill converts amongst their own subject peoples, the Yadji persecute them, and some other Gunnagalic peoples spurn them.

Plirism is still slowly growing. This is not least because once a population has become majority Plirite, they are very unlikely to revert to other faiths. This is part of the Plirite teaching that other religions increase discord and suffering; any would-be converts are discouraged through passive or active means. Plirite peoples are also inclined to speak out against their own people if they believe that a particular person is not living according to the Path. After all, anyone who steps off the Path is, in their way, increasing the suffering of others.

Still, after 1618, Plirism will have deal with a religious challenge greater than any which it has so far experienced.

#18: Of Factions, Farmers and Forests

Look back, if you will, into the past of a history that was not. You might see a city built on what appears to be a large hill. Tjibarr, its inhabitants call it, which in their language means "the place of the gathering." The heart of the city is built on what seems to be a natural mound raised above the surrounding countryside.

In fact, this mound is not natural. Tjibarr is an ancient metropolis, the oldest continually inhabited city on the continent, and this mound shows the accumulation of history. Level after level of the city has been built over the ruined foundations of its predecessors, in a series which stretches back more than four millennia.

The city's inhabitants are aware of some of that long history. Their historical memory does not stretch back as far as the city has been inhabited; the most ancient times have been lost in the mists of myth and pre-literacy. Still, they remember the past, and draw from its lessons to understand their present.

Water surrounds Tjibarr on all sides. To the north lies the Nyalananga, the Water Mother, the greatest river which the people of Tjibarr know. To the east lies a natural lagoon which has been expanded by human actions, and beyond that the Anerina [River Loddon]. To the west and the south lie more lagoons, these wholly artificial. The lagoons act as a defence, as a source of food, and for flood control since they can absorb some of the rising waters of the Nyalananga. Roads lead through the lagoons, yet they can be easily flooded if the need arises. While some goods do move by road, the bulk of trade moves by boat, so even being fully surrounded by water will merely inconvenience its inhabitants.

Oft times the city has been surrounded by water for months, either when enemy armies threaten, or when the Nyalananga floods. This matters little to the people of Tjibarr. What they care about is inside the city itself. Here is the Thousand-Fold Palace, where it is said that a thousand kings have reigned from within its walls and then been interred in stone within its foundations. Here is the Plaza of the Four Moons, the grand square which is at the heart of the city, lined with statues of monarchs and other important beings, both historical and spiritual. The Plaza is an important gathering point when the rulers call the people together, and hosts the main markets of the city, where its inhabitants fondly believe that they can find anything worth buying.

Here is the Hall of Rainbows, an elaborately-constructed building with eight wings around an octagonal centre. Each of these wings has been carefully measured to be of equal area. The eight-sided central complex is where the elders of the factions meet to discuss matters of common concern, while above them towers the marble spire which is the tallest point in the city. Here are the several carefully cultivated fields where the factions play out their rivalry. On the largest of those sports arenas, the Field of Champions, twenty thousand people can gather to watch their faction's sporting heroes demonstrate their skills. Here are a myriad of temples and shrines, offering their own form of testament to the diverse views encapsulated in Tjibarr's syncretic religious outlook. It is said that Tjibarr has a shrine on every street corner, and this is not far from the truth.

Here, too, are all of the less prominent but equally essential buildings needed for a thriving city. Tjibarr throngs with people, both residents and visitors, for it is both an important trade nexus and manufacturer of specialty goods. The workshops, the schools, the warehouses, the docks, the houses, and other buildings of Tjibarr are less spectacular in their construction, but equally important for the city's functioning.

* * *

Tjibarr is not the largest city on the continent, but it is the oldest. It forms the spiritual heart of the kingdom which bears its name, thanks to its ancient legacy of sacred places and religious traditions. These days, other cities are nearly as important in terms of economics or population, especially Tapiwal, but Tjibarr remains the official capital and most frequent residence of the royal family. The city of Tjibarr is often called Tjibarr-of-the-Lakes, to distinguish it from the kingdom which bears the same name.

The inhabitants of Tjibarr and its surroundings call themselves the Gunnagal, a name which future linguists and anthropologists will give to all of the languages and peoples descended from the first yam farmers who lived around Tjibarr. In 1618, though, the name Gunnagal simply refers to the speakers of a related series of dialects around Tjibarr and its environs. They are the largest ethnicity within the kingdom's borders, although far from the only one. Several other Gunnagalic-speaking peoples are subjects of Tjibarr, and even a few hunter-gatherer peoples along the driest reaches of the Nyalananga are also more or less willing servants of the king.

The heartland of the kingdom of Tjibarr is the middle stretches of the Nyalananga, which it has controlled since time immemorial. The other borders of the kingdom have expanded and shrunk over the centuries, as rivals have emerged or subject peoples have revolted.

In 1618, Tjibarr shares control of the Five Rivers with two other kingdoms: Gutjanal on the upper Nyalananga, and Yigutji which controls most of the course of the most fertile tributary river, the Matjidi. The most powerful rival of all is to the south; the Yadji Empire has long fought with Tjibarr. Over the last two years, Tjibarr's armies have been victorious over the Yadji; driving them from the mouth of the Nyalananga, and bringing the rich territories of the Copper Coast[82] under their sway.

Whether this victory will endure is difficult to be sure; even some of the Gunnagal generals are not optimistic. The Yadji have always been a difficult foe, and the other neighbours of Gutjanal and Yigutji are sometimes foes and sometimes allies, as the tides of war and politics shift. The last war which Gutjanal and Yigutji fought was against each other, while in the war before that, Gutjanal fought with Tjibarr against an alliance of Yigutji and the Yadji.

Still, of all the threats to the recent conquests, the greatest probably come from within Tjibarr itself. Tjibarr is nominally a kingdom, but the monarch's power is far from absolute. The internal politics of Tjibarr are convoluted, based on a system of semi-hereditary factions whose relations are byzantine in their complexity. The monarch is personally revered, but to most of the kingdom's inhabitants, their loyalty to their faction matters much more than their relationship to the monarch.

The ancient institution of the monarchy had long been seen as serving a role of balancing the factions. With the shifting spiritual tide, some new ideas have penetrated from Plirism, even though the majority of citizens do not follow that religion. The ruler is seen as the essence of harmony, whose role is to maintain balance within the kingdom. Often, this means that the ruler does not have to do much, but simply to be there. This suits the factions, who conduct

---

[82] The Copper Coast is the region which in historical terms stretches from the Murray Mouth to Port Augusta, or in allohistorical terms from the Nyalananga Mouth to Dogport. The Gunnagal call it the Copper Coast for reasons of historical memory; it was the most important ancient source of copper. While the metal is still mined there, it has become less important since the Gunnagal learned the arts of ironworking; iron is mined in the Copper Coast (some small deposits) and other locations throughout Tjibarri territory. To the Tjibarri, the Copper Coast is more valuable for its agricultural produce than its mining.

much government business amongst themselves. But the ruler is expected to act to preserve the balance, live an orderly life, and deal with outside threats.

* * *

The Gunnagal who live in the heart of Tjibarr still preserve the names of the *kitjigal*, the ancient system of social groupings which had evolved in the Formative days of their distant ancestors. However, while the name remains, the *kitjigal* have evolved into a form which those long-departed ancestors would barely recognise. The ancient *kitjigal* formed a hereditary system whose leaders filled a combined role of priests, oligarchs, merchant princes, and military commanders. People were born into a particular *kitjigal*, could only marry certain other *kitjigal*, and their children changed *kitjigal* according to strict patterns.

In 1618, the *kitjigal* have evolved into a more fluid system of what are called factions. The factions are social groupings whose activities are intertwined into many aspects of daily life, but which do not have the same hereditary or universal basis as the ancient system. There is no equivalent of the old pattern of people moving between *kitjigal* over generations; people often remain as members of the same faction as their parents, but they can and sometimes do change between factions[83].

The factions serve many functions in Gunnagal society, but their most visible role is as competitors and supporters of sports. The sports fields of Tjibarr and some other leading cities within the kingdom host regular contests of a kind of football, which evolved out of their old systems of ball games. Gunnagal football involves a combination of kicking and throwing a ball, with the rules allowing them to hold the ball and pass or kick the ball and move. Competition between the factions is intensive, leading to a

---

[83] The factions have preserved the old colour names: grey, white, black, gold, blue (i.e. medium and dark blue), azure (light blue), green and red. Aside from some occasional decorative motifs, they have lost the connection with the 'totems' which their ancestors used.

myriad of arguments, rivalries, and sometimes outright rioting based on game results.

The rivalry amongst supporters of the factions spills over to most aspects of daily life. The Gunnagal often dress themselves in the colours of their factions, argue endlessly about the results of past games and the skill of individual players, and choose their friends and socialise based largely on faction. The rivalry links to trade and commercial operations; people buying from a merchant of their own faction can expect a better price, in some cases, or at least better treatment and prompter service. Broader cooperation between traders, shippers, and other commercial operations is also often conducted amongst people of the same faction, or at least with a friendly faction.

The factions no longer have any formal role in religion, unlike their role in the ancient system, but they are an integral part of the aristocracy. Gunnagal aristocrats are expected to be supporters of one faction or another, and this is much closer to being a hereditary system than amongst regular supporters. For the nobility, the rivalry amongst the factions is much more about trade and land control than it is about sports, although many individual aristocrats are just as avid football supporters as commoners. Each of the factions also has its own internal politics, with rivalries and personal conflicts being common, especially about which aristocrat keeps control of a given portion of land, or who is allowed to represent the faction when negotiating or arguing with the other factions.

In land control, the faction system has become an integral part of government. Each faction holds rights to use different areas of land, although they do not own the land in the strict sense of the word. (In theory, they hold it in trust for the monarch.) In most cases, the land is worked by tenant farmers who serve one or another of the factions, and who deliver an agreed portion of their harvests in exchange for this right to work the land. For some specialty crops, the factions do not use tenant farmers, but appoint specialist land managers who can draw on the services of farmers who are effectively hired to work the land for an arranged payment, but who do not directly receive any portion of the harvest. Arguments over land control, farming, and the like form another major part of the rivalry between the factions; in extreme cases it is possible for a faction to be stripped of the right to work a particular area of land.

The faction system also extends to providing justice. If there is a crime committed between two people in the same faction, then it should always be resolved by internal methods. It is considered extremely uncouth for outsiders to become involved. Even in disputes between two factions, it is often preferred for leading members of the two factions to arrange a solution. The government can become involved in such cases, although sometimes private vendettas are used to resolve even the most serious crimes.

The role of the monarchy in this system is thus often to act as an arbiter, although the government administration does perform some other functions. Construction and maintenance of major waterworks and aquaculture is under government control, for instance, and the government bureaucracy calls on workers based on need, usually during the downtime of the harvests. The government also maintains a standing army, although the factions each have their own armed militia; another reason why sporting arguments often become quite intense. Having armed members of the factions around is often useful, since they will help to defend a city or region in time of war, but it is also means that unpopular monarchs face armed opposition. If the factions act together they can depose any ruler. A skilful monarch usually finds that the best way to survive is to keep a certain tension amongst the factions.

Of course, often monarchs have little difficulty keeping tension amongst the factions, because they argue so much amongst themselves. Gunnagal are notoriously argumentative; it is said in the Five Rivers that the hallmark of achievement is getting three Gunnagal to agree about anything. Visitors usually conclude that their disputativeness stems from two causes; one being their concern over perceived status, and the other over an extreme obsession with precision and details.

Concern over their reputation and rank is certainly a matter of considerable concern to most Gunnagal. The rivalry between and within the factions contributes to their strong views about perceived status, although there are other factors involved. For instance, one of the customs inherited from the Imperial days relates to the importance of the First Speaker, which was the literal translation of the Emperor's title. While this originally mattered for religious purposes, the Gunnagal have come to use speaking first as a measure of primacy at gatherings large and small. Interrupting each other is a sign of dominance, and so can produce some heated responses when done.

In large formal gatherings, everyone is expected to remain silent until the leading person gets to speak. They have developed some social rules about how to avoid this, such as for instance not being officially at the gathering until they sit down, and so they can thus speak without offering technical insult to the leading person. This also means that they have developed a form of sign language which they can use to convey meaning without officially speaking.

The other aspect of the argumentative Gunnagal nature comes from what they think of as a concern for accuracy, although outsiders often take it to be pedantic nitpicking. In a discussion, they will explore even minor points in great detail. The Gunnagal often focus on a point to the point of obsession; they will argue a point not only to death, but past its death and keep arguing even after its funeral[84]. This is partly a case of curiosity; the Gunnagal are intensely interested in new ideas and new methods, and partly just a concern with being completely right.

---

[84] If the Gunnagal believed in angels, they would not just argue over how many angels could fit on the head of a pin, but what their names were, what they were wearing, and which direction the pin was pointing.

* * *

The Gunnagal obsession with precision is reflected in many other aspects of their society. The one which is best known to their neighbours is the intricacy of their metalwork and other forms of manufacturing. The Gunnagal are the premier artificers on the continent in their jewellery, their finely-detailed sculptures, and in their metallurgy. Craft objects of wood, stone or metal made in Tjibarr are widely exported throughout the continent, carried by the inland trade routes or via the Islanders at the mouth of the Nyalananga. They are also experts at intricate decorations; the interiors of their buildings are often covered with elaborate frescoes and enamelled tiles.

Even much of their bulk metalwork is similarly intricate. Gunnagal smiths learned the art of working iron from a few Atjuntja who travelled on Nangu trade ships and settled in Jugara. With their intense curiosity and willingness to experiment, it did not take the Gunnagal long to develop new forms of working with iron. This led them to develop a form of mail[85], which is now the basis of their armour.

Their smiths also know how to work in other metals; silver and gold are common for jewellery and other decorative work. Jewellers incorporate a variety of other materials into their designs, especially precious stones such as opals, sapphires and carnelian, and even some animal materials such as turtle shells from their artificial wetlands. They have also become experts in working with brass. Brass is used for ornamentation at shrines ant temples. They also use brass in a number of medical instruments such as forceps, and in a wide range of musical instruments. Gunnagal musicians use a combination of brass horns, gongs, cymbals, and a four-valved instrument which is similar to a trumpet.

The Gunnagal obsession with detail has also manifested in their mathematics and calendric system. Their

---

[85] Or chain mail, as it is sometimes anachronistically called.

mathematics uses a base twelve system, because of the way they mark numbers counted. When counting on their fingers, the Gunnagal do not use both hands, but instead use only a single hand. They count with their thumb, using it to count the joints on each of their other fingers. This meant that they counted twelve joints, and this became the foundation of their mathematical system.

The Gunnagal have developed a considerable body of knowledge about mathematics, particularly when applying it to fractions and counting time. Their calendar is based on a series of twelve-day cycles, which can be roughly translated as their week. Each of these days has a different name, and the twelve-day cycles are repeated thirty times throughout their year (i.e. 360 days). They have also developed a month, whose name translates as 'two times and half a time.' That is, two twelves and half a twelve (six), which makes for a thirty day month. They have twelve of these months in a year. The remaining intercalary days (5 or 6) occur at the end of their year, and they have special names for those days.

The Gunnagal calendar is an ancient system, and has been adopted by many peoples across the eastern half of the continent. The Gunnagal themselves, though, have been more concerned with precision of measurement. They are acutely aware of the irregular nature of the year, and add 5 or 6 days as necessary to align the calendar with the sun and stars. They have also developed more detailed methods for keeping track of time. Most peoples of the continent rely on sundials, but the Gunnagal have created complex water clocks with feedback systems and intricate gearing to ensure that time is accurately recorded.

Within each day, the Gunnagal divide time into twelve "hours," counted from sunrise to sunrise. These "hours" are divided into twelve units called *buyu*, which are approximately 10 minutes. The *buyu* are further subdivided into twelve "minutes," of approximately 50 modern seconds. These correspondences are not exact, because the Gunnagal calibrate their clocks each sunrise.

The "minutes" are also more theoretical than real; while well-constructed, Gunnagal water clocks are not precise enough to record time so finely. This combination of resetting clocks daily and a lack of precise accuracy about their "minute" leads to many arguments, as can be expected from a people who are keen to get in both the first and the last word.

Their close recording of time has become linked to their development of currency. This started because each of the factions kept their own stores of yams and wattleseeds from the harvests they control. These stores became a source of wealth which could be traded for other purposes. To spare themselves the inconvenience of transporting large weights of wattleseeds or yams when trading, they developed a system of carefully marked clay tokens which were used as receipts. Yams or wattleseeds which were deposited at warehouses were issued these receipts, and the tokens could be traded as a form of currency[86]. Unlike some other forms of currency, however, the value of a token decreases over time, since stored food diminishes due to consumption, rot and pests.

The receipt and food storage system is divided into two classes of token. Those representing stored yams are initially worth more, since their flavour is preferred. However, their value decreases quickly, since like all root crops they are more prone to rot. Stored wattleseeds are of less initial value, but they decline much more slowly in their worth.

The receipt tokens are used as a currency where they are traded between people to simplify exchanges of goods. However, they are limited in that they can only be redeemed in the same warehouse where the food was stored, so that they can be checked against the warehouse records to reduce fraud. They cannot be redeemed in other cities in

---

[86] A similar system was used in ancient Egypt, although through the temples rather than any equivalent of the factions.

the kingdom, or even in other warehouses of the same faction in the same city. The tokens are still sometimes traded at different cities, but the value of these tokens depends on both their age and how far they are from their home city. Not all the tokens are from the factions; Plirite temples operate a similar system, based on their donations of goods and food provided by the devout.

* * *

While the Gunnagal will argue about almost anything, there is one group of people they rarely argue with: their doctors. The best doctors on the continent live in the Five Rivers. In some respects, their physicians are better than European doctors in the same period. This is largely because the Gunnagal are the heirs of a wholly different medical tradition, which does not include many of the errors of European medicine at that time. For instance, the Gunnagal were fortunate not to inherit any belief in the value of bloodletting or of the widespread use of leeches. While Gunnagal medical tradition has its own mistaken beliefs and ineffective practices, few of those are as likely to harm their patients as bloodletting.

The main Gunnagal medical tradition originated with physicians who lived in the early Imperial period and afterward, when the spread of literacy allowed ideas to be communicated over wide distances. Several early physicians conducted systematic studies of people with a variety of diseases, injuries, and other conditions. Physicians emerged as a separate social class during the Imperial period, and have remained so ever since. They move freely amongst all the Five Rivers kingdoms, maintain contact with their fellow physicians and monitor their treatments. This is mostly because poor physicians can be ostracised and punished, but it also allows them to share knowledge of new discoveries.

Gunnagal physicians have an established knowledge of pathology. They have categorised and recognised a variety of diseases, with their usual symptoms and prognosis. They have a basic knowledge of epidemiology; they understand that epidemics can occur, and recommend quarantine to prevent the spread of disease. However, their knowledge is far from perfect; they also recommend quarantine for some diseases such as cataracts which are not contagious.

Gunnagal doctors have a reasonable knowledge of anatomy. Several physicians have performed dissections over the years, and made some accurate deductions about some aspects of human physiology. Still, they have no concept of using autopsies to identify the cause of death of any particular disease.

When treating illnesses, Gunnagal physicians draw a sharp distinction between two kinds of sickness. These can be approximately translated as "natural" and "supernatural" illnesses. They believe that natural illnesses have physical causes and be treated as such, while supernatural illnesses can only be cured by spiritual treatments.

Natural illnesses include injuries, rashes, and other diseases with clear external symptoms. Supernatural illnesses include diseases where the symptoms are either less obvious or completely internal, such as some cancers. Sometimes, according to Gunnagal physicians, natural and supernatural illnesses coincide, and separate treatments are used for each. Fever without any other obvious external symptoms is considered to be a supernatural illnesses, although fever associated with a rash, cough, sore throat, or other respiratory infection is considered to be a natural illness.

This means that someone who catches the worst epidemic disease, Marnitja, is considered to have suffered a combination of natural and supernatural illness. The first stage, pink cough, is considered to be a natural illness, while the later fevered delirium is considered to be a supernatural illness which is beyond the power of any physician to heal.

Supernatural illnesses are treated by a special class of priest-healers, who are distinct from physicians and generally look down on them. The priest-healers' remedies do not involve anything as mundane as touching the patients or prescribing physical remedies. Their methods involve a combination of chanting, invocations, prayer, and spiritual communion with the patient. These treatments do not do much harm, but then they do not do much good either.

In some cases, the priest-healers' methods have some slight benefits. By talking with the patients and encouraging them, they sometimes strengthen the patient's own sense of self-belief, which occasionally encourages healing. On the other hand, some of their methods include keeping people awake for long periods, since this is thought to allow communion with the person's spirit. In fact, depriving patients of sleep can sometimes weaken their immune system instead of allowing them to fight off diseases.

For natural illnesses, Gunnagal physicians have a wider variety of treatments, some of which are actually effective. They can perform some simple surgery, ranging from minor draining of abscesses up to amputation of limbs. However, they have only limited methods of stopping blood loss, so many surgeons' patients do not survive. Some physicians are experts at dentistry, including the extraction of teeth and their partial or full replacement by gold teeth. Of course, only the truly wealthy can afford to use gold teeth.

A variety of treatments are based around the application of plant and animal products. In many cases, these products are in fact useless. A wide array of ointments, lotions, and other products are applied to irritated skin and eyes, or inhaled as nasal decongestants. Noroon [emu] fat is a popular treatment as an ointment, although it does not do any good. Physicians also recommend a number of plant-based tonics to promote general good health. Most of these treatments are of limited practical benefit, save as placebos, but they don't do any actual harm, and so their use has persisted.

A few of the plant-based treatments do have some efficacy. Sweet sarsaparilla is a plant native to the east coast, but the spice trade had long ago brought it to Tjibarr.

This plant has roots and leaves which are turned into a tonic which helps to treat chest infections, inflammations, and which can also prevent scurvy in drought times or after bushfires. It is also used to alleviate the symptoms of some skin diseases, although with less effectiveness, and is sometimes drunk as a cure-all to ensure good health[87].

Corkwoods are a group of small trees which the Gunnagal find invaluable. One species (*Duboisia hopwoodii*) has become known to them as *kunduri*, since it is the primary component of the drug. Snother species of corkwood (*D. myoporoides*) contains a number of alkaloids in its leaves which the Gunnagal use to produce some effective medications. An extract from the plant's leaves can be used to treat disorders of the digestive system, such as ulcers, inflamed stomach, and colic. Another extract from the leaves can also be used as a pain treatment, especially during childbirth. Unfortunately, there are occasional medical lapses with corkwood extract. Like most early painkillers, physicians found it difficult to get the dosage right, and overuse can sometimes harm or kill mothers[88].

---

[87] Sweet sarsaparilla (*Smilax glyciphylla*) is a close relative of Jamaican sarsaparilla (*S. regelii*). The Jamaican plant has been used as a flavouring and medicine in much of the world, and the Aururian version has similar properties. Sweet sarsaparilla is native to the east coast, but it is easily cultivatable over a wide range of habitats. In historical Australia, the plant was used for medicinal purposes by early European colonists, particularly for treating scurvy. It was also one the first native Australian plants to be exported in quantity; for a time in the nineteenth century, it was exported to China for use in traditional medicine.

[88] In historical Australia, this species of corkwood (*Duboisia myoporoides*) is commercially grown today as a source of several alkaloids used to make modern pharmaceutical products. In addition to the uses listed above, it can also be used to treat motion sickness and in various psychiatric uses, such as a rapid-onset sedative or to alleviate Parkinson's disease.

Gunnagal physicians have also made several technological advances. One of the most significant of these is distillation. This was originally a chance discovery from one of their oldest medical treatments. Since pre-farming days, steam baths had been used to alleviate illnesses such as headaches or colds. In the simple form, these consisted of boiling up the leaves of a chosen plant over a fire, with the patient inhaling the steam. Usually this was done for individuals, but with growing urban population, some physicians started to use communal steam baths.

Depending on the particular illness, a variety of plants could be used in steam baths, especially eucalypts. Another of the popular plants used for this purpose, the ti tree (*Melaleuca linariifolia*), originally came from the eastern coast, but was grown further west both for medical and perfume uses. Ti tree leaves were among the various plant remedies used for skin irritations when applied directly, but they were also used in steam baths.

The use of communal steam baths meant that the oil from ti tree leaves would often condense on the roof as the steam cooled. Alert Gunnagal physicians noticed that the condensing steam on the roof contained a stronger smell of ti tree than the natural leaves. In time, this led to the development of distillation techniques to extract ti tree oil from the leaves.

Ti tree oil itself was of limited value[89], but distillation offered other benefits. A variety of medicines could be extracted via distillation. Physicians did their best to

---

[89] Historically, ti trees were an important component of traditional Aboriginal medicine. Today, the commercial extraction of ti tree oil from plantations has become a significant industry. Claims have been made that it is useful as an antiseptic and anti-fungal agent, amongst other uses, although medical evidence is mixed at best. Allohistorically, the ti tree oil which the Gunnagal use comes from a species called the narrow-leaved paperbark (*Melaleuca linariifolia*). This is a different species to the main source of commercial ti tree oil in historical Australia (*M. alternifolia*), but the properties of the oil are more or less identical.

control knowledge of distillation, but have been only partially successful. Distillation is still not common knowledge in Tjibarr, and distillation of alcohol is still unknown. However, perfume-makers learned about the technology over a century ago, and use it as part of a substantial industry in perfume-making and related aromatic products.

* * *

In its agriculture and cuisine, Tjibarr is at the crossroads of the continent. Many crops have been domesticated here or obtained from other lands. Even some plants which cannot be grown along the Nyalananga are imported from elsewhere for the kingdom's inhabitants to consume. For the Gunnagal have the greatest preference for variety and flavouring in their foods of any people on the continent. The elites, in particular, enjoy having a wide choice of foods, and often encourage some use of irrigation to grow small amounts of crops which would otherwise be unsuitable in the dry lands along the Nyalananga.

For all of their new crops, the single largest source of calories still comes from staple root crops. The red yam is their most important crop, as it has been for four millennia, and murnong is an important secondary crop. Whether baked, roasted, fried, boiled, steamed, grated, mashed or pounded into a paste-like porridge, the Gunnagal have long made root crops the basis of their cuisine.

Other root crops have spread along the trade routes in recent years, bringing new options for Gunnagal chefs. Lesser yams have spread from the tropical north. Contact with the Patjimunra on the east coast brought sweet potatoes, known by their Māori name of kumara, and which ultimately originated in distant South America. From the western Atjuntja lands came two other root crops, the warran yam and the bush potato, long cultivated in the western lands, then adopted by the Islanders and then spread up the Nyalananga[90]. None of these crops gave yields as large as the red yam, and the sweet potato in particular required more labour since it needed irrigation and was an annual plant, unlike most native perennial crops. Still, they brought new flavours to the cuisine, and the royal family of Tjibarr have been noted consumers of sweet potato for the last few decades.

The other staple crop is wattles, the wealth-trees, the plants of multitudinous uses. Eight main species have been domesticated, with the Gunnagal domesticating the first three and in time acquiring most of the others from elsewhere[91]. The nature of Aururian farming means that at least two species are usually cultivated in any given area, so Tjibarri farmers make use of a wide range of wattle crops. Cultivated wattles and their products have a myriad of uses: timber, dyes, adhesives, soil revitalisers, a source of bark-skin paper, mulch, tannins for leather, scents in perfumes, and many more.

From a culinary perspective, the main use for wattles is the production of wattleseeds, with a secondary production of wattle gum. The different species of wattleseeds offer some minor differences in flavouring but are broadly

---

[90] The lesser yam (*Dioscorea angustus*) is a hybrid of red yams with another native yam species, the long yam (*D. transversa*). It needs somewhat higher rainfall and/or irrigation and produces smaller yields than red yams, and is thus a secondary crop. (It is more important in the north, since unlike red yams, it can grow in the tropics.) Warran yams (*D. hastifolia*) are another native yam species which can be grown in areas of moderate rainfall. "Bush potato" is a name which has been applied to several Aururian plants. The one referred to here is *Platysace deflexa*, which is unrelated to yams but which has quite a distinctive sweet taste.

[91] The various kinds of domesticated wattles differ in their productivity for seeds, the time of flowering (early or late), how much wattle gum and/or tannins they produce, and their rainfall requirements. The most important wattle crop throughout most of Aururia is the bramble wattle (*Acacia victoriae*), although the sallow wattle (*A. longifolia*) is more intensively grown in the higher-rainfall areas along the eastern seaboard and in Aotearoa.

similar. Wattleseeds can be eaten whole like a cereal, but they are usually ground into flour. Wattleseed flour lacks gluten, and so it does not rise when baked. It is most commonly cooked into a variety of flatbreads. Some varieties of wattles have been bred where the seeds are eaten in their pods while still immature, similar to green beans.

Noodles are another common culinary practice for wattleseed flour, made by boiling the flour either alone or with duck or noroon eggs. The first visiting Europeans who tasted these products will call them black noodles, because of the distinctive dark colour of wattleseed flour. The Gunnagal also grow a few other crops which produce edible seeds, such as purslane, native flax, or spiny-headed mat-rush. These seeds are also ground into flour, and used either in combination with wattleseed flour for additional flavouring, or as their own distinctive crops.

Besides staple crops, the Gunnagal grow many other plants as delicacies, nutritional supplements, condiments or for non-food uses. Fruits and nuts are much favoured, and the Gunnagal have access to a variety of them. Many of these fruits were domesticated early in the history of Aururian agriculture, and are widespread in Tjibarr and elsewhere in the Five Rivers. The most commonly grown fruits are those which can be grown without irrigation: quandongs, desert limes, and native raspberries. Some other fruits require irrigation and are thus either imported or grown as rare delicacies or for the social elite; the most notable of these are muntries, native passionfruit, and apple berry[92].

In recent times, the Gunnagal have domesticated some additional fruits to add to their cuisine. Australian boxthorn (*Lycium australe*) is a relative of the wolfberry or goji berry (*L. barbarum* and *L. chinense*) which was first

---

[92] All of the fruits listed here are plants which have been domesticated or otherwise cultivated in historical Australia; quandong (*Santalum acuminatum*) is perhaps the most widespread. Aururia has several native species of passionfruit; the one described here is *Passiflora herbertiana*.

domesticated in China. Australian boxthorn is a small, hardy shrub which produces small orange-red berries, and had long been collected by Aururian peoples. The early Gunnagal also collected the wild plants, sometimes for their fruit, but more often for using their leaves or root bark as part of traditional medicines for treating sore eyes, inflammations, and skin diseases. This process slowly led to the domestication of the plant, which they called *yolnu*.

In part, the Gunnagal use cultivated *yolnu* for medicinal purposes, but they have discovered a much more pleasing use. The Gunnagal had long produced *ganyu* (yam wine) from fermenting yams and flavouring it with the juice of desert limes. *Yolnu* has a nut-like taste which neatly complements the flavour of *ganyu*, and so now most of the fruit harvest goes for this purpose.

Another plant which the Gunnagal have recently domesticated is the bush pear (*Marsdenia australis*), a native vine which is widespread across the interior. It is most common in arid areas, away from the main farming cultures, and thus was not domesticated early. It started to be cultivated during the unusual climatic conditions of the ninth and tenth centuries AD, when farming peoples moved into the Red Lands beyond the Anedeli and became more familiar with some of the desert plants. Domesticated bush pears spread out from the Red Lands to the other farming peoples of the Five Rivers, including Tjibarr.

The bush pear is a drought-hardy vine of which almost all parts of the plant are edible. It produces a pear-shaped fruit with a great many seeds inside; the fruit pulp is sweet, and the edible seeds are reminiscent of peas. The leaves and stems of the plant are equally edible, and are collected and roasted whenever the vines are pruned. The flowers can be collected and cooked. The vine also produces an edible tuber which the Gunnagal chefs collect and roast along with yams and murnong. The Gunnagal name for the bush pear translates – for very good reason – as "many vine."

The settlement of the Red Lands also led to the domestication of the kutjera or desert raisin (*Solanum centrale*). A relative of tomatoes and tamarillo, this plant produces a small fruit with a strong, pungent taste. It is widespread across the arid regions of the continental interior. In the wild, it fruits prolifically in the year after fires or good rains. When farmers moved beyond the Anedeli, they discovered that they could mimic these effects by a little judicious irrigation. This led to the domestication of kutjera. The strong taste of the fruit means that it is commonly used as a condiment in sauces and dressings, particularly to give a hint of sourness; it is only rarely eaten fresh.

Besides their new fruit crops, the people of Tjibarr and elsewhere in the Five Rivers have also benefitted from the spread of two new nut crops. Macadamia trees are native to the higher rainfall areas of the eastern seaboard, and produce a nut which for a long time was wild-gathered as a favoured food.

Over time, this led to the domestication of the macadamia amongst the ancestors of the Kiyungu in the distant Coral Coast. Cultivation of the macadamia spread along the tin routes until it arrived in Tjibarr. However, growing of macadamias is on a small scale, since they require irrigation. Macadamia nuts are only eaten by the social elite, since they control the limited supply[93].

The other nut crop which the Gunnagal sometimes use is unusual in that it has not, strictly speaking, been domesticated. The bunya tree (*Araucaria bidwillii*) is a conifer which produces very large cones full of edible nuts, similar to pine nuts, which can be eaten raw or roasted, or ground into flour and cooked into bread. The bunya is erratic both in its germination and its seed production; cones are not formed every year. To hunter-gatherer

---

[93] Macadamias are the most widespread domesticated native crop in historical Australia. The modern crop is mostly a hybrid of two macadamia species (*Macadamia integrifolia* and *M. tetraphylla*). The allohistorical Aururiancrop is derived solely from *M. tetraphylla*; this was the more widespread plant and was thus domesticated.

peoples, the intermittent fruiting of the bunya tree (usually every third year) was a sacred occasion. Disputes were halted by truce and runners carried message sticks from band to band, leading to great gatherings (corroborees) where many peoples came together to feast on the abundant harvest. The bunya tree itself was regarded as sacred.

The veneration of the bunya tree was one belief which withstood the tide of the Great Migrations. When Gunnagalic farmers first entered regions where the bunya trees grew, they acquired the same view of the tree as sacred. Since they were already growing their own food, the fruiting of the bunya no longer brought about the same gathering of people, but it was still regarded as a time where disputes should be put aside. Sacred bunya trees also spread south along the tin routes, even to the drier regions where they required irrigation to grow. The trees have not changed in any significant way from their wild ancestors, and are thus not truly domesticated, but they are still cultivated widely. Amongst the Gunnagal in Tjibarr, the fruiting of the bunya trees is a time of truce amongst the factions, when disputes are set aside and the bunya nuts are handed out freely for all to consume. The tree itself is also revered; it is considered extremely poor manners to have any arguments or violence while close to a bunya tree.

Gunnagal cuisine also incorporates a range of other plants which have some nutritional or taste benefits. They have a variety of crops which are grown partly or primarily as leaf vegetables; warrigal greens, purslane, and scrub nettles are among the most common. Native flax is grown both for its edible seeds and as a source of textile fibre. Several thousand years of selective breeding means that some varieties of native flax now have very large seeds. These are often pressed to extract a form of linseed oil which is used in cooking. They grow beefsteak fungus and several species of mushrooms, which are carefully cultivated on mulches of wattle timber and leaves enriched with manure.

Of all the plant products available to the Gunnagal, though, none are more treasured than those used as drugs or spices. The most basic spice is a sweetener, wattle gum. One of the many uses of this gum is to dissolve it in water and use it to sweeten drinks or as part of sauces and dressings on food. Wattle gum is relatively cheap to obtain. It is tapped from wattles by cutting notches into the bark once the summer heat has faded, and returning a few weeks later to collect the large lumps of gum which exude from the notches.

The other main sweeteners which the Gunnagal use derive from tufted bluebell flowers. Ever since the Empire popularised the use of this flower, it has been an integral part of Tjibarri cuisine. Tjibarr continues the old imperial practice of having public flower gardens where people can collect the flowers in their season; every town of any size in Tjibarr has one or more bluebell gardens open to the public. Unwritten rules apply about any one household collecting too many of the flowers, rules which if broken tend to attract significant punishment from factional leaders. Of course, the genuinely wealthy have sufficient private gardens of their own that they will not suffer personally if someone overharvests from the public gardens.

The main way in which the Gunnagal use bluebell flowers has not changed since ancient times: steep them in water and then use the blue-water produced as a flavouring and sweetener. Sometimes the flowers or petals are eaten directly, particularly by the wealthy. One process which has changed with developing technology is that bluebells are sometimes distilled as part of perfume manufacturing. The by-product of that distillation also produces a sweet-flavoured liquid, stronger than normal blue-water. Wealthier Gunnagal, or those who are on good terms with perfume-makers, use this as their preferred sweetener.

The Gunnagal use a variety of herbs and spices as part of their cuisine. Some are grown locally in dryland agriculture or through irrigation, while others are imported along the trade routes from north, east or south. Many of the locally-grown spices have been modified by thousands of years of selective breeding into much stronger, more consistent flavours than their wild ancestors.

The most commonly used local spices are river mint, mintbushes, and mountain pepeprs, which are all easily cultivatable using dryland agriculture or light irrigation[94]. Eucalyptus leaves from several species of local gum trees are also used to flavour food; the most commonly cultivated species are blue-leaved mallee (*Eucalyptus polybractea*) and peppermint gum (*E. dives*). Sea celery, a close relative of common celery, is grown as a herb and condiment. Lemon-scented grass (*Cymbopogon ambiguus*) is used as a herb in cooking [like common lemon grass], and is also occasionally used to make a lemony tea.

Some spices which were originally native to the eastern coast are now grown in considerable quantities in Gunnagal lands. Native ginger (*Alpinia caerulea*) is a shrub whose berries, leaf tips and roots produce subtly different gingery flavours. Gunnagal chefs choose which sort of ginger to use depending on their preferences, and their general attitude is that no good roast is complete without being flavoured by some form of native ginger. The roots, shoots and berries of sweet sarsaparilla (*Smilax glyciphylla*) are also used by Gunnagal chefs to flavour drinks and soups. As well as being a seasoning, sweet sarsaparilla is an important element of Gunnagal medicine.

The most valuable spices are those which are too difficult to grow in the dry, occasionally frost-prone lands

---

[94] River mint *(Mentha australis)* is a true mint, with a flavour reminiscent of peppermint. Mintbushes, also called native thyme, are restricted to Aururia. Their flavour is somewhat akin to true mints, but remains a distinct taste. The main cultivated mintbush is the roundleaf mintbush (*Prostanthera rotundifolia*), although several other mintbushes in the *Prostanthera* genus are also exploited as spices. Three species of sweet peppers are known to the Gunnagal, each with their own distinctive taste, but mountain pepper (*Tasmannia lanceolata*) is by far the most common, and the only one grown within Tjibarr.

along the Nyalananga. These spices the Gunnagal need to import from elsewhere, usually from the damper areas in the eastern mountains or even the eastern seaboard. The overland spice routes are ancient, with some of them having been used for two millennia. Some of these spices routes have been partly replaced by seaborne trade on Nangu ships, but many of the spices grow best in more northerly regions where the Nangu rarely visit. The two most important areas of spice production are Daluming and the Kingdom of the Skin.

Of the spices imported from the east coast, the greatest quantity and the greatest prices are both commanded by myrtles. These are several species of trees whose leaves contain distinctive flavours. On the eastern coast these leaves are normally used fresh, but they are also easily dried and traded overland. Lemon myrtle (*Backhousia citriodora*) is the most common, with a sweet blended flavour which the social elites in Tjibarr consider as superior to any lemon-flavoured alternatives[95]. Aniseed myrtle (*Syzygium anisatum*), cinnamon myrtle *(Backhousia myrtifolia)* and curry myrtle (*B. angustifolia*) also have highly-valued flavours, and are traded over the mountains in considerable volume. Apart from myrtles, another common spice is the strawberry gum (*Eucalyptus olida*), whose leaves are dried and used for similar purposes as a sweet spice.

The other two spices which are commonly imported from the east coast are two other forms of sweet peppers. These are the species which the Gunnagal call bird-peppers

---

[95] Australia has several cultivatable plants which produce lemony flavourings. As well as lemon myrtle and lemon-scented grass, there is also jeeree, which in real history is called lemon-scented tea tree (*Leptospermum petersonii*) which can be used to make a lemon-flavoured tea. Allohistorically, all of these are cultivated on the eastern coast as flavourings, and jeeree has become a cultural icon. However, to peoples in the Five Rivers, jeeree has never held much interest, and lemon myrtle is considered superior for flavouring purposes.

[Dorrigo peppers, *Tasmannia stipitata*] and the even rarer and more expensive purple pepper [*T. purpurascens*], which has the hottest taste. Bird-peppers are imported from Daluming, while purple peppers are imported from the Kingdom of the Skin (Murrginhi). All Aururian sweet peppers have high water requirements, even mountain peppers, and the other sweet pepper species have such high water requirements that they have never been reliably grown within the Five Rivers, and so need to be imported.

Apart from their many spices, the plants most important to the Gunnagal are those which are used to make their main drug, *kunduri*. By far the preferred plant for this purpose is corkwood. For centuries Garrkimang had an effective monopoly on corkwood production, but it has now spread throughout the Five Rivers, including to Tjibarr. *Kunduri* is a nicotine-rich drug formed by mixing corkwood (or a substitute) with wood ash from wattle trees, which is then chewed[96]. It acts as a stimulant, creating a sense of wellbeing, and in mild doses it can suppress hunger and thirst. In particularly strong doses, *kunduri* can act as a sedative or a hallucinogen.

Those Gunnagal who cannot afford *kunduri* have to rely on the old standby of alcohol. The most expensive form is gum cider, which needs to be imported from the Cider Isle [Tasmania]. This is rare and expensive in Tjibarr, and virtually unavailable further upriver. The best locally-produced form of alcohol is *ganyu*, a form of yam wine mixed with other fruit flavourings such as desert limes or *yolnu*. For those who cannot afford *ganyu*, the alternative is a kind of yam beer which has only a weak alcohol concentration and no additional flavourings. The Gunnagal

---

[96] Australia has a variety of plants which have nicotine. Aside from corkwood, there are also a variety of native tobacco plants in the *Nicotiana* genus (relatives of domesticated tobacco). *Kunduri* can be made from any of those plants (and was done so in historical Australia), but corkwood (*Duboisia hopwoodii*) was the preferred species whenever it was available.

do not have access to distilled spirits; knowledge of distillation is still restricted to doctors and perfume-makers.

In terms of meat and animal products in their cuisine, the Gunnagal in Tjibarr and elsewhere in the Five Rivers have not changed much since their early ancestors. They still maintain artificial wetlands as a source of fish and waterbirds. Their key domesticated animals for meat are noroons and ducks, with dogs an occasional delicacy. Duck and noroon eggs are used in their cuisine almost as much as the meat of those animals. However, they have not yet obtained the domesticated geese which are used by some peoples on the Cider Isle and other south-eastern regions.

Meat products are often consumed fresh, but not always. Smoking meat is an ancient preservation technique which the ancestors of the Gunnagal learned long ago from the Junditmara. With domesticated wattles, they have abundant fuel available, so meat is often smoked for preservation. The Gunnagal being who they are, they often choose smoked meats for flavour as much as for preservation.

For flavouring, the Gunnagal have developed something new to make from fish. They use a variety of sauces made from fermented fish, known by the general name of *wineegal*. These sauces are sometimes made from whole fish, and sometimes just from fish intestines which would otherwise be discarded. The fish or fish products are mixed with brine, pressed, and allowed to ferment slowly. The longer the fermentation time, the richer and more intense the flavours produced. The finished product adds a savoury, umami flavour to foods.

The Gunnagal obtain several kinds of fish from their artificial wetlands, and in turn use these to produce a variety of different types of *wineegal*, with different flavours depending on the types of processing and sometimes different spices which were added during production. *Wineegal* makes a useful commodity for any estates with wetlands available to obtain the fish, and is exported around the Five Rivers, or more rarely to the Island or the Yadji lands[97].

When consuming food, the Gunnagal have a variety of eating utensils. By far the most common method is a combination of knives and fingers, where they simply cut the food and lift it into their mouths. They sometimes use a two-pronged analogue to a fork to help them hold meat while they cut it, although this is not commonly used to convey food to the mouth. Soup and other liquid foods are usually sipped from bowls. Spoons are known, but are used mostly by the upper classes, where they are used at all.

* * *

For more than two thousand years, the Gunnagal and their ancestors have used a perennial system of agriculture. Cyclical experience with droughts and loss of soil fertility taught them the importance of systems which could replenish the land, and which could prepare for downturns. Sometimes this involved crop rotation or companion planting. Sometimes it involved developing methods of food storage which would last for a decade or more[98]. Sometimes it meant selection of crop species which could survive the trials of drought, flooding, or bushfires.

All of these practices had one factor in common: they required the Gunnagal to think about the longer term. These agricultural requirements have contributed to the

---

[97] *Wineegal* production is similar to some fish sauces used historically, such as fish sauces used in East Asian and Southeast Asian cooking, and to *garum* and *liquamen* which was used in classical Greco-Roman cuisine.

[98] The Gunnagal are fortunate that their main long-term food storage is of wattleseeds. These seeds naturally have thick, impervious coats which allow them to survive in soil for a very long time. In the wild, wattleseeds usually rest in the soil and do not germinate until a fire goes through an area. This means that wattleseeds need to remain viable for over a decade; in some species, they can remain viable for up to fifty years. Luckily for the Gunnagal, this means that stored wattleseeds can keep for a very long time if they are simply sealed in an airtight container or room.

broader development of a long-term mindset amongst the Gunnagal, both in terms of government planning and individual decision-making. They are not conservationists in the modern sense of the word; they still see the natural world as something to be exploited. Still, they think in terms of what an action will mean, not just for today, but for the future. They also are more alert to gradual shifts in climate, in soil fertility, or other developments.

For instance, in their creation and maintenance of artificial wetlands, and their designation of royal hunting grounds, Gunnagal government and faction planners think in terms of sustainability. Catches of waterfowl and fish are subject to quotas, and only chosen hunters are allowed to catch gupas [kangaroos] in designated hunting areas.

When it comes to planting and maintaining forests, the Gunnagal adopt a longer term view. They can obtain plenty of small-scale timber from their planting of wattles, but their main domesticated wattles do not grow tall enough to supply really large logs. For this, and for other tree-related products, the Gunnagal have turned to plantation systems, coppicing, and managed woodlands. They maintain plantations of a number of fast-growing eucalypts such as blue gums, which they cut down every ten or fifteen years, and then leave to regrow. This gives them a useful source of larger timber for construction, boat-building, and other purposes, and sometimes as a source of large-scale charcoal production for fuel.

The Gunnagal also maintain suitable trees for the production of silk. At the time of the Empire's collapse, domesticated moths were only available along the Matjidi, in what became the kingdom of Yigutji. Over the centuries, the Gunnagal have obtained sufficient quantities of moths for some silk production of their own. The trees which they use for silk production – mostly varieties of eucalypts – are integrated into their broader system of woodland management.

In other woodlands, the Gunnagal also think in terms of managing the environment for more thorough exploitation.

They will selectively burn or uproot weed species in favour of plants which they find more useful. They sometimes make small clearings to allow favoured understorey plants to appear, particularly those which produce seasonal fruits or other flavoursome products. These plants are not domesticated as such, but the Gunnagal still rely on gathering their products[99]. Anywhere near where the Gunnagal live, no area is truly a wilderness, even if it only rarely has people in it.

Some of the trees which are planted and managed in this format are not used for timber, but for more valuable products. The Gunnagal around Tjibarr have developed substantial plantations of black and white cypress pines, two relatively drought-tolerant conifers native to their homeland[100]. The cypress pines are eventually harvested for high-quality timber, but throughout their lives, they are tapped as a source of resin. The Gunnagal use this resin for many purposes, such as a varnish and adhesive, for soap-making, an ingredient in ink, and as a component of incense.

Their most valuable use of resin, however, comes from the application of another Gunnagal discovery: distillation. Gunnagal perfume makers have learned how to distil resin and other plant products to produce essential oils. While

---

[99] This approach is in some ways similar – although more extensive - to what happened in parts of medieval Europe and elsewhere in the world. In medieval Europe, several fruit-bearing plants such as raspberries and blackberries were not yet domesticated. Woodlands were managed in ways which encouraged their growth, and gathering of wild berries produced considerable harvests. Likewise, coppicing trees was a useful source of timber and charcoal.

[100] The black cypress pine (*Callitris endlicheri*) and white cypress pine (*C. columellaris* or *C. glaucophylla*, depending who you ask) are native Aururian conifers which grow reasonably well even in drought-prone areas. Historically, the white cypress pine in particular has flourished since European arrival. The distilled oil from these pines is used today as a basis of perfumes and other products.

these have other applications, the main use of these distilled products comes from the production of perfumes. While several peoples across the continent manufacture perfumes from crushed herbs and plant products, only the Gunnagal know how to distil resin, flowers, and leaves to obtain more concentrated fragrances.

Gunnagal perfume makers use a variety of blends of distilled resins, flowers (especially wattles), and other aromatic parts of plants to produce a diverse range of perfumes. These scented products are sometimes used for religious purposes, and are also a significant part of Tjibarr's exports. The most expensive of all perfumes are those made using a form of musk. Gunnagal perfume makers collect this product from the musk duck, a bird which frequents their artificial wetlands. The rights of harvesting musk ducks are one of the most contentious of economic issues that the factions argue over; musk is the most expensive animal-based product on the continent. The complex, earthy fragrances of musk-based perfumes are the most highly-favoured scent on the continent[101].

* * *

In 1618, as the isolation of the island continent comes to an end, all of its inhabitants will face immense challenges. Contact with the outside world, with its new technologies, faiths, diseases and ideas, will change the fate of the island continent. Still, of all of the peoples who cultivate yams and wattles, the Gunnagal are perhaps the most fortunate. With their immense curiosity, ruthless exploitation of any possible advantages, and mindfulness of the longer term, the

---

[101] Musk was until recently an extremely valuable product harvested from various animals in Eurasia, particularly the musk deer. Until the development of synthetic musk, the collection of musk from musk deer produced what was one of the most expensive products in the world; by weight, it was sometimes worth more than twice as much as gold. In allohistorical Aururia, the musk duck (*Biziura lobata*) – a bird endemic to wetlands in the south-eastern part of the continent – will be similarly prized for the fragrance it yields.

Gunnagal may be the best-placed to exploit the threats and opportunities which they will encounter in the decades ahead.

#19: Life Among The Rivers Five

Allohistory calls the region the Five Rivers. That name is a misnomer. Many more than five rivers can be found in the region, while of the five rivers which gave the region its name, the Anedeli [River Darling] is only considered part of the region in its lowermost reaches, and the Pulanatji [Macquarie] is no longer considered part of the Five Rivers.

Whatever it might be called, the Five Rivers is the wealthiest and one of the most densely-populated parts of Aururia. The foundation of this prosperity comes from the more than five rivers which flow through the Five Rivers. Foremost of these is the Nyalananga, the great river which rises in the shadows of Aururia's highest mountains then runs for 2500 kilometres through mostly flat, low-lying country until it finally empties into the Bitter Lake, where its waters slowly mix with the sea. The Nyalananga runs through one channel for most of its length, but in part of its midway journey through the Five Rivers, it divides into three rivers which the local people call the North Channel [Edward River], Middle Channel [Wakool River] and South Channel [Murray proper]. These branches of the Nyalananga serve valuable purposes to the people of the Five Rivers, since they give additional transport routes and sources of irrigation.

Besides the Nyalananga itself, several of its tributaries are also significant to the prosperity of these lands. First amongst these is the Matjidi [Murrumbidgee], itself nearly 1500 kilometres long, and with an importanttributary of its own, the Gurrnyal [Lachlan]. The Dulabul [Goulburn River] is the longest left bank tributary of the Nyalananga, with the Anerina [River Loddon] and Wandilwang [Ovens River] being other significant rivers.

The Nyalananga and its tributaries thus form the Five Rivers, a region of slow-moving rivers and managed artificial wetlands. The tributaries are often only navigable during winter and spring when water levels are at their highest. Even the major rivers can have some difficulties with navigation, particularly with sunken logs which can snag passing boats. However, the local peoples have long since learned to manage these problems. In a land where the only other mode of transport is vehicles pulled by people or dogs, even sometimes-troublesome riverine travel is far cheaper and faster than the alternatives.

The peoples of the Five Rivers are divided into three kingdoms, Tjibarr, Yigutji and Gutjanal. Each of these kingdoms grew out of a founding city which gave each kingdom its name. Each of these founding cities has been given a more descriptive name to distinguish them from their realm: Tjibarr of the Lakes, Yigutji of the Eagles, and Gutjanal of the Clay. The Five Rivers is also divided into speakers of three main languages, Gunnagal, Biral and Wadang. Despite these divisions of language and politics, the ease of transportation and strong trade links means that in many ways the Five Rivers form a common cultural zone.

* * *

In the Classical period of the Nyalananga peoples, the place which would someday become the great city of Gutjanal was a village of no particular consequence in the great kingdom of Gundabingee. After the Imperial conquest, the site of Gutjanal was chosen as a suitable site for a Biral garrison-colony.

This location offered several advantages. Gutjanal was in the low foothills of the Spine, toward the limit of where even small boats could sail up the Nyalananga. It was well-placed as a point for collection and basic processing for the timber and sweet peppers harvested from further upriver. It also made a useful place to watch for potential revolt in conquered Gundabingee.

Gutjanal gradually grew in prominence throughout the Imperial era. It operated as an urban centre that both processed and supported the work of people living upriver. Many of its population worked in the saw pits where logs that were floated downriver were riven and cut into boards. In turn, this supported a thriving manufacturing base of shipbuilders, carpenters and other woodworkers. Gutjanal also operated several bronze foundries, where copper mined further upriver was smelted with tin brought from downriver and turned into bronze. In turn, this bronze was used for tools both within the urban industries and for the lumberjacks and miners who lived upriver. The waste wood from the saw pits also made convenient fuel for the foundries.

Gutjanal also had another resource which its inhabitants learned to exploit: clay. Abundant deposits of clay could be found both at Gutjanal and at other places along nearby tributary rivers. These clays were suitable for making into fine ceramics. While pottery had been made along the Nyalananga for millennia, this was porous earthenware which could not hold liquids properly without glazing. With the abundant timber for fuel and examples from metalworkers of how to build hotter fires, the potters of Gutjanal learned to build more efficient kilns which allowed clay to be fired into stoneware. These fine ceramics were impermeable to liquids, harder than earthenware, and regarded as being of higher quality. Gutjanal stoneware grew to be exported throughout the Five Rivers and sometimes beyond. These ceramics were useful for storing the myriad aromatic compounds such as incenses and resins made elsewhere in the Five Rivers, and also prized for their aesthetic qualities.

With these thriving industries, Gutjanal quickly outgrew its origins as a Biral colony. While the Empire maintained a garrison, the majority of the city's population were Wadang speakers who lived in the surrounding Upper Nyalananga.

Over time the garrison were largely assimilated until they thought of themselves as belonging to Gutjanal rather than the Empire. When broader Imperial authority crumbled in the mid-eleventh century AD, Gutjanal's local governor Julanoon found it convenient to declare himself a monarch of a new kingdom. He already spoke better Wadang than Biral, so his new kingdom adopted a new language of administration but otherwise had a great deal of continuity.

Gutjanal has been the capital of an independent kingdom ever since.

* * *

The city of Yigutji was founded during the Classical era of the Nyalananga kingdoms. Yigutji was formed as a small colony of ethnic Biral who moved upriver from the great city of Garrkimang, during the time when Garrkimang was one kingdom amongst four and not yet an empire. The site of Yigutji was founded as one of several upriver agricultural outposts to supply food for the growing city of Garrkimang further downstream. It marked a location where the Matjidi could be conveniently forded, but otherwise had no particular significance and was just one agricultural centre among many.

Like Gutjanal, Yigutji gradually developed into something larger. Its early growth came when the kingdom of Garrkimang started to cultivate *kunduri* at several locations along the Matjidi. Yigutji's alluvial soils were well-suited to growing *kunduri*, although this was true of many locations along the river. Yigutji started to grow as a town because it was the largest town of any size along the Upper Matjidi, and so was the most convenient point to process all of the *kunduri* which had been grown further upriver. Over the Classical era and into the early Imperial period, Yigutji grew into one of the more noteworthy *kunduri* towns.

Yigutji developed further after the domestication of the ribbed case moth (*Hyalarcta nigrescens*) and thus more reliable production of silk. Yigutji was one of five towns along the Matjidi which the Empire designated as silk-producing regions. Silk production was lucrative but labour-intensive, which gradually drew migrants to the city and its hinterland. The trees chosen for moth production were sited further from the river, and the processing into raw silk was conducted in and around those farms. Yigutji functioned as the main centre for silk-weaving into finished cloth.

Even while the Empire shrunk, Yigutji expanded. The lure of *kunduri* and silk meant that by AD 1000, Yigutji had grown into the fifth-largest town along the Matjidi. However, the events which catapulted Yigutji into prominence came from an accident of birth, not from its wealth.

Yigutji was the home city of an ambitious man named Duntroon. Duntroon was born in Yigutji in AD 1079, in the dying days of the Empire. The year after his birth, a series of revolts along the Upper Matjidi meant that these regions broke from imperial rule, reducing the Empire to a shrunken remnant which consisted of little more than the city of Garrkimang and its surrounding agricultural district. The rulers of Garrkimang still claimed the prestigious title of First Speaker, but in their actual authority they were nothing more than a glorified city-state.

At first, the revolts which brought independence to the Upper Matjidi did not produce a unified kingdom, just a loose alliance of city-states who hated the First Speakers only slightly more than they hated each other. Inevitably, that led to squabbling and eventually warfare between the city-states. Duntroon joined Yigutji's armies as a common soldier. Through a combination of luck, tactical sense and personal charisma, he rose through the ranks until he was appointed Yigutji's highest military commander in 1115. The next year, the petty king of Yigutji died – sources differ on whether his death was assisted – and Duntroon claimed the title of king.

Over the next few years, Duntroon united all of the cities of the Upper Matjidi by a combination of battlefield success and adroit diplomacy, so that by 1123 he was the uncontested ruler of a sizeable kingdom. With this accomplishment, he asked the First Speaker of Garrkimang to adopt him as imperial heir. Adoption had been a recognised part of imperial succession for centuries. The First Speaker refused, though again sources differ as to the reason; perhaps pride, perhaps preferring his biological son, or perhaps just dislike of Duntroon.

The long-standing tradition around the office of First Speaker was that it belonged to the imperial family and could not simply be claimed by outsiders. However, Duntroon was not a man who would be casually denied. He is reported to have said, "If I cannot be the next First Speaker, then no-one will be." He invaded Garrkimang the following year and deposed the First Speaker, bringing the Empire to an end.

Duntroon incorporated Garrkimang into his new kingdom, but retained Yigutji as the capital city, since it was his birthplace and he did not want to be overshadowed by the imperial legacy. Yigutji has been the capital of an independent kingdom ever since.

* * *

The Five Rivers kingdoms have a long history of interactions in both peace and in war, and this common history means that they have many cultural similarities, despite differences in other areas. For example, all three kingdoms have a shared medical tradition and respect for physicians. Their physicians travel freely amongst all three kingdoms, even in times of war, and share their knowledge and treatments with each other. These exchanges of knowledge also mean that some non-medical technologies such as distillation have been shared between the three kingdoms.

Similarly, many technologies and customs are shared across the Five Rivers. The three kingdoms have a shared monopoly on production of *kunduri* and silk, both of which are valuable export commodities that are traded across the agricultural regions of Aururia and even into Aotearoa. All three kingdoms similarly have long traditions of fine and skilled metalworking in iron and gold; their arms, armour and jewellery are all of exceptional quality by Aururian standards.

Even when these kingdoms have shared heritage, the details often differ. Tjibarr is renowned for how football has become part of its way of life, with virtually every non-royal adult identifying with one of the football factions. The interrelationships between the factions dominate political and economic life in that kingdom. Similar forms of football are played in both Gutjanal and Yigutji, but in those two kingdoms football is merely a sport; its supporters do not have any wider connection to political and economic life.

Cuisine, too, is an area where the three kingdoms have much in common, thanks to many shared crops that have spread across the Five Rivers, and access to a variety of imported spices. Here, though, the kingdoms have stereotypes of their neighbours. The people of Tjibarr and Yigutji stereotype the cuisine of Gutjanal as relying on the pure heat of sweet peppers, and lacking subtlety. To the people of Gutjanal, the cuisine of Tjibarr and Yigutji is bland and lacks the pleasing numbness created by sweet peppers, which in turn makes other flavours easier to appreciate. Both of these stereotypes have an element of truth. Sweet peppers are more abundant in Gutjanal because of the higher rainfall and closeness to the highlands where sweet peppers grow even more vigorously. But Gutjanal is further from the main trade routes for the more exotic spices, with these needing to pass through either Tjibarr or Yigutji.

In their economic links, too, the three kingdoms have differences in details even when they have much in common. Gutjanal is still known for its production of ever-finer ceramics which are traded throughout the Five Rivers and beyond. Yigutji still produces the greatest quantity of raw silk and is renowned for its finely-woven silk products, although cultivation of silk continues to expand across the three kingdoms. On the whole, Tjibarr produces the most and highest-quality aromatics of perfumes, resins, incense and related products.

In some aspects, the kingdoms of the Five Rivers remain distinctive despite their shared heritage. One of these significant areas is in their political organisation. Although all three kingdoms emerged out of the collapse of the old Empire, they did so in different circumstances. Tjibarr was an old city which had been at the heart of its own kingdom before imperial rule, and retained many of its old political traditions even after regaining independence. Gutjanal and Yigutji were new cities which grew into prominence during the imperial era, and developed their own political traditions during and after the collapse of the Empire.

In its political organisation, Tjibarr is divided into the eight factions. The monarch in Tjibarr is about as far from an absolute monarch as it is possible to get; the Tjibarri kings mostly perform the role of umpire between the factions.

The monarchy in Gutjanal is based more on the absolutist tradition established under imperial rule. The kings of the Julanoon dynasty claim supreme power over all of their subjects. The truth is often far from this claimed ascendancy, depending on both the character of the monarch and the strength of the local aristocracy, but in general the kings of Gutjanal wield far more power than their counterparts in Tjibarr.

The aristocrats in Gutjanal do retain one official power: that of naming the next monarch. The Council of Elders is a body composed of the twenty or so greatest landholders – the number has varied over time – who between them have the authority to name the next monarch. Their choice is by tradition limited to adult males of the Julanoon family. Sometimes this decision is no choice at all, being a mere *pro forma* anointing of the preferred royal heir, but on many occasions the will of the Council does matter. Yet the Council has power only to choose a monarch; it has no authority to remove one.

The monarchy in Yigutji is different again. Where Gutjanal and Tjibarr both have forms of elective monarchy, the monarchy of Yigutji is decided by inheritance or, on one or two unfortunate occasions, by warfare. The king of Gutjanal claims to be an absolute ruler, but the king of Yigutji is much closer to that in truth.

Yigutji's political traditions were first shaped by Duntroon, when he removed the First Speakers but made a deliberate attempt to preserve many of the old imperial institutions and traditions. One of his first proclamations after deposing the First Speakers was to declare that the old Empire had been corrupted, but that Yigutji was where the best part of the Empire would be preserved.

Within Yigutji the monarch explicitly retains the privilege of speaking first at any event, and the customs and ceremonies associated with the monarchy are likewise a continuation of those developed in imperial times. More substantially, the monarch of Yigutji claims supreme political and religious authority; while there is an aristocratic class in the kingdom, it has very little effective political power and is subordinated to the monarch and royal officials.

In their views on religion there are likewise significant differences between the three kingdoms. In Tjibarr and Gutjanal, the majority of the people continue to follow traditional Gunnagalic beliefs. These are not a codified religion but a group of related beliefs within a shared conceptual universe, with a variety of religious ceremonies and practices being observed by individuals or families.

In both of these kingdoms, Plirite minorities have become part of the social fabric. In Tjibarr there are different Plirite schools associated with different factions, particularly the Blues where following their school of Plirism is expected. In Gutjanal, Plirism has become largely assimilated into their traditional religion, to the point where later scholars will refer to the religion of Gutjanal as Pliro-Gunnagalism. Several kings of Gutjanal have individually converted to Plirism and followed its practices, but none have tried to impose widespread conversion on their people.

In Yigutji, religion is considerably more distinct. Duntroon and his successors imported the old religious tradition of the First Speakers being the ones who interpreted the cosmos. The monarch of Yigutji is regarded as having a direct connection to the cosmos and to its divine beings. Proclamations from the king of Yigutji have the full force of both religious and political authority.

The priestly system of Yigutji is also highly structured. In Tjibarr and Gutjanal the priestly classes effectively answer only to themselves. In Yigutji, the different priestly groups have codified doctrines and are organised under the control of the monarchy. There is a system of recognised temples which receive royal patronage, with any private temples being strongly discouraged. There are a few small Plirite groups within the kingom, which are tolerated provided that they do not proselytise too openly.

Still, of all of their traits, perhaps the most notable is their shared history of warfare. Gutjanal, Tjibarr and Yigutji have been both allies and enemies many times over the centuries. These shifting alliances are influenced not just by developments within the Five Rivers, but with the Yadji to the south.

Gutjanal and Tjibarr have a long history of warfare with the Yadji. Both kingdoms have been at war with the Yadji for almost as many years as they have been at peace. In both cases, the prize being contested is lucrative border territory. With Tjibarr that means the valuable trade through Jugara and the wealthy Copper Coast beyond, while with Gutjanal the prize is some fertile agricultural land and the gold mines which lie near the ever-shifting border.

Of course, for all that they have the Yadji as a common enemy, Tjibarr and Gutjanal have fought many wars between themselves. The prize there has been the verdant, wealthy lands along the Nyalananga and its side channels.

The borders between Tjibarr and Gutjanal often shift with the fortunes of war.

In these shifting alliances, Yigutji's role has often been the deciding factor. Yigutji has seldom held long-term alliances with any of the other states. On the occasions when Tjibarr and Gutjanal are at war with the Yadji, Yigutji has often made common cause with the Regents. On the occasions when Tjibarr and Gutjanal are at war with each other, Yigutji might support one or the other or remain neutral. On very rare occasions, Yigutji has fought alongside both Tjibarr and Gutjanal in wars with the Yadji; this has usually been when the Yadji hold enough of the Copper Coast that Yigutji deems them too great a threat.

* * *

So in 1618, the Five Rivers remains a region which has much in common, and much that is distinct among the three kingdoms. As a region it is the wealthiest part of Aururia, but it is about to be exposed to cultures who are even wealthier. It remains to be seen how successfully the three kingdoms can face this new challenge, and whether they will be able to do so together or whether they will continue their warfare amongst themselves.

#20: Among The Seven Sisters

History calls this country the Eyre Peninsula, a triangular block of land jutting out into the waters of the Great Australian Bight. A thinly-populated country named for one of the first Europeans to venture there; a land known mostly for its agricultural fertility and for the seafood collected from around its shores. A land with abundant mineral reserves, including some of the highest quality iron ore in the world, which was used to form the steel for the oddly-shaped bridge which is the most well-known landmark in Australia.

Allohistory calls it the Seven Sisters. A region named for a probably-legendary group of seven women who were the first farmers to move into the land. A small region of agriculturally productive land which is separated by barriers of desert and water from other farming peoples. A region which in terms of agriculture, population and wealth has always been on the fringes of the much wealthier and much more populous lands further east.

The people who dwell in the Seven Sisters call themselves the Mutjing. They consider this land their eternal possession, and claim that no other humans ever dwelt there before them, only mythological beings. Later archaeologists will deny that claim; abundant surviving evidence shows that hunter-gatherers dwelt in the Seven Sisters long before farming. But it is clear that the Mutjing have dwelt in the Seven Sisters for a very long time, since well before the beginning of recorded history.

* * *

As with most farming peoples in Aururia, the tale of the Mutjing begins with the Great Migrations; the era when Gunnagalic-speaking peoples were spreading over much of the continent. The region which would come to be called the Seven Sisters was amongst the most isolated target of these migrations. The Seven Sisters is only a fertile land in its southern half. The northern half of the peninsula is covered with dry desert, with minimal water even for travellers, let alone productive agriculture. The waters of the Turtle Gulf [Spencer Gulf] provided their own form of isolation too; the early Gunnagalic peoples were not seafarers in any meaningful way.

The ancestors of the Mutjing were among the many peoples displaced during the Great Migrations. Later archaeologists will speculate endlessly about whether the Mutjing came to the Seven Sisters by land or by sea; the land route is considered extremely diffucult, while the sea route is considered unlikely because there is minimal evidence of seafaring.

As it happens, the land route is the true answer. The forefathers and foremothers of the Mutjing had heard enough tales from the hunter-gatherer peoples to know that the Seven Sisters existed, and of the difficulties of reaching it. The chaos of the Migration era meant that the isolation of the Seven Sisters was extremely appealing; the further that the Mutjing could get away from their former neighbours, the happier they would be. So they risked the privations of a desert migration for what they believed would give them security.

In that judgement, the ancestors of the Mutjing were largely proved correct for a long time. The Seven Sisters remained a land apart for a very long time. They were organised into city-states and had no larger system of political organisation. They farmed the land, fished the coastal waters and occasionally fought amongst themselves, but they had limited interactions with the peoples further east. Over time, they learned to build small boats which they used for fishing and very occasional contact with the peoples on the eastern side of the Gulf. Since neither their boatbuilding nor navigation were very advanced, such contact remained quite limited.

Isolated behind their shields of desert and water, the Mutjing were for a long time spared from the expansive conquests which marked the rise of the Watjubagan Empire. The Empire went through its largest period of expansion from AD 588-822, and during that era the Mutjing were never contemplated as targets for imperial conquest. The Mutjing were isolated enough that they did not even face the common imperial "requests" for tribute from peoples near the borders of the Empire. They had some occasional contact with the imperial outpost at Dogport where they traded for opals, but otherwise they were still largely left alone.

The Mutjing's isolation came to an abrupt end in 916 when Tjangal took the throne in distant Garrkimang. Tjangal was a young prince who had seen the Empire humiliated during his childhood, with the subject peoples of the Junditmara and Patjimunra both successfully breaking away from imperial rule in the last couple of decades. Tjangal believed that the Empire had lost its sense of purpose, and that new conquest was needed to restore the faith of the people. As First Speaker, he chose as his target the only remaining independent agricultural region which had never been part of the Empire but where conquest was at least potentially possible.

The imperial campaign to conquer the Seven Sisters lasted a decade, from AD 917 to 926. The Empire was declining, but when compared to the Mutjing it still had effectively inexhaustible manpower. The Mutjing city-states were outnumbered and technologically outmatched. They had no history of co-operation that might have enabled them to work together to repel the imperial armies, and even if they had combined their armies, they would still have struggled to maintain their independence. Their only defence was to withdraw behind their city walls and hope that the Empire lost patience with the sieges.

With Tjangal as First Speaker, the Empire would never run out of patience. The Mutjing city-states capitulated one by one, with the last to fall being Luyandi [Port Kenny] in the far northwest of the Seven Sisters. Tjangal had his conquest, though it did not bring him satisfaction for long; he died of suspected food poisoning in 930. The Empire rotted quickly after his successors; within two decades of his death imperial rule was effectively over everywhere outside of the Five Rivers heartland, the Copper Coast, and the recently-conquered Seven Sisters. The Mutjing city-states rose in rebellion in the late 960s, killing or expelling all imperial colonists. A brief reconquest attempt between 972-4 failed, and the Seven Sisters remained independent from that time onward.

For the Mutjing, imperial conquest cost them much in short-term bloodshed, but brought some longer-term benefits. The imperial administration introduced writing, transplanted a greater range of crops (though not the imperial monopolies of silk and *kunduri*), and encouraged greater economic links between the Seven Sisters and the Copper Coast. The post-imperial Mutjing were no better boat-builders than they had been before imperial rule, but now that that they knew that profits could be made, they traded by sea (and occasionally by land) with the peoples of the Copper Coast. And, in time, with the Island.

* * *

When the first Europeans come to visit southern Aururia, they will view the Nangu as the pioneers and master shipbuilders, thanks to their maritime trading network which stretches around the southern half of the continent. What will be less obvious, however, is that the Nangu would never have developed into what they became without the resources of the Seven Sisters to fuel their growth.

The Nangu and Mutjing had been making sporadic visits to each other since time immemorial; both peoples were capable of building boats and sailing between their two lands, which were not too far apart. Of the two, however, the Island had more advanced shipbuilding techniques, originally developed for them to enter the tin and bronze trade with the Cider Isle further east.

From about AD 1050 onward, Nangu trading-captains started to visit Pankala [Port Lincoln] regularly enough to appear in the records of that city. They were attracted by one commodity above all: salt. The Mutjing in Pankala and several other coastal towns had long produced salt by evaporation at coastal ponds. The Island had more difficult geography which made it harder to establish salt ponds, and the Nangu found it convenient to trade with Pankala to obtain salt to use as both flavouring and preservative.

From that time onward, the Mutjing and the Nangu had ever-strengthening trade links. Salt remained a core part of that trade, with Mutjing salt being sold on via Jugara and the Yadji ports for distribution inland. Over time, as the Island's population expanded, it also came to rely on food imported from the Mutjing; the Seven Sisters were referred to quite accurately as "the granary of the Island." As the Island gradually used up its convenient lumber sources, the Nangu also turned to the Seven Sisters as a supply of timber and, sometimes, as a place for shipbuilding.

Contact with the Nangu also brought the faith of Plirism to the Seven Sisters. The Nangu converted *en masse* to Plirism in AD 1240, and they soon became enthusiastic missionaries in seeking to spread their faith through their trade contacts with their neighbours, including the Mutjing. In turn, the Mutjing gradually converted to the new faith. This conversion was a combination of pragmatism and genuine belief. Some Mutjing converted because they accepted the message of the Sevenfold Path. Others converted because it gave them access to better trade opportunities; the Nangu preferred to trade with fellow Plirites because that meant trade contracts would be more likely to be honoured.

* * *

In 1618, the Mutjing of the Seven Sisters are a people united in faith but divided in politics. They have virtually all converted to Plirism, but they remain as politically divided as ever. The Mutjing are ruled by what they call city-kings, who rule from the larger cities and contest with each other for control over the smaller towns and surrounding lands. As a result, the Mutjing city-kings are in a state of intermittent low-level warfare with each other for territory.

These wars rarely escalate into peninsula-wide warfare, due to the influence of the Island. The Seven Sisters are under the loose colonial hegemony of the Nangu. The Nangu control is partially religious and partially economic. Trade with the Nangu and the wealth they can bring is essential to the power of the city-kings, since it is what enables them to pay for their wars and maintain their status. The religious authority of the Island is equally strong, with senior Nangu priests being well-respected in the Seven Sisters as mediators of disputes and promoters of harmony. Between these twin pillars of influence, the Nangu can usually steer the Seven Sisters away from full-scale warfare.

All of the greatest Mutjing city-states are on the coast because that gives the best access to trade with the Nangu; while there are a few mid-sized towns inland, these are all in one way or another subject to the control of the coastal city-kings. The relative power of the city-kings has varied over time, with some diminishing and new rulers emerging at different ports. As of 1618, the most powerful city-kings are Pankala, Yorta [Coffin Bay], Munmee [Cowell], Luyandi [Port Kenny], Nilkerloo [Elliston] and Yarroo [Port Neill]. A dozen lesser city-kings also rule at some coastal and inland cities, usually in formal or informal dependency on the greater six.

The old semi-isolation of the Seven Sisters has long since faded. The Mutjing are an integral part of the trade links which span southern Aururia. Most of their exports remain raw materials; the old staples of food, salt and timber have been joined by lesser quantities of copper, dyes and spices.

The other common export is people. Mutjing priests frequently travel to the Island to study, and often to other Plirite temples within the Five Rivers and Copper Coast. Individual Mutjing often sojourn or permanently emigrate as workers to the Island or other places within its colonial influence. Many of the sailors on Nangu ships or timber workers on the Cider Isle are Mutjing by birth, though only rarely do they rise to be trading-captains of ships.

Notably, the Mutjing also export soldiers. Many of the Mutjing are military veterans, thanks to their regular warfare. In times of peace, or just when lured by wealth from abroad, Mutjing soldiers have often operated as mercenaries. The Island has long made extensive use of them as bodyguards, or occasionally to intervene in disputes between some of the peoples of the east coast of Aururia. Sometimes the request for Mutjing mercenaries has come from other peoples; the Tjunini and Kurnawal of the Cider Isle often request Mutjing mercenaries when their wars grow bitter, and some of the eastern coast peoples who have converted to Plirism have also sought Mutjing mercenaries to aid in their own struggles.

So, in 1618 the Mutjing are a thriving people. With the coming of the Raw Men, however, the Seven Sisters will find themselves with a new challenge. For if the Europeans sail east of the Atjuntja realm, the next agricultural people they will encounter will be the Mutjing. The Mutjing will need to decide how to balance their desire for harmony with the Nangu with the new opportunities and threats which the Europeans will bring.

#21: My Highland Home

Aururia is the flattest and most low-lying continent in the world. It has few mountains, and most of those are hills in comparison to those on other continents, or even those on the failed continent whose highest regions rise above the waves to form Aotearoa.

Yet Aururia does have a few highland regions. The largest of these is the region which another history will call the Monaro and Errinundra plateaus. Nestled below the highest peaks on the continent, these highlands are the source of the largest rivers in Aururia, the Nyalananga and Matjidi. The height of these peaks catches enough rainfall and winter snowfall so that the Nyalananga and Matjidi, unlike many Aururian rivers, almost never run dry.

The reliability[102] of the Nyalananga meant that, over thousands of years, the dwellers alongside its banks were able to gradually domesticate one plant that they found there: the red yam. The slow, unconscious process of domestication meant that those lowland dwellers became semi-sedentary, and then in time they domesticated an entire package of crops. They became pioneering farmers. In time, their descendants would expand over much of the continent, bringing their crops and languages with them, and displacing the hunter-gatherers who formerly lived in those regions. Their crops would spread even further, to the south-west of Aururia, and to Aotearoa.

---

[102] Always a relative term when describing Aururian waterways.

The highlands, though, were another matter. The key crop of lowland agriculture was the red yam. While that plant gave excellent yields in the lowlands, it required a long growing season for best results. It could tolerate snow cover during winter, but it needed a reasonably early melt in spring to start its growth. The altitude of the highlands meant that the early varieties of red yams could not get reliably established there.

Despite several attempts, early Gunnagalic farmers could not maintain themselves in the highlands. Some migrants passed through the highlands to the low-lying coastal regions beyond, but they could not remain in the high country. For several centuries after farming was spreading across lowland Aururia, the highlands remained the preserve of hunter-gatherers who spoke other languages: Nguril and Kaoma.

Farming came late to the highlands, and largely through a stroke of chance. The red yam was the earliest and most important root crop in the lowlands, but not the only one they cultivated. Murnong is another staple Aururian root crop, whose above ground growth looks like a dandelion, but which produces edible tubers. The plant is more tolerant of cold than red yams, and there is an alpine-adapted variety of wild murnong which already grew in the highlands. In the upper Matjidi valley, a chance cross-breeding between a domesticated lowland murnong and a wild upland murnong produced a new strain of murnong, one which was suitable for farming even in the highlands.

The spread of upland murnong was slow; after all, it did not form a complete agricultural package. But cultivation of murnong allowed the highland dwellers to become hunter-gardeners, with food storage letting them support an increased population. Cold-adapted versions of wattles followed over the next couple of centuries, together with several supplementary crops such as scrub nettles for leaves and fibre, and different strains of flax which yielded either large edible seeds or fibre. With these, the Nguril and Kaoma had adequate crops to become mostly sedentary farmers. Eventually, a cold-adapted version of the red yam was added to their farming package, but this occurred a couple of centuries after the highlanders were already farmers.

While the Nguril and Kaoma had adopted farming, their agriculture was never as productive as that of the lowlands. The red yam had been adapted to a shorter growing season at the cost of a smaller tuber. The most important staple remained the lower-yielding murnong. The soils of the uplands were poorer, too. Farmers they were, but bountiful farmers they were not; they continued to gather more in the way of wild foods than lowlanders. Agricultural surpluses were smaller, and the population density was always lower than in the Five Rivers lowlands.

The character of agriculture led to vastly different societies for highlands and lowlands. In the lowlands, large agricultural surpluses were combined with convenient riverine transport networks. The agricultural surpluses allowed a significant proportion of the lowland population to be non-farming specialists, while the ease of moving food by water allowed those specialists to live in several large cities and towns.

In the highlands, not only were agricultural surpluses smaller, they were less reliable from year to year. Without water transport or any beasts of burden other than dogs, moving food around was slow and expensive, and famines more common. The highlanders thus did not dwell in cities or large towns. They built some small villages where they met seasonally for markets and other commerce, and where a few specialists lived, such as smiths, leatherworkers and the like. But even those specialists would continue their activities from farms as often as not. Those agricultural surpluses which did exist were converted into caches of food held in dispersed locations to protect against crop failures or bushfires. Or, after states emerged in the lowlands, as protection against invasion.

Invasion from the lowlands was a common feature of highland life, though it must be said that in turn, the hill men did plenty of raiding of their own into the lowlands. The states based along the Nyalananga and Matjidi often sent armies into the highlands. The names of those states sometimes changed – the Classical great cities of Gundabingee, Weenaratta and Garrkimang; the Imperial power of Watjubaga; the post-Imperial states of Yigutji and Gutjanal – but the drive into the highlands never seemed to end.

Yet while lowlanders could send armies into the highlands, converting that effort into a successful invasion was another matter. The highlands had no waterways to send food for an invading army, and what the highlanders called roads were nothing but muddy tracks. Nor were there much in the way of real targets to conquer. The highlanders tended to scatter rather than come to pitched battle. Deploying troops into the few small towns was easy enough, but keeping them there for long was nothing but an invitation to starvation when food ran out. Tracking down the caches of food was challenging; the hill men concealed both caches and themselves well.

Invasion of the highlands was further complicated by the different timing of the seasons. The main campaigning season for lowland armies was during the winter. Then, the main root crops had died back to the ground, with their tubers harvested and replanted for the following year. The next harvest, of early-flowering cornnarts, would not begin until late spring. Winter was when food supplies were at their largest and the greatest part of the population could be spared from agricultural duties and levied into armies. But this was the time when snow covered the highlands, making an invasion foolhardy. Any would-be invaders had to wait until late spring, or better yet summer, when they had more reduced manpower and lower supplies of food to bring with them to the highlands.

Time and again, invading armies came to the same conclusion: easy to burn a few towns and farms, declare victory, and then head home; almost impossible to attain a lasting conquest.

* * *

The closest any lowlanders came to conquering the highlands was during the height of the Watjubagan Empire, under the First Speakers. After many previous failures, in the mid-eighth century the imperial armies succeeded in imposing a degree of control over the highlands. In keeping with imperial practice, this largely consisted of demanding tribute from local leaders. Such tribute would be regularly if grudgingly paid when imperial power was strong. But whenever the imperial power weakened due to rebellion, war, civil strife or simply a weak First Speaker, tribute payments ceased quickly, as the local leaders who had been paying tribute either led a revolt or lost their lives to revolts they could not stop. A fresh invasion would be required each time, beginning the difficult process over again. After about a century of intermittent control of the highlands, the imperial armies were pushed out in a rebellion in AD 887, and they would never again have a lasting presence in the highlands.

The final lapse of imperial control over the highlands ushered in an era of the hill-men's favourite pastime: raiding. This was an art form which the highlanders had practised long before the Empire appeared, but which was now encouraged because even the limited imperial rule had given the hill-men a taste for many of the goods available in the lowlands. Acquiring these goods through commerce was difficult for the highlanders. Their only significant export goods were sweet peppers which grew better in the highlands than in the lowlands. However, there were never enough of these to buy everything that the hill-men wanted. Instead, the highlanders often turned to a more ancient form of commerce, that known as "you get what you grab."

The art of raiding was well-suited to the highlanders' social structure, since this form of artistry was one which they practised on themselves as much as on the lowlanders. For the hill-men had some sense of commonality, in that they viewed themselves as separate from the lowlanders, but that did not make them friends. The hill-men gladly raided each other as much as they raided the lowlands.

Highland life was one of frequent raids, or at least the possibility of such raids. This led to a culture where all able-bodied men were expected to carry weapons and know how to use them, and who mostly had experience in carrying out raids or defending against them. This meant that in proportion to their population, the highlanders could mobilise much larger fighting forces than lowlanders, and do so at short notice. And most of those men[103] would be veterans.

Of course, the highlanders could not mobilise such forces for long. The demands of upland agriculture meant that most workers were needed in the fields for much of the year. But as with the lowlands, there was a campaigning season. In the lowlands, this season fell during winter. In the highlands, it was summer. For highland agriculture, early-flowering cornnarts were harvested in late November and early December, and the next harvest of late-flowering cornnarts did not begin until the end of February or early March.

This left a summer campaigning season where the hill-men could mobilise and go raiding. They usually took advantage of that opportunity. The highlanders could not sustain a long-term invasion of the lowlands, but they could and did make many raids.

* * *

Culturally and for the most part genetically, the hill-men are descendants of the old Nguril and Kaoma-speaking hunter-gatherers who slowly took up farming during the era when Gunnagalic speakers were expanding across the continents. As speakers of non-Gunnagalic languages, they are in a

---

[103] Or mostly men, anyway. Highlander women are often familiar enough with weapons to defend themselves on raids, but it is extremely rare for them to be permitted to "take up arms", i.e. to be called to take part on a raid.

distinct minority; only four such languages survived within the region which later history would call Gunnagalia.

The Nguril language, spoken mostly in the northern half of the highlands, is distantly related to the Mungudjimay language, whose speakers live a third of a continent away along the eastern coast. The Kaoma language, spoken mostly in the southern half of the highlands, is a linguistic isolate. No related languages survive; presumably they were swallowed during the Gunnagalic expansion. A couple of later linguists will claim that they find evidence of a Kaoma-related language as a substrate in the Wangalo language in the neighbouring eastern lowlands around Yuin-Bika [Bega, NSW], but those linguists will usually be dismissed as cranks.

Socially, the hill-men were long divided into a complex system of lineages and kinship groupings. These were viewed as being part of shared descent from famous named ancestors (some almost certainly mythical), and sometimes were linked to political leadership, but mostly dictated rules around intermarriage. Men from one lineage were forbidden to seek out wives from the same lineage, but could choose from a set of other acceptable lineages. Usually on marriage a wife was considered to adopt her husband's lineage, but there were provisions for some occasions where a husband would adopt the wife's lineage, such as occasions when a leader of repute had only daughters.

Individual lineages were also considered part of larger kinship groupings, for which the Nguril and Kaoma names are usually translated as "tribes". There were five of these groupings. Intermarriage was usually only permitted between lineages of the same tribe, although there were a few special exceptions where particular lineages had for some historical reason or other[104] allowed intermarriage

---

[104] Usually where a successful warleader had a bastard child with a mistress of another lineage, and still viewed that child as kin, and so arranged a deal where the warleader's own lineage recognised intermarriage with the other given lineage.

with one or two lineages from other tribes. The main reason why the distinction between Nguril and Kaoma languages was preserved was because the two largest tribes were predominantly Nguril speakers, while the remaining three tribes were mostly Kaoma speakers, and intermarriage between them was so restricted that they remained linguistically separate (and mostly genetically, too).

In the late fourteenth century, the hill-men experienced their greatest social change since the end of imperial influence. In that era, the new Yadji Empire was emerging from its feudal predecessor, the Empire of the Lake. That empire had an old military caste, the *briyuna*, who were being forcibly retired from service by the new Yadji Regents [Emperors]. Many of them accepted that retirement, but some refused to give up their old ethos, and fled instead. Most of those exiles ended up in the highlands, where they became part of the hill-men.

The *briyuna* brought with them their own code of appropriate behaviour for warriors. Their ethos had also included the expectation that a *briyuna* would be literate, and they brought that view with them to the highlands. More importantly from the highlanders' perspective, they also brought with them much better knowledge of iron-working, armour and weapons than the hill-men possessed on their own.

The *briyuna* integrated into highland society reasonably well. The intermarriage prohibitions of the highlands applied to their own lineages; lowlanders were outside those lineages, and while there were few examples of intermarriage with lowlanders, they were not forbidden. Many of the *briyuna* found local wives. Even where they did not, their ethos still lived on via the hill-men they taught.

With the *briyuna* influence, the hill-men were still raiders, but they now viewed raiding as being as much for glory and honour as for plunder. The hill-men gradually adopted codes of how a warrior should behave while raiding, although the strictest aspects of those codes applied to raids on other highlanders; the view of which codes applied to lowlanders was much looser. Thanks to *briyuna* influence, the hill-men also acquired a dislike of the Yadji realm, and they gradually increased their raids into imperial territory.

Some of the effects of *briyuna* influence were more symbolic. In their old realm, they adopted a system of banners to mark their allegiance, and as a rallying point in battle. While the hill-men did not adopt banners in the same way – they were of less use in the sort of raids the highlanders preferred – they did adopt a code of symbols for their men, to represent leader and lineage, modelled on the symbols of the old *briyuna* banners.

Politically, the government of the highlands has not changed that much even with the integration of the *briyuna*. The hill-men are mostly organised at the level of a village or small region controlled by a "chief," or respected warleader. Most of the followers of a chief will be of the same lineage, although there are many examples of chiefs who have followers from many lineages, and even sometimes from different tribes.

Given the ever-shifting risks and endemic raiding of the highlands, a successful chief is one who has obtained the most glory in leading raids, and in protecting against raids on his own people. With the *briyuna* ethos gradually permeating the highland psyche, a leader is also viewed as one who behaves appropriately as a warrior, at least when dealing with other highlanders.

Swift indeed is the fate of a leader who fails in raids or becomes perceived as weak. This is an ancient tradition; even during imperial times, a leader who had been forced to concede tribute to the Empire would quickly lose his life if a revolt began and he did not join it. If a chief falls, new chiefs will quickly emerge to replace those who have lost power and life.

The highlands have no enduring political organisation above the level of chief. Sometimes more powerful chiefs manage to impose a level of control on neighbouring chiefs, whether through sheer prestige, or collaboration if lowlander attacks grow more threatening. Such control rarely lasts beyond the lifetime of a given chief, however; the power of a chief relies so much on personal prestige that it seldom transfers to a successor.

* * *

In 1618, the highlanders continue life as they have lived for the last centuries: dwell in their high plateaus and rarely visit the lowlands unarmed. Their separation from the coast and limited interaction with the lowlanders means that they will be among the last agricultural Aururian peoples to hear about the arrival of Europeans, let alone have contact with them. Yet sooner or later, the highland life will be changed with the arrival of Europeans, too.

#22: Children of a Failed Continent

"Te amorangi ki mua, te hapai o ki muri." (The leader at the front and the workers behind the scenes.)
- Māori proverb

* * *

Seven continents provide the large majority of the land surface of the globe. Or six continents, or five, or four, or even eight, depending on who provides the definitions. Regardless of their number, all of the continents have one thing in common: they are composed of masses of ancient rock which are light enough to float above the rest of the earth's crust and provide land above the waves.

One continent, though, is a failure. It is heavy enough and unstable enough that most of its surface does not provide a continental land mass above the ocean waves, but has sunk into the depths below.

A few fragments of that failed continent still project above the surface of the ocean blue. The two largest of these fragments form islands that preserve relicts of ancient times, carrying on their soil plants and animals whose relatives have vanished from most of the rest of the globe.

For this failed continent was, like the other continents of the southern hemisphere, once part of the supercontinent of Gondwana, and some of that ancient landmass's survivors found a new home within these more limited confines. The forests that cover these islands have relatives that persist in other southerly landmasses. The animals that live on these islands are likewise distinctive. None more so than the tuatara, an innocuous three-eyed creature that appears to be a kind of lizard but is in truth the last survivor of an ancient lineage.

The two islands are dominated by mountains that have been raised up recently in geological time, as forces beneath the crust move in new patterns, thrusting up a range of high peaks. Erosion has done much to wear down these new mountains, creating some fertile plains, but much of the geography of these two islands is still marked by these high peaks or other rugged, hilly terrain.

Distant from any neighbouring landmasses, these two main islands and myriad smaller offshore islands were inaccessible for most of human history. Reaching them required mastery of shipbuilding and oceanic navigation, to say nothing of determination.

The first visitors to these islands were the Polynesians, a people who sailed from island to island and explored a third of globe using stone and wood, their wits, and a lot of coconut fibre. To this people of explorers, the smallest of islands was worth fighting over and settling, even tiny outcrops of limestone and coral sand which could not hold permanent fresh water. History does not record, but imagination can supply, their delight at finding the two massive, forest-clad, well-watered main islands of Aotearoa which appeared to be more wealth than should be contained anywhere in the world.

Such a wealth of land must certainly have drawn quick Polynesian settlement, once they were aware of it. The first Polynesians to come here called themselves by various names, but in time they would come to think of themselves as the Māori.

The first settlers built villages which clung to the coast. Their own tropical-suited crops barely grew in these temperate lands, but the early Māori still found food in abundance. Amidst the dark, ancient forests of the interior dwelt the moa, massive flightless birds which provided an abundance of meat for any hunters who sought them. When not hunting moas inland, the early Māori hunted seals – another valued meat resource – and gathered food from the sea, as their forefathers had done since time immemorial.

Acclimatising to this new land of Aotearoa still presented some challenges to the early Māori. The sea voyages to their old islands were long indeed, enough that most domesticated animals could not survive the trip. Their Polynesian forefathers had raised pigs, chickens and dogs, but only the dogs survived the journey to Aotearoa. The kiore [Polynesian rat] came with the first voyagers, too, and quickly established itself on the main islands of Aotearoa, but that provided only a nuisance to the Māori. With only dogs for domesticated animals, the Māori were dependent on the moa and seafood for their protein, which would present problems if the moa were ever hunted out.

In their cultivation of fibre crops, the early Māori were more fortunate. Their traditional fibre crops were coconuts and pandanus, used for ropes and sails among much else, but neither of these plants grew in cooler Aotearoa. This new land offered a more than adequate replacement, however. The plants which they called harakeke and wharariki [New Zealand flax] could be harvested wild, and their leaves yielded a fibre which was superior to anything that the Māori had seen before[105].

With the vast expanse of their new islands, the early Māori did not truly need to keep exploring for new lands; Aotearoa held more wealth than any other land the Māori or their ancestors had found for millennia. Such a tradition

---

[105] Harakeke (*Phormium tenax*) and whararaki (*P. cookianum*), historically known in English as New Zealand flax, provide some of the best natural fibres in the world. The fibres from their leaves can be readily worked into a wide variety of textiles, ropes, sails, and other products, and were a major part of the traditional Māori economy. In historical New Zealand after European contact, the plants would also find willing international customers; the Royal Navy, for instance, traded muskets and other products for ropes of New Zealand flax since it was stronger by weight than their other customary fibres such as hemp.

of exploration, however, would not fade so quickly. A few Māori kept voyaging back and forth to their ancient islands, while more explored in other directions. Their early explorations were largely unsuccessful, finding only other small islands which were of little use to a people who knew the land of Aotearoa[106].

In 1310, the first Māori explorers sailed far enough west to find a land which made Aotearoa seem small, albeit also a land rather dry and fire-prone. Its inhabitants called this land by many names, but the Māori who learned of its seemingly endless expanse called it Toka Moana[107].

In Toka Moana, the early Māori came into contact with people who possessed many arts which their ancestors had lost over the long migrations which brought them to Aotearoa, and had other things which no peoples outside of that island continent had even seen. The Māori kept sailing back and forth between Aotearoa and Toka Moana, gradually exploring more of the country and learning of its peoples, and beginning a process of cultural exchanges which would transform the lives of peoples on both sides of the Grey Sea [Tasman Sea].

To their western neighbours, the early Māori gave some of their own crops, most notably kumara [sweet potato] and taro. They shared, with varying degrees of enthusiasm, some of their knowledge of shipbuilding and navigation. From their western neighbours, Māori explorers and traders acquired crops which were much more suited to their

---

[106] It is not known how long the Māori historically kept up their tradition of exploration and long-range navigation, but it's likely to have been until at least AD 1500, when the Chatham Islands were first settled. The Māori also likely discovered and settled other island groups such as Norfolk Island and the Kermadecs, although those settlements eventually failed.

[107] Originally, toka moana meant a rock which stood firm in the wildest seas, but its meaning evolved to mean a rock so big (ie land) that it took longer to cross than the ocean. To later Māori, the name will usually if somewhat inaccurately be translated as the Land Ocean.

temperate lands, most notably red yams, wattles, murnong, scrub nettles, purslane, and fruits such as muntries and apple berries. They acquired domesticated birds – ducks, noroons [emus] and geese – to provide a protein source to replace the dwindling moa. In time, they acquired many new skills from the westerners, such as knowledge of pottery, bronze working and eventually writing.

After this, the Māori would never be the same again.

* * *

1618: the eve of the first tentative Dutch contact with the western extremities of Toka Moana. On the eastern coast, the Māori of Aotearoa have been visiting Aururia for centuries. The voyage across the Grey Sea is a long one, but shorter than the journeys which brought their ancestors to Aotearoa from distant Hawaiki. What can be found in Toka Moana is certainly worth the travel.

From early in their contact with Toka Moana, the Māori explored much of the eastern coast. They still visit parts of that occasionally, but their main sustained contact has been with the Cider Isle [Tasmania] in the south. Here, they can find the commodity which they prize above all: tin ore. Their own islands lack any meaningful native source of tin, and the arts of iron working have not yet spread far enough east for the Māori to learn to work that metal. Bronze is the metal they know and treasure most; while they have local copper sources, they must import all of their tin from the Cider Isle, or sometimes trade for bronze in its finished form.

To the Cider Isle, then, the Māori come to trade for tin ore, and sometimes for *duranj* [gum cider] and gold, too. In exchange they provide jade, textiles of harakeke and wharariki, and sometimes other goods such as kauri gum or finished crafts. When the Māori visit further north, they mainly trade for spices such as myrtles or sweet peppers, or occasionally for finished bronze goods.

In Aotearoa itself, the demand for all of these goods is high. For there are a great many Māori now; numbers which their ancestors could barely have imagined when they landed their first canoes on Te Ika a Maui [North Island]. Food is abundant, thanks to the crops from Toka Moana. Red yams grow well in Aotearoa, except in the uttermost south, and even then wattles and murnong can be cultivated. The new crops have flourished so well, in fact, that the Māori have abandoned their original crops from Polynesia. What need to grow a kumara through laborious construction of north-facing gardens and end up with a tiny tuber the size of a man's thumb, when a handful of buried red yam seeds will yield tubers the size of a man's forearm?

Likewise, domesticated birds from Toka Moana have become an integral part of Māori life. Noroons, ducks and geese graze their fields, supplying fertiliser and providing a welcome source of meat and eggs. Domesticated quolls were originally brought across to control the pesky kiore. While good at that task, they are also excellent at surviving on their own; quolls have turned feral and destroyed much of the native bird life. Nor are quolls the only species from Toka Moana to cause an ecological catastrophe. Domesticated wattles have spread wild, too; the rapidly growing trees crowd out much of the native flora and transform the landscape into one where many of the native birds can find nothing to eat.

Perhaps the greatest ecological catastrophe came from the Māori themselves, though. Human hunting ravaged many of the native birds, particularly the giant moa. Slow-growing, lacking any familiarity with mammalian predators, the moa made easy targets; the process had been well advanced even before the first Māori visited Toka Moana. At least ten species of the flightless birds dwelt on Aotearoa before human arrival; barely a century later, they had all been hunted to extinction.

In Aotearoa, at least.

For while the Māori exterminated the moa in its native country, they were not the only people to glimpse these massive birds before they vanished from the fragments of the failed continent. In the early days of contact with Toka Moana, some of the westerners took passage on Māori ships and came to visit Aotearoa. Among those visitors was Burrinjuck, the High Chief of the Jerrewa people [who live around Batemans Bay, NSW].

Like most of those visitors, Burrinjuck found the giant moa to be hugely impressive. Also like many of the people of Toka Moana, Burrinjuck had a great passion for hunting; his people preserved large rangelands around their home country which were open for kangaroos to graze and, in turn, be hunted. In common with most visitors, Burrinjuck thought that moa would be excellent for hunting back in Toka Moana.

Unlike most of those visitors, though, Burrinjuck had the authority to do something about his desires. He asked to have stocks of the largest moa [*Dinornis novaezealandiae*] established in his home country, where they might be preserved for hunting. His hosts were willing to accommodate this fancy, in exchange for certain understandings of a bronzed nature, and arranged to capture some young moa chicks and ship them back to Toka Moana.

There, in the Jerrewa lands, Burrinjuck established the moa in his private hunting preserve. A very special preserve, where only the High Chief's kin were permitted to enter, and only the highest class of chiefs were permitted to hunt. Protecting the moa has taken vigorous effort over the generations, but the chiefs of the Jerrewa like their privileges, and enforce the death penalty on any commoner who kills a moa within their hunting grounds. Any moa who wander away from these lands will usually be killed, but within these lands they are well-protected. So a few moa still survive in 1618, one last fragment of Aotearoa preserved across the sea.

* * *

Unlike the true continent which forms its western neighbour, the failed continent of Aotearoa is a well-watered, fertile land. Toka Moana is geologically ancient, with poor, eroded soils and no high peaks; Aotearoa is rugged and often mountainous, and the mountains thrust up by tectonic forces are being continually weathered and their rocks washed down to the plains to enrich the soil. Toka Moana sits firmly in the desert latitudes and is the driest inhabited continent; Aotearoa lies in temperate latitudes with regular chilling winds that bring abundant moisture with them.

The relative benefits of climate and geology can best be summed up thus: in 1618, Aotearoa sustains nearly half the population of Toka Moana in a land surface barely 3.5% of its size. The population density is higher on Aotearoa than virtually anywhere on Toka Moana, except the heartland of the Yadji realm.

Crowded into such a relatively confined land, the Māori have developed what are in many ways more elaborate and more organised social systems than most of the Tauiwi, their counterparts on Toka Moana[108]. With higher population density has come more intense competition for resources; when combined with their ancient traditions inherited from Polynesia, the Māori are in most respects more warlike and hostile to foreigners and each other than the peoples across the Grey Sea. It also allows them to support some social institutions to a much greater degree;

---

[108] Tauiwi, originally *tau iwi* (roughly translated, strangers), is the generic Māori name for the people of Toka Moana. It can be used either as a catch-all for all of the westerners, or simply in cases when the Māori don't know the names of the individual peoples across the Grey Sea. The Māori are quite familiar with the distinction between the three peoples of the Cider Isle, know about the Islanders, but often do not bother to distinguish between the other peoples.

among other things, the Māori make much more use of slavery than the Tauiwi[109].

The heart of Māori social organisation has developed around three levels of relationships which define all Māori's interaction with each other. These are ancient classifications which dated back to the earliest days of settlement in Aotearoa, and which were originally methods of tracing kinship, but which have become more general forms of social structure.

All Māori are first of all members of their local *whanau*, which originally meant extended family, but now generally refers to all of the people who were born or married into a particular locality. Members of the same *whanau* still consider themselves as relatives of a kind, and intermarriage amongst people of the same *whanau* is considered to be incest. All of the warriors who defend a particular region and serve its leader are drawn from the local *whanau*, or sometimes adopted into it.

Every *whanau* is part of a *hapu*, a word which can be variously translated as clan or subtribe. Like the *whanau*, a *hapu* was originally a genealogical term, in this case indicating a more distant but still significant relationship amongst the various *whanau* that it included.

Time and social construction has changed the nature of a *hapu*, though. Now it simply serves as a term for the fundamental political unit of Māori society. All *hapu* are ruled by a prominent leader, usually an accomplished warleader (or sometimes a priest) with his own sworn

---

[109] Slavery does exist in Toka Moana, but it is not a major component of their social systems. Most Tauiwi peoples rely on corvees or other forms of drafted labour for part of the year. Permanent slavery on Toka Moana is generally confined to household domestics and for unpleasant tasks such as mining. Amongst the Māori, who are much more warlike (and thus obtain prisoners) and have a much higher population density (and thus uses for forced labour), slavery is much more common. One of its principal uses is in the harvesting of fibre crops and weaving of textiles, which is a labour-intensive but vital task.

warriors, and who acts as a protector of all the *whanau* who have sworn to him.

Usually the member *whanau* of a *hapu* are close together geographically, since the main function of the *hapu* is to provide mutual defence and cooperation against enemies. They are not always contiguous, however. This is particularly important since individual *whanau* can choose to change their allegiance to the leader of a rival *hapu* within the same *iwi* [tribe or kingdom].

The process of changing *hapu* is part of the broader political and military struggles within Māori society. If the leader of a different *hapu* is deemed to have greater *mana* [standing, reputation, charisma, psychic power], or is a more accomplished warleader, then other *whanau* may choose to transfer their allegiance to his service, and thus gain his protection and hopefully some of the benefit of his *mana*. With raids a common part of Māori life, a warleader who can offer protection is something to be treasured.

The largest political unit in Māori society is the *iwi*. The word can be variously translated as clan or people, but in practice it refers to what amount to Māori kingdoms. An *iwi* is composed of multiple *hapu* who reside in a given region, and who are a people who can trace their descent to named ancestors who reached Aotearoa on one of the ancient canoes. All members of the same *iwi* are thus theoretically related, although in effect they are citizens of the same kingdom. An *iwi* controls a recognised territory, although given the more or less continual warfare of Māori society, the borders of an *iwi* often shift in line with the tides of war.

Leadership at all three levels of Māori society is in theory elective, based on the *mana* of the leader and the acclamation of the people in the next rank. *Ariki* (leaders) are normally chosen for life, although particularly egregious deeds or failure in warfare (those often being synonymous) may see a leader abandoned by his followers; his name cast out and forgotten. A son may succeed a father, but in most kingdoms, this is not guaranteed.

The basic customs and traditions which surround Māori leaders do not vary significantly at each rank. The same word, *ariki*, is used for all leaders, distinguished only by the name of the particular social unit they lead. An *ariki whanau* leads an extended family, an *ariki hapu* leads his group of *whanau*, and an *ariki iwi* is more or less the king. All *ariki* are expected to conduct themselves according to the same social mores and to maintain and build their *mana*.

Each *ariki* draws their power from the same symbolic source, their *marae* or meeting hall, the ritual centre of their leadership. The Māori use the same word to refer to the dwellings of all three ranks of leaders, although naturally the form of the *marae* depends on a leader's power. An *ariki whanau* may simply have a hall at the centre of his *pa* [stockade, fortification], while the *ariki iwi* may have a *marae* which is a palace or a virtual town unto itself.

Regardless of its outward form, each *marae* has one room which always serves the same function: the room which contains the heart stone, the *toka atua* [literally, god stone]. The *toka atua* is the most sacred symbol of a leader's *mana* and power. Traditionally carved from granite or some other hard stone, it will be inscribed with a symbol chosen by the leader's ancestors, and passed down through the generations. All warriors who swear service to a leader do so to this stone, ritually binding themselves to the leader's *mana* and to that of all of his ancestors.

The *toka atua* must be defended above all else; to lose it to an open raid is the greatest possible blow to a leader's *mana*, and one from which few can recover. To have the stone stolen by stealth is shameful, but not an irreparable blow to a leader's prestige, and it may be recovered in kind.

Besides their *marae*, all leaders also maintain one or more *pa* [fortifications]. These defensive structures are essential given the warlike nature of Māori society. All leaders maintain a warband of sworn warriors, and most adult Māori males can use weapons at need, if only a staff, or sometimes a *taiaha*[110]. Lesser leaders will call out their warriors if a greater leader calls, or often go raiding of their own accord. Raids are commonplace, sometimes even within the same *iwi*, although it is rare for leaders of the same *hapu* to raid each other.

Indeed, warfare is an integral part of Māori life, and it is intertwined with their conception of *mana*. That word has many nuances in Māori life: authority, reputation, conduct, prestige, influence, honour, charisma, psychic force. All warriors, and to a lesser degree all Māori men and higher-class women, seek to gain *mana*, and to avoid activities which would weaken their *mana*.

For warriors, demonstration of their *mana* includes a formal list of the deeds which they have accomplished. All sworn Māori warriors have an account of their deeds which is recited on formal occasions during their lives, and ultimately at their funerals. Their mana is also represented in the *moko* which all warriors have carved onto their faces[111]. These designs mark a warrior's *mana*, and particularly accomplished warriors will often have additional *moko* marked on their faces or bodies. Among men, only sworn warriors are permitted to wear *moko*, although some higher-status women are also permitted to use it.

Whether a warrior or not, all Māori acknowledge the central role of *utu*, of reciprocation and balance, in maintaining *mana*. All actions, whether friendly or

---

[110] A *taiaha* is a traditional Māori weapon shaped from hard wood, usually with one end decorated, and the other with a flat, smooth blade. Sometimes this blade will be made from wood, although better-equipped Māori will often use a bronze blade instead. Although visually it is similar to a spear, a *taiaha* is a close-quarters weapon designed to be held with two hands and wielded using short, calculated blocks, thrusts and strikes.

[111] *Moko* is a traditional Māori form of tattooing, where grooves are cut into the skin with chisels and then marked with pigments, rather than the punctures of standard tattooing.

unfriendly, demand an appropriate response. A kind deed should be repaid, in one way or another, and revenge should be sought for hostile actions. This principle brings both benefits and problems for Māori society; kindness is encouraged, but it also brings about a near-endless cycle of revenge between some groups.

In such an often hostile society, various rituals and customs have developed to help maintain some order. Leaders have an essential role to play in maintaining these customs, particularly those involving hospitality rituals. People who first visit the *marae* of a particular leader will usually be invited to go through one of a variety of forms of hospitality rituals, involving exchanges of gifts and stylised challenges from warriors. After going through such a ritual, the participants will be under the protection of the local *ariki*. This means that they cannot be killed without cause, although in some cases the definition of just cause can be very broad.

The hospitality rituals are usually mandatory for the first visit to a new region, but the protection usually holds for further visits, unless the leader explicitly revokes the protection. For leaders of *whanau* and some of the less influential *hapu*, the challenges and other rituals are generally carried out in person by the local *ariki*. For leaders of *iwi* and more prominent *hapu*, the ceremonies will usually be carried out by a relative on behalf of the *ariki*, except for particularly high-status guests.

Of course, no amount of rituals can prevent all forms of hostility, not with warfare a fundamental component of Māori life. The nature of war varies immensely, from minor raids for *mana* or revenge, to larger campaigns to secure prisoners, to major wars to capture resources or territory. Early Māori warfare often involved cannibalism of the fallen, partly as a source of protein but mostly to gain some of the *mana* of the defeated enemy. While the practice is much rarer in modern Māori society, ritual cannibalism is still sometimes part of contemporary warfare, traditionally involving consumption of the heart and arms of defeated warriors.

* * *

In 1618, while centuries of warfare have led to some political consolidation, the Māori are still divided into a number of competing *iwi*. They are often hostile to strangers even within their own *iwi*, and extremely wary of visitors from other *iwi*. Their default attitude to foreign visitors is similarly hostile. The only people who visit them with any regularity are the Islanders, some of whom have succeeded in gaining protection. The Māori still have a few sporadic visitors from Polynesia, and the occasional very lost ship from westerners who had been meaning to sail up or down their own east coast.

The Māori themselves still keep up their own trading contacts with the Cider Isle, and some Islanders have occasionally found it profitable to bring tin, bronze or *kunduri* to Aotearoa[112]. Bronze is by far the good most in demand in this trade, since the Māori supply of the metal is ultimately dependent on imported sources.

Fortunately for the Māori, bronze is an alloy which can be almost endlessly recycled and reforged for new purposes. The Māori are assiduous in their pursuit of collecting abandoned or damaged bronze objects for reforging; the metal is too valuable to be allowed to go to waste. One of the privileges of controlling a battlefield in victory is to scavenge for abandoned or damaged arrowheads, spearheads, shields or armour and reclaim it. So while the Māori do not import much tin in any given year – the sea lanes are long, after all – they have accumulated a significant amount of bronze over the centuries.

---

[112] Islander visits are uncommon both because of the distance, and because the Nangu trading network is centred on the Island itself. Most of their goods are brought back to the Island to be exchanged there, except for short-distance trips such as between the Cider Isle and the Yadji realm.

So determined are they in their recycling, in fact, that future archaeologists will find precious little evidence of bronzeworking amongst the Māori, finding mostly abandoned tools of copper or stone. This will lead to vigorous scholarly debate about how extensive the Māori use of bronze was during the precontact period.

The same Islanders who occasionally export bronze to Aotearoa have also sometimes tried to export Plirism to the Māori. This has met with only modest success. Only two of the western *iwi*, the Te Arawa [in Westland, South Island] and Ngati Apa [in Taranaki, North Island][113] have significant numbers of Plirite converts, and even then not a majority. No Māori *ariki iwi* has yet accepted the faith, although a few *ariki hapu* have done so.

The Māori's own religion is derived from that of their eastern Polynesian ancestors, centring on their belief in the interrelatedness and common descent (*whakapapa*) of all life, and its links to the gods and heroes of legend. This link to the past is part of what gives a Māori his or her *mana*, and any Māori of status can recite their genealogy back to one or more ancestors who sailed from Hawaiki, or from other great figures[114].

Some of these figures include: Tangaroa, who personifies the seas and is the origin of all fish; Tane, who embodies the forest and is the origin of all birds; Kupe, who in some traditions first explored Aotearoa; and Kawiti, who in most

---

[113] The names of the *iwi* listed here all existed historically, being peoples who still existed at the time of historical European contact. The changed patterns of warfare and migration, though, mean that they inhabit different areas than they did historically.

[114] Although whether these genealogies are accurate is far from certain. Even where there have been no creative interpolations, literacy did not spread immediately to the Māori. While modern Māori have written records of their genealogy, in written form these usually do not go back much over a century.

traditions was the discoverer of Toka Moana[115]. With this link to the past an essential part of their *mana*, relatively few high-status Māori have been willing to adopt the new faith of Plirism, for fear of angering their ancestors and breaking the sacred connection.

For all their hostility to outsiders and ambivalent views of foreign religion, the Māori in 1618 may soon find themselves exposed both to more outsiders and another religion.

---

[115] Whether Kupe and Kawiti are genuine historical figures will be the source of much scholarly argument. The Māori lacked writing when settling Aotearoa, and neither the Māori nor the Raduru (the people they first contacted in Toka Moana) had writing at the time of contact. Regardless of their historicity or non-historicity, Kupe and Kawiti remain important cultural figures among the Māori.

#23: Content To Lie In the Sun

Imagine, if you would, that you can step into a machine unparalleled in the history of the world. One which can travel not only back in time, but into worlds that history has sidestepped, where the river of time has followed a new course. The worlds of if.

If you could step through such a machine, you would find a place which the history you know calls south-eastern Queensland, but in allohistory is called the Coral Coast[116]. This is a narrow band of coastal lands east of the continental divide [the Great Dividing Ranges], fringed by warm seas. With a subtropical climate, the Coral Coast is a land of frequent sun, lush plant growth, more fertile soils and heavier rainfall than most parts of this driest of inhabited continents. Sometimes the rains fall so heavily that the coastal rivers rise in quick, devastating floods.

While long inhabited by hunter-gatherer peoples, the first Gunnagalic-speaking farmers arrived here during the Great Migrations, around 500 BC, and began to gradually dominate this land. The process of displacing the earlier peoples was slower and less complete than in most other areas touched by the Great Migrations; there were still hunter-gatherers living in parts of the Coral Coast over four hundred years after the first Gunnagalic farmers arrived.

---

[116] The Coral Coast corresponds roughly to the historical regions of Gold Coast, Moreton Bay and Sunshine Coast in south-eastern Queensland, although it stretches slightly further north and south.

The land which these ancient farmers established was in some ways welcoming, in others restricted. The mountains to the west were both a barrier to exploration and a defence against other newcomers; beyond them lay the sweeping, thinly-populated region called the Neeburra [Darling Downs]. To the east lay the sea, at this time untouched by any other people. Further south along the coast dwelt the Mungudjimay, a people who would later develop into head-hunting raiders, but who at this time were largely inward-looking. Further south inland were the highlands which formed ancient Aururia's key source of tin for bronze-working. To the north lay warmer lands where their ancient staple crops of red yams and murnong could not grow[117].

These early farmers gradually evolved into the people who called themselves the Kiyungu. Located at the northernmost extremity of Gunnagalic farming, they were for a long time largely insulated from developments further south; one later scholar of the Kiyungu famously remarked, "History mostly passed them by."

The Kiyungu were never completely isolated, of course. Long ago, they learned to sail the coast further north to places where they could dive for corals, which served as a valuable trade good both within Kiyungu society and when trading further south. Their proximity to the sources of tin meant that they had abundant bronze tools. From their hunter-gatherer predecessors, they acquired a belief in the veneration of the bunya tree, and both the belief and the tree itself would spread south along the trade routes[118].

---

[117] Red yams do not grow in tropical latitudes due to insufficient shortening of days to trigger their tuber formation. Murnong is too heat-sensitive to grow so far north, except in highland areas (which this region mostly lacks).

[118] The bunya tree (*Araucaria bidwillii*) produces erratic but large yields of edible seeds. Its veneration is an ancient phenomenon, and the occasions when it produces seeds are times for celebration among the Kiyungu.

Still, for so long the Kiyungu were a people content mostly to live under the subtropical sun, divided into city-states which squabbled amongst themselves. With mountains to the west and hunter-gatherers to the north, they did not have any major external enemies, and they were not very warlike. In their distant location, they were protected from the greatest changes that affected the south; the Empire never reached this far, and the ancient Kiyungu were only barely aware of its existence.

Change first came to the Kiyungu through political and religious developments among their neighbours. The Mungudjimay to the south gradually consolidated into the kingdom of Daluming, and began to expand their head-hunting raids, which started to touch the Coral Coast around AD 1300. Soon after, the followers of Tjarrling spread to the Yalatji who lived beyond the western mountains, and some of those peoples made religiously-inspired visits further east, including some missionaries-in-force.

Fresh inspiration came to the Kiyungu around this time, too, with the first visits from Māori explorers around 1350. These contacts were few and did not endure, since the Kiyungu lands were distant even by Māori navigators' standards, and the two peoples had no goods which the other valued enough to sustain long-term trade.

Still, they had one important effect. Of all the Aururian peoples, the Kiyungu were the keenest sailors apart from the Nangu, and had a strong interest in the Māori vessels. Like the Nangu before them, the Kiyungu adopted lateen sails, twin-hulled ships and some knowledge of navigational techniques. Unlike the Islanders, the Kiyungu did not develop these techniques much further, since their interest was initially limited to better ships for reaching the coral reefs to the north, and for more reliable fishing.

The greatest change which came to the Kiyungu was not from politics or religion, but from the appearance of new, tropically-viable staple crops. The initial contact with the Māori was limited enough that the two peoples did not exchange crops, but the Māori's crops of kumara [sweet potato] and taro were adopted by peoples further south. These crops gradually spread north along the coast, reaching the Kiyungu around 1450.

About half a century before that, a new crop had appeared of its own accord in Kiyungu fields: a new form of yam. It was smaller than the common yams, and needed to be cultivated through cuttings, since at first it did not develop seeds. The Kiyungu never noticed that it needed more rainfall, too; that was not a problem in the lands along the Coral Coast.

What mattered to the Kiyungu was that they found that these new yams were easy to grow without the stunting problem that sometimes troubled their common yams. That gave them reason to grow it, and this motivation only increased when they realised that the lesser yam could be grown further north, too. There was, in fact, no apparent limit to where it could be cultivated.

The first lesser yams were planted further north in small fields adjacent to ports, to provide food for the ships of coral-divers. But it would not take long for the Kiyungu to find motivation to plant them even further north. This motivation, too, would only increase when kumara and taro reached the Kiyungu.

* * *

When it comes time for future linguists, anthropologists and other -ists to study the Kiyungu, they will note that these are in many ways the most distinctive of all the Gunnagalic peoples, in their language, their religion, and their broader culture.

Linguists will note that the Kiyungu still speak a language related to the other members of the Gunnagalic language family. Nevertheless, its grammar, vocabulary and even phonology differ significantly from its linguistic cousins. While the majority of its words and grammatical features have equivalents elsewhere, a significant minority of its basic words have no equivalent in other Gunnagalic languages. Most notably, most word roots relating to water, boats and fishing are unique to the Kiyungu, as are many words related to hunting. Even the names of many familiar animals have changed; most Gunnagalic languages have related words for animals such as kangaroos and wombats, but the Kiyungu words are distinct.

This shift in vocabulary will be inferred (correctly) by future linguists to be the result of a substratum of word roots which have been borrowed from a now extinct language or languages; the peoples who lived along the Coral Coast before the ancestors of the Kiyungu reached there.

Most Gunnagalic peoples displaced their predecessors during the Great Migrations, but the less effective agriculture in the north meant that the early Kiyungu mingled much more considerably with the previous inhabitants. This included a substantial portion of their vocabulary, particularly that which related to hunting and fishing.

The intermingling of peoples influenced the Kiyungu in other notable ways, particularly religion and social structures. Later scholars of Gunnagalic studies would note that the Gunnagalic peoples share more than just a common ancestral language; they have also inherited some significant common social structures and, in many cases, common religious beliefs. The ancient social divisions into *kitjigal* were represented in one form or another in most later Gunnagalic peoples. The Kiyungu, however, preserved no trace of those ancient institutions; a sign that their social system had been influenced by other cultures. Likewise, their own tradition of mentorship with Elder Brothers and

Elder Sisters[119] found no comparison amongst other Gunnagalic peoples.

For religious beliefs, students of comparative mythology would later note the common deities and common myths believed by many of the Gunnagalic peoples. Many scholars could compare equivalent gods (including similar forms of their names), identify the ancestral forms, and recognise the places were earlier myths were adapted into later structures.

The Kiyungu mythology would be amongst those which later scholars would identify as having many points of comparison with other Gunnagalic peoples. However, they would also note one significant feature which is unique to the Kiyungu, and which they will again assume (correctly) to be the result of non-Gunnagalic influence.

While most of the Kiyungu deities were recognisably derived from ancient Gunnagalic beliefs, none of them had related names to their Gunnagalic counterparts. Most of the deities had common attributes and myths, but their names were distinct. Instead of related names, Kiyungu deities have titles which sound as if they were originally used as euphemisms or praise-names, with the original names for the deities later being lost. To the Kiyungu, the Rainbow Serpent is called the Curved One, the Twins (or Fire Brothers) are called Firstborn and Secondborn, while the Green Lady is called the Wanderer. By comparing the changes in the Kiyungu language, scholars are able to identify the original Kiyungu names for these deities, but the

---

[119] This institution of mentorship in the Kiyungu involves an older man (or more rarely, woman) taking on responsibility as the guardian, guide and lover of a younger person of the same gender. The Kiyungu view this as the best way for a person to learn about love, life, proper values, and social order. It usually involves teaching a valuable craft skill, too. The formal role as Elder Brother or Elder Sister ends when the younger is deemed ready for marriage, although the elder party will usually still provide advice to the younger throughout their lives.

names themselves are not attested in the Kiyungu mythology.

Still, despite the best efforts of later scholars, for one important Kiyungu deity, they cannot find a counterpart in other Gunnagalic cultures. This is a deity who is considered a troublemaker, a negative influence, a source of much discomfort in the world. This is also a deity who is apparently alien to the common Gunnagalic religious heritage; it must have been a pre-Gunnagalic deity who was believed in fervently enough to be absorbed into Kiyungu religious beliefs.

Unfortunately, where the names of the other Kiyungu deities can be deduced by comparison to other Gunnagalic languages, the name of this deity is lost to history. Without the Kiyungu preserving the name, it can never be known. All that remains is the euphemism for this deity; the Kiyungu title translates literally as He Who Must Be Blamed.

* * *

By 1618, the Kiyungu have put to good use the new crops which they acquired over the last few centuries. They now inhabit over one thousand kilometres of the Aururian coastline, stretching from their northernmost major city of Quamba [Mackay, QLD] to Woginee [Tweed Heads, NSW] in the south. This expanse marks the greatest geographical distance inhabited by any one people in Aururia. Yet the Kiyungu are scattered, without any true political unity, and only the vaguest sense of common identity.

Kiyungu-inhabited territory is not contiguous. Their northward expansion has been largely by sea, and so even in 1618, Kiyungu farmers have not entirely displaced hunter-gatherers along the coast. They have established outposts at all of the convenient ports, but in the more rugged coastal areas, some non-farming peoples still occupy the land.

The Kiyungu are also confined in their landward advances, since the continental divide is never too far inland. Kiyungu do not venture west of the mountains in any significant numbers, since there is little to interest them inland. They prefer to fish for their meat, rather than farm noroons or hunt wild animals. The sea provides both their most convenient transportation and their best source of wealth; while the Kiyungu harvest a variety of spices which more distant peoples would value, to the Kiyungu themselves, these are commonplace.

Most of the Kiyungu live in or near city-states along the Coral Coast or the more northerly cities. In the northern Kiyungu outposts, political organisation is confined to this level, as indeed it was amongst all Kiyungu cities until relatively recently. The Kiyungu are ruled by monarchs who come from the same (very extended) family, and who were usually able to maintain order in their own cities, but never really capable of building larger states. The perpetual problem was one of control; collecting tribute from another city-state was easy enough, but conquest required appointing a viceroy, who in time would be likely to declare independence on their own.

Recently, this trend has been partly altered amongst the southern Kiyungu. The need for common defence against Daluming raids and Yalatji proselytisation has led to the development of the League, a loose alliance which exists to resolve disputes amongst member states and encourage mutual defence against enemies. The League is not a solid alliance, but the threat of ostracisation or joint attack from its neighbours is usually enough to bring member cities into line when there are disagreements.

The Kiyungu population density, even in the south, remains reasonably low. Their overall population is growing rapidly thanks to the potential of sweet potato and lesser yams to secure their food supply, but northward expansion offers a population growth outlet. Most of the more adventuresome or simply down-on-their-luck types amongst the Kiyungu choose to strike north to acquire land, potentially new wealth, or just a fresh start. The northward march continues even in 1618; some pioneering farmers are pushing north past Quamba. There is no geographical barrier to stop them until they reach what another history would name Torres Strait.

For those Kiyungu who are settled, though, both in north and south, they still have much of the old laidback attitude of their forebears. They fish, they dive for coral, they eat spicy food, and they do, in fact, like to lie in the sun. Life usually finds its own pace amongst the Kiyungu. Like most Aururian farming peoples who use perennial crops, they have a labour surplus, but as often as not they are content to use the time simply to relax rather than find some industrious pursuit.

The Kiyungu are not completely isolated from other farming peoples, but virtually all of their contacts are with the often-unfriendly Yalatji to the west, or the less organised peoples to the south who are also victims of Daluming raids. They live close enough to the ancient sources of tin that they can still import as much of that metal as they need to make bronze, an alloy which suits all of their metalworking needs. In 1618, they have had only the most sporadic contact with the Islanders, and none of their immediate neighbours use iron to any meaningful degree, so the Kiyungu remain firmly in the Bronze Age.

Collecting coral has been a Kiyungu habit for nearly two millennia, and their taste for it has not diminished. Their sailors still search the Inner Sea [the waters inside the Great Barrier Reef] for some of the more valued and colourful types. It is the basis of much of their own jewellery and ornamentation, and the main trade good which they exchange further south for tin. Most of their other main ornamentation comes from gold. The Kiyungu no longer have any active gold mines, but their ancestors discovered and exploited several small alluvial gold fields in earlier times[120]. Much of that gold remains in Kiyungu jewellery, although some has been traded further south.

---

[120] The largest of these was in historical Gympie, Queensland, which was the site of a gold rush in early colonial Queensland.

Thus, in 1618, the Kiyungu are a people who have lived on their own nearly independent path for a long time, and have no inclination of the storms gathering beyond their mental horizons. Given their distance from the first point of contact with the Raw Men, though, it remains an open question whether the first great changes will come to the Kiyungu from the Raw Men, or other Aururians.

#24: Burning Mouth, Burning Rocks

"This is a land of burning ground. The people dig up rocks and burn them. Even what grows from the ground burns your mouth."
- From a Yigutji traveller's account, after visiting the Kuyal [Hunter Valley, NSW] during the fourteenth century.

* * *

History may be written by the victors, but only if they have a tradition of writing history in the first place.

The art of writing history is not an advanced practice in Aururia. In so far as it has developed, it is practised most frequently by the peoples of the Five Rivers, the ancient heart of Aururian agriculture and still overall the most economically productive part of the continent.

Before their contact with the Raw Men from beyond the known world, historians of the Five Rivers – and their peoples generally – viewed only four political entities as being properly civilized. These were the "four states"[121]: the three kingdoms of the Five Rivers themselves, namely Tjibarr, Gutjanal and Yigutji, and the Yadji Empire.

The Five Rivers historians regarded every other people on the continent as being primitive, barbaric, or disorganised, or some combination of the three. The Atjuntja of the far west were viewed as barbaric, the Nangu

---

[121] The Gunnagal phrase which is usually translated as "four states" may also, depending on the ideological views of the author, be translated as "four nations".

of the Island were regarded as too disorganised to count as a state, while the Kurnawal kingdom of the Cider Isle was regarded as primitive.

In their categorisation of the rest of the continent, Five Rivers historians held particularly low opinions of the eastern coast. They viewed the cultures there as having achieved the trifecta of primitivism, barbarism and disorganisation.

Of course, Five Rivers historiography, such as it was, took no account of geography or biogeography. Farming did not develop on the eastern coast; all of the founding crops for Aururian agriculture were found west of the continental divide, in the Five Rivers. In addition to the great ranges of the continental divide acting as a barrier to the first farmers, the terrain on the eastern seaboard is generally more rugged, divided into a few farmable areas which are also difficult to travel between even when moving north and south. The rivers of the eastern coast are short and usually unnavigable, in stark contrast to the rivers which supported early transportation and commerce in the west.

Together, these factors meant that agriculture was slower to get established in the east, and that societies there were more fragmented, with a much lower population density. There were more distinct languages spoken amongst east coast farmers than in all of the other agricultural peoples combined, despite the lower population.

With no beasts of burden other than the dog, and the general geographical barriers, there was only slow transmission of ideas and innovations across the mountains or even between eastern cultures. Writing spread only slowly to the eastern coast, and while there were a few instances of traded iron tools, no eastern culture had adopted meaningful iron working in the pre-Houtmanian era.

Regardless of these reasons, the Five Rivers peoples held a low view of easterners. "*If not for spices, there would be nothing worthwhile in coming to the sunrise lands*," as one traveller wrote, epitomised westerners' view of the eastern peoples.

Spices, of course, were a very big exception. All Aururian farming societies used spices to some degree. In many cases those spices could be grown locally. The Five Rivers states cultivated a great variety of herbs and spices, including some such as white ginger and sweet sarsaparilla which were originally native to the eastern seaboard.

The most valuable spices, though, were grown only on the eastern coast. Indeed, their value was high *because* they only could be grown in the east, particularly in the more northerly parts of that region. The higher rainfall, the lack of frost for some frost-sensitive species, and in some cases just natural rarity, limited those spices to the eastern fringes of the continent.

Seven main spices grown on the eastern coast commanded interest from westerners. This includes the aromatic leaves of four related trees which another history would call myrtles, but which allohistorical Europeans would name verbenas: lemon, cinnamon, aniseed and curry verbenas. Some of the verbenas had restricted natural ranges, but their value as spices saw them spread along much of the eastern coast, even when they could not be grown inland.

The fifth spice was strawberry gum, another leaf spice[122] whose flavours were used to improve food or *ganyu* (yam wine). The sixth and seventh eastern coast spices were different species of sweet peppers. One was known to Aururians as bird-peppers, with a flavour that was both

---

[122] In historical culinary usage, "herb" refers to using the leaves of plants for flavouring, while "spice" refers to any other part of plants, such as seeds, fruit, roots or bark. In allohistorical usage, this distinction is blurred because many of the Aururian spices made from leaves resemble flavours that in other parts of the world come from spices, such as cinnamon, aniseed, and pepper. The Aururian products will still be classified as spices.

hotter and more complex than common sweet peppers. The other spice was one which later Europeans would call purple (sweet) peppers, because of the colour of their fruit. While the kind called common sweet peppers was ubiquitous across the farming regions of Aururia, purple peppers were more drought-sensitive and very restricted in their natural range. They were still sought out as trade goods because purple peppers provided the most intense flavour of any Aururian peppers[123].

While spices were cultivated in most eastern coast societies where the climate was warm enough, two regions were particularly prominent for their spices. One was the kingdom of Daluming, which was close to the ancient sources of tin, and had long been connected to those old trade routes, so forming one of the eastern ends of the Spice Road.

The other region was the River Kuyal [Hunter River]. The Kuyal is one of the longer rivers on the east coast, and its valley has some of the most fertile soils on the continent. The river itself is suitable for transportation along much of its length, although the river mouth has treacherous sandbars which make access difficult for oceangoing vessels. The Kuyal Valley has a decently well-watered climate by Aururian standards, and is the southernmost region that is warm enough to grow the eastern spices. Around the headwaters of the Kuyal, the western mountains are low and easily crossed in several places, which permitted easier trade with the west than for most other eastern coast societies.

These qualities made the Kuyal Valley the other main eastern end of the Spice Road.

* * *

---

[123] These two species are historically called Dorrigo peppers (*Tasmannia stipitata*) and purple pepperbush (*T. purpurascens*). Dorrigo peppers require intense rainfall and purple pepperbush even more so. That, together with their restricted natural range, has meant that their cultivation has not spread west.

The history of agriculture in the Kuyal began around 500 BC. In that era, the time of the Great Migrations, Gunnagalic-speaking farmers originally from the Nyalananga basin were expanding across the continent, driven by drought and warfare to seek out new lands.

Thanks to the ease of crossing the mountains, the Kuyal Valley was one of the first eastern coast regions to be settled by the migrating farmers. The rich soils of the Kuyal were well-suited to the farmers' crops, and their population expanded rapidly after they established themselves. The previous hunter-gatherer inhabitants were absorbed, leaving only a small genetic contribution to the later inhabitants, providing a few new words to the farmers' language, mostly place names, and a predilection for gathering certain wild plants, particularly sweet peppers.

The people who inhabited the Kuyal Valley came to call themselves the Patjimunra. As with all the other migrants, they inherited much from their Gunnagalic forebears: a complex system of perennial agriculture, the social system of kinship groups called *kitjigal*, and common heritage of religion with deities and associated myths. And in common with the other migrants, that legacy developed in its own direction in the new lands the Patjimunra had occupied.

Unlike other eastern coast peoples, however, the Patjimunra were less isolated from the westerners. The ease of crossing the mountains at the head of their valley, together with the desire for the spices which they had long traded west, made the Patjimunra a target for conquest during the days when the western societies were united into one empire. One of the most ambitious and successful imperial generals, named Weemiraga, conducted his great March to the Sea in AD 821-822, conquering what were then the Patjimunra city-states. They were the only eastern coast people to be formal tributaries of the Watjubagan Empire.

As per normal practice for tributaries, imperial rule over the Patjimunra principally consisted of demanding tribute from the Patjimunra city-states, and maintaining the peace between them. The Empire maintained two garrisons, whose role was largely to collect the tribute and be a deterrent for potential revolt or warfare between city-states. Governance was largely left to the city-states themselves, with only occasional "advice" from the military governors. Tribute was usually paid in spices sent back to the imperial heartland.

True imperial rule over the Patjimunra endured for barely half a century. In 872 the Kuyal flooded prodigiously, devastating crops over a wide region, and the city-kings pled poverty rather than pay tribute that year. They used the same excuse the following year, with less credibility, but this too was largely accepted. From that time on, the Patjimunra mainly sent excuses rather than tribute. Imperial rule had been weakened by a devastating civil war in the 850s and a failed conquest of the Kurnawal [in Gippsland, Victoria] in the 860s, so there was little imperial interest in stirring up a fresh revolt.

The already-vague imperial authority was further weakened by another failed conquest in the 880s, when an attempted second march to the sea to conquer the Mungudjimay was defeated, and then by a disputed imperial succession in the 890s. Emboldened by this, and after two and a half decades of paying little tribute, the Patjimunra states issued a joint declaration in 899 that they would no longer pay any tribute. The Empire was in no condition to reassert its authority, and withdrew its garrisons. With other pressing military problems, and since the Patjimunra were perfectly willing to sell spices at reasonable prices, the Empire never attempted a reconquest.

From this point on, the Patjimunra largely developed on their own.

* * *

In the early Gunnagalic farmers, the elaborate social system of the *kitjigal*, or skin groups, dominated interpersonal relationships. The ancestral Gunnagal divided themselves into eight kinship groupings (*kitjigal*), with all members of the same *kitjigal* being considered related. Membership of a *kitjigal* changed over the generations in a complex pattern. Elaborate rules covered marriage, inheritance, and other individual and political relationships, based on the *kitjigal*. Each of the eight *kitjigal* had their own associated colours and totem animals.

The Patjimunra inherited the system of *kitjigal*, but it evolved a new name and new functions in their land. The old pattern of the *kitjigal* was based on a sense of interrelatedness because of the generational change in membership, and it was egalitarian in that no *kitjigal* was considered innately superior to any other.

During the settlement of the Kuyal Valley, and the absorption of the previous inhabitants, a new pattern emerged for the *kitjigal*. They became gradually linked to occupations, more than interpersonal relationships. In this new system, the pattern of generational change became unacceptable, because the more common expectation was that children would take up the occupations of their parents.

So the old system changed into an occupational-based code. This still dictated rules of intermarriage and inheritance, but now intermarriage was expected to be within a *kitjigal*, rather than requiring intermarriage with other groups. Inheritance also followed within the same group. The old code had dictated rules of social interaction where members of certain *kitjigal* would avoid certain others; in the new Patjimunra occupational-based code, this morphed into a hierarchy of groups where those which were ranked too far apart would not interact with each other.

The code which developed amongst the Patjimunra originally had some flexibility in moving between groups, but it gradually became more rigid. By the post-imperial era, the code had settled into what future anthropologists would call its "mature form": a rigid social structure which defined all interactions between people in Patjimunra society.

In the mature form, Patjimunra society was divided into five *ginhi* –a word which literally means "skin", but which will usually be translated as "caste". Future students of Gunnagalic studies will find the *ginhi* to be invaluable when seeking to reconstruct the ancient system of the *kitjigal*. The name itself is a linguistic descendant of the Proto-Gunnagalic word for *skin*. The names of the *ginhi* are equally instructive: in three cases, the names are clearly linguistic descendants of the proto-Gunnagalic words for colours (green, gold and blue), while the Patjimunra dialects have adopted unrelated words to replace those missing colours. The names from the remaining two *ginhi* are likewise descended from the proto-Gunnagalic words for kinds of animals (brusthtail possums and grey kangaroos) which were totems for two other *kitjigal* (red and grey, respectively), and again the Patjimunra words for those two animals are unrelated to proto-Gunnagalic roots. The three remaining *kitjigal* have vanished, presumably lost during the migrations or integrated into other *ginhi* over the centuries.

The five *ginhi* are:

(i) *Dhanbang* [Greens]. This is the "noble" caste of rulers, warriors, administrators, and secular teachers. They believe they are the highest caste.

(ii) *Warraghang* [Golds]. This is the "spiritual" caste. This is the smallest caste and mostly involves priests, spiritual teachers, doctors and advocates, plus a few smaller occupations which are considered spiritually related, e.g. hunting big animals (but not trapping or fishing) and raising ducks (which are considered sacred). They also believe they are the highest caste.

(iii) *Baluga* [Blues]. This is the "agricultural" caste. This involves farmers, hunters and trappers of small game, and those who wild-gather some foods (such as berries, other fruits, and spices) or manage woodlands (e.g. when coppicing wood, or loggers). It also involves a few related urban pursuits such as selling "unprepared" food (e.g. eggs, fruit). This is generally viewed as the lowest caste.

(iv) *Paabay* [Greys / grey kangaroo]. This is the "service providers / common craftsman" caste. This involves most labourers and town dwellers, house workers and servants, anyone who digs for a living (except coal miners), fishers and sellers of fish, boat-builders, making and selling prepared foods (e.g. bakers), leather workers, millers, and other occupations which are considered common crafts. It also includes a couple of distinctive subcastes: merchants, which to the Patjimunra means anyone who travels to trade; and a group of transient workers / rural labourers who follow seasonal work (e.g. fruit picking, pruning) or short-term urban labouring duties, but who do not permanently own agricultural land. This is generally viewed as the second lowest caste, although sometimes the transient worker subcaste is viewed as lower than the agricultural caste.

(v) *Gidhay* [Reds / brushtail possum]. This is the "higher craftsman / non-physical worker" caste. This is a smaller caste which pursues a range of occupations which are seen as higher status than common crafts. It includes scribes and related occupations that require literacy but are not performed by nobles or priests. It includes bronzesmiths, jewellers and any other workers with metal, carpenters, stone masons, and a few other specialty occupations. It also includes anyone who works with coal, including mining and transportation. This is generally believed to be ranked third highest (or third lowest) among the castes.

Movement between *ginhi*, including intermarriage, was theoretically forbidden in the post-imperial Patjimunra society. In practice the *ginhi* were never completely closed, with a few people managing to move between castes, or more commonly between subcastes, but this became increasingly rare. The Warraghang (priests) were the most strictly concerned with social movement, and cases of people moving into or out of that caste were almost unknown. The most flexibility was between the so-called lower castes of Baluga (agriculturalists) and Paabay (service providers), where intermarriage or even just a new job opportunity would sometimes allow movement.

Patjimunra customs imposed a wide range of requirements and prohibitions on the various *ginhi*. For instance, literacy was notionally required for the two upper castes, permitted for the Gidhay (higher craftsmen), and prohibited for the lower two castes. In practice this was sometimes circumvented by the lower castes, especially merchants, while plenty of warrior Dhanbang would struggle to recognise more than their own name in writing.

Bearing arms was something which was permitted only to nobles and priests. This rule was somewhat more strictly enforced, although in practice a weapon was defined as being a metal weapon. So swords, long knives and metal-headed spears were forbidden to the lower three castes. Wooden weapons such as staves were not affected by the prohibition, and even bows were known among the lower castes.

The rules for *ginhi* also regulated contact between the different social classes. In general, this meant that contact between the different castes was more restricted with greater distance between them in the hierarchy, and that any interaction which did take place would be within the strictures of the system. For example, contact between the Warraghang (priests) and the three lower castes was acceptable in the context of visiting a temple during services or festivals, or for the Plirite minority when they were visiting for spiritual counsel, but social contact outside of those prescribed roles was not acceptable. The priests and nobles generally had the most interaction of any two castes, due to their mutual belief that they are of the highest rank, but even then social contact was usually limited.

Similarly, the strictures of *ginhi* also imposed physical separation between the castes. They generally lived within different districts within the cities, and for the Baluga (agriculturalists) even living within a city was discouraged, except for those subcastes which had urban occupations. Even when some lower castes were required to live in the same dwellings as the higher castes, such as servants, there were strictly demarcated areas within dwellings that the servants lived in during their (usually very limited) non-working time.

The complex rules of *ginhi* also affected how they viewed outsiders. Anyone who was not a Patjimunra was viewed as *gwiginhi* (skinless) and outside of the proper social system. The usual Patjimunra practice was to deal with outsiders when required, such as merchants trading for spices or warriors conducting raids, but otherwise to have limited engagement with them. Social interaction with the skinless was not forbidden, but largely discouraged outside of the usual hospitality offered to guests. Intermarriage was strictly forbidden, and while it sometimes happened despite this, this almost always meant a Patjimunra who left their lands for the marriage. Having outsiders marry into the local *ginhi* was forbidden, and any illegitimate children produced were spurned.

This view of outsiders led to the near-legendary insularity that they displayed when they came into contact with other societies. The Patjimunra happily traded their spices to anyone who came to buy them. In exchange, their most preferred commodity was *kunduri* from the Five Rivers, and tin or bronze from both the Cider Isle and the Gemlands [New England tablelands]. They also valued the silk, dyes, perfumes and resins of the Five Rivers, and the gold of the Yadji and Cider Isle. But while they took these commodities, they remained an inward-looking people who cared little for what happened beyond their borders.

Despite the thriving spice trade with the westerners that had been ongoing for many centuries, and more recent seaborne trade with the Nangu and Māori, the Patjimunra remained resolutely uninterested in the wider world. Very few non-merchants ventured out of their homeland, and rarely did the Patjimunra adopt any new technology or other learning from outside. Matters among the skinless simply held little interest for them. For instance, they remained bronze workers and had never acquainted themselves with iron working. The Nangu, more persistent than most, had some success in spreading their Plirite beliefs, but even there the Patjimunra adapted it to their own society.

* * *

As with their social structure, the Patjimunra religion developed from their ancient Gunnagalic heritage, but it has been adapted to their new homeland. The old Gunnagalic mythology included a considerable number of beings of power and associated tales about them. The Patjimunra have translated this into a celestial pantheon of twelve deities, the six greater and six lesser gods, each of whom has their representatives among the priestly caste.

The Patjimunra deities are viewed as paired; each greater god has their counterpart among the lesser. Broadly speaking, the greater gods are seen as more distant and forces of nature, with the lesser gods being more concerned with the affairs of humans[124].

The twelve deities are:

(I) Water Mother (greater). In ancient Gunnagalic mythology this referred to the deity who was the Nyalananga (River Murray). Among the Patjimunra, this name has been transferred to a goddess who dwells within the waters of the Kuyal and its tributaries. With the frequent, prodigious flooding of this river system, the Water Mother is seen as powerful and often detached from human affairs: her waters bring both life and death with equal indifference.

(i) Crow / The Winged God (lesser). This god is seen as the most cunning and unpredictable of all deities. He is mercurial in his moods, rarely dwelling in one place for long, and often meddling with human affairs. Fickle in his

---

[124] The original Patjimunra words which are translated as "greater" and "lesser", or alternatively "elder" and "younger", do not have a connotation of different *power* among the deities, or of any hierarchy, but of differences in *focus*. The greater gods are those that look at a broader range of things, and so do not look so much at humans in particular, while the lesser gods are those who look more closely at humans but do not do as much for the broader natural world.

attention, he often plays tricks on people, though sometimes he rewards them too. Many of Crow's associated tales describe him playing tricks on those who are seen as lacking in virtue, particularly those who are too proud or lack generosity. Some tales say that it was the Winged God who first stole the secret of fire from the Fire Brothers and taught it to men, although other tales credit the Sisters of Hearth and Home for the same feat.

(II(a) and II(b)) Fire Brothers (greater). The Fire Brothers are twin gods which represent the creative and destructive aspects of fire: destruction from what is fed to fire, and creation from the regrowth after fires have passed. The Patjimunra view these as two halves of one whole deity.

(ii(a) and ii(b)) Sisters of Hearth and Home (lesser). These goddesses are viewed as maintaining the fires which are used for cooking and heat, and by extension for all aspects of life within houses. The names of the sisters are descended from two unrelated beings in traditional Gunnagalic mythology, but they have been twinned together in the Patjimunra religion, perhaps to balance the Fire Brothers.

(III) Green Lady (greater). The wandering creator of life from the soil. She is viewed as responsible for the vitality of all plant life, and in a land where even the best-watered lands can experience drought or soil infertility, she is pictured as a wanderer who moves where she wills regardless of human concerns.

(iii) Man of Bark (lesser). The personification of trees, the source of all the goodness that comes from in wattleseeds, wattle gum, the soil replenishing characteristics of wattle farming, and more broadly associated with all forms of timber and nuts. The patron of construction and of transportation; the latter is because of his association with the development of timber boats and travois which are used to move goods.

(IV) Lord of Lightning (greater). The ruler of storms, bringer of thunder and (obviously) lightning. This god is seen as a distant force whose storms can wreak havoc, and who follows his own whims in how he brings them. He is also, more paradoxically, seen as the patron deity of coal, which the Patjimunra believe to be lightning which has been trapped within the earth.

(iv) Windy (lesser). The goddess of wind and (non-stormy) rain. She is viewed as more benevolent than the Lord of Lightning, bringing nourishing rain to the land, but also capable of being angered and withholding rains or sending punishing winds, particularly those that fan bushfires.

(V) Nameless Queen (greater). She who must not be named, lest speaking her name invoke her presence. The collector of souls. The queen of death.

(v) The Weaver (lesser). The judge of the dead, the arbiter of fate. This god is also known by the euphemism of the White God, a name which developed because of the association of a white (blank) tapestry before he wove the fates of men into it in colour. This deity is also more generally associated with law and justice; advocates swear to be faithful to the White God.

(VI) Rainbow Serpent (greater). The shaper of the earth, driver up of mountains, carver of gullies, punisher of wrongdoers, and patron of healing. He is sometimes described as the creator of all. In ancient Gunnagalic mythology, the Rainbow Serpent was also associated with bringing rain, but in the Patjimunra pantheon that role has been taken by other deities.

(vi) Eagle (lesser). She is seen as watching over all the world, seeing all and knowing all. This is symbolised (naturally) by the wedge-tailed eagle (*Aquila audax*) which flies everywhere; while most of the ancient totemic connections to animals have been lost among the Patjimunra, they still see eagles as sacred. Travellers often invoke Eagle for her guidance and protection on their journey (sometimes together with the Man of Bark). Scholars and teachers also see themselves as guided by the Eagle.

Each of the twelve deities has their own associated myths, practices, and duties for their priests to perform. In most cases, there are also festivals and other services held in the deity's honour, which the people are expected to attend. Apart from priests (and advocates, who are also of the priestly caste), most Patjimunra do not regard a particular deity as their patron, and will attend ceremonies for most deities, as time permits.

Religion in Patjimunra society is being slowly changed by the spread of Plirism. This new faith has been spread by the Islanders who come in trade, speaking of their religion as they visit. So far only a small number (less than 10%) of the population has converted, and further growth is slow.

Most converts do not abandon their old faith entirely; rather, they integrate Plirism into their existing religious practices. They still view themselves as members of the same castes, and usually attend many of the same celebrations and ceremonies as their old religion. The converts tend to identify their old gods with the related figures in the Islanders' Plirite traditions. A few Warraghang (priests) have adopted Plirism, and they provide the counselling and guidance that other Plirite priests do in other societies.

The spread of Plirism, and to a lesser degree the increasing contact with outsiders, has brought some minor change to Patjimunra society. Some converts are discontent with the old religion and its strictures, and have advocated more substantial change. So far, this has mostly been manifested in more Patjimunra trying to change occupations, and occasionally being successful, together with some other Patjimunra who have left on Islander ships or over the western mountains.

* * *

The Kuyal Valley has other natural resources besides fertile soils. Beneath the ground, and sometimes right at the surface, is an abundance of what the Patjimunra call "the black rock that burns." Coal was so abundant and prominent in the valley that the first Europeans to visit the land in another history would name it the Coal River.

Somewhere back in the lost mists of unwritten history, some early Patjimunra discovered the flammable properties of the black rock. Perhaps they were trying to use the traditional "hot rocks" method of cooking, and discovered that the black rocks got rather hotter than expected.

However they managed it, the early Patjimunra learned the flammable qualities of coal. At first, they held it to be a sacred rock. The earliest archaeological traces of coal usage will be associated with funeral pyres; high-ranking Patjimunra nobles were cremated on fires fuelled (at least in part) by coal. The practice became more widespread amongst members of the nobles and priestly castes, until it was the norm for them to be cremated. The lower castes continued to be buried rather than burned.

Over the centuries, the practice of cremating the dead was abandoned. Despite this, or perhaps because of it, coal became used for other purposes. Bronze workers used coal to fuel their forges, while the wealthy used coal to heat their homes in winter. While timber and charcoal could be used for these purposes, coal was better-suited for metallurgy, and required less use of valuable land than the production of charcoal. Other Aururian civilizations used elaborate systems of coppicing and charcoal production to provide sufficient quantities of fuel, but the Patjimunra used their timber for construction instead, and increasingly relied on coal for fuel.

The first workers of coal were able simply to pick the coal from the ground, thanks to the suitable surface deposits. Because it did not require digging (a lower-caste occupation), and because the black rock was sacred, working with coal came to be considered a higher-caste occupation. The distinction remains, with coal miners and workers being viewed as Gidhay (higher craftsmen), even though the work now involves digging for coal.

When the surface deposits of coal were largely exhausted, the Patjimunra turned to mining. Their mining techniques were not particularly advanced. The Patjimunra mostly used drift mining where they followed surface seams of coal horizontally further into the rock, or some small-scale shaft mining where they dug downward for coal. The main problem was drainage, since they had only very basic pumping methods to remove water. Patjimunra coal mining was thus limited to those locations where the water table was low, or conducting the mining during times of drought. Flooding of mines required long periods of pumping and waiting for the water to subside before they could resume extracting coal.

Despite the limits of their mining technology, coal is abundant enough in the Kuyal Valley that the Patjimunra now use it in considerable quantities for heating and fuel, particularly in metallurgy.

* * *

Agriculture in the Kuyal Valley involves many of the ancestral crops developed by westerners, but some of their cuisine now features some other distinctive crops, either native to their own region or imported from elsewhere than the Five Rivers.

On the east coast, the annual rainfall was much higher than in the natural homeland for their ancestral crops, and the soils were often less well-drained. This sometimes created difficulties when cultivating the traditional staple root crops, such as red yams and murnong, which could rot or yield more poorly in imperfectly-drained soils. Such problems did not occur every year or in every place, but they were frequent enough in some regions that the early Patjimunra adopted additional crops.

In the lower reaches of the Kuyal, flooding was particularly frequent and severe, and many soils remained waterlogged afterward. In these conditions, the earliest Patjimunra farmers often turned to gathering some plants, usually ones which they had been taught about by the previous hunter-gatherer inhabitants. For the best of these plants, they continued to gather them in later years, especially during flood years.

The result was the adoption of the only native Aururian domesticated cereal: a plant which they called weeping grass, and which another history would call weeping rice (*Microlaena stipoides*). Weeping grass is a perennial cereal which provides a reasonable grain yield over a wide range of conditions, and is much more tolerant of waterlogged soils than root crops, although it requires more water[125].

The Patjimunra cultivate weeping grass in the most flood-prone and poorly-drained soils, particularly in the lower reaches of the Kuyal. It is only rarely grown elsewhere, since away from waterways the soil usually drains well enough for the higher-yielding red yams to be cultivated. The rainfall is also lower in the upper reaches of the Kuyal, and so the plant is only rarely grown there. Weeping grass has spread to some neighbouring areas of the east coast, but its cultivation has not spread further west.

The Patjimunra are also starting to make more extensive use of a plant which they know as kumara (sweet potato), which they adopted from the Māori. Kumara requires much more rainfall than the red yam, but it also yields highly, so use of this crop is still expanding in the Patjimunra lands.

The Kuyal valley was also the site of another key domestication: the plant which the Patjimunra named jeeree[126]. This is a small tree whose leaves can be used to make a lemony tea. The Patjimunra long ago acquired a taste for this hot drink, which they considered calming (it

---

[125] Weeping grass is a cereal which has been recently domesticated in historical Australia, where it is marketed as "alpine rice". Despite the name, it occurs naturally in a wide range of conditions, in both highlands and lowlands. In historical Australia, it also serves a dual purpose because once the grains have been harvested, the plant can be used as a grazing crop. The natural range requires rainfall of about 600mm or higher.

[126] Jeeree, historically known as lemon-scented tea tree (*Leptospermum petersonii*), has a flavour which is reminiscent of lemon, but lacks the tartness.

has a mild sedative effect), and it has been integrated into their culture. The practice of drinking jeeree spread along much of the east coast, and even to a couple of peoples in southern Aururia, but it has never become commonplace in the Five Rivers, whose inhabitants prefer other beverages such as *ganyu* (spiced yam wine).

Of all the plants which the Patjimunra cultivate, though, none is more distinctive to their cuisine than the plant which Europeans will come to call purple sweet pepper. Historically called purple pepperbush or broad-leaved pepperbush (*Tasmannia purpurascens*), this plant has the most intense flavour of any Aururian sweet pepper.

In its native range, the purple sweet pepper is found only in two small subalpine areas in the upper reaches of the Kuyal Valley. These areas are both relatively cool (being subalpine), and extremely well-watered. Cultivation of the purple sweet pepper was more difficult than other sweet peppers because of its extremely high water requirements. To the Patjimunra, though, the heat and flavour provided by this plant were highly desirable; enough to make it worth obtaining despite the difficulties.

Early Patjimunra settlers wild-harvested the purple sweet pepper, a practice they adopted from their hunter-gatherer predecessors. In time, they mastered the practice of cultivating it using collected rainwater or irrigation systems. While it remains a finicky plant, the Patjimunra make extensive use of both its stronger berries and milder leaves in their cuisine, which has a reputation for being the hottest in the known world[127]. The dried berries of the purple sweet pepper also make for one of their more valuable export spices.

* * *

---

[127] And, if anything, more heat would be welcomed. When the Patjimunra come into contact with the chilli pepper, they will welcome it as much as rifle-carrying soldiers welcomed the machine gun. (Provided those soldiers were behind the machine gun, and not in front of it.)

The Patjimunra live almost exclusively in the Kuyal Valley, together with the neighbouring coastal regions. Their largest city is Kinhung [Maitland], at the head of oceanic navigation for the Kuyal. The city is the largest simply because their relatively primitive nautical technology makes it much easier to bring food and other goods downriver rather than upriver, and so that city benefits more from trade than more upriver locations. Gogarra [Newcastle], at the mouth of the Kuyal, is the key emporium for oceanic trade with the Islanders and Māori, but a lack of suitable fresh water has prevented it growing into a truly large city. The largest other cities along the Kuyal are Wonnhuar [Raymond Terrace] and Awaki [Whittingham]. Guringi [Denman] is the westernmost town of any size, and is the start of the main overland trade roads with the Five Rivers. All of the cities and towns along the Kuyal have strong city walls, which are used as much for flood control as for defence.

The Patjimunra have also settled some of the neighbouring coast both north and south of their riverine homeland. To the north, their territory stretches to a northerly harbour which they call Torimi [Port Stephens, NSW], although they also use this name for the main city built on the shores of the harbour [Corlette / Salamander Bay]. To the south, they have settled around the great saltwater lake that they call the Flat Sea [Lake Macquarie]; their largest city there is Enabba [Toronto], with their southernmost outpost at Ghulimba [Morriset / Dora Creek].

In their political organisation, the Patjimunra were long a people of competing chiefdoms and city-states. They remained in that condition until the imperial conquest in the early ninth century AD. The example of centralised imperial rule offered some inspiration to the more ambitious Patjimunra kings, and following the expulsion of imperial forces in 899, several monarchs sought to unify the Patjimunra. These initial efforts largely failed, but more ambitious monarchs did not stop trying.

Eventually the first unified monarchy was proclaimed under Yapupara, King of the Skin. He claimed all of Patjimunra-settled territory, and even a little beyond in some regions around the Flat Sea. During his lifetime, he even exercised power over those regions.

Unfortunately, the successors to the King of the Skin were often unable to impose similar authority. The Kings of the Skin have continued to rule from Kinhung, but the amount of power they exercise has waxed and waned over the centuries. War, revolution, or a series of natural disasters (floods or earthquakes) is often enough to break the people's trust in the ruler, and to claim independence. The priestly caste is particularly prone to decrying the authority of a King of the Skin of whom they disapprove, and this sometimes leads to rebellion.

On the eve of their first contact with Europeans, most of the Patjimunra were united once more under the rule of the King of the Skin. This included all of the Patjimunra living along the Kuyal itself. Their kingdom is known to themselves as the Kingdom of the Skin, or in their language, Murrginhi.

Three traditional Patjimunra territories remain outside of the rule of the king at Kinhung. The wealthy city-state of Torimi in the north had maintained independence since 1582. The upland city-state of Gwalimbal [Wollombi] had been independent for even longer, since 1557. The southern city-state of Ghulimba has been independent of the King of the Skin's rule since 1602.

In their relations with the wider world, the Patjimunra remain inward-looking. They have traded with the skinless for many centuries, but are still uninterested in the wider world. They trade with the Māori, the Nangu and the Five Rivers peoples, and will be equally accepting of Europeans who come to trade. But they care nothing for what other peoples do in their own lands, except for any territorial disputes with their immediate neighbours.

Of course, no matter how much the Patjimunra refuse to look outward, that will not stop other people looking at them.

#25: The Bones Of The Earth

Step back far enough into the vanished aeons, and you will come to a time when the continent which will someday be called Aururia is just one portion of a much larger landmass. In that time, titanic forces moved beneath the crust of the earth, buckling the surface and pushing up rocks into a range of mountains which at their formation would have towered above the modern Andes.

Yet the forces that buckled the earth and lifted up those mountains have long since ceased. The epoch of mountain-building in Aururia ended when dinosaurs still walked the land. Geological forces still worked beneath the surface, but with different effects. Now, the currents beneath the crust worked to break apart the land, not to push up mountains.

Fragments of the ancient landmass separated one by one. Africa had started to rift away even while the mountains were still being driven up in what would become eastern Aururia. South America separated next, in a slow, drawn-out process which would not see it break away completely for tens of millions of years. Another fragment broke off from eastern Aururia, moving further east and then mostly sinking beneath the waves. Only a few elevated portions of that fragment would remain above the waves as isolated islands, the largest of which would come to be called Aotearoa.

The fragment that would become Aururia slowly separated from the southern remnant of the old landmass that would come to be called Antarctica. Aururia gradually drifted north toward the tropics, and most of this new island continent slowly dried out under the searing forces of the desert sun.

During the eons of continental shattering and tectonic movement, the ancient mountains in eastern Aururia were exposed to the forces of weathering. The slow but inexorable actions of ice, water and wind scoured the mountains, wearing down the once-towering peaks. Those ancient mountains, those bones of rock which had been driven to the surface, were stripped of their covering. Mighty rivers flooded east, fed by glaciers and snowmelt, carrying immense burdens of rock and soil out to the sea to be turned into endless deposits of sand. The flesh of the mountains was stripped away. All that remained were eroded remnants, weathered and rugged. All that was left was the bones of the earth.

As Aururia drifted further north, the sea levels rose and fell in concord with the formation of colossal ice sheets on many of the world's continents. Most of the island continent was too dry to form such large sheets of ice, although more glaciers formed in the ancient mountains, wearing down the bones even further. During one of the more recent times of ice, the first humans crossed the narrowed seas and spread across the continent.

When the sea levels rose once more, there was one place where the rising waters lapped directly against the bones of those once-mighty mountains. One place where the bones of the earth were directly exposed to the sea. The people who lived in this area called it Yuragir [Coffs Harbour], and they called themselves the Mungudjimay. They did not know about the aeons which had preceded them, but they were quick to recognise the eroded bones. In the weathered and contorted shapes of the remaining mountains, they saw their own ancestors, and named the surrounding peaks after celebrated heroes from their legends.

For millennia, the Mungudjimay were just one group of hunter-gatherers among many. They hunted, fished and managed the bounty of the earth, just as their neighbours did. Sometimes they raided and fought with those neighbours, and sometimes they were at peace. They were fortunate enough to live beside one of the few natural harbours on the eastern coast of Aururia, but otherwise there was nothing to suggest what they would someday become.

Far to the southwest of the Mungudjimay and their lands, other peoples were learning new methods to control the bounty of the earth. Those distant peoples slowly bred a range of crops which let them ensure that the earth brought forth produce in its seasons. In time, those early farmers migrated across much of the continent, in most cases displacing or absorbing the peoples who had lived there before them.

The Mungudjimay were fortunate enough, or astute enough, to be spared displacement by the Gunnagalic farmers expanding across the south-eastern regions of the continent. They accepted the first band of farmers who carried yams, wattles and flax into their lands, and mingled their blood and their learning.

A new people arose from this union, who preserved the name and the language of the Mungudjimay hunter-gatherers who had dwelt around Yuragir since time immemorial. They preserved many of their own beliefs, too. From the Gunnagalic settlers who had merged with them, they learned the arts of farming, and of working with metal. Their beliefs mingled, too, particularly those among the Mungudjimay who remembered the bones of the earth.

With a much increased population and the encouragement of immigrants who had built in stone, the early Mungudjimay farmers found a new way to honour their ancestors. With religious dedication, stubborn determination, and many thick flax ropes, they dragged large lumps of basalt into prominent positions in the mountains. These were well-chosen sites, usually overlooking cliffs or other positions where they were visible over long distances without being directly exposed to rain overhead.

From here, the Mungudjimay carved and worked the basalt into the form of heads which were meant to honour their ancestors. The basalt heads had distinctively rounded forms; the Mungudjimay masons tried to avoid anything representing a straight line on any of these heads. Carved basalt heads were created over a period of about five centuries, starting not long after the Mungudjimay took up farming. Eventually, changing religious views, a lack of nearby suitable sites, and social disruption caused by the first blue-sleep epidemic [around AD 365] meant the abandonment of the practice.

While the knowledge of head-carving itself faded, the veneration of the early heads continued. The Mungudjimay flourished as a people, expanding north and south along the coast. They were quick to acquire new technology; given their location just east of the first tin mines, they were among the first peoples to work with bronze. Yet through all of this development, they did not forget the looming round heads which stared down at them whenever they ventured inland into the eroded remnants of the ancient mountains.

The passage of time and the ravages of the elements would damage many of the basalt heads. Some were weathered so badly that their original carvings were difficult to discern. Some were washed out of their original positions and shattered or damaged by falls. Yet some remained nearly intact, and would still be standing in their original positions when the first Europeans visited the region over fifteen centuries after the first heads had been carved. The Mungudjimay still considered those heads sacred then, although their explanations of their origins had been woven into legend. The sons and daughters of the Mungudjimay came to view these heads themselves as their ancestors.

The basalt heads of the Mungudjimay would inspire considerable later speculation about possible contact with cultures in other parts of the world, such as the Tamochan [Olmecs] or Easter Islanders, even though their styles were wholly distinct. These speculations were completely unfounded; the basalt heads were an independent invention, and no meaningful contact occurred between Aururian farming peoples and outside peoples until the first Māori visited the east coast in the early fourteenth century. Despite archaeological evidence which would find that the basalt heads were carved locally and long before Polynesians or other peoples could have visited the region, the speculation would never completely end.

For the Mungudjimay themselves, the basalt heads were simply an unusual part of their heritage. Their veneration of these supposedly ancestral heads, and the mountains which held them, led them to a new conclusion about the nature of the soul. The Mungudjimay came to believe that the soul was contained entirely within the head, and that what happened to the body did not matter. From the stone head their ancestors had sprung, their own heads were what felt and saw, and only the soul contained in the head would endure beyond death.

The alien nature of their religion was only one factor which separated the Mungudjimay from their neighbours. All of their surrounding peoples spoke Gunnagalic dialects or languages which were similar enough that they could learn each other's' speech without too much effort. The Mungudjimay language was completely unrelated, as were many of their traditions and outlooks. The Mungudjimay had no equivalent to the *kitjigal* social divisions of their Gunnagalic neighbours, and they found that system alien and distasteful.

Of all the factors that separated the Mungudjimay from their neighbours, the most important was their own sense of independence. By 886, the Watjubagan Empire had gained control of most of south-eastern Aururia, and appeared to be at the height of its power. Its emperor commanded the conquest of the Mungudjimay lands, but his armies were utterly repulsed. This victory would become an integral part of Mungudjimay mythology; when they coalesced into a united state, they would date their calendar from the year of that great battle.

While separated by barriers of language, religion and geography, the Mungudjimay were never completely isolated. Some ideas and technology inevitably penetrated from neighbouring peoples. Writing spread to them by the early tenth century, although its use would largely be confined to their priestly classes. They acquired knowledge of better bronze weapons and tactics while fighting the Empire and its successor peoples to their west, and they would put this knowledge to good use in war.

Before the attempted conquest by the Empire, the Mungudjimay were politically organised into clustered groups of city-states and related farming communities established along the coast. They had fought among themselves as much as their neighbours. After the defeat of the Empire and the introduction of writing and new military technologies, they gradually consolidated into more unified governments.

By 1020, the Mungudjimay had united into two main states. The northern state was named Yuragir, after the ancestral harbour site which became the capital. The main rival was the kingdom of Daluming further south. This kingdom was named after the major river which flowed through its territory; the River Daluming [Macleay River] was surrounded by a region of very fertile soils which allowed it to support a substantial population.

For two centuries, the northern and southern Mungudjimay kingdoms had a complex relationship; sometimes at peace, but often at war. Their wars were often more intended for tribute, prisoners and sacrifices than for conquest. During this time of struggle, the northern kingdom of Yuragir became popularly called the Blue Land because it controlled the best harbour. Daluming became known as the White Land because of the abundant sand deposited by its eponymous river, both at its mouth and along its banks.

The two kingdoms were united in 1245, ostensibly by a dynastic marriage where the king of Daluming married a Yuragir princess and merged the kingdoms. In practice this was accomplished more by a military coup, with the remaining Yuragir royal family given the opportunity to find out firsthand whether their beliefs about the afterlife were correct. However, the new monarch moved his capital to Yuragir soon afterward, and while the kingdom kept the name Daluming after the old dynasty, the political and cultural capital became established at Yuragir. The old divisions were preserved in some names and symbols in the kingdom, such as the king's staff of office, which was topped with a blue sapphire and white pearl to signify the old Blue and White Lands.

After the unification of the kingdom, the Mungudjimay became raiders and conquerors on a much larger scale. Their main cities were along the coast, although they had a few inland settlements in key areas. Their northernmost city of importance was Ngutti [Yamba], although they claimed much further north. In the south, they had a thriving city established at Tarpai [Port Macquarie], again with lands claimed further south but mostly raided rather than controlled. In the west, the mountains for long defied any long-term conquest. However, in 1592 Mungudjimay soldiers conquered the region around Anaiwal [Armidale], which they still held in 1618.

* * *

In 1618, the Daluming kingdom is the largest state on the eastern seaboard of Aururia. It claims more land than it controls, but its soldiers raid even further than it claims. Daluming soldiers raid for tribute, glory, and religious satisfaction; their boldest soldiers have reached as far north as the fringes of Kiyungu territory, and as far south as the frontier of the Kingdom of the Skin.

In its geography and fertility of its soil, Daluming is a fortunate kingdom. The bones of the earth to the west are much eroded, but they still reach high enough to make clouds condense and bring an abundance of rain.

Occasionally there is too much rain; Daluming is just far enough north that it is occasionally flooded by wayward cyclones.

For most of the time, however, the rain is enough to water their crops and allow them to farm the soil much more intensively than their neighbours inland. They have access to spices and other plants which will not grow inland, such as myrtles and other spices which they export, and fruits such as white aspen, lemon aspen, and riberries which are consumed locally. Occasional contact with the Māori in the south-east has brought the new crops of kumara [sweet potato] and taro which grow well in their lands.

Politically, Daluming is a nearly homogenous society under a semi-divine king who has absolute control over the life and death of his subjects. They are nearly all Mungudjimay speakers, apart from a few Gunnagalic subjects in the outlying territories. The monarch is revered and lives a life of semi-seclusion; common people rarely see him except on great state or religious occasions, and then only from a distance. The monarchy is nominally elective amongst any member of the royal family, although in practice the priestly hierarchy usually decides the successor. Once crowned, monarchs do their best to impose their will over the priestly classes, with varying degrees of success.

In its technology, Daluming has usually been like most of the peoples on the eastern coast; most of its knowledge has been acquired through technological diffusion rather than local invention. In one area, however, they have become the premier manufacturers on the continent. For the Mungudjimay have found a use for the eroded flesh of the earth, which has been scoured from the mountains, carried out to the sea, and then washed up on their shores. For they take this sand and turn into the jewels of their world; they make glass, an art in which the Mungudjimay outmatch all others on the continent.

Glassmaking developed several centuries ago in what was then the Yuragir kingdom, and the art has improved since the Daluming conquest. The technology has diffused elsewhere, but the Mungudjimay are the most accomplished artisans. They use sand, wood ash from wattles, limestone, and other local materials to make glass of a variety of hues. In the last two centuries, they have also developed techniques for making colourless glass, although what they make is not completely transparent, and they have not discovered the techniques of glass-blowing.

The Mungudjimay make extensive use of coloured glass beads for jewellery, and this glass has also been exported widely across the continent. They shape a variety of vessels out of glass, such as beakers and bowls. They have made a few glass mirrors, although these are rare enough to be available only to the royal family and a few favoured priests. The Mungudjimay are fortunate that the sand along their coast is naturally replenished, allowing them to continue drawing from it to make ever more frequent use of glass[128].

Of all their uses for glass, though, none will amaze European visitors than the combination of glass and religion.

* * *

In the Daluming kingdom, the Mungudjimay inhabitants still hold to their old belief that the soul is contained only within the head. They think that the rest of the body is only used in this world, and that once a person is dead, the rest of the body might as well be abandoned. As such, they sever heads for separate collection and honour, and do not

---

[128] For the Mungudjimay, sand is effectively a renewable resource. Sand is continually drifting north along this area of the east coast, being accumulated across beaches and then pushed up the coast by the process of longshore drift. The town at the same location in historical Australia, Coffs Harbour, is an artificial harbour built by connecting two offshore islands to the mainland, and this process has interfered with the natural sand drift along the coast. The beach to the south of Coffs Harbour now has an ongoing accumulation of sand, which is causing problems with the harbour.

bother to bury the body with full rites. Headless bodies are sometimes simply interred somewhere out of the way, and sometimes cremated. If someone is killed in battle, even an enemy, the Mungudjimay will simply remove the head and let the body rest where it fell.

Their practice of head-collecting is something which their enemies often find disconcerting. Yet there is no malice involved. To the Mungudjimay, the collection of heads is an essential component of funeral rites. They collect the heads of enemies fallen in battle, and treat them with the same respect as they do those of their own kin. Having severed heads rotting around doorways is not always pleasant to newcomers, but the Mungudjimay do this both for defeated enemies and their own people.

Head-collection was an ancient Mungudjimay practice, but the priesthood of the unified Daluming kingdom built it into a dramatic representation of their religion. For one of the strangest sights in Aururia can be found in Yuragir. This is what the Mungudjimay call the Mound of Memory, but which later English explorers will call Glazkul, and it is that name by which it will become known around the world.

On the easternmost point of their mainland[129], the Mungudjimay have built a pyramid. This is a step pyramid about 100 metres high, although the staggered structure means that it contains much less rock than the Egyptian or Mesoamerican pyramids. This pyramid is partly built on a natural rocky outcrop which supplies much of the volume of the pyramid; the other necessary step levels have simply been built around the rock.

As a pyramid, Glazkul offers an imposing sight in itself. Built to catch the morning sun as it rises over the eastern sea, Glazkul will appear lit up and shining. The stone

---

[129] This point lies just opposite the island that is historically called South Coffs Island; that island has now been reclaimed to the mainland in modern Coffs Harbour.

pyramid itself was built over a period of nearly sixty years, with rocks being transported from the nearby bones of the earth and shaped into a new pyramid. Yet that accomplishment was only the beginning of the true completion of Glazkul.

The pyramid is shaped into ten steps, and each of those steps is formed into what is mostly a flat level. Except that on the outer rim, at the top of each level, niches have been left in the stone. These niches were left vacant when the pyramid was constructed; they needed to be filled in later.

Each of the niches has been built to hold a skull. A skull which has been carefully cleaned of all flesh, placed into a setting of bronze, then fitted into the niche. Each niche has then been sealed with a block of translucent glass. Here, rocks which once formed part of the bones of the earth have been eroded into sand, then melted into glass and used to seal true bones.

Not all of the niches have been filled; the uppermost levels are still empty. For the niches cannot be filled merely by any available skull. The pyramid of Glazkul, the Mound of Memory, is central to the priestly rites of the Daluming. The yearly round of festivals must be observed from its summit; the equinoxes, solstices, and the celebrations each new moon.

For such a sacred site, the skulls which are placed there must be from worthy donors. There are two sorts of people considered worthy. Those who are of royal blood are automatically considered worthy, and their heads are added to Glazkul upon their deaths. The other, more common way of adding a skull to the niche is that it must come from the head of what the Mungudjimay call a *meriki*, a word which is usually translated as "blooded warrior." This refers to anyone who has a military calling and who has killed at least one person in honourable combat – battle or a duel – and who has in turn died in combat. The heads of blooded warriors who died of old age are not acceptable.

To have one's skull added to Glazkul is considered a great honour, at least by the Mungudjimay. Their neighbours may not always agree, but then the Mungudjimay have never really cared what their neighbours think. Many of their raids are fought with the objective of adding skulls to Glazkul. Of course, raids which kill meaningless people are of no use. The only acceptable skulls are those of enemies who have been observed to kill a Mungudjimay in battle first, or those of their own blooded warriors who have fallen in battle.

With no niche open to Mungudjimay warriors who die of old age, few of them opt to let themselves reach such an end. For those Mungudjimay warriors who reach a veteran age, a custom of duelling has developed. These duels are sacred events, often held in the shadow of Glazkul. It is not unknown for both duellists to wound each other so severely that they both die and have their heads added to Glazkul.

With the strict restrictions on which skulls are worthy of admittance, the pyramid of Glazkul has taken a long time to fill. Yet the priests and warriors of the Mungudjimay have been dedicated in their service. The first eight levels are completely full, the glass glistening in the morning light or reflected at night by the torches lit on solstices, equinoxes and each new moon. The ninth level is nearly full, and only the tenth level remains. Once that is finished, then it will be the time of the Closure, when the legends of the Mungudjimay say that a new world will begin.

#26: Worlds In Collision

August 1619
D'Edels Land / Tiayal [Western coast of Australia]
Commander Frederik de Houtman stood at the summit of a hill in a new land, surrounded by two dozen sailors and three kinds of trees he had never seen before. Scorching heat and waiting had been the features of most of his morning. The sun beat down here, even when it was winter in this hemisphere. At least the air was dry when compared to what he would find when he sailed north to the Indies.

He had to wait, of course. He had decided to keep his men in the shade of this hill until they saw the natives coming out to meet them. He did not want to alarm the natives by coming too close to their town unawares, and he also wanted to keep his ships in sight. This hill was not very high, but it was tall enough to allow him to see the *Amsterdam* and the *Dordrecht* waiting at the nearby inlet. The other ships of his expedition were further out to sea, as he had ordered. All to the good.

"Need we wait here all day?" Pieter Stins said.

"If the natives don't come out by mid-afternoon, we'll go back to the boats," said de Houtman.

Not all of the sailors appeared happy at that announcement, but he ignored their discontent. If one of them wanted to say more, he would answer, but he would prefer to stay alert rather than be distracted by argument.

De Houtman went back to watching the native town. The distance made fine details impossible to pick out, but he had always had keen eyes, so he could see the broad form of things. The town was small; it probably held no more than five hundred people. Oddly, it had no walls. He wondered whether that meant that these natives had no enemies – which would be strange, if true – or if something more complex underlay that decision.

The town had three small docks jutting out into the river. A few small boats were moored on those docks, and some smaller vessels which looked almost like canoes were pulled up onto the banks. Impossible to be sure from this distance, of course, but he doubted that those boats were very seaworthy. That would explain why all of those docks were here in the shelter of the inlet, rather than out facing the open sea.

While they waited, the sailors started to speculate amongst themselves about the nature of this strange people. De Houtman half-listened while he watched the town, without speaking his own thoughts. No-one knew much of anything about these people, of course, but that just added to the wildness of the speculation. From what they had seen of the natives from a distance, they were dark-skinned, darker than anyone who lived in the Indies. Maybe even as black as Africans.

One of the sailors pointed to the large birds which crowded a couple of the fields nearer the town. "This must be like Africa. It has blacks, and ostriches."

"Those are no ostriches," another sailor said. "Wrong colour, not quite the right shape. Besides, we're too far from the Cape."

De Houtman did not bother speaking, but of course the second sailor was right. This land had strange crops and trees, and they had seen several kinds of brightly coloured birds flying around. Yet it was not Africa. A few Company ships had touched along this land's western coast from time to time, even if they had found naught worth the visit. This must be a whole new land. After all, no-one had properly explored all of the Spice Islands yet; this could be just the southernmost and largest.

The sailors kept arguing amongst themselves. Eventually, the conversation shifted to what de Houtman had already considered: whether this was one of the Spice Islands. That led them to wonder whether they would be able to speak with the natives. If this land had some contact with the more northerly Indies, that might be possible. The languages of the Indies were closely-related; de Houtman himself had learned Malay and published a dictionary on their language.

With any luck, there would be a few people here who had learned Malay or a related language from traders. If not, then possibly they had encountered shipwrecked Dutch sailors; there were certainly enough reefs and shoals along this dangerous coast. Failing that, then they would have to use sign language and gestures. Hardly ideal, but it would have to suffice until they could learn the natives' speech.

"Captain, do you know what these trees are?" Pieter Stins' voice cut through de Houtman's reverie.

Stins gestured to the trees which the sailors sheltered under. Small as trees go, with grey-green leaves and twisted bark. De Houtman had wondered what these trees were, but the natives had only planted a few at the hilltop and occasional scattered ones lower down. He had been more interested in the two kinds of smaller, more numerous trees planted along the hilltops and at the edges of the fields on flatter ground. Those trees were abundant, and one kind was started to sprout golden flowers. He wondered what kind of fruit it produced.

Stins said, "I knew I'd seen something like this before, but couldn't remember where. In Pallaicatta [Pulicat, India]. It's not quite the same, but I'd swear that this is a kind of sandalwood."

"Sandalwood," de Houtman repeated, vaguely aware of the silence that had descended over the sailors. Sandalwood. Source of wood, incense and fragrant oil, and one of the most valuable spices in India. "Are you sure?"

"Not completely, but..." Stins reached out and broke off a twig. He had a quiet discussion with another sailor who had a tinderbox, and after a few moments they had the twig alight. Stins sniffed the smoke rising from the twig, grinned, and passed it to de Houtman. "Smell it for yourself."

De Houtman needed only a quick whiff to recognise sandalwood. Maybe not quite the same as Indian sandalwood, but close enough. "I do believe we've discovered a reason to come back to this land," he said.

The sailors went back to talking among themselves, leaving de Houtman to watch the town, and wait. He was now even more willing to wait, though the delay was frustrating. He had already realised that this town and whole new land offered opportunities. Now he wondered what else it contained beside sandalwood.

He hoped he would have time to find out. He had already sent a group of four sailors back to the ships to report on what had happened, and they had come back with word that Jacob d'Edel approved of waiting. For now. He could change his mind, of course. Always a risk with having a Councillor of the Indies along on your expedition.

A few moments later, one of the sailors said, "Men coming out of the town!"

De Houtman followed the sailor's gaze, and saw a group of people leaving the western edge of the town. Impossible to count exact numbers at this distance, but there looked to be at least thirty of them. More than his group of sailors, but not so many that he was inclined to withdraw back to the ships.

"Down to the base of the hill, then we can wait for them there," he said.

As it happened, he had the sailors stop a short distance up the slope. Better to watch the natives coming, and the higher ground should give them some advantage if attacked.

After a while, the group of natives appeared in the distance, walking along the shore of the river.

"What do you want us to do, sir?" Stins asked.

"Load your muskets, and make sure your cutlasses are where you can reach them quickly," de Houtman said.

Wheel-locks were much better muskets to fire than the old matchlocks, and could be kept prepared for firing. Still, if it came to a fight, his men would probably only have time for one shot. After that, it would be steel on steel.

"Best if we don't fight," Stins said.

"Indeed. If we must fight, though, best that we win," de Houtman answered. "Anyway, I hope to persuade a couple of the natives to come with us." That would be the best way to learn the natives' language, assuming that none knew Malay. And even limited knowledge of their speech would let the natives tell them much about this new land.

"And if they don't want to come?" Stins asked.

"We'll see," de Houtman said.

When the natives drew close, he saw they were divided into two groups. The leading group, about twenty men, were soldiers. They wore armour of iron scales that ran from their shoulders to their knees. The scales were fixed to some form of cloth that extended slightly past their knees. Their shoulders were covered with two large metal plates that fitted around their necks. The soldiers' helmets were iron too, shaped to rise to a simple conical peak, with a noseguard attached. They carried large oval wooden shields. All of the soldiers had an axe slung over their backs, and he glimpsed a few with sheathed swords at their sides, too.

The soldiers were all dark-skinned, and to a man had full black beards. Standing just behind the soldiers was a man who was obviously an officer or other high-ranked personage. He had the same dark skin and full beard, but wore clothes made of some blue-purple cloth. His only armour was a helmet, which shone as if with polished steel. Around his neck, he wore some kind of neck ring; it was too far away to make out the details, but the gleam of gold was unmistakeable.

The other group of people looked to be servants, or at least were plainly-dressed. Their clothes were made of light-coloured cloth wrapped around their bodies and arms, which left most of their legs exposed. Where all of the soldiers were men and had black hair, about half of the servants were women, and all but one of them had blonde hair, even though their skins were equally dark. None of the servant men wore a beard, either.

As the natives came near, de Houtman said, "Don't shoot unless they're about to attack us, but if it comes to a fight, shoot their leader first."

The soldiers stopped about twenty paces away from the nearest sailors. The front rank drove their shields into the ground in front of them, almost in unison, forming the shields into a wall.

The neck-ringed leader stood in the middle of the group of soldiers, just behind the first rank. At this distance, de Houtman saw that he had a golden bracelet on his right wrist, and a matching silver one on his left. The leader shouted out a few words in a language which made no sense whatsoever.

"We are Dutchmen," de Houtman shouted back, in Dutch. The natives showed no signs of recognising the language.

The leader shouted something else. Most of the words were different; the only word he recognised from both times sounded something like "tiajal."

"We are Dutchmen," de Houtman shouted, this time in Malay. Again, the natives showed no sign of recognition.

The native leader barked a single word in a commanding tone. The front rank of soldiers pulled their shields up, took two steps forward, then drove them back into the earth. Again, they acted in almost perfect unison.

"Damnation," de Houtman muttered. He did not like how close these soldiers were coming, not at all. "If they come in closer, shoot them. Aim for the leader."

The sailors started to turn the wheel-shafts of their wheel-locks; a series of clicks announced that they were ready.

The native leader shouted more demands, in the tone of one used to being obeyed. De Houtman held his hands palm upward in what he hoped was a gesture of peace. No way to tell whether they would take it as that; these natives looked as if they were keen for a fight.

"Come no closer!" he shouted, in Malay. Again, no sign of understanding from the natives.

The native leader shouted out another command, and his soldiers picked up their shields again. That did it. "Fire!" de Houtman bellowed.

Fire and smoke belched from the muskets in an irregular cacophony. Shots flew through the air toward the ranks of natives. The native leader collapsed to the ground, along with several other soldiers. Some of the standing soldiers turned and ran, but a few pushed aside their shields, pulled out their axes, and charged at the Dutch sailors.

Most of the sailors dropped their muskets, drew their cutlasses, and ran to meet them. De Houtman stayed back, along with half a dozen other sailors who were frantically reloading their muskets. De Houtman had a cutlass himself, but he did not plan on drawing it unless he had no choice.

Fortunately, he did not need to. The native soldiers had the look of veterans, but they probably had never seen guns before, judging from their reactions. Whatever the reason, they had been broken by the first volley of musket fire, and were badly outnumbered. Some died, a few fled. After a few moments, the only natives left alive were four servants who had fallen to the ground rather than flee.

"What should we do now?" Pieter Stins asked. His voice held more than a touch of reproach. Two Dutch sailors were down, moaning and bleeding. One more would never have a chance to moan again; an axe blow had nearly severed his neck.

"Catch those servants, before they flee too," de Houtman said. No need to tell the sailors to see to their comrades; they were already doing what they could. Whether that would be anything useful was another question entirely, but they would make the effort.

The four servants did not attempt to flee. Instead, they rose and walked hesitantly toward de Houtman, when the sailors gestured for them to do so. There were three men and one woman. Most looked young, except for one man whose receding hair had turned white. The others all had blonde hair, which up close looked even stranger against their dark skins.

De Houtman assigned six sailors to guard the servants, and six more to carry their dead and wounded comrades back to the ships.

"We need to move quickly," he said. That town was large enough to contain more soldiers, and who could say how many more would be brought in from further afield? "First, though, see what's worth taking from those dead soldiers." A few samples of their weapons and armour, naturally. Their leader's gold jewellery would become de Houtman's personal prize, at least for now. And who could say what else these native soldiers would have on them?

* * *

Namai, scion of the noble family of Urdera, second only to the imperial family itself in its prominence[130], had long wondered what he had done to anger the King of Kings. He had never learned why; the King of Kings' choices were ineffable. That had not stopped Namai from pondering the reasons why he had been exiled to the governorship of Archers Nest[131], rather than dwelling in the White City, as was his right of birth.

Now, though, he thought he might have found the first thing that made it worthwhile to be sent to govern this place so far from the White City.

This field at the edge of the Goanna River [Swan River] amounted to little in itself. It was next to Sea-Eagle Tree, a minor town that had no virtue other than being near to Archers Nest. Still, standing here in the morning light from the Source, after this strange visitation from the ever-ocean,

---

[130] In the opinion of the Urdera family, anyway.

[131] Archers Nest is historical Redcliffe, a suburb of modern Perth.

this field held strange promises. Or was it just strange dangers?

At first, he had thought this tale of giant ships and raw-skinned men to be nothing but the warped hysterics of a Djarwari peasant woman. Surely this was just a misguided report of Islanders who had broken the King of Kings' edict and sailed around Sunset Point[132] to seek trade with the western shores. It would have made much more sense.

Alas, he had clearly been mistaken. Namai still could not find out exactly what had happened here, but what he could see from his own eyes was clear enough. His brother-cousin-nephew Atjirra had brought twenty good Atjuntja soldiers to this field to investigate the report of strangers. Now Atjirra lay dead, along with the majority of the soldiers and two peasants.

That much was certain. If only he could be sure about anything else.

He had reports, of course, from the four peasants and seven soldiers who had survived the encounter, and who he had brought back here with him. Yet that told him less than he wished. He had been given eleven confused accounts which left him little clearer as to what had happened. He had heard conflicting descriptions of what the strangers looked like, how many they were, and what they wore.

All of the descriptions agreed that the strangers had this striking pink-white raw skin. But then, the tales had told of that even before he arrived here. What he most wanted to know about were the strangers' weapons, and here, he did not know whether to trust what he heard. If these accounts were true, these strangers had weapons which could chain *kuru* to drive metal balls to incredible, deadly effect.

---

[132] Sunset Point is historical Cape Leeuwin, the south-westernmost point on the Australian mainland. The Atjuntja Emperor has an edict preventing the Islanders from sailing past that point, so that they cannot disrupt the internal trade between the Atjuntja western and southern coasts.

Maybe this was so, but the contradictory accounts of sounds of thunder, swirling dust, and belches of flame left him unconvinced. No soldiers ever liked to admit that they had been defeated. Maybe they had just invented an explanation about strangers who could reach across the great water's eternity and drag *kuru* into the mortal lands to serve them. Perhaps.

The strangers did use metal balls in some form, yes. That much, he had seen with his own eyes, for a few of them had been left behind. Unfortunately, nothing else had been. The strangers had collected everything, including their own dead and wounded, however many they had been. They had taken all of poor dead Atjirra's ornaments, including the sun-kin [gold], and weapons and armour from the other fallen soldiers, too.

Whatever else these strangers might be, they were definitely looters of the dead. Extremely abhorrent. But then the Islanders were distasteful in their way, and the King of Kings had agreed to tolerate them. Would he decide the same thing was true here, if the strangers wished peace?

That went to the heart of the most serious question of all, even more than that of what weapons these strangers used. What had caused this meeting to turn into a skirmish? Were the strangers hostile, or was Atjirra a hothead, as he so often could be? Was this bloodshed the workings of some malevolent *kuru* or worse yet, some twist of the Lord's will?

After a moment, Namai nodded to the most senior surviving soldier. "Are you sure that these men attacked first?"

The soldier hesitated, then said, "These are not men, but *kuru*. No mortal men could strike as they did."

"Do not give me stories about these raw-skinned men being *kuru*. No *kuru* are visible to mortal eyes," Namai said, his tone harsh enough to make the other man step back.

The soldier doubtless thought that only *kuru* could bind lesser *kuru* into weapons, and so concluded that these strange-looking men must be *kuru*. Still, he should have known better. Few people could ever glimpse *kuru*, or even hear them, and not without consuming special substances. In any case, he refused to believe that any of these confused soldiers and peasants possessed the Sight.

"Ah, these... men shouted challenges. When our noble leader told us to move closer to show we were uncowed, they released the thunder from their bound *kuru*."

A couple of the other soldiers started to speak, most likely to contradict the senior soldier. They stopped when Namai held up a hand. He needed to think. Even before he came here, he knew that these strangers had stood for many hours at the top of the nearby hill, in the shade of the sandalwood trees. They had only come down when the soldiers approached. Perhaps they had needed the shade. Not for themselves, but if their weapons did chain *kuru* somehow, the shade would be necessary. No *kuru* liked to be in the direct light of the Source, and lesser *kuru* such as those that might be bound into weapons would soon be consumed by the light.

If so, that would explain part of the strangers' actions. A small part. For the rest, though, he could not decide it himself. And that, after a moment, let him realise what he needed to do next.

Namai ran his gaze over the gathered soldiers, peasants and assorted functionaries, then clenched his left hand into a fist and smacked it against the open palm of his right hand. That ancient gesture meant: *I will brook no further argument*.

"The families of the two dead peasants will be exempt from all tributes and labour drafts for the next, hmm, four years. So let it be shown on the nearest land-stone to their homes."

After some more thought, he continued, "The priests in Archers Nest will sacrifice to appease the Lord and to honour the Lady. We will wait to see if they receive any messages or if the *kuru*-listeners hear any omens."

He beckoned to the two nearest scribes. When they came forward, he pointed to one. "You will prepare a letter to Star Hill. Tell them what has happened here, and ask what omens the heavens reveal." That scribe bowed and withdrew.

To the other scribe, Namai said, "Record what I say." The scribe shook his head, and produced two wax-covered tablets and a stylus. "To his exalted majesty the King of Kings, from your servant Namai Urdera, governor of your garrison-city of Archers Nest: May the Lady continue to honour you and bring you good health and fortune. May the earth continue to yield its bounty, that you may receive your due."

He paused. Choosing which of the ritual formulas of greeting to use was easy enough. Deciding what he actually wanted to say was harder. "Strangers have come across the great storm road from the west in great ships. They are not Islanders. They have killed your servant Atjirra Urdera and thirteen of your soldiers, then fled in their ships. It is not yet sure whether they meant to kill or whether the Lord's will brought the deaths. More will be said once more is known."

He gestured to show he had finished dictating, then said, "Set that to parchment and seal it. Let the post-runners carry these letters to Star Hill and the White City."

With that done, he decided, he could only wait, to see what word came back. And he would watch, to see if these strangers sought to come back to the Middle Country.

#27: The Third World

"My intention is to demonstrate briefly and clearly that the Dutch – that is to say, the subjects of the United Netherlands – have the right to sail to the East Indies, as they are doing now, and to engage in trade with the people there. I shall base my argument on the following most specific and unimpeachable axiom of the Law of Nations, called a primary rule or first principle, the spirit which of which is self-evident and immutable, to wit: Every nation is free to travel to every other nation, and trade with it."
- Hugo Grotius, *Mare liberum*, 1609

* * *

To his exalted majesty's servant Namai Urdera, governor of the garrison-city of Archers Nest, from Birring Gabi, Chief Watcher of the West and Seventh Councillor [of Star Hill]: May the fortunate stars watch over you and the wanderers [planets] bring you joy and prosperity. May you know your path as it stretches out before you in this life, your lives past, and your lives yet to come.

Take heed and beware: on the night these raw-skinned strangers arrived, four stars were ripped from the Python[133]

---

[133] The Python is more or less the constellation of Scorpio, although it includes a couple of stars in its "tail" from Sagittarius.

and descended to the earth. Know this to be true: four greater *kuru* have crossed over into the mortal realm. Consider and understand: this augurs a time of great consternation, of potent forces at work.

Answers may be found, if you contemplate the Python. Prey it finds, dangers it dispatches, not by poison or by swift strike, but by the slow embrace of the crushing death. If war the raw-skins offer, resolution will not be found in one swift strike. Measured, persistent, and unyielding action must be your response. If peace the raw-skins offer, likewise let the wisdom of the Python guide your steps, while considering always that even the pacifistic may cause harm through mischance or greed.

* * *

December 1619
Batavia Fort, Java

Rain poured onto the roof, a steady drumbeat of water which had started a month before and which would continue for several more months – the annual rhythm of the monsoons. This building, the new residence of the Governor-General of the East Indies, had been thrown up hastily, from the look of it. As Commander Frederik de Houtman walked in, with Councillor Jacob d'Edel at his side, he could only hope that the rapid construction had been enough to withstand the endless rains.

Of course, if he had had his way, he would have met with Governor-General Jan Coen months earlier, before the monsoon started. Alas, fortune had conspired against him. Earlier this year, Coen had moved the headquarters of the Company to Batavia from its old site of Ambon. De Houtman had not known that before he left the Netherlands, and so he had first taken his ships to Ambon, and then needed to resupply before he could come to Batavia.

"Have you met Coen before?" Jacob d'Edel asked, while they waited to be brought in to meet the Governor-General.

De Houtman shook his head. He had seen Coen occasionally, at meetings of the Lords Seventeen in

Amsterdam and Middleburg, but had never spoken with him.

"From what I hear, he's sharp of both tongue and mind, and demands respect and strict obedience from all who serve him. Be careful what you say and do."

De Houtman nodded absently. He was more concerned with how long it had taken Coen to meet them at all, even after they reached Batavia. Apparently the Governor-General was more concerned with rebuilding the town, which had been burned in the fighting, and negotiating with the English, who were being more troublesome than usual[134].

Governor-General Coen rose to greet them as they entered his office. He dressed as a gentleman should, in a full coat topped by a broad white ruff. He had a narrow chin beard below a wider moustache, and his dark brown hair had been cut short to better suit the Indies' heat.

They exchanged perfunctory greetings, then Coen said, "So, Commander Houtman, you've found something you're proud of."

A blunt man, indeed, de Houtman thought. Still, Coen had the trust of the Seventeen Lords, so he was not a man to be crossed. And de Houtman suspected that Coen would also be prepared to put whatever effort was required to achieve something, if he decided that it needed to be done.

De Houtman said, "We have found a whole new world, as isolated behind its oceans and deserts as the Americas were before Columbus. The peoples who live there are as unknown to us as-"

---

[134] Anglo-Dutch relations in the East Indies at this point were sometimes hostile, sometimes cooperative. In the following year, diplomatic agreements between Amsterdam and London would allow closer cooperation. In the historical East Indies, this cooperation broke down in 1623 with the Dutch executing some Englishmen (and others) accused of treason. Things may change in the allohistorical East Indies, though, since both countries will soon have other things to worry about.

Coen's chuckle cut him short. "And you consider yourself the next Columbus, no doubt. I know that you styled yourself as Captain-General on your voyage here, even though you were never granted that title."

De Houtman started to speak to defend himself, but Coen waved him to silence. The Governor-General continued, "You may have earned that rank, *if* this new land brings rewards worth the visiting."

"It does," d'Edel said.

"Indeed?" Coen steepled his fingers, and looked over them at the two men. "Tell me, or better yet show me: what does this land produce that is worth the Company sending more ships there? The reports from previous ships have not been encouraging."

De Houtman placed two bracelets on the table, one of gold, one of silver. He had taken those from the dead native leader. Along with a larger neck-ring made of two pieces of gold twisted together, but Coen did not need to know about that. The neck-ring would remain in de Houtman's personal possession, until he could present it to the most important people he could meet back in the Netherlands. For preference, to the Stadtholder, Maurits van Nassau, or at least to the assembled Lords Seventeen.

He said, "One of the natives' nobles wore these. The natives we brought back with us have confirmed that they mine gold and silver somewhere in their lands, although being peasants, they are too ignorant to tell us exactly where."

Coen smiled.

Well he might, too, de Houtman thought. Not only were gold and silver valuable in themselves, they were needed to buy the spices which the Company shipped back to Europe. Using bullion of silver or gold, Company traders could buy spices which were worth more than the metals themselves.

"Gold would indeed be excellent, if we can obtain it usefully. Is there anything else?"

"The natives have spices. We have not found out how many kinds, yet; we do not know enough of their language to understand the spices which the natives know of. Still, we can be sure of at least two."

De Houtman placed a small twig on the table. One of many samples; he had had his sailors cut down one of the sandalwood trees and bring it with them before they left d'Edels Land. "This is a kind of sandalwood. Not quite the same as that which comes from India, but still valuable, I dare say."

He waited while Coen found a tinderbox, lit the twig, and inhaled the smoke. The smile which lit the Governor-General's face was perhaps not as wide as the first one, but still, he clearly approved of the fragrance.

"And the other spice?"

De Houtman said, "Sadly, we could not bring any samples, but the natives know of tobacco. They recognised it when they saw our sailors smoking it, and begged to be allowed some themselves."

He shrugged. "They did not smoke it, though. They mixed it with ashes from the ship's ovens and chewed it. As far as our sailors can understand their language, they liked it, but said that it was inferior to what grew in their homeland."

This time, Coen's expression was one of calculation, at least as far as de Houtman could judge. Tobacco grew mostly in Brazil and the Caribbean islands, although sailors almost everywhere smoked it. A new source of tobacco could be promising indeed, especially if it truly was superior to that grown in the Americas. Or it might turn out to be useless; de Houtman did not know, but he wanted to find out.

"So, you have found a land of gold and spices. What of the natives themselves? A brief account only, if you please; if I want more details, I will ask for them."

De Houtman gave a short account of the inlet in d'Edels Land, the strange plants, and their skirmish with the natives. He continued, "We brought the natives back to the ships with us. There were four, but one of them decided to jump off the ship and drown herself in the open sea rather than come with us." Actually, he suspected that the native woman had been raped by sailors, despite his strict orders to the contrary. He could not prove that, though, and even if he could, he would not have admitted the failure here.

"A few sailors have learned something of their language, and we've started to teach them Dutch. Their knowledge is still limited, so we don't know much what their country is like. They do know nothing of the Indies, though, or anywhere else in the world other than their own southern land. They have some sort of king or lord at a place they call the White City, but we need to know more of their language to find out much about that city."

Coen said, "Would they be interested in trade? Especially for gold."

De Houtman glanced over at d'Edel. Being a Councillor of the Indies, d'Edel was in a better position to deliver ambiguous news. "We don't know, yet," d'Edel said. "The natives we have are peasants, from what I can gather. They babble about traders who visit somewhere to the south, but not the whys and wherefores. To know more about the potential for trade, we'd need to find some natives of good standing."

"We'll have to find out, then," Coen said. "If they are unwilling to trade, can gold be easily seized?"

De Houtman said, "Difficult to say. They know nothing whatsoever of muskets, nor of horses. The natives were horrified when they first saw horses in Ambon. But we don't know how large their armies are. Their fighting spirit is not to be despised; they killed two of my sailors, one immediately and a second who died of his wounds."

Coen said, "I will think more on this. Please send me a full written account of your meeting with these natives and everything which you have learned from them. Thank you, Councillor, Commander; we will speak more of this soon."

* * *

To his exalted majesty's servant Namai Urdera, governor of the garrison-city of Archers Nest, from his exalted majesty's servant Lerunna Mundi, chamberlain of the palace: May the Lord turn his eyes away from you. May you know friendship and honour all the days of your life.

His exalted majesty Kepiuc Tjaanuc has heard your words and has instructed me to reply in his name. Your vigilance is noted; your dedication is to be praised. The death of your noble kinsman is to be mourned; may the Incarnator guide his spirit to a suitable rebirth. His exalted majesty's soldiers have died in his service, and deserve to be honoured. Send to me a full list of their names and kin, that their names can be revered at the next equinox parade along the Walk of Kings, and that their kin may be rewarded from his exalted majesty's storehouses.

His exalted majesty is pleased that all of the Middle Country recognises his supremacy, thanks to the Lady's blessing and the Lord's assent. Always must this supremacy be preserved, whether from treachery or from rebellion or wanderers from the treeless lands or Islander mutterers [ie priests] or wind-blown visitors from the west. You are instructed to keep watch, and respond to these strangers as you see fit if they return, provided that you always honour and uphold his exalted majesty's supremacy.

* * *

Instructions for the yachts *Hasewint, Assendelft* and *Wesel*[135] having destination jointly to discover and explore the South-Land, 23 April 1620

Inasmuch as Our Masters [i.e. the Seventeen Lords] earnestly enjoin us to dispatch hence certain yachts for the purpose of making discovery of the South-Land; and since moreover experience has taught by great perils incurred by sundry of our ships - the urgent necessity of obtaining a full

---

[135] Yachts were the preferred vessels for exploration since they had very shallow drafts and thus could explore much closer to shore than larger transport ships. Dutch yachts of this era still had substantial crews; usually over a hundred men.

and accurate knowledge of the true bearing and conformation of the said land, that accidents may henceforth be prevented as much as possible[136]; besides this, seeing the late reports and accounts of the last ships to explore the said coast, it is highly desirable that an investigation should be made to ascertain which parts of these regions are inhabited, and whether any trade might with them be established[137].

Therefore, for the purpose before mentioned, we have resolved to fit out the yachts *Hasewint*, *Assendelft* and *Wesel* for undertaking the said voyage, and for ascertaining as much of the situation and nature of these regions as God Almighty shall vouchsafe to allow them.

You will accordingly set sail from here together, run out of Sunda Strait, and steer your course for the South-Land from the western extremity of Java, keeping as close to the wind as you will find at all possible, that by so doing you may avoid being driven too far westward by the south-easterly winds which generally blow in those waters. You may therefore run on as far as the 32nd or 33rd degree, if

---

[136] By 1620, Dutch ships had actually been touching parts of the western coast for several years, and had prepared charts showing parts of the coast. These charts were not always accurate, however; a regular complaint from Dutch captains in this period was that they were striking land in places other than where their charts indicated that this should be. In historical Australia, this would largely be corrected by voyages in the late 1620s and early 1630s. In allohistorical Aururia, de Houtman's report of 1619 inspires earlier charting.

[137] While Governor-General Coen does not entirely disbelieve de Houtman's account, he suspects a certain amount of exaggeration. This is because other Dutch ships which had been visiting parts of Aururia during the last four or five years had universally reported that the coast was barren and the natives were "savages", when they found inhabitants at all. Coen is unaware that the previous Dutch ships made landfall in the north-western parts of Aururia, which are quite hostile country and inhabited by hunter-gatherers. De Houtman's expedition was the first one to make landfall far enough south to contact the farming peoples of the south-western corner of the continent.

you do not fall in with land before that latitude; having got so far without seeing land, you may conclude that you have fallen off too far to westward, for sundry ships coming from the Netherlands have accidentally come upon the South-Land in this latitude; you will in this case have to turn your course to eastward, and run on in this direction until you sight land.

When you shall have come upon the South-land in the said latitude or near it, you will skirt the coast of the same as far as latitude 50 degrees, in case the land should extend so far southward; but if the land should fall off before you have reached the said latitude, and should be found to trend eastward, you will follow its eastern extension for some time, and finding no further extension to southward, you will not proceed farther east, but turn back. You will do the same if you should find the land to turn to westward. In returning you will run along the coast as far as it extends to northward, next proceeding on an eastern course or in such wise as you shall find the land to extend: in which manner you will follow the coast as close inshore and as long as you shall find practicable, and as you deem your victuals and provisions to be sufficient for the return voyage, even if in so doing you should sail round the whole land and emerge to southward.

The main object for which you are dispatched on this occasion, is, that from 45 or 50 degrees, or from the farthest point to which the land shall be found to extend southward within these latitudes, up to the northernmost extremity of the South-Land, you will have to discover and survey all capes, forelands, bights, lands, islands, rocks, reefs, sandbanks, depths, shallows, roads, winds, currents and all that appertains to the same, so as to be able to map out and duly mark everything in its true latitude, longitude, bearings and conformation. You will moreover go ashore in various places and diligently examine the coast in order to ascertain the nature of the land and the people, their towns and inhabited villages, the divisions of their kingdoms, their religion and policy, their wars, their rivers, the shape of their vessels, their fisheries, commodities and manufactures, but specially to inform yourselves what minerals, such as gold, silver, tin, iron, lead, and copper, what precious stones, pearls, vegetables, animals and fruits, these lands yield and produce. In all of these regions, you will diligently inquire whether they yield anywhere sandalwood, nutmegs, cloves, tobacco or other spices; likewise whether they have any good harbours and fertile tracts, where it would be possible to establish settlements, which might be expected to yield satisfactory returns.

To all of which particulars and whatever else may be worth noting, you will pay diligent attention, keeping a careful record or daily journal of the same, that we may get full information of all your doings and experiences, and the Company obtain due and perfect knowledge of the situation and natural features of these regions, in return for the heavy expenses to which she is put by this expedition.

To all the places which you shall touch at, you will give appropriate names such as in each instance the case shall seem to require, choosing for the same either the names of the United Provinces or of the towns situated therein, or any other appellations that you may deem fitting and worthy. Of all which places, lands and islands, the commander and officers of these yachts, by order and pursuant to the commission of the Worshipful Governor-General Jan Pieterszoon Coen, sent out to India by their High Mightinesses the States-General of the United Netherlands, and by the Lords Managers of the General Chartered United East India Company established in the same, will, by solemn declaration signed by the ships' councils, take formal possession, and in sign thereof, besides, erect a stone column in such places as shall be taken possession of; the said column recording in bold, legible characters the year, the month, the day of the week and the date, the persons by whom and the hour of the day when such possession has been taken on behalf of the States-General above mentioned. You will likewise endeavour to enter into friendly relations and make covenants with all such kings and nations as you shall happen to fall in with, and try to prevail upon them to place themselves under the protection of the States of the United Netherlands, of which covenants and alliances you will likewise cause proper documents to be drawn up and signed.

Any lands, islands, places, etc., which you shall take possession of, as aforesaid, you will duly mark in the chart, with their true latitude, longitude and bearings, together with the names newly conferred on the same.

According to the oath of allegiance which each of you, jointly and severally, has sworn to the Lords States General, His Princely Excellency and Lords Managers, none of you shall be allowed to secrete, or by underhand means to retain, any written documents, journals, drawings or observations touching the expedition, but every one of you shall be bound on his return here faithfully to deliver up the same without exception.

For the purpose of making a trial we have given orders for various articles to be put on board your ships, such as diverse ironmongery, cloths, coast-stuffs [from Coromandel in India] and linens; which you will show and try to dispose of to such natives as you may meet with, always diligently noting what articles are found to be most in demand, what quantities might be disposed of, and what might be obtained in exchange for them; we furthermore hand you samples of gold, silver, copper, iron, lead, pearls, sandal-wood, tobacco, nutmeg and cloves, that you may inquire whether these articles are known to the natives, and might be obtained there in any considerable quantity.

In landing anywhere you will use extreme caution, and never go ashore or into the interior unless well-armed, trusting no one, however innocent the natives may be in appearance, and with whatever kindness they may seem to receive you, being always ready to stand on the defensive, in order to prevent sudden traitorous surprises, the like of which, sad to say, have but too often been met with in similar cases, specially in the late landing of the ship *Amsterdam*. And if any natives should come near your ships, you will likewise take due care that they suffer no molestation from our men.

In a word, you will suffer nothing to escape your notice, but carefully scrutinise whatever you find, and give us a full and proper report on your return, by doing which you will render good service to the United Netherlands and reap special honour for yourselves.

In places where you meet with natives, you will either by dexterity or by other means endeavour to get hold of a number of full-grown persons, or better still, of boys and girls, to the end that the latter may be brought up here and be turned to useful purpose in the said quarters when occasion shall serve.

The command of the three yachts has been entrusted to Frederik de Houtman, who during the voyage will carry the flag, convene the council and take the chair in the same, in virtue of our special commission granted to the said de Houtman for the purpose.

Given in the Fortress of Batavia, this 23rd of April, AD 1620.[138]

---

[138] In historical Australia, similar instructions were given in 1622 to the captains of two Dutch yachts, the *Haringh* and *Hasewint*. (A translation of these instructions has been adapted into these allohistorical instructions, suitably modified given the changed circumstances of de Houtman's encounter.) Their expedition did not go further than the Sunda Strait, since they were diverted to join the search for a missing ship (the *Rotterdam*).

#28: The Voyage of Tales

"These Wesel Landers have the most unpleasant looks and the worst features of any people that I ever saw. Black and naked of skin, hair frizzled, their frames tall and thin, their face and chests painted white with lime or some similar pigment, their appearance is altogether distressing and unwelcoming.

They are the most wretched people in the world. They lack for houses, garments of cloth or even of animal skin, they keep no sheep, poultry, or beast of any kind. Their food comes from country that yields only meagre fish and roots that they dig wild from the earth. They have no herbs or pulses, no grains or fruit that we saw, and lack the tools to catch the wild birds and beasts."

Or so wrote Jan Vos, captain of the *Hasewint*, one of the three yachts in de Houtman's expedition, sent to explore the western coast of what would come to be called Aururia. He wrote this unflattering depiction of the inhabitants of what they had called Wesel Land; the first land they had sighted since passing through the Sunda Strait between Java and Sumatra[139].

His descriptions were harsh, but his disappointment was perhaps understandable. He and his fellow captains had heard wild tales of the land which they were to explore. De Houtman had been reasonably circumspect in his descriptions, but he had still spoken of a land of gold, sandalwood and tobacco, where the iron-using inhabitants had endless fields of yams and strange flowering trees. The tales told by his sailors were more exaggerated, and grew in each telling and retelling in Batavia in the months between the *Dordrecht*'s arrival and the departure of the new voyage.

Instead of the expected land of abundance, their first landfall at Wesel Land (named after one of the expedition's ships) found only an eroded, infertile country of coastal sandplains. The hunter-gatherer inhabitants did not know how to work metals and had no native crops that the visitors could perceive[140]. Most of their tools were of stone; only occasional metal tools of copper or rusted iron had been traded through many hands from the farming peoples further south, although the Dutch sailors did not yet know this.

---

[139] De Houtman's expedition first touched land about halfway between the locations of the historical towns of Port Hedland and Karratha. The region which they call Wesel Land is semi-arid country covered in spinifex grass and scattered trees. It is too close to the equator for Aururian crops to grow, and in any case the rainfall is so low that any farming would be extremely marginal. The negative statements which Vos is depicted as recording about the inhabitants are adapted from similar sentiments which William Dampier recorded historically in his account of visiting New Holland (Australia).

[140] Vos did not understand the complex land management practices which the local peoples used to ensure that they could obtain food without exhausting natural resources. He was not alone in missing this; many later Europeans would also fail to grasp it, both in Aururia and in real history.

Instead of the sandalwood and spices they had been expecting, the local peoples had nothing to offer in trade. They recognised iron and tobacco from the samples which the expedition brought, but could not supply either of those in any quantity. Worse, the Dutch could not even communicate with them; the people here had no language in common with the native interpreters which de Houtman's expedition had brought.

The voyage, though, continued. From their initial landfall they sailed west, skirting and charting an island-studded coast with occasional bays and harbours, but no large rivers or fertile tracts of land. Their instructions were to search these latitudes for any sign of the most valuable spices – sandalwood, cloves, nutmeg – which might grow there wild or domesticated, or for arable land where spice plantations could be established. They found neither, only continued disappointment.

After several days of careful sailing through shallow seas and numerous islands, the coastline to their south opened into a wide gulf [Exmouth Gulf] with mangrove-lined shores and filled with sea turtles. However, the shores of this gulf were dangerously shallow, and the surrounding lands dry and uninviting, so de Houtman marked the gulf on his charts as Turtle Sound and ordered his ships around its western extremity.

Here, for the first time the coastline turned south, which was the flotilla's expected direction. The southward voyage soon brought them into a region of the coast which was already sketchily marked on their charts; it was called Eendrachtsland, named by a Dutch explorer who had visited this region four years before.

Yet even here the disappointment continued, for an extensive coral reef along the shore [Ningaloo Reef] prevented them from coming close to the shore or making any further contact with the natives. The expedition skirted wide of the coral-lined coast, and did not make landfall again until they had cleared the reef and came to the north point of a sand-dune covered island.

Here, they made a remarkable discovery. A pewter plate had been nailed to a tree on this island. Its inscription announced that this island had been visited by Dirk Hartog on the ship *Eendracht* in 1616[141].

De Houtman noted the discovery of the plate in his journal, and mentioned the shallow waters of the bay further inland, although he did not give it a name. Because of the shallow water and unpredictable currents, he ordered his ships not to enter the bay, and after resupplying with water, they continued their journey south.

De Houtman would never find out that he had bypassed the northernmost Atjuntja outpost, which the locals called Dugong Bay. A penal colony established to mine salt and collect pearls, this outpost lacked sufficient water to sustain any substantial agriculture; being appointed as governor of Dugong Bay was a punishment reserved for Atjuntja nobles who had gravely displeased the King of Kings.

Once past the island, the expedition drew near a more familiar section of coastline. Here, only the year before, de Houtman had discovered a series of low-lying islands with coral reefs surrounding them, which he had called the Abrolhos[142]. Because they had no high points or headlands to make them visible from a distance, he had almost lost a ship to the reefs the year before.

This time, because he knew of their location, he deliberately ordered his ships to stay closer to shore, making careful progress while charting the coastline. Their caution meant that while they sighted the mainland coast many

---

[141] In historical Australia, the Dirk Hartog plate was rediscovered in 1697 by another Dutch captain, Willem de Vlamingh, who replaced it with another pewter plate of his own and took the original back to Amsterdam. The Hartog Plate is the oldest known European artefact associated with Australia.

[142] Those islands still bear that name in historical Australia; formally they are called the Houtman Abrolhos, which is usually shortened to Abrolhos.

times, they did not attempt to land until they reached a locale where they were sure that there was a useful harbour or other safe landing.

After slow progress against unfavourable winds and contrary currents, de Houtman's three ships reached a large promontory jutting into the Indian Ocean. The shelter of this promontory created a reasonable harbour. In this, they found several wharfs and jetties built into the water, with several small boats and canoes anchored. On the shore beyond, they saw the first houses of wood and stone, and knew that they had found what they sought.

The houses which clustered around the docks were those of the artisans, fishermen and common folk of the Binyin people who dwelt in this region. Beyond those houses, de Houtman's sailors found field after field filled with workers. They watched as the workers methodically dug out the yams, cut off the main part of the bulky tuber, replanted the remnant of the tuber and refilled the hole. Thus, they became the first Europeans to witness a yam harvest[143].

Once they had bargained for safe travel, de Houtman's sailors also became the first Europeans to glimpse an Atjuntja garrion-city. Inland, beyond the docks and the low houses, rose walls of pale orange sandstone, a statement both of defence and authority. This garrison-city of Seal Point was the residence of the Atjuntja governor of this region, as well as housing the administrators who oversaw life here, and the soldiers who enforced their will.

De Houtman's expedition had brought two interpreters with them, peasants who had more or less voluntarily accompanied de Houtman's sailors on his first visit to the

---

[143] Red yams are harvested in late April-May, when the tubers are at their largest and the above-ground portions of the plant are starting to wither and die back in preparation for the coming winter.

South Land[144]. These peasants were of the Djarwari people who dwelt further south, but their dialect was close enough to the locals to allow communication.

Contact was wary, but peaceful. The Atjuntja governor had been forewarned by post-runners, who carried word from further south of the brief skirmish near Archers Nest [Perth]. He did not allow any of the Dutch sailors inside the walls of Seal Point, but they were permitted to visit the local town which had grown up outside the walls. The Dutch found the town-dwellers to be quite friendly, especially some of the local women.

Although the Dutch did not know this at the time, this friendly contact would have unfortunate consequences for both sides. De Houtman's ships had already sailed on when the Dutch sailors started to fall ill with a strange form of influenza which brought quick fatigue and turned faces and lips blue. In time, this illness would claim the lives of seventeen Dutch sailors, including Captain Jan Vos of the *Hasewint*, and weaken many more. Their interpreters recognised the disease and called it "blue-sleep," but the Dutch sailors christened it sweating-fever.

While they were in Seal Point, however, de Houtman and his sailors knew nothing of this. In accordance with his instructions, he offered the Atjuntja governor the friendship and protection of the United Netherlands. When that offer was translated and understood, it produced nothing but raucous laughter. The governor of Seal Point explained that friendship was all very well, and not to be despised. Yet all of the Middle Country was under the rule of the King of Kings, who lived in the White City at the centre of the universe, and who needed protection from nothing in the mortal realms.

---

[144] De Houtman had brought three captives back to Batavia, but only two had been sent back with him. The third was kept in Batavia to learn more Dutch, and as a safeguard in case something happened to de Houtman's exploratory voyage.

With this exchange, de Houtman finally began to grasp the extent of the nation he had contacted. He had made landfall at a place more than 400 kilometres further north than his first visit, only to be told that it was under the rule of the same King of Kings in a distant city. He knew that the Atjuntja lands extended some distance further north and an indeterminate distance to the east, and now he was reminded that the White City was somewhere far to the south, too.

When his diplomatic advances came to naught, de Houtman and his fellow captains explored a matter which was even closer to their hearts: trade. The Company had been generous in supplying them with samples of trade goods: iron and steel manufactures; linen and other textiles; Coromandel goods such as lacquered boxes, screens and chests[145]; metals, gems and similar such as gold, silver, lead, tin, pearls, and coloured glass; and very limited quantities of spices such as nutmeg, mace, sandalwood, tobacco and cloves.

To their delight, the Atjuntja governor and his administrators recognised most of their trade goods. Gold and silver they acknowledged, although they did not appear greatly impressed. Lead they viewed with disdain as commonplace; pearls and glass interested them more. Textiles and lacquer work interested them even more, as did some of the iron cookware and utensils[146].

---

[145] These lacquered products were mostly manufactured in China, but the trading networks saw them re-exported to the Coromandel Coast of India, and this became the common name for them.

[146] They would have been even more impressed by muskets, but de Houtman had prudently ordered his sailors not to fire muskets except at uttermost need, or describe their function. He wanted them to be a surprise if they were attacked. The Atjuntja had heard exaggerated tales from the south that these raw-skinned strangers could chain *kuru* and throw thunder balls, but did not recognise the muskets for what they were.

Of the most valued goods, the spices, though, the Atjuntja recognised tobacco but treated it as nothing of consequence, and they thought that the Indian sandalwood was inferior. Alas, of the other spices, they knew nothing, and appeared to care but little.

To de Houtman's frustration, the Atjuntja governor bluntly refused to conduct trade. He explained that everything valuable in the Middle Country belonged to the King of Kings, and that it would not be traded without his permission. Everyday items such as food, wood and tobacco could be exchanged as gifts between friends, and some of them had already been supplied to the visiting Dutch. However, items of value such as gold, silver, sandalwood, "worked goods" and *kunduri* were part of the tribute owed to the King of Kings, and could not be exchanged elsewhere without his approval.

The Dutch disappointment was almost palpable; severe enough that de Houtman took some time before he remembered to ask what *kunduri* was. His interpreter refused to relay the question, saying that would be like asking a man to explain what water was. Instead, the interpreter simply explained that *kunduri* was to tobacco what yam wine was to water.

After three days of explanation and frustration, de Houtman decided that they had found out all that they could from Seal Point. Privately, he told his captains that he hoped to find a place further south where the natives would be willing to trade, no matter what restrictions their emperor might have placed on them.

From Seal Point, the expedition continued southward, charting the coast and noting as they explored that the shore country was becoming ever more fertile. De Houtman and his captains named many geographical features, with no regard whatsoever for what the natives called them.

The captains knew both elation and frustration as they ventured ever further south. Elation, because their methodical progress permitted them to draw extremely accurate charts of the coastline, currents, and other features of interest. Frustration, because the fever claimed too many of their crew, and because further visits to the coast provided exchanges of food but met the same absolute refusal to trade any goods which the natives deemed valuable.

Before too much longer, the expedition struck trouble. The three ships were nearing the latitude where de Houtman had made landfall on his last visit. Mindful of the bloodshed on this previous occasion, he had planned to avoid any contact with the natives in this region. Alas, weather and ocean currents interfered with his plans. Overnight, the wind shifted to a land breeze, and unknown to his captains, an eddy in the current pushed their ships further out to sea[147].

The *Wesel*, at that point the lead yacht in the expedition, struck rocks near an offshore island. De Houtman had known of this island, naming it Rottnest on his previous expedition, but had not been able to warn the other ships in time. Taking on water, the *Wesel*'s new captain had no choice but to bring the vessel into sheltered water to effect repairs. There was only one suitable anchorage on the mainland; a narrow inlet which they had called Swan River, and on whose shores Atjuntja and Dutchmen had first shed each others' blood.

Despite de Houtman's misgivings, the Atjuntja did not attack them on sight. The immediate problem was preventing their interpreters from fleeing home. Once that was under control, they met a deputation from the Atjuntja governor, who reported that they would be permitted to anchor in the river, and would be provided with gifts of food and some timber to help them repair their vessel. De

---

[147] The currents on the coast of western Aururia are quite complex. There is a major warm water current which moves south (historically called the Leeuwin Current), but it is bracketed by cold-water currents which move north. This is one of the many features which make navigation along the western Aururian coast so troublesome.

Houtman, who had by now gained some understanding of how Atjuntja society worked, responded with gifts of his own, including iron cooking utensils and tobacco to the families of the peasants and soldiers who had been killed in the last skirmish.

Repairs to *Wesel* took nearly two weeks. They could have been hurried, but de Houtman did not urge his sailors to make haste, since he decided that staying here would allow him to fulfill more of his instructions. Governor-General Coen had ordered his expedition to survey what vegetables, animals, fruits and other produce could be obtained in the South Land. While a few sailors worked on the *Wesel*, the rest were rotated through visits ashore, learning what they could of the region which they called d'Edels Land.

Thus, the sailors of de Houtman's expedition were the first to learn much of what Aururia produced and how its inhabitants lived. They saw Archers Nest, another garrison-city, but built away from the coast in a reminder that the Atjuntja did not look to the sea. They saw the many fields of what the Atjuntja called wealth-trees, and asked what these trees could produce that was so valuable. The Atjuntja responded by giving their Dutch guests an ample supply of wattleseeds and wattle gum. De Houtman ordered that some of these seeds be brought back to Batavia, along with some of the ubiquitous yams, in case they would prove suitable to grow there[148].

The Atjuntja crops presented their Dutch visitors with a strange combination of the familiar and the exotic. Flax they knew; while the Atjuntja species differed in its appearance, it produced similar fibres and seeds. De Houtman also noted in his journal: "they grow a variety of indigo here, which produces a dye as fine as anything I have

---

[148] Red yams, at least, will not grow so close to the equator. Wattles are not quite as sensitive to latitude, but the Dutch will still have difficulty getting the main domesticated species to grow properly in a tropical climate.

seen from India. Yet their indigo plant is more versatile, for by different preparations they may use the same leaves to produce either the true indigo colour, or an excellent green, or a brilliant yellow[149]."

Other Atjuntja crops simply left the Dutch perplexed. They recognised the timber of eucalypts as being extremely useful; those were the main source of the wood they used to repair the *Wesel*. Yet the smell of eucalypts was like nothing they had ever encountered before, and reminded them that this land was an exotic place. Likewise, the local dried fruits offered tastes unlike anything which the Dutch had known; after sampling dried quandong, de Houtman recorded in his journal that he wished that he had visited the South Land when these fruits were in season.

Still, no crops offered such a complete mix of the familiar and exotic as tobacco and related crops which the Atjuntja used. Tobacco was something with which every Dutch sailor was familiar. So, indeed, were most European sailors; they had been spreading tobacco around the world since their first contact with the Americas. The Atjuntja tobacco crops were distinctive in their appearance, but could still be recognised as forms of tobacco[150].

Yet while the Atjuntja grew and used tobacco, they universally told the Dutch sailors that this tobacco was merely an inferior product. The drug of choice was *kunduri*. This time, de Houtman overrode the wishes of his interpreters and asked the Atjuntja governor what *kunduri* was and why it was so valuable. The governor replied that

---

[149] This plant is native indigo (*Indigofera australis*), a relative of true indigo (*I. tinctoria*). Native indigo is widespread across much of the continent, and in historical Australia it was used in early colonial times to dye wool.

[150] Native Aururian species of tobacco have been used as narcotics for tens of millennia; the main one cultivated by the Atjuntja is *Nicotiana rotundifolia* (sometimes classified as *N. suaveolens*). This is similar to common tobacco in its cultivation, although the Atjuntja only chew tobacco (mixed with wood ash); they do not smoke it.

kunduri was what every Atjuntja man would use if he could, but that it was rare and came from beyond the sunrise. He had a reasonable quantity, but few of his soldiers or administrators were so fortunate.

In what was an extremely generous gesture, although de Houtman did not yet recognise it as such, the governor of Archers Nest sent for some of his personal supply of *kunduri* and offered a sample to de Houtman.

The appearance of the *kunduri* was unremarkable; dried leaves and plant stems which did not look much like tobacco. Still, following instructions, de Houtman mixed the *kunduri* with wood ash and chewed it. He described the resulting sensation in his journal: "I chewed this *kunduri* for several minutes, and a sensation of bliss and relaxation came over me. I no longer cared who was in the room, nor what they might say or do. The effect was akin to the euphoria I might feel after several glasses of good French wine[151]."

The Dutch sailors found the same mixture of familiar and exotic in the Atjuntja domestic animals. Dogs were familiar, except that the breeds which the Atjuntja had developed had no European equivalents. Ducks they knew, although again, the breeds were unfamiliar. Captain de Vries of the *Assendelft* recorded in his log that "they use ducks in as many numbers and varieties as Dutch farmers use chickens." Quolls were an exotic animal, but the Dutch did their best to link them to more familiar forms; they referred to domesticated quolls as pole-cats. To the Dutch,

---

[151] This is de Houtman's introduction to the drug known in historical Australia as *pituri*. John King, the only survivor of the Burke and Wills expedition of 1860-61, reported a similar reaction when he first experienced *pituri*. Allohistorically, *kunduri* is grown in parts of the Nyalananga [Murray] basin and exported to many parts of the continent; it reaches the Atjuntja via Islander trading ships. It does have a stronger effect than tobacco; the nicotine content of *kunduri/ pituri* is up to four times stronger than that of modern commercial tobacco. The drug also contains other alkaloids such as hyoscyamine and scopolamine, which add to its potency.

noroons were the most exotic of the domesticated animals; oversized flightless birds with voracious appetites and booming calls which could be heard over a mile away. The captains' journal entries indicated bemusement about whether the noroons would be of any worth as poultry in Europe.

Before leaving Archers Nest, de Houtman recorded in his journal that he believed that this was the most promising site yet for a trading post, if the Atjuntja could be persuaded to permit one. He also recorded his frustration at convincing any natives to come voluntarily, and noted that he did not want word to spread ahead of his voyage that the Dutch were kidnappers. He wrote that the time to kidnap natives would be at the last place they visited.

As the three ships sailed south of Archers Nest, their journal entries grew increasingly enthusiastic about the merits of d'Edels Land. The land was well-watered, the vegetation grew ever more luxuriant, with some towering forests visible along the shores.

The expedition continued its diligent work of charting, but for some time after visiting Archers Nest, de Houtman did not allow any extensive visits ashore. He had by now become obsessed with sailing to the Atjuntja capital. And while his peasant interpreters did not have a detailed understanding of the geography, they had reported that he needed to pass a major landmark called Sunset Point [Cape Leeuwin] and sail east along the "great storm road" to reach the White City.

As it happened, for all of his conscientiousness, de Houtman would never sight Sunset Point, although he believed until his dying day that he had done so. Sunset

Point was one of the world's three great capes[152], marking the merging of two oceans, but was also surrounded by several rocks and small islands which reached further into the ocean. De Houtman steered the *Hasewint* clear of those rocks, missing the cape itself, and brought his ships east in the strong winds of the Roaring Forties.

At every town which he visited along the southern coast, he had his interpreters ask if he had reached the White City. Three times, he visited a city or town and was disappointed when he received a negative answer.

On 26 July, the *Hasewint* sailed into a wide natural harbour, and then further into an inner harbour. De Houtman saw crowded docks, a towering row of statues behind them on the shore, and beyond that twin mountains with colossal edifices built into their sides, and he knew that he would not need to have his interpreters ask the question again.

---

[152] The three great capes are three major landmarks in the Southern Ocean. Cape Horn in South America divides the Atlantic from the Pacific, the Cape of Good Hope in South Africa is the traditional sailing landmark (though modern oceanography sets the dividing point for the Atlantic and Indian Oceans further east at Cape Agulhas), and Sunset Point/Cape Leeuwin in south-western Australia divides the Indian Ocean from the Pacific.

#29: The City Between The Waters

"She is mine own,
And I as rich in having such a jewel
As twenty seas, if all their sand were pearl,
The water nectar, and the rocks pure gold."
- William Shakespeare, *The Two Gentlemen of Verona*, Act II, Scene IV

* * *

Excerpts from "My Life in the South-Land". Written by Pieter Stins, a sailor who served on de Houtman's first and second voyages to what would come to be called Aururia.

Our ships sailed into the harbour of Witte Stad[153] on 26 July. Even before we came ashore, we knew we had reached a city like no other in the South-Land. Buildings covered the shore, some in a large city in the main harbour, and a smaller quarter across the water. Neither quarter had walls. Even from a distance it seemed as if everything had been built on a colossal scale.

There were docks aplenty; unlike the smaller cities, Witte Stad had boats in abundance. A few boats moved in the harbour, most of them small vessels like those of the

---

[153] *Witte Stad* is Dutch for White City. It acquired this name because the native translators have a habit of translating the meaning of names, where they have such meanings, rather than transliterating them. So they consistently translated the city's component words into Dutch as Witte Stad. Thus, this became the name by which the White City would become known in the wider world. (For a time, at least.)

other cities. One was larger and completely strange; twin hulls, lateen rigged, steered with a rudder rather than steering oar. One of our translators said that this was an Islander ship, from some subject people who live in the east and who sail west to trade and to honour the native emperor.

The city officials had known we were coming. They declared that only Captain-General de Houtman and thirteen other men could come ashore into the main city at any one time. The rest would have to stay at the foreign quarter across the water.

The Captain-General did not trust them, and had our ships stay well out to sea in the main harbour. The natives were meticulous in watching and counting who came and went; throughout our time there, we would only ever have fourteen men ashore at any one time. I was fortunate enough to be among the thirteen whom the Captain-General chose to accompany him into Witte Stad...

My memories of Witte Stad are confused in their order and their sense. Throughout my time there, especially the first few days, it felt as if I were walking through a dream. This is a city like no other, the jewel of the Orient, a place of mystery, splendour and horror combined. Here, the native emperor has gathered everything important in his realm into one place; gold, stone, gardens, animals, men, and heathen gods.

Everything in the city has been built to be larger than life. A man cannot walk down any street without being dwarfed by statues, whether of men or idols, looming over him wherever he walks. It is crowded, thronging with men from all quarters of this realm. I know not the numbers, but there must be tens of thousands, or hundreds of thousands. More men and women dwell here in any city of the Netherlands, or any European city I have seen. Some cities of the Orient may be larger, but none that I have seen or heard of have been built on this scale designed to make men feel like mice[154].

Two sounds I always remember from my time in Witte Stad. One is the noises of construction and maintenance. Seldom can a man walk far in this city without witnessing the toils of those who serve their emperor. Men labour to move materials, to shape and repair statues, to smooth and maintain the roads, to build in wood and stone, to clean and polish buildings[155]. When their work itself is silent, then the natives provide their own noise, chanting and singing as they labour. I could not decide whether the music is because they are joyful to work or to take their minds from their endless labour.

Another sound I will never forget is the endless sound of water. It is not as loud as the toils of labour, but it is always present. Rare is it indeed to find a place in the city where a man cannot hear the sound of water, whether flowing, cascading, bubbling from fountains, or dripping from the mouths of statues.

The natives adore the sound of water, and devote much of their labour to ensuring that it can always be heard. Fountains are numerous throughout the city. Sometimes water spouts from elaborately carved statues, sometimes it cascades over rocks in melodies which the natives find

---

[154] Amsterdam, the largest city in the Netherlands at this time, had around 50,000 people. Rotterdam was smaller. The White City at its fullest holds around 200,000 people, and this expedition is visiting at a time when workers are not needed in the fields, so most of the drafted labourers are in residence. There were actually many cities larger than the White City at this time, even in Europe; London was slightly larger, and Paris about twice the size. However, the scale on which the White City is built makes it seem much larger than the relatively cramped, crowded European cities.

[155] The construction and repair of the White City is not always this laborious, but de Houtman's expedition visited during the peak season of the year, when drafted labour is present in large numbers, and when most of the maintenance is performed.

pleasing, and often it fills basins where a man can drink his fill whenever he chooses.

Nowhere do the natives use water more lavishly than the place they call the Thousand-fold Garden[156]. This is a veritable wonder of nature, of carefully shaped stones and plants. An endless array of trees and shrubs, a maze of flowers and beauty, trod by ducks with feathers of a thousand hues. Amidst the Garden is always the sound of water; cascading over rocks, flowing down falls, or bubbling from artfully arranged fountains that mimic the natural world...

When I first witnessed the Garden, I thought that the natives must have heard of Eden as God made it in the beginning, and that they had done their best to create a replacement for it in this fallen world. Alas, I soon learned how mistaken I was in this regard.

The natives' beliefs are a corruption of Christianity. They refer to the Lord, but believe that they must make endless sacrifices. They know not that Christ died for all our sins, and kill men or shed their blood slowly in the name of pain. I will not commit to paper a full report of the bloodthirsty abominations they commit in the name of their perverted gospel. Theirs is a heathen religion of torture, the twisted worship of a false Christ, a malformed degradation of all that is good and holy...

The natives of Witte Stad are divided into two peoples. The people who call themselves the Atjuntja are the rulers; not all the people of this stock are considered noble, but they all think of themselves as better than their subjects. In skin and in features, there is naught to distinguish an Atjuntja from their subjects, but all of their men wear full beards, and they do not permit the same to their subjects. Most all of the Atjuntja have black hair.

---

[156] This name is a mistranslation from the real Atjuntja name, which would be more accurately translated as the Garden of Ten Thousand Steps. The native translators did not yet have a complete grasp of the Dutch language.

Their subjects go by a variety of names; the one most common I heard was Yaora, but sometimes they call themselves Yuduwungu and Madujal[157]. Most of these Yaora have blonde or light hair, though their skins are much darker. With some of the Yaora men, their hair is darker, especially those who have grown older, but not yet old enough for their hair to turn grey or white. The men among them do not all shave, but those who have beards keep them trimmed short. Our native interpreters told me that among the Atjuntja, light hair is considered a sign of common blood, although the other Yaora do not care about it in the same way...

While Witte Stad is unlike the smaller towns and cities of the South-Land in many ways, it seems to me that most of all it is designed to be a spectacle. In its construction, its waters, and its streets, it is shaped to ensure that all who visit here know that this is the residence of their emperor.

It is kept that way by most careful arrangement. For these Atjuntja do not even allow animals to wander free and disturb the streets. While these people know nothing of sheep, horses or pigs, they have noroons [emus], dogs and ducks, but they do not allow them to roam the streets, except for the multi-hued ducks in the Garden. They even keep out the pole-cats [quolls] that they use to hunt vermin. Perhaps animals are kept away because they are so fastidious about keeping their streets clean; I do not know. But I do know that this city is a place of wonder.

* * *

---

[157] Stins has misunderstood the relationship between the peoples of the Middle Country. Originally, Yaora was the collective name for all of the related peoples who occupied the south-western portion of Aururia, including the Atjuntja themselves. The name is still sometimes used in that sense, but the more common modern usage is to refer to any non-Atjuntja subject people within the Middle Country. Yuduwungu and Madujal are the names of two of the subject peoples, and who are numerous enough that they make up the most common labour draftees to the White City.

July-August 1620
Witte Stad / Milgawee [White City]
D'Edels Land / Tiayal [western coast of Australia]

A cool breeze swept across North Water into the Foreign Quarter. Standing on the shore, looking west to the twin peaks at the heart of the greatest Ajuntja city, Yuma thought that the wind was most appropriate. It brought the tangy aroma of salt water, diluted slightly by fragrances of eucalypts and shrubs, a silent reminder that these Atjuntja worshipped nature instead of understanding it. Still, more important than the smell, the wind blew from the direction of the three strange ships that waited silently in the other harbour, West Water.

Yuma, third-most senior trading captain of the Tjula bloodline, was not usually a man given to indecision. Few Nangu trading captains were. In a world where the greatest profit went to the boldest, a captain who hesitated would be lucky if his bloodline elders did not strip him of his command or find his crew deserting for captains who earned greater wealth and glory.

Now, though, he had found himself watching for two days, and he had still come no closer to a decision. He was the captain of the last Nangu great-ship of the winter's trading fleet to remain in Milgawee. The rest had departed over the last two weeks. Those with better captains carried cargoes of sandalwood, spices, gold and fragrant oils; those with weaker captains bore mostly iron, silver, or dyes.

Yuma himself had brought his ship, the *Restless*, to these western lands with a cargo of *kunduri*, Tjibarri jewellery, and gum cider. He had carefully negotiated a series of exchanges of most of this cargo for sandalwood and gold. He could have finished his trading a week ago, but had held on to the rest of his loading of *kunduri* to see if he could bargain for a better deal once the Atjuntja realised that the other ships were gone and that no more *kunduri* could be had until the next trading fleet arrived months later.

Thanks to that delay, and perhaps the guidance of the sixth path, he had been the first Nangu captain to glimpse these strange ships enter the harbour. Ships larger than even the finest Nangu great-ship. Perhaps not as manoeuvrable, but an intimidating sight nonetheless. He had known instantly that these were foreigners; the pitiful Atjuntja knowledge of shipbuilding would not allow them to build anything remotely approaching the quality of these ships.

Word from across the water at the main quarter of Milgawee brought endless rumours of the strangers who used these ships. Raw-skinned men from beyond the world, as the Atjuntja understood it. Men with strange skills and crafts, none more awe-inspiring than that they could bind thunderbolts and use them as weapons. Men who had visited the western coast the previous year and killed Atjuntja soldiers, but who had returned speaking of peace. Apparently the commander of these raw-skinned men had been admitted to the Palace of a Thousand Rooms to meet with the King of Kings.

Yuma doubted that last part of the rumours, at least. The myriad complexities of Atjuntja protocol would not allow the King of Kings to meet with any stranger so easily. Not that it would matter; the Atjuntja conducted such negotiations through intermediaries.

Still, no matter what the Atjuntja babbled about, he knew that these strangers must be men like any other. No-one had ever heard of any western islands worth visiting before, and the King of Kings' edict against western exploration meant that few Nangu had tried to find such islands. But it was only sensible that such lands existed. After all, if the Māori came from Aotearoa beyond the sunrise, why should there not be other islands beyond the sunset?

Which left Yuma in an odd position. He was, for now, the only Nangu trading captain to know about these strange ships from beyond the west. A few Nangu lived here permanently, but they were of no consequence for his purposes. No-one else back on the Island would hear word of these strangers for months unless he carried it.

So he had to decide whether to approach them, and how to find out what he could. If these raw-skins were wealthy, trade with them could prove to be very valuable. Unfortunately, there was another problem. The bearded Atjuntja buffoons were always wary of any Nangu captains who sailed further west; they preferred trade to flow through their home ports. They would be very suspicious of anything which they saw as an attempt to bypass them.

Then he had to consider these strangers themselves. They had been told that they could dock in the Foreign Quarter, if they wished, but they had chosen to keep their ships well out in the harbour. These actions spoke of a people who were full of suspicion. Any surreptitious attempts to sail to those ships would be more likely to bring an attack than a conversation. And the few strangers who went ashore to the main quarter of the city were being closely watched, he was sure. It would be difficult to speak to them without the Atjuntja finding out.

As he stared across the water, Yuma decided that for now, it would not be worth his while trying to contact these raw-skinned strangers. They were only three ships in one visit; they would not have that much worth trading for directly. Better to finish his own trading for now and sail back to the Island.

Once back home, he could consider other ways to take advantage of this new discovery. Perhaps take a great-ship further west into the sunset, to see if he could find these stranger's home islands. Or he could bring a more carefully-chosen cargo next time, with more samples of many goods, to find out what these raw-skinned strangers wanted to trade for.

For now, though, he decided these strangers should be left alone.

*

Lerunna Mundi, chamberlain of the palace, most favoured servant of the Floral Throne[158], reached for the

---

[158] In his own mind, at least.

kunduri pouch at his waist. Only a small ball, of course; enough to relax, not to stupefy. During an important negotiation, only a fool would drop a boulder into the stillness[159].

Still, he welcomed the double blessing the *kunduri* brought. For one, he had a pleasant break while he rolled the ground leaves into ash from a lantern, shaped them into a ball and chewed them. That let him force the raw-skinned commander – dee Ootman, he called himself – into blessed silence for a few moments.

For another, the blissful relaxation of *kunduri* let him rebuild the aura of calm and relaxation which His Exalted Majesty had ordered in all dealings with these Raw Men. Oh, this dee Ootman was not a complete fool, as far as such things went. But this outlander was so wrong-headed in his expectations that the difference was sometimes difficult to remember.

With the *kunduri* chewed and his spirit's essence restored, Lerunna turned his attention back to the outlander. As patiently as he could, he said, "You will not be admitted to see the King of Kings. You are not of the blessed; you cannot hear his voice."

How could even an ignorant outlander have so much difficulty grasping such a fundamental truth? No-one would be allowed to hear the Voice of Divinity without being of the right birth. Being an outlander was a disadvantage, but not an insurmountable one. Some of the Thousand Rooms had hosted outlanders as imperial guests, usually some desert chieftain who needed to be pacified, or occasional eastern delegations from the Islanders, Mutjing or Gunnagal. "If your western sta-tjol-der comes himself or sends one of his kin, perhaps His Exalted Majesty will grant his blessing and allow an audience."

---

[159] This Atjuntja metaphor can be approximately translated as "only a fool would cloud his sense."

The peasant interpreter looked worried when he had to translate that. The conversation between the two went back and forth for some time; Lerunna supposed that the interpreter was taking the opportunity to explain some truths to dee Ootman.

Taking advantage of the pause, Lerunna made a closer study of this outlander. His clothing was a mixture of marvel and stupidity. Made of some fibre called *wool*, or so he understood from the previous conversations, that was suppler than even the finest linen. Yet it was woven into strange tubes wrapped around arms and legs, and belted closely at his waist, in a form that seemed far too hot and uncomfortable.

This dee Ootman knew enough of proper appearance to wear a full beard, yet several of the outlanders with him did not. All of these men had pink skin which showed when they flushed. Likewise, his beard and hair were coloured orange-red; an odd hue for a commander. Some of his men had dark hair, and others had blonde, but the colour of their hair did not appear to correspond to any difference in rank.

Odd, very odd. Easterners all had dark hair, so they could not use that to distinguish amongst themselves. These westerners, though, had different classes and different hair colour. Why did they not use this information?

After the interpreter finished explaining a few truths, dee Ootman said, "If your King of Kings will not meet me, how can I be sure that he has agreed to terms of trade?"

Even the bliss of *kunduri* could not stop Lerunna from nodding in sheer disbelief at this outlander's ignorance. He composed himself, then said, "His Exalted Majesty has chosen me to speak on his behalf. I bear his message, I speak with his words. His Majesty is minded to permit trade, or he would not invite me to speak with you at all."

As the interpreter laboriously relayed his words into the outlander tongue, Lerunna reflected how frustrating it was to work through a peasant interpreter. Not to mention another sign of this dee Ootman's wrong-headedness. Any outlander who came to the White City to trade and negotiate should have taken the time to learn the Atjuntja tongue. The Islanders, warped through they were in other ways, had long known that. So did the few desert chieftains who had been permitted into the White City. Why did these raw-skinned outlanders not do the same?

Maybe, Lerunna wondered, dee Ootman was more cunning than he appeared. Maybe this bearded commander had learned the Atjuntja language, but chose not to reveal it. So far, dee Ootman had not shown any signs of understanding when he heard Lerunna speak, but maybe that was a ruse. Perhaps this outlander kept silent because he had more time to think while the interpreter relayed the words, or in case he overhead conversations. Lerunna decided that he would have to be careful speaking in the Atjuntja language in the presence of any outlanders, even if the interpreters were not present or not translating.

Dee Ootman said, "Your King of Kings' willingness to trade is welcome. Yet it is frustrating that we have had to wait so long before we could meet anyone to discuss trade."

Again, Lerunna wondered how this outlander could misunderstand something so simple. "You are in the dominion of the King of Kings, who fears nothing in the mortal realms. Here, you will follow his timing and his wishes. If you were in the realm of your sta-tjol-der, then you would do as he pleased. Here, you will wait on our pleasure."

Dee Ootman nodded when that was translated. The interpreter hastily explained that amongst these outlanders, a nod meant agreement rather than distrust or disapproval.

After that, they settled down to discuss trade terms. The negotiations were leisurely, drawn out over three days of production of samples, exchanges of gifts, presentation of food, and other appropriate courtesies. Dee Oootman learned quickly; by the end of the negotiations, he had become much more polite in his dealings.

The terms of trade which they eventually agreed were much as Lerunna had expected, of course. For all of the courtesy, exchange of gifts and marvellous products which these outlanders offered, they were strangers to this land. They had to accept His Exalted Majesty's terms if they wished to trade at all.

As per his instructions, Lerunna thus secured agreement to trade terms barely changed from what the Islanders followed. Trade was to be conducted at two ports on the western coast, with the land for the trading posts negotiated with the local governors. These outlander ships were not to make landfall anywhere other than the two trading posts, except in emergency if they needed food or repairs. If their ships had to land, then they should stay no longer than needed for repairs, food, or favourable weather for sailing.

Only the named trade goods were to be exchanged at the trading posts, and nothing else of value. If the outlanders had new goods which they wished to trade, they must first gain the approval of His Exalted Majesty or one of his governors. The outlanders could live and worship within the bounds of the trading posts, but when venturing outside, they would not speak of their own faith or seek to convert any of the King of Kings' subjects.

In all of the negotiations, only two matters gave Lerunna any real surprises. The first was when he stated that while the outlanders could build their own dwellings within the trading posts, they could not build any fortifications.

"What if we are threatened?" dee Ootman asked. "There are other nations whose ships may try to attack our trading posts."

A meaningless answer, as far as Lerunna was concerned. The whole of the Middle Country lived under the King of Kings' peace, and his sovereignty. His Exalted Majesty would protect people, and he would not suffer walls to be built around subject cities which might be used to support rebellion. The only exceptions came in frontier areas where the desert dwellers might raid. Even then, any wall-builders were carefully watched.

He said, "If you fear for your safety, ask of the governors, and they will provide Atjuntja troops for your protection."

The other surprising matter came when dee Ootman wanted to write the terms of the trade agreement. Very good to want it in writing, of course. Yet he presented some flimsy stuff which he called *paper*, and wanted the trade agreement written on that. Lerunna threw back his head and laughed at that nonsense. Oh, this lightweight material might perhaps be more useful than parchment for everyday messages and records, but what kind of fool would present it as a binding pact of trade?

He said, "What use have we for that material which is even more crumbling than parchment? No treaty set on parchment will last. Our agreement will be written in stone here in the White City, and repeated on land-stones at the sites of your trading posts."

*

Captain-General Frederik de Houtman stood on the stern of the *Assendelft*, watching as Witte Stad faded into the distance. First the trees and flowers blended into the background, then the shapes of the statues became impossible to discern, and then the docks blurred into insignificance. His last sight of Witte Stad was of the Twin Peaks, clad in green and stone, slowly vanishing in clouds that blew in from the west.

With the great city fading, de Houtman allowed a broad smile to creep across his face. "I do believe we will be congratulated for what we've accomplished here."

Captain Cornelisz de Vries nodded. "So we should be. A city like that... As God is my witness, never have I been so bittersweet about leaving a port. How can those people combine such wonder with such depravity?"

De Houtman shrugged. "They won't inflict their heathen rites on us." Of all the astonishing things in this city of wonders, the greatest was that the victims of this sacrificial blood-letting had all freely volunteered. "I'm not happy to witness those events, but it won't stop us trading with them."

Negotiating a trade treaty had taken much longer than it should have, especially the endless frustration of never getting any meeting with their emperor. Still, he had achieved the most important part of his mission: a trade agreement.

And what riches it would bring!

He knew, now, what trade goods would be preferred here. Even if when finding out, the Atjuntja had refused to call what they did trade. They had called it exchanges of gifts, since trade was only permitted to Dutchmen on their western coast. For now, anyway; that prohibition would not last forever.

The exchanges had been an acceptable substitute for trade, and had told him what he needed to know. These Atjuntja had been impressed with cotton textiles, with tin and steel, with rum, and most of all with the lacquered chest from Coromandel. They were not at all impressed with Brazilian tobacco, but then he did not like their version of tobacco, either. He had seen that some of it was brought on his ships anyway, naturally. Maybe others would find it more palatable. If not, sometimes any tobacco was better than none. Besides, he had a few samples of their *kunduri*, which was better than tobacco, in his estimation. Even if the Atjuntja had been horrified when he tried smoking it.

Regardless of how valuable this *kunduri* might prove to be, this land had many other goods of worth: gold, silver, sandalwood, indigo and other dyes, and salt. Some of their other produce might be valuable, too. The gum of their wealth-trees resembled gum arabic; perhaps it could be sold for a suitable profit. Their peppers had a hotter taste than any which de Houtman had ever experienced; maybe they, too, could be sold as a spice.

De Vries said, "Are you sure you want to sail no further east?"

"Quite. We have fulfilled our instructions," de Houtman said.

Enough of the instructions, at least. He had explored, charted, recorded and negotiated. He had secured a trade agreement and permission at two sites to be chosen – no doubt this Archers Nest, and somewhere else he would leave to the Governor-General to consider. He had met with a few of these Islanders who lived in this city's foreign quarter, and who had mentioned something of their own lands far to the east[160]. He had brought enough gold and silver to pay for the cost of this expedition, even if everything else he had found turned out to be worthless.

Oh, he had not quite fulfilled everything. He had not secured any of the natives by force, judging that it would do too much harm. One of his sailors had brought back a native mistress, but that woman would hardly be available for the Company's use. Nor had he extended the Netherlands' protection to these Atjuntja, but no-one could have achieved that.

He had accomplished everything that the Company could have hoped for, and more besides. As the three Dutch yachts navigated out of the harbour and began the slow journey west, de Houtman could only look forward with eager anticipation to the new tomorrows which awaited him.

---

[160] De Houtman successfully sent some sailors to land in the Foreign Quarter of the White City. Those sailors met with some of the Nangu who lived there and learned some things about them, although all of the Nangu trading ships had left before de Houtman's sailors visited the Foreign Quarter.

#30: Of Traders, Treasures and Trailblazers

"Portugal and Spain held the keys of the treasure house of the east and the west. But it was neither Portugal with her tiny population, and her empire that was little more than a line of forts and factories 10,000 miles long, nor Spain, for centuries an army on the march and now staggering beneath the responsibilities of her vast and scattered empire, devout to fanaticism, and with an incapacity for economic affairs which seemed almost inspired, which reaped the material harvest of the empires into which they had stepped, the one by patient toil, the other by luck. Gathering spoils which they could not retain, and amassing wealth which slipped through their fingers, they were little more than the political agents of minds more astute and characters better versed in the arts of peace... The economic capital of the new civilization was Antwerp... its typical figure, the paymaster of princes, was the international financier.

Convulsions of war and tides of religion unseated Antwerp from its commercial throne, the city besieged and its dissenting inhabitants dispersed. While force of arms might move borders, wealth migrated according to its own dictates, not the whims of princes. As the seventeenth century neared, international commerce continued in Amsterdam from where it had halted in Antwerp..."

— J S Stanhope, *Religion and the Birth of Capitalism*[161]

* * *

Captain-General Frederik de Houtman's second voyage to Aururia was, for the Dutch, a shining success. A trade agreement had been negotiated, and a valuable collection of sample trade goods had been brought back to guide the Company's merchants in their pursuit of profit. Better yet, the expedition had brought back a host of information in charts, logs and journals to aid in the planning and conduct of further ventures.

The descendants of the Atjuntja and the other Aururian peoples would not have quite the same view of de Houtman's voyage. Of course, that was hardly something that concerned Governor-General Coen or the other senior officers of the *Vereenigde Oost-Indische Compagnie*. De Houtman and his fellow captains were showered with honours on their return.

Along with the honours, Jan Pieterszoon Coen gave the captains and their crews strict orders not to talk about their new discoveries. All had sworn oaths to the Company and to the United Netherlands, and those oaths had to be obeyed. They were to reveal nothing of this new South-Land, particularly about its wealth, and most particularly its location.

This order lasted about as long as it took the Dutch sailors to reach the nearest tavern.

The Dutch sailors did not intend to tell foreigners the secrets, exactly, but alcohol and secrets rarely go together. Mostly, they talked to other Dutchmen, who in turn repeated rumours to other compatriots. The taverns of Batavia were not the exclusive preserve of Dutchmen; apart from the local Javanese, this was a trading post sometimes

---

[161] Historically, the first paragraph of this quote was taken from RH Tawney in *Religion and the Rise of Capitalism*. Allohistorically, another author has expressed similar sentiments but with further details about how events shifted from Antwerp to Amsterdam (the second paragraph of the quote).

visited by Englishmen, and occasionally by the Portuguese[162].

The Dutch sailors did not give detailed directions, but, inevitably, they talked. Within a few months, the Javanese, English and Portuguese knew that the VOC had discovered some fantastical new land somewhere to the south. Or was it to the east? Rumours spread, no two of them the same, about where this new land was and what it contained. The stories spread to Timor, to Malaya, to Surat, and in time to London, Lisbon and Madrid...

* * *

With the prestige secured from his second voyage, de Houtman successfully manoeuvred for command of the third expedition to the South-Land. He obtained appointment to the task of negotiating for the construction of the first Dutch outpost on the South-Land, and overseeing the first trade conducted there.

De Houtman set about his new task with enthusiasm. With a fresh fleet of ships loaded with carefully-chosen supplies, he returned to the South-Land in 1621 to establish a trading post. His chosen site was familiar from two previous visits: the Swan River. Given that he had already secured the permission of the King of Kings, it did not take long for de Houtman to negotiate the local governor's agreement to set up his new trading outpost.

De Houtman had chosen a site on the south bank at the mouth of the Swan River, at a distance he thought was about fifteen miles from the local garrison-city. He optimistically called the site Fort Nassau [Fremantle], even though his trade treaty stated – and the governor had reiterated – that no fortifications were to be built. His

---

[162] Strictly speaking, these Portuguese visitors would have been considered Spanish; those two countries had had a unified crown since 1580. Most of the trade in the East Indies was conducted by the Portuguese, however. At this point, Spain-Portugal and the Netherlands had a truce, and there was still some contact between traders on both sides. (The truce was due to expire in March 1621).

sailors were set to the task of constructing houses and other key dwellings. De Houtman used a few judiciously-chosen gifts to obtain the assistance of some local labourers to speed the process. Fort Nassau was developed into a useable state and declared open after three months, although completing some stone buildings would take over another year.

Atjuntja nobles and merchants (often the same people) had already started to gather before Fort Nassau officially opened. The samples of Dutch trade goods the previous year had attracted a great deal of interest, and de Houtman assured all arrivals that they would be given the opportunity to bargain for similar goods. De Houtman had always been an astute bargainer, and he was in a particularly favourable situation here. In most cases, the Atjuntja merchants bid against each other to obtain the most favoured goods.

Even with his previous experience of the White City, he was surprised by some of the priorities they set. The most highly-prized items were anything which showed great craftsmanship; lacquered goods, richly-decorated textiles, and the like. Steel ingots were worth half their weight in gold, and tin ingots only slightly less valued. Rum and brandy were held in similarly high esteem, especially after de Houtman's traders generously provided some free samples. Wine, though, they would not accept. Nor, despite his best efforts, could he persuade any Atjuntja to trade lead ingots for anything.

In exchange, de Houtman's trade ships were laden down with the commodities he had most desired. Gold and silver in abundance. Sandalwood in smaller quantities but, if anything, greater value. Dyes, especially their magnificent indigo. Considerable quantities of their mints and peppers and lesser spices, brought mostly to see if they could be resold for greater value. Yet despite his best efforts, he could not persuade any Atjuntja to offer *kunduri* at a price he would accept. Instead, he received many variations of responses which amounted to, "*Kunduri* is not something we trade, it is something we trade *for*."

Still, after de Houtman concluding his trading, he had the ebullient feeling that he had accomplished as much here as in his previous voyage. He left Fort Nassau in the command of a junior officer, and sailed for Batavia. There, he received another hero's welcome. As de Houtman had expected, Coen was well-pleased with him.

Unfortunately, Coen would not stay pleased for long.

* * *

With trade expanding between Batavia and the South-Land, the rumours of newfound Dutch wealth spread ever further. They caused some consternation in London, where the governor and directors of the East India Trading Company had been considering a delicate situation.

An opportunity had arisen in the Middle East, where Persia had declared war on Spain, and was besieging the Spanish garrison on the island of Kishm, near the vital Spanish-held island of Hormuz. That port had been in Portuguese and then Spanish hands for nearly a century, and offered a gateway to Persia. The Persian commanders had requested English help in capturing Kishm and then Hormuz, and had offered to allow English merchants entry into the valuable silk trade.

Alas, opportunity was balanced by danger, namely, the risk of outright war with Spain. England and Spain had been at peace for nearly two decades, and the Company might find that its pursuit of profit in the Gulf would cause a broader war. The heads of the Company were minded to ignore that risk, trusting to Providence and the good offices of King James I to ensure peace was preserved.

However, now the governor and directors had a new risk to consider: the rising power of the Dutch, and more precisely that of the VOC. The two companies had been rivals in the East Indies for two decades, until they negotiated a recent truce. Now, if the VOC had found a spectacular new source of wealth, could they be trusted to hold to that truce? If not, perhaps it would be better to cooperate with Spain against the Dutch, rather than starting what could become two wars.

The directors considered this dilemma for a few days. In the end, they decided that the immediate opportunity was worthwhile. Trade with Persia would be a valuable new market. Besides, the Spanish were Catholics, and not to be trusted. So they accepted the proposed alliance with the Persians, and decided that they would deal with the consequences when they came.

The planned attack on Kishm Island went ahead two weeks later than originally planned. The English fleet bombarded the fort and quickly forced the Spanish garrison to surrender; the assault sustained very few casualties[163]. Bolstered by this success, the English and Persian forces conducted a joint operation against Hormuz, with the Persians attacking by land while the English scattered the Spanish fleet and bombarded the castle.

Hormuz surrendered on 7 May 1622, and the Persians took control of the island, while the Spanish retreated to a secondary outpost at Muscat. Honouring their agreement, all Christian prisoners were repatriated to England, and plans began for the exchange of English cloth for Persian silk. Spain was outraged, and the Company was forced to pay ten thousand pounds each to James I and the Duke of Buckingham in compensation for the efforts they went to in preserving peace[164].

* * *

Frederik de Houtman was an extraordinary man. An explorer, but also a self-promoter and liar. An astronomer

---

[163] The similar historical attack which happened a couple of weeks earlier was also successful, but one of the (few) casualties was the notable English explorer William Baffin. Baffin had made his name exploring the artic regions of North America, going further north than any before him while searching unsuccessfully for a passage to India. He had recently joined the East India Trading Company, and was present for the assault on Kishm, where he met an untimely end. With the allohistorical delay to the attack, Baffin survives.

[164] This is essentially the same outcome as happened historically, although the historical date for the fall of Hormuz was 22 April 1622.

and a visionary, recorder of constellations unknown and charter of lands unvisited by Europeans. A linguist who recorded the first European dictionary of the Malayan language, and an optimist who always trusted that fate would reward him. An opportunist with an eye for the main chance, but whose vision ultimately deserted him.

After his three voyages to the South-Land, de Houtman was eager to return to the Netherlands to describe in person what he had found. And, of course, to receive the adulation he believed he deserved for his discoveries.

Governor-General Coen willingly allowed de Houtman to return home, but was dismayed by what happened when the explorer made it to the Netherlands. De Houtman took the opportunity to describe his triumphs *ad nauseum*. He was careful enough to present his tales only to those who could be relied upon to keep the details secret: Company lords and officers, the Stadtholder, and other government officials.

Unfortunately, that was the limit of de Houtman's discretion. To hear him speak, a listener would believe that his actions alone had been responsible for the discovery of the South-Land. And that no-one else had the wit to recognise the opportunities. To add to his misdoings, de Houtman presented a magnificent golden neck-ring to Maurice of Nassau, Prince of Orange, and Stadtholder of Holland, Zeeland, Utrecht, Guelders and Overijssel. This neck-ring was a prize which de Houtman had collected while in the South-Land, but he had retained it rather than giving it to the Company.

De Houtman's generous gift endeared him to the Stadtholder, but it enraged the Lords Seventeen. Combined with his ever more frequent self-promotion, it ensured that he would never be trusted by the Company again. De Houtman was denied any further commissions, and lived out the remainder of his life in Europe. While he died a rich man, he never again set foot on the South-Land.

* * *

As the years turned, despite de Houtman's departure, and regardless of the distant battles and manoeuvring in the Gulf, the Dutch were busy shipping goods to and from their newly-discovered land. A few outbound fleets from the Netherlands were ordered to stop at Fort Nassau on their way to Batavia, conducting trade with the Atjuntja merchants. Prices had fallen after the initial novelty – no longer did the Atjuntja value steel as half the worth of gold – but any Dutch ship which stopped to trade at Fort Nassau always left with more valuable cargo than when it arrived.

Fortunately for the Dutch, the Atjuntja and the rest of the world, the long shipping times meant that most diseases were not exchanged between the two peoples. Incubation periods were mostly too short; a disease would burn its way through a ship's crew either before it reached the South-Land, or before the departing ships made their next landfall at Batavia.

Not all diseases were contained by the ocean barrier, of course. The first venereal diseases had been left behind at Seal Point in 1620 when de Houtman's expedition visited there. Blue-sleep was an ever-present threat to Dutch sailors when they came ashore; many of them caught the illness. Yet this was a fast-burning disease; while many sailors fell ill and some died from it, it ran through a ship's crew before they reached the Indies.

The greatest threat awaiting the Dutch in the South-Land was the malady called the Waiting Death. No epidemic of Marnitja had swept through the Atjuntja lands in the last decade before the Dutch arrival, so they were safe, for now.

The isolation of the seas would not last, of course. Eventually an asymptomatic carrier would make the journey, or a fast ship would carry disease to a new shore. If nothing else, some maladies would linger in blankets or textiles and bring Eurasian diseases to the South-Land, or Aururian diseases to the Old World, but that time was not yet.

* * *

While the Company officers were glad of the profitable trade they had found at Fort Nassau, they were eager to discover more. The first visit to the White City had told them that the Islanders lived far to the east, but not the details of how to travel there.

So a few of their officers did some exploration by land along the Atjuntja road network. That was tolerated, up to a point, provided that they did not attempt to trade. Yet they were always watched, and discouraged most strongly from coming by land to the White City or any other place where they might encounter Islander traders. The King of Kings did not wish his two trading partners to contact each other directly, realising full well the problems that this would bring for the carefully controlled Atjuntja internal trade and tribute networks.

Thus, the Dutch land explorations gave them some grasp of the geography of the Atjuntja dominions, but did not let them explore any further trade. Some inland regions were also expressly off limits, such as the vicinity of Star Hill or the main gold mines at Golden Blood. To build new trade networks, they would have to venture along the seas.

In 1622, Governor-General Coen ordered the first voyage be sent to explore past the Atjuntja dominions in pursuit of new trade markets. Pieter Dirkzoon was named captain of the *Leeuwin*, with the yacht *Nijptang* accompanying, and given orders to explore the southern coast of the South-Land. He was instructed to explore east past the White City, in the hope of reaching the Islander homeland and determining whether it was worthwhile establishing direct trade with this barely-known people.

Mindful of the Atjuntja watchfulness, Dirkzoon led his two ships from Batavia to Fort Nassau, where they resupplied before steering well south of Cape Hasewint [Cape Leeuwin]. His ships stayed out at sea until they had passed what they judged to be the easternmost Atjuntja dominion, Pink Water [Esperance], then turned north.

As it happened, Dirkzoon was correct in his navigation, and he brought his ships close to the shore at what were no longer Ajuntja lands.

Unfortunately, these lands were devoid of Atjuntja for good reason. The endless westerly winds gave the Dutch ships great speed, but the coast they faced was the bleakest that any of them had ever seen or heard of. This barren stretch of coast consisted of seemingly-endless sea cliffs, imposing bulwarks of stone which reached 300 feet high or more, stretching from horizon to everlasting horizon. Above the cliff-tops was nothing at all but featureless emptiness; no trees, no rivers emptying, nothing but hundreds of miles of unwelcoming hostility.

The coast was ever-intimidating, never approachable. Besides the fierce winds pushing them against the cliffs, the seas themselves were a threat. Immense wind-driven swells broke endlessly upon the sea-cliffs, slowly eroding their bases, with force that would shatter even the largest ship to driftwood and splinters in an instant.

In an unusual display of originality, since new lands were normally named after high-ranking Company officers, Dirkzoon christened this endless barrenness as Kust van de Nachtmerrie [Nightmare Coast].

With such an unwelcoming and dangerous coast, Dirkzoon could not keep his ships constantly in sight of the shoreline. To do so risked disaster, since a gust of wind or more than usually potent set of swells would destroy his ships in a heartbeat. Thus, while he maintained enough sightings of the cliffs to know that they continued, he missed the one small break in the cliffs which marked a lonely Islander settlement that the locals so aptly christened in their own language as Isolation.

Dirkzoon kept on, doggedly persistent, until his expedition reached a point where the sea cliffs turned to the south-east. This was the worst possible direction, since it would force the ships ever further away from Batavia. His orders had anticipated sailing around the South-Land and back up to tropical latitudes, where he could return to Batavia in relative safety.

Alas, he now faced seemingly endless sea-cliffs stretching away in the wrong direction. For all Dirkzoon knew, the bleakly featureless cliffs stretched all the way to the South Pole. While he knew that the Islanders lived here somewhere, he did not know how far, or how friendly they would be. With dwindling supplies, hostile seas, and the prospect of a very slow voyage back west against the wind, he was minded to turn back.

Decision time came when the two ships reached a couple of small islands off the coast. The seas calmed enough to allow a few boats to venture ashore and confirm that these islands were uninhabited. The sailors replenished their supplies of fresh water from the islands, but otherwise found that these isolated rocky outposts had nothing to commend them.

While Dirkzoon's ships lingered at these two islands, a rare shift in the wind saw the breeze come from the east. This fortunate change was enough to convince Dirkzoon to turn back; he might not get another such opportunity. So he ended his exploration and brought his two ships back to Batavia, where he provided them with charts and descriptions of bleakness, but not the new trading markets which Coen had sought[165].

* * *

With the failure of Dirkzoon's 1622 expedition, Coen and the VOC decided to focus other priorities, rather than further exploration. War had broken out with Spain-Portugal in 1621. The Company concentrated its efforts on

---

[165] The progress of Pieter Dirkzoon's exploration is similar to that of the historical exploration of Francois Thijssen in the ship *Gulden Zeepaerdt* in 1627; he charted much of the southern coast of Australia but turned back when the coast started to stretch to the south-east. The islands which Dirkzoon discovered are in historical Australia still called the Nuyts Archipelago, which Thijssen named after a high-ranking passenger on his ship.

protecting its Far Eastern holdings and seizing other places of known value, rather than diverting valuable ships for another costly, challenging, and probably fruitless expedition. Instead, in accordance with their treaty, they built a second trading post near the Atjuntja garrison-city of Seal Point, which they called Fort Zeelandia. Being nearer to the salt-harvesting regions, this new outpost saw greater trading in salt, but otherwise its goods were similar to Fort Nassau.

Coen knew that the South-Land contained other nations and markets. However, he had also learned that gold and sandalwood, the most valuable goods of the South-Land, were what the Islanders came to Atjuntja lands to trade for. They would not find these goods if they ventured further east. The only known trade goods from further east were *kunduri* and gum cider. Gum cider was of little value to the Company. *Kunduri* was spoiled in Coen's eyes for another reason: when he had first tried smoking it, he had inhaled so much of the stronger substance that it had caused him to vomit. He refused to try *kunduri* again, and decided that it was worthless. While some other Company officers had sampled the drug and now savoured it, Coen was too stubborn to change his mind.

Thus, over the next four years, Coen ordered that Company ships focus on the known rewards of gold, sandalwood and sweet peppers[166]. This provided valuable capital for supporting Company activities elsewhere in the Orient, particularly for building new ships and recruiting mercenaries for garrisons and raids. The wealth of Asia beckoned; Coen hoped to monopolise shipping between the nations. The commodities of the South-Land were merely building blocks in the corporate edifice he wanted to construct.

---

[166] Sweet peppers are what the Dutch call the various cultivars of mountain peppers that the Atjuntja cultivate (*Tasmannia lanceolata*). Per weight, the berries have about ten times the spiciness of common peppers, and they are developing into a profitable spice which the VOC exports to Europe.

The Company only decided to change its policy when it received direct word from the Islanders. In late 1625, a Nangu trading captain named Yuma Tjula discreetly arranged for some Djarwari labourers returning to their homeland to pass on an invitation to the commander of Fort Nassau. This gave the Dutch enough of a description of the southern coast of the South-Land to know how to sail to Islander-held territory.

With this inspiration, the Lords Seventeen commissioned a new expedition of discovery. They sent three ships, under the command of François Thijssen in the *Valk*, to make contact with the Islanders. Unlike his predecessor, Thijssen was given explicit orders to explore further east, to find a way around the expected edge of the South-Land and return to Batavia by a more northerly route.

So, in 1626 and 1627, François Thijssen commanded an expedition which some would later claim to make him the greatest European explorer of Aururia. Even those who did not give him that rank placed him a close second behind Frederik de Houtman.

Thijssen did not visit set out from Fort Nassau as his predecessor had done, but came directly from Europe via Mauritius. Knowing that the winds were more reliable in higher latitudes, he sailed well south of Cape Hasewint, and did not turn north until he judged he had neared the longitude where Dirkzoon had turned back.

Thijssen had, in fact, gone further east than he intended, and by the time he sailed north he made landfall near the tip of what would come to be called Valk Land [Eyre Peninsula, South Australia]. He followed the coast until he reached the Mutjing city of Pankala, where he and his sailors were the first Europeans to contact a Gunnagalic people in their own land.

From here, Thijssen charted some of the coast, then crossed over to the Island, where he spent a few days at Crescent Bay before sailing on to Jugara on the mainland. Here, among many other accomplishments, he became the first Dutchman to visit the kingdom of Tjibarr, and the first to trade for a significant quantity of *kunduri*[167].

Due to warnings from both Tjibarr and the Islanders, he avoided any efforts to contact the Yadji. Instead, he sailed further south, where he explored much of the south and east coasts of an island which would later be named for him, although he called it New Holland [Tasmania]. Here, he became the first European to contact the Kurnawal, and the first to be utterly confused by attempts to translate their allusion-laden poetry.

In keeping with his orders, Thijssen sailed further east across a great expanse of sea, until he made landfall on the western coast of the southern island of Aotearoa [New Zealand]. The local Māori king ordered his sailors to depart or be killed, saying that they had no interest in visitors. Thijssen decided that combat was pointless, and withdrew. He sailed up the western coast of Aotearoa, meeting with similar hostility and sometimes violence whenever he made contact with the Māori kingdoms. So he confined himself to mapping the western coast of the two islands (although he believed they were a single island), and sailed north into the Pacific.

Thijssen's expedition went much further north, visiting Tonga before turning west, sailing north of New Guinea, and returning to Batavia in November 1627. Here, he had a wealth of tales which he planned to tell.

Unfortunately, the world had changed by then.

* * *

"Sire, Your Majesty finds yourself in a situation in which no part of your dominions is not under attack from your enemies, in league and conspiracy so extensive that one can without any exaggeration say that the whole of the rest of

---

[167] Some influential (or, perhaps, influenced) historians would argue that his establishment of trade in *kunduri* was more important than his contact with Tjibarr.

the world is turned against Your Majesty alone, in Asia, Africa and Europe."

- Gaspar de Guzman, Count-Duke of Olivares to Philip IV of Spain (and Philip III of Portugal), 26 July 1625

#31: The Gates of Tartarus

"And I looked, and beheld a pale horse: and his name that sat on him was Death, and Hell followed with him. And power was given unto them over the fourth part of the earth..."
- Revelation 6:8

* * *

Infectious diseases are the greatest killers of humanity throughout history. In war and in peace, diverse infestations of diseases have ravaged the world's population time and again. Effective treatments have been rare until the last couple of centuries of human history, and even today many diseases can only be prevented, not cured.

Yet, as is well-known, while epidemic diseases can kill humans wherever on the globe they may live, the diseases themselves did not originate from all parts of the world. The Old World had more than a dozen major killers which were transported along with Old Worlders to the other continents and islands, but the rest of the world did not have any major killers awaiting Old Worlders when they arrived[168].

So, as Europeans reached other parts of the world, they brought a host of diseases with them. Smallpox, measles, typhus and influenza are usually considered the deadliest global killers, but malaria, yellow fever, tuberculosis,

---

[168] With the disputed exception of syphilis, which probably originated from the New World.

whooping cough, diphtheria, (bubonic) plague, mumps, typhoid, chickenpox, rubella, and other diseases were also major scourges.

Look into the depths of allohistory, however, and this exchange of diseases was not always one-way. In the continent which history calls Australia, and allohistory calls Aururia, the inhabitants have long suffered from a variety of diseases. Many of these are minor, non-fatal, or otherwise constrained by geographical and biological factors to the continent itself. Still, the Aururian continent holds three diseases with the potential to become worldwide killers: blue-sleep, swamp rash, and Marnitja.

Blue-sleep is a form of avian influenza, which originated from migrating birds that travel between Aururia and parts of Asia and Europe. Like all forms of influenza, it is airborne, highly contagious, and mutates rapidly, making long-term immunity impossible, although people who have survived a previous infection are unlikely to die from a re-infection. Infected victims quickly experience fatigue and have their faces and lips turn blue, but in other respects the disease is similar to common influenza.

Being derived from avian influenza, blue-sleep has extreme potential to turn into a pandemic. The worst influenza pandemics in both history and allohistory originated from avian forms of influenza, and blue-sleep is no exception. The historical Spanish flu pandemic of 1918 is estimated to have killed about 5% of the global population, and blue-sleep has a similarly lethal potential.

Blue-sleep is infectious and common enough that it afflicted Dutch visitors as early as de Houtman's second expedition to Aururia. Fortunately for the rest of the world, blue-sleep spread very rapidly amongst ship crews, and the main Dutch trading post at Fort Nassau was a considerable sailing time from the next port of call at Batavia. This meant that while Dutch sailors regularly caught blue-sleep, transmission of the virus across the oceans was much more difficult.

Swamp rash is a mosquito-borne virus which evolved from the historical Barmah Forest virus. It produces chills, fever, fatigue, swollen joints, and a blistery rash which spreads over most of the body. While most of the victims recover, in some cases the infection enters the lymphatic system, leading to painfully swollen lymph nodes and eventual death.

Swamp rash is not a continent-wide disease. The virus is mostly confined to the artificial wetlands in the Nyalananga [Murray] basin, although it has recently spread to the wetlands in the western regions of the Yadji lands [southwestern Victoria]. For it to spread further, however, is unlikely. The mosquitoes which carry swamp rash are short-lived species, and the birds which are its other natural hosts do not migrate beyond the continent. While it would not be impossible for the virus to spread overseas, it would be unlikely.

The mortality rate of swamp rash varies. The peoples who live along the Nyalananga itself have evolved some natural resistance to the virus, and so their mortality rate is only about 5% for children and less for adults. For visitors from elsewhere in the continent, or overseas, the mortality rate is about 10% for adults, and worse for children.

Of all of the afflictions found on the Aururian continent, however, none is deadlier than what the locals call the Waiting Death: Marnitja, in the Gunnagal language. Marnitja is an allohistorical henipavirus, related to the historical Hendra and Nipah viruses, and more distantly to measles and mumps. Marnitja originated as a bat-borne virus which spread via domesticated dingos and ultimately evolved into an exclusively human epidemic.

People infected with Marnitja show a distinctive two-stage set of symptoms. The first stage is a haemorrhagic infection of the lungs called the "pink cough," where the fevered victims experience severe coughing and other breathing difficulties. They also suffer from fatigue, fever, and sometimes blood loss and renal (kidney) failure. Some survivors of the pink cough have life-long breathing problems.

Survivors of the pink cough, however, are not yet free of Marnitja. While they are no longer infectious, they may still be afflicted with the second stage of the virus. This is a form of encephalitis, an infection of their central nervous system which leads to fever, seizures, delirium and almost inevitable death. Survivors of the pink cough have to endure an interminable wait to find out whether they will succumb to the delirium; the usual period is two to three months, but on rare occasions it can take as long as three years[169]. This lingering period of uncertainty is what led the survivors to christen the disease the Waiting Death.

The fatality rate of Marnitja varies considerably, depending on a population's previous exposure to this virus or to infectious diseases in general. Amongst the Aururian peoples, each epidemic usually kills less than 5% of the population. For Eurasian peoples, the virus would kill anywhere between 10-15% of the population, depending on their nutritional levels and general health. For peoples with insufficient exposure to epidemic diseases – which in the early seventeenth century includes most of the New World – the fatality rate is likely to be in excess of 20% of the population.

Given the shipping times between Aururia and the East Indies, Marnitja is also unlikely to be transmitted by direct infection. However, one of the distinctive features of Marnitja is that it produces a relatively high proportion (up to 0.5%) of asymptomatic carriers. Anyone who becomes an asymptomatic carrier will be infectious for life, and it will only take one such person to travel from Aururia to the rest of the world for Marnitja to become a global problem.

* * *

---

[169] This waiting period is mirrored in the historical counterparts to Marnitja, named Hendra virus and Nipah virus. For those viruses, in some cases those diseases have taken over 4 years for the viral encephalitis to appear.

The first European exposure to Marnitja was in April 1625, when a Dutch trading fleet arrived in Fort Nassau [Perth] after sailing from the Netherlands. The Waiting Death burned through the ships *Dordrecht* and *Sardam* as they sailed to Batavia, but the pink cough had run its course before the ships reached the East Indies. While some of the sailors would later die in a fevered delirium, by this stage they were no longer infectious. One of their Yaora mistresses recognised the Waiting Death and described it to the Dutch, but they did not pay it much heed. They treated this malady as simply one more in a long list of tropical diseases which often struck Europeans who visited the Spice Islands.

They would soon learn the gravity of their mistake.

Centuries later, a collaboration of three authors – an epidemiologist, a linguist, and a historian – would trace the path of the first Marnitja epidemic as it burned across the globe. Their efforts were dedicated, their report exhaustive, and it would eventually be published in three languages on as many continents.

This report marked the authors as the first to accomplish many things. They were the first to trace the oldest references to the virus. They were the first to recommend the application of what would become the near-universal name for the disease (Marnitja), replacing the host of appellations which the disease had carried before that: the Dutch curse, the dying cough, the sweating sleep, the unholy death, and many more.

What these authors would not do was discover the name of the first Dutch asymptomatic carrier who carried the disease to the world. History would never record that name. Yet these authors gave this carrier a name anyway: Patient Zero.

The authors discovered that Patient Zero was a sailor aboard the Dutch merchant ship *Vliegende Hollander*, which landed at Fort Nassau on 15 October 1626. Several sailors caught Marnitja on this visit, and many of them died from it. As before, the Dutch assumed that this was another tropical malady, and after conducting normal trade, set sail for Batavia. The *Vliegende Hollander* was one of four ships in this trading fleet, but after its arrival, it was the only one to be reloaded with gold and spices for a quick return to the Netherlands, along with five other ships making the voyage home.

The authors presumed that Patient Zero stayed on the *Vliegende Hollander* for most of the unloading and reloading, for there is no record that Marnitja spread from him to anyone in Batavia. The *Vliegende Hollander* and its fellow ships sailed west with the November monsoons. While crossing the Indian Ocean, the *Vliegende Hollander* became damaged in a storm, and had to put ashore on the eastern coast of Madagascar for repairs. Relations with the locals were peaceable enough after the captain provided a few gifts, and the repairs were effected over the next few weeks. The *Vliegende Hollander* departed the island for Amsterdam, some time behind its fellow ships. However, it left a legacy behind.

Madagascar became the first region of the Old World to know the scourge of Marnitja. In 1627, the affliction burned its way across the island, earning it the name of "burning lungs." It left behind a legacy of fevered, coughing victims, survivors with breathing difficulties, and other survivors who did not yet know the doom which awaited them.

The Mozambique Channel presented no barrier to an epidemic of the Waiting Death. Madagascar had long been a hub of traders coming to and from East Africa; the Portuguese who had begun to establish colonies along the coast were only seeking to break into a much longer-established market. From Madagascar, trading vessels carried the new affliction near-simultaneously to the Portuguese outposts at the Island of Mozambique and Zanzibar.

Once established on the African mainland, Marnitja spread rapidly both north and south. It left a deadly passage as far south as the Cape, devastating the Bantu and

Khoisan peoples of southern Africa. To the north, it spread more slowly, reaching Ethiopia in 1628 and then Egypt in 1629. Seaborne trade carried it to the Persian Gulf in 1628, striking first at Muscat, then spreading along both shores of the Gulf and into Persian lands.

Marnitja reached Mecca in time for the annual *hajj* in 1629. Among the victims were a few pilgrims who believed that they had been spared from the visitation of this new malady, when in fact they would be bearing the disease home with them. From Egypt, Mecca and Persia, the disease was poised to spread over the rest of the House of Islam. However, it did not spread much into Christian Europe, for by this time the Waiting Death had already reached that continent by another route.

From Ethiopia, Marnitja did not just spread north; it also burned its way west across the Sahel. In time, it devastated all of the West African peoples, including kingdoms such as Allada, Oyo and Kaabu. As well as the suffering inflicted on these regions by the disease itself, the first wave of Marnitja also struck the European slave-trading outposts in West Africa.

Unfortunately, this was not enough to destroy the slave trade entirely, not with sugar planters in Brazil and the Caribbean with a seemingly endless demand for more labour. In 1630, among the unfortunate slaves crammed into European trading vessels were three asymptomatic carriers, two bound for Brazil, the other for Hispaniola. From here, the disease spread rapidly throughout the Caribbean and Portuguese Brazil, and more slowly into Mesoamerica, through Central America, and down into Peru. All of the heavily-settled parts of New Spain were also struck by the virus. The main wave of infection burned out in the northern deserts of New Spain and did not penetrate into most of North America. However, over the next few years, secondary waves of infection struck the European colonies on the eastern seaboard, and spread to the neighbouring Amerindian peoples.

Europe itself first felt the Waiting Death thanks to Patient Zero. On 21 August 1627, the *Vliegende Hollander* sailed into Amsterdam, where its crew disembarked. One week later, the first Dutch men and women developed fevers and chills, followed quickly by a hacking cough which grew ever worse.

Two days later, Marnitja caused its first deaths on the European mainland. The first of uncountably many. Many prominent Dutchmen died, including Frederik de Houtman, the discoverer of the South-Land, who succumbed to the pink cough on 1 October 1627[170]. Still, Frederick Henry, the Prince of Orange, survived the disease without any apparent ill effects.

At this time, Europe was nine years into a war which another history would call the Thirty Years' War. The Dutch Republic was not involved in the main part of this struggle, although it had been at war with Spain-Portugal since 1621. Its neighbours were at the forefront of the fighting, though; the Holy Roman Empire was the key battleground, and Christian IV of Denmark had led his kingdom into the war two years earlier.

In 1628, Marnitja spread rapidly through war-ravaged Germany, killing both sides indiscriminately. Recognising where it had come from, if not the cause of the disease, the Germans referred to the epidemic as the Dutch curse. It was a curse which would kill many of their people in the days to come, including several of the leading political and military figures of the day.

Like so many of his subjects, Ferdinand II, the Holy Roman Emperor, was afflicted by a severe bout of the pink cough. While he survived, he was gravely weakened, with breathing difficulties which would persist for the remainder

---

[170] This did not shorten de Houtman's life by very much; in real history he died only a few weeks later.

of his truncated life. Left more vulnerable to other infections, he would succumb to pneumonia in 1631[171].

The Catholic forces had two leading generals at this time. One, Johann Tserclaes, Count of Tilly, died in a fevered delirium in February 1628. The other, Albrecht von Wallenstein, also caught the Dutch curse but escaped with only mild symptoms. However, the deaths and disruption caused by the disease meant that he had to abandon his plans for a siege of Straslund, the last holdout Protestant port on the southern Baltic coast.

On the Protestant side, the most prominent casualty of the Dutch curse was John George I, Elector of Saxony. Christian IV of Denmark survived, although he lost several of his children, including Prince Frederick [who would later have become King Frederick III]. His designated heir, Christian, survived Marnitja but experienced severe scarring of his lungs, which would later shorten Christian's life.

Most other major Protestant rulers survived, although Georg Wilhelm of Brandenburg-Prussia was permanently invalided by breathing problems caused by the pink cough. The effective governance of his state passed to his Catholic chancellor, Adam, Count of Schwarzenberg.

The Dutch curse could not, of course, be confined to the combatants in what would now not be called the Thirty Years' War. It crossed the Rhine and swept into France around the same time as it was ravaging Germany. Here, Cardinal Richelieu had taken personal command of the royal armies besieging the Huguenots in La Rochelle. In April 1628 he died coughing up blood, and the Dutch curse took so many soldiers with him that the government forces abandoned the siege. The epidemic spread from here into Spain, where it took a heavy toll of the population, including several prominent nobles, although Felipe IV survived.

---

[171] In real history, Ferdinand died in 1637.

The Dutch curse spread eastward and southward from the Holy Roman Empire. In 1629, Victor Amadeus I, Duke of Savoy, became one of the rarest of survivors, one who suffered but survived the delirium of the Waiting Death. Unfortunately, it left him with severe paralysis and impaired speech. His Francophile wife Christine Marie, the Duchess consort, was then pregnant with the future Louise Christine, and became the *de facto* regent of Savoy. Further south in Rome, Pope Urban VIII survived the curse, although several of his most prominent cardinals did not.

In its eastward spread, the Dutch curse cut a deadly path through Poland-Lithuania; the monarch Zygmunt III survived, but lost one of his sons, Aleksander Karol. The disease spread on into Muscovy, as well as passing south into the Ottoman-ruled Balkans. Sultan Murad IV survived without apparently even catching the disease, although it struck his court. The most prominent casualty in the Sublime Porte was the Grand Vizier, Gazi Ekrem Hüsrev Pasha. From here, it combined with the other wave of infection coming through Persia and Arabia, and burned its way across the length and breadth of Asia.

One final tendril of infection went north from Lithuania into Swedish-ruled Estonia, and thence into peninsular Sweden in 1630. This was a secondary wave of infection, since the disease had already entered Sweden from Denmark in 1628. However, among those who had not caught Marnitja during the first wave was the Swedish king, Gustavus Adolphus. He caught the pink cough in May 1630, and survived. By this time, though, word from the Netherlands (via several Aururian mistresses) meant that the Swedish monarch knew that he still needed to wait to see whether the delirium would take him. He might succumb in any time up to three years.

Gustavus Adolphus decided that if he did die, he would leave a legacy worth remembering.

* * *

Blue-sleep took longer to expand its deadly reach out of Aururia. Confined by sailing times from their trading posts, no early Dutch ship would bring the disease back to the Indies.

However, the Dutch were not the only early explorers of Aururia.

Portugal and England knew of the Dutch discovery of a new land near the Indies; word had not taken long to spread. Tthe VOC had been assiduous in restricting knowledge of charts and other important navigational details, so other nations were not sure exactly where this new land could be found, or how to navigate it safely. England soon found other concerns besides the distant rumour of gold, but Portugal had a greater presence in the Indies. And, due to a combination of religious concerns and an ongoing war with the Dutch, a greater motivation to explore these new lands.

Father António de Andrade was a distinguished Portuguese Jesuit who had spent two and a half decades as the Society of Jesus' chief missionary in the Indies. He had been recalled to Goa in 1624, but he retained an interest in affairs in the Indies. With ever-growing rumours of the new land which the Dutch had discovered, he decided to return there and explore this new land to see whether he could spread the Word of God to the new peoples.

De Andrade returned to Flores in the Indies in 1629 along with his brother, Manuel Marques, and arranged for a ship to be sent to explore these new lands. Under de Andrade's guidance, the ship sailed to the south-east and explored part of the South-Land. They called this region Costa Problematica [Troublesome Coast], for what they found was a barren, forbidding land, with the "natives" being very reluctant to approach. De Andrade persisted, and had some brief encounters with some of the natives, but was unable to induce any of them to return to Flores on board the Portuguese ship.

De Andrade's visit marked the first Portuguese exploration of Aururia. It failed in terms of direct conversion, but he had always known that was unlikely on a first visit. The expedition did develop some useful charts of parts of the new land. Unfortunately, the sailing times were quick enough that it also brought back something else with it: blue-sleep. A sailor had caught the disease during one of the meetings with the Aururians, and it spread amongst the crew on the voyage back to Flores. Several of the sailors were still infectious when it reached the Portuguese colony.

Once a disease such as blue-sleep was established in the Indies, it inevitably spread. Airborne, easily transmissible and often lethal, blue-sleep followed the trade routes throughout the Indies and onto the Asian mainland. From here, it burned across the length of Asia and on into Africa and Europe.

Blue-sleep ravaged Europe in 1631-2. While the overall toll from this disease was lower than that of Marnitja, the greatest proportion of the deaths was among young adults[172]. This meant that it killed many young men of military age, which had considerable effects on the armies then fighting across much of the continent.

The disease took its toll of prominent members of European society, too. Perhaps the most notable victim was Charles I of England, Scotland and Ireland. His death left his infant son Charles II as nominal sovereign and his dominions to be governed by an uncertain regency, with the claimants including George Villiers, Duke of Buckingham[173] and Thomas Wentworth.

In Poland-Lithuania, King Zygmunt III still survived, but the royal family lost another prominent member. The most

---

[172] In this regard, blue-sleep is much like a historical avian-derived influenza virus, the Spanish flu pandemic of 1918. That disease, too, was most deadly for young adults.

[173] Historically, Buckingham was assassinated in August 1628 by a disgruntled soldier; here, the dislocation of diseases means that he was not in the vicinity of his would-be assassin, and so survives for the time being.

prominent prince, Wladyslaw [who would have become King Wladyslaw IV in 1632] succumbed to blue-sleep.

The Austrian branch of the House of Habsburg suffered a severe toll due to an unfortunate confluence of timing; the children of the Holy Roman Emperor Ferdinand II, and many of the other leading members of the House, were at the most vulnerable age. Ferdinand III had only succeeded his father for six weeks when he succumbed to blue-sleep on 18 October 1631. His only brother, Archduke Leopold, had died two weeks before, leaving no direct male heirs. He had only two surviving sisters, and one of them, Cecilia Renata, died in early November.

Worse, there were now no suitably-aged close male relatives amongst the Austrian Habsburgs. The closest male-line relative was the three-year-old Ferdinand Charles, Archduke of Further Austria, and cousin of Ferdinand III. Ferdinand Charles had himself been born posthumously; his mother had been pregnant when his father Leopold, the old Emperor's last surviving brother[174] had died from the Dutch curse in April 1628.

The only other alternative was to find a husband for the last surviving daughter of Ferdinand II: Archduchess Maria Anna of Austria. She was reportedly intelligent, stern, driven, opinionated – and an extremely attractive political prize. The intrigues started before Ferdinand III's body had a chance to grow cold.

* * *

The seventeenth century was already a time of global upheaval. The European powers had begun their assault on the globe which would see them establish colonial control over most of the world's surface in the next few centuries. The deepening climatic effects of the Little Ice Age brought famine and other agricultural problems to much of the planet.

---

[174] Yes, another Leopold. Like many European royal families, the Habsburgs had a habit of recycling names.

The Americas were in the midst of the largest population replacement of the modern era. Japan was nearing the time when it would have chosen to close itself off from all but carefully regulated contact with the rest of the world. In China, the worsening climatic conditions brought about social unrest which would have led to the collapse of the Ming Dynasty and its replacement by the foreign Manchu. In Europe itself, the continent convulsed as old political and religious certainties crumbled.

In these volatile times, the twin waves of Aururian epidemics could only add to the upheaval. Collectively, they killed 19% of the global population - over 100 million people - and their effects did not stop there. Marnitja, in particular, would recur every generation and depress the global population growth rate for centuries. The world which followed would be an emptier place.

More, the deaths and devastation had inevitable effects on the world's psyche. A new age had dawned, or so some later historians would say, when describing the changing attitudes to religion, to labour, and to social and political institutions.

Of course, some of those historians would argue that, for all of the death and upheaval which Aururian diseases caused, that this was not the greatest effect which the discovery of Aururia would have on the rest of the world.

#32: The Sounds of Harmony

"The greatest of leaders speaks the least, and inspires the most. He does not *demand* obedience, he *receives* it. A lesser leader seeks respect, a greater leader knows that he will earn it. The grandest deeds of a leader are those which his followers perform without needing his instructions."
- From *Oora Gulalu* [The Endless Road], a text composed in Tjibarr in the fifteenth century, and widely respected by both Plirite and Tjarrlinghi believers

* * *

Serpent Day, Cycle of Salt, 382nd Year of Harmony (4.10.382)[175] / 10 July 1621
Crescent Bay, The Island [Kingscote, Kangaroo Island]
Wind blew steadily from the north, swirling an irregular course across the city streets, up the hill slopes, and through the open doors of the temple. With it came the tang of salt, a reminder of the seas that formed the livelihood of all the Nangu. Perhaps it carried the sounds of the city streets, too, but they could not be heard. As with all proper houses

---

[175] The Gunnagalic calendar (adopted by the Nangu) divides the year into 30 cycles of 12 days, with an additional 5 or 6 intercalary days at the end of the year. Each of the days and cycles are both named and numbered. So 4.10.382 is the fourth day in the tenth cycle of the year 382, ie Serpent Day in the Cycle of Salt. There are also "months" of 30 days, which overlap this timing and are used for some social and religious purposes, but which are not used in the standard version of naming and numbering days.

of harmony, the Temple of the Five Winds supplied its own sounds.

Tinkles, ringing and thuds came from the chimes that hung on every exterior wall and in some of the open passages inside; a soothing irregular melody born of the endless breeze and marked in sounds of brass and wood. Underlying the loud but unpredictable chimes came the softer but steadier beat of hands striking stretched noroon skin; the reliable rhythm of temple drums.

Yuma Tjula let the noises of the temple wash over him, cleansing his mind and bringing him closer to a state of harmony. So it always was when he came here. He was not a devout man, either in his own estimation or that of the priests who remarked on his attitude. Still, he had attended the Temple of the Five Winds since childhood, when duty called or when he needed guidance.

Such as now.

Yuma knelt in the north-easternmost chamber of the temple. Closest to the sun, given where it stood in the morning sky, and its light flowed into the room through the half-moon windows spaced along the walls. Beneath those openings, shapes had been carved from wood and attached to each wall; stylised depictions of a myriad of divine beings.

In the centre of the chamber, a gilded statue loomed large, but Yuma gave it little heed. The Good Man had mastered wisdom, but he had much loftier concerns than intervening on behalf of one repentant trading captain. Instead, Yuma had taken up a position beneath the ornately-carved forms of the Fire Brothers; ruby-eyed Carrak stood with burning sword held aloft, while diamond-eyed Burrayang knelt to turn over ashes into new life.

Head bowed, knees aching but ignored, Yuma shaped the litany of his soul into fitting words, that the Fire Brothers might hear his misdeeds and grant him guidance. He explained his inaction in the White City, far to the west.

How the giant ships of the Raw Men had appeared in the harbours while his own vessel was there to trade.

His voice growing softer, his tone more despondent even to his own ears, Yuma admitted how he had failed to follow the third path, the path of decisiveness. He could have taken decisive action by contacting the Raw Men directly, or he could have waited properly, until they had the chance to contact him. Instead, he had taken a half-measure, neither truly decisive nor truly inactive, by finishing his trade and then departing. He had thought, in his own misguided mind, that he could return next season to make proper contact.

Instead, he had learned that in his absence the Raw Men had visited the Nangu who lived in the Foreign Quarter. They had spoken briefly to the resident Nangu, then departed. Their new trade agreement, proclaimed in stone in the White City, announced that the Raw Men were restricted to ports beyond Sunset Point, where they could not contact the Nangu.

Oh, the lost opportunity! Since that time, Yuma had come to the unfortunate realisation that his actions had been *waal* [bringing discord], due to his lack of proper decisiveness. No point asking the Fire Brothers to correct his mistake; if they were prepared to intercede and change the past, then it would have already been remade. Instead, he asked for them to guide him in proper decisiveness in the future. There would be more chances with these Raw Men, if he sought them, and if he acted properly when the moments were granted.

His prayers concluded, Yuma waited in silence for a long moment, straining to hear if he would receive any instructions. He heard nothing, no still small voice whispering beneath the sounds of harmony. All as he had more than half expected. If the Fire Brothers were going to guide him along the path, then he would need to be alert in the future; they offered nothing immediate.

Of course, he would also need to consider his own actions, and build his own knowledge of the paths. So it always was; the search for self-insight and greater understanding was a lifelong endeavour. He would not need to come to a temple for such striving, though. He would reflect on his own deeds, and ensure that he was guiding his own steps along the paths.

With his main purpose completed, Yuma rose, glad to give his weary knees rest. He moved to stand with bowed head beneath the statue of the Good Man, and muttered a few invocations of respect for his exalted knowledge. He walked around the statue to face west, then added a brief prayer of respect for all of his ancestors and descendants.

Yuma ambled silently through the corridors of the temple until he reached the eastern entrance. He exchanged a few polite, ritualised phrases with the two priests seated on either side of the doorway, then strode down the hillside path toward the main buildings of Crescent Bay.

As he hurried down the path, he still found time to look over the town, and the shining blue seas beyond. Crescent Bay itself had the look of stone and all too precious wood, while the sparkling water beyond was decorated with a half-dozen ships. Yuma classified them with an ease born of much experience at sea.

The one ship sailing in from the east was a day-farer, an ancient design whose shallow draft allowed it to be pulled up on any beach in case of a change in the weather. Its crew would have taken it on a fishing voyage to bring in some of the sea's bounty. Hardly the grandest use of a ship, but one which might return a slight profit. The other five ships were sailing in from the north-west. They were all double-hulled regular ships, heavily laden with yams and other essential food from Pankala or some other Mutjing port.

Yuma's own bloodline had ships taking part in that trade, he presumed, although he had not bothered to check any time recently. Like most Nangu sailors, he had learned his craft on the regular round trips between the Island and the Seven Sisters [Mutjing lands]. As soon as he became a captain, though, he took his ship elsewhere. No captain could earn a decent profit trading for food.

As he descended from the hill and strode through the town, people stepped out of his path. Not all of them would know him by name or sight, though he thought that most would; perhaps he flattered himself. Still, all of them could see the headwreath that held his hair back from his face. Made of Five Rivers silk, dyed with sea purple[176], woven with Yadji gold-thread and studded with Māori jade and river sapphires, it proclaimed that he was a captain of great wealth and substance. Men blocked his path at their peril, and fortunately everyone today recognised it.

The white-grey granite walls of the Council Hall loomed large above him as he neared. Naturally, they lacked the ornateness of the Temple of the Five Winds, or most any other temple on the Island. Few elders would allow their bloodlines to spend much of their hard-earned trading wealth for a building which those elders usually visited only once a year. Yet pious captains and elders would lavish much more of their fortunes to support the priests who balanced the harmony that allowed the Nangu to flourish.

The guards at the doors of the council chamber admitted him with nothing but a brief nod. All as it should be. As the third-most senior captain of the Tjula bloodline, Yuma had the right to attend any meeting of the Council, and hear what the elders decided. Perhaps even speak to influence them, given the opportunity.

Inside, a series of tables had been arranged into a rough circle. The tables displayed more wealth than the rest of the chamber, since they were made from jarrah wood which

---

[176] Sea purple refers to a dye made from the large rock shell (*Thais orbita*), a relative of the Mediterranean sea snails that produced purple and blue dyes which were extremely valued commodities in classical times. Even to the Nangu, sea purple is a rare and valuable dye; while there are no formal restrictions on who can wear it, the price it commands means that only elders, the greatest trade captains, and their most favoured wives and mistresses can afford to do so.

had been shipped back from Tiayal [Atjuntja lands]. Twenty-one seats were arranged around these tables; one for the elder of each of the surviving bloodlines. Everyone else in the room had to stand behind.

Seven of those seats were still empty when Yuma entered the room; those elders had yet to enter the chamber. Perhaps not all of the elders would be near the town to attend. Today marked an almost unheard of event; the Council had been called together outside of the usual annual meeting at the spring equinox, halfway through the year. A sign of the importance which had been attached to the news out of the west, and another reminder to Yuma of the blunder he had made in committing a half-measure.

Yuma exchanged greetings with Wirnugal, elder of the Tjula, and with three other senior captains who had gathered for this meeting of the Council. Keeping his voice low, he asked, "Are all the other elders expected?"

Wirnugal said, "The Manyilti and Wolalta elders will not be attending; they are both off the Island. All of the others should arrive soon." His voice had an undertone of frustration; presumably the late-arriving elders were seeking to show their status by making others wait for them.

Yuma also wondered, absently, why the Manyilti and Wolalta elders were not anywhere on the Island. Elders rarely left the Island except for one of two reasons: to visit some holy sites in the Five Rivers, or to personally oversee some important trading venture.

Neither of those two elders was particularly pious, so Yuma doubted that their absence had anything to do with religious visits. That meant some new trade coup might well be in the offing. The port-captain [mayor] of Jugara, the gateway to the Five Rivers, was of the Manyilti bloodline, so perhaps their elder was negotiating new trade terms with some Tjibarri faction. Wolalta captains had won their greatest trading coups in voyages to the Spice Coast [eastern Australian coastline]; might they have made some new discovery there?

His musings were cut short when a group of five elders arrived together. Suspicion hardened in his heart. Perhaps these elders had waited to enter together as a group to avoid any concerns of status. Or, more likely, they had been conducting private negotiations. Very unfortunate, in that case, since these elders also represented some of the most powerful bloodlines.

He knew them all, of course. Such as the most senior of the elders, titled the Lorekeeper because of his twin roles as rememberer of Council decisions and adjudicator of disputes. It made sense for him to arrive late. But the others did not have his seniority, only their pride and their wealth. It was not fitting for them to keep the rest of the elders waiting.

Punalta Warrikendi ambled to his seat, as if he would never be hurried. Probably not an act, in his case. Punalta was renowned as the most devout elder. He might almost have been a priest himself, and occasional rumours suggested that he planned to retire to one temple or another. It had never happened, though. Yuma suspected that Punalta preferred to remain on the Council and focus their minds on proper questions of harmony and perseverance.

The third elder wore a full beard, which was so rare for a Nangu that he was near universally known as the Beard. He had picked up that habit when he was a trader who lived for many years in the Foreign Quarter of the White City. That time had given him many valuable connections amongst the Atjuntja. Under his aegis, the Kalendi had become one of the wealthiest bloodlines.

Still, Yuma thought that the Beard had become too much like an Atjuntja, and not just in ways as trivial as appearance. Rumours were rife that the Beard had acquired some of the other distasteful Atjuntja habits. If true, though, he indulged those habits only behind the closed walls of his city residence or in his manor overlooking the Narrows, and neither he nor his Mutjing mistresses spoke openly of his habits. The Beard also possessed a powerful rage which he used when challenged. So not even the priests dared to call him out on those rumours.

The fourth elder to take his seat had lighter skin than the norm for a Nangu, and a coarseness to his features which proclaimed his foreign heritage. Nakatta was the only elder who was not Island-born. A native Gunnagal from upriver Tjibarr, he had been adopted into the Muwanna bloodline and rose to prominence after several bold trading coups with his former countrymen. Under his auspices, the Muwanna continued to negotiate favourable trade terms with the ever-shifting factions of Tjibarr.

The fifth elder, Burra Liwang, had a peculiar way of stepping, moving his feet so silently and delicately that he gave the impression of sliding rather than walking. His effortless pace allowed him ample time to look over the room, offering friendly smiles to most of the elders, including Wirnugal. Those smiles offered some reassurance that the five elders had not been conducting private negotiations to the disadvantage of the other bloodlines.

Of course, Burra often played the role of peacemaker among the bloodlines. The role suited his temperament, and he was also helped by his bloodline's holdings. The Liwang had relatively few trading ships. They obtained most of their wealth because they had the largest holdings on the Island itself, and controlled the largest proportion of local spice and dye production. Their main trade was with other bloodlines who would then export the dyes and spices. They had found it more convenient to establish a reputation for equal dealing with all other bloodlines, rather than needing to outdo rivals in foreign trade.

When Burra was seated, the Lorekeeper moved to his own chair. He nodded to the two empty chairs and said, "With your elders absent, will the most senior captains present of the Wolalta and Manyilti sit on their behalf?"

As the two captains moved into chairs, the Lorekeeper met the gaze of the black-clad priest who stood just inside the door. The priest moved to stand beside the Lorekeeper, and offered an opening invocation for the meeting, calling for all present to remember the wisdom of the Good Man and conduct themselves in accordance with the Sevenfold Path.

Servants moved around next, pouring gum cider into silver goblets for each seated man. It had to be gum cider, of course; offering any lesser beverage here would be an insult.

The Lorekeeper said, "The Council has been called together out of season to discuss this news of outlanders." He provided a brief summary of the contact between these Raw Men, the Atjuntja, and the Nangu in the west. "So the Council must decide whether restrictions should be placed on contact and trade with these Raw Men."

"A captain has the right to trade wherever he wishes," the Beard said.

Contentiousness rang clearly in his voice, offering a warning. In some bloodlines, the elder was simply one strong voice among many. Among the Kalendi, though, the Beard's word was absolute. If he took offence at an action, a feud could follow, or worse yet a vendetta.

"There is precedent for binding the bloodlines," the Lorekeeper said, his voice calm. "In 183 [AD 1422], the Council agreed to restrict all contact with the Atjuntja to their designated trade ports, and to punish any captain who sought to trade elsewhere. That edict was allowed to lapse in 211 [AD 1450], and has been enforced by custom ever since."

All as it should be, Yuma thought. Custom and familiarity made it easier for men to walk the right paths, which was why they were usually followed. Of course, the custom was adhered to in this case due to the unspoken threat that any bloodline who broke the Atjuntja trade edict would find every other bloodline turning on them.

The Lorekeeper added, "But the Council has that authority, if it so chooses."

The Beard grunted, rather than offering any substantive answer. That was an even more ominous sign that he was determined to force his own way. He had the determination to push that into feud or vendetta, too.

Yuma hoped that the Beard could be persuaded to show restraint. Once there had been twenty-four bloodlines on the Island. Three had been destroyed utterly in vendettas, and over the centuries some others had come close to destruction. Bloodlines always competed with each other in commercial rivalries, but sometimes those rivalries became matters of pride or hatred. In those cases, a feud or vendetta could follow, with the knife replacing the trade bargain. No matter how much the priests decried them for bringing discord, vendettas could still be called, and inevitably turned out deadly for both sides. Not to mention for outsiders caught up in the chaos.

When he spoke, Nakatta's voice still had a slight rasp which betrayed his foreign origins. "Before we consider that, we must know more of these far westerners. What has been seen of them?"

"Only their one visit to the White City," said the Lorekeeper. "Everything else is rumour and wild tales."

"One should never give too much heed to rumours," the Beard said. That remark produced a number of carefully blank faces around the chamber.

"These Raw Men are real," said Punalta. "Yet they are also strange. Strangeness leads to uncertainty, to tale-mongering, and to exaggeration. Rumours are inevitable, in such circumstances. We must not allow wild tales to lead us to discord."

"It is the nature of their strangeness that concerns me," Nakatta said. "Every people have their own customs which appear strange to others, especially peoples who have not learnt the paths of harmony. Are these Raw Men strange only because they are different, or because they have crafts and knowledge that we lack, as our forefathers did not know of the working of iron before we learned from the Atjuntja?"

A sign! Yuma realised, at that moment. The Fire Brothers must have been listening after all, and allowed him to see it. He tapped his foot on the stone floor, a polite way of signalling that he wanted to speak.

Wirnugal, fortunately, was alert. "I wish one of my captains to be permitted to speak," he said.

The Lorekeeper glanced around the elders. When none of them objected, he signalled for Yuma to proceed.

Yuma thought for a moment, considering how much information he should reveal. Knowledge was a trade good, often the most valuable of all. Yet he needed to be decisive, and knowledge was of no use if it was never acted on. "These Raw Men have some crafts which we lack. Shipbuilding, of a certainty, and perhaps others. I have seen their mighty vessels in the White City, large enough to make a great-ship seem small. Of the other rumours I cannot speak with assurance, but they are said to have great knowledge of weapons, too."

"How fast are those ships?" asked the captain sitting for the Wolalta elder; Yuma did not know his name.

"I cannot be certain; I saw them only within the harbour. Their sails are large, though. I expect that they can run very fast with the wind. Into the wind, I think that our ships would be more agile."

"How would they have built ships so large?" another elder asked, but the Lorekeeper signalled for silence.

The Lorekeeper said, "These questions should be answered, but not in this time and place. Thank you for your words to the elders, Yuma Tjula."

Nakatta said, "Shipbuilding or not, we must know these Raw Men's interests. Have they comes as wanderers [explorers] or as traders?"

"Both, so far as we can tell," the Lorekeeper said. "They have concluded a trade agreement with the King of Kings. But they came first as wanderers, and wanderers they will no doubt continue to be."

"Will they wander to the island, then?" Nakatta asked.

That question provoked some heated discussion. The Beard led a group of about a third of the elders who exclaimed about the myriad opportunities available for trade with these new Raw Men, whoever they were. Nakatta led a similar number of elders who pointed out the threat of competition, and the dangers of having these outlanders sail directly to the Island.

Yuma wondered about the dangers himself. The only other true seafarers in the world were the Māori, and they did not sail further than the Cider Isle. That had always left the Nangu free to trade and sail elsewhere, whenever they pleased. Without competition, and without threat.

Still, if these Raw Men had such marvellous trade goods, the wealth that they could bring would be fantastic. Even if they had superior knowledge, well, the Nangu could learn from them. They had learned ironworking from the Atjuntja, and, if the old stories were true, other arts of seafaring from the Māori. They could learn again, if needed.

After the elders had argued for a while, Punalta said, "This debate ignores the essential question. Do these Raw Men know of the Good Man and the Sevenfold Path?"

The Lorekeeper said, "No, not according to the reports. They worship three gods like the Yadji, not two like the Atjuntja. They think that their gods' will is absolute, that nothing men can do will change their destiny. They are even worse than the Atjuntja, apparently, for they believe that all men are depraved and will act to bring discord."

"Then they must be taught the truth," Punalta said. "If we do not teach them to act according to the Sevenfold Path, then the consequences of their disharmony will not be limited to them; they will bring chaos and disruption to us all."

"So, then, we must contact and trade with them," the Beard said.

"And invite them to bring their disharmony to us?" Nakatta answered.

Burra Liwang, who had been silent throughout the long argument, tapped his foot on the stone. An unusual action for an elder, but it got everybody's attention. Burra said, "These Raw Men will come anyway, whether we hide or not. They already know we are here. The Atjuntja would have told them of us even if they had not met our own people. They are wanderers, so they will come. If so, better that we contact them in the west than on our own Island."

As he usually did, Burra had found a way to bring the elders to agreement. With him guiding the discussion, the Council agreed to circumspectly search for a way to contact the Raw Men's trading posts in the western Atjuntja lands, when they were established.

If that failed, then captains would be permitted to sail into the west beyond Sunset Point, if they wanted to brave the endless winds. Any captains who wanted to do so could see if they could sail directly to the Raw Men's homelands. However, the Council ordered that any west-venturing captains must make absolutely certain that they gave the Atjuntja no warning, and that they did not land anywhere on western Atjuntja lands. That would break the Nangu's own trade agreements with the Atjuntja, and in a way which brought no gain.

With that agreement, the Lorekeeper called the Council meeting to an end.

Yuma kept his face carefully impassive, but he now knew what he had to do.

#33: Amidst The Falling Stars

"When tillage begins, other arts follow. The farmers, therefore, are the founders of human civilization."
 - Daniel Webster, "Remarks on Agriculture"
* * *
Second Harvest Season, 23rd Year of King of Kings Kepiuc Tjaanuc [November 1625]
Near Seal Point [Geraldton, Western Australia]
Cerulean skies above, the boundless light of the Source unmarred by clouds. The bountiful illumination stirred the heat from the soil and drove any meddlesome *kuru* into refuge of shadows or underground hideaways. Warmth filled the world from horizon to endless horizon in all the sweat-inducing heat of second harvest, if not quite the baking dryness of full summer[177].

A golden time, or so it should *be*, thought Ngutta son of Palkana. With his family, he stood among the wealth-trees [wattles] on the western edge of their holdings. No longer did the trees bloom golden, but their fallen petals still coated the ground in a reminder of the faded flowers. New shoots sprouted from where the flowers had been, small branches which ended in long pods. The pods were light

---

[177] The Atjuntja divide the calendar into six unequal seasons. Second harvest is from late October to mid-December, and corresponds to the time when they collect the seeds from late-flowering wattles (mostly *Acacia victoriae*). The Atjuntja summer starts from mid-December and runs until roughly the end of February.

green except where they had started to turn brown at their edges, and stood out in contrast with the much darker green of the tiny leaves.

Gold still sparkled from the wealth-trees, occasional flashes from where the first drops of gum oozed from the bark of the trunk and lower branches. After the main harvest had been completed, Ngutta would return with his sons to prune the trees and cut gashes into the bark at carefully chosen points, to return a much larger yield of gum. For now, though, they had other work to do.

After so many years, Ngutta and his family went about their tasks in smooth routine. His two youngest daughters – the only ones left in his household after their elder sisters had departed on their marriages – and his younger wife laid down mats around the base of one wealth-tree, then moved on to the next.

Behind them followed his elder wife and the two youngest of the four sons who still lived beneath his roof. They used long hooked poles to shake the branches, releasing the pods to fall to the waiting mats. A few stray leaves, twigs, insects and other detritus fell with the pods. The pole-carriers ignored that, simply making sure that all of the pods had been shaken loose before moving on to the next tree, where more mats waited ready for them.

Ngutta followed with his eldest and third eldest sons. He still missed his second son, who had gone to Seal Point to work for the Atjuntja and find a town-born wife, despite Ngutta's misgivings. But that absence would not impair the harvest; his remaining sons knew their roles.

He and his elder sons collected the mats, and shook them carefully. The mats had been woven with small gaps, so that most of the leaves and other small material fell through the holes. They emptied the seed pods into canvas bags, and handed the mats to his younger sons, who had returned to collect them and carry them ahead. Then Ngutta and his elder sons carried the bags to the next tree to repeat the process.

When all of the bags were full, the whole family would gather to carry them back to the nearest storehouse. There the seed pods could be held until they popped open in a few weeks, with the wealth-seeds going into storage and the empty pods used to feed ducks and noroons [emus].

The rhythm of the tree harvest was ancient. Ngutta had learned it from his father, who had learned it from his father before him, and so on back an uncounted number of generations. It had served him well all his life. Even in drought years, the wealth-trees still produced a harvest of seeds, albeit a smaller one.

Now, though, he wondered if all their labour would be futile.

Ngutta had always thought of himself as a successful manager of his family's holdings. He knew how to divide his lands and rotate his crops so that he always received a good harvest of two kinds of wealth-seeds, of red yams, and warran yams. Depending on the year and his needs, he ensured yields of flax, of indigo, or quandongs. When there were problems with fire, drought or poor soils, he knew what to plant or what to leave unharvested so that the bounty of the earth would be sustained.

For the first time, though, his biggest problem was not harvesting crops, but storing crops.

The last few years had been strange ones. Rumours permeated the Middle Country, speaking of raw-skinned strangers who had come from the west, and who had brought goods with them to match anything provided by the Islanders. With the strangers had come other tales, of new maladies that claimed lives or left their victims disfigured, of ill-favoured omens witnessed among the stars, of displaced *kuru* crossing over from the liquid eternity, and about the Lord turning more of his attention to the King of Kings' dominions.

Ngutta did not know how much credence to give those rumours, but he knew the affliction which was ruining his family's holdings.

Rats.

Rats had always been a problem of sorts for raiding stored food. But their numbers could usually be contained by farm quolls and occasional hunts by himself and his family when farm work permitted.

A new kind of rat had appeared around his farm this year, though. Black and alien. No larger than the more familiar kinds, but much less shy around people, and much more numerous. The farm quolls ate until they were full, gorging themselves on rats, but the rats kept breeding, and kept eating. Much of the first harvest of wealth-seeds had already been damaged, and Ngutta had little more confidence for this crop. As for what he would do when the Atjuntja came to demand their tribute, he did not know.

As he laboured to collect the wealth-seeds, Ngutta had an even more unwelcome thought. When ill fortune became prevalent enough, the Atjuntja would think that the Lord had turned more of his attention toward the King of Kings' dominions. If that happened, then there would be calls for volunteers for sacrifice. Many volunteers. And if volunteers were not forthcoming, what would the Atjuntja do?

Ngutta did not know, but despite the heat of second harvest and of his labour beneath the Source, he still felt chilled.

* * *

"In nothing do men more nearly approach the gods than in giving health to men."
- Cicero

* * *

Eagle Day, Cycle of Life, 387th Year of Harmony (12.21.387) / 27 November 1626
Milgawee (White City) [Albany, Western Australia]
Tiayal (the Middle Country) [western coast of Australia]
Lopitja, called the Red by some, had travelled far and wide within the Five Rivers, and even beyond. It was both a privilege and a necessity for one of the most acclaimed physicians in the world. In his travels he had seen many things, and accomplished many things.

Yet never had he travelled so far, seen so much, or, in his own estimation at least, accomplished so much.

A few months before, Lopitja had visited the Island to seek the wisdom of the priests at the Temple of Broken Chimes. A rare visit for a Gunnagal, but then he had always followed the Sevenfold Path, even if not in quite the same way as the Islanders, and he had found the priests' advice useful in the past.

The visit had been purely for Lopitja's own insight. Rarely if ever did the Islanders bother to consult Gunnagal physicians – which was their loss – and in any case, few physicians were willing to leave the Five Rivers to provide medical treatment elsewhere. So Lopitja had been astonished when one of the Islander elders had asked for his professional advice.

He had been tempted to refuse, since the request had involved much more than a simple consultation. Even among the few physicians who travelled beyond the Five Rivers, none in living memory had committed to the risks of a long Islander voyage. The Islanders were seafarers like no others within the circles of the world, but even their ships sometimes failed to reach their destinations. Especially into the winds and storms of a voyage to the far west.

The Islander elder had been persuasive, though. He was Gunnagal-born himself, and he understood the value of physicians, as did anyone who came from the Five Rivers. Lopitja had accepted, out of a combination of curiosity, lucrative compensation for his time, the chance to extend his learning, and the knowledge that having an Islander elder owe him a favour was no small blessing.

So Lopitja had found himself in the White City, the place beyond the western storms. Tales of that distant city had been exaggerated, or so he had always thought. He had found out how wrong he was. The White City was larger even than Tjibarr of the Lakes, more ornate than Garrkimang with its ancient glories of the long-vanished Empire. A tribute to the boundless power of the King of

Kings, who wielded so much more authority than any monarch in the Five Rivers, or even the Yadji Regent.

Still, for all of the splendour of the City Between The Waters, he had come here to examine people, not buildings. A new affliction had struck the Atjuntja lands, one severe enough that the Islanders had thought it worth sending for a Gunnagal physician.

And so Lopitja had come. Now he had accomplished something which no other physician had achieved since the great Dulabul: he had diagnosed the symptoms of a new bushfire disease [epidemic disease]. The corpus of physicians' knowledge included many maladies, but most of those were slow-burning, afflicting only a few individuals but persisting for years.

Bushfire diseases were, fortunately, much rarer. When they struck, they spread very quickly, burning their way across the world and killing thousands or tens of thousands. So far as Lopitja had known, so far as any Gunnagal physician had known, there were only two: blue-sleep and Marnitja.

Now there was a third.

Hundreds, perhaps thousands were dying in the White City from this new affliction, and an uncountable number in the countryside beyond. Local rumours linked this bushfire disease to many sources, but Lopitja cared nothing for rumours, and still less for the misguided Atjuntja belief that any ill event was due to the Lord's will.

This new bushfire disease was a severe affliction, but it had nothing to do with the actions of some god. Like all maladies, it was indirectly an effect of discord somewhere in the world, but the disease itself was simply a physical manifestation of that discord. All physical aspects of the world could be understood, and in the case of diseases, sometimes even contained or treated.

A bell rang three times. Among the Atjuntja, that was a polite way of announcing that someone of great importance had arrived and wanted to be admitted. The Islanders who lived in the Foreign Quarter had adopted the same habit, it seemed.

Lopitja left the sickroom where the last afflicted survivors had been gathered to rest and recover their strength.

Inside the antechamber of the sickhouse, the Islander elder, Nakatta, waited with barely-concealed impatience. After a brief exchange of polite greetings, Nakatta said, "You now understand this malady?"

"With as much wisdom as the Good Man can grant in such a short time of learning," Lopitja said. He paused, wondering how many details he should inflict on the elder.

"I have called it swelling-fever," he said. The Atjuntja gave it many other names, but it was a physician's privilege to name a new illness which he described. "It is marked by severe swelling, like so" – he gestured to show swelling which started on both cheeks and ran down under the chin – "and pain in the jaw and head. Some men swell around their manhood, too. Many recover after that. Those who do not recover will suffer fever, afflictions of the head, and sometimes of the intestines, leading to vomiting. Some will die of the fever, or in delirium which is like a lesser form of Marnitja."

"Will this affliction spread to the Island?" the elder asked.

Lopitja said, "I cannot be sure. But I can tell you that if any men on your ships show the signs which I have described, you must not allow that ship to land. It must remain offshore until a cycle [twelve days] has passed after the last person has shown any of the signs of swelling-fever. Only then can the passengers be allowed to return to the shore."

Nakatta said, "Will that be enough?"

"I hope so," Lopitja said, but he could offer no stronger reassurance.

* * *

"Sacrifice still exists everywhere, and everywhere the elect of each generation suffers for the salvation of the rest."

- Henri Frederic Amiel

* * *

August 1631
The White City, Tiayal

Drums beat out a slow two-beat, the rhythm echoing back and forth across the Third Audience Hall. The hall's purpose was exactly as its name signified, the third-largest audience chamber in the Palace; the King of Kings had ordered its name changed from the former title of Hall of Lorikeets.

The Third Hall could hold over two thousand people who had come before the King of Kings. Only a relative handful of nobles, officials and attendants were gathered here today. Namai of the Urdera, governor of Archers Nest, waited in their midst. He vaguely thought that it would be better to hold this audience in one of the many smaller chambers in the Palace. But then, apart from his oddly prosaic preference in names, the King of Kings had always thought that something which was worth doing was worth overdoing.

The echoing drums shifted to a three-beat, a warning of who approached. Namai lowered his head slightly in preparation.

A few moments later, the drums changed to a staccato four-beat, and the herald proclaimed, "Lower your eyes! He comes among you! Lower your eyes! He comes among you, the blessed of the Lady, the Voice of Divinity, the mightiest in the mortal realms, the occupant of the Floral Throne, the one who has no equal, the King of Kings, his exalted majesty Kepiuc Tjaanuc!"

Namai lowered his head until he saw only the floor in front of him. Around him, everyone else did the same. He heard, rather than saw, the King of Kings enter the chamber and sit on the less ornate representation of the true Floral Throne. While he did, he strove to keep his breathing soft and regular. No matter what fate the King of Kings had in mind for him, he would not reveal any fear or uncertainty.

The herald announced, "Namai, scion of the Urdera, you may raise your eyes and approach the throne."

As Namai walked toward the King of Kings, he struggled to keep his footsteps steady. The herald had not called him the governor of Archers Nest. That omission could hardly be accidental. Namai had always thought his governorship in such a distant garrison-city had been a sign of the King of Kings' disfavour, being banished from the glories and comforts of the White City. Even having first choice of the Raw Men's trading goods did not alleviate his sense of exile. Still, how much worse could things be if he was to be stripped of the title in such public circumstances?

Namai stopped seven paces from the throne, and raised his head to meet the King of Kings' gaze.

His exalted majesty, Kepiuc Tjaanuc, wore clothes and head-dress of perfumed splendour, as he always did. Namai knew better than to look for any meaning there. But he noticed the grey in the King of Kings' beard, the increasing web of lines which marked his forehead and cheeks. Time was always both friend and foe; it wore a man down to nothing, and then allowed him rebirth. For this life, though, it had become the King of Kings' enemy.

The King of Kings kept his face expressionless, and gave no word of greeting. Instead, he made some gestures with his right hand. Lerunna, the chamberlain of the palace, stepped forward to stand beside the throne. "His exalted majesty asks you to tell him the state of his country of Archers Nest."

Oh, the humiliation! Namai made an effort to keep his face still, but he doubted that he succeeded. The King of Kings had refused to speak directly to him! Namai was of the blessed; as a scion of a noble house, it was his birthright. He was permitted to hear the Voice of Divinity... yet the King of Kings would not countenance it. And again, there had been no reference to Namai's rank of governor of Archers Nest.

Nor could Namai tell the King of Kings anything which he did not already know. Namai had been astute in sending parchments – and more recently, paper traded from the Raw Men– advising the White City of the troubles which plagued Archers Nest and its environs.

"Archers Nest is both favoured and afflicted. The ships of the Raw Men call there often, engaging in the trade which your exalted majesty has permitted. They have brought many wondrous new things – steel, cotton cloth, donkeys, Coromandel works. Yet strange new afflictions have come with them, claiming the lives of many of your exalted majesty's subjects. A swelling sickness – the little death [mumps]. Plagues of sores, rashes, and fevers, leading to broken men [syphilis]. The red cough [tuberculosis] spreads through the country. Many fields lie untended or have been abandoned for want of workers. Endless infestations of rats have ruined many storehouses. The tribute to your exalted majesty has been reduced."

Lerunna glanced at the King of Kings, then said, "These plagues have not all been confined to Archers Nest. Perhaps you have suffered worst, but all of his exalted majesty's dominions have been afflicted. What have *you* done to protect his exalted majesty's interests?"

"Everything I can," Namai said. "I have consulted the omens, and been diligent in following them. I have ordered more quolls bred, and more ratcatchers trained. Builders have been ordered to strengthen storehouses and leave other construction work for a more auspicious time. I have released more peasants from garrison labour to help harvest the fields."

"Yet the troubles continue," Lerunna said.

It was not a question, so Namai simply raised his right palm to show agreement.

The King of Kings gestured again, then Lerunna said, "The Lord has turned his attention to the mortal realms. Many sacrifices have been made, but the troubles continue. His exalted majesty asks what should be done to appease Him."

Namai shivered, despite all of his efforts at self-control. He had grown up with the language of the court, even if he had not been able to put this knowledge to proper use during his long years of exile. He knew a call for a volunteer when he heard one. And with the troubles which afflicted Tiayal, this would not be a call simply for a sacrifice to the pain.

No, this was a call for a sacrifice to the death. That much, Namai was not willing to do. His long years in exile had been sacrifice enough, as far as he was concerned. He would prefer to let other nobles sacrifice themselves when the blood of peasants had failed.

Except that the King of Kings would not be satisfied with that. Clearly, Namai was the chosen sacrifice, and the alternative was to be publicly humiliated by being stripped of his rank as governor. Unless...

Namai said, "It is these Raw Men who have brought the Lord's attention."

Lerunna said coldly, "His exalted majesty will not order the Raw Men to trade no more with the Middle Country."

Namai noted that the chamberlain had not bothered to consult with the King of Kings before answering that question. That made him wonder what other politics troubled the court. The plagues were worst around Archers Nest, but they had also reached the White City. The people must be unhappy. Were the nobles, too? Yet the nobles were also the ones who received most of the wondrous new goods from the Raw Men, and would be greatly aggrieved if they lost this source of wealth. If the King of Kings ordered trade cut off, how secure would he be on the Floral Throne?

Still, that would not help his own situation. Namai said, "If the Raw Men are the ones who have brought the Lord's attention, then it can only be their blood which appeases Him."

That suggestion brought the King of Kings' eyes back to meet Namai's gaze. "No outlander has ever been called to sacrifice himself to the Lord," the King of Kings said.

"No outlanders have ever brought the Lord's attention to the Middle Country before," Namai said.

The King of Kings remained silent for a long moment. Eventually, he spoke in a raised voice which carried clearly across the Third Hall. "Nami of the Urdera, governor of Archers Nest, you are ordered to return to the garrison-city. Once there, you will ask the Raw Men to provide three volunteers to be sacrificed to the death in the House of Appeasement, that the Lord's attention may be turned away."

Namai lowered his eyes to the floor. "I hear and obey."

#34: Cruel World

"According to the judgement of all knowledgeable people it is considered certain that the war in this land will neither cease nor be ended as long as the king of Spain remains peaceably in possession of the kingdom of Portugal and that kingdom's East Indian dependencies; and of the West Indies, which have made him powerful and rich such that he can afford to continue the war here in the Netherlands."

- Anonymous pamphlet printed in Amsterdam in the early 17th century

* * *

Renewal Season, 29th Year of King of Kings Kepiuc Tjaanuc / August-September 1631
Archers Nest / Fort Nassau [Perth & environs]
Tiayal / D'Edels Land [western coast of Australia]

"Land ahoy!" came the cry from somewhere far up amongst the sails of the *Wapen van Hoorn*.

Lars Knudsen uttered a silent prayer of thanks. He heartily despised long sea voyages. This leg of the journey from the new settlement at Port de Warwick [Mauritius] had been especially difficult, with endlessly strong winds, immense waves and storms. Two of the other ships in the fleet had been scattered by the inclement weather; no way to know whether they had been wrecked in the endless seas.

He stood with a hand against a mast to steady himself. Sailors claimed that all men could learn to balance themselves on a rolling ship's deck, but he had never acquired the art. One more reason to dislike sea voyages, along with boredom, risk of shipwreck, seasickness, ever-present danger of scurvy, and so much else. If not for the riches to be found here at the far end of the world, he would never have accepted this commission.

The ship's rocking lessened as it drew nearer to the shore. Behind him, Knudsen heard the ship's officers shouting orders about turning to port and changing sails, but he gave it little heed. It was the captain's job to command the ship; he would only interfere if he asked questions or watched too closely.

Besides, he had much more interest in what could be seen on this new land. He made his unsteady way to the right side of the ship – sailors called it starboard, but he cared little for sailors' talk – to look out over the land. To his disappointment, he was too far from the shore to see much other than glimpses of cliff faces interspersed with occasional beaches. No sign of the natives, or their wealth.

"They are nearby," he murmured, only half-aware that he had spoken aloud.

The land he saw now, however imperfectly, was the land which had sustained his hope throughout the rigours of the journey from Amsterdam.

A land with many names, and many promises. D'Edels Land. The South Land. Teegal. A land of gold and sandalwood, of exotic animals and plants, of strange crops and stranger men. Smaller but more alien even than the first discovery of the Americas.

A land of promise, balanced by horrors. A scourge had come out the South Land which ravaged Europe, felling monarchs and commoners alike. Calls had come both within in the Netherlands and from elsewhere in Europe – including his own Danish homeland – for closure of all contact with this land.

The Company had refused those demands. So far, the Dutch Republic backed them. The South Land simply offered too much profit, and the Company and the Netherlands had great need of its wealth. Spain assailed the Dutch at home and around the globe. The South Land's gold could pay for their homeland's defence, and support Dutch actions in eliminating their Catholic enemy's colonies wherever they could be reached.

More, the English were reportedly gazing longingly at the Dutch outposts, too. Fellow Protestants they might be, but under the aggressive guidance of their new Regent, they were looking remarkably unfriendly. If war came, then there would be even more need of the South Land's gold to pay for driving out the English, too.

The *Wapen van Hoorn* sailed steadily north. Knudsen kept his place at the ship's side. His broad-brimmed hat spared him from the sun, both its glare and its burning touch. He caught impressions of the features of the land as the ship passed: long beaches with sand stretching on sand; small, empty islands; and occasional signs of cultivation.

The cultivation interested him most, for what it might tell him about the natives. Unfortunately, he could not recognise much of consequence. None of the fields had familiar crops or animals– no grain, no horses, no cattle. Of course, he had known that this land had strange crops. Many of the fields were empty, while others were covered with strange trees. The trees intrigued him; many of them bloomed with an abundance of yellow flowers, so that whole fields looked golden. He hoped that was an omen of what he would find when the ship reached Fort Nassau.

As the day faded into afternoon, the *Wapen van Hoorn* rounded a large island and sailed into calmer waters. Soon afterward, Knudsen had his first glimpse of Fort Nassau.

"Doesn't look much like a fort," he murmured. A cluster of buildings constructed from stone and timber, nestled in a triangle of land formed by sea and the inlet of a river. The buildings sprawled back out of sight, but there were no walls or other signs of fortifications. Only a rather impressive collection of docks – even the largest of Company trading fleets could anchor here – and the construction beyond.

As the ship docked, Knudsen made a closer inspection of his new home. There was a sort of order to it; a broad cobbled avenue separated the docks from an open square behind, and a cluster of buildings in stone. That avenue looked as if ran around all of the stone buildings. Within that avenue, most of the people he saw were Dutchmen, or at least others of white stock. Outside of that avenue, away from the docks, most of the buildings were timber, and built up against each other in a slap-dash manner. All of the men he saw there had dark skins, like the natives here were reported to have. It looked as if the Company had built its own premises, and then the natives had decided to live nearby.

I'll have to check whether my command runs to those native buildings, he thought. He was, or rather was about to become, the governor of Fort Nassau. But how could he govern properly if Company authority did not run to the natives who lived right next to his hometown?

Men on shore helped the *Wapen van Hoorn* to dock, but the current governor did not seem to have come out to greet the new arrivals. Maybe the current governor ran a lax fort. Knudsen hoped that was the reason, since anything other explanation would be worse – it would mean that he had arrived to face a major problem on his first day of his new governorship.

Knudsen made sure that he was one of the first men ashore. Someone did step forward to greet him, then, a thin-faced man with pockmarks that showed he had survived smallpox. He bowed, ever so slightly. "I am Piet Janszoon. And you are...?"

Impolite man, I will remember you, Knudsen silently promised. True, the other man did not know his rank, but he should have shown more deference to someone who was clearly of high rank.

Knudsen pitched his voice to make sure that it carried. "Lars Knudsen, by the grace of God and the commission of the Lords Seventeen appointed to the governorship of Fort Nassau!"

Stillness descended around him, as sailors stopped whatever errands or tasks they were performing to look at him. All as he had hoped.

The thin-faced man, though, just nodded slightly and said, "Welcome, governor. We'd heard you were coming, but yours is the first ship from the Netherlands that we've seen in over three months."

Knudsen said, "Never mind that. Just take me to the former governor."

Janszoon said, "Governor Hermanszoon is at church, or he would have greeted you himself. Would you like to join him there, or wait for him at the governor's residence?"

"Take me to the governor's house," Knudsen said. He had lived in the Netherlands for fifteen years, and worked for the Company in one role or another for ten, but he still followed the Lutheran creed of his youth. He had no interest in attending a Calvinist service except where protocol required it.

The thin-faced man bowed, barely deeper than last time, then snapped a quick order to one of the sailors to make sure that Knudsen's goods were brought to the governor's residence. Evidently Janszoon could organise things, even if he lacked politeness.

The governor's residence turned out to be just across the avenue and main square. Judging by the men constantly entering and leaving, the single-floored building served as the centre of administration too. That was reasonable enough; Fort Nassau was not that large, and the wealth it earned would be better used paying for the Company's operations elsewhere than in building an opulent governor's residence. For his own part, Knudsen expected to earn much from his tenure as governor, but he would take that wealth back home with him, not spend it here.

Inside the governor's house, Janszoon showed him to a comfortable room to wait. Perhaps an hour later, a tall, full-bearded man strode into the room and gave a quick bow. "Governor Claes Hermanszoon. Welcome to Fort Nassau."

Knudsen returned the bow. "Governor Lars Knudsen... or I should say, Governor-to-be."

Hermanszoon waved a hand. "However you like. The appointment is yours. I have served my five years and more. I will leave for Batavia whenever the next ship is ready."

He took a seat.

Knudsen returned to his, then said, "I will have questions for you first. Many questions. I've been told much by the Company before I left Amsterdam, but I'm sure there's much still to know."

"Indeed." The former governor tilted his head. "*Duguba jangganyu ngarru, wirri*[178]?"

Knudsen said, "*Warari.*" He repeated himself in Dutch: "Some."

"Learn more," Hermanszoon said. "A few of these Atjuntja understand Dutch, but they will usually not deign to speak it. Be careful, too. A few of the craftier natives will listen when you speak with each other in Dutch, or have interpreters with them who do. The better to help them trade."

"Trading is hardly my role," Knudsen said. Apart from ensuring that he collected his rightful share of the profits, but that was another matter. "The factors will handle that, surely."

"The factors will be with you, of course, but the natives here have strange expectations. Most of those who you will be trading with are nobles – the nobles are usually the merchants here, too, with a few exceptions. Atjuntja nobles always expect to have what they think of as a man of substance present at any negotiations. Factors won't count, I'm afraid. It has to be you, as the governor. Even if the factors do most of the talking, the nobles will refuse to speak with them unless you're nearby."

---

[178] This is an Atjuntja phrase which means "Speak you the true tongue, honoured one?"

Knudsen nodded. No-one back in Amsterdam had seen fit to mention that to him. Perhaps they didn't know, or just assumed that he would learn it when he came out. They had chosen him in part because he had a gift for learning languages, so maybe they did know a little.

"Still, if the factors are doing the bargaining, why do I need to know the language?"

"Anything you can do will help," the former governor said. "Some of the natives are sharp negotiators."

"I'd heard that they were easy to bargain with."

Hermanszoon frowned. "At first, yes, but some of them have learned. They have a good idea of the value of our goods. You will strike a great deal if you bring something exotic or unfamiliar, but if it's something they recognise, then they will often bargain hard."

"Anything else I should know about bargaining with them?"

"Yes. Grow a beard." Hermanszoon saw the look which Knudsen directed at him, then said, "The nobles here respect beards, although they won't allow the peasants to grow them. Not full beards, anyway – the peasants have to trim theirs short."

The former governor paused, then added, "Your black hair will be an advantage here, too. I wouldn't be surprised if that's why the Company sent you here."

Knudsen raised an eyebrow.

"The Atjuntja equate black hair with being of their race, not their Yaora subjects. Not all of their nobles have it, and a few non-Atjuntja do, but still, it is never far from their minds. They will respect you more for it."

Knudsen considered that. It was not the most welcome of thoughts. No-one back in Amsterdam had mentioned this, either. He had believed that he had won appointment to the governorship because they had recognised his talents. No doubt that was true, in part, but how much of a factor had been the simple fact of his black hair?

Something of his disappointment must have shown on his face, since Hermanszoon laughed and clapped him on the shoulder. "Don't worry about it. When fortune deals you a card, you play it."

"I suppose. Apart from the trading, what are the biggest problems with governing this fort?"

"Obtaining native labourers to do much of anything. You can't just pay them wages to work for you. The natives have no idea of coinage. Payment of everything is in kind, and labour is usually commanded by their own governor, off to the east. You can sometimes bid for workers by negotiating with the nearer holdings – they will use our goods to meet their tribute. If not, you will have to work with the native governor for the use of their labour. I've done both, but it can be difficult. Sometimes they demand more valuable goods for their labour than I'd like to pay them – those are trade goods which could be put to better use. Expect the Governor-General to write you some threatening letters from Batavia condemning your wastage of trade goods. But it's a price of doing business here. What we earn in gold and sandalwood more than makes up for it."

Knudsen nodded. "What about local news? Has anything important happened here?"

"Recently?" The former governor shrugged. "The native governor has gone back to the White City for some reason. I don't know why; it's never happened before in all the time I've been here. It makes things difficult, since whenever I need any workers the natives just look blank and say I have to wait for the governor to return."

Hermanszoon drummed his fingers on his chair, then said, "Not much else worth mentioning. A couple of sicknesses have afflicted the locals – mumps, I think – but nothing for us to worry about. Oh, and two ships have recently gone missing along the coast of the South Land. I've ordered other ships to search for them, and apparently Batavia has done the same, but without any success so far."

"Ships sailing north, I presume," Knudsen said, keeping his voice carefully neutral.

"Yes. Our treaty with the Atjuntja forbids us from trading further south. We've sent a couple of ships south anyway and made contact with the Islanders further east, but no-one's got around to establishing proper trade with them."

Knudsen nodded, although he had in fact already known that. One part of his instructions in Amsterdam – rather more secret than the rest – had been to do what he could to establish more regular contact with these Islanders and find out how to trade with them, bypassing the Atjuntja. He knew that the explorer Thijssen had made contact with them back in 1626, but the disruptions of war and plagues had meant that the Company had not yet put proper resources into trading with the Islanders. Now that things were stabilising, that would become more of a priority.

Hermanszoon said, "How about your voyage here?"

"Two ships scattered in storms, and the rest half a day behind us, we think. Hopefully they'll arrive soon. Some sailors dead of scurvy, I hear, and many sick, as can only be expected."

"That can be dealt with." The former governor rang the bell beside him. A moment later, Janszoon reappeared. "Send word to the new-come ship to have all of the sufferers of scurvy report to the hospice immediately. Their captain may not know about it."

The thin-faced man nodded and left.

Knudsen looked a question at the former governor.

Hermanszoon explained, "The natives have a very good remedy for scurvy. A kind of sarsaparilla which can be turned into a drink that will relieve scurvy very quickly. We give it to all of the ship captains who visit us here[179]."

"Useful," Knudsen said. "Many things for me to learn about this place, then."

He settled down to question Hermanszoon in much greater detail.

Knudsen had a week to familiarise himself with his new duties as governor. In that time, four more ships from the fleet arrived in Fort Nassau, including one of those which had been scattered in the earlier storm. He watched the native nobles begin to gather to trade with the fleet, although on the former governor's advice, he did not let the trading begin yet. Better to wait until there were as many nobles present as possible, so that the natives could compete with each other for Company goods.

Unfortunately, he also found that Piet Janszoon had the best command of the Atjuntja language of any European at this outpost. Removing him from office would hinder the efficiency of operations at Fort Nassau. Janszoon probably knew that, too; it would explain his attitude. Knudsen decided that there was nothing he could do about Janszoon for now, but he would remember.

A week into his tenure, a native messenger came to Fort Nassau to tell him that the Atjuntja governor had returned to Archers Nest, and summoned him to attend.

He thought the demand sounded ominous. Hermanszoon was of no real help, saying that the message could simply be because the Atjuntja governor wanted to meet the new fort governor, or it might mean something

---

[179] As has happened in many other cultures around the world, the Atjuntja have identified plants with high levels of ascorbic acid (Vitamin C) which can be used to cure scurvy. The particular plant which is being used here is sweet sarsaparilla (*Smilax glyciphylla*), native to the east coast of Aururia but easily cultivatable elsewhere. While the local peoples mostly use it as a condiment, it is also helpful for relieving scurvy when people are on land. Unfortunately, the ascorbic acid contained in sweet sarsaparilla cannot be viably stored for long-term on board ships.

more dangerous, since the native commander had just come back from conferring with their Emperor.

In any case, Knudsen knew he had to attend. He wanted to bring Hermanszoon with him, but the former governor declined, saying that would simply confuse the issue of who was the true governor of Fort Nassau. "The Atjuntja don't like ambiguity," Hermanszoon said, as if that was sufficient answer.

Instead, Knudsen took Janszoon with him. Insubordinate the man might be, but a fluent speaker of the Atjuntja language would be extremely helpful. There were native interpreters available, both in Dutch employ and those which the Atjuntja used, but Knudsen did not trust them, and he was not yet completely confident in his command of the Atjuntja language.

A Dutch boat took them up the river, then they had to walk the remaining distance to Archers Nest. A fortified city, of course. With towering walls of grey stone, topped by crenellations. The natives built fortifications, but they denied them to Fort Nassau. He would have to see what could be done to change that, after he had met the Atjuntja governor.

Once at the gates, they were quickly ushered in to meet the Atjuntja governor. Janszoon murmured, "This is unusual. Normally he would make us wait for hours."

Knudsen did not take much notice of the buildings or the people. Time to think about them later. For now, he had to prepare himself for meeting with the native governor – Namai, if he remembered the name properly.

Namai proved to look much like any of the Atjuntja: tall, skin almost as dark as an African, black beard growing far down his chest. The shape of his clothes was similar too: cloth wrapped around his body and arms, leaving most of his legs clear. But everything about him was much more ornate, from the intricately-dyed patterns of blue and scarlet on his clothes, to his gem-studded gold neck-ring and bracelets.

Namai spoke in Atjuntja. Knudsen followed most of it, but he still turned to the thin-faced man for a translation.

Janszoon said, "He offers you greetings in the name of his Emperor, and calls the blessing of the Lady on your term as governor." The thin-faced man paused, then added, "The Atjuntja worship two deities: a good goddess and an evil god. He is offering you his best wishes, in effect."

"Return my best wishes in whatever manner is polite among these Atjuntja," Knudsen said. He could have done that himself, but he thought it would be better to let Janszoon do it. That would let him hide his own knowledge of their language, for now. Besides, the thin-faced man would have more understanding of the natives' protocols.

Janszoon spoke, and then Namai looked directly at Knudsen. His words came slower than before, enough that Knudsen could understand without translation. "I have a request of you, on behalf of the King of Kings."

Knudsen waited for Janszoon to murmur a translation, for the look of the thing, then said, "Tell him to ask."

Namai's next words sounded ritualised and formal, enough that Knudsen could not follow them entirely. He did recognise the Atjuntja word for sacrifice, though, and that was enough to make his stomach start to knot. He knew – all of the Dutch knew, by now – that the natives of the South Land were as bloodthirsty as the vanquished natives of the Americas.

Janszoon turned paler than usual while he offered the full translation. "He says that, in the name of his Emperor, he asks you to send three Dutchmen to the White City to be sacrificed in their heathen rites."

"No," Knudsen said, automatically, and then realised that he had answered in the Atjuntja language.

Namai answered, "I did not hear you."

Knudsen opened his mouth to repeat himself, but Janszoon touched his arm. "He heard you perfectly. That is the polite Atjuntja form for showing that he does not accept your response, and gives you a chance to make another reply."

"There's only one answer to that heathen murderer," Knudsen said. Namai's eyes narrowed at that, perhaps at the tone, or maybe he understood more Dutch than he showed, too.

"We need to give him a more diplomatic answer than that," Janszoon said.

"Any suggestions?"

"These Atjuntja will only sacrifice volunteers. You could say that you will ask, and then a few days later say that no-one volunteered."

"That only puts off the problem," Knudsen said. "But it gives us some time, I suppose. Tell him that I'll ask."

Through Janszoon, Namai replied, "You have thirteen days. Leave me now, and return on the thirteenth day with volunteers."

Knudsen hurried out, before the Atjuntja governor could add any more demands.

*

Namai of the Urdera watched the new Raw Man governor scuttle out like a rat when a quoll stepped into its sight. Not for the first time, he was glad that he had troubled himself to learn the basics of their strange language. So, they would simply play for time and then refuse the King of Kings' wishes, would they?

"Attend me," he said, and the three available scribes stepped forward. "Orders to Fingerman Nagan: he is to move his Fist to Sea-Eagle Tree, and conduct manoeuvres outside the town for the next thirteen days."

That town was the nearest to the Raw Men's trading post. It would mean that they would know that the warriors were nearby, but not so close that their presence would be threatening. Let that be a warning to the Raw Men, if they were astute enough to understand it. Hopefully, it would be enough to make them see reason.

It was not.

Thirteen days later, when the Raw Men returned, it was the same two men, the appropriately-bearded governor and the strangely pock-marked scribe-translator who accompanied him. After the customary greetings, Namai said, "Where are the three men you have brought to be sacrificed to the Lord?"

The scribe said, "The honoured governor expresses his regrets, but no men offered themselves up for the Appeasers."

Namai said, "Tell him that I did not hear his answer."

The scribe said, "The honoured governor expresses his disappointment, but no men would volunteer for sacrifice to the death."

Impertinent outlanders, who stand on the soil of the King of Kings but do not heed his will! Still, however much it troubled him, Namai knew not to say that. The Raw Men needed to be treated with care, for they had much knowledge, and many goods that the Middle Country needed. "Tell him that your people have brought the Lord's attention to this land, in plagues and famines. It is up to you to appease this affliction. Only blood can divert the Lord's attention. If men will not volunteer of their own will, persuade them to volunteer."

The scribe translated that, then the two outlanders had a heated argument in their own language. Namai followed only the gist: that the scribe wanted to make another delaying response, and the governor wanted to make an outright refusal.

Their argument ended when the governor, Nuddhin, asserted his authority. He spoke in the true language: "It is against the law of *our* Lord to give up any man for sacrifice."

The scribe added, "The honoured governor asks whether your King of Kings will refuse us trade because we refuse sacrifices."

Namai said, "I do not speak for his exalted majesty. The land-stone permitting trade still stands. Unless he orders us to destroy it, trade is allowed."

And if Namai understood the political situation in the White City correctly, then the King of Kings did not dare to close off trade entirely. Perhaps he would subject it to restrictions, or perhaps not.

"Your short-sightedness disappointments me. Death is part of the order of the world. If you choose not to conduct it properly through sacrifices, you will find that it comes anyway. Your inaction has brought affliction to the Middle Country, but it will come to your lands, too."

The scribe started to translate, but Namai spoke over him. "Nuddhin, I know you understand me. Leave my presence now. Your servant can interpret for you later, and may you consider my words and choose the path of wisdom instead."

When they left, Namai released a sigh he had only barely known he was holding. The Raw Men were great craftsmen, but it seemed that in their understanding of the divine order they were as ignorant as Islanders. They would have to learn wisdom through more direct attention from the Lord. He just had to hope that the lessons would not make the Middle Country suffer too greatly in the meantime.

The first lesson came much sooner than he had expected.

Five days later, an exhausted messenger arrived at Archers Nest. He was one of the soldiers in Nagan's Fist, and he had run all the way from Sea-Eagle Tree. He gave a confused tale of new outlander ships appearing in the sea, and using chained *kuru* to throw thunder at the Raw Men's outpost, bringing fire and death. Outlander soldiers had landed from these ships to attack; strange new raw men who were enemies of the more familiar Dutch. Fingerman Nagan had responded with commendable urgency, leading his Fist to fight alongside the Raw Men, and sending the messenger back for reinforcements.

Namai sent out orders for every available soldier to gather for a march to battle, save for one Fist retained to defend the walls of Archers Nest in case those ships came up the Goanna [Swan] River. The rest, five Fists strong, were at his command. *If* they could reach the Raw Men's outpost – Fort Naddu, they called it – in time to matter.

A column of smoke rose from the western horizon as the army set out. Despite forced march pace, no enemies remained by the time Namai and his soldiers reached Fort Naddu. Instead, he looked out over the ravaged ruins of what had been a thriving trading outpost only hours before.

One of the Raw Men's ships still burned beside the docks. The docks themselves had been badly damaged. Many of the grand stone buildings had smoke rising from their interiors, too. Some had walls collapsed, as if struck by some great force. Maybe the invaders here truly could chain *kuru* to serve their needs; the power to smite stone so effortlessly certainly appeared divine.

The Djarwari peasants who had taken up residence outside the trading post proper had suffered even worse. Many of their timber homes were aflame. Without Namai needing to give any orders, the Fingermen ordered their Fists to help put out the fires and collect the dead – Atjuntja, Raw Men and peasants – whose bodies were scattered around.

Finding out the details of what had happened took longer. Fingerman Nagan had survived, it turned out, along with many of the nobles who had been here waiting to trade. From what he could gather, Atjuntja soldiers had fought alongside nobles retainers and Raw Men guards against the enemies from the sea, who were another kind of Raw Men. They had come to raid and destroy, and carried away as much sun-kin [gold] and other goods as they could find.

Namai ordered that some of the soldiers be sent to patrol outside Fort Naddu while the rest contained the fires and collected the dead. That done, he brought Fingerman Nagan with him and eventually found the Raw Man governor, Nuddhin, and his scribe-translator.

"Who were these raiders?"

"They are called Pannidj," Nuddhin said. "We have been at war with them for years, but I never expected that they would come here."

"They were led here," Namai said.

"How could that be?" Nuddhin said. "We have been careful not to let the Pannidj or anyone else know exactly how to sail here."

"As I warned you, violence will come with the Lord's attention. You have not turned His gaze away with sacrifices, or allowed us to do the same. So He turned his gaze here, and He has called these Pannidj in to make sacrifices for Him."

Nuddhin did not look convinced, but for now Namai did not care. The warning had been delivered; it would take time for the Raw Men to understand it. He had other things to worry about, such as how the King of Kings would respond to this latest affliction. He could only hope that his exalted majesty's decisions did not include compelling Namai to volunteer for sacrifice to the death.

#35: The Lord's Will

"You are to proceed to the southward in order to make discovery of the continent abovementioned [Aururia] until you arrive in the latitude of 40 degrees, unless you sooner fall in with it. But not having discovered it or any evident signs of it in that run, you are to proceed in search of it to the eastward between the latitude before mentioned and the latitude of 35 degrees until you discover it."

- Instructions issued to William Baffin by the Directors of the East India Trading Company in July 1635, prior to his first expedition to Aururia[180]

* * *

Summer, 29th Year of King of Kings Kepiuc Tjaanuc [December 1631-February 1632]
Milgawee (White City) [Albany, Western Australia]
Tiayal (the Middle Country) [western coast of Australia]
Water, water everywhere. Not plunging uncontrollably from the sky, or bubbling from the secret places beneath the earth, but flowing according to the desires and for the pleasures of men.

Or were these bearded Atjuntja truly men? Might they not be spirit beings who lived in the spirit time as much as in the present time?

Attapatta, chief of the Wurrukurr, could not decide the answer to those questions, much as he wondered. Before he

---

[180] The wording of these instructions is based on the historical instructions given to Captain James Cook in 1768.

had come to Milgawee, he had been confident that these Atjuntja were men like any others, even if possessed of different Dreamings.

The Atjuntja knew different skills than the desert-dwelling Wurrukurr[181], but they still had their limits. Or so it had seemed. He had been invited to some of their smaller cities, earlier in his life, and seen that the Atjuntja had different knowledge. The Atjuntja could work metals and make food grow from within the earth, but they did not know how to listen to the world around them and were almost incapable of hunting properly.

Now, though, he had seen Milgawee, the place of stone and water and boundless vegetation, and he could not decide whether these Atjuntja were truly men. The first time he had seen an Atjuntja city, he had called it a big place, but the local Atjuntja had just laughed. Now that he had seen the place they called the Centre of Time, he understood their reactions.

Here at Milgawee, it was as if the spirit time still endured, where the ancient spirit beings had never stopped their work of shaping the earth[182]. Here walked men – or perhaps more-than-men – who had the powers to call forth stone and water according to their desires.

And they had welcomed him! The Wurrukurr came from a hotter and harsher land, where the sun burned brighter and water was life. Attapatta had guided his people through the challenges of that life, but he had never expected to be welcomed by spirit beings.

---

[181] The Wurrukurr are a people who live north of the Atjuntja domains, along the coast near historical Carnarvon, Western Australia.

[182] The beliefs of the Wurrukurr have some similarities to beliefs held by some historical Aboriginal peoples, but the Wurrukurr beliefs are not the same as that of any historical people. The millennia of changes in the altered history of Aururia means that beliefs have changed considerably too.

Attapatta had been given rooms in their palace to live, and gifts of iron and clothes made of *linen*. Those were marvellous enough. The Atjuntja had even called him one of the *blessed*, who was permitted to hear the voice of their great ruler, the Many-King[183] who commanded all the spirits of this place.

Still, for all of these wonders, nothing matched the Garden. Here, the sounds of water were everywhere. Here was a truly sacred place created by the most powerful of Dreaming. Back in the hot lands of his home, the growth of plants was a rare, infrequent thing, in a land which had been baked red. In the Garden, though, water flowed everywhere, and the growth of plants was commanded entirely at the wishes of the Atjuntja.

Here, too, was where Attapatta had been invited to meet with Lerunna Mundi, the voice of the Many-King, to discuss whatever reason they had for inviting him to travel so far.

Lerunna said, "Your Wurrukurr people follow your lead, I know. How much do your neighbours heed your words?"

Attapatta frowned, trying to follow the import of the question. He said, "I am chief, not a... king. All of the Wurrukurr elders have a voice, and our people will listen to them. As for our neighbours, we talk with them, but no-one can command another people. They do as they wish in their country, as we do in ours."

Lerunna said, "So long as you talk with them, that is enough for his exalted majesty's wishes."

"Of course we talk with them. A people should always heed their neighbours."

Lerunna smiled. A normal expression if he was a man; perhaps the same held true for spirit beings. "His exalted

---

[183] This misinterpretation comes from the language of the Wurrukurr, who double most words to indicate plurals. When Attapatta hears a reference to the King of Kings, he interprets this to mean Many-King.

majesty offers you gifts – iron knives and tools, linen and *kunduri*."

"What does the Many-King want from us, that he offers such gifts?" Attapatta said. He knew that desire stirred in his voice; the gifts which he had already received were incredible.

"Your scouting, and your warning. His exalted majesty knows that the Wurrukurr understand how to move through the red lands [desert] without being seen, when you need. He asks that you send word to our soldiers if you or your neighbours learn of ships coming from the sea."

"Ships?" Attapatta said.

"The ships of the Raw Men, who come out of the sunset."

"Ah," Attapatta said. He had heard word of this from the Atjuntja near his homeland, although he had never seen a ship himself.

"There are two kinds of Raw Men. The Nedlandj [Dutch] are our sometimes friends. Tell us if they come. The other kind are called the Pannidj, and they are our enemies. Do not threaten them, for their weapons are powerful. But his exalted majesty wants to know if their ships come. If they try to build outposts in your country, send word to us, and his exalted majesty's soldiers will capture the Pannidj for you."

"If they are so powerful, we should be wary of their anger," Attapatta said.

Lerunna said, "The Pannidj can be killed. His exalted majesty's soldiers killed them when they attacked our friends the Nedlandj. But we will need your people to guide us. You know the red lands better than anyone, and you can bring our soldiers close to the Pannidj without being seen. If they come, we will defeat them."

An easy proposition, as far as Attapatta was concerned. The risks lay with the Atjuntja, not with his own people. "It is agreed," he said.

* * *

From: "The United East India Company [Dutch East India Company]: Reflections on the Golden Age"
By Alexander Boniface

The first decade of the Company's deeds in Aururia was shaped by priorities set elsewhere in the world. Company merchants acquired Atjuntja gold and sandalwood as an excellent source of wealth, but they spent the profits of that trade elsewhere.

During the tenure of Governor-General Coen, the Company's efforts in the Far East were focused on building up an inter-Asian trading network whose profits would supply the spice trade to Europe. Aururian gold provided the capital to finance this trading expansion, but for the first ten years, Aururia itself formed only an isolated outpost on that trading network.

In particular, under Coen's leadership the Company did not seek to become deeply involved with the Atjuntja. Despite the consternation caused in Europe by accounts of Atjuntja religious practices – often exaggerated, but the reality was bad enough – or the frustration of Atjuntja trading restrictions, Coen did not wish any disruption to such a valuable source of gold.

So for the first few years, the Company simply traded with the Atjuntja and complied with most of their restrictions. Where convenience allowed and the risk was low, the Company did ignore their treaty obligations, such as by sending ships to explore further east in Aururia. Blatant interference, however, remained forbidden...

A variety of factors combined to change the course of the Company's involvement in Aururia. With the passing of Jan Coen in July 1631, the prime focus was no longer building up inter-Asian shipping; a task which had in any case been largely completed by that time. His successor Hendrik Brouwer had a much greater interest in exploration of new markets and trade goods.

Aururia offered an inviting temptation for renewed exploration. François Thijssen's voyage [in 1626-27] had offered tantalising hints of the potential new markets which could be found there. Action on these hints had been delayed by Coen's Asian focus, and the chaos caused in Europe by the first sweating sleep [Marnitja] epidemic meant that no-one in the Netherlands had overruled him. With Coen gone and the situation in Europe stabilising, further exploration of Aururia became a much higher priority.

Concerns about the security of their Aururian outposts also became an increasing source of friction between the Company and the Atjuntja. The Spanish raid on Fort Nassau in 1631 exacerbated these underlying tensions, since the Company now wished to fortify and garrison their outposts properly, but the Atjuntja administrators refused to allow fortifications.

The infamous demand of the Atjuntja governor Namaidera [Namai Urdera] for Dutch sacrificial victims has been much-cited as bringing about the collision between Company and Atjuntja interests, but in truth this was but one symptom of an underlying conflict. Eurasian diseases and rats were causing increasing problems in Tiayal, and the flood of Old World trade goods caused economic disruption amongst the local aristocracy.

With such growing sources of friction, it was inevitable that the Company would need to take more active involvement in Aururia. The critical moment came in 1632, in the aftermath of a new wave of disease, when the first epidemic of chickenpox swept across Tiayal...

* * *

The man called Nyumbin would become one of the most disputed figures in accounts of Aururian history, and indeed across the world. Over the centuries, a plethora of writers, historians, social activists, nationalists, revolutionaries and other figures would depict their own views of Nyumbin. Many would cite him as inspiration for their own deeds, many would condemn his actions, while a few offered a more nuanced view of his life and deeds.

To some, Nyumbin would be seen as the first great Aururian patriot, a cultural hero who offered the first resistance to foreign influence. Others would see him merely as a nationalistic rebel, fighting for the Inayaki people against the Atjuntja, while being totally ignorant of the wider clash between Europeans and Aururians. Still others would view him as simply an aristocratic opportunist, who sought to take advantage of the arrival of the Dutch to obtain greater personal wealth and power by replacing Atjuntja rule with his own.

In time, Nyumbin would be viewed by some as a bloodthirsty would-be tyrant who sought to oppress everyone. Some would see him as a traitor whose rebellion allowed the Dutch to impose control over the Atjuntja. Others would see him as an avatar of the Lord, sent to bring bloodshed and chaos into the mortal realms. A few more controversial historians would see him as demonstrating the first stirring of class-consciousness in Aururia.

In the welter of accounts, the truth about Nyumbin is almost impossible to discern. Still, some facts are relatively undisputed. Nyumbin was born into one of the old Inayaki noble families. As was so often the case, his family had been partially assimilated into the Atjuntja hierarchy, and were recognised as noble, but they preserved their own language and something of a separate sense of culture.

Of the man's appearance and character, the tales naturally vary, but through all accounts, some features are often highlighted. Nyumbin was a man of dark skin even by the standards of Tiayal, with the black hair that was so expected of Atjuntja nobility, but rarer amongst their subject peoples such as the Inayaki. He is reliably reported as a man who kept himself in prime physical condition: tall, well-muscled, flexible, and an expert with sword or spear.

One seemingly minor point about his appearance will cause endless acrimony amongst scholars and in popular culture. Some descriptions of Nyumbin assert that he never wore the full beard so heavily associated with Atjuntja nobility, that he had always kept himself clean-shaven to distinguish himself from the Atjuntja overlords. Other descriptions claim that he had worn a full beard to fit with Atjuntja expectations – as did most of the other semi-assimilated nobility in the subject peoples – and that he only shaved his beard when he began his great rebellion. The point matters greatly to those who view him as a lifelong patriot and nationalist, or to those who see him as a mere opportunist, but it will never be truly settled.

Whatever else Nyumbin may have been, he was certainly a gifted military tactician and a charismatic leader. Even hostile accounts of his life usually agree that he was a man of immense personal presence and charm, with an extremely persuasive way of speaking. His military talents were demonstrated first when he acted for the Atjuntja to lead raids against eastern desert peoples who had started to impinge into farming lands during times of drought[184]. In time, they would be demonstrated when he acted against the Atjuntja.

Nyumbin's deeds were ostensibly triggered by the passage of the chickenpox epidemic which swept through Tiayal in 1632 and claimed the life of the King of Kings, Kepiuc Tjaanuc. Certainly, he must have had some motivations which had been building for longer than that, but which of these reasons is seen as his true motivation depends on which later figure is offering an account of his life.

It is known that Nyumbin had some resentment of the main Atjuntja noble merchants who came from the White City to trade with the Dutch at Fort Nassau. The Atjuntja aristocracy controlled the supply of gold which was the most valuable good to trade with the Dutch. Nyumbin and the other non-Atjuntja nobles had to trade using lesser goods such as sandalwood and sweet peppers, and it was a

---

[184] The desert peoples Nyumbin fought against were inland dwellers of the eastern desert, not the northern coastal dwellers such as the Wuurukurr.

source of offence that he was not treated as being as good as an Atjuntja noble.

Nyumbin may also have had a personal hatred of the local Atjuntja governor, Namai Urdera. Many stories will describe quarrels between the two. Some of those are undoubted later embellishments, but it is known that Nyumbin did not have a good opinion of the Atjuntja governor.

Nyumbin would certainly have been aware of the increasing discontent among the populace, due to inflexible Atjuntja tribute demands – or oppression, as some would later call it. The Atjuntja had long maintained a system of tribute and labour drafts on their subjects, based on carefully-calculated census records.

The tribute payments were usually set at a level which farmers and workers could pay without too much difficulty. Infestations of introduced rats consumed many farmers' harvests, and the deaths from Eurasian diseases cut into the available labour both for farming and for meeting Atjuntja labour draft requirements.

Fearful of arousing the wrath of the King of Kings, Atjuntja governors did not lower their demands for tribute or labour. As farming yields declined, the populace were increasingly hard-pressed to meet the Atjuntja requirements. The farmers were placed under the greater pressure, but by some reports even the local nobility were feeling the strain. Some later sources will conclude that Nyumbin wanted to lift the oppression of the people, some will assert that he feared for the loss of his own wealth, and some will claim that he cared nothing for the suffering of the people.

Whatever his reasons, Nyumbin would lead the greatest rebellion which had been seen in Tiayal since the earliest days of the Atjuntja empire.

Nyumbin launched his rebellion in May 1632. He acted two weeks after word came of the death of the King of Kings, when the Atjuntja governors had gone to the capital to attend his funeral, and before the kings[185] in the White City could decide which of the many sons of Kepiuc Tjaanuc most deserved the imperial dignity. Whether by intelligence or good fortune, his timing was impeccable. Late May marked the start of the campaigning season, when workers had finished the harvests and would normally be called to serve on labour drafts for the next three months[186].

Nyumbin called on these workers to fight instead, in the name of the Inayaki and the Djarwari peoples. He found plenty of volunteer militia to supplement his personal troops. He put his rebel troops to immediate use, gathering them around the garrison-city of Archers Nest and storming it using a combination of surprise and well-crafted ladders. The captured Atjuntja, both soldiers and non-combatants, were massacred, except for a few of noble blood who were kept as hostages. The Dutch at Fort Nassau maintained wary neutrality, and he ignored them as posing no threat.

Following this success, Nyumbin marched east to capture the major garrison-city of Verdant Valley[187]. In the absence of the governor, who perhaps would have been more judicious, the local military commander decided to engage Nyumbin's numerically superior forces outside the city's walls, rather than settling into a defensive siege.

---

[185] The "kings" amongst the Atjuntja are the heads of the thirteen greatest noble families, and who are responsible for naming the new King of Kings. Usually this is a formality, since the last monarch will have designated a successor, but Kepiuc Tjaanuc was better at encouraging competition amongst his sons than choosing one to be his heir.

[186] The military campaigning season in Aururia is usually in the southern hemisphere's late autumn and winter. The weather is usually cooler, and the harvests have just been collected. This allows both the conscription of farmers as additional soldiers or labourers, and ensures the largest possible food supply to support the armies.

[187] Verdant Valley is the historical town of Northam, Western Australia.

The Atjuntja commander trusted his troops' discipline and superior armour to carry the day, but Nyumbin relied on a tactic he had learned when desert hunter-gatherers used against him: feigned retreat. He used his best-trained personal troops to stage an apparent retreat, and then others hit the pursuing Atjuntja in the flank. The Atjuntja army broke and fled the field, leaving Nyumbin's forces to occupy Verdant Valley, where he conducted a similar massacre of all Atjuntja within its walls.

In the space of two weeks, Nyumbin had captured two Atjuntja garrison-cities, when even capturing one had been a rare feat in previous rebellions. These triumphs attracted a flood of support for Nyumbin's cause, both from peasants and other non-Atjuntja nobles.

Nyumbin sent some of his newly-raised troops east to capture the next major garrison-city of Spear Mountain, although that venture simply resulted in a long siege which would eventually be abandoned when word reached the besiegers of events elsewhere. However, the presence of those troops meant that the Atjuntja dominions were now cut in half, since the rebels controlled all the major roads north.

Leaving his eastern forces to continue the siege of Spear Mountain, Nyumbin marched northwest to the next major northern garrison-city, Lobster Waters. The commander here had the good sense to avoid battle too, with his troops defending the walls instead. However, they were betrayed from within, thanks to some local Inayaki servants who opened one of the smaller gates during the night, allowing the rebels into the city. This time, Nyumbin ordered only the soldiers killed, and spared all non-combatant Atjuntja to act as hostages.

Nyumbin's triple success at capturing garrison-cities and victories in the open field naturally provoked terror in the White City. No rebel leader before had been so successful. However, the capture of Lobster Waters did not give the same boost to Nyumbin's cause as his previous victories. He had already attracted most of the available support from the Inayaki and Djarawari subject peoples. The Binyin people who lived further north were much less inclined to support him, thanks to a legacy of old hatreds and fear that they would simply be replacing Atjuntja dominion with Inayaki overlordship.

Without additional support, Nyumbin was forced to return south to prepare for any Atjuntja counter-attacks. While he had gained control of considerable territory, the bulk of the Atjuntja armies were further south and east, in their old heartland. They did not march quickly to oppose him, but their threat remained significant.

With his return to Archers Nest, Nyumbin had three choices. He could march south to try to capture the next coastal garrison-city of Corram Yibbal, although a siege risked becoming bogged down. He could go east to Verdant Valley and then take the major road to the White City, which was sure to bring about battle with the main Atjuntja armies. Or he could remain where he was, consolidate his control over his territory, and stage some meaningless negotiations with the Atjuntja while he tried to train and equip his soldiers up to Atjuntja standards.

In the end, Nyumbin chose a middle course, opening negotiations with the Atjuntja over the possibility of recognition of his conquests, while he sent a portion of his forces south to besiege Corram Yibbal. The Atjuntja nobility sent representatives to conduct a pretence of discussing terms, but neither side treated these negotiations as anything other than a delaying tactic. The Atjuntja rarely bargained with rebels – and then only when they could find religious justification – but they welcomed the chance for a truce while they settled their own arguments about who should become the next King of Kings.

The rebels and imperial forces clashed several times while these negotiations were taking place, but Nyumbin himself did not take the field until early in 1633, when he apparently felt confident enough to march on the White City. There were Atjuntja forts along the way, each of which would take some time to capture.

Nyumbin never reached the White City. While he was besieging the third Atjuntja fort on the road there, he received word of disaster in his rear. Atjuntja troops had landed by sea, supported by men armed with strange thunder-weapons [ie cannon] that broke men and stone with equal ease. Archers Nest and Verdant Valley were quickly recaptured by imperial troops, destroying his supply lines.

Nyumbin was forced to withdraw back toward Verdant Valley, only to be caught between imperial forces advancing from both directions. He accepted battle against the odds, and his rebels were systematically cut to pieces by Atjuntja soldiers. Nyumbin himself died in battle, preferring that fate to capture. His last words, according to most accounts, were to curse the Raw Men whose ships and thunder had brought about his failure.

* * *

From: "The United East India Company: Reflections on the Golden Age"
By Alexander Boniface
In the aftermath of Nyumbin's rebellion, the Company was quick to collect on the debt owed by the Atjuntja government. They were granted permission to establish a third trading outpost, which would later become Coenstad [Esperance, Western Australia]. All restrictions on fortifying and garrisoning their outposts were lifted. The Company obtained the right to sail east of Tiayal, although this was merely acknowledgement of a practice which had already begun.

Further concessions followed, inevitably. Ostensibly little had changed after Nyumbin's rebellion, since there was again an undisputed King of Kings ruling over Tiayal. In truth, the Company had been handed a wedge which it was quick to apply. The efficiency of Dutch shipping had been demonstrated, and the Atjuntja nobles continued to clamour for unrestricted trade.

With those advantages, it took only a handful of years for the Company to demand unrestricted trade access, with the right to visit any Atjuntja port and trade in any goods they desired. For the Atjuntja monarchy, this had short-term benefits, since it placated an increasingly unruly aristocracy. In the long-term, though, it would benefit only the Company, since it disrupted the previous land-based Atjuntja internal trade networks, and destroyed the careful control of resource production which had been maintained by the Kings of Kings...

* * *

Third Harvest Season, 1st Year of King of Kings Manyal Tjaanuc [April 1633]
Milgawee (White City) [Albany, Western Australia]
Tiayal (the Middle Country) [western coast of Australia]
Silence around him, at least as far as sounds carry to his ears. Namai Urdera lies in the centre of the public arena of the House of Pain, with twenty thousand people watching him, but he hears no noise save for a faint whispering on the breeze.

He has been placed on a raised wooden platform, his wrists and ankles chained to four stakes. There is not much spare movement in the chains; his arms and legs are both spread wide. He has been left only a loincloth to wear, although he does his best to bear himself with dignity. His beard and head have been shaved, silent testament to the fact that this is no ordinary sacrifice.

It is an execution.

Namai has been condemned for failing to secure sacrifices from the Nedlandj, and for failing to prevent the rebellion of that infuriating man Nyumbin. He did volunteer to be sacrificed to the death, but that does not erase the condemnation. The King of Kings' blessing has been withdrawn; Namai is no longer permitted to hear his voice or speak directly to him.

Namai would not argue with the new King of Kings' decision, even if he could. The Lord has been greatly angered, with what He has inflicted on the Atjuntja; only blood can answer the call. Namai does think, though, that his sacrifice will not be enough. Given the magnitude of the disasters, only royal blood can appease the Lord. The new King of Kings has about fifty surviving brothers. One or more of them must be sacrificed to the death.

A shadow passes above him. The Appeaser is ready. No words are spoken, for none are needed.

Namai does not know exactly what is coming, since every Appeaser has his own methods. He knows enough, though, after watching countless sacrifices, and now he will become one.

The first cut is faint, oh so faint. Barely a touch of the knife. The second is slightly deeper, on the other side. The third cut is shallow, too, as far as he can tell.

Something burns against him, the feel of hot metal. Air escapes his lips, but he does not scream. He will hold out against that for as long as possible. The more resilience he can show, the more that the Lord will be appeased.

The Appeaser continues his work, slowly increasing the intensity of his efforts. Most of the cuts are shallow, and quickly burned afterward, to prevent too much blood loss. Namai knows this technique, too; he has witnessed it often enough.

He blocks out the suffering as best he can, even when he feels the first of his fingers severed. Worse follows, but he tries to find a place inside himself. The pain becomes background to him, changing in form, slowly growing.

It seems to Namai that the sky is slowly turning from blue to white. Intense white light, shining down on him. He knows what the Appeaser is doing, but it is as if the knife is being thrust into someone else. The white light grows, surrounding everything, replacing everything.

Namai's last thought, as the whiteness embraces him, is that no matter that the King of Kings has withdrawn his blessing, he has still been blessed, for he has been shown the colour of eternity.

#36: Shards of Pangaea

"For all mankind that unstained scroll unfurled,
Where God might write anew the story of the World."
 - Edward Everett Hale

* * *

**From: "Three Worlds in Collision: The Globe in Upheaval"
By Shimon Grodensky**
Step back in history for a millennium, and the blue-green globe we call Earth was not, in truth, one world. Mankind had reached all of the habitable portions of the globe save for a few scattered islands, but the planet remained divided. Not one world but three, each following separate paths.

The Old World, with the four united continents of Europe, Asia, India and Africa and outlying islands, contained the bulk of the world's area and population, the earliest agriculture, the earliest civilizations, and the most advanced technology. With their common geography, the fates of these four continents had been entwined since the emergence of the human species.

The New World, with the continents of North and South America joined at the Isthmus of Panama, accompanied by the isles of the Caribbean, reached from the tropics to both poles. While smaller in area than the Old World, and only reached by mankind ten or so millennia before, it still provided a third of the world's habitable land surface and supported substantial human civilizations.

The Third World, the island continent of Aururia and the then-uninhabited islands of Aotearoa, held only a small fraction of the world's area and an even smaller fraction of its population. In its flora and fauna, though, it had followed an independent path for so long that the first explorers who saw its plants and animals believed that it was the product of a separate creation.

One thousand years ago, these three worlds had developed largely according to their own destinies, with only occasional contact which did not significantly affect their isolation. The Old World and the New saw limited crossings of peoples across Broch Strait [Bering Strait]; the Old World and the Third encountered each other in hesitant interactions across Torres Strait.

In the course of the last thousand years, these three separate worlds were forged into one globe with a unified destiny. Still, the first efforts at fusion were abortive. Pioneering Austronesians had anticipated the joining of the worlds, visiting Aururia long enough to leave behind dogs, and visiting South America to swap chickens for sweet potatoes. Yet these landmark contacts were not sustained. Norse settlers colonised Greenland and landed on North America, only to be driven out by the indigenous inhabitants. The ancestors of the Māori colonised empty Aotearoa and then crossed the Tethys Sea [Tasman Sea] to encounter the Aururian peoples, but then lost contact with their relatives in Polynesia.

Sustained contact, and the global unification which this would produce, awaited the birth of more determined explorers. Christopher Columbus's discovery of the Caribbean islands set in motion a course of events which would join the Old World to the New. While Columbus was not the first to discover the Americas[188], his accomplishment was in making sure that this contact would

---

[188] Of course Columbus was not the first to discover the Americas; for a start, they had already been discovered by the Americans themselves.

endure. A century and a quarter later, Frederik de Houtman created a place for himself in history when he achieved a similar feat in discovering Aururia. Again, de Houtman was not the first discoverer of the island continent, but he was the first man to ensure that Aururia would not return to its isolation.

The three paths of human existence came together in a crossroads forged by two men. The expeditions first of Columbus and de Houtman started to bring the three worlds together; two voyages which marked the first tremors of exchanges that would shake the globe.

The Columbian Exchange and the Houtmanian Exchange were the most significant events in human history. They transformed the globe over the course of the last five centuries; no corner of the planet was untouched by the events set in motion by Columbus and de Houtman. The modern world as we know it was in large part created by the consequences of these two exchanges.

The Exchanges marked an immense transfer of people, diseases, plants, animals, and ideas between the three previously separate worlds. These exchanges had massive effects on every human society on the globe. New diseases spread around the world, devastating many societies. Large-scale migrations transformed or replaced many cultures. The spread of new plants and animals marked a more beneficial aspect of the Exchanges; more productive or more resilient crops allowed increased human populations...

Of all the changes to human ways of life which the Exchanges brought, none were more profound than the spread of crops and livestock. New staple crops transformed the diets of peoples on every continent, as much larger growing regions were opened up for cultivation. The spread of domestic animals revolutionised transportation, farming practices, and entire ways of life of peoples around the globe.

Consider, for instance, that maize and cassava, when introduced into Africa, replaced the former dietary staples to become the premier food crops on much of the continent.

Red yams and cornnarts [wattles] became the highest-yielding crops around most of the Mediterranean. South American potatoes had never been seen in Europe before 1492, but within three centuries they became so important in Ireland that potato blight threatened mass starvation on the island; the dire situation was only averted by expanding cultivation of another imported crop, this one from the other end of the globe: murnong.

Horses had never been seen in the New World before Columbus, but they spread throughout the North American prairies, leading entire cultures to abandon farming and turn to a nomadic lifestyle. Coffee and sugar cane were native to the Old World, but the Columbian Exchange saw their cultivation expand to massive plantations in the New. Rubber was native to the New World, but its greatest use has now become in plantations in the Old. *Kunduri* was native to the Third World, but during the Houtmanian Exchange it became cultivated in plantations in both the Old and New Worlds, while cultures throughout the globe were transformed by the influence of *kunduri*...

Some crops and animals which spread during the Exchanges have become so iconic to distant regions that it is hard to imagine that five hundred years ago, the peoples of those regions had never seen or heard of them. Who can imagine Tuscany without tomatoes, Ireland without potatoes, Sicily without red yams, Thijszenia [Tasmania] without apples, Tegesta [Florida] without oranges, West Africa without peanuts, Costa Rica without bananas, Maui [Hawaii] without pineapples, or Tuniza without quandongs? What would Bavaria be without chocolate, South Africa without *kunduri*, or France without the klinsigars [cigarettes] produced from it? Or who can picture Tejas without sheep, the Neeburra [Darling Downs, Australia] without horses, or Argentina without wheat and cornnarts and the immense herds of cattle they sustain?

Indeed, the list of exchanged plants and animals that have become naturalised in new regions could be expanded almost endlessly. Before de Houtman, Ethiopia had no noroons [emus] and no murnong, Brittany had no sweet peppers[189], Portugal had no lemon verbena [lemon myrtle], and Persia had no lutos [bush pears]. Before Columbus, there were no chilli peppers in Siam and India, no coffee in New Granada, no vanilla in Madagascar, no sunflowers in Daluming, no avocados in Ceylon, no rubber trees in Africa, and no oca in Aotearoa...

Nothing offers greater testament to the agricultural benefits of the Exchanges than a comparison of the origins of the modern world's major crops. The world's agriculture is dominated by a mere twenty crops. They are the titans of the plant kingdom, which between them contain the best-suited staple crops for all of the diverse climes around the globe. Together, these crops account for around nine-tenths of the tonnage of all crops grown under human cultivation.

Six of these foremost crops come from the New World (potato, maize, cassava, sweet potato, tomato, chilli & bell pepper), eleven are from the Old World (rice, sugar cane, grape, wheat, soybean, barley, orange, onion, sorghum, banana, apple), and three are from the Third World (red & lesser yam, cornnart, and murnong). Today their cultivation is global, but a millennium ago each of these crops was confined to one of the three worlds, and often had restricted range even within their native world...

The two Exchanges have much in common in their effects on the globe: they transformed agriculture and cuisine, and made each world's resources available to a much larger area. Still, the two Exchanges had distinctly different characters, particularly in their relative effects on the Old World, and in the fates of the peoples and cultures in the two smaller worlds.

In the Columbian Exchange, many major crops moved in both directions, and Eurasia swallowed many of the New

---

[189] The plants which are here called sweet peppers are pepperbushes (*Tasmannia* spp) from Aururia. They are not the historical plants which are called sweet peppers, bell peppers or capsicum (which allohistorically are usually called bell peppers or pimentos).

World's resources. In most other aspects, however, the Columbian Exchange was in effect unidirectional. In the movement of diseases, Old World epidemics devastated the populations of the New World, while not a single significant human disease made the reverse journey back across the Atlantic to Europe or elsewhere in the Old World. The Americas did not provide a single major domestic animal that greatly transformed Old World societies – cavies, llamas, turkeys and muscovy ducks were only of minor importance – while Eurasia provided horses, cattle, sheep, pigs, and chickens which all transformed life in the New World. The shifts of language and peoples in the Columbian Exchange were all cases of Old World peoples expanding at the expense of the native languages and peoples of the New World. And while the resources of the New World would feed the burgeoning commerce and ultimately manufacturing of Europe, no significant changes to Old World religion or science came about as a result of Columbus's contact...

In the Houtmanian Exchange, as in its Columbian predecessors, major crops were exchanged in both directions. Yet the Third World did not provide as many resources to feed Europe's growth, mostly because of the much smaller size of Aururia and Aotearoa.

De Houtman's legacy saw a true exchange of diseases between the Old and Third Worlds, although the character of this interaction was markedly different from that which followed Columbus. Aururian diseases were much swifter in their effects on the Old World (and the New), due to their individual nature and the facts of geography which made them easier to transmit around the globe. The effects of Old World diseases on Aururia were slower, more insidious and ultimately much more destructive.

In the exchange of domestic animals, the Old World again provided many more kinds of livestock which would transform the societies of the Third World – horses, camels, donkeys, pigs and chickens. Nonetheless, the Third World provided one domestic animal, the noroon, whose arrival changed human ways of life in a substantial part of the Old World.

In the transfer of peoples and language, the Houtmanian Exchange was more complex than the Columbian, but ultimately bidirectional. Likewise, while the flow of ideas was largely a tide flowing from the Old World, contact with Aururia did lead to significant developments in the history of religion and science...

* * *

From: "Europe's Assault on the Globe"
By Hans van Leeuwen
Chapter 7: Drive to the East

Europe's interest in the East began long before Columbus inadvertently began the European assault on the West; indeed, the misguided Genoan had intended to reach the East by sailing west. The lure of spices had inspired the Portuguese to explore Africa and round the Cape before Columbus set foot on the isles of the Caribbean, and even those intrepid explorers were merely seeking to gain easier access to Eastern goods which had previously passed through Muslim and Venetian hands.

Vasco de Gama reached India a handful of years after Columbus's wayward voyage led him to what he had fondly believed was the Spice Islands. In this era, Spanish conquistadors followed in Columbus's wake, pursuing gold and visions, and delivered the first blows in what would become Europe's assault on the Americas. With Spain thereby distracted from Eastern ambitions, it fell to Portugal to become the vanguard of Europe's drive to the East...

While the East held and holds many diverse regions, the early aims of the Powers were focused on four prizes that held the greatest rewards to match Europe's interests. Cathay, then the most advanced nation on the globe, source of much silk and porcelain (and later tea), and an endless sink for bullion. The East Indies, politically divided and often unwelcoming, but the source of many of the most valuable spices in the world. India, dominated by the expanding might of the Great Mughals, had long been the emporium of the world, attracting many other goods even from the prizes of the East, and which offered cotton, dyes, silk, and saltpetre. Aururia, isolated, divided and primitive, but with supplies of gold and silver to rival the resources of the West, home to and at first the exclusive supplier of *kunduri*, a rival supplier of silk, and a source of new spices, some of which offered new markets, and others which would ruin the market for what had until then been the most valuable spice in the world.

These were the four prizes which lured the Powers to explore the vastness of the globe, and whose wealth drew individual Europeans to make long voyages even at the risks of privation, disease, and far too common death. Unlike in the West, where military might was quickly aimed at the native inhabitants, in the East, the early Europeans came as traders more than as conquerors. To be sure, European powers fought in the East where it suited their purposes, but their aims were not conquest, but access and ultimately control of trade markets. Commerce was their aim, military force merely their tool. In the East, when Europeans turned to force of arms, as often as not their targets would be other Europeans, not the Eastern peoples...

Chapter 10: In Pursuit of Gold and Spices

In Aururia, as elsewhere in the East, the early Powers who descended on the continent were the Dutch, Portuguese and English. Unlike the other Eastern prizes, in the South Land the Dutch were the pioneers, and the other Powers were the ones seeking to unseat them.

As in the rest of the East, though, the Powers were competing for wealth. There was not yet any thought of major settlement, even though parts of this island continent were as empty as much of the Americas. Lucre drew them, not land, for the shipping distances were far longer and the diseases much more formidable, even in those parts of the continent where the natives were not yet any more advanced than the Red Indians. For those Europeans who wanted land, the Americas were closer and more welcoming. Those who were prepared to travel across half the world wanted something much more rewarding for their endeavours...

The Dutch, in the guise of their trading company, had little difficulty establishing the first European trading outposts in western Aururia. Mutual trade suited both Dutch and natives, profitable enough to thrive despite the first ravages of Aururian plagues across the world and the first of many Eurasian epidemics in Aururia.

The problems which the Dutch faced would derive from their rival Powers, not the natives. Rumours of gold spread even faster than the dying cough [Marnitja]. The Portuguese were the Power keenest to heed these rumours, and with the fortunate capture of a Dutch ship, received access to excellent charts, and were informed of the unprotected Fort Nassau. The temptation was overwhelming, the lust for gold insatiable, and Portugal launched the first strike in the European struggle for control of Aururia. There could hardly be a more telling omen of the fate that awaited the Land of Gold than that this blow had been delivered by one European power upon another...

#37: An Aururian Miscellany

October 1629
Crescent Bay, The Island [Kingscote, Kangaroo Island]
The last curve of the sun's fire glowed above the western horizon as the day began its descent into night, while in the east the first stars were emerging to complete that transformation. Almost directly overhead, the moon cast down its own incomplete light; this was the half-moon, perfectly balanced between the fading of the last new moon and emergence of the next full moon.

In short, a most auspicious time, a time of perfect balance in the endless cycles of the world. This was a time when a man could hear the harmony of the world reflected within himself, if his mind and soul were properly ordered, and when he could use that wisdom to guide himself during difficult decisions.

Lalgatja, elder of the Wolalta bloodline, needed a time such as this. Wisdom had always been the most valuable of commodities, and unlike anything else, he could not send out his trade captains to collect it. Guidance he needed, in this time when the Nangu were divided amongst themselves worse than any other time in living memory, with troubles afflicting the Island and the nearer parts of its hegemony, while an unknown people moved around the world in a way which could bring great profit or great destruction.

The last light of the sun faded into the west while Lalgatja contemplated, and his three senior captains waited in fitting silence. He had chosen this site at the western door of the Temple of the Five Winds, and the priests had wisely left them alone. As they should; with the generous gifts which the Wolalta had given to this temple, time for private contemplation was the least they deserved.

The Raw Men, he realised. It had all begun with them. The consequences of their arrival had rippled across most of the world, as consequences always did, but everything had begun with the Raw Men.

Thanks to the Raw Men, the Nangu bloodlines had fallen back into the old ways of feud and rivalry. The Raw Men had arrived at the western edge of the world, showed magnificent goods which drew the interest of every true-blooded Nangu... and then refused to trade with them!

Instead, the Raw Men had established trade with the Atjuntja, foolishly adhering to their pact with those bloodletting savages, and not sending their trade ships further east. A few of the Raw Men's goods had reached the Island after being traded on by the Atjuntja, but those few items which had come at great cost did nothing but arouse competitive passions amongst the bloodlines.

The Raw Men themselves had remained tantalisingly distant. Some of the bolder Nangu captains had sailed into the far west in the hope of discovering the Raw Men's homelands. Those voyages had ended in disappointment for the fortunate and death for the rest. The arguments over those voyages – particularly the bloodlines who suspected each other of destroying their ships – had begun the first of the feuds which now troubled the Island.

Other Nangu had sought to establish contact with the Raw Men via intermediaries, a course which risked arousing the anger of the King of Kings. One attempt had succeeded, that Lalgatja knew of; one of the Tjula captains had invited the Raw Men at their trading outpost to send a ship to visit the Island. That should have been a triumph for the Tjula, but once the other bloodlines had learned of this visit, the Manyilti had led a faction who blamed them for acting without the Council's approval, and threatening all trade with Tiayal. Another feud had been born out of that dispute, adding to the Island's troubles.

The Raw Men had eventually heeded the Tjula's call, sending a fleet of three ships to wander [explore] the seas, and visited the Island. One fleet only, with small quantities of valuable goods and only limited interest in trading[190]. The result had been endless disagreements among the Nangu, as the bloodlines competed in a most undignified manner to secure some of the Raw Men's goods.

That had been the first great warning, as far as Lalgatja had been concerned. He had ordered his captains not to trade with the Raw Men at all. His judgement had been that any price paid would be too expensive, and that being involved in the bargaining would only attract the hatred of other bloodlines.

Events had proved him right; more feuds had grown out of the Raw Men's visit than any of the earlier troubles. So far none of those feuds had turned into a full vendetta, but the risk remained. Especially with almost three years passing, and no sign whether the Raw Men would ever return. The bloodlines grew ever more fractious, with whispered rumours accusing others of warning off the Raw Men, or of concluding secret agreements for exclusive access.

Other troubles had followed in the wake of the Raw Men's visit. Disease had struck; a new malady called swelling-fever [mumps] which had first appeared amongst the Atjuntja, and then in time followed the trading ships back to the east.

Swelling-fever had struck first in the Seven Sisters [Eyre Peninsula], then on the Island. Many men had died of this new affliction. This had happened despite the best

---

[190] This was François Thijssen's 1626-7 voyage to Aururia and Aotearoa. He did not actually have limited interest in trading with the Nangu *per se*, but he had only a few samples of trade goods. He did not want to exchange them all with the first people he met, preferring to keep most of them if he encountered other peoples further east.

precautions of the Nangu, who had acted on the advice of Nakatta, elder of the Muwanna bloodline. Nakatta had advised of the need to quarantine any ship whose crew showed symptoms of the swelling-fever. That quarantine had been enforced, but the disease still spread to the Mutjing and then to the Nangu[191].

The failure of Nakatta's advice had discredited the Muwanna bloodline, but that had only been the start of the problems. The Lorekeeper, most senior elder in the Council, had been among the victims of the swelling-fever. With his departure to join his kin, the bloodlines had lost their most respected adjudicator, which had only worsened the feuds.

Trade had suffered, too. With the deaths of so many farmers amongst the Mutjing, the price of yams, wealth-grain [wattle seeds] and other foods had risen. That always made the Nangu uneasy. The Island depended on importing food from the Mutjing, and paying more for it cost trade goods which had to be obtained from elsewhere. So far, prices had not risen unbearably, but the fact that they had increased at all had worsened the tension amongst the bloodlines.

Even lesser events seemed to conspire to bring misfortune to the Island. From the mainland, word had come that the Yadji Regent [ie Emperor] was dead of the swelling-fever. Privately, Lalgatja suspected that the priests had simply used a convenient excuse to rid themselves of a mad Regent. Regardless of the reason, however, the Land of the Five Directions [Yadji lands] drifted leaderless while the priests squabbled among themselves.

Normally, chaos among the Yadji would have been a welcome sign that the security of the Island was being maintained. Not now, though, when it let Tjibarr

---

[191] The quarantine has failed because mumps produces a significant proportion of asymptomatic carriers, and some of them have carried the disease past the quarantine.

consolidate its decade-old conquest of Jugara and the Copper Coast. The safety of the Island had always rested on the balance between the Yadji and Tjibarr, so that both of them were too busy looking at the other to threaten the Nangu. Now it looked as if that might no longer hold. Worse, in the short term, the unrest in the Yadji lands meant that their rulers were disinclined to trade, which wove another thread into the tapestry of Nangu troubles.

On the Cider Isle, worse than unrest had come; the Tjunini and Kurnawal had started another cycle in their endless war. Many times, such news would have had the trading captains flocking to their shores to profit from trading with both sides. Alas, this war had been more destructive than most, with cider gums deliberately burned, and gold mining curtailed while both sides focused on mining tin to make bronze for weapons. There was little worth trading for in the Cider Isle, until the war was done.

So, in the midst of this time of troubles, Lalgatja had come to seek wisdom, to chart a course for his bloodline through rough waters. The Island afflicted by disease and riven by feuds, the world growing unsettled, and the Raw Men both mysterious and enticing beyond the fringes of the world.

As he considered matters, he realised that he had already been given the most important insight. The Raw Men were the key. Know them, understand them, and the path would become clear. The other troubles would come and go, but they were merely ripples in the cosmos.

"We *must* reach the Raw Men properly," Lalgatja said, the first time he had spoken aloud since he reached the temple. "If they will not come to us, we must find a way to go to them."

With that invitation, his captains now knew that they could speak. If they had anything worth saying.

Werringi, the second-most senior captain, said, "We cannot reach the Raw Men if we sail west. Most of the other bloodlines have tried and failed, even with captains and crews whose skills are not to be despised."

Lalgatja said, "That truth we knew before coming here."

"The truth we knew, but not what follows from it. The Raw Men come from the west, but when they have traded with the Atjuntja, they do not sail west again."

Now, *that* was a new thought. If true. "Are you sure?"

"They go north. So agree those who have been to the White City," Werringi said. "And we all saw the ships which the Raw Men brought to the Island. They cannot sail into the wind as well as our ships can, even if they are faster with the wind behind them. If the western winds have defeated our captains, then the Raw Men *must* be sailing north."

Kunyana, the most senior captain, said, "That will not let us sail after them. To voyage along the western coast of Tiayal is difficult, since we cannot secure landfall without being asked very demanding questions. Our ships would have even more troubles if they wander beyond Atjuntja lands. Going north, it is easy to sail away but hard to sail back, which makes it very difficult to judge how far a ship can safely sail before turning back."

Werringi said, "So we must sail east first."

Lalgatja raised an eyebrow. "You would reach the Raw Men by sailing further away from them?"

"It is the route which the Raw Men took after visiting here. They would not have sailed there if they did not know that the voyage could be done."

Werringi stood, his enthusiasm carried in his voice as he spoke. "It would be a great voyage, but not an impossible one. I have sailed to the Spice Coast, to the Patjimunra lands and even once to Daluming. That is the way which the Raw Men must have gone, and they would only have sailed there if they knew that they could find their homeland again. So I will take a ship east, then north, and sail west where I can, until I can find where the Raw Men go after they leave Tiayal."

Kunyana said, "Boldness is good, but suicide is not."

"It is the third path [decisiveness]," Werringi said. "This is a time of great change; we will not succeed by taking half-measures."

Lalgatja gestured for Werringi to sit again, then let them wait in silence while he thought. After a time, he said, "Do as you will, Werringi. I will not sanction your voyage, but neither will I oppose it. If you can persuade your crew to sail with you, and perhaps find another captain willing to take his ship with yours, then I will pray to Eagle for your success."

* * *

This section is a summary of the key domesticated Aururian plants and animals and what effects they might have on the rest of the world. This is not a comprehensive list of all such plants and animals; it only includes some of those which have potential to be exported to the rest of the world and make a significant difference there.

In this list, the allohistorical name is given first, if it differs from the historical name. Where there is more than one important allohistorical name, the name which is used is the one by which the plant or animal will be most widely known in English.

Staple Crops

Red yam (*Dioscorea chelidonius*) is a perennial vine which produces large, edible tubers, and for cooking purposes can be used much like a potato. It grows well in semi-arid conditions between latitudes of 25 to 45 degrees. Can grow in areas of higher rainfall, but does not tolerate waterlogged soils. Widely-grown throughout subtropical and temperate Aururia, and has excellent potential to be exported to other parts of the world. It will grow well in areas of Mediterranean climate and other mid-latitude regions, but will not grow in the tropics. It has a reasonably high agricultural yield, although on fertile, well-watered soils, crops such as potatoes would be superior.

Lesser yam (*Dioscorea chelidonius* var *inferior*) is a hybrid of the red yam and the related long yam (*D. transversa*). It has a lower yield than the red yam, and has higher water requirements, but unlike the red yam, it can grow in the tropics. The plant is cultivated mostly in the northern fringes of Aururian agriculture [east-central Queensland], but if exported, could grow well in many drier areas of the tropics.

Cornnarts / wattles (*Acacia* spp) are fast-growing trees which produce large quantities of edible, high-protein seeds and can be tapped to yield gum aururic [wattle gum]. As legumes, they also replenish soil nitrates. About ten species of cornnarts have been domesticated. Cornnarts are mostly suited for low-rainfall climates in the middle latitudes, although some of the domesticated species can grow in the tropics or cooler climates, and some can also tolerate higher rainfall.

Murnong (*Microseris lanceolata*) is a perennial crop which produces edible tubers, which are used similarly to red yams or potatoes. Murnong does not tolerate excessive heat, and in lowland regions it cannot be grown as close to the equator as the red yam. However, it is more tolerant of cooler climates, poorer soils and shorter growing seasons, and can be grown at higher latitudes than the red yam. It also does not have the red yam's problems with tropical day length, and can be grown in cool highlands within the tropics.

Aururian flax / native flax (*Linum marginale*) is an Aururian relative of common flax (*L. usitatissimum*). Like the Eurasian plant, it is used to make fibre (linen, textiles, rope), and its seeds are edible or can be used to create a form of linseed oil. It does not grow as large as common flax, but if carefully harvested it will regrow from its roots for up to five years without needing reseeding. If exported, it will need lower rainfall or need less irrigation than common flax, although it will not yield as much fibre per acre. This will allow expansion of textile production by allowing linen to be grown in wider areas, although the Aururian fibre is still quite similar to common flax, and lacks the flexibility of some other plant fibres (such as cotton).

Quandong (*Santalum acuminatum*) is a desert tree which produces large, sweet fruit (including an edible nut at the centre of each fruit). Itparasitises the roots of other trees, and so needs to be cultivated in mixed orchards with other trees. Choosing different host species produces different fruit flavours (cornnarts are normally used in Aururia). Grows well in hot, relatively arid regions, and would be suitable for cultivation around much of the world, particularly zones of Mediterranean climate.

Luto / bush pear (*Marsdenia australis*) is a desert vine where almost all of the plant is edible. The pear-shaped fruit has a sweet pulp and edible seeds. The leaves and stems are edible and used for flavouring. The vine also produces an edible root tuber. A drought-hardy species, the luto will grow even in relatively poor soils and semiarid climates throughout much of the world. In Aururia, it is nicknamed the "many-vine" for the range of flavours which can be produced from its various parts, and some other countries will incorporate the luto into their cuisine when it is eventually exported.

Spices

Lemon verbena / lemon myrtle (*Backhousia citriodora*) is a tree whose leaves produce a sweet, strong lemony flavour. While it tolerates low levels of some nutrients, overall it needs better soils, warmer weather and higher rainfall than most Aururian plants. In pre-Houtmanian Aururia, lemon verbena's cultivation was largely confined to the subtropical eastern coast, but it was traded across the continent. Lemon verbena has considerable potential to be exported as a spice, and could be grown in areas of similar climate around much of the world. The potential is similar for several other spice trees which grow on the subtropical east coast, aniseed myrtle (*Syzygium anisatum*), cinnamon myrtle *(Backhousia myrtifolia)* and curry myrtle (*B. angustifolia*).

Sweet peppers / pepperbushes (*Tasmannia* spp) are shrubs whose leaves and especially berries have an intense peppery taste. All of the sweet pepper species tolerate reasonably poor soils and frosts. The most widespread species, common sweet peppers / mountain peppers (*T. lanceolata*) is grown across much of the southern half of Aururia, although it often needs some small-scale irrigation. The hotter and more flavoursome species, bird-peppers / Dorrigo peppers (*T. stipitata*) and purple sweet peppers / broadleaf pepperbush (*T. purpurascens*) are restricted to small regions on the east coast. Sweet peppers have considerable potential for export; the berries of the common sweet pepper have, per weight, up to ten times the heat of the more common black pepper (*Piper nigrum*), while the other species are even hotter.

Ovasecca / desert raisin (*Solanum centrale*) is a desert shrub related to the tomato, which produces a fruit with a taste reminiscent of tamarillo and caramel. The fruit conveniently dries while still on the stalk, making for easy transport and storage. The plant tolerates dry conditions and poor soils. In the wild it only fruits after heavy rains; in cultivation this is mimicked by judicious irrigation. Ovasecca is cultivated in the Five Rivers and nearby areas as a condiment, and has the potential to be cultivated in semiarid regions around the world where there is access to irrigation.

White ginger / native ginger (*Alpinia caerulea*) is a shrub whose fruit, new shoots and tubers have gingery flavours. Native to the warmer areas of the eastern Aururian seaboard, it can be grown much more widely with irrigation. It is cultivated intensely in the Five Rivers, and less commonly elsewhere, as a spice. White ginger can be cultivated in subtropical climates around the world with reasonable rainfall and/or irrigation, and has some potential as a spice for export.

Others

Kunduri / corkwood (*Duboisia hopwoodii*) is a shrub whose leaves contain high levels of nicotine and other alkaloids, and provide Aururia's drug of choice. The cultivated form of kunduri is grown in the Five Rivers, and is their most valuable export to the rest of the continent.

Although Eurasians who first encounter kunduri will often find it too strong a drug (due to the elevated nicotine levels), it has very strong long-term potential for export and will influence the world (in several senses of the word). Kunduri could also be cultivated in subtropical arid or semiarid areas around the world (with irrigation).

Green indigo / native indigo (*Indigofera australis*) is a relative of true indigo (*I. tinctoria*), which produces a similar dye to the more familiar (to Eurasians) plant. Green indigo is more versatile than true indigo, since by various treatments to the leaves, it can produce not just the true indigo colour, but a brilliant yellow and a distinctive green. Green indigo was cultivated over most of the farming areas of Aururia in the pre-contact period. The plant can grow in poorer soils and drier climes and further into subtropical latitudes than true indigo, and so has considerable potential both for export from Aururia and for cultivation around much of the world. The name green indigo will be given because of the green dye which can be produced from it.

Jeeree / Lemon-scented teatree (*Leptospermum petersonii*) is a tree whose leaves produce an intense, lemony taste. It can tolerate reasonably poor soils, but needs reasonable rainfall and is sensitive to frost. In Aururia, it is grown almost exclusively on the eastern coast, where its leaves are used to make a lemon tea-like beverage that is popular amongst all of the eastern cultures, though it is only used in limited areas on the rest of the continent. Jeeree has some potential for export as an exotic "tea", and can be cultivated in most subtropical latitudes where there is reasonable rainfall or access to irrigation.

Noroon / emu (*Dromaius novaehollandiae*) is a large, flightless bird which is Aururia's prime domestic animal. A fast-growing bird, it is a useful source of meat, leather, fat and feathers. In comparison to big Eurasian domestic animals (such as cattle), the noroon is less efficient as a grazer, but when grain fed, produces more usable meat in proportion to the amount of grain. The noroon has reasonable potential for export to subtropical and tropical latitudes, particularly since as a bird it is unaffected by some tropical diseases which afflict domesticated mammals.

Pole-cat / tiger quoll (*Dasyurus maculatus*) is a marsupial equivalent of the cat, domesticated to serve a similar rat-catching role. Pole-cats are widely distributed among the farming peoples of Aururia, who find them an invaluable asset for controlling native rodents and other pests. The pole-cat is not quite as efficient a rat-catcher as cats, but it still has some potential for export as an exotic pet, and it may also become an invasive species if introduced into some environments.

Silk-bagger / ribbed case moth (*Hyalarcta nigrescens*) is a domesticated species of moth whose caterpillars produce a fine cocoon which can be used to extract silk. Silk-baggers are found exclusively within the Five Rivers, principally within the kingdom of Yigutji, although silk cloth is exported throughout the farming regions of Aururia. The silk-bagger produces silk of comparable quality to domesticated silkworms (*Bombyx mori*) from historical China. Rearing of the silk-bagger in its cocoon is easier than that of silkworms, since it is less sensitive to temperature and will feed on a greater variety of plants. However, the extraction of silk from the cocoon is slightly more labour-intensive than that from silkworms. This is likely to mean that silk can be more widely-cultivated in some regions where silkworms cannot grow, but will not reduce the price of silk to any significant degree since the overall cost of production will be similar.

* * *

In Europe, the course of what another history would call the Thirty Years' War would be changed by the ravages of Marnitja in 1628. At this time, the imperial forces under Albrecht von Wallenstein had made Christian IV of Denmark regret his intervention in the war, defeating Denmark's allies and ultimately overrunning Jutland. To threaten the Danish capital on Zealand, though, the imperial forces needed a Baltic fleet, and plans were made to besiege the port of Stralsund.

The effects of Marnitja changed that. The preparations for besieging Stralsund were abandoned amidst the disruption. While both sides suffered casualties from the epidemic, the Danish forces were in a better position to liberate much of Jutland, since they could draw on local support while the imperial forces were operating on hostile territory.

A year of manoeuvring on Jutland followed, with a number of engagements which saw imperial forces pushed out of part of the peninsula, but never decisively defeated. By this point, both sides were inclined to seek peace. Diplomatic manoeuvring replaced its military counterpart, and by April 1630 the two sides had agreed on terms.

By the terms of the Treaty of Lübeck, Jutland and Royal Holstein were restored to Denmark, while the Duchy of Holstein was granted joint overlordship of Hamburg. Prince Ulric, a younger son of Christian IV, was named Prince-Bishop of Verden, and Bishop of Schwerin, and was designated as the heir of the Lutheran Prince-Archbishop of Bremen, when the current incumbent died. The Dukes of Mecklenburg were restored, including the estates which Wallenstein had confiscated. In exchange, Wallenstein was granted estates around Stettin in central Pomerania, which allowed him to collect tolls from trade along the River Oder. As part of the treaty, Christian IV agreed to withdraw all Danish forces from elsewhere in the Holy Roman Empire, and not to provide any further support to Protestants in Germany.

So, in April 1630, it appeared that the war which had begun eleven years earlier might finally come to an end.

Other events, though, changed that.

In Sweden, Gustavus Adolphus caught Marnitja in May 1630. He survived the pink cough, but now faced the prospect of waiting to see whether he would be claimed by a fevered delirium. Gustavus did not plan to wait passively for death to claim him, but decided that if he would die, he would leave a legacy behind. He wanted to make sure that his name would be remembered.

The previous year, Sweden had ended its war with Poland by signing a seven-year truce, the Truce of Altmark[192], which gave Sweden control of Livonia and some Baltic ports. Gustavus Adolphus was not inclined to break that truce in pursuit of further gains.

Instead, he looked south. As he saw it, the Protestant cause in Germany had been betrayed by Denmark, but here was an opportunity to secure his legacy. Germany was in chaos, the Protestants needed support, and glory beckoned. Swedish forces landed near Stettin in June 1630, with Gustavus Adolphus at their head and conquest on his mind. He knew that landing here would inevitably draw the forces of Wallenstein, the greatest surviving general of imperial forces, and hoped that defeating Wallenstein would rally Germany's Protestants under his banner.

Gustavus Adolphus did not just hope to secure glory through victory in Germany, though. By now, Europe was rife with rumours of the wealth to be found in colonies, with the Spanish long ago acquiring dominions in the Americas, and the Dutch finding a new fortune in the distant South Land. Gustavus Adolphus chartered a new company, based in Gothenburg, with orders to explore North America and find a suitable place for founding a new colony there that would bear his name.

---

[192] This truce was somewhat more generous to Sweden than the historical equivalent (which only lasted six years). Under the treaty, Sweden has control of Livonia, some coastal cities in Prussia, and a substantial share of the tolls from trade passing through Poland's Baltic ports.

#38: The First Seeds

"Satisfaction comes from doing the proper works of a man."
- Plirite maxim
"A man's worth is no greater than the sum of his ambitions and his balance."
  - Nangu saying

* * *

Werringi, or so his parents named him. One man among many born to the Wolalta bloodline, which itself was one bloodline among many which vied for wealth and pride in the endless struggle of the Nangu.

Werringi would make a name for himself, though, as a sailor and as a trading captain. And, in time, much more. Before he breathed his last on this mortal world, where by his devoutly held Plirite beliefs he would in time be reborn according to the balance of his own actions and the ripples in the wider cosmos, he had earned another epithet.

Kumgatu, he would later be called, a name which meant "the Bold". Awarded for the deeds he performed during his life – one in particular – it was the name by which he would be known in Aururia and, afterward, elsewhere.

* * *

April 1630
Inner Sea, Southeast of Quamba [Mackay, Queensland]
Stillness surrounded the *Dawn Seeker*; cloudless, almost windless sky above, and still, deep water below, so clear that it seemed as if the boat itself was floating in the sky.

"Perfect weather," Ouraidai said, from his place beside the steering oar. The same thing he usually said whenever he took the *Dawn Seeker* out to dive for coral. Of course, if it had not been a perfect day, Ouraidai would not have brought the twin-hulled vessel out of Quamba.

Quailoi approved of that caution, naturally; Ouraidai had been his Elder Brother[193], and taught him so much of what it meant to be a man, including the need for prudence. Even now that Quailoi had married, the two men remained firm friends, and worked the Inner Sea together. Quailoi worked as the coral diver; Ouraidai now deemed himself too old for that kind of work, and steered the boat, watched the rope and helped from the surface.

Ouraidai had steered the *Dawn Seeker* to the right location; a place where the water was shallow enough to let them see down to the sea floor below, but still deep enough to yield a particularly prized kind of scarlet coral. Any fool could harvest coral from the reefs which marked the boundary of the Inner Sea; finding a valuable sort in the depths was another matter entirely.

Quailoi took his position on the poles which joined the *Dawn Seeker*'s two hulls together, and secured the rope to the poles in preparation to dive. Before he could enter the water, though, Ouraidai called out for him to wait.

Quailoi followed the other man's outstretched finger. Boats had appeared to the south. Three boats with sails of a proper triangular shape but with sails dyed a most peculiar shade of teal that nearly blended into the sea and

---

[193] Elder Brother (or, more rarely, Elder Sister) is a social institution amongst the Kiyungu which involves an older man (or woman) assuming a role as a mentor and lover of a younger person. The mentor is always of the same gender as the younger, and it is considered a valuable way of teaching about love, life, proper values, the social order, and often a craft skill. The formal relationship is ended when the younger gets married, although usually the elder party will still be available to provide advice to the younger for the rest of their lives.

sky. Doubtless that was why they had not noticed the boats before.

"Have you ever seen boats with sails like that?" Quailoi asked. It was a proper question to ask an Elder Brother; for a moment, it felt as if he was back in his youth, seeking guidance.

"No. What proper Kiyungu would waste good dyes on a sail?" Ouraidai said. "Especially such an inauspicious colour."

Quailoi nodded. Sometimes Kiyungu from the southern cities were strange, but surely not so foolish as that. Still... "Yet who else sails the Inner Sea?"

"None that I know of," Ouraidai said. "Head-taking Daluming raiding the League cities in the south, yes. But I've never heard of them coming this far, and they prefer to strike by land anyway."

Quailoi could only agree. The Daluming could not be here, and no-one else could sail on the Inner Sea. To the north lay only barbarians who knew not how to farm; better to look for wombats to fly than for them to build boats with sails, let alone ones touched by dyes. But who did that leave? "Is there anyone else who might sail so far?"

Ouraidai did not answer immediately; doubtless considering the question.

While the other man thought, Quailoi looked at the boats again, and realised that they had sailed noticeably closer. Fast movement for ships in such a mild breeze; their sails must truly catch the wind.

Now that the ships were closer, he saw more about them. They were double-hulled, like all decent boats, and large enough to carry several men. The sails were not just dyed teal, either. Each of them had a large hollow circle in the centre, coloured a brilliant yellow.

"That pattern is to *identify* the ship," Quailoi said. "It must be. The colours are to announce who the ships belong to. Like a banner, but without needing to attach it separately."

"It could be," Ouraidai said. "Doesn't tell *us* who they are though. Maybe, just maybe, they're Māori from Aotearoa. They'd be from a long way away, but the Māori are said to sail to south of Daluming. Maybe they've decided to come further north."

Quailoi looked south again, to where the ships had come noticeably closer. They were truly moving quickly, even with the poor wind. "Well, we'll soon find out."

Conversation faded then, as both men watched the strange ships narrow the gap. Gradually Quailoi made out the forms of men on the approaching vessels. On the lead vessel, one man stood at the front of the left hull, his arm outstretched as if trying to touch the *Dawn Seeker*.

The foreign ships hove to a little out of reach of the *Dawn Seeker*. The man at front called across the gap. "Peace and fortune be upon you!"

No matter how strange it was to hear the proper forms of greeting from someone who was obviously not Kiyungu, Quailoi gave the proper reply. "And health and life upon you."

Ouraidai said, "Who are you, strangers?"

The man said, "I am Werringi of the Wolalta. From the Island."

"Which island?" Ouraidai asked.

"Our homeland. A long voyage south and then west from here."

"Why have you come to the Inner Sea?"

Werringi grinned. "I have come to sail around the world."

* * *

By 1629, Werringi had earned his path to the second-most senior trading captain of the Wolalta bloodline. His main voyages were to the eastern seaboard of Aururia, to what the Nangu called the Spice Coast, for the much-valued lemon and cinnamon verbena and other spices grown there. His main destination had been the caste-ridden, inward-looking Murrginhi, the Kingdom of the Skin, but he had visited further north, too.

In 1629, he found a new inspiration: to discover the homeland of the Raw Men who had come to visit the Atjuntja in the west. These Raw Men had made one brief visit to the Island in 1626, but now seemed to have spurned any further contact.

Werringi decided that if the Raw Men would not come to the Island, then he would go to them. He had recognised that the Raw Men sailed north from Atjuntja lands, and knew that when they had visited the Island, they had continued east to visit the Cider Isle [Tasmania], and had then apparently turned north. So he reached the somewhat incorrect conclusion that the best way to reach the Raw Men's homeland was to sail north along the Spice Coast and then on to unknown regions northward, turning west at some undiscovered point to sail west to the Raw Men's homeland.

Organising the voyage took several months, as Werringi sought to persuade other captains to join him, to find out what tales he could from people who had sailed north (or who claimed they had sailed north), gather provisions, and choose the most suitable ships.

While as a senior captain he had a great-ship to command, Werringi chose to yield that ship and use a smaller vessel. Nangu great-ships could carry more cargo than any other ship, but they had a deeper draft and could not be pulled ashore on a beach at need, unlike the smaller Nangu trading ships. Given the risks and hazards of exploring such completely unknown waters, Werringi preferred to use a vessel which could land without needing a port.

In time, Werringi persuaded two other Wolalta captains to join his voyage, and prevailed upon the Wolalta elder to promote another would-be captain to command of his own vessel. So, on what another calendar would call 14 February 1630, he set out from the Island, leading an expedition of four ships.

The first part of the voyage was rapid, as Werringi guided his fleet through the familiar waters of the Narrow

Sea and then north to the Spice Coast. The fleet resupplied at the Patjimunra city-state of Torimi [Corlette, Port Stephens], a destination which Werringi had visited many times before, and which usually represented the northernmost limit of Nangu voyages.

After leaving the Patjimunra, the expeditions proceeded north more cautiously. Werringi intended not just to reach the Raw Men's homeland, but also to obtain a very detailed knowledge of the journey. After passing the Patjimunra lands, he started to chart the coastline, recording the general shape and key features, and keeping written records of the important events and what he and his crew had seen, including the shifts in the stars.

The expedition visited Yuragir, the capital of Daluming. Werringi had been to the kingdom before, but never as far north as the capital city. Here, he hoped to find out what the Mungudjimay knew about the geography and peoples further north.

Instead, he experienced his first major misfortune. Due to a misunderstanding over cultural expectations[194], the Nangu sailors were challenged by a group of Mungudjimay warriors, and fled for their lives. Werringi himself narrowly escaped capture, but several of the sailors died, and Mungudjimay warriors boarded the last Nangu ship as it left shore. With a fight raging, the Nangu sailors fired their ship and abandoned it for the waves, swimming to the other ships and leaving the armoured warriors the choice of burning to death or drowning.

After this escape, Werringi was careful not to land anywhere else in Daluming, although he maintained his careful charting of the coast. When he reached the Kiyungu lands of the Coral Coast, he found a much warmer

---

[194] That is, the Nangu sailors thought that the best place for their heads would be still attached to their bodies, while the priests of Daluming thought that those same heads would be of more use in niches in the Mound of Memory, ie the great pyramid where the heads of many notables are kept behind glass.

welcome. Never any friends of Daluming, the southerly Kiyungu city-states had established a loose alliance to defend against raids from Daluming, and, in another form, proselytisation from the Yalatji people in the interior, who were increasingly strident advocates of their Tjarrling beliefs.

The southern Kiyungu gave Werringi's expedition a friendly reception, particularly the Kiyungu women, and this delayed the voyage for several days while the two peoples interacted. Werringi tolerated the delay because it served several purposes. It boosted the morale of his sailors, it let them learn the basics of a language which some of the other peoples further north might also understand, and it let him and his fellow captains find out what the southern Kiyungu knew about the world further north.

After leaving the southern Kiyungu, the expedition passed west of Heaven of Sand [Fraser Island] and entered the Inner Sea. Here, they faced a new danger: coral reefs. They had been given sketchy descriptions of the region by the southern Kiyungu, and the reefs had been the feature which had most impressed Werringi. He ordered that their ships sail only during daylight and near low tide, so that they had the best chance to see any reefs, and if they did strike one, they could be carried off it by the rising tide.

With these instructions, progress was slow within the Inner Sea, but much safer than could have been otherwise. The expedition made contact with some of the northern Kiyungu towns, including their northernmost major city at Quamba. These contacts were equally friendly, and led Werringi to recognise the value of sweet potato and lesser yams as tropical crops; the Nangu knew what they were, but had never seen them growing in the warmer climates to which those plants were most suited. However, these contacts did not add much to the expedition's knowledge of the world further north[195].

After leaving Quamba, the expedition reached truly unknown lands. The peoples who dwelt along the shore were mostly hunter-gatherers who were only slowly acquiring crops and domesticated animals from further south, while the waters were warmer and more filled with corals.

Werringi ordered his ships to take even more care. He also decided that for the rest of the expedition, his ships would need to make regular stops along the shore to identify potential resupply points and ports. If possible, they should also establish relationships with the locals, and learn whether they would be amenable to ongoing contact. For the distance his ships were sailing had started to give him some appreciation of how far it might be to the Raw Men's homeland, and if this were to become a regular Nangu trade route, outposts would need to be established along the way.

The voyage amongst the reefs of the Inner Sea was arduous, but Werringi had never lacked for persistence, and kept his captains and crew motivated. In time, they found the reefs fading into the depths beneath them, and felt winds and currents coming out of the west. All of the seasoned Nangu sailors recognised this as a new sea, or at least a new strait, and Werringi ordered his ships to turn to the west, believing that at long last he was nearing the Raw Men's homeland.

In fact, the distance he still had to travel was greater than that which his ships had covered. After negotiating their way through several islands, the expedition found that the land now turned to the south, more than the west.

---

[195] At this time, the northern Kiyungu are slowly expanding their areas of settlement along the coast, thanks to the new crops of sweet potato, taro and lesser yams which let them farm the tropics. The process is relatively slow, though, since the Kiyungu don't have much cultural drive for exploration or expansion.

Disappointed, Werringi could only order that the ships continue to follow the coast, and make regular stops to ascertain the nature of the country and the people.

Discouragement followed disappointment as the great exploration continued. Werringi's ships explored what their maps eventually let them realise was a great gulf in the mainland [Gulf of Carpentaria], and then kept going west. On one beach which he would name Blood Sands [on Melville Island, Northern Territory], his ships were attacked by the locals one night when they were beached, leading to a fight with several casualties on both sides, before the locals were driven off.

Enough Nangu sailors were killed in that battle that they did not have enough crew to operate all three ships properly. Werringi made the reluctant decision to burn the third ship, and the surviving sailors crowded into the two remaining vessels.

After Blood Sands, the expedition faced an even more difficult choice. The land started to turn southward again, and there was no indication whether it would ever continue northward. Werringi had to decide whether to strike out to sea and hope that he could find the Raw Men's homeland out over the open ocean, or continue following the coast toward what would, most likely, eventually lead them to the Atjuntja lands.

Had Werringi but known it, if he had sailed a few days across the open sea, he would have reached Timor and probably come into contact with the Portuguese. After much discussion with his fellow captains, however, he decided to continue following the coastline. The expedition had already lost half its ships, and losing another would mean that their sailors could not all make their way home even if they survived the ship's destruction. Even if the Raw Men's homeland could not be discovered on the first voyage, what his expedition had discovered so far would be invaluable to allow further expeditions. And if all else failed, the Raw Men had outposts in the Atjuntja lands; perhaps they could be visited there.

So Werringi's ships followed the coastline west and south with their usual slow, methodical progress. In time they reached peoples who had knowledge of the Raw Men; enough to recognise what ships were, even if not much more than that. That did not make Werringi change his mind; he still believed that the best course was to follow the coast, rather than strike out to wherever these ships sailed.

And so, on 18 September 1631, Werringi's two remaining ships anchored off the shore of the Middle Country, at a Raw Men outpost which its inhabitants called Fort Zeelandia...

* * *

18 September 1631
Fort Zeelandia [Geraldton, Western Australia]
Sails on the western horizon, or such had been the warning. That had been enough for Governor De Vries to order every available man with a musket to the docks, in preparation for whatever raid might be coming. Word had come by runner – Atjuntja runner; for once their roads brought word faster than ships. The Spanish had raided Fort Nassau a few days before, bringing fire and blood with them. If they planned to do the same here, then De Vries would make sure that they did not find easy pickings.

When the two ships came closer, though, he saw that they could not be Spanish. Twin hulls, triangular sails dyed blue-green with a golden ring in the centre. Smaller than he had expected, too. Certainly not big enough to mount many cannon or carry a large group of sailors. Even if this were somehow a Spanish ruse, so few men would not pose a danger.

"What sort of ships are they?" De Vries asked. "The Atjuntja can't build anything remotely like this."

Pieter Willemszoon, next to him, said, "Can never be sure, but I think that they're Islander ships."

"*Islanders*? Here?" De Vries said. "The Atjuntja forbid them to come here." A great pity, that, and a greater shame that Governor-General Coen had not pushed more vigorously for trade with the Island. From what De Vries had sampled of their *kunduri*, in particular, he thought that was a great loss.

Willemszoon shrugged. "The Atjuntja forbid us to sail east of Cape Hasewint [Cape Leeuwin], too, but that hasn't stopped us."

"I suppose. Still, I'd have expected them to go to Fort Nassau before coming here." He paused. "Before the Spanish raided, at least."

The two ships quickly neared the shore, even with the breeze blowing out to sea. They tacked effortlessly, it seemed, and sailed closer to the wind than any ships which De Vries had ever seen.

When the two ships were almost to shore, the crew on one pulled down the sail and threw a rock over the side, with a rope tied to it.

"Anchoring off shore?" Willemszoon murmured.

"Only one," the governor said. The other ship kept on coming, straight to an open place on the dock. As if it had every right to do so.

This close, he could make out the men easily enough. Dark skins like the natives here, although all of them had dark hair, too. That settled it. Nothing the Spanish could have done would have let them send these men here in a ruse. It had to be Islanders, and clearly coming to parley. Prudent, too, to keep one ship out to sea so that it could run for home with word if the first ship were attacked or its crew imprisoned.

"When the Islanders land, send their leaders to my residence," De Vries said. "With an armed escort, of course."

"Sir?" Willemszoon was usually efficient, but he did not follow the governor's train of thought this time.

"They want some sort of bargain, or they wouldn't be coming. Better to discuss that in comfort in my residence than at the docks when surrounded by armed men, don't you think?"

Willemszoon nodded.

Some time later, with De Vries sitting comfortably in his favourite chair, Willemszoon re-appeared. Along with three of these Islanders, dressed in a rather poor state, but then they had surely been sailing for a while. And five Dutchmen, all with muskets and swords. The Islanders did not carry anything more dangerous than knives, but better to take no chances.

One of the Islanders, obviously the leader from the way the others regarded him, spoke in heavily-accented Atjuntja. "May this meeting bring harmony to both our peoples, with the guidance of the Good Man."

The words sounded stylised and formal, even through the heavy accent. It took De Vries a moment to realise that they were a blessing of sorts. Well, he had already known that the Islanders were no proper Christians. Hopefully their pagan gods weren't as bloodthirsty as those of the Atjuntja.

"May God smile on us," he said, also in the Atjuntja language. Except that he used the proper Dutch word for God. He would not deign to invoke the name of the heathen Atjuntja deity, even indirectly.

"My name is Werringi. I am of the..." He paused, and had a rapid exchange of words with one of his fellow captains. "Your pardon, but this Atjuntja language does not have the right word. I am a captain of the *great family* Wolalta."

"I am De Vries, governor of Fort Zeelandia." He also noted that while this Werringi used the Atjuntja language, he was not very fluent in it. In fact, De Vries thought that he spoke it better than the Islander captain. A puzzle, perhaps, but one to be considered at another time. "Be welcome here, although I am surprised that you have come."

Werringi said, "Your people did not come back to our Island, so we decided to come to you." He had a sly smile as he spoke.

"I understand that the Atjuntja forbid you to sail past... Sunset Point," he said, remembering the Atjuntja name for Cape Hasewint.

"Our agreement with the King of Kings forbids us to sail *west* past Sunset Point," the Islander said. "So I did not sail that way. My ships came here from the north."

"That's impossible!" De Vries snapped. In Dutch, he realised a moment later, but the other man clearly understood the tone if not the words.

"A bold feat, yes," Werringi said. That sly smile returned at the word *bold*. "But we have mastered a feat of navigation to match that which you Raw Men have done."

That smug overconfidence needed to be punctured. If not, De Vries would not have revealed something he had always been ordered to conceal. "Not by a tenth, I think. Sailing to the Netherlands, our homeland, takes up to a year, most of it across the open ocean far out of sight of land."

That news weakened the Islander's confidence, sure enough. "A year?" he asked, his smile falling into a frown. Then he and the other two Islanders broke into a heated argument.

De Vries let them argue volubly for a time, as he considered his own position. Orders against revealing anything to do with navigation existed for a reason, although he supposed that mentioning that the voyage took a year would not do any great harm.

Still, the Islanders would certainly have more questions. Unless he could distract them with something more important. He said, "You have truly sailed around all of this land?"

Werringi said, "I said it, and it is true."

"What did you discover? What lands did you find on this voyage?" he said.

Werringi said, "Offer me a cloak for a spar, or a spar for a cloak."

"What the... What do you mean?"

Werringi frowned. "You Raw Men are traders. You know that knowledge comes with a price. You do not ask for a gift of knowledge. Especially not something as valuable as our maps and tales."

Charts? De Vries had not even realised that these Islanders made charts. He wondered, for a moment, what else they knew. "You want to bargain for maps?"

Werringi shook his head. Among that Atjuntja, that was a gesture of agreement. Apparently the same held true for the Islanders, for he said, "I offer a copy of my maps and records of my voyage around the world. In exchange for charts and tales of your own. You will tell me about the land you Raw Men come from, and how you sail here."

This time, De Vries needed to consider for even longer. Charts were protected documents for very good reason; the Company hid its navigational knowledge to gain an advantage over rivals. Still, the bargain was extremely tempting. Learning about the geography of a whole new continent, and of the peoples who lived there, could be invaluable.

Worth trading for knowledge of our own charts and voyages? Yes, he decided, after a while. If he told these Islanders how to sail to the East Indies, that would be nothing which the English and the Spanish did not already know... and the Spanish knew how to sail to the South Land too, now.

In any case, he would not have to tell the Islander captain everything. And no matter what he told them, he doubted that these pagans would traverse the world's oceans and sail to Amsterdam. To Batavia, perhaps, which might be a problem, but hardly any worse than the English who already sailed there.

"Let us discuss this further," he said, and they settled down to bargain.

* * *

With his landing at Fort Zeelandia, Werringi became the first Nangu captain to seal a trade bargain with the Raw Men. Or the Nedlandj, as he now knew that they were called. He was fortunate, too, that the Atjuntja governor was far too concerned with manoeuvring his soldiers against a possible Pannidj threat to argue much over the presence of Islanders in forbidden country. The Atjuntja governor simply informed him that what he had done was not forbidden this time, so he could visit provided that he did not attempt to trade, and that word would be sent to the King of Kings. It might prove that the treaty with the Nangu would be revised to forbid any travel to the western shores of the Middle Country, regardless of the route.

Werringi quietly avoided mentioning the knowledge exchange, but simply resupplied his vessels with food, which was permitted under the treaty, then set out again. He kept his ships well out to sea this time, rounded Sunset Point, and visited the White City long enough to leave another copy of his charts and journals with the Wolalta who lived there, in case of misfortune on the final leg of the voyage. Then he took his remaining two ships into the seas of endless winds, and returned to the Island. There, his voyage quickly won him a new name...

* * *

Taken from: "A History of the Dutch-Speaking Peoples"
By Hildebrandt van Rijn

The Cape marked a great landmark to the intrepid navigators who first explored the world's oceans, but as a land for settlement, it would take much longer to gain notice. The native Hottentots were not welcoming of outlanders, and the Portuguese who first explored the Cape had no interest in displacing them. The Portuguese established supply stations further east, and left the Cape largely neglected.

As Dutch and English trade with the Orient expanded, the Cape became a useful stopping point for ships whose crews suffered from scurvy or other malnutritions. It lay at a convenient midpoint between Europe and the Indies, and so by the turn of the seventeenth century, the Cape was regularly visited by European ships.

With the United [Dutch] East India Company's trade with the Orient booming, by 1635 the Lords Seventeen approved the establishment of a permanent settlement at the Cape[196]. The original intent was not for large-scale colonisation, just for a suitable harbour for ships avoiding bad weather or needing repairs, and to allow sufficient provisions to resupply passing ships.

The first expedition reached Table Bay in 1637. The early efforts proved to be a failure. European crops and farming techniques were poorly suited to the lands around the Cape, and food had to be brought in to resupply the settlement[197]. The Lords Seventeen were not pleased to have a victualling station which in fact could not supply victuals to passing crews.

Plans were made to abandon the settlement, until a returning Councillor [of the Indies] who stopped at the Cape noted that the climate there was very similar to that in much of Aururia. He suggested that perhaps crops from the northern hemisphere did not grow as well in the southern, but that Aururian crops would provide a useful alternative.

Given that this particular Councillor[198] was about to join the Lords Seventeen, his idea was well-heeded. The only difficulty was that the Dutch-speaking peoples at this

---

[196] This decision has been taken about fifteen years ahead of when the VOC would historically decide to approve a settlement on the Cape. The earlier settlement is because the VOC's trade is both more profitable and higher volume than it was at the same point in OTL. Even with the casualties from the plagues, Aururian gold, silver, sandalwood, sweet peppers, and first shipments of *kunduri* have significantly boosted revenues.

[197] The historical settlement of Cape Town experienced similar early problems, although they were eventually resolved by better strains of European crops.

[198] Van Rijn is being coy about naming the Councillor because the person in question happens to be one of his ancestors, and he considers it immodest to name him.

time had very little knowledge of how to farm Aururian crops. There had been previous sketchy attempts to introduce various crops to both Amsterdam and Batavia, which had until then been unsuccessful except for some small success in growing murnong in the Netherlands.

So the Company decided to procure both crops and workers from Aururia. Two hundred Mutjing men and women from Valk Land [Eyre Peninsula, South Australia] were persuaded[199] to settle in the Cape in 1640, and ample supplies of seed for their preferred crops were brought with them.

In line with the Councillor's expectations, the new crops thrived in the Cape. The first red yams were supplied to ships in the first year, and bountiful harvests of cornnarts [wattle seeds] from 1642. Harvests of their variety of flax were also plentiful, which laid the foundations for a weaving industry to supply new ropes and sails to damaged ships.

The endeavour was successful enough, even after some conflicts with the Hottentots, that in 1643 another forty Mutjing families were invited to abandon their struggling homeland and move to the growing settlement at the Cape...

The first significant problems arose in 1645. An outbreak of measles killed nearly a quarter of the Mutjing farmers. The distraught people turned to a religious explanation; they blamed the epidemic on the lack of guidance in how to avoid bringing disharmony. They demanded that the Company bring in a Plirite priest and allow them to build a small temple for him.

The Company officials at the Cape knew that allowing the establishment of a heathen temple in a Dutch colony would not be viewed favourably in Europe. However, to a Company pragmatic enough to maintain trade with the Atjuntja, overlooking the presence of a Plirite priest or two

---

[199] For a given value of persuade, that is.

in one of their distant outposts would be no difficult task. Keeping the Cape settlement functioning properly was deemed to be the greater priority, and a Plirite priest was duly invited from Valk Land. They expected, with some justification, that in time the Mutjing farmers would convert to Christianity.

So the first Plirite temple was founded at the Cape in 1647...

Interlude: The Portuguese Yam

Taken from Intellipedia.
Red Yam
The red yam is a starchy, tuberous crop from the perennial *Dioscorea chelidonius* of the Dioscoreaceae family (also known as the bread vines)[200]. The name red yam can refer to the plant itself, as well as the edible tuber. The name is also sometimes misleadingly used to refer to the related crop *Dioscorea angustus*, properly known as the lesser yam. However, in Portuguese, no such ambiguity arises, since the same name, *inhame vermelho*, is used to refer to both species. [citation needed]

In southern and eastern Aururia, there are other closely-related wild yam species, none of which are cultivated. However, the warran yam (*Dioscorea hastifolia*), native to the south-west of the Third World [this phrase has been reported as offensive: discuss] has been cultivated[201]. Despite having first been introduced outside of Aururia four centuries ago [dubious: Aotearoa is not in Aururia!], red yams have today become a fundamental component of much of the world's cuisine. Today, the red yam is the world's fifth-largest food crop, after rice, wheat, potato and maize[202].

---

[200] "Red Yams: Notes". Jessup University Department of Landscape Architecture.

[201] Tjula, D.S. "100 Recipes for Warrans".

[202] FABSTAT.

Related *Dioscorea* (yam) species are distributed through tropics of the globe, and a few extend into temperate latitudes. However, domesticated yams are derived only from the Old World and Aururia; no yam crops have been domesticated from the Americas. [citation needed] The red yam (and lesser yam) is by far the most widespread and commercially significant domesticated *Dioscorea* crop. However, other yam crops are equally important to the peoples who cultivate them, particularly white and yellow yams in West Africa [irrelevant addition: discuss].

Based on historical records, local tradition, and genetic analysis, the red yam is known to have been first domesticated in the Nyalananga basin. Although the precise location has not been identified. Archaeological evidence has clearly demonstrated that domesticated red yams were grown by 2500 BC[203]. However, the red yam was cultivated as long ago as 10,000 years ago[204] [unreliable source].

Introduced to the world by the Netherlands after 1619, the red yam was then distributed by mariners to territories and ports throughout the globe. Hundreds of varieties remain in Aururia, where a single agricultural household may grow half a dozen cultivars. Once established across the globe, the red yam soon became an important staple crop, particularly in the Mediterranean littoral and the subtropical Americas.

Characteristics

Red yam plants are herbaceous perennial vines that grow up to 6 m long (depending on variety), with the yam stems dying back in late autumn. They bear purple, white, pink or yellow flowers. Red yams are cross-pollinated mostly by insects, including bees and moths, which carry pollen from other red yam plants, although a few cultivars are capable

---

[203] Hylla S.A., Dusel F (eds). "Aururia in Prehistory"

[204] Meyer, J.B., personal communication

of self-fertilisation. Tubers form in response to decreasing day length, although a few commercial cultivars start forming their tuber earlier than the summer solstice.

After red yam plants flower, some cultivars produce small fruits, although these are toxic. All new red yam cultivars are grown from seed. Any domesticated red yam variety can also be propagated vegetatively by planting the tuber, or the uppermost portion (called the head) [citation needed]. Red yams can also be bred from cuttings, which are most commonly used in greenhouses. A few commercial cultivars cannot produce seeds, and are cultivated only from cuttings or tuber heads. However, the "Sombra" cultivars of red yams, bred in Portugal, are grown for ornamental purposes. Sombra yam vine stalks grow year-round, and are much-favoured for decorating buildings in Lisbon and the Algarve, but do not form viable tubers.

Genetics

The major species grown worldwide is *Dioscorea chelidonius* (a tetraploid with 160 chromosomes), and modern varieties of this species are the most widely-cultivated worldwide. There are also three hexaploid species, most notably the lesser yam *D. inferior*, and the less widespread *D. stenotomum* and *D. siliqua*[205].

Including the hexaploid subspecies, there are about a thousand genetically distinct varieties of red yams globewide[206]. Seven hundred or so are confined to Aururia and Aotearoa, and about six hundred of those are exclusively found within the Nyalananga basin. No truly wild form of *Dioscorea chelidonius* survives today; genetic pollution and habitat destruction has meant that all surviving wild varieties of red yam contain some introgression of domesticated genes. Archaeological digs

---

[205] Burani, K. "Molecular description and similarity relationships among native yams"

[206] Schultz, K.G., Thiele, A.M. et al "*Dioscorea* Taxonomy Reconsidered: Insights from Genetic Similarity Testing"

have recovered the genome of apparently wild forms, and Hani Tarun, a genetic pioneer, is actively leading research into identifying genes from preserved varieties of wild red yams which can be used to enhance cultivated forms for better growth or resistance to disease and pests [this appears to be a personal advertisement: flagged for removal: discuss].

History

Red yams yield abundantly with little effort, and with appropriate care and replanting after harvest an individual plant can be made to yield tubers for up to a decade. They are best suited to moderately dry climates, and together with cornnarts are the most water-efficient of staple food crops. Red yams are vulnerable to moulds and rotting if stored in damp or humid conditions, although their thick skins mean that they are less vulnerable than other major root crops such as potatoes or sweet potatoes. Red yams can rarely be stored for more than a year except in specialised conditions, in contrast to cereal crops which can be safely stored for several years.

Aururia

The red yam originated in south-eastern Aururia, somewhere on or near the Nyalananga, although the precise location remains disputed. Red yams were first domesticated sometime between 3500 and 2500 BC, and spread over the southern half of the continent before 1 AD. They formed the basis of native Aururian agriculture, providing the principal energy source for the Atjuntja, Yadji and Tjibarri states, and their predecessors and successors. Even today, red yams provide the single largest source of food energy for Aururia.

Aotearoa

Red yams spread to Aotearoa, together with other Aururian crops, sometime before AD 1350. Its properties were so respected by Māori farmers, and its cultivation so widespread, that it completely displaced the Polynesian crop package which the Māori had brought with them. Sweet potatoes, taro and Asian yams were cultivated during the early days of Māori settlement, but were abandoned before first European contact in 1627. They survived only in archaeology and where they were imported into Aururia. However, some have argued [who?] that without the Māori bringing sweet potatoes to Aururia, the northern half of the continent would have been largely empty until European invasion [this term has been flagged as offensive: discuss].

Africa

Red yams were introduced to southern Africa in 1640, with the first Cape Maddirs who were forcibly deported from their homelands [citation needed]. Plirite missionaries carried red yams along with their faith beyond the borders of Dutch control, until the missionaries reached the Tropic of Capricorn. The missionaries progressed further, but the red yam did not. However, the *D. chelidonius ssp. inferior* varieties of red yam spread along the eastern coast of Africa, until by the mid-eighteenth century they were being grown as far north as the Habeshan highlands...

Europe

Dutch East India Company sailors brought red yams with them back to the Netherlands in the 1620s, but the crop did not grow well at such northerly latitudes[207]. The red yam was first introduced into Europe in 1648 by the Portuguese sailor Miguel Ferreira do Amaral, who successfully replanted red yam tubers which he had taken on as food at the Cape. Mastering the cultivation of this native Aururian crop would have been impossible without the help of Yadilli farmers who willingly shared their knowledge with the Portuguese despite being forcibly brought to Europe [citation needed].

The red yam spread to Spain and then to Spain's dominions in Sicily and elsewhere in Italy, and from there to Venice and the Turks. During the later seventeenth century and the early eighteenth century, the red yam became

---

[207] Boniface, A.E. "The United East India Company: Reflections on the Golden Age"

integrated into Mediterranean farming, particularly given its ability to give good yields even on poor, parched soils in southern Italy. Sicily grew so many red yams that even today, many Mediterranean countries call the plant the Sicilian yam. Historians believe (Kant, 1987) that the red yam-fed population boom in Sicily led to social tension over land tenure and inheritance, and ultimately to the Advent Revolt which replaced Spanish rule with the native Piazzi dynasty...

Elsewhere

Historical records of red yams in South America date to the late seventeenth century. Contact is presumed to have been via the Cape, where some Portuguese ships resupplied, or Spanish ships during times of peace with the Dutch. Buenos Aires is noted as an early centre of New World red yam cultivation, and from there the red yam spread throughout the Spanish Americas [citation needed].

Role in World Food Supply

The Food and Agricultural Bureau reports that the red yam plays a vital role in maintaining and expanding the global food supply in subsistence economies. Although mechanised farming of the red yam remains problematic, its qualities as a perennial, low water demand crop mean that is suitable for low-capital agriculture and intensive dryland farming...

#39: Sprouting Stalks

"The Nedlandj are covetous and cunning, loud and quickly-spoken, and sail to the uttermost reaches of the world. Of balance they know nothing, for they proclaim for one god yet ignore his rules in pursuit of gold."
 - Anonymous Nangu sailor, describing the Dutch after visiting Batavia

* * *

Azure Day, Cycle of Clay, 392nd Year of Harmony (3.22.392) / 30 November 1631
Crescent Bay, The Island [Kingscote, Kangaroo Island]
"This place is no longer what it once was," Yuma Tjula murmured.

He needed only to feel the extra weight on his shoulders to know that, or glance at the men escorting him. Once, Yuma had walked alone anywhere on the Island wearing whatever sumptuous clothes he liked, armed with nothing but the common Nangu dagger which was as much tool as weapon.

Now, he did not dare. Whenever he set foot on the streets of Crescent Bay, or almost anywhere outside of the lands of his own bloodline, at least four men came with him. Four men armed not with the usual knife but with swords and maces. Four bodyguards. It seemed surreal, even now, like something out of the old days of vendettas.

Those old days had returned, though. Yuma no longer wore a gem-studded headwreath to proclaim his wealth. Instead, he protected himself with a bronze helmet of

Tjunini manufacture, traded despite the war which consumed the Cider Isle. To protect his body, he wore an iron skin: Tjibarri mail, obtained in Jugara at a greater cost in dyes and spices than he cared to think about.

Security had replaced ostentation. Oh, not entirely. He had still found time to have the helmet adorned with a few black and fire opals around the rim, and he still pondered what could be done to improve the appearance of the mail. But the fundamental problem remained: with the Island consumed by feuds, he had to protect himself, or the only adornment he wore would be blood.

He guided his bodyguards past the docks, warily watching if any people in the crowd tried to press too close and slip in a knife. That was how the Beard, the elder of the Kalendi, had been hastened to his next life.

Given the rumours of how the Beard had behaved in life, Yuma thought that his fate was an inevitable consequence, but the Kalendi did not see the outcome that way. They had declared a vendetta on the Nyumatta bloodline, the first called on the Island for many years. Inevitably, further death had followed in the wake of that call.

As they neared the shipyards beyond the docks, Yuma saw that two ships were being built. Great-ships, from the size of the timber that had been assembled for the construction. Strange, indeed. Most ship-building had moved to the Seven Sisters or the Cider Isle, since wood on the Island was more valuable for other purposes.

Yuma almost stopped to see what purpose these new great-ships were meant to serve. Until he saw the banner hung between the ships, a scarlet triangle with stylised bone-white forked lightning in its centre. The symbol of the Manyilti bloodline. Who had declared a feud with his own Tjula bloodline, over Yuma's actions in inviting the Raw Men to visit the Island. No, he did not dare go there. He was not yet ready to reach his next life, and the Island did not need another vendetta such as would follow from his death.

Instead, he directed his bodyguards to step away from the docks and the water, into a street which ran between two warehouses. He wanted to keep well away from the Manyilti and their knives.

In any case, he could guess why they were building new ships, if not why construction was taking place on the Island. Word of Werringi's return was spreading, and the Manyilti must expect more trade as a result. They might even be right; the Raw Men were said to love *kunduri*, as their first visit had confirmed. The Manyilti were well-represented in the trade with Tjibarr, which would let them obtain it to trade to the Raw Men.

Yuma stopped at an unremarkable stone building a short walk beyond the warehouses. Four more armed men stood at the front door, another reminder of how times had changed on the Island. This building was the official town residence of the elder of the Tjula, and served as the town headquarters for the bloodline.

The residence was built of undecorated stone. The lack of ostentation suited its purpose. Almost all of the bloodlines, including the Tjula, maintained grand buildings and estates out in the country. A legacy of the old times when most of the Islanders lived in country holdings, not in the new cities. Those days had long passed, but most bloodlines chose to spend their wealth in country dwellings, not in the crowded environs of Crescent Bay.

Inside waited Wirnugal, elder of the Tjula, and a half-dozen other trading captains. Wirnugal half-rose from his seat to acknowledge Yuma's entrance. "Be welcome in my house, most senior of my captains."

Yuma returned the greeting with equally polite forms, but those words still brought a twist to his heart. Once, not so long before, Yuma had been only the third most senior of the Tjula captains. That had been before the swelling fever [mumps] and the red breath [tuberculosis] swept through the Island. Now the bloodline had been deprived of the knowledge and skills of those former two most senior captains, at a time of great troubles.

For that matter, Wirnugal himself bore the marks of struggle; his face had more lines, his hair was white, and his voice lacked its former power. He had survived the red breath, but his days in this turn of life grew few. Which left Yuma feeling even more uncertain. He had always wanted to lead the Tjula, given time, but not so soon, and not this way.

Wirnugal said, "You have all heard, by now, of what Werringi claims to have done."

"A very bold move, to sail around the world," one of the captains said.

"*If* he speaks truth," another captain answered.

"If what he says is true, he has not sailed around the world at all," Yuma said. "He has only sailed across a small part of the world."

Werringi had been coy about many of the things which he had discovered on his voyage. Doubtless he had carefully prepared charts, and those would be shared only amongst his bloodline's friends. He had met with the Raw Men, and maybe he had established private bargains and obtained other secret knowledge.

But what Werringi had revealed had been amazing enough. Yuma was still trying to fit his head around the idea of how big the world might be. A *year* to sail to the homeland of the Raw Men? Twice that, or more, to sail around the world?

Oh, he had always known that the world was round, as did any learned captain or other great man. To see that, a man only needed to stand on the hill of the Temple of the Five Winds and watch distant ships disappear below the horizon, their hulls vanishing first and only afterward their sails and mast. The scale, though...

"Can that be true?" said Njirubal, now the second-most senior Tjula captain, and a man who Yuma thought had reached that rank too soon.

Wirnugal provided the answer, though. "It can be. The world curves beneath our feet; this we have always known. Perhaps the Raw Men have told only half the truth, and they exaggerate the size of the world to dishearten us from sailing to their homeland. But this much my heart knows to be true: the world is much larger than we have ever known, and there are peoples whose wealth and power dwarfs that of the Yadji or Atjuntja."

The pause which followed was long. Each man filled it with his own thoughts. Yuma wondered how the Raw Men had so much decisiveness, that they could sail so far. The others, no doubt, had other things in mind.

Sure enough, one of the captains said, "If we find them, the trade which would follow would surpass anything which the Atjuntja have, too."

"Or it may bring us nothing but torment instead," Njirubal said. "Witness how the Island seethes with feuds since the Raw Men first visited."

That thought was more worthy of the second-most senior trading captain. Yuma added, "And what if some kinds of Raw Men would bring war to the Island? The White City is full of stories of the war-making brought by some new group of Raw Men."

Wirnugal said, "My heart tells me that the Raw Men will come to us again, no matter what. Better that we find them, too, no matter what else may happen. To act otherwise would bring only discord from their visits, without any counterbalance to bring harmony."

Yuma nodded. As always, Wirnugal saw clearly. But then, what else was an elder expected to do? He said, "We need only decide, then, how best to contact the Raw Men." Remembering Wirnugal's words about balance, he added, "And whether to do it alone or in alliance with other bloodlines."

Wirnugal frowned. "Truth indeed. Feuds bring disharmony. Perhaps only through joint action can we bring back balance on the Island."

The Tjula settled down to discuss how best to reach the Raw Men.

* * *

For the first decade after de Houtman landed on the western shores of what they now called the South Land, the Dutch had only limited contact with the eastern inhabitants of the continent. Failures of early exploration, the intransigence of Governor-General Coen and the disruption of the plagues combined to delay any regular contact with the east.

Motivation for more extensive contact came from several sources: the shock of the Spanish raid on Fort Nassau in 1631, obtaining copies of the charts of the first Islanders to circumnavigate the continent later that same year, and a growing appreciation of the native drug called *kunduri*. Rumours of more gold, silk and spices to the east only added to the growing desire.

Lars Knudsen, the governor of Fort Nassau who had taken office in 1631, had been instructed as part of his orders to establish trade links with the Islanders and any other peoples of commercial interest in the east. While he spent most of his time rebuilding the damaged outpost, he also discreetly gathered what intelligence he could obtain about the eastern peoples, their languages, and their habits.

By a stroke of good fortune, one of the labourers obtained to help rebuild Fort Nassau had previously been drafted to work in the Foreign Quarter of the White City, and had gained a basic knowledge of the Islander language. With the help of generous gifts of steel, Knudsen arranged for the labourer to work permanently for the Company.

With this, copies of charts obtained from the Islanders, and other information garnered from Atjuntja sources, Knudsen decided that he knew enough to organise another expedition to the east. Using authority which was not formally his, he redirected two of the next group of ships to visit Fort Nassau, the *Fortuin* and the *Zuytdorp*.

The two ships were loaded with a variety of trade goods, particularly steel swords and other metal goods, textiles, and two rather expensive clocks procured by Knudsen after their original owners failed to interest Atjuntja merchants in trading for them. Knudsen had a hunch (correctly, as it turned out), the eastern peoples might find them of more value.

Knudsen gave command to Willem Cornelis, a young man[208] who showed talent, and gave him the services of several interpreters, most of whom spoke only the Atjuntja language, but included the one Nangu speaker available. The governor issued only broad orders. Renew contact with the Islanders and their neighbouring peoples. Validate the charts which the Company has received. Explore the potential for extending the Netherlands' protection to any of the eastern peoples you may visit. Obtain a good price for the trade goods which you have been provided, and gather information about what goods are in most demand and of highest value in the east. Establish trade agreements or at least ongoing trade relationships, particularly for *kunduri*.

The two ships left Fort Nassau in February 1632, just as a chickenpox epidemic was sweeping through the Middle Country, brought either by those ships or others in the same fleet. After a quick voyage in strong winds, they reached the coast of what the Dutch knew as Valk Land [Eyre Peninsula], a shoreline dominated by bleak cliffs but with occasional openings. Venturing into one of those openings, they discovered a sheltered bay [Venus Bay] with tidal flats, islands and lagoons, but enough deep channels to let them sail further in.

On the shore, they discovered a city and port nestled among flat expanses of yam and cornnart [wattle] fields. The city's inhabitants proved friendly enough, and through the Nangu-speaking interpreter, explained that this was the city-state of Luyandi [Port Kenny, South Australia]. Its elected ruler was named Maralinga, and he offered warm greetings to the newcomers, along with an invitation to trade food for any goods they might have to offer.

---

[208] The Company has a lot of young men in its service at this time, since many of its more experienced employees have died of the plagues.

Luyandi was a Mutjing city-state, and like all of those cities it was under the economic hegemony of the Islanders, although it took some time for the Dutch to discover this fact. Islander hegemony had never been exercised through direct rule, only through trade contacts, religious pressure where required, and through mediating disputes between the Mutjing cities.

Always a man with an eye for opportunity, Cornelis extended a tempting offer to Maralinga: gifts of steel and textiles in exchange not just for food, but for a trade agreement with the Company. The Lords Seventeen are powerful, he explained, and their influence reaches across the world. They offer you their friendship, and more besides. Exclusive access to these trade goods, the only Mutjing city which would be granted that privilege. And protection from your enemies, if needed.

To cement his offer, Cornelis provided a demonstration of what sort of protection the Company could offer: first muskets, then cannon. Maralinga was most impressed, and indicated that he would welcome a trade agreement. With one codicil: Luyandi would not fight against the Island, and if the Dutch attacked the Island, the trade agreement would be void.

The Company offers only friendship and trade with the Island, Cornelis assured Maralinga. Wars are nothing but trouble and interrupt peaceful trade.

So Willem Cornelis became the second Company officer to strike a trade agreement with a South Land people, and started what would become a very long period of Company presence in Luyandi.

After sailing on from Luyandi, the expedition charted the coast of Valk Land, making brief contact with other Mutjing ports, but without attempting to engage in further trade. Cornelis steered his ships along the eastern side of Valk Land, in the gulf which opened before him [Spencer Gulf], and thus he and his crew became the first Europeans to discover Dogport [Port Augusta] at the head of the gulf. This ancient port linked to the opal mines inland, and while the surrounding countryside was under Tjibarri rule, the city itself was controlled by the local Nangu port-captain. Here, Cornelis traded for opals and other goods, and found that textiles and steel were again profitable trade items, but he received only evasions when he tried to set up any more lasting trade agreements.

Sailing down the eastern shore of the gulf, which he named Brouwer Gulf after the new head of the Company in Asia, he had more contact with areas which were genuinely ruled by Tjibarr, but had no more fortune in securing trade agreements. Whenever he tried to find out who ruled any particular city, he would provoke an argument amongst the inhabitants, which would usually never be resolved.

He only had more success when he worked far enough along the coast to reach Jugara [Victor Harbor], a port which had previously been visited by François Thijssen in 1626, and where the Nangu port-captain was only too eager to allow trade. The local Gunnagal factions quickly bid against each other to obtain European goods, and most particularly the two clocks. The holds of the *Fortuin* and *Zuytdorp* were nearly emptied and refilled with a large weight of *kunduri*, and smaller amounts of Gunnagal jewellery, silks, perfumes, dyes, sweet peppers including small quantities of varieties unlike those in the west [bird-peppers and purple peppers], and a new spice somewhat reminiscent of ginger [native ginger].

With his trading triumph, Cornelis deemed this an auspicious time to visit the Island, where he planned only to renew contact before sailing west for home. His reception on the Island was much less welcoming than he had expected. The Islanders had heard of his visits to Valk Land and Jugara, and expressed opinions varying between puzzlement and resentment about why he had not reserved his best goods to trade on the Island. Cornelis had held a few goods back, but they were the least valued of his ships' contents, and the astute Islander captains recognised it. He secured some vague agreements from some of the bloodlines to consider his goods next time, but for the immediate moment, most of them refused to take trade goods which they viewed as leftovers.

Worse was to follow. Cornelis wanted to sail directly home from the Island, but to do that, he needed a favourable wind. The prevailing winds blew out of the west, and his ships could not sail effectively into those winds. He waited for what he hoped would be a brief time, but week after week passed, with no sign of a change in the winds. His ships remained effectively trapped in Crescent Bay, unable to return to Fort Nassau.

The Islanders' reactions changed from resentment to amusement, and in time to mockery. Cornelis and his crew were held on the Island while Nangu trading ships set out, week after week, including the departure of the main trading fleet to the Atjuntja lands. One less than tactful captain asked Cornelis how he expected to trade if he had only ships which were at the mercy of the winds[209].

Still, the time his expedition spent in Crescent Bay was not wasted. Cornelis was not idle; he learned much of the Nangu language, and studied their customs and beliefs. He evinced a polite interest in Plirism, enough to visit several of their temples, and established friendly relations with some of the priests. He built his knowledge of the bloodlines and the commercial rivalries which dominated Nangu society, and he kept detailed descriptions of what he had seen.

After four months on the Island, Cornelis in increasing desperation began to consider even sailing east around the South Land and returning to Batavia that way. He was spared that decision when, a few days later, the winds changed to blow steadily out of the northeast, and he launched the *Fortuin* and *Zuytdorp* back into the west. He returned to Fort Nassau after a total of eight months

---

[209] The Nangu ships use a variation of the Polynesian crab claw sail (adopted from the Māori) which allows them to tack easily even into strong winds.

voyage, much longer than he had originally planned, and with a much greater appreciation for Islander seamanship.

* * *

Serpent Day, Cycle of Falling Stars, 394th Year of Harmony (4.12.394) / 3 August 1633
Pankala, Seven Sisters [Port Lincoln, Eyre Peninsula]
Men crowded the royal hall, clustered onto benches around the tables. Tables which were empty of food but full of ceramic goblets with *ganyu* [yam wine]. The *ganyu* was full of blandness, to Dandhal's palate, but he suspected that he was the only man to notice. Proper *ganyu* should be flavoured with a blend of spices, not this insipid beverage without discernable taste.

Serving women moved between the benches, keeping the *ganyu* flowing. King Darruk might have been miserly with the quality of *ganyu*, but he had been generosity personified with the quantity. Perhaps the monarch knew his guests; while Dandhal found the drink forgettable, no-one else seemed to care.

Dandhal sat on one end of a bench, slowly sipping at his goblet, and watched the men around him continue their loud, blissful journey into drunkenness. If he was more silent than most, none of the men around him noticed. Perhaps the women did, for they did not rush to refill his goblet as they did for the others, but none of them commented.

"You would be Dandhal," a voice said.

Dandhal turned in his seat, to see a man standing close behind him. A man wearing lustrous silk dyed with sea purple. Only a priest or royalty could afford such sumptuous wealth – and Dandhal knew all of the royals here in Pankala. "I am, harmonious one."

The priest smiled. "You are polite. Yet you are not celebrating the peace-feast."

"Each man celebrates in his own way," Dandhal said.

"No man drinks *ganyu* like that if he thinks there is something worth celebrating," the priest said. He had the crisp accent of the Island-born. One of the Island's priestly delegation then, who had come here and negotiated an end to the war between Pankala and Yarroo [Port Neill].

Dandhal disliked lying, especially to a priest, but he did not have to tell the whole truth, either. "A few moments of contemplation."

"Peace is worth contemplation," the priest allowed. He sketched a bow toward Dandhal, then moved on around the hall.

Peace is worth contemplation, if you are a priest. Dandhal did not detest the Island-born, exactly, but they were too quick to force an end to war. The squabbling between Pankala and Yarroo had been the perfect opportunity for Dandhal and his group of warriors to earn glory and wealth. Until the priestly delegation from the Island had arrived, bringing about an immediate truce, and now a negotiated peace which this feast was meant to celebrate.

Dandhal took a brief sip of the *ganyu*; bland or not, he could not face the prospect of peace without something to drink. War was what he lived for. He had led his band of warriors to war all over the Seven Sisters. In his youth, before he became a leader of warriors, he had even fought on the Cider Isle, when there was no war here. Some of his warriors had even fought as mercenaries in the Sunrise Lands.

Peace here was a disappointment, he realised, but not a permanent one. There would be another war soon, here or elsewhere. There was always another war.

#40: Intermission

17th Year of Regent Boringa Yadji [June 1629]
Kirunmara [Terang, Victoria]
Land of the Five Directions (Yadji Empire)
Drums beat, voices chant. Sunlight spills over feather-bedecked, thread-of-gold wearing priests and singers. Leather shoes click on tiles; the floor awaits its mistress.

Lenawirra glides into the centre, her movements sinuous, her limbs moving in patterns shaped in memory and in song, never resting. One step flows into the next, arms and shoulders matching in counterpoint. Stillness cannot prosper, jerkiness would be betrayal. All must be continuous, her body as fluid as the water which drives history. Only the ears can distinguish the separation of her movements, her shoes falling in a staccato of their own, the tap of leather on ceramic.

In the centre she halts, the pattern suspended to await command. Before her rests a cushion, in the hands of one she dares not name, even in the sanctity of her own thoughts. He is the... No, think not of him. Look instead at the object that awaits.

A shape of gold and feathers, a mask that conceals the face and will reveal the soul. Two golden rings to surround her eyes, with a leather strap at their sides to fasten around her head, while the shape of the mask below the eyes first expands slightly, then closes in a wedge that will fit just below her chin, with delicate feathers carved into its shape. She has been honoured beyond words with this gift; no-one else in the court is permitted to wear the shape of the eagle[210].

Gleaming is the mask, polished of gold, a mirror of power. Visions are blurred, in feathers and shapes, but herself she sees, imperfectly yet fittingly. Her skin dark of nature, her hair green of artifice, her clothes woven of determination.

"Wear what calls to you, fear it not," he says, the man before her. Look at him now she must, for all that she would declaim that privilege. His name she still will not think, for to speak it while he yet lives is to bring misfortune or worse upon oneself.

The Lord of All is he, the Regent of the Neverborn, the supreme ruler of the Land of the Five Directions, the first above the earth. His name belongs to himself alone, and it will not be spoken by another living being until he goes to fight his Last Battle [dies], where if he is victorious he will hear a voice calling to him: "Truly fought, my noble Regent, but now seek rest; your Emperor awaits you."

That voice has not yet called him, but another voice calls to her. It is the Regent, speaking not according to the forms, but outside of them. "Take up the mask, Lenawirra. It belongs to you, if it belongs to anyone."

With such a command, she cannot refuse, even if it brings her pain. Coherent now, the Regent sounds. Such a division it brings, the two sides of her heart beating against each other. Better if he were consumed entirely by madness. A fully insane Regent would have forced the priests to resolve the situation. Where sanity flits like a banner caught in the wind, how can anyone know whether to honour the Regent or mourn him?

---

[210] The largest Aururian eagle, the wedge-tailed eagle (*Aquila audax*) has an extremely distinctive wedge-shaped tail which is easily recognised in flight. The wedge-tailed eagle is associated with royalty and power amongst eastern Aururian peoples, including the iconic representation of a wedge to show its tail.

Take the mask, she would prefer not, yet. Right yet, the time is not. The sun shines on the floor, but not yet on her.

Commands the Regent, though, and obey she must. Rhythm returns, hands moving in the pattern that has become part of her soul. Don the mask she does, the drums beat again, and the chanters raise their cries. The music dictates her movements, Lenawirra steps outside of herself, and the Mask Dance consumes her.

Woe is unto the night, or so comes the chant, and her limbs move in accord. Flowing, outstretched arms circling her, above and below, banishing the darkness.

Goanna steps into the sun. The dance shapes into a new rhythm, balancing her as she leans back, as if she were poised on two legs and tail.

Owl lands on the tree. Arms outstretched again, swooping down this time, coming into what would be a perfect landing and then stillness, except that the dance calls her into the next steps.

Sun glints off the waves. Undulating patterns of arms, legs, chest and head, dipping and raising, circling slowly around the motionless figure of the Regent.

Whirlwind calls to the dust. Arms upraised above her, still for the first time in the dance, her body twirling in not-quite-circles as she mimics the unpredictable shifting of the eddies of the call of the Lord of Night.

Duck takes to flight. A gliding crouch she shapes, rhythmic and sensuous, with arms calling to the wind in ever-increasing flaps.

Dingo calls the hunt. Circles again, she does, with arms folded and mask uplifted, evoking the cries of the wild dogs now more memory than presence.

Echidna protects itself. With practiced sweeps of her feet she suggests the exploring snout of the spiny totem, and curls her head down into a roll which brings her body briefly into the shape of a ball, as the echidna protects itself. The roll brings her to the feet of the Regent, where she stands with secreted knife now clasped in hand, and plunges it into the Regent's chest.

Move she will not, as agonised cry comes from the Regent's throat, overwhelmed at first by the chants. Soon those fade as witnesses observe, the criers falling silent, the drums ceasing their beat.

Confusion and shouts, anger and despair, all beyond her. Lenawirra removes the mask, and she returns to herself. The rhythm has fled, the pattern broken, the Regent gone to a contest he must face alone.

"It had to be done," she says, words that he can no longer hear, and which no-one else cares to know. Where sanity is an occasional refuge, the Land of the Five Directions leaderless, no man dares to take up the knife, to her it has fallen.

It is a crime beyond redemption, they will say. The Lord of the Night has taken on womanly form, they will declare. She cares not. Blame her they will, but praise the outcome they must. Where lunacy ruled, now a new Regent must be named to reign.

The dance of her life has ended, but may the rhythm of the Land of Five Directions resume, moving always until the end of time when the Neverborn breaks free from the earth to claim His own.

#41: Blooming Flowers

"The Nangu fear neither God nor danger. They care for naught but lucre and glory."
- Vasily Mikhailovich Stolypin

* * *

The 1632 voyage of Willem Cornelis to Valk Land, the Copper Coast and the Island marked a watershed in the history of eastern Aururia. Its long isolation from the rest of the world had been broken; from this time forward, it would remain in contact with the wider world, and in particular with Europe.

For the investors of the United East India Company, the promise of new wealth in the Orient appealed, particularly given their unstable situation at home. Europe still reeled from the aftermath of a wave of epidemics whose combined death toll was exceeded only by the Black Death as the greatest plague in history[211]. The shock of those plagues had destabilised a continent already in upheaval, and set it aflame with religious and trade wars. The situation had grown unfortunate enough that one English statesman saw fit to remark: "it is as if a ring of fire has encircled the Continent."

---

[211] Across the world as a whole, the Aururian plagues have inflicted a higher absolute death toll than any previous epidemic in history, although the Black Death and some earlier plagues were worse in proportional terms.

Still, for all of Europe's troubles, markets remained for Oriental goods. Cargoes of silk, porcelain, peppers, cloves, nutmeg, and other spices continued to command high prices. The Company had to pay higher wages to attract employees from Europe to make the voyage to the East, but it remained a highly profitable enterprise.

Into this volatile environment, Cornelis's voyage offered new opportunities, such as dyes, opals, novel spices, and additional sources of gold and silk. Above all, though, ranked *kunduri*. The natives chewed the drug with wood ash, but the Dutch sailors quickly discovered that it could be smoked, to most pleasing effect. Its effects were both like and unlike tobacco; more intense per weight, usually with a calming effect, but in large doses, it acted as a hallucinogen.

Kunduri created a new market for the Company, in the Indies, in India, and potentially in Amsterdam and Europe. Unfortunately, obtaining a reliable supply of the drug initially proved to be a difficult enterprise. Sailing to eastern Aururia was easy enough, with Dutch ships driven by the seemingly endless winds of the Roaring Forties. Sailing back to Batavia from eastern Aururia, though, posed more problems. It required waiting a long time for a change in the winds, or a long voyage around the east of the Great South Land. These difficulties were particularly galling when the Islanders were effortlessly able to sail west from their homeland to the Dutch trading posts on the western edge of the continent.

In time, these problems were resolved, and trade in *kunduri* boomed. With the booming trade, however, came competition.

* * *

Taken from: "People of the Seas: The Nangu Diaspora"
By Accord Anderson
New London [Charleston, South Carolina], Alleghania: 1985
Chapter 2: Early Ventures

Venturesome yet restricted, the Nangu had been. Confined by a horizon of misknowledge, their voyages had been begotten of the possible, not the unknowable. Where rumours or faint existing knowledge preceded them, the Island's trading captains had ventured in search of profit. Yet restrained they were by falsity of belief, by unwholesome fondness for the notion that all the tradeworthy civilizations were confined to the southeast and southwest of the continent. Beyond those confines, the Nangu ventured not.

Kumgatu [Werringi the Bold] shattered those old limits with his first great feat. Circumnavigation of Aururia beguiled the Island, yet his true accomplishment lay in the relocation of the horizons of knowledge. The Nangu learned of the great expanse of the globe. With the barriers of the mind now lifted, the trading captains could venture forth.

Truly great voyages could not yet be made, until sufficient Nangu acted in *dandiri* [bringing harmony]. From first knowledge of the Dutch and their goods, disharmony had been the reaction, with feud and vendetta the consequences. Bereft of balance and committed to *waal* [bringing discord] were too many, Nangu both high and low, those who listened not to better counsel, and those who followed where the imbalanced led.

Mistrust fed among the bloodlines in the early years, a poison on the Island. Rivalry had been ancient, competition and striving for achievement a mark of men of decisiveness, yet most Nangu had forgotten the need for balance with cooperation. Bloodline had always sought to undercut bloodline, but not where this meant weakening the Island against the world.

With the wealth and diseases of the wider world, too many Nangu forgot the old lessons. Feuds ruled the bloodlines, knives ruled the cities, and desperation ruled trade. *Waal* became the norm, the Council an argument rather than a mediator, and bloodlines sought to outbid each other at the expense of the Nangu.

Bought at unreasonable prices were Dutch goods, captains most astute at bargaining with Atjuntja or Yadji or Tjunini slavered over steel and cottons. Marked the purchases were in unrealistic hope, that an excessively-priced commodity bought now could be resold at a price truly exorbitant to a greater fool. While plentiful the world supply of fools has been, it is not truly limitless; the overbidders found in time that they ran out of greater fools to resell to.

Contest and discord at home made for inaction abroad. Long had the Mutjing looked to the Island. Now they started to turn away. The Dutch called, found the Mutjing willing. Help did not come enough to those Mutjing who resisted Dutch influence. Decisiveness could have restored the drifting Seven Sisters to the Nangu orbit, yet hesitation and squabbling marked the Island's response.

Inevitable were the consequences, in an Island where struggle predominated. Disharmony ruled too many, bringing them to ruin; time would bring an extinction to many ancient bloodlines.

Yet as each man's fate is a balance between his own actions and the ripples of the cosmos, so the Island itself shook on waves born on another shore. Calamities afflicted the Island, many consequences of the Dutch. While misguided reactions to doom consigned many bloodlines, gravely troubled even the most harmonious still would have been.

Outlander goods, ships and merchants gravely weakened the old Nangu trade monopolies; Atjuntja gold and sandalwood increasingly sold north to Batavia, not east to the Island. Dutch ships ventured east in numbers ever greater; even if inferior in sailing technology, superior still in armaments and in cargo capacity. *Kunduri*, the greatest trade good of all, lost its exclusivity, Jugara witnessing Dutch merchants bidding, often with Atjuntja goods brought east on Dutch not Nangu ships.

Superior westward-sailing ships preserved much Nangu advantage, granting them some wealth still, buoyed by the foresight of Gunnagal who refused to sell all of their greatest harvest to the Dutch. Bold Nangu captains brought *kunduri*, spices and silk to the White City, although the fading authority of the King of Kings still stretched far enough to forbid the Nangu to sail around Cape Sunset to Fort Nassau. Yet still the old trading roads[212] were gravely weakened.

Plague and illness marked Dutch contact; death stalked ahead of them. Mumps, tuberculosis and chickenpox were scourges early and heavily felt; worse than one in ten Nangu died on the Island from the marks of the Dutch. Knowledge faded, labour grew scarce, markets grew smaller; scarcity brought its own consequences.

Discord reigned, yet not all bloodlines let feud consume them. The more aligned sought return to the old, better ways; competition between bloodlines, but cooperation between Nangu. Desperation and astuteness combined purposes to shape alliances.

Most determined, and most astute, was Kumgatu and his Wolalta bloodline. Negotiations opened with Yuma, elder of the Tjula, with bargaining most astute leading to pact. Old knowledge of cooperation forged with new concepts acquired from the Dutch. The outcome a syndicate, with proportional sharing of profit from all trading voyages that ventured further afield than Cape Sunset in the west or east of the River Gunawan[213]. The benefits obvious to anyone who heeded the counsel of the priests and sought harmony, two other bloodlines swiftly joined the syndicate.

---

[212] The Nangu word translated as "road" has a much broader meaning than the modern historical English equivalent.

[213] The River Gunawan is the Snowy River in historical eastern Victoria. In allohistorical Aururia, this marks the effective eastern border of the Yadji Empire. (The Yadji claim further, but have no meaningful rule past that point). The Wolalta and Tjula have made, in effect, a trading company which will share profits anywhere outside of the core areas of Nangu trade.

Under the aegis of cooperation, the Nangu became venturers again...

* * *

The first sustained contact between Nangu and Nedlandj influenced both peoples. The Nedlandj were influenced by what they found – particularly *kunduri* – and were quick to report back on the wealth which could be found in what Cornelis's report called "a land of gold, and more than gold."

What the Nedlandj were slower to grasp was that in the Nangu, they had found a people unlike any they had met before. A people who were not content merely to trade with the Nedlandj, but prepared to sail out in search of new trade markets, and to seek to control trade on their own terms. A people of an alien faith whose priests sought, politely but persistently, to persuade all Nedlandj visitors to adopt their creed.

A people, in short, who would be influenced by the Nedlandj, but on their own terms.

The early Nangu reactions to the Nedlandj activities were a combination of concern, bemusement, and desire for the new opportunities. Concern, because the Nedlandj had started to displace Nangu influence in the Seven Sisters, with the potential to interfere with the food imports which sustained the Island. And because the Nedlandj trading directly at Jugara threatened to cut the Nangu entirely out of the *kunduri* and silk trades.

Bemusement, because for all of the apparent wisdom of the Nedlandj, their ships could not manage as simple a task as sailing into the wind. And because of some of the prices the Nedlandj were willing to pay for commonplace goods, such as indigo and (especially) sweet peppers.

Desire, because for all of the factionalism and disease-induced strife which troubled the Island, the Nangu had never been a people to pass up on an opportunity. The sight and tales of European ships inspired the Island's shipbuilders, and several bloodlines started to build bigger ships even before Cornelis's visit.

Those efforts were intensified in the months after Nedlandj contact. Most of the bloodlines intended only to move larger volumes of cargo west to Atjuntja lands to trade with the Nedlandj. One group, though, had more ambitious ideas.

During the Nedlandj visit to the Island, many curious Nangu asked questions about the nature of this "Company" that the Nedlandj all obeyed – or was it worshipped? The answers were puzzling and misinterpreted in part by the Nangu; joint-stock companies were not a concept which mapped easily onto their worldview. Collaborative trade and profit-sharing, though, they understood easily enough, even if to most of the bloodlines, three centuries of rivalry prevented them putting it into practice.

Some, though, applied the new lessons.

Werringi the Bold wanted to build on his first circumnavigation of Aururia, while Yuma, the new elder of the Tjula bloodline, knew that his bloodline's experience trading with the Atjuntja was obsolete with the new rush for direct trade with the Nedlandj. The Tjula had wealth and ships, the Wolalta had the knowledge and contacts with the eastern peoples to make truly long-range voyages possible.

A pact of cooperation and profit-sharing suited both of the bloodlines, and the terms were quickly and discreetly negotiated in 1633. Over the next year, two further bloodlines were quietly recruited to join the syndicate. The Muwanna bloodline were discredited politically within the Island, but preserved excellent contacts with the kingdom of Tjibarr, which promised access to large yields of *kunduri*, silk and dyes. The Nyugal bloodline had voyaged to the Spice Coast almost as much as the Wolalta, and were willing to bring their own ships and wealth to the new syndicate.

The syndicate had one major goal: to establish direct trade with the Raw Men in their trading posts in the Indies. They knew of the Nedlandj at Batabya [Batavia], and their rivals the Pannidj who had an outpost somewhere east of that land [Timor]. Werringi argued – and his collaborators agreed – that despite the risks, such voyages would allow much better terms for trading *kunduri* than bidding against other bloodlines to bring the drug to the White City.

Werringi first negotiated a treaty with the Patjimunra city-state of Torimi, which was ideally placed to serve as a safe harbour and resupply point on voyages north. With the support of the Nyugal bloodline, he established a broader treaty with the Kiyungu city-states further north. The pact with the Kiyungu involved supplying iron weapons and armour, in exchange for spices and for farmers who would serve for several years at the more northerly resupply port which the syndicate planned to establish.

With Kiyungu support secured, the syndicate set up a new victualling and repair station in the northernmost reaches of Aururia, at a place which Werringi called Wujal [Cooktown, Queensland]. Here, on his first voyage north, he had found a natural harbour with suitable land for farming, and whose river offered easy inland access for any timber required to build or repair ships. The new outpost had a Wolalta port captain, a handful of permanent Nangu residents who were mostly carpenters and loggers, and a larger number of Kiyungu recruits sworn to serve five-year terms as farmers of kumara [sweet potato], taro, lesser yams, and wattles.

By 1635, Werringi was confident enough in his ships and knowledge of the sea routes to undertake a new long-range voyage. With four great-ships – one from each bloodline – and a few smaller vessels, his second great voyage set out from the Island with a cargo of previously-acquired *kunduri* and silk. They sailed east and then north along the Spice Coast, including a visit to the Kiyungu to trade the silk for additional cargo of eastern spices: lemon verbena, cinnamon verbena, aniseed verbena, and strawberry gum.

After visiting Wujal, they passed through the strait which Werringi had named the Coral Strait [Torres Strait], and sailed west and north toward the islands which they knew only as the Indies. Astute interpretation of the Nedlandj charts, combined with traditional Nangu stellar navigation, let them recognise the larger islands. Werringi led his ships through the Lombok Strait and then west along the north coast of Bali and Java until he arrived at Batabya.

The presence of Nangu traders in Batabya itself caused consternation, both amongst the Nedlandj and the local Javanese who lived around the port. The Governor-General of the Indies, Hendrik Brouwer, wondered for some time about how best to respond to these audacious Nangu.

Profit won in the end, though; the first shipments of *kunduri* to Europe were already earning marvellous prices, and having the Nangu ship them to Batabya would avoid the complication of sending ships to the eastern reaches of the South Land and having to deal with the difficulties of coming back[214]. The new spices which the Nangu brought offered intriguing potential too, especially since the Javanese had experimented with lemon verbena and were effusive in its praise.

So the Nedlandj and Nangu concluded their first trade deal outside of Aururia, and Werringi the Bold led his ships back east laden with wealth. They sailed from Batabya via the Coral Strait and the Inner Sea, south against the prevailing winds, until they arrived at Torimi to resupply.

Other strange ships waited in that harbour: large multi-masted vessels which were recognisably ships of the Raw Men, but flying an unfamiliar flag. These were the ships of William Baffin, sailing for the English East India Company.

* * *

12 April 1636
Amsterdam, United Netherlands
A dimly-lit room, with comfortable but widely-spaced chairs whose occupants can make out only outlines of each

---

[214] That is, the Dutch ships would need either to wait an interminable length of time for the prevailing winds to change, or sail all the way around eastern Aururia and New Guinea (or the Torres Strait) to come back to Batavia.

other. This is not a place for men to know who speaks to each other. What they discuss here is not treason, precisely, but it will gravely anger powerful men when it is revealed. If it is known too soon, the endeavour will fail.

Pieter Nuyts stands in the middle of the circle of chairs; *he*, at least, does not fear if his identity is known. Those same powerful men have already judged him and cast him out; he no longer fears their displeasure[215].

"A new world beckons," he says. "A new people in a land of gold. Yadji, they are called. A people with more gold and silver than the Atjuntja, or the Mexicans [Aztecs] before them."

---

[215] Pieter Nuyts (senior) in actual history was a Dutch diplomat, explorer and politician. He was on the first Dutch expedition to visit southern Australia in 1626-7, where several geographical features are named after him today. After that expedition, he became a Dutch emissary to Japan, and governor of Formosa (Taiwan). He proved to be a failure both as diplomat and governor, angering the Japanese when he was there, causing resentment amongst the Taiwanese, and eventually taking some Japanese merchants hostage. Nuyts's eldest son Laurens was one of the Dutchmen taken hostage by the Japanese in retaliation; Laurens died of dysentery in 1630 while still in Japanese imprisonment. Nuyts was so despised that he was extradited to Japan in 1632 to be punished there for his actions, and was imprisoned there for four years before his release was negotiated. When he returned to Batavia, he was given a large fine for his part in the whole mess with Japan, and sent back home.

In allohistory, Nuyts's 1626 voyage never makes it to southern Aururia, since like most VOC expeditions by this time, it stops off at Fort Nassau instead to resupply. Here, Nuyts keenly noticed the wealth of gold in this new, barbaric land. (In both real history and allohistory, Nuyts had a low opinion of "natives".) He still went to Formosa to serve as governor, where while the details were different, he bungled relations with Japan badly enough that he was still packed off to Japan for punishment. The disruptions of the Marnitja and blue-sleep plagues, and a wealthier VOC being better able to negotiate, meant that Nuyts was released two years earlier (1634), and he was also fortunate that Laurens survived with him. Nuyts was still fined heavily and sent home to the Netherlands. In allohistory, though, he has found a suitable way to take revenge on the Company.

"Trading for gold would violate the Company's monopoly," someone says.

"The Company has ignored the Yadji and their gold," another speaker says.

"Even so, to trade for gold would invite their retribution," the first speaker answers.

"Let the Company keep their trading licence," Nuyts says. "What I plan is more direct."

Several of the occupants make polite enquiries.

Nuyts says, "The Company scratches around for gold, and for goods they can trade for it. They find some... but there is so much more to be had in the South Land. Why pay for eggs when you can own the chicken?"

That brings about a rustling of bodies on chairs, and quiet mutterings. At length, one speaker ventures, "You want to *conquer* the Yadji?"

Nuyts nods. "Indeed. Bring them to their knees, and their gold will be ours for the taking."

"You think you can conquer their Empire?"

"It can be done," Nuyts says, every word dripping with confidence. "Cortes broke the Mexicans. Pizzaro conquered the Inca. Both with only a handful of men."

That produces a long, thoughtful silence. He knows what must be filling their thoughts: visions of gold. Is it time to make those visions more real? No, not yet. Let them consider for longer first.

A speaker says, "The Indians fought with stones. These South-Landers have iron."

"Iron, yes, but not steel," another speaker says.

Nuyts says, "The Yadji are a pagan rabble. They know not gunpowder; they lack both cannon and muskets. They have no cavalry. Given me a thousand good men, armed and trained, and I will have the Yadji bowing to me, and their wealth will give you recompense a hundredfold."

"Bold, if it works. Foolhardy, perhaps, to strike at a land so far away," says one speaker.

Another says, "The Company has allies nearby... Valk Land, is it called? Perhaps we could operate from there. If not, there is the Island. They will do anything for lucre."

The first speaker says, "Even if so, how can a thousand men overrun an Empire? Cortes did not fight alone. We must have local allies, if this is to work."

Nuyts smiles. "The Yadji rule over alien subjects. A people called the... Yadilli on their border, who embrace the same pagan faith as the Island. They yearn to be free of the Yadji, and will surely help us. Better yet, the Yadji fight among themselves. Their last emperor was assassinated. His sons contest over his legacy."

"Are you sure about this?" the first speaker asks.

"Quite. The one who slew their emperor wore this."

He pulls the cloth from a podium beside him. This is the one place where there is bright light in the room, the better to reveal the golden eagle mask. Feathers delicately traced, fitting over a shape of gold, gleaming in the light. A worthy treasure in itself, but an auspicious omen of what can be found among the Yadji.

"They see this mask as damned, now; it was traded to the Yadji's enemies the Tjibarri, who sold it to the Island, and then to us. But the Yadji still fight among themselves. They are weak, and ripe for conquest. Who wants to be part of this endeavour?"

This time, there is no pause, just enthusiastic acclamation.

#42: Breeze Ruffles The Petals

"For then there will be great tribulation, such as has not been from the beginning of the world until now, no, and never will be."
  - Matthew 24:21
* * *
Year of the Twisted Serpent [June 1629]
Kirunmara [Terang, Victoria]
Land of the Five Directions (Yadji Empire)
Without any false modesty, Gunya Yadji knew that he looked splendid today. Of course, he had no modesty in him, false or otherwise. But then, today of all days, he had to appear in his finest attire.

Gunya wore his most splendid tunic, woven from a base of dog-wool collected from the packs of hair-dogs maintained on the royal estates to the east of Kirunmara. The dog-wool had been carefully dyed into a pattern of azure and scarlet. Around his chest, golden thread had been woven into the pattern, and four small silver plates studded with freshwater pearls. The weight of his *anjumi* [headband] spoke of the gold thread which had been used in that, too. Fortunately, the lorikeet feathers which decorated his *anjumi* were as light as they were spectacular.

He strode out of his private chambers, where his scale-armour-clad bodyguards awaited him. The four bodyguards went down on one knee and ritually pressed their lips against the cold floor tiles.

"Obey me," he said, using the ritual words, and they rose to stand around him.

"To my cousin's chambers," Gunya added. The first bodyguard led the way toward the private chambers of the Regent, who was after all the only cousin whom Gunya would never refer to by name.

They never reached the Regent's chambers, of course. All as Gunya had known, or rather, hoped. If Gunya's mad cousin who called himself the Regent could still be found in his chambers, or even found breathing at all, then events had gone terribly wrong.

Jirandali, Third Watcher of the Dreams [a senior priest], intercepted him about halfway to the Regent's chambers. Jirandali wore finery almost a match for Gunya's own: a single gold plate adorned with polished rubies and diamonds covered his chest, and his *anjumi* was decorated with tanned goanna-skin leather. An unusually splendid outfit, which meant that the priest must have been attending the Mask Dance.

Sure enough, Jirandali said, "I bear the gravest of news."

The man used the neutral version of the pronoun when referring to Gunya[216]! Either he was distressed enough to commit a major social blunder, or he presumed far above his station. Gunya was a prince of the royal family, who even his worst foes admitted was second in line to the succession – and in his own opinion, first in line. No priest could claim him as an equal!

Gunya did not answer, waiting for Jirandali to admit the gravity of his error.

The priest did not appear to notice. He looked instead to the bodyguards. "This news should not be overheard."

---

[216] All Junditmara pronouns and personal titles come in six versions: dominant, submissive, masculine, feminine, neutral, and familiar. A complex set of social codes dictates which form should be used in which circumstances. In this instance, Gunya is concerned because the priest used the neutral form, which suggests either that he does not know whether Gunya is a superior or not, or that they are of equal rank.

After such an insult, Gunya was not of a mind to make even minor concessions. He inclined his head to his bodyguards and said, "Speak of this to no-one without my permission."

Jirandali fixed him with a level stare. Gunya matched it.

After a moment, the priest relented. "Your cousin, the Regent, has been hastened on his journey to join your royal ancestors."

"That is an abomination," Gunya said. He carefully did not pretend to show shock at the news. Astonishment would be expected, in one sense, since this was a crime which had not happened since far beyond living memory. In the more important sense, though, showing surprise would also show weakness. "Which man has served the Lord of Night with such a deed?"

"Not a man. A woman. Lenawirra, who was to perform the Mask Dance, stabbed the Regent."

"This will not be publicly announced," Gunya said, using the commanding form of the verb[217].

"Quite. Let it be said that the swelling-fever [mumps] has claimed him," the priest said.

"Well-chosen. The sickness caused by these strange Raw Men is believable," Gunya said.

Such a good answer, in fact, that suspicion stirred in Gunya's heart. How did Jirandali have such a plausible excuse so ready to bring out? Perhaps the priests had been making plans of their own.

Well, I'll have to see about that. "No matter how the truth is concealed from the world, *we* must find it. How convenient it is that the... now-departed? Yes, good, the now-departed Lenawirra was able to conceal a knife? Who

---

[217] In the Junditmara language, most verbs have two flavours, which can be broadly categorised as "directive" or "suggestive". Directive implies command that something *must* be done, or in other circumstances, indicates that a person is certain that something *was* done. Suggestive describes a request or a preference, or in some cases, indicates that a person is uncertain whether something happened in a particular way.

was responsible for searching her before she came into the presence of my cousin?"

"I do not know," Jirandali said, using the commanding form of the verb. Interesting.

"Find out, then, and quickly," Gunya said.

In truth, he neither knew nor cared exactly how Lenawirra had concealed the knife. It may well have been that respect for the dignity of the woman chosen to dance the tribute to the Regent [perform the Mask Dance] had kept anyone from searching her. But asking the question would make the priests uncomfortable until they had an answer. Anything which gave discomfort to the priests was valuable, and doubly-so at a time when he would need them distracted.

All that Gunya cared about was that he knew that the trail would not lead back to him. He had nothing to do with the means Lenawirra had used, only her motivation. It had taken considerable effort to bring her to think of the need to commit this deed. No doubt she even thought to her dying moment that it was her own idea. Her own inception.

Gunya knew better, of course. His departed, unlamented cousin Boringa had been only an occasional guest in the halls of sanity. That had suited the priests well. Far too well, since they could claim to speak for him, and ignore the wishes of those who knew better how to renew the vigour of the realm.

The Land of the Five Directions had drifted leaderless for too long, weakened inside its borders. While outside the treacherous Tjibarri had seized the wealth of the Copper Coast, and the mercurial Gutjanalese had seized the northern gold mines of Djawrit [Bendigo]. A firm hand was needed, one which could slap down the priests and then strike the enemies abroad.

"I will ensure that an investigation is undertaken," Jirandali said. "Questions will be asked, as vigorously as needed. In the meantime, who will oversee the rites for the Regent?"

A dangerous question, that one, and another reminder that the priests must be playing games of their own.

"*I* will do that," Gunya said, as he had long been planning.

"Then I leave it to you to inform Bailgu Yadji," Jirandali said, then turned smoothly on one heel and withdrew.

Gunya decided, then, that Jirandali would have to suffer the same fate as his recently-departed cousin. Such a barb, such insolence, could not be tolerated. Well, there were many ways that a man could die.

Bailgu! How dare that turbulent priest speak of him now? Bailgu had far too much ambition – everyone knew it – and would surely bid to follow Boringa into the Regency. He would have to be dealt with, one way or another, but Gunya did not need the priests interfering.

"To the Eagle Tiles[218]," he said. "Much must be done."

* * *

The Yadji Empire had long been ruled by the family of the same name, but in the centuries of its existence, it had never solved two fundamental questions: how the royal succession should be determined, and what the relationship should be between royal princes and senior priests.

The royal succession was complex since there had never been any formal system of primogeniture. Any close male relative of the current Regent could be chosen as successor. Yadji stability relied on the authority of the current Regent to name a preferred heir, which would usually be honoured after his death. Occasionally the succession had been challenged, but the only serious bloodbaths had been fought when the succession was unclear.

The relationship and lines of authority between senior priests and the royal princes was equally complex. Priests in the outlying towns were little more than extensions of the Regent's will, and relocated regularly to prevent them establishing a local power base. Senior priests were another

---

[218] ie the room where the Mask Dance is performed.

matter entirely; their tenure in the capital was usually for life.

During times of a strong Regent, senior priests in Kirunmara were often given considerable *de facto* authority, since they were perceived as more reliable than often quarrelsome princes. In times of a weak Regent, the senior priests sometimes had even more authority, since they were able to persuade a Regent to follow their lead. When the Regent was gone, the senior priests often had some influence over his successor.

Nevertheless, no matter how much unofficial power the priests had, no priest could ever formally rule the Land of the Five Directions. All authority ultimately derived from the Yadji family, from the descendants of Narryani. The royal princes might seek the support of the priests, or the priests might find a means to use a royal prince as a figurehead, but the princes could never be ignored entirely.

With the assassination of Boringa Yadji, and an investigation into his murder which would ultimately prove fruitless, the worst aspects of the Yadji power structure were now brought to the fore.

No clear successor existed. Boringa had never fathered a legitimate child. Nor had he named a chosen successor. Given that he had been known to speak as the interpreter for his pet rock, any designation of a successor would likely have been ignored anyway.

Without a son, the most likely candidates for the succession were the two oldest cousins, Gunya and Bailgu Yadji. Neither had a clear advantage over the other. Gunya was elder, but was the son of Boringa's youngest aunt. Bailgu was younger, but was the son of Boringa's elder aunt. Both believed that they had the strongest claim, and both were prepared to fight to back their claims.

Worse, the senior priests were bitterly divided about which prince to support. The arguments turned into recriminations, which turned into rows. Ultimately, the Yadji succession would be determined on the battlefield.

* * *

"In battle, never a step backward."
  - Yadji saying

#43: The Time of Troubles

"Nothing is stronger than the bond between brothers, except the hatred between brothers who have fallen out."
 - Batjiri of Jurundit [Koroit, Victoria]
* * *
Year of the Twisted Serpent [August 1629]
Kirunmara [Terang, Victoria]
Land of the Five Directions (Yadji Empire)
Around him, the familiar stone of the House of the Dawn[219]. Much less splendid than his own chambers in the great palace, but much safer. Gunya Yadji did not risk setting foot inside the palace these days, unless surrounded by a host of bodyguards.

"I welcome you," Gunya Yadji said, using the masculine form of the pronoun.

"You are generous[220]," said Bidwadjari, his guest, shaking his head[221].

---

[219] The House of the Dawn (several exist in most Yadji cities, despite the singularity of the name) is a place where people go to hold vigils for fallen comrades. It is considered the utmost in sacred ground, even more than a temple. Staying there serves Gunya two purposes: implying he is still holding a vigil for his assassinated cousin, and means that not even the most determined of enemies would send someone to assassinate him.

[220] Because Gunya used the masculine form to imply informality and near-equality for the purposes of the meeting, rather than the dominant form which would have showed clear superiority.

Gunya raised a palm, acknowledging the statement, then picked up a ceramic flagon and filled two goblets with a *ganyu* [yam wine] spiced with cinnamon verbena and limes. He raised his goblet and announced, "To the memory of my departed cousin Boringa. Whatever his faults in life, may he find rest after fighting his final battle."

Bidwadjari held up his goblet in turn, repeated the invocation, and they both drank.

After a moment, Bidwadjari said, "And with your cousin now consigned to memory, you" – he used the masculine form of the pronoun, too – "want to secure his legacy. With my aid."

"You are direct," Gunya said, with what he hoped was a convincing imitation of surprise. He knew how Bidwadjari conducted himself; the general's reputation preceded him. "But largely correct."

Bidwadjari frowned. "Soldiers have a saying: Safer to step barefoot into a pit of tiger snakes[222] than play in the politics of princes."

"With what is coming, all men must choose where they stand," Gunya said.

Bidwadjari said, "I would stand apart. I will lead the Fronds [his army group] wherever the chosen Regent commands, but I would not become involved in the choosing."

"These are not usual times," Gunya said. "Omens stir, new plagues come out of the uttermost west, and a Regent has been slain. What would in ordinary times be most

---

[221] In most Aururian cultures, including the Yadji, shaking the head is a form of emphasis or agreement, not denial.

[222] The tiger snake (*Notechis scutatus*), one of the most venomous land snakes in the world. It is abundant in southern Aururia. Its preferred habitats include wetlands and small creeks, including the extensive Yadji artificial wetlands. Tiger snake bite is a frequent cause of death among the Yadji.

proper deference will in this time become impossible, for now there may not *be* a chosen Regent."

Bidwadjari stirred in his seat, then. Not standing, exactly, but flexing the heavily-muscled shoulders which had borne armour for longer than most men had lived. His hair – or what was left of it – had gone white, but he remained a most formidable figure of a man. Not to mention the most experienced army commander in the Empire; a man of such reputation that he could speak his mind to anyone he wished, without fear of retribution.

At length, the soldier said, "It is for princes to decide which of them believe they should be the most worthy Regent." He paused, then added, "Which, in your opinion, would be you."

"Of course I believe I would make the best Regent, or I would not have invited you here," Gunya said. "Unfortunately, the first of your statements is incorrect."

Bidwadjari raised an eyebrow.

"If it were *princes* who decided who will be Regent, I would not need to ask where you stand," Gunya said. "But now priests interfere in the business of princes."

"Do you doubt their wisdom?"

Gunya felt his lip curl. "Too many of our priests grew used to speaking for the Regent."

"Someone needed to rule while a mad Regent reigned," Bidwadjari answered, his tone cool.

"If they had ruled properly, I would not be concerned," Gunya said. "Look at what happened while Boringa whispered and the priests claimed to interpret his words! Tjibarr seized the Copper Coast, Gutjanal took the gold of Djawrit, and the hill-dwelling savages grew restless on our eastern frontier[223]. All this happened, and the priests cared not."

---

[223] ie the Nguril and Kaoma of the Highlands [Monaro plateau], who sometimes raid into the Nyalananga basin, and sometimes into the Yadji's eastern provinces.

"Our armies were not idle during those defeats, nor lacking in courage," Bidwadjari said.

"No man could ever doubt your valour, or that of our soldiers," Gunya said. "What you lacked was support. The priests cared for nothing outside of Kirunmara's walls, and did not send you what was needed."

Bidwadjari had met Gunya's eyes only briefly during the whole of the conversation, as was proper. Now, he turned his gaze squarely on Gunya. "You believe that if you become Regent, our armies will be victorious?"

The old soldier had a truly penetrating gaze, when he chose to use it. Gunya did not hesitate before it, though. "I cannot promise that. What I *do* know is that they will not lack the support they need."

"And you think that your cousin will not do the same?"

Gunya snorted. "Bailgu listens too much to the priests, and cares for naught but pleasure. He will not attend to the defence of the Empire. Oh, he can command armies – do not underestimate him – but he is lazy. A wastrel. He will be happy to sit in Kirunmara eating fish, drinking gum cider, and surrounded by concubines, while the priests rule and the Empire's glory rots."

"I will consider this," Bidwadjari said, his tone as neutral as the form of the pronoun he used. He rose to leave, and Gunya made no move to stop him. The great commander would decide alone which way he moved; no further persuasion would be effective.

*

Silence. Far too much silence.

Immense though the royal palace might be, it had always seemed too small to contain the sounds of the people who filled it. Regents, princes, priests, cooks, soldiers, scribes, cleaners, and an endless stream of others moved in and out as duty demanded, and were rarely silent when doing so.

Now, though, Bailgu Yadji found himself overwhelmed with silence. Many people had abandoned the palace, with no Regent to steer the Empire on its proper course. Those who remained trod lightly and carried out their duties as quietly as they could, as if fearing that someone would notice them and order them to depart. When they had to speak, it was usually with lowered voices and brief sentences, as if every surplus word would become a fresh weapon raised against them when they went to fight their final battle.

For himself, Bailgu Yadji cared nothing for the silence. He spoke as loudly as he always did. Louder, if anything. Let the fools and cowards mutter in their meanderings. He had a Regency to win; an Empire to put to rights. He strode the corridors of the palace, speaking to people whenever he could, reminding them of his existence while his foolish cousin had fled under the excuse of conducting a long vigil for the fallen Regent.

This morning, he had one of the more devout priests awaiting him, so he kept his conversations briefer than usual. He did not want to keep one of the Neverborn's more pious followers waiting too long.

Still, one of the men he passed made him pause longer than usual. A man busily writing at a table hardly made for an unusual sight in the royal palace. Until Bailgu noticed the checked pink and grey pattern on the man's *anjumi* which proclaimed him as a death warrior.

There's an incongruous sight. Rarely would a literate man be one who embraced the frenzied glory of the death cult. Nor was it common to see a death warrior without the white dye[224].

Intrigued, Bailgu coughed to indicate his presence. The death warrior looked up, and said, "A moment please."

The death warrior wrote rapidly until the ink in his pen was exhausted, then rose.

---

[224] Death warriors who are going into battle dye their face with white dye in a pattern which makes it look like a skull. Most death warriors keep that dye on all the time.

Bailgu said, "What is your name, sworn one?" He used the neutral form of the pronoun[225].

"Batjiri of Jurundit," he said. "Of the Fearless."

"Did you learn to write before you took the oath?"

"Afterward," Batjiri said. "So I could read the Nine Classics[226]."

"Oh." Strange. A man who waited calmly for battle and a frenzied death did not strike him as a man who should trouble himself to know the Nine Classics. Bailgu nodded at the writing table. "Are you preparing a new copy?"

"No, I am writing a new text. I hope that someday it may be considered the Tenth Classic."

"Ah... Ah, that is... not what I would have expected from a man whose oath means that at any time he may be called to battle to chant his name until he is ready to make the ultimate sacrifice."

Batjiri shrugged. "Every man will go to fight his Last Battle sooner or later. They know not when it is, but act as if it will be far into the future. For me, the difference is that I accept that I could die at any time, if I am called. Even if my classic is unfinished, what I have written will still be worthy."

"A commendable ambition," Bailgu said, carefully keeping his face blank. He understood what drove most

---

[225] All death warriors are referred to using the neutral form of the pronoun, except among themselves. This is because death warriors are treated as being outside of the social order, with neither dominance nor subordination to others. Those who swear the oath of a death warrior are treated as dead in law for most purposes, with their worldly goods handed over to their kin. The death warriors are then supported by the temples and the royal family.

[226] Nine venerated texts among the Yadji, regarded as the epitome of literature, both for the quality of their written language, and the virtues espoused within them. Most of the Nine Classics date back to the days of the feudal Empire of the Lake, and were written by or about (sometimes both) *briyuna*, the sworn warriors of the feudal lords.

death warriors, but this man...? He gestured to the writing desk. "If you want to resume your writing..."

Batjiri's lips twisted into a smile, one which did not touch his eyes. "If the oath has taught me one thing, it is the value of time." The death warrior sat back down again, and Bailgu hurried on.

Soon enough, he reached the chamber where Jirandali, Third Watcher of the Dreams[227] awaited him. Polite greetings took up some time, with mutual invocations of good health, long life, and listening to the voice of the Neverborn.

After that, Jirandali said, "It is certain: your cousin met with the Head of the Fronds this morning."

If he had not been in the presence of a priest, Bailgu would have muttered a curse. Clenching his fists made for a poor compromise. "Bad enough that he meets with other Yadji [princes]. If he is trying to sway soldiers... Do you know if they reached any agreement?"

"No-one is certain. If so, neither of them has said anything about it where our listeners can hear."

"Do *you* think that Bidwadjari would side with Gunya?"

The Watcher looked thoughtful. "I think that he would prefer that a Regent is chosen quickly, without bloodshed."

"Which won't happen," Bailgu said. "I will not stand by and let *that man* lead the Land. He thinks only of this world, and cares nothing for preparing the Land for the world to come."

---

[227] The rank of Third Watcher of the Dreams originally meant a priest who was charged with interpreting the omens contained in the Regent's dreams. There were four such priests, each serving for one month in four, in succession. (The priests were equal in rank; the number simply indicates which months each priest would serve). The role of Watcher has gradually evolved into a more general spiritual counsellor and adviser for the Regent. While there are several priests whose formal rank is higher than the Watchers, the direct access to the Regent gives the Watchers significant informal authority.

"All truth, and truth which you have said before," Jirandali said. "Yet will it convince enough of your family?"

Bailgu said, "I fear that too many of them share his obsession. Gunya thinks only of recapturing the Copper Coast." He waved a hand in dismissal. "A folly believed only by those who cannot see clearly. We have fought Tjibarr for centuries, and never defeated them badly enough to hold onto the Coast for more than a generation. The blood and treasure we pay to take it are greater than the province is worth. Better to let Tjibarr have it, and the joy of holding it."

Alas, despite the self-evident truth, too many princes refused to see it. Gunya and his ilk cared more for glory than for reality. Perhaps the Empire should fight more for Djawrit and its gold, but the Copper Coast was worth nothing. Better secure borders for the Empire than endlessly trying to extend them. Then he could concentrate on holding the peoples already within the Empire, and preparing for the Cleansing, when the Neverborn would break free from the earth to claim his dominion.

"If so, we must prepare for war," the Watcher said.

"Perhaps it can still be avoided, but yes, preparations are essential," Bailgu said. *And, my dear cousin Gunya, there you will be defeated.*

* * *

Civil war: almost an impossible proposition to consider for the Yadji, a royal family who had prided themselves on their ability to present a united front to their subject peoples. Rebellions against the Yadji were common enough, but rarely was there a Yadji at their head.

Disputed successions were reasonably common, but were usually resolved by politicking or the intervention of the senior priests. Only in a few instances had this led to combat between princes. Even then, on most of those occasions, the conflict had ended quickly when it became clear that one prince had much more support than the other, or was a better general.

When it was clear that one prince was superior in support or in martial skills, the traditional solution was for the other prince to swear the oath of a death warrior. Taking this oath meant that the defeated prince was dead in law, no longer considered part of the Yadji family, and could not inherit the Regency. Depending on the generosity of the new Regent, the new death warrior sometimes found himself fighting in every battle on the Tjibarri frontier until he had fulfilled his oath, or sometimes was allowed to live out his life in reasonably comfortable exile in a distant city.

The Time of Troubles (1629-1638), known to the Yadji of the time as the Year of the Twisted Serpent[228], was an unfortunate exception to the usual practice. Gunya and Bailgu, the two main princes involved in the struggle, were bitterly opposed both in pride and in policy. Both could draw on considerable support from their fellow princes, from the priests, and from the generals. Politicking failed to resolve the impasse, and the outcome was civil war.

For a war fought at least nominally for ten years, the destruction was not as severe as might have been expected, particularly in comparison to European wars of the time. Wanton destruction was uncommon; both sides exercised restraint since they wanted to have a well-populated, prosperous empire to rule afterward.

Gunya's forces won the first great battle, near Jerang [Lorne], and after that, Bailgu's main force retreated into fortified positions. For most of the war, the focus was on sieges of key enemy cities. These typically involved long periods of boredom followed by brief periods of intense interest.

The death toll for sieges was usually low. The Yadji had traditionally maintained large stores of food – one reason the sieges lasted so long – and their siege weaponry was not

---

[228] The Yadji traditionally name their years for the current Regent. When there is no Regent, another name is used for the period in question. The Year of the Twisted Serpent was thus rather a long year.

particularly advanced. In a disease environment less hostile than the Old World, great disease outbreaks during sieges were also relatively unknown[229]. Even when sieges were successful, the civilian population of the captured town was usually spared; after a couple of early massacres failed to intimidate other besieged towns into surrender, both Bailgu and Gunya largely abandoned the practice, except on a couple of occasions when attacking troops got out of control.

---

[229] The Aururian disease environment is more hostile than that of the New World, but considerably less so than that of Eurasia (or worse yet tropical Africa). There are diseases and waterborne parasites around which can cause problems for besieging armies, such as Marnitja, but the overall effects of these is less than in comparable sieges in the Old World, where the disease toll in sieges could be horrific. The Yadji are also fortunate in that the main sieges in the Time of Troubles were in the central and eastern provinces. This meant that that they were spared a heavy toll from the worst siege-related disease in Aururia, swamp rash.

Swamp rash is a mosquito-borne disease which for centuries has been endemic in the artificial wetlands along the Nyalananga. It has recently spread to the western wetlands of the Yadji Empire, and is slowly expanding east. Swamp rash does not usually cause epidemics, being more of an endemic disease afflicting people who are exposed to mosquito bites. However, it does have the potential to cause epidemics if besieging armies are encamped near wetlands.

Swamp rash is also one Aururian disease where the mortality rates vary considerably between Aururian peoples. The Gunnagal and other peoples who live along the Middle and Upper Nyalananga have had centuries of exposure to the virus, and have evolved some natural immunity. The Yadji (and other non-Five Rivers peoples) have no such resistance, and their mortality rates from the disease are roughly twice those of the Gunnagal. The endemic nature of swamp rash also means that most Gunnagal will have been exposed to the disease in their childhood, and thus (if they survived) will be immune to an outbreak as adults. This means that when Tjibarri and Yadji armies fight, an outbreak of swamp rash will take a significant toll of the Yadji armies but have little effect on Tjibarr's forces. (This is one factor which has helped Tjibarr defend its core territories from Yadji invasion.)

This practice of restraint during sieges was only consistently violated during another odd example of the conventions of Yadji politics: the response to the Kurnawal uprising early in the Troubles.

In 1631-1632, the Kurnawal [inhabitants of the easternmost Yadji province] tried to take advantage of the civil war to assert their independence[230]. Regardless of how much the two imperial pretenders despised each other, there were family dictates to be honoured. The two quarrelling princes negotiated a temporary truce, assumed joint command of their armies, and marched east to subdue the Kurnawal.

Here, they ended sieges with fire and blood, the better to force the rebels back under imperial control. When the Kurnawal were reconquered, as per the terms of the truce, the two princes' armies returned to their former positions[231] and resumed their civil war with mostly the same restraint as before.

Of course, for all that the two princes tried not to undermine the foundations of the Empire, the effects of so many years of warfare were considerable. A significant portion of the Empire's soldiery died, and many of the valuable food stores were exhausted. While both sides did not directly interfere with the harvests, and famines were rare except inside besieged cities, disruptions were inevitable with soldiers called to war.

For most of the Time of Troubles, the course of the war still hung in the balance. Gunya's forces were generally more successful in open battle, but that led in turn to them conducting more of the sieges and losing relatively more men in assaults. The outcome of the war was still in doubt

---

[230] Or, more precisely, to assert their independence from Yadji tribute-collectors, particularly those seeking to pay for the civil war.

[231] More or less. Both sides resumed control of the same ground as before the truce. They still took advantage of the truce to resupply and move troops into better positions within their current territory.

in April 1636, when William Baffin's ships sailed into the harbour of Gurndjit and became the first Europeans to make direct contact with the Yadji Empire.

#44: Ripening Pods

"No matter what their course in life, all men will fight one battle at their death."
- Batjiri of Jurundit [Koroit, Victoria]

* * *

London, 1635. A city less crowded with people than ten years before, but it seems that it has become more crowded with rumours to make up the difference. Tales and gossip abound in the English capital; accounts factual and fanciful of the intent of their rulers, and of the world beyond the shores of their island.

Stories abound of the grand designs which the Duke Regent[232] has whispered into the ears of the infant

---

[232] The Duke Regent is William Cavendish, 1st Duke of Newcastle-upon-Tyne. Historically, he was an accomplished soldier, equestrian, diplomat and politician, whose close relationship with the Stuarts saw him awarded a series of titles, including Earl of Newcastle in 1628, and he was named a Duke after the Restoration in 1660.

In allohistorical Britain, the first wave of the Aururian plagues swept through Britain in 1628, causing considerable deaths among British notables, although ironically enough sparing George Villiers, 1st Duke of Buckingham, who would have been assassinated by a rogue soldier in August. In the nobility-deprived days after the first plague, Cavendish rose quickly in the favour of Charles I, along with Thomas Wentworth, although Buckingham remained the most prominent favourite. Cavendish was promoted to Duke of Newcastle in October 1630, and Thomas Wentworth was named Earl of Strafford in February 1631.

monarch. Of plans for intervention on the Continent, in Germany or France or Spain. Rumours are rife of the inexorable fate that Sweden faces after its royal lion finally succumbed to the Waiting Death. Some gossipmongers claim that France itself will finally join the war on the Continent.

The wildest and most oft-repeated tales, though, are of a far more exotic locale. They feature the newer new world that the Dutch have discovered. Ten thousand rumours fill the streets, it seems, each one stranger than the last. The recently translated account "My Life in the South Land", written by a Dutch sailor, has only added to the gossip.

The South Land. The Great Spice Island. Teegal. A land of strange crops, strange people, and stranger animals. A land of wealth and mystery, where even the most commonplace thing becomes part of the bizarre. A place where the trees keep their leaves on their branches all year round, while their bark falls off every winter. Or peppers which are first sweet to the tongue, then burn hotter than the most intense peppers ever known before.

A place of exotic mystery, a blend of promise and terror. Trees which smell like they come from another world, maybe hell, for they fuel fires that can consume the landscape in a heartbeat, while the trees themselves then regrow within weeks. A land inhabited by beasts of mystery. A race of half-men, half-rabbit creatures which can hop like rabbits but stand upright like men. A duck-otter with fur, a duck's beak and which lays eggs.

Charles I died in November 1631 during the second wave of Aururian plagues. This left an uncertain regency, since the infant Charles II did not have any of the close male relatives who would have been a natural choice as regent. Buckingham intrigued to be awarded the position, but by this time he was despised enough in Britain that Wentworth and Cavendish were able to defeat his manoeuvres. Cavendish was named Duke Regent, although Wentworth retains a powerful influence.

Tales most of all about wealth for the taking, of spices and sandalwood and bullion. A drug so fine that it makes tobacco seem like sawdust. A land where the people have battled so intensely over the centuries that their blood has stained the dust red. But gold, above all there is gold. Gold so common that the natives use its dust to dye their hair blonde.

The directors of the English East India Trading Company have heard all of these rumours. Indeed, they have started a few of their own over the years, judiciously calculated to add to the interest in London for foreign ventures. Yet for all of their knowledge, they have not been in a position to act.

Ever since a truce signed in this very city in 1619, the English East India Company has been officially at peace with its Dutch counterpart, and claims a share of the trade from the Spice Islands. The peace has been strained at times, but not yet formally broken[233]. Alienating the Dutch risks losing a guaranteed share of the sure wealth of the Spice Islands; particularly concerning for a company which needs to rebuild after the strains on manpower and finances caused by the plagues. So the directors have never acted, especially since the rumours seem so fantastic that they must be more myth than truth.

That peace, though, grows ever more precarious. The directors have heard, through sources much more reliable than the word on the street, that the new Duke Regent shares their frustration with the Dutch. That there has been discussion of alliance with Spain against them.

---

[233] Historically, the Anglo-Dutch Treaty of Defence in 1619 was irrevocably strained by the Amboyna massacre in 1623. Allohistorically, the different circumstances of Dutch discovery of Aururia meant that they were more focused on this new prize, and not quite as suspicious of English involvement in Ambon Island. There has been no equivalent to the Amboyna massacre. While the Dutch and English are still trading rivals and frequently accuse each other of bad faith, there has been no formal breach as of 1635.

Word has come, of course, of what Spain achieved in their raid on the Dutch outpost in the South Land. Of what wealth it brought them. Now the Dutch grow ever more protective of their self-asserted monopoly... but thanks to the belligerence of the Regent, the directors wonder whether it is time to challenge the Dutch.

After much discussion, they decide to take the crucial first step. Commission a fleet to explore where the Dutch do not wish other Europeans to be. If they are discovered by the Dutch, well, they will have to deal with that problem then. It is time to find out how much truth lurks within these rumours.

The captain they choose for their fleet is named William Baffin.

* * *

Year of the Twisted Serpent [April 1636]
Gurndjit [Portland, Victoria]
Durigal - Land of the Five Directions (Yadji Empire)
"We draw near to Gurndjit," the Islander said, in his passable Dutch.

William Baffin glanced port-side, following the Islander's gaze, and saw nothing but waves and high clouds to the north. "How can you be sure?"

The Islander nodded, a gesture which Baffin had come to learn meant disbelief to these strange men. "How can you Inglidj sail so far around the world, and yet be blind to something so plain?"

Baffin shrugged. The Islander, who answered to the name of Jerimbee Manyilti, had an often-frustrating manner. In the voyage from the Island, he had been sometimes impressed by what he saw, but often contemptuous. His views of navigation were only the most recent example. Jerimbee had been effusive in his praise of the compass, but dismissive of the English charts as lacking details such as currents, and openly mocking of the English lack of knowledge of the stars.

Still, after all that, how could he be so sure that the *Intrepid* and the other Company ships were nearing the Yadji port? "What should I see?"

"Watch the waves," Jerimbee said. "Can't you see how they change when they pass the..." He paused, as if his Dutch had run out. "The shallowing shore?"

Baffin looked, but he could not see what the Islander meant. The waves were not breaking at all, and he could make out no pattern in the swells. Of course, this Islander had led ships along this route for years, according to his claims. Perhaps he knew the route better. "So should I turn the ship north?"

"Not yet," Jerimbee said. "This is a dangerous shore. The winds and waves will drive your ship into the cliffs if you draw too near, and your Raw Men ships cannot sail properly into the wind."

"When should we turn?"

"Soon," replied Jerimbee. "I will tell you."

Baffin shrugged again; it was something he found himself doing often around the Islander. Jerimbee asked many questions, and sometimes dismissed the answers, but remained endlessly curious. He was worth tolerating, since he revealed a wealth of knowledge about this Great Spice Island. He could also serve as an interpreter; his Dutch was if anything better than Baffin's own, and other Dutch-speaking sailors were on hand to clarify words if needed.

This time, though, Jerimbee stayed silent, watching the waves, and sometimes glancing up at the sun. Judging its height, if Baffin understood that gaze properly.

"We near the cape," Jerimbee said. "Turn north."

Baffin snapped out orders, and the *Intrepid* started to turn to port. Trailing behind, the other ships of his fleet – *Godspeed*, *Lady Harrington* and *Delight* – did the same.

The breeze blew steadily off the port quarter, driving the ships easily before it, toward the north shore. Where the greatest empire in this South Land awaited them. The Yadji. A people both capricious and wealthy, according to all reports.

Back on the Island, most of its people had told him he was a fool for sailing there without invitation. Fortunately, one of their captains had thought otherwise. And been willing to join his voyage, in exchange for a rather heavy price. Still, some prices were worth paying.

Land appeared to the northwest, a rugged, cliff-lined shore. "Steer around the cape," Jerimbee said, waving vaguely to starboard. "Gurndjit is in the bay behind."

Sure enough, the rocky faces of the cliffs gave way to sandy beaches, then, as the ships steered further to port, to where a natural headland had been extended by a stone breakwater. The sheltered bay beyond it looked to offer protection against even the fiercest storms.

"A safe haven," he murmured, and then realised he had spoken in English.

The Islander recognised the word *haven*, though; it was close enough to the Dutch word for port. "The Yadji built that sea wall because we asked them to," he said. "It makes this a safe port; something they would not care about otherwise."

"They build a port like this and then do not sail from it themselves?" Baffin asked. As the *Intrepid* tacked into the bay, he saw a few ships tied up at quays, but they looked to be tiny, primitive boats. Nothing like the relatively elegant Islander ships.

"Oh, a little here and there, but they know nothing of navigation," Jerimbee said. "They fish, and move a few things along the coast, but they fear to sail at night." He nodded. "The Yadji are a peculiar people. There is nothing they do not know about building with water, or building *in* water, but they fear to sail into deep water. They think they will be separated from their god within the earth."

"So this port is for you Islanders?" Baffin asked. It looked to be an impressive construction for a people who would not use it themselves.

Jerimbee laughed, as if he had discerned the intent behind Baffin's words. "Yes, built for us. The Yadji are master builders; what they can accomplish with stone and water is without equal."

Baffin held up a hand, and gave quick orders for the helmsman to anchor the *Intrepid* within the bay, but away from the docks. He did not want to be trapped here, not yet, and boats could take them to shore. Then he turned back to the Islander. "It still seems... strange."

The other man just smiled. "Trade matters to all men, does it not? Strange though the Yadji can be, they still know its value. So they built Gurndjit into a better port for us."

"How many more ports have they built?" Baffin said.

"None quite like this," the Islander answered. "There are three ports in all the Yadji lands which can safely harbour a great-ship. Or your Raw Men *fluyts*[234]. Other ports can hold smaller vessels, safely up on a beach or in sheltered coves."

Baffin briefly wondered which other Yadji ports offered such a safe haven, but filed the question for later. "We are safe from storms here, but are you sure that the blue flag will keep us safe from the Yadji themselves, when we seek to land?"

Jerimbee shook his head. "Simple as getting a Gunnagal to argue. So long as it is dark blue[235], as you would say, you will be greeted with words, not swords."

"That guarantees safety?" Baffin asked. The Islander had assured him of that point before they left port, but he still wondered, given how many of the man's compatriots had warned him against coming here.

---

[234] *Fluyts* is a Dutch kind of sailing vessel designed for maximum cargo volume in trans-oceanic voyages. The Nangu have adopted this name as a generic name for any large European ship.

[235] To Gunnagalic-speaking peoples, including the Nangu, blue and azure (light blue) are separate colours, similarly to how red and pink are treated by English-speakers.

"It will keep you from being attacked simply for landing on Yadji soil." Jerimbee chuckled. "Nothing is a complete guarantee of safety when you visit the Water People."

"And you can do nothing more to keep us safe amongst the Yadji?" Baffin said.

The Islander raised an eyebrow. "Reward comes hand in hand with danger. A man who risks nothing earns nothing."

Baffin kept his voice as calm as he could, telling himself that the Islander brought benefits, too. "What should we do when we land, then?"

"Be careful. These Yadji are strange. Even stranger than you Inglidj, in many ways. They expect everyone to think as they do, and will not hesitate to call you out for not agreeing with them."

Beside them, the first boat was being prepared. Baffin gestured for the Islander to walk ahead of him to the boat. Perhaps being on a boat might make him more useful. "Warn me if I am about to offend them, then."

"I will, as much as I can," Jerimbee said.

Two boats full of sailors rowed toward the nearest quay, both with blue flags held aloft, and with Baffin and Jerimbee in the leading boat. Anchoring on the quay was simple enough. They could have landed directly on the beach, since the bay had wide stretches of sand to choose from, but the quays would be better with no other foreign ships likely to visit now.

A party of men awaited them at the quay's end. With slightly darker skin than the Islanders, unless he missed his guess. The men wore a diverse mixture of garments, in a multitude of hues, but one and all they bore elaborately-patterned headbands. About half of the men had spears, too, but they were held aloft. So far as he could tell – which probably wasn't far, given what the Islander claimed – they did not look hostile.

"Greet them in whatever manner is polite amongst the Yadji," Baffin said.

Jerimbee talked with the Yadji at some length, with words going back and forth a few times. It seemed too long for a simple greeting, but perhaps these Yadji were as strange as the Islander claimed.

Eventually, Jerimbee said, "It is strange. We are not being greeted in the name of their priests."

"What about their priests?"

Jerimbee said, "The Yadji priests command their people, not guide them as proper priests should."

That helped not at all. The Islander said something similar at every opportunity. Then Baffin recalled that among the many long diatribes which Jerimbee had made about the priests, had been one about the ritual of offering the twelfth after being greeted in the name of their head priest, and then attending the temple.

The twelfth he had prepared for as best he could. Before leaving the Island, Jerimbee had warned him that the Yadji temples demanded a twelfth of all trade goods from a ship as tribute to the temple and their king, before they would deign to trade at all.

Trying to refocus the conversation, he said, "Who *is* greeting us, then?"

"A man of... stature, would you say? The... most prominent man of good birth."

Baffin shrugged. "The headman."

"Headman, yes, thank you. He gives commands to these Yadji as if he were their royally appointed priest. Most unusual."

Baffin said, "Offer their headman my greetings, then, if you haven't already done so. And ask if he invites me to meet him." After a moment's thought, he added, "Without offering the twelfth, unless they ask for it."

Jerimbee spoke again to the Yadji. The exchange was quicker this time, but long enough for Baffin to notice that the language which Jerimbee used with the Yadji – and which they answered – sounded exactly like the Islander tongue.

640

"Is the Yadji language close to your Islander speech?" he asked. Better for English traders if it was; easier to learn one new language than two.

"No, the Yadji language is nothing like ours. Alien, alien. Even the Atjuntja tongue is easier to learn than theirs[236]."

Baffin said, "Why not use their language? You said you could speak to the Yadji."

Jerimbee shook his head. "I can. I have traded with the Yadji for years. I know how to speak with them."

"No, why..." Baffin paused, wondering whether the problem was translating his question into Dutch, or just Islander deviousness. "Why don't you know the Yadji language, if you have traded with them for years?"

"Only a fool tries to speak to the Yadji in their tongue," Jerimbee said. "They are capricious, their language intricate, and to use it incorrectly can be taken as a mortal insult. Better to use another language which does not offer the same risks. The Yadji understand Nangu, usually. Or Gunnagal, sometimes."

The Islander turned back to the Yadji, who appeared not at all worried about the lengthy delay. After a brief

---

[236] When the Nangu think of how close languages are, they mean more than whether languages are closely-related. They also think in terms of ease of learning. In that sense, Atjuntja is easier to learn than Junditmara (the Yadji language), since it does not have the same intricate social customs which govern its usage.

In a linguistic sense, the Atjuntja language is in a different language family to the Nangu language. The Atjuntja language is part of a widespread family of languages across much of the continent, which later linguists will name Wuri-Yaoran, though amongst all of the Wuri-Yaoran speakers, only the peoples of the Atjuntja Empire have adopted agriculture. Nangu is one of the Gunnagalic languages of the eastern agricultural regions. The Junditmara language is a linguistic isolate; while it did formerly have related languages nearby, those were all extinguished during the Gunnagalic migrations of 900 BC – AD 200.

exchange, he said, "Their headman invites you to meet him, if you wish. And they have not mentioned the twelfth."

"Lead on, then."

Striding through the roads of Gurndjit, Baffin was struck by a sense of orderliness. Of careful organisation. Both of the city itself, and the people who inhabited it. The streets were wide and paved with black basalt fitted together in regular patterns. The inhabitants moved quietly on those streets, rarely obstructing each other, and with none of the arguments or tempers he would have expected to see in an English city.

It took him longer to realise what else was strange about Gurndjit: the smell. Or, rather, the lack of stench. Oh, the city had odours – the smell of salt wafting up from the bay, of bread or something like it being baked in a couple of buildings which they passed. But none of the smell of refuse or excrement which would have been normal in an English city. The people here did not empty chamber pots into the streets. He wondered, briefly, what they did with them[237].

The Yadji led them to a building complex surrounded by a low wall constructed from some pale yellow stone. The wall looked to be more ceremonial than functional; it was only about three feet tall. About half a dozen buildings stood within the complex, and beyond that was a lagoon.

The Islander muttered something in what sounded like his own language, although it was too quiet for Baffin to be

---

[237] At this time, sanitation was not an advanced concept in England. (Or indeed anywhere much in Europe, with some slight exceptions such as Paris, and even then the main purpose of Paris's sewer system was to remove stormwater). London's sewers were open ditches designed to carry waste into the Thames. The unhygienic consequences were inevitable.

In comparison, the Yadji and their predecessors have used covered sewers for centuries. In the upper class houses, they even have flush toilets (something which the English do know of, but are not so effective at putting into practice).

sure. The Islander continued in Dutch, "Very strange. This is their main temple... but with no sign of any priests."

"Where could they have gone?"

Jerimbee said, "To await rebirth, probably. I know nothing else that would remove all the priests."

"Won't they tell you?" Baffin asked. It would help to know just who he was negotiating with.

"Do not ask! Never risk that kind of question with the Yadji. That is true at any time, and doubly so in a civil war. That's why I haven't asked which prince they back for the throne."

"The winning one, surely," Baffin said.

Jerimbee said, "Gunya, probably – he is said to mistrust priests. But for now, simply talk to their headman as if he is the ruler, and you should do well."

Inside the temple, he found it easy to believe that anyone who lived here was a ruler. It seemed as if gold glinted everywhere. Gilt lining to the shutters on their glassless windows. Gold ornamentation on vases, columns and statues. Most of all, gold as personal decoration – most of the people they passed wore some form of gold, either as jewellery or woven into the threads of their clothing or headbands.

The headman himself outdid his fellows, naturally. Gold and silver armbands, gold and pearl-studded silk tunic, a single thread of gold in his headband, and some staff in his hand which had a golden orb at the top.

The headman sat on a chair, but there was nowhere else to sit in the chamber. Did that make the chair a throne? Baffin considered asking that question, but the headman started talking, and then Jerimbee translated.

"He bids you welcome to Gurndjit, but does not offer his name," the Islander said.

"Why does no name matter?" Baffin asked.

Jerimbee muttered something in his own language again, then went on in Dutch. "The Yadji do not speak the name of their king while he lives. It is as if this headman claims the royal privilege."

Baffin shrugged. While he wanted to know who he was negotiating with, he cared little for the intricacies of Yadji customs. "Tell him that I am Commander William Baffin, sailing for the East India Trading Company."

The Islander relayed that, then said, "He asks if you are of the same people he has heard tales of from the far west. The Nedlandj, he says."

"Tell him no, we are Inglidj. We know of the Nedlandj, but we are not of their kind."

Through Jerimbee, the question came back, "Are you friends of theirs?"

A good question, Baffin thought. Part of his orders were to do what he could to loosen the Dutch grip on the South Land, but he did not know if there were already relations between these Yadji and the Dutch. If they were already established friends, then denying Anglo-Dutch friendship would annoy the Yadji. If the two were enemies, then he would be missing out on an opportunity.

In the end, he said, "Tell him we and the Nedlandj have been both friends and enemies in the past."

"A good answer," the Islander said, before he translated it. "The headman says that he would like to hear more about the Inglidj, and invites you to eat with him."

"Tell him yes, of course," Baffin said.

The headman barked what were clearly commands, even though Baffin understood not a word. Two men at either side of him hurried out. More plain-clad men and women entered the chamber, carrying linen-lined cushions which they handed to Baffin, Jerimbee, and the dozen sailors with them.

The cushions were surprisingly soft; Baffin could not guess what filled them. The two dozen attendants around the headman sat, too, leaving only a handful of guards and servants standing.

Food arrived soon thereafter, carried on wooden plates, and accompanied by knives as the only utensils. The centrepiece of the meal was some sort of fish, cut into long fillets, baked dark, and covered with some sort of thick, peppery sauce. It was accompanied by some odd long, black, thin creations of dough [egg noodles], and what looked for all the world like chopped celery.

After the headman invited them to eat, the Islander cut one slice of the fish, and his eyes widened. "This is an honour!"

"We are honoured by being served fish in a port?" Baffin said. Personally, he would have considered a fine cut of beef a greater honour, but the South Land had no cattle that he had heard of.

Jerimbee made a dismissive gesture. "This is not sea-born fish. The fishing is very poor in Yadji waters, anyway[238]. The Yadji grow their fish in lakes and ponds which they build for themselves. Fish here is under noble control. And this fish is eel, the most prized of all."

During the meal, the headman asked a variety of questions about England, about its people, and about why Baffin had come. He gave general answers as best he could, not wanting to reveal too much. He explained that he was here to explore, not to trade, and offered gifts as a sign of gratitude for the welcome he had received. He explained that he sailed on behalf of a company, not a king. The headman did not seem to grasp this concept at all – although Baffin noted that the Islander looked much more interested when translating it – and Baffin ended up by saying that he sailed in the service of a group of powerful men.

In time, the headman asked what else Baffin planned to do among the Yadji. Jerimbee took the opportunity to add a few words of his own as advice. "Make it plain that you are not going to interfere in their civil war. Not in any way."

---

[238] Fishing in Aururian waters is poor at the best of times. It is even poorer off Yadji waters since their various kinds of dams and artificial wetlands mean that most sediment gets deposited again before it reaches the sea. This means that Yadji coastal waters are relatively nutrient-deprived, and even more barren of fishing than they were historically.

"Why not?" Baffin had been contemplating the idea, although his four ships did not carry much in the way of cannon or anything else which might help. These South Landers knew nothing of guns, though; perhaps something could be made of that.

"Yadji are mistrustful of outsiders, always. Prince Bailgu has already turned down offers of assistance from Gutjanal. Even if you are offered a pact, that will likely alienate many of the other... royal men, who will turn to the other prince."

That sounded strange, to Baffin's way of thinking, but this was why he had the Islander here. "What do you suggest, then?"

"Stay out, as we of the Island have done." Jerimbee's eyes narrowed for a moment. "Most of us on the Island. But let one prince win, then negotiate for terms."

Sound advice, but Baffin doubted he would still be here whenever the Yadji princes finally settled their differences with pact or with blood. Or perhaps when Tjibarr invaded from the northwest. That was one other idea which he had considered; much talk back on the Island had been about whether Tjibarr would take advantage of the confusion to invade the Yadji. He had considered contacting Tjibarr instead of sailing here, but had decided that there were more advantages here.

Wait. Perhaps there is a way. "Do not mention it to him yet, but do you think that this headman would agree to let some of my men wait here – in peace – until I return?"

Jerimbee looked surprised. "Perhaps, for the right gifts. And if you offered the right reason."

"If I explain that I would like to leave men behind... while my ships return home to discuss possible trade. That I do not offer trade now, just friendship, but trade can follow in time, if he is willing, and after I have carried his words to my powerful men."

The Islander looked unconvinced. Baffin wondered, for a moment, if Jerimbee had planned to throw in some trade negotiations of his own with the Yadji; he still did not fully trust the Islander, and he knew that all of that man's people had a lust for profit.

"How long would your men need to say here?" Jerimbee said.

"Until my ship returns to my homeland, and another comes in its place." Well, perhaps his ships would only need to return as far as India before the Company sent out another ship. No need to reveal just how far away England was, either. "A year, perhaps two. It depends on the winds and God."

The Islander frowned. "That I could never translate. Best not to mention to the Yadji that you fear interference from a god."

"There is but one God," Baffin said. He was far from the most pious of men, but still, some things could not be denied.

Jerimbee did not reply directly to the statement, but looked thoughtful for a long moment. "You would need another interpreter here, if I am to sail on east with you to the Cider Isle."

"Could you bargain for one of your kinsmen to come here and translate for us, if the headman accepts?"

The Islander frowned. "Perhaps one would be willing to take the risk. For the right price."

Baffin recognised the opening for another trade negotiation, and it was one he would be willing to pay. The more he thought on the idea, the more he liked the opportunity to have some men dwell here among the Yadji. With another interpreter, they could manage. They would learn the Islander tongue, at least, if not the Yadji one.

More, this place offered so many opportunities. What the headman and other people wore here made it plain that wealth was here for the offering. Gold in abundance here, just as the Dutch had already found in the west.

"A land of gold," he murmured. A fitting name for this place, perhaps. No, it would be best in Latin, so that all men understood it.

"Aururia," William Baffin said.

#45: Shaking the Branches

"Hope is the delusion of fools. Acceptance is the choice of wisdom."
- Batjiri of Jurundit [Koroit, Victoria]

* * *

Picture, if you will, a plain outside a city, leading down to a gently sloping beach. The city is one which its inhabitants call Coonrura, and which another history will call Kingston [Kingston SE, South Australia]. At this time, the city is inhabited mostly by a people who call themselves the Yadilli and who follow the wisdom of the Good Man [Plirites], but it is ruled by the Yadji. Or it would be, if the divided Yadji could ever end their seemingly endless civil war and decide on a single Regent.

On the plain outside, an army is encamped, watched over by strange ships anchored offshore in the bay. An army unlike any which has ever been seen before in the Land of the Five Directions. A force composed mostly of men with strange, half-coloured skin as if they had been pulled out of the oven too early.

Under the command of Pieter Nuyts and his son Lauren, they have come in the name of gold. Thirteen hundred foot soldiers with arquebus and pike. Three hundred cavalry, all veterans of the long war which is slowly grinding to a halt in Europe. Not all of their horses survived the voyage here, and some of those which did are in a poor state, but still, these strange four-legged giant beasts have both impressed and terrified the Yadilli. Accompanying them are two dozen cannon of varying calibre, brought most astutely by the elder Nuyts, who had heard of the impression which those weapons have made among the Aururian peoples further west.

With these Raw Men march allies. Five hundred mercenaries of the Mutjing, veterans of their own people's endless squabbling. None of the Yadilli have taken up arms yet, but Nuyts is making most valiant efforts to persuade them to join him.

The Nedlandj invasion has begun.

* * *

Founded by the teachings of the Good Man, Plirism is both united and divided. United in its acknowledgement of the wisdom of its founder, divided in both polity and its interpretation of how that wisdom should be applied.

The Nangu branch of Plirism is the most widespread of those interpretations, thanks to being carried afar by the Island's merchant venturers, but it is not universal, and not even the eldest interpretation. Another, older interpretation is cherished by the people who call themselves the Yadilli.

The Yadilli hold that the Good Man revealed that true harmony can only be found in the Evertime, and that this world is inherently disharmonious. Anyone who is born into this world is only here because they are originally ejected from the Evertime due to being disharmonious. The Yadilli hold that people on this world are trapped in a cycle of reincarnation until they have become harmonious again, at which point they will return to the Evertime and no longer be reborn in this world.

The Yadilli are among the most ancient of Gunnagalic-speaking peoples. Their ancestors settled on the lower reaches of the Nyalananga in the earliest days of Aururian agriculture. Their ancestors were quick to adopt copper-working, and were the first to learn the art of working arsenical bronze. It was the vigorous pursuit for mining that metal which led to uprising, and indirectly to the collapse of the Formative Gunnagal culture which will so puzzle future archaeologists.

The ancestors of the Yadilli were among those who had burned the ancient great city of Goolrin, triggering the Interregnum. They fled across the mighty river to the south. There they found that for days and days of travel, they were cut off from the sea by a series of long, bittersweet lakes with sand dunes beyond[239]. The water there promised fishing and waterbirds for food, but it did not offer safety for people who still feared being forced to work in mines and out of the sun.

They fled further, until they arrived at a region where the lakes disappeared, to be replaced by a wide sheltered bay with glistening white beaches, and where the shape of the coastline protected it from the worst weather of the southern ocean[240]. Here, they felt safe. Here, they settled, and would remain for a very long time.

The Yadilli have long believed themselves to be a people apart. They did not expand much further from their ancestral lands, and they have lost even legends of that far-off time when they migrated from across the Nyalananga. But they maintain a strong sense of their own identity.

The Yadilli have preserved their language and culture through more than two millennia of local and foreign rule. They survived the chaos of the Great Migrations. They endured the rule of the First Speakers. They had a short time of independence where they adopted the faith of the Good Man before being conquered by the growing might of the Yadji. For some brief periods, their lands have been

---

[239] This is a series of lakes along the coast of historical south-eastern South Australia, which are an extension of the Nyalananga Mouth, and separated from the sea by a long series of sand dunes created by silt deposited by the great river. They are a mixture of fresh and salt water, depending on the balance of rainfall and river flow. The nature of the coastline makes settlement by the sea itself difficult, although it provides for good fishing.

[240] This is Lacepede Bay, which is not a completely sheltered harbour, but whose geography protects it from most weather except when the wind is blowing directly out of the west.

claimed by the kingdom of Tjibarr, although the Yadji have ruled them for the last half-century.

Now, in the year which another continent's calendar calls 1637, they face a new challenge.

* * *

A small scroll of wattle-bark paper is carefully unrolled. The ink markings on it[241] are clumsily-drawn, as if the writer had only rarely used a quill. Which is indeed the case, as the reader knows.

This scroll has come from a listener [spy] assigned to Coonrurua. That listener knows only the basics of writing, and indeed has used far more pictographs in his message than should be properly used, including a few employed incorrectly.

Still, the gist of the message is clear enough:

"Strangers have come on ships. Not Islanders or Tjibarri. Men uncooked. Led by One True Egg[242]. Some ride giant dogs. Summon thunder and throw iron balls like the breath of the Rainbow Serpent. One True Egg urges Yadilli to rise against the Neverborn. Their elders have not announced yes or no."

With a muttered curse against the Lord of the Night, the reader rises. He wonders whether he can find another to bring this news to the prince.

* * *

The Time of Troubles, as it will later be known, or the Year of the Twisted Serpent, as the Yadji of the era call it. Either way, it is finally nearing its end. The largest civil war in the history of the Yadji Empire has been traumatic, bloody, and

---

[241] Aururians use ink made from a combination of soot (from burnt wattle wood) mixed with wattle gum (as a binding agent – much as gum arabic was used elsewhere in the world). The Yadji take this one step further by writing on a kind of paper made from the boiled inner bark of wattles. Wattles: the trees with one thousand and one uses.

[242] By a coincidence of language, to Junditmara speakers the name Pieter Nuyts sounds similar to the words for "one true egg."

lengthy, but now, in the year which the visiting Raw Men call 1637, the end is in sight.

Or so it should be.

Gunya Yadji and his commanding general Bidwadjari have fought a long war. Despite superiority of numbers and force of arms, his great rival Bailgu Yadji has refused to submit under any terms. It has taken siege after long siege to bring Bailgu's supporters into submission.

The core of the Land of the Five Directions has been cleansed of Bailgu's taint. The greatest province, the Lake Country, is entirely cleared, while in the western province of the Red Country, two cities have recently fallen, and only one last holdout remains at Balam Buandik [Beachport, South Australia]. Only in the farther reaches of the Golden Country and the even more distant White Country does Bailgu have any strong remaining presence, and even then his remaining outposts in the Golden Country are under siege.

Bidawdjari has judged that, barring the intervention of the Lord of Night [ie misfortune], most of the remaining enemy strongholds should have fallen within another year. Capturing the rest would take longer, but it is possible that seeing Bailgu facing annihilation will make his remaining royal supporters abandon him. Particularly if they can secure a pardon if they change sides; Gunya has already begun to make some efforts along those lines.

If only all of those plans had not been halted by the news out of the west.

* * *

Taken from:
The Tenth Classic
A novel by Duarte Tomás

"Report," Lauren Nuyts said crisply.

The scout dismounted, passed the reins to a waiting attendant, and then nodded. "All as expected. The *kuros*[243] are encamped for the night. A few scouts for warning, but they're not wandering far."

"Numbers?"

"Maybe five thousand," the scout said.

"Good work," Lauren said, then turned on his heel and walked back into the camp.

Finding the command tent was a matter of moments, even with the gathering darkness. His father waited inside, looking composed as ever. Madjri was still beside him; Lauren thought he had never seen the local headman anywhere else since they had struck the alliance to bring down these heathen Yadji.

Not that the Yadilli creed is any better, Lauren mused. But they will be our subjects soon. Time enough after to bring them to Christ.

The head of the mercenaries was there, too, along with a few of the senior Dutch soldiers.

"Scouts are back," he said. "Yadji army is bedded down for the night. About eight or ten thousand of them. They'll attack tomorrow."

"Of course they attack," Madjiri said in his broken Dutch. "They say leave or die, you stay, they attack."

"I'd rather know *how* they will attack," his father said. "We know so little of Yadji tactics."

"With straightforward courage," observed Dandal – at least, that was the closest Lauren could come to pronouncing the name of the Mutjing mercenary leader. "Not all Yadji soldiers seek death, but none of them fear it. They will see that they outnumber us, and they will aim for our centre and seek to crush us."

---

[243] *Kuro*, an allohistorical Dutch term for Aururian peoples, was first used by Pieter Nuyts and his son Lauren. It is derived from the Japanese word for black; the two Nuyts learned that term during their imprisonment in Japan, and use it to distinguish dark-skinned Aururians from even darker-skinned Africans.

"Good thing they not know we have thunder, eh," Madjiri said, the whiteness of his teeth amazingly bright against his black skin.

His father shrugged. "We have steel and horses. I would fight even without cannon."

"But how best to use the weapons we have?" asked Colonel Michel. "Bombard them with cannon balls as they march on us, or give them a volley of muskets when they are near?"

"Your thunder will break the Yadji armies either way," Dandal said.

"Panic is good, but with cannon, they will flee before we can close with them," his father said. "I think that we should keep our cannon for another time. Let them feel the weight of shot and musket."

The conversation grew intricately involved with battle plans and deployment after that. Lauren listened with only half an ear. He needed to hear these things, but he did not pretend to be a master tactician. That was why they had recruited the German and Dutch soldiers in the first place.

No, what intrigued him more was how the Yadji would react after they were defeated. They were here to conquer an empire, after all, as Cortes and Pizzaro had done before them. Winning the battles was important, but more would need to be done afterward.

In time, the soldiers settled on a battle plan which would require the Dutch troops to hold a solid centre and face the main Yadji charge. The Mutjing mercenaries would protect the left flank, while the cavalry would be on the right flank with the most open ground and the chance to pursue the enemy when they broke. The Yadilli militia were to be held in reserve. His father explained that this would be for pursuit, too, but the unspoken message was that the Yadilli would not yet be trusted.

Once the battle plans were settled, Lauren asked Dandal to translate his words into a form which the Yadilli would understand; he did not trust Madjiri's broken Dutch for these questions.

Via Dandal, he asked, "With the Yadji defeated here, what will they do next? Will their emperor submit?"

Madjiri laughed. "Were you not listening? Yadji will not fear death, but welcome it. To them, this invasion will be part of the end of the world, when they must fight utterly until their over-powered god is released."

Of his own initiative, Dandal added, "Prince Gunya is a man of great drive. He has fought his brother for ten years and more. He will not stop until he has no armies left."

Not the most cheering of thoughts, Lauren mused.

*

Smoke still hung over the field of battle. The air hung still and hot, with no waft of breeze to clear the haze or mask the noises. Lauren's ears still brought him the sound of screams, and more distant shots and shouts as the cavalry and Dutch infantry pursued the remaining *kuros*.

Before him, though, was a more urgent problem.

A couple of hundred Yadji had surrendered, whether through injury or lack of courage. Some of the Yadilli militia had been assigned to guard them while his father oversaw the pursuit.

Madjiri said, "What good keep Yadji alive? No need prisoners. That not..." He went back and forth with a Mutjing mercenary who was assigned as an interpreter. "Lack decisiveness."

"You can't just kill prisoners," Lauren said. Well, it could be done sometimes, depending on the bitterness of the fighting. Such a wholesale bloodlust struck him as excessive, though.

"Not kill all of them," Madjiri said. "Spare... one in hundred, send back to tell of their defeat. Rest must die – only way to bring balance."

Lauren started to argue, then stopped. These Yadilli had been only half-hearted supporters until now. Some had agreed to join to fight, yes, but many more had stood aside. Victory now would inspire the rest. No need to antagonise them over this when the Dutch needed local allies.

"So be it," he said.

#46: The First Pods Fall

"The wars of mankind today are not limited to a trial of natural strength, like a bull-fight, nor even mere battles. Rather they depend on losing or gaining friends and allies, and it is to this end that good statesmen must turn all their attention and energy."

- Count Gondomar, ambassador to London, to Philip III of Spain, 28 March 1619

* * *

Taken from:
The Tenth Classic
A novel by Duarte Tomás

Darkness outside, kept at bay by flickering of lanterns and tallow. Coolness in the air, not the harshness of a Dutch or Japanese winter, but a welcome relief from the heat of the day.

"They not give us food, then they will have no food," Madjiri said. As always, the Yadilli commander had a disconcertingly bright smile, thanks to teeth polished God only knew how.

Lauren Nuyts shrugged. The Yadilli rebels had a way of warfare which made even the most long-serving veterans of the German war uneasy. Massacre of prisoners with not even the possibility of ransom or exchange. Now this, too.

"Why antagonise the locals needlessly?" He took in their confused expressions, and said, "I mean, why upset them."

"I understood," said Dandal, the Mutjing mercenary commander. Madjiri shook his head, suggesting that he also followed.

"Not your words that puzzle me, but your meaning," Dandal added. Which made sense; these *kuros* had proven to be extremely quick in picking up the gist of Dutch. "These villagers have food, but they will not open their storehouses to us. If they will not open their storehouses, then they should have no houses."

Lauren absently swatted a mosquito that had been buzzing around his ears, then said, "Destroying this entire village would get us food here, but it would make enemies of everyone else who hears of it."

Madjiri chuckled; it was not a pleasant sound. "It will make them think that maybe they should obey us."

Dandal said, "If we let this village refuse us, we will never receive food or aid from any others. We must show them what we are. War is not a time for half-measures."

Lauren looked to his father, who had been conspicuously silent throughout this discussion. He ventured a question in Japanese, a language which they had both perforce learnt during their exile [ie imprisonment] there. "I know we need to make an example of these natives, but wouldn't that go too far?"

The elder Nuyts said, "Heathens know heathens best." He switched back to Dutch. "Let them know our anger."

* * *

Year of the Twisted Serpent [1629-1638 AD]
Balam Buandik [Beachport, South Australia]
Land of the Five Directions (Yadji Empire)

Balam Buandik: a place with nothing left to recommend it.

In happier times, it would have been a place to treasure. A town on an isolated neck of land beside a rich, teeming lake [Lake George]. The lake had been one of the most prized of waters, a mix of true and bitter water, where waterfood could be found in abundance[244].

The lake was useless, now. The besieging army had blocked the channels which brought true water into the lake. Now it was a drying wastewater with more salt than the sea. Useless for food, useless for transport, leaving only glistening salt plains behind as the waters receded.

The town of Balam Buandik remained, despite the best efforts of Gunya's besiegers. Its location on the narrow lands meant that it could be protected by one short wall on the main landward approach, and a longer wall across the dunes on the western side. With enough canoes bringing in fish from the sea, and enough land within the walls to allow gardens for yams and wealth-trees [wattles], it could never be starved into submission.

The valuable location meant that Balam Buandik had held out for Bailgu Yadji even while the other western strongholds had fallen, one by one. So far as Warmaster Reewa knew, Balam Buandik was the last stronghold to remain west of the White Country.

How much longer he could keep this town intact, though, he wondered. Food was not the problem. Water was abundant enough from wells and cisterns, too.

No, the problem was piling up almost beneath his feet.

The walls of Balam Buandik had withstood all attempts to storm them, so far, but his opposing commander had been doggedly persistent. Rather than continue with futile

---

[244] Historically, Lake George is one of a series of coastal lakes created through the accumulation of sand dunes on their seaward side. Most of these lakes (including Lake George) have no natural outlet to the sea, and are hypersaline due to water being lost only to evaporation and thus accumulation of salts. Lake George had a drainage channel dug to the sea early in the twentieth century, which reduced the salinity and turned it into a useful fishing area. Allohistorically, Yadji engineers have developed a much more complex series of water inflow channels and a dammed exit which maintains the water level, and have stocked the lake with their favourite fish to encourage its productivity.

efforts of ladders and ropes, he had resorted to a more long-term solution.

Every night, enemy soldiers came under cover of noroon-hide shields and dropped loads of earth and rock beside the wall. There were too many of them standing with bows ready to permit the defenders to dislodge the growing pile during the day. Every night, the mound of earth and rock grew larger. It was slow work, but the enemy commander proved to have the patience to carry it out.

The mound almost reached the top of the walls, now. It would not take many more nights before the enemy soldiers could climb directly onto the wall. When that happened, everyone inside would fight a last battle, and then their Last Battle.

"Warmaster, see!"

The voice broke Reewa from his reverie. Outside of bow range, one of the besieging armies held up a banner of unmarked blue.

They want to parley now? Strange, so very strange. Now that they held an inexorable advantage, why would they bother with that? They knew full well that Reewa would never surrender unless ordered to by Bailgu Yadji himself.

"How should we answer?" the nearest soldier asked.

"Colour a blue flag with one white dot," the Warmaster said. Whatever words needed to be said would be between him and the enemy commander alone. No-one else should overhear.

After his orders had been carried out, the enemy forces replied by pulling their banner down and raising it with a single white dot, too.

"Find a rope to lower me onto their mound," he said. "May as well get some use out of their work, yes? And make sure that archers are ready to kill the enemy commander if I am attacked out there."

When he had started to descend, one man stepped out from the enemy lines. Even at a distance, the shine on his armour was obvious.

They met roughly in the middle, of course, as custom and honour required. The man was indeed the enemy commander, with armour which must have been specially polished for this purpose. No sign of gold anywhere, though.

"I am Illalong," the enemy commander said, using the neutral form. No mention of his rank, either. Clever fellow, if that meant he was trying to avoid sounding either of higher or lower status.

"I am Reewa," he replied. "Have you invited me out here to gloat, now that your mound is nearly finished?"

"No, I invited you to parley because I have been so ordered by Gunya Yadji himself."

Reewa managed a slight chuckle. "Nice to hear that your prince cares so much about capturing Balam Buandik."

"To be frank, I think that he would be content to let you rot inside your walls until he has taken the crown," Illalong said.

"Why bother me, then?"

The other commander frowned. "News from the north. The Yadilli rise up in revolt, aided by Mutjing mercenaries and strange men from the uttermost west, beyond the seas."

News indeed, if it was true. Reewa suspected it was; Balam Buandik was hardly such a prize that Gunya Yadji would resort to a ruse to capture it. "Does your prince propose a truce to defeat them, as was done with the Kurnawal?"

"Not that he has told me," Illalong said. "Only that your prince needs to hear this news. And to believe it. Gunya Yadji thinks that he will be more likely to accept it if is delivered by your troops being given safe passage to one of the fortresses he still holds."

"You ask me to abandon my duty to hold this place?"

"I ask you to make your prince fully advised of this new threat," Illalong said. He shrugged. "It is I who am deprived, anyway. Without this order, I would have taken Balam Buandik within a week."

Reewa thought he heard exaggeration there; the mound would not be completed that quickly. Still, the words held enough truth for him to shake his head. "And if I refuse?"

"If you have not accepted by tomorrow's dawn, I will attack as soon as I can. There must be no secondary threat when Gunya Yadji marches to defeat these rebels."

"The decision will not take that long," Reewa said. In truth, he was already minded to accept. He had been offered an honourable course to preserve his soldiers. Still, it would not do to appear too hasty. "If I accept, I will raise a black banner above the walls before sundown. And if so, my soldiers will be ready to march at first light tomorrow."

"So be it." Illalong sketched a slight bow, then turned and strode away.

* * *

September 1637
Gurndjit [Portland, Victoria]
Land of the Five Directions (Yadji Empire)
Another day with no sign of cloud or ship.

For over a year and a half, Maurice Redman had been the commander of this most isolated of Company outposts. So isolated, in fact, that the directors of the East India Company might not yet know that they possessed this foothold in a new world. A *new* New World.

By now, he hoped, Baffin had brought his ships back to a Company outpost in India, or perhaps even back to England itself. He had four ships; surely at least some of them should have survived. When the Company knew what it had here in Aururia, it would send a relief ship, or perhaps even a trade ship or two.

If all of Baffin's ships had been wrecked during the voyage, well... there would be time to deal with that later. Perhaps they could build a ship; they should have sufficient tools, if the Yadji would supply the iron and timber required.

If not, perhaps he could bargain with their Islander interpreter about hiring an Islander ship to sail to Surat[245]. The Islander ships were capable of the voyage, he was sure; smaller than most English ships, but sturdy enough. The Company would not be happy that the Islanders had been shown the way to India, but the news of Aururia should make up for that.

In the meantime, though, he needed to wait. And wait. Depending on what else happened on his voyage, Baffin's ships might be delayed for quite a long time, and the voyage from England to Aururia could take a year in itself. He would have to allow at least another year from now before he sought other ways of getting word back to the Company.

"At least there are things to learn here," he murmured. Both about the Yadji and the Islanders.

He had already acquired a good grasp of the Islander language; he had passed some of the waiting by writing a book of comparative words and grammar.

No-one tried to learn the Yadji language anymore. Not after the Yadji headman ordered Charles executed for using the wrong word when attempting to speak to him. That had only been the most unpleasant of the incidents which confirmed that the Islanders had not been joking about Yadji touchiness.

Redman shook his head, realising he had been letting himself grow mental cobwebs, and returned his attention to the latest entry in his word list. *Dandiri* was a multifarious Islander word; trying to understand all of the shades of

---

[245] Then the site of the largest English trading outpost in India.

meaning which the Islanders imparted to it could give a man nightmares[246].

Before he could find another equivalent to that annoying word, he found another, more genuine distraction. One of the other Englishmen came in to report that Redman had been summoned to attend the local headman.

"What does that bloody devil want with us?" Redman muttered, but he hurried outside, anyway.

Eighteen months in Gurndjit, and he still couldn't find *anyone* who would say the headman's name. That was meant to be a sign of royalty around here, but this headman definitely reported to Gunya Yadji, who claimed their capital even if the civil war still continued. The Yadji were beyond strange, sometimes.

After he entered the former priestly temple, the headman gave him his usual greeting. Superior to inferior, from what he understood of Yadji ways, but he could live with that.

The headman said, "Gunya Yadji summons you to Kirunmara. You will attend with all haste."

A dozen questions came to Redman's lips, but he swallowed most of them again. Questions could be dangerous with the Yadji, as he and his countrymen had discovered. "I will attend. Does the prince require just me, or my countrymen also?"

The headman smiled; a question which sought further instruction was the least likely to anger a Yadji. "You, and any of your men who know about war. Especially anything about your *cannon*."

Redman shook his head; that meant agreement among the Yadji.

"You will follow the Royal Road. You are expected, and will find succour in any town you pass."

---

[246] This is because *dandiri* is a word used in Plirism to mean bringing order or harmony. Given how the faith intertwines with their lives, the Islanders use it in many different senses, although its most common non-religious meanings are to indicate approval or to describe prosperity or good fortune.

Redman bowed, wondering to himself what the devil had brought this about, after so long being ignored by the Yadji rulers.

* * *

Darkness, or so it seems. He can feel heat on his skin, and worse than heat beneath his skin, but no light.

Are his eyes not working? The question takes a long time to come to his mind, and longer to answer. Something is blocking them. Whether it is swelling – his face feels light and puffy – or something placed over his eyes, he cannot work out.

Voices sound in his ears, faint as if they are floating through mist. Sometimes the meaning registers, sometimes it does not.

"This is my son you're talking about," a voice says. He knows that voice. It is his father, although right now he cannot picture a face to match the voice. He lacks the concentration required.

"We talk about, but not to," another voice says. One of the natives, he thinks, but cannot place which one. "No point talking to him. Swamp rash reach that stage, only thing a man can do is bring his mind into balance."

"A doctor could..." His father's voice trails off.

"No doctor here. Gunnagal doctors not come among Yadji."

"Could they do something?" his father asks, an edge of something in his voice. "Not just for Lauren. A quarter of our men – yours and mine both – lie abed with this affliction, and many of them will die. Can these... Gunnagal doctors save them?"

"Some can, or so it is said," the native says. "No help now. Too far away, even if they would come among Yadji."

"God help me, there must be something we can do," his father's voice says, but it seems to come from even further away.

The voices keep talking, but he is no longer able to understand them.

#47: Drumming the Pods

"I stood on the royal road to Kirunmara
And saw a pillar of fire, even as a wheel
Of flame descending from the abyss [heavens].
It spun from west to east, the sun turned backward
Consuming land, tree and beast alike in fury untamed
As abyss and earth prepared for the Last Battle."

- Yadji verse describing the coming of the Nedlandj under Pieter Nuyts, and comparing it to their religion's view of the apocalypse. Attributed to Prince Gunya Yadji, just before the battle of Kirunmara (1638)

* * *

Water falling from the abyss; the steady dripping that fed the Land and its waterworks, but made for bad listening.

Usually, Bidwadjari, senior commander of the armies of Prince Gunya Yadji, had little use for rain. It mattered to farmers, but its infrequent visits made battle manoeuvres far more difficult, and interfered with transportation anywhere off the royal roads.

This evening, though, with the news from the west, he welcomed the rain. It would delay the invaders. The seemingly invincible Raw Men. The pink men who had chained the thunder of the abyss into weapons.

At first, Bidwadjari had thought that these Nedlandj were just trouble-makers, foreign mercenaries who had been come to support the Yadilli in rebellion, and claim some of the gold of the Land. His prince had thought the same.

Now, he knew better. These Nedlandj and their leader One True Egg were the true drivers. They brought their thunder and their beasts with them, and they stirred up revolution. Whether for gold or for some other reason, they brought war to the Land. A new and terrible form of war. A form he had to learn about.

"You tell me not enough of how the battle fared," Bidwadjari said.

The handful of men he spoke to were all survivors of the second great battle with the Nedlandj. It had gone no better than the first. Thunder, fire, giant beasts, unknown manoeuvres, defeat, and massacre of the survivors. The Nedlandj were emboldened, and had found more allies. The Yadilli, the Mutjing and now the Tiwarang[247] joined them. For plunder, surely, with the Tiwarang, not the Plirite bleating which had lured the earlier allies.

"I must know," Bidwadjari added. It could not be due to incompetent commanders. Not twice. Illalong was a good warmaster, and he had certainly led more men than the Nedlandj and their rebel allies, but he had found only defeat.

"Their soldiers know no fear," one said.

"They bring thunder and hard iron where they march," another said.

"Not their character. Speak of how they deployed in battle," Bidwadjari said.

"In a wall of smoke," one said. Another added, "Riding giant dogs down one flank, and a wall of hard iron along the other."

Piecing the details together took too long. There were too few survivors, and it sounded as if they had seen little of the battle anyway. The Nedlandj on their strange big dogs could run too fast, and cut down too many as they fled.

---

[247] The Tiwarang are a Gunnagalic people who live in the north-westernmost reaches of Yadji territory, around historical Naracoorte and Penola in South Australia.

These survivors had only escaped because there were so few Nedlandj on dogs and so many men fleeing in panic that not all of them could be caught.

Still, after much going back and forth, Bidwadjari began to understand something of the battle. The Nedlandj had formed a line of battle with a core of their own men on a low hill. Their raw soldiers wore hard iron and wielded weapons which belched smoke and spit thunderbolts that could kill at a hundred paces or more. On the hilltop, they had strange carts[248] that used chained thunder to hurl balls of solid iron fast enough to dismember men.

On the flat ground, they used their Mutjing and Yadilli allies to form a defensive line. That Plirite rabble were not soldiers to match proper Yadji warriors, but they were good enough that they did not break instantly. That let the Nedlandj use their iron-hurlers to hit the back Yadji ranks – and then their dog-riders to hit the flanks of the engaged soldiers, breaking them. Illalong had been ridden down somewhere in that mass of men, and most of the survivors were those who had been held in reserve, then fled.

As to what the Nedlandj had done after their victory... there, he did not need to hear from the survivors. His own scouts – those that had returned – had reported that the Nedlandj had turned off the royal road before Gurndjit. The rain would slow them down, there, but it made him wonder what they wanted.

The royal road was paved against the worst of weather, but following it would also mean that the Nedlandj had to capture or bypass town after fortified town. So did they fear the fortifications, did they manoeuvre to receive reinforcements from the Tiwarang, or were they just

---

[248] The Yadji have invented the wheel, although with no real beasts of burden larger than dogs, they do not have that many uses for it. "Cart" is the best approximation of a Yadji word which describes almost any wheeled vehicle; their most common forms are carts drawn by hand or by teams of dogs.

contemptuous enough of Yadji arms that they thought that a march straight on Kirunmara would bring them conquest?

"Did anyone hear tale of the parley before the battle?" he asked. If there was one, of course.

That produced another round of argument. No-one had witnessed the parley, but rumours about what was discussed had spread. The soldiers talked about how the Raw Men had admitted to being part of the Cleansing. That this time of blood and fire marked the first blow fought by the servants of the Lord of Night, as time marched to its end.

All meaningless speculation, as far as Bidwadjari could tell. None of the soldiers had heard, so they gossiped. He doubted that this involved the end of time. For all that Gunya Yadji had ordered priests killed for spreading rumours, for all that this was a time of strangers and strange weapons, he doubted that this marked anything supernatural. These Nedlandj had the feel of men to him, more alien than the Tjibarri or the folk of the Cider Isle, but men in search of plunder and conquest. That much, he understood.

He just wished he could think how to stop them.

* * *

Maurice Redman thought that he should have been more impressed by the Yadji royal palace.

The Yadji could build wonders. He had expected that from his first glimpses of the temple at Gurndjit. It had been confirmed by his journey to the royal city, with the endless dams, canals, lakes and swamps which the Yadji maintained for no good reason. Fish was a decent enough meal, if hardly worth so much effort, but it demonstrated the Yadji construction talents. Even their royal road was an impressive highway: wide, well-paved, and well-maintained.

The Yadji ruler – Gunya, although no-one uttered that name in his presence – offered an impressive sight, too. Some sort of woollen tunic dyed into a bright pattern of blue and scarlet, with gold, silver and pearls decorating his chest, and a headband of gold decorated with brilliant feathers.

So why in the name of all that was good and holy did he rule from so plain a building?

A palace should have been larger, especially for a people as wealthy as the Yadji. It should have been filled with gold and ornamentation and all the other splendour which he had witnessed on a smaller scale in the temple in Gurndjit. It should not be a small place of largely plain stone, apart from a few tapestries hung from the walls[249].

Why would the Yadji royal residence show such a lack of magnificence[250]?

Redman knew not to ask that question aloud, but he doubted anyone would have answered him anyway. This was supposed to be an audience with the Yadji emperor, but some old soldier in front of him just asked a lot of questions, while Gunya listened in the background.

The old soldier – nameless, like his ruler – wanted to know much about European weapons and tactics. He asked about horses, about steel, but most of all about gunpowder.

"What drives the thunder of your stringless bows?" the old soldier asked.

---

[249] What Redman thinks of as tapestries are not actually much like European tapestries, being made of linen rather than wool. They are also a sign of great wealth in Yadji culture; the effort required to create them means that only the wealthiest can afford to use them, and then only in the most valued locations. The Yadji tapestries here are actually more valued than most other forms of ornamentation.

[250] This is because Gunya chooses not to occupy the royal palace, but the House of the Dawn; the most sacred ground in Yadji religion, and usually only occupied to hold a vigil for a departed comrade. Gunya claims that he rules from here in honour of his departed cousin. This is a break with tradition, but one which he has so far maintained because of his claim that his cousin is not truly laid to rest until his successor has been named. Of course, no-one among the Yadji would bother explaining this to an outlander such as Redman.

After some back and forth, Redman realised that he meant the gunpowder in muskets. "A black powder that burns," he said.

"You make thunder from fire?" the old soldier said, a sharp edge to his voice.

"From this special powder, yes," he answered. "It burns fast enough to push out objects. Small pellets in muskets, or large balls in cannon."

That produced an even longer exchange where Redman had to explain that muskets and cannon both fired solid objects.

After that, the old soldier said, "Where do you find this special powder?"

"It is not found, it is made," Redman said. He did not want to reveal much more. Knowledge like that should not be given away for nothing. It sounded as if selling guns and powder would be a major market with these Yadji, if the Dutch raiders could be driven off. In any case, he did not know the exact formula of gunpowder, only that it involved some mixture of brimstone, saltpetre and charcoal.

"How is it made?"

"I am not entirely sure. I know how to use muskets, not how to make powder."

The old soldier gave him a long stare. He had a most penetrating gaze, firm and full of suspicion.

Redman offered, "I know that it involves charcoal" – a word which needed further explanation – "but not what else is required."

The questions kept coming, but eventually the soldier accepted that Redman knew nothing useful. The questions moved on to more general military tactics, of which he knew less, but where he was more willing to answer.

The old soldier said, "Can spears be used to hold off... horses?"

Redman nodded, then remembered himself and changed it to a shake of his head. "They can, if used properly." Pike was not a word he knew how to say in the Islander language. "Only if their lines remain unbreached. If the horsemen break into the line, then spears do not work much."

"Or if *cannon* break our soldiers' lines apart," the old man said. "Or fire from a line of your *muskets*."

This soldier is no fool, Redman realised. Of course, this man commanded the side which was apparently winning the Yadji civil war. Perhaps he was the reason for that success.

"How do your armies fight against foes with cannon, muskets and horses?" the old soldier asked.

"Mostly, by having cannons and muskets of our own," he said, which got him another sharp look. "I am not a soldier, so I do not know for certain, but I know that weight of numbers can account for much."

"Truth," the old soldier said. After a few moments, he added, "This black powder burns, you say? How does it fare in rain?"

"It will not burn if it is too wet," Redman said. "Fighting battles is much harder in damp conditions."

The old soldier smiled. "That gives me much to think about."

Only then did Gunya Yadji speak. "Your words have been heard, man of the Inglidj." He clapped his hands, and a servant stepped forward, carrying some form of cloth. "Give this to the masters of your *Company* to mark my gratitude."

The cloth was a long rectangle of white and gold background, with a dark bird woven into the centre. The bird looked like an eagle, he thought. When he took the cloth, Redman felt the weight, and he realised that the golden colour in the cloth came from woven gold thread. *God preserve me!*

He bowed his head. "I will give this to them, along with your words." Unless he could figure out a way to use this gift to escape on his own. No. Baffin would be back, and the Yadji ruler would be sure to ask what happened to his gift.

Gunya said, "I will not send you or your countrymen back to Gurndjit yet. For your safety, you must remain here in Kirunmara."

The old soldier said, "We have not heard that these rebels are on the royal road, but they may move quickly. Once these Nedlandj have been defeated, you can return to await your ships."

* * *

When the Inglidj soldier had departed, Gunya gestured for the other servants and soldiers to depart, too. Only Bidwadjari remained.

"Will his words help you prepare for the great battle?" he asked.

The old general said, "I will consider them. Fortune may favour us. Particularly if rain comes on the right day."

Gunya's lip curled. "The Neverborn has other things on his mind to organising that, I expect. Or so his priests would assure me. Those who still remain."

"Bailgu brought too many priests with him," Bidwadjari said. "Even if all of the others had fought their last battles, we would not be spared the bleating of these newcomers."

"Let them talk, for now," Gunya said. He risked much on this one gamble. A great battle here, if won, would end the civil war. Bailgu's position was already weakened, and a victory here would ensure that the other princes abandoned him. Even if Bidwadjari could not arrange for Bailgu to be among those who died in the battle.

Gunya added, "What the priests say will matter for naught if you can bring victory against these Raw Men."

Bidwadjari said, "Much I have to consider. Numbers may be the answer, but if your soldiers stand too close together, more will die from this black powder. If they stand further apart, fewer will die from this black powder, but they will not do well when they reach the Nedlandj lines if they are too far apart. If we attack them from the flanks, we risk having their *horsemen* grind us from front and rear."

Gunya said, "I would not complain if you deployed Bailgu's troops to the front line, in merit of their courage."

Bidwadjari said, "Alas, he has so little trust as it is. He would recognise it as a ploy to get them killed."

"Truth," Gunya said, although he hated to admit it. "But I am sure of one thing: there is no better commander in the Land than you. If you do not discern how to defeat these Nedlandj, none of us will."

#48: Seeds of the Wealth-Trees

"Any weapon you hold at your death will still be in your grip when you step beyond the grave."
- Batjiri of Jurundit [Koroit, Victoria]

* * *

25 January 1638
Near Kirunmara [Terang, Victoria]
Durigal [Land of the Five Directions]
Evening drew near its end, with the first stars appearing in the fading light. Proof that even the too-long summer days in this land of upside-down seasons did not last forever. The moon had not yet risen, but it was drawing near to the three-quarter mark which their Yadilli and Mutjing allies insisted was a sacred time of danger balanced with opportunity.

Hans Scheer sat holding a cup of the sweet lemony tea which the Yadilli had given him[251]. He would have preferred ale or wine, but these South-Landers knew nothing of those beverages, and he could not stomach their spiced *ganyu* [yam wine]. The lemony tea was an acceptable compromise.

---

[251] This is jeeree, made from the leaves of the lemon-scented tea tree (*Leptospermum petersonii*). This plant is native to the east coast of Aururia and is mostly cultivated there, but has spread to some of the Yadji lands. The ruling class and most of the dominant ethnic Junditmara do not care for it, but some of their subject peoples do, including the Yadilli in the west and the Kurnawal in the east.

Eight other soldiers sat nearby, clustered around the very small fire which they had made for light and to brew the tea. The ground had been carefully cleared around the fire to make sure that the flames did not spread. They had witnessed only one of the wildfires which came to this land in summer, but it was not an experience he would ever want to repeat.

Someone strode up to the fire, and Hans stiffened when he recognised Colonel Michel.

"Easy, boys," Michel said, holding up a hand. "No need for ceremony here. Just here to hear if you want to say anything before the morning."

"Everyone's ready, sir," Hans said. He still missed Johan and Ludwig, one dead of swamp rash after the first battle, and the other dead in the second, but everyone else kept their courage.

"Excellent," Michel answered. "It's time to give these pagan *kuros* another dose. We've beaten them twice already, but it seems that they don't learn their lessons easily."

"We'll teach them," Hans said. "No better teachers than musket, pike, cannon and cold steel."

The men laughed.

The colonel clapped him on the shoulder. "Too true. Rest well, men, and tomorrow we'll kill thousands more of these pagans."

He rose and strode off to the next fire.

Hans took another sip of the tea, and grinned to himself.

*

An assemblage of men, six hundred or so all told. Two banners worth of death warriors. Men who were dead in law, men who for one reason or another had taken the oath that could never be unsworn. Men whose faces were dyed white in a pattern which resembled a skull. Men whose ornamentation proclaimed them death warriors on the eve of a battle.

Batjiri of Jurundit stood among them, toward the front. He was one of the most senior death warriors, who had held to the oath for more than ten years. Much longer than he had expected, but then no man could second-guess fate.

Now, their prince addressed them for the first time in years. "My friends, I have erred," Bailgu Yadji said.

Cries of denial rose from the throats of the assembled death warriors. Batjiri's voice sounded loud among them.

Bailgu held up a hand. "Not in my choice of soldiers. I could have asked for none finer."

This time, the death warriors cheered.

"For so long I have held your banners in reserve, awaiting the time of a final battle when you would be called to fulfill your oaths. This much of my anticipation was true: the final battle would be fought."

Bailgu smiled. "My mistake was that I thought it would be against my cousin. That the final battle would be of prince against prince."

The prince held up both hands. "It is not so. The final battle comes, but this is not a war between Yadji. The Cleansing is at hand. Time marches toward its end. The final battle will be of Yadji against the allies of the Lord of Night. In tomorrow's battle, your deaths will prepare the way for the rise of the Neverborn."

Shouts of acclamation answered him.

* * *

26 January 1638

Near Kirunmara, Durigal

Darkness still hung over the encampment when Hans Scheer rose. Dawn must be a ways off – he had no clock to be sure – but they would need to be prepared to move at short notice.

Dressing could be done in the dark, fortunately. Pants, shirts, boots, belt, blood-red tabard – Nuyts's suggestion, to quickly tell their own side in the battlefield – and hat. The hat was perhaps what he valued most, save his musket itself. The sun in this land burned far too hot, especially in midsummer.

He had powder and musket ready where he had left them last night, but Hans did not move to pick them up yet.

When it came time to move, that would be soon enough. This would be his third battle on the soil of the South Land, and the eighth in his life, not counting minor skirmishes. He had learned the value of patience.

Raised voices carried to him, and he emerged from his tent. "What's happened?"

A sergeant stood outside, surrounded by several of Hans's campmates. "Water on the battlefield."

"Rain?" Hans asked, before realising how foolish that sounded. The ground here was still dry.

"The God-damned Yadji have released one of their dams. That flooded the ground we need to fight on."

"Those pig-faced eel-fuckers!" Hans paused a moment while he recovered his cool. "How bad is it?"

"Water's gone down, but it destroyed some of the powder we had in place for the cannon. Ground's still muddy, too, and it's ruined the trench we had ready to protect us."

"Christ. Does that change the battle plan?"

The sergeant shrugged. "Yes, but not sure how yet. Except that we need to be there first, in case the pagans try something clever. Grab your equipment; we'll be marching soon."

*

Night drew near to an end. Probably the last night Batjiri would ever see, unless he lost his Last Battle after death and was called to the minions of the Lord of Night.

He sifted a few ashes from the wealth-tree [wattle] ash in front of him, and rolled it into a ball with the crushed leaves of alertness-weed[252]. Soon it was ready to chew; he popped the ball into his mouth to start working on it.

The effects were quick: a slight deadening of his body, as the world became more distant. He still knew where he was

---

[252] Alertness-weed is what the Yadji call a couple of the Aururian species of tobacco (*Nicotiana suaveolens* and *N. velutina*) that death warriors chew as part of their preparation for entering their battle trance. These are close relatives of domesticated tobacco, and have stimulant properties.

and what he was, but he felt lighter, more alive. While it was not obvious yet, he knew that pain would be weakened if he felt it, and fatigue banished from him.

He rose, picked up the pages of his manuscript, and went to look for his fellow death warriors.

*

Mud underfoot in the blue hour [morning twilight] was not Hans's idea of the best way to prepare for a battle, but it would have to do. They were almost in place at the low rise which the commanders had picked out to defend. Fortunately, the mounted scouts had reported that there were no other Yadji dams nearby which could be broken to flood the field again.

He had his musket in place beside him. His lovingly-treasured flintlock. All of the men in his ten-strong front rank of musketeers had these new, wonderfully fast muskets. Some of the musketeers still fought using the older snaphances, which was why they were deployed to the flanks and rear of the formation.

The pikemen were in the centre, twenty wide, with another rank of musketeers on the other side. More pikemen were on his left, and another group of musketeers further past that. The same pattern would be duplicated on the other side. He could not see that far, even with the higher ground, but he knew the deployment. It was the same that the Colonel had ordered in the last two battles, with the cannon on the even higher ground behind them, and the cavalry off doing whatever Nuyts deemed best.

Now all they had to do was wait for their allies to arrive – they would be delayed by their morning prayers – and then for the enemy to attack.

*

Raw mushrooms were being passed around. Batjiri took two of them, and sent the platter on to the next warrior. He popped the first in his mouth, chewing it quickly, and swallowed. Then he consumed the second.

His armour was laid out before him, as standard for a death warrior in preparation for fulfilling his oath. The writing table and pen beside it were not standard, but Batjiri wanted to write whatever inspiration came to him before his departure.

Chanting started up around him as the death warriors started to dress. He joined in with the familiar chants, the ancient words coming to his lips almost without conscious thought. Recited so slowly, oh so slowly.

"The path opens, the path opens..."

He put on the padded undershirt first, left sleeve first, then the right.

"The journey begins, the journey begins..."

He tightened and tied the strings at the front, those designed so that the wearer could fit them himself.

"The first step is the hardest..."

He picked up his armour, with fish-shaped scales fastened to a jacket of noroon-leather hide. A weight of metal in his arms, his last great burden to be fastened to him in this life.

"To make your oath true..."

He fitted the left sleeve first again, feeling the weight on his arm and shoulder as the jacket settled into place.

"Once on the road, once on the road..."

He closed the right sleeve around his arm, and pulled the jacket tight as the armour fitted around him.

"You will walk ever onward, ever onward..."

He signalled for his neighbour to tighten the straps for his jacket, to bring the armour into maximum protection.

"To the end that lies beyond..."

He closed his neighbour's armour too, fixing it so that the straps closed at his back where they would be best defended.

"Go armed, go armed into the mist of decision..."

He pulled on the leather leggings, reinforced with only light scales which offered lesser protection, but which allowed freedom of movement and reduced weight.

"Battle to the death, battle to the death..."

He finished tying the leggings at his waist, and reached for his helmet.

"So that you can fight on after it!"

He placed the helmet on his head, his final protection, as the chant started again, the pace quickening slightly this time.

"The path opens, the path opens..."

He checked his shield, running his finger around the edge for flaws.

"The journey begins, the journey begins..."

He started to feel more detached now, as the mushrooms began to take effect inside him.

"The first step is the hardest, the hardest, to make your oath true..."

He strapped his shield onto his back, where it would be ready to carry into the battle.

"Once on the road, once on the road..."

He reached for the dagger and belt, and fixed them around his waist.

"You will walk ever onward, ever onward..."

He checked his sword too, blade and hilt, but did not move to put this on, not until he marched out.

"To the end that lies beyond..."

Words were being shaped by his lips, but others now brewing inside his head. Now, he knew how to finish his classic.

"Go armed, go armed into the mist of decision..."

He inked the pen and crouched over the table. Writing was awkward in armour, but he had written so many words during the long wait that he was sure he would manage now.

"Battle to the death, battle to the death, so that you can fight on after it!"

He wrote the words that concluded his work: *Care not how you die. Care how you live.*

The writing finished, Batjiri joined fully in the chanting, as the words were repeated again and again, gaining slightly in tempo each time.

*

The sun rose gradually higher in the sky as Hans waited with his compatriots. He silently blessed his hat. Back in Germany that would often have been merely decoration, but here it would be a stone-cold blessing as the day heated.

Movement on either side showed him that the Mutjing and Yadilli allies were moving into place. Slower than he liked, on a day like this. The Yadilli in particular had always put him ill at ease, with their persistent attempts to convert him and his fellows to their pagan faith. But no-one could doubt Yadilli courage.

There would be no parley today. Perhaps demands had been heard discreetly over the last couple of days, but by now every man knew that the Yadji would never surrender until they had been utterly defeated. Today would have to be one more lesson.

As the sun rose higher, the Yadji eventually came. Units of the enemy marched across the open ground in front of them. Many units of men, seeming to stretch from horizon to horizon. As they neared, he could pick out the distinctive two-part Yadji banners, with a square section hanging from the top and a smaller downward-pointing triangle below. He had no idea what the different banner designs meant, but noticed how many of them were being carried.

"So it begins," he murmured.

*

Drums beat to his left and right. Batjiri marched on according to the demands of their rhythm. He was in the front rank of the Spurned, his banner of death warriors.

But not in the front rank of the whole army, as he might have expected. Units marched in front of the death warriors. Not in the usual tight formations that prepared for a charge. Small columns of men, two or three wide, with gaps between each column. The units had been separated, as if to weaken them. Or to make space. Who knew why Gunya Yadji had given his orders?

The ground beneath his feet held some mud, but not enough to trouble him. This part of the battle was one he understood. The order had gone forth that the muddy ground would weaken the Raw Men. That their thunder balls would be harder to fire, that their dog-riders would find manoeuvre more difficult, and that the eggs from their thunder-carts would be less effective in the mud.

The drums continued their slow beat, and the death warriors marched on toward the enemy.

*

Cannon belched somewhere behind and above him, their balls landing among the approaching Yadji. Faint words carried across the narrowing gap; the Yadji seemed to be singing as they charged. He had never heard that before.

Regardless of the enemy actions, Hans knew what he had to do. A discipline born of long practice consumed him. He bit down on his first paper cartridge, ripping it open with his teeth. He pushed the frissen [striker] forward and tipped a small dose of powder into the revealed flash pan.

The singing grew slightly louder as he pushed the frissen back to close the flash pan. He tipped the musket vertically, the barrel held upward, and emptied the main dose of powder into the barrel. The ball went in next, before he pushed in the wadding formed from the cartridge paper. He took the ramrod from its position beneath the barrel, and pushed it into the barrel to compact the wadding, powder and ball into a mass ready for firing.

Ignoring the sounds of the approaching enemy, he replaced the ramrod and raised the musket ready for firing. The butt fitted against his shoulder as he pulled back the hammer.

The mass of enemy soldiers were close enough now, despite the strange gaps in their ranks. He aimed as best he could, readying himself for the order.

"Fire!" came the cry, somewhere behind him.

Smoke belched from the musket as he and his fellow musketeers fired. The thunder of the powder firing was followed by some screams that carried across the gap from the charging pagans. He ignored that as best he could, kneeling down to let the second rank fire, and tried to keep the powder cartridges dry and clear of the mud while he repeated the process to reload.

When he stood to fire again, he vaguely glimpsed many of the front rank of Yadji down, but more of them kept coming. The gap closed, and he fired again.

A third volley followed, then a fourth. The Yadji died in numbers, but they kept coming. It was as if they cared nothing for whether they died.

"Pikemen forward!" came the order.

Pikes were lowered as the men stepped forward, around Hans and his fellows. The approaching Yadji were close, so close now, and breaking out of their columns now that the musket fire ceased.

With the first two ranks of pikemen in front of him, Hans reloaded at a less frantic pace, waiting to fire over their shoulders when an opportunity presented itself.

*

Soldiers ahead fought and died. Smoke rose like mist from the battlefield, obscuring the enemy ranks and those who had come closest to them.

A few regular soldiers broke and ran, but the death warriors paid them no heed. Batjiri and his fellows cared nothing for those who fled death. An ending came to all men. All that mattered was how they faced it.

The beat of the drums quickened, and Batjiri shifted from a walk to a jog.

Ahead, a few more of the thunder-sticks belched lead and smoke. More of the enemy seemed to be fighting in hand to hand, at least as far as he could tell through the smoke.

The drum beat quickened again, and Batjiri shifted into a run. Thunder sounded, and somewhere off to his left, he heard screams as a large ball struck the ground. He focused more ahead than anything else. Between the smoke, he could see some of the enemy soldiers thrusting their very long spears to keep the regular soldiers at bay. Others fired more of their thunder-sticks.

The drum beat intensified, and Batjiri broke into a sprint. For now, he could concentrate only on frenzy and the charge.

*

Hans stood, waiting for a gap in the pikes, and fired. A Yadji soldier dropped to the ground. Whether dead, injured, or just out of fear, it mattered little. All that was important was keeping the enemy far enough away to keep the pikes intact.

So far, it remained unbreached, at least in front of him. He could not see or hear other parts of the battle, but since they were not being pressed from either side, events could not be going too badly.

As he crouched for yet another reload, he heard a sound which carried over the immediate clash of battle. Drums, growing louder and faster, and then a mighty shout that overcame even that sound.

When he rose again, he saw a fresh round of enemy soldiers drawing close. They carried two banners that he could see, and they moved at an incredible pace. He fired again, along with some other musketeers around him, but those two banners kept coming closer, and the drums kept sounding.

*

Nothing matters now, nothing except the charge. Other warriors march beside him, crying out fragments of one chant or another. He hears them not, his focus is on what lies ahead.

Many enemy long-spears, but not an unbroken wall. Enough of the regular soldiers have reached the enemy ranks that there are gaps here and there. That is all he needs, as he runs into one of those openings, right up to the spear-wielders.

The nearest soldier wears scale armour, but Batjiri hardly notices. He runs right up, with a thrust of his sword that brings down the scale-armoured man. The one behind him wears brighter colours, though that barely registers too. He has a sword, but still in position to fight the soldier who just died. Batjiri's thrust catches the man in the shoulder, and the enemy falls. Batjiri's boots land on the man's jaw as he steps forward, to face another brightly-coloured enemy.

*

Hans drops his musket hurriedly, and reaches for his rapier. "God preserve me!" he says.

The second wave of Yadji soldiers have devastated the front ranks. He knows he shot at least one, and others within his sight fell from other muskets or impaled themselves on pikes. Even those gruesome deaths have served the enemy's purposes, since others pushed into the gaps left when their fellows fell to the ground and carried the pike heads with them.

No matter how many of them died before they came close, once they reached the lines, the rest have fought with the fury of dragons. Nothing is left of the front two ranks of pikeman before him, and he has only been saved by other pikemen who pressed forward after dropping their pikes and drawing their swords.

Now, it is his turn. One of those frenzied maniacs is clashing with another German, sword on sword. Hans steps forward when he sees an opening, and strikes the maniac in the side. It does not kill him, or even pierce his armour, but the distraction lets the other German strike a deadlier blow.

"They die!" Hans shouts.

He never sees the blow that comes from his left. Or anything again after that.

*

Batjiri strikes again and again, sword on sword or armour or shield. He does not hear anything. Noise is naught but background in his frenzy. All that matters is what he sees, and what he sees, he attacks.

He is not capable of counting how many of the enemy have fallen. Or even of distinguishing between friends and enemies, except for those who wear the white dye. Anyone else is a foe to be cut down.

And cut them down he does, until a pistol shot he never sees blasts through his armour, and he falls to the ground. Even then, prone on the ground, he manages to draw his dagger and thrust it at the nearest foe, though he will never know if it causes any damage.

Behind him, as he the world fades around him, sounds register again. A fresh sound of drums.

Batjiri has gone to fight his Last Battle before a third wave of regular Yadji soldiers charges in. The embattled Raw Men are too busily engaged in melee to use their pikes or muskets to hold off this wave.

After that arrival, only one fate remains open.

* * *

27 January 1638
Kirunmara, Durigal

Row after row of soldiers, lined up for Gunya Yadji to inspect. His soldiers, now, one and all. Far too many have died in subduing the Raw Men and their allies and rebels. So many widows will weep tonight.

Yet for all of the cost, this is a victory he will treasure for ever more. The seemingly-invincible Nedlandj have been defeated, by the courage of the death warriors and by Bidwadjari's cunning, and ultimately by weight of iron and blood. His cousin Bailgu is most lamentably not among the dead, too, but even the best of battle plans do not accomplish everything.

He completes his inspection of the soldiers, walking past the front rank of each unit, to cheers and acclamation. This is *his* victory.

Bidwadjari and his other senior commanders await him in the centre of the field. The other princes stand behind them, too, except for now-departed Bailgu.

After a moment, he shouts, "Bidwadjari, my right arm, and all of my soldiers: praise be unto you for the glory you have won."

He waits, for the soldiers to shout on the message in relay until it has been carried to all units.

Before he can go on with his speech, Bidwadjari drops onto one knee. "The glory is yours, my Regent. Command me and I shall obey, in all things, until the Neverborn breaks free of the earth and reclaims his dominion."

The ritual announcement leaves Gunya momentarily lost for words. The throne belongs to him, of course, but it is not something he has expected to claim just yet.

The commanders around Bidwadjari match the announcement, and then the soldiers behind. Making the most of the unplanned moment, Gunya turns to the princes, to await their response. One by one, they do the same. The slowest are those who had been backing Bailgu, but even they submit.

Such an acclamation expects that he will now give commands worthy of a new Regent. Fortunately, he already knows what he wants to order. One part had already been planned whenever he declared victory in this battle, while the other simply awaited his assumption of the Regency to say what has long been in his heart.

Gunya says, "Hear my commands. Prisoners we have seized from the Nedlandj and the rebels. When they captured honourable Yadji soldiers in their uprising, they slaughtered them. It is only fitting that our response be the same. Death for death, sword for sword. Kill all of the prisoners, sparing only those drove the thunder-carts [cannon]."

"It shall be done," Bidwadjari says.

"For those few who escaped on their giant dogs, do not kill them all, so long as they flee," Gunya says. "Harry them, chase them, kill a few, but do not destroy them. Drive them from the Land, and let them carry word of their defeat. Let them carry word of the might of the Yadji."

That draws forth cheers, as the words are relayed to the soldiers.

After the orders have been relayed, Gunya speaks again. This time, he adopts his most formal tone. "Hear the words of your Regent: the Nedlandj are enemies of the Neverborn. They are not to be harboured. They must not be welcomed. The Nedlandj are to be killed on sight, by any man or woman who holds to honour. The Land of the Five Directions must be free of their taint. Never can they be permitted to set foot here, until the Neverborn comes and Cleanses all the world."

* * *

Riding, endless riding, punctuated by moments of too-short sleep.

Twenty horses trail behind Pieter Nuyts. Only fifteen carry riders. The other horses are there as remounts and carriers of the few remaining provisions and other supplies which the escapees have managed to bring with them.

Worse, this small band of sixteen men are less than half of those who fled from the battlefield beside the Yadji capital. They had still numbered twenty-four when they reached Coonrura, only to find that their ships had fled before their arrival, giving up the promise of gold out of fear of the Yadilli who had turned on their former allies. Now, they number only sixteen men fleeing north-west out of the Yadji lands, with the fear that every skirmish with their pursuers will cost them more blood.

Another hill, another declining slope, as they urge their horses on, with Nuyts still at the lead. Strength has failed them in the Yadji empire, but for now, he will run. After that... he will have to see.

On the downslope, the grass gives way to a scattering of these strange, sharp-smelling, fire-loving trees which are so characteristic of this land. The trees gradually grow closer together, but there is a trail through here, too. Not a well-used one, by the looks of it, but wide enough for two horses to ride side by side.

Further down, the ground flattens out, and the trees open up into one of those wide swathes of open, slowly-regrowing land which mark the passage of one of their wildfires. Nuyts signals for the horsemen to ride four abreast. Not that he expects much danger ahead, since the Yadji have been trying to pursue them on foot, but it will be safer nonetheless.

Or so he thinks.

When they are nearly across the open ground, men emerge from the trees beyond. Sunlight glints off metal as they emerge. Not scaled armour like the Yadji prefer, but something else. It looks like mail, with rings reflecting the sunlight.

He almost signals for an attack, since only about two dozen men who have stepped out from the trees. Then he notices that more men are standing at the edge of the trees. Many more men, at least twice as many as the mail-clad warriors. Men who carry some sort of bows. Why didn't he notice them earlier?

Nuyts has drawn his horse to a halt, as have those with him. The mail-clad warriors make no move to attack them, either, although the ones behind have their bows out where they can nock arrows quickly.

One of the mail-clad men steps forward slightly. His gaze lands on Nuyts.

"Pieter Nuyts, I presume," the man says, his Dutch accented but understandable.

"So I am called," he says. "Who are you, to ask that of me?"

"I am Wemba of the Whites," the other man says, and sketches a bow with left arm across his stomach and right arm extended, for all the world as if he is a Dutch gentleman.

Nuyts wonders, almost abstractly, why the man calls himself a White. His skin is a few shades lighter than that of a typical Yadji, but still dark in comparison to any man not born in Africa[253]. "You are a... Gunnagal?"

The man nods. "Of course."

---

[253] Strictly speaking, there are other non-African peoples whose skin tone could be considered as dark as the Gunnagal (eg some Melanesian peoples). Nuyts is not really aware of those, though; at this point New Guinea and the Solomon Islands had only limited contact with Europeans.

It takes Nuyts a moment to realise that Wemba has nodded to mean the affirmative, something which no other *kuro* has ever done. And there is the way he bowed, too. Just how much does this man know of Dutch ways?

Wemba says, "But the archers behind me are not Gunnagal. They are Palawa. One Palawa with a greatbow can hit a duck at two hundred paces. I have fifty Palawa behind me. Consider this carefully as you listen to my next words."

A shiver passes through Nuyts, despite the heat. "I'm listening."

"Pieter Nuyts, you are summoned to Tjibarr," Wemba says. He holds up a hand, and the archers behind him move as one to seize arrows and nock them into the bowstrings.

Will those arrows pierce steel armour? If they are anything like the longbows which the English are said to have used in the past, they may well. Anyway, the horses have no protection.

Despite the danger, though, Nuyts still does not want to agree. Being ordered around so arrogantly grates at him. "And if I refuse to come?" he asks.

Wemba grins, or at least his mouth is open and his teeth are showing. "If you are summoned to Tjibarr, you will come." His grin widens. "As to whether you are dead or alive when you arrive – that is your choice."

Epilogue: The Dance of Football

Sometimes, it is hard to decide if you are a guest or a prisoner.

Willi Schröder had come to this new South Land as a soldier of fortune, in pursuit of gold and glory. The invasion force he joined had failed. He had been among the fortunate few escapees who outran the vengeful pursuit of the native armies. Only to fall into the hands of another group of natives.

Gunnagal, these natives called themselves. They had invited the refugees to come to Tjibarr, their greatest city. An invitation which could not be declined without ceasing to breathe, but an invitation nonetheless.

The refugee Germans and Dutchmen had duly come to Tjibarr, Schröder among them. Now he and his fellows still could not decide whether they were to be honoured as guests or kept as prisoners. They had been hosted in what would have been considered a luxuriously-furnished house even back in Hamburg. Yet they had also been surrounded by guards and not permitted to leave or to have others enter.

At that time, Schröder had said, "These guards are here to keep us prisoner."

The lord who hosted them – or who was their head captor – called himself Wemba of the Whites, despite having a skin as dark as the rest of the natives here. He said, "These guards are to assure the safety of my guests. Your deeds during your invasion have displeased many, both amongst we of the Gunnagal and our neighbours. Best not to risk what mischance might befall without protection."

"Protection for us or for protection for you?" Schröder had persisted.

"Yes," Wemba had said.

Their former leader, Pieter Nuyts, had been removed when they arrived at Tjibarr. Perhaps he still lived, and was housed separately. None of these Gunnagal would say anything about that, one way or the other. Schröder did not care so much about what had happened to Nuyts – the man had failed in his invasion, and was unworthy of further leadership – but he wanted to know whether these Gunnagal were inclined to kill. If Nuyts had been killed, the same thing might happen to others.

Now, several days later, Wemba had returned, together with a retinue of a large number of men and a smaller number of women. All were dressed in clothes coloured white, or mostly white. The quality of the clothes varied from as ornate as Wemba's to shapeless masses of fabric, but the colours were the same: white.

Wemba said, "Today the football season opens. The Reds challenge the Whites. I have reserved a seat for one of you."

"I'll go," Schröder said quickly. Whatever form of football the natives played here in the South Land, it would be better to see it than remain in this gilded prison. Maybe he would even have a chance to escape being a guest of the Gunnagal.

None of the other refugees contested his acceptance, so Schröder left with Wemba and his retinue of white-clad natives.

Wemba walked alongside Schröder, speaking pleasantly as they travelled. Wemba spoke fluent Dutch, if anything better than Schröder's own grasp of that language. Remarkable, given the Dutch had only been trading with this part of the South Land for a handful of years.

"What is this football, your football I mean?"

"Nothing like what you know in Europe," Wemba said. "Your football would involve the whole town playing and played throughout the town, or so I have been told."

"Many rules in many towns," Schröder said. "It is all different."

"For we of the Gunnagal, football has one set of rules throughout the nation." He smirked. "Though men still endlessly argue about the interpretation of the rules."

"Sounds important."

"It is the game of games, the heart of life. It is said that one cannot understand the Gunnagal unless one understands football."

"Do you believe that?" Schröder asked.

"As with most proverbs, they simplify a more complex truth," Wemba said.

They had been walking steadily as they talked, through this city's streets that had people in abundance but no donkeys or cattle or horses. The natives here lacked all of those.

"Where is football played?" he asked, as he realised that they were still within the heart of the city. Schröder had expected that this football would be played at some common land or field outside the city walls, if it was not played with the town itself as the field.

"At the Field of Champions. Not much further now. You can see part of the Field, up over there."

Ahead, Schröder saw what looked like a towering wall, which stood far above the surrounding buildings. "That is a field?"

"That is part of the... I do not think that the Dutch have a word for it. The seating. For where the wealthier can sit to watch the football."

"A football game where men sit to watch?" Schröder asked in disbelief. "Who would... I have never heard of such a thing."

"Football is important here," Wemba said. He added some more comments to the natives in his retinue, which he did not bother to translate.

The Field of Champions turned out to be immense. A very large field, with the grass cut short enough that it would have required many men with scythes working a long time to accomplish it. A very long rope had been laid around much of the field, in a near-perfect circle. Some more open grass surrounded the rope, then there was a low wooden fence, also in a near-perfect circle.

Past that... men and women crowded onto ground which sloped gradually upward, so that all could watch the game. Around about one-quarter of the boundary, the seats that Wemba had mentioned rose in tiers built into stone. Canvas had been hung from long poles that stretched out over those seats, offering shelter from the sun and perhaps even from rain. Though rain was a rare feature here in the South Land.

The men and women who crowded around the field were mostly clad in either red or white. They stood in distinct clusters of the same colour, either white or red. Some people wore other colours, and they stood in no obvious pattern.

"How many people are here?" he asked in wonderment.

Wemba shrugged. "Not a large crowd for this match. My Whites performed well last season, but the Reds did not, so few of the other factions have attended. Perhaps eight thousand here to watch."

"*Eight thousand men*? To watch football?"

Wemba chuckled. "I told you, football is the heart of life in Tjibarr. The Field of Champions can hold twenty thousand or so, depending on how they crowd in."

"This city has so many people who come to watch football?"

"Not all are from the city. Many are visitors. People travel the length of the nation to attend football season."

Schröder shook his head in disbelief.

Wemba's retinue pushed down through the crowd to the boundary fence, then over the fence and around the edge of the field toward the seating. Then Wemba led the way up into the seating, choosing some which were three tiers back.

Glancing around the seated natives, he realised that they were neatly divided in half. The half including Wemba wore white, while the other half wore red. "Do you... Gunnagal always wear the colours of your team?"

"When watching football, it is customary. At other times, it is common, but to a person's choosing."

Colours. Some people here wear other colours. "How many teams... factions, you said, play football?"

Wemba smiled. "Eight. Each with their own colour, naturally, and each with their own customs in life. Such is the... again, I think that Dutch has not the word. *Jingella*, we would say. The... endless dance."

"The dance of football?"

"The dance of life. Football is the heart of the dance, but the Endless Dance is something which a man steps through wherever he is, whatever he does."

Schröder shook his head again; it was something he found himself doing far too often with these Gunnagal. For all that Wemba spoke fluent Dutch, sometimes his meaning was impossible to follow.

He opened his mouth to ask a further question. A roar interrupted him, the sound of thousands of voices raised in acclamation.

Two lines of men were walking through two gates in the boundary fence. One group wore white, while the others wore red. Of course.

More than twenty-five men stood in each line; Schröder could not count the precise number. Once all had entered the field, each group started to walk around the circle in opposite directions, waving to the people watching outside. The roars of the crowd grew louder as the men circled the field.

Another group of men walked into the centre of the field. Musicians, carrying a variety of instruments both like and unlike those he knew from Germany. All were made of brass. Some carried cymbals, or something very much like them. Others carried horns, and a strangely-shaped tube that reminded him of a trumpet.

The musicians played in the centre of the field as the football players walked around. The music may have appealed to the natives, but Schröder found it simply loud with a difficult rhythm to follow.

The two teams finished their circuits of the field, and clustered around the musicians. With the crowd quietened – slightly – Schröder took the opportunity to ask, "How is your football played?"

Wemba said, "I could spend the rest of the day explaining the rules to you, and I would still not be finished. But in short: you see the scoring posts in each quarter of the field?"

The native lord gestured in turn to four pairs of poles, standing just behind the boundary rope to north, south, east and west on the field.

"Each team can score at two of those pairs of poles, north and south or east and west, and must protect the other two. A ball must be kicked between the two poles to score. A ball which bounces before it goes through scores one point. A ball which is kicked through without bouncing is worth two points. Each team has one player who stands behind each of the four pole-pairs, to attack or defend. If the attacking player catches a kicked ball from their own team without it bouncing first, that kick is worth three points. If the defending player catches a kicked ball before it bounces, or touches a bouncing ball before it passes the boundary fence, then no points are scored."

Schröder felt the faint beginnings of a headache. "Our football is much simpler, I think."

The football players had scattered over the field, usually with a white man paired with a red. A cluster of them stood in the centre, other near each of the pairs of scoring-posts, and others in different places for some purpose which no doubt made sense to them.

A brown-clad man stood in the centre of the field. He held out a ball, circled it around his body three times quickly by flicking it from hand to hand, then threw it high in the air.

What happened after that made very little sense to Schröder. The players sometimes kicked, sometimes threw one-handed, and sometimes jumped on top of each other to take kicks. One thing he did grasp was that if the ball had been caught from a kick without bouncing first, the player who caught it had time to prepare for another kick without the opposing team interfering with him.

In time, he asked, "Are there rules for when a man may kick or throw the ball?"

Wemba laughed. "This is football. There are rules for everything. But in short: the ball may be caught with both hands from a kick, but only one hand from a throw. It can only be thrown one-handed. When a ball is caught then the player may not advance toward the nearest goal if they are making a throw or kick while holding the ball. They may drop the ball to the ground, and once there they can kick it freely, but not pick it up again. If a kicked ball is caught without touching the ground, the opposing team may not advance any closer to the player who caught the ball."

Schröder rubbed his temples. "How does... can you... never mind. I'll just watch."

He studied the football players going around the field, with the ball bouncing and kicking and occasionally thrown. The players were agile, of a certainty. Past that, he could not say he understood this game, or even fathomed why these natives liked it so much.

"Why is this game the heart of life? Football is just football," Schröder said.

"Every Gunnagal supports one of the eight factions, the eight teams which play football. Well, all save the king and royal household, who are neutral. During football season, the factions compete with each other on the field, for the rest of year they compete in life."

"In life?" he asked. Once more came the feeling that Wemba spoke words which individually could be understood, but together made no sense.

"Compete in everything. In land, in commerce, in status. All is part of the Dance. Stand together against outsiders, when needed. Other times, the factions compete with each other for advantage. Cooperate when required, naturally, but always seeking advantage."

Schröder said, "You make it sound like the factions rule the kingdom, not the king."

Wemba laughed again. "Of course the factions rule. The king in Tjibarr is... how do you say it in Dutch?" The native lord pointed to the brown-clad man in the centre of the football field. "You see that man in brown? He is the judge, would you say? He starts the game, he enforces the agreed rules, but he does not decide who wins. The players decide who wins."

"The referee," Schröder said.

"Referee, thank you," Wemba said. "The king in Tjibarr is like the referee. He helps to keep the balance, but he does not decide for all or rule for all."

"I don't understand."

Wemba looked at the football field, then back to Schröder. "Let me try with an example. You and your countrymen are wanted men. Our neighbours have demanded your return or execution. We of the Whites have decided to offer you our hospitality instead. We negotiated with the other factions, and they agreed to let us make you our guests. The king had no part in that process; the factions decided."

"So thanks to football, I am a prisoner?"

"Thanks to football, you are *alive*. Go to a kingdom where there is a king who rules, and they would return you to our neighbours for execution. Thanks to football, we can keep you as a guest instead. You should honour football for your hospitality."

Sometimes, Schröder realised, it is hard to decide if you are a guest or a prisoner.

Appendix: Maps

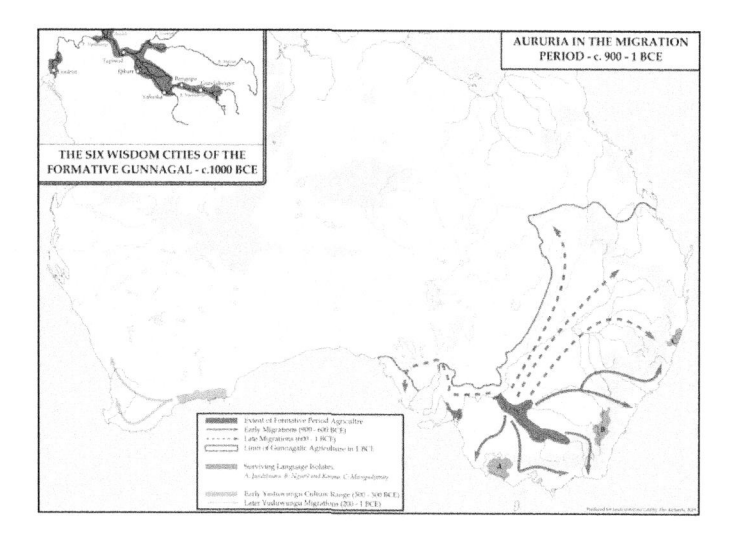

WATJUBAGA EMPIRE

THIJSZENIA IN 1618

Incorporating the history of the colonisation of the Cider Isle by Gunnagalic peoples in the Pre-Houtmanian Epoch

- Tjunini Lands
- Kurnawal Lands
- Former Kurnawal lands lost to the Tjunini

Note: Highlands within Gunnagalic lands are shown in stripes

Produced for Lands of Red and Gold by Alex Richards, 2009

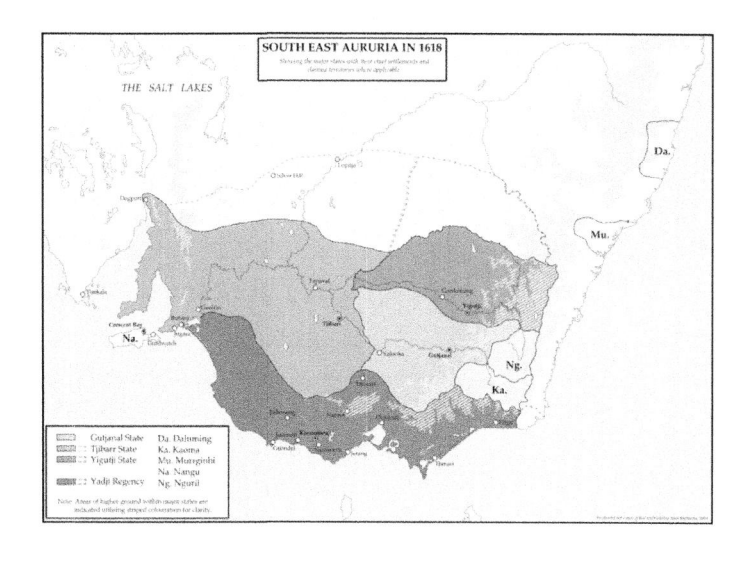

SOUTH EAST AURURIA IN 1618
Showing the major states with their chief settlements and claimed territories where applicable

THE SALT LAKES

Da. Dahoming
Ka. Kaoma
Mu. Mutgimbi
Na. Nangu
Ng. Ngurú

- Gutjanal State
- Tjibarr State
- Yigutji State
- Yadji Regency

Note: Areas of higher ground within major states are indicated utilising striped colouration for clarity.

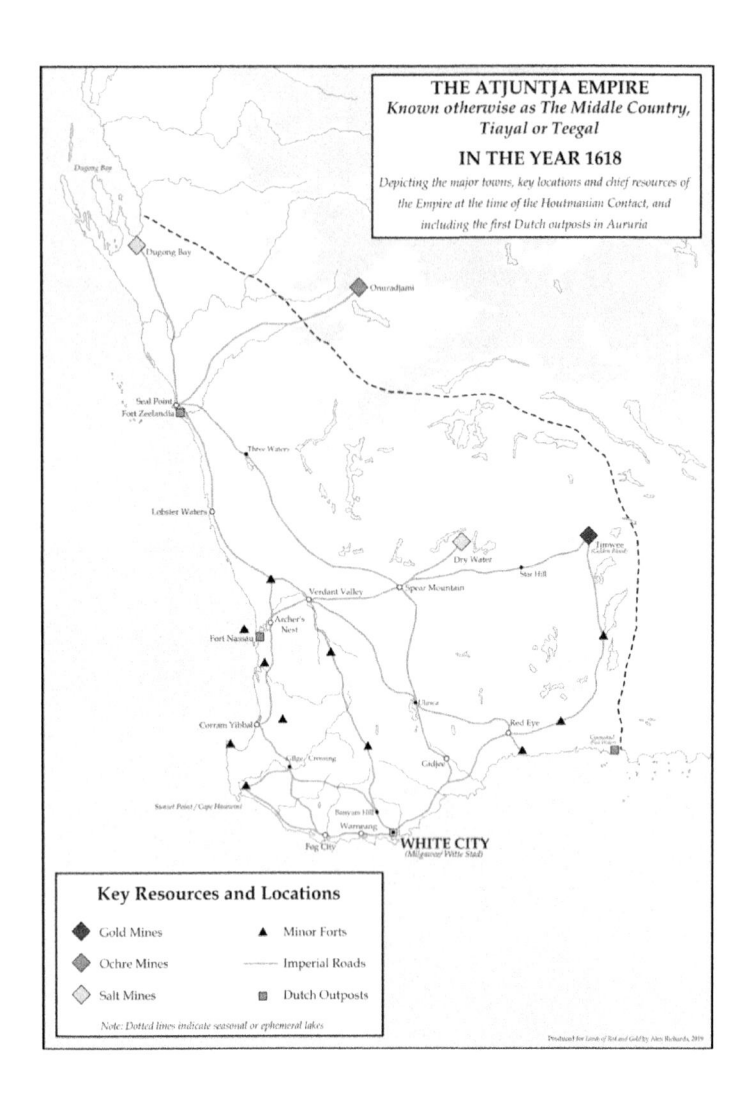

THE NANGU THASSALOCRACY IN 1618

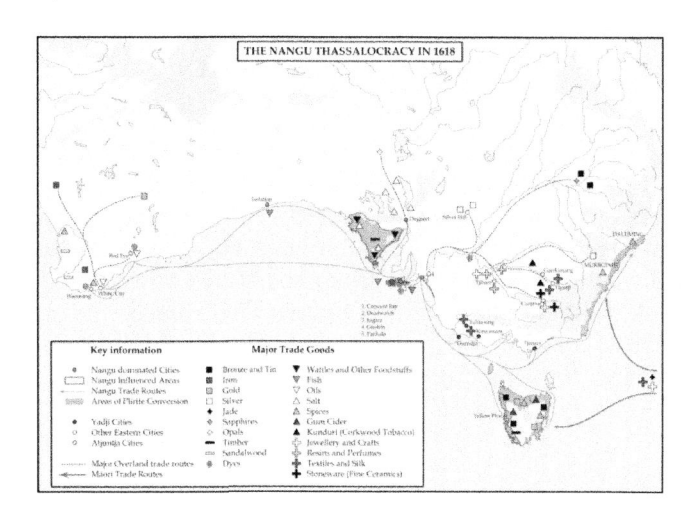

Key information	Major Trade Goods		
● Nangu-dominated Cities	■ Bronze and Tin	▼ Wattles and Other Foodstuffs	
▭ Nangu Influenced Areas	▨ Iron	▽ Fish	
— Nangu Trade Routes	▣ Gold	△ Oils	
▨ Areas of Plirite Concession	☐ Silver	▲ Salt	
	◆ Jade	△ Spices	
◆ Yadji Cities	◇ Sapphires	▲ Gum Cider	
○ Other Eastern Cities	◇ Opals	▲ Kunduri (Corkwood Tobacco)	
○ Atjuntja Cities	— Timber	✦ Jewellery and Crafts	
	∽ Sandalwood	✚ Resins and Perfumes	
----- Major Overland trade routes	● Dyes	✚ Textiles and Silk	
←— Maori Trade Routes		✚ Stoneware (Fine Ceramics)	

Acknowledgements

I would like to acknowledge the many contributions made by readers at the online forums AlternateHistory.com, Sufficient Velocity, the Sea Lion Press Forum and the now sadly-defunct Usenet newsgroup soc.history.what-if. This book would not be what it is without their valued input and feedback over several years. I would also like to thank Alex Richards for designing the maps in this book.

Afterword

The *Lands of Red and Gold* series is, first and foremost, a work of fiction. None of the cultures depicted in this tale are meant to be representative of any real Aboriginal peoples. While I have taken some broad inspiration from various Aboriginal cultures, I have deliberately changed the details of the fictional cultures. This represents how different cultures might have emerged if history had taken a different path.

Lands of Red and Gold was written over more than ten years, and involved lots of discoveries along the way. In particular, I would like to acknowledge the work of Bruce Pascoe in *Dark Emu*, who provided much more information about the many ways in which Aboriginal peoples managed the land, cultivated, stored and traded food than I was aware of when I started writing this series.

In writing *Lands of Red and Gold*, I have explored how things might have developed differently if there had been a plant in Australia which encouraged the adoption of something closer to European methods of farming, though of course still not the same. This is not meant to denigrate the extensive farming and land management methods used by Aboriginal peoples in real history.

In this series, I have used the term *hunter-gatherer* to represent the fictional cultures which continued to use land management methods similar to those used by Aboriginal peoples in real history. While I have some reservations about the term, I have opted to use it because it is most familiar to readers around the world, and for lack of a suitable alternative. But I emphasise that the lifestyle of these fictional cultures still involves active management of the land. The distinction drawn here is between cultures who have developed methods closer to European styles of farming, and those who use different methods of cultivating and managing the land.

Sea Lion Press

Sea Lion Press is the world's first publishing house dedicated to alternate history. To find out more, and to see our full catalogue, visit **sealionpress.co.uk.**

Sign up for our mailing list at **sealionpress.co.uk/contact** to be informed of all future releases. To support Sea Lion Press, visit **patreon.com/sealionpress**

Printed in Great Britain
by Amazon